W9-AQJ-354

Great
Ghost
STORIES

Great Ghost Stories

101 TERRIFYING TALES

COMPILED BY STEFAN DZIEMIANOWICZ

FALL RIVER PRESS

New York

FALL RIVER PRESS

New York

An Imprint of Sterling Publishing Co., Inc.
1166 Avenue of the Americas
New York, NY 10036

ISBN 978-1-4351-6231-0

Manufactured in the United States of America

13

sterlingpublishing.com

Contents

Introduction

Ghost stories have been with us ever since human beings began pondering the significance of death and wondering whether there might be an afterlife in which vestiges of mortal existence persist. Although ghosts have haunted the literature of all nations for thousands of years, the ghost story as a form of popular fiction first came into vogue in the late eighteenth century, when the gothic novel was ascendant and specters of the dead were just one of many affronts to the rational conjured in tales of supernatural horror. The era of traditional gothic fiction peaked in the early 1800s before giving way to other literary fads, but the ghost story lived on and flourished in the flickering shadows of the gothic twilight.

Great Ghost Stories draws from the wealth of ghost fiction written between the early-nineteenth and early-twentieth centuries—arguably the golden age of the ghost story, and certainly the era in which modern ghost fiction acquired the shape and structure that it has today. In the earliest such stories ghosts played a largely passive role: simply by manifesting or otherwise revealing themselves they struck terror into the hearts of people who considered themselves above the primitive superstitions on which belief in the supernatural was founded. Of course, it was not the intention of all of these ghosts to be frightening. Some made their presence known to reassure the living that death was not the end for the dear departed. Others continued in the benevolent manner that their living hosts had served, finishing tasks whose completion is crucial to the welfare of those left behind, or perhaps steering them to a treasure or other unknown enrichment, the revelation of which had been forestalled by their host's passing.

While there are several stories of this type to be found in *Great Ghost Stories*, most take their direction from the stories of M. R. James who, in the preface to his collection *More Ghost Stories of an Antiquary* (1911), outlined basic tenets for the telling of an effective ghost story, as distilled from his own writing and the best ghost stories of the nineteenth century that had served as its models. The first was that "the setting should be fairly familiar and the majority of the characters and their talk such as you may meet or hear any day." To James's way of thinking, the contemporary reader who appreciated the familiarity of the setting and characters of the ghost story was more likely to feel that "If I'm not very careful, something of this kind may happen to me!" Perhaps even more critical, James stressed the importance of ghosts being "malevolent or odious." "Amiable and helpful apparitions are all very well in fairy tales or in local legends," he wrote, "but I have no use for them in a fictitious ghost story."

Far from limiting the creative range of the tale of ghostly horror by reducing it to a set of formulae or narrow rules, James, through his guidelines, encouraged writers to seek all manner of identities and motives with which ghosts might engage and disturb the living. The ghosts who parade through this volume are a testament to the imaginative possibilities that the short ghost story can accommodate. Bernard Capes, in "Dark Dignum," presents a terrifying ghost hell bent on personal revenge for the wrong that ended his life. The ghost who appears in John Kendrick Bangs's wryly amusing "The Water Ghost of Harrowby Hall" is the avatar of an ancestral curse inflicted on members of a family regularly over the generations. By contrast, the intentions of the ghost who manifests in Jerome K. Jerome's "The Haunted Mill; or, The Ruined Home" are inscrutable—although, for his human victim, no less bedeviling. The victims of ghostly encounters in E. and H. Heron's "The Story of the Spaniards, Hammersmith" and G. M. Robins's "The Man with No Face" seem simply to have been in the wrong place at the wrong time, whereas those in Ford Madox Ford's "The Medium's End" and Edgar Jepson's "Mrs. Morrel's Last Séance" openly invite horrors from the spirit world by foolishly delving into the unknown. The ghosts in Ralph Adams Crams's "In Kropfsberg Keep" manifest to re-enact the horrifying dance of death that played out in a castle centuries before. In several of the stories, however, there is no visible presence of the ghostly—only the paranoid sense of an unseen intruder, as in William Fryer Harvey's "The Clock," or the suffocating depression that perfuses the atmosphere of a room imbued with the spirit of a suicide in Algernon Blackwood's "The Occupant of the Room." And not all ghosts in these stories assume recognizable human forms: the shadowy entities that scuttle through William L. Wintle's "The Spectre Spiders" are all the more horrifying for their inhuman shapes and behaviors, while W. C. Morrow's "The Haunted Burglar" terrifies with its notion that a phantom limb can develop a will independent of its host's.

The stories collected in this volume show the great variety of ghostly experience as conceived by some of the greatest weird fiction writers of all time. You don't *have* to believe in ghosts to enjoy these stories—but you dismiss their power to terrify you at your own peril.

—Stefan Dziemianowicz

New York, 2016

Across the Moors

William Fryer Harvey

It really was most unfortunate.

Peggy had a temperature of nearly a hundred, and a pain in her side, and Mrs. Workington Bancroft knew that it was appendicitis. But there was no one whom she could send for the doctor.

James had gone with the jaunting-car to meet her husband who had at last managed to get away for a week's shooting.

Adolph she had sent to the Evershams, only half an hour before, with a note for Lady Eva.

The cook could not manage to walk, even if dinner could be served without her.

Kate, as usual, was not to be trusted.

There remained Miss Craig.

"Of course, you must see that Peggy is really ill," said she, as the governess came into the room, in answer to her summons. The difficulty is, that there is absolutely no one whom I can send for the doctor." Mrs. Workington Bancroft paused; she was always willing that those beneath her should have the privilege of offering the services which it was her right to command.

"So, perhaps, Miss Craig," she went on, "you would not mind walking over to Tebbit's Farm. I hear there is a Liverpool doctor staying there. Of course I know nothing about him, but we must take the risk, and I expect he'll be only too glad to be earning something during his holiday. It's nearly four miles, I know, and I'd never dream of asking you if it was not that I dread appendicitis so."

"Very well," said Miss Craig, "I suppose I must go; but I don't know the way."

"Oh, you can't miss it," said Mrs. Workington Bancroft, in her anxiety temporarily forgiving the obvious unwillingness of her governess's consent.

"You follow the road across the moor for two miles, until you come to Redman's Cross. You turn to the left there, and follow a rough path that leads through a larch plantation. And Tebbits' farm lies just below you in the valley.

"And take Pontiff with you," she added, as the girl left the room. "There's absolutely nothing to be afraid of, but I expect you'll feel happier with the dog."

"Well, miss," said the cook, when Miss Craig went into the kitchen to get her boots, which had been drying by the fire; "of course she knows best, but I don't think it's right after all that's happened for the mistress to send you across the moors on a night like this. It's not as if the doctor could do anything for Miss Margaret if you do bring him. Every child is like that once in a while. He'll only say put her to bed, and she's there already."

"I don't see what there is to be afraid of, cook," said Miss Craig as she laced her boots, "unless you believe in ghosts."

"I'm not so sure about that. Anyhow I don't like sleeping in a bed where the sheets are too short for you to pull them over your head. But don't you be frightened, miss. It's my belief that their bark is worse than their bite."

But though Miss Craig amused herself for some minutes by trying to imagine the bark of a ghost (a thing altogether different from the classical ghostly bark), she did not feel entirely at her ease.

She was naturally nervous, and living as she did in the hinterland of the servants' hall, she had heard vague details of true stories that were only myths in the drawing-room.

The very name of Redman's Cross sent a shiver through her; it must have been the place where that horrid murder was committed. She had forgotten the tale, though she re membered the name.

Her first disaster came soon enough.

Pontiff, who was naturally slow-witted, took more than five minutes to find out that it was only the governess he was escorting, but once the discovery had been made, he promptly turned tail, paying not the slightest heed to Miss Craig's feeble whistle. And then, to add to her discomfort, the rain came, not in heavy drops, but driving in sheets of thin spray that blotted out what few landmarks there were upon the moor.

They were very kind at Tebbits' farm. The doctor had gone back to Liverpool the day before, but Mrs. Tebbit gave her hot milk and turf cakes, and offered her reluctant son to show Miss Craig a shorter path on to the moor, that avoided the larch wood.

He was a monosyllabic youth, but his presence was cheering, and she felt the night doubly black when he left her at the last gate.

She trudged on wearily. Her thoughts had already gone back to the almost exhausted theme of the bark of ghosts, when she heard steps on the road behind her that were at least material. Next minute the figure of a man appeared: Miss Craig was relieved to see that the stranger was a clergyman. He raised his hat. "I believe we are both going in the same direction," he said. "Perhaps I may have the pleasure of escorting you." She thanked him. "It is rather weird at night," she went on, "and what with all the tales of ghosts and bogies that one hears from the country people, I've ended by being half afraid myself."

"I can understand your nervousness," he said, "especially on a night like this. I used at one time to feel the same, for my work often meant lonely walks across the moor to farms which were only reached by rough tracks difficult enough to find even in the daytime."

"And you never saw anything to frighten you—nothing immaterial I mean?"

"I can't really say that I did, but I had an experience eleven years ago which served as the turning-point in my life, and since you seem to be now in much the same state of mind as I was then in, I will tell it you.

"The time of year was late September. I had been over to Westondale to see an old woman who was dying, and then, just as I was about to start on my way home, word came to me of another of my parishioners who had been suddenly taken ill only that morning. It was after seven when at last I started. A farmer saw me on my way, turning back when I reached the moor road.

"The sunset the previous evening had been one of the most lovely I ever remember to have seen. The whole vault of heaven had been scattered with flakes of white cloud, tipped with rosy pink like the strewn petals of a full-blown rose.

"But that night all was changed. The sky was an absolutely dull slate colour, except in one corner of the west where a thin rift showed the last saffron tint of the sullen sunset. As I walked, stiff and footsore, my spirits sank. It must have been the marked contrast between the two evenings, the one so lovely, so full of promise (the corn was still out in the fields spoiling for fine weather), the other so gloomy, so sad with all the dead weight of autumn and winter days to come. And then added to this sense of heavy depression came another different feeling which I surprised myself by recognizing as fear.

"I did not know why I was afraid.

"The moors lay on either side of me, unbroken except for a straggling line of turf shooting-butts, that stood within a stone's throw of the road.

"The only sound I had heard for the last half hour was the cry of the startled grouse—Go back, go back, go back. But yet the feeling of fear was there, affecting a low centre of my brain through some little-used physical channel.

"I buttoned my coat closer, and tried to divert my thoughts by thinking of next Sunday's sermon.

"I had chosen to preach on Job. There is much in the old-fashioned notion of the book, apart from all the subtleties of the higher criticism, that appeals to country people; the loss of herds and crops, the break up of the family. I would not have dared to speak, had not I too been a farmer; my own glebe land had been flooded three weeks before, and I suppose I stood to lose as much as any man in the parish. As I walked along the road repeating to myself the first chapter of the book, I stopped at the twelfth verse:

"'And the Lord said unto Satan: Behold, all that he hath is in thy power . . .'

"The thought of the bad harvest (and that is an awful thought in these valleys) vanished. I seemed to gaze into an ocean of infinite darkness.

"I had often used, with the Sunday glibness of the tired priest, whose duty it is to preach three sermons in one day, the old simile of the chess board. God and the devil were the players: and we were helping one side or the other. But until that night I had not thought of the possibility of my being only a pawn in the game, that God might throw away that the game might be won.

"I had reached the place where we are now, I remember it by that rough stone water-trough, when a man suddenly jumped up from the roadside. He had been seated on a heap of broken road metal.

"'Which way are you going, guv'ner?' he said.

"I knew from the way he spoke that the man was a stranger. There are many at this time of the year who come up from the south, tramping northwards with the ripening corn. I told him my destination.

"'We'll go along together,' he replied.

"It was too dark to see much of the man's face, but what little I made out was coarse and brutal.

"Then he began the half-menacing whine I knew so well—he had tramped miles that day, he had had no food since breakfast, and that was only a crust.

"'Give us a copper,' he said, 'it's only for a night's lodging.'

"He was whittling away with a big clasp knife at an ash stake he had taken from some hedge."

The clergyman broke off.

"Are those the lights of your house?" he said. "We are nearer than I expected, but I shall have time to finish my story. I think I will, for you can run home in a couple of minutes, and I don't want you to be frightened when you are out on the moors again.

"As the man talked he seemed to have stepped out of the very background of my thoughts, his sordid tale, with the sad lies that hid a far sadder truth.

"He asked me the time.

"It was five minutes to nine. As I replaced my watch I glanced at his face. His teeth were clenched, and there was something in the gleam of his eyes that told me at once his purpose.

"Have you ever known how long a second is? For a third of a second I stood there facing him, filled with an overwhelming pity for myself and him; and then without a word of warning he was upon me. I felt nothing. A flash of lightning ran down my spine, I heard the dull crash of the ash stake, and then a very gentle patter like the sound of a far distant stream. For a minute I lay in perfect happiness watching the lights of the house as they increased in number until the whole heaven shone with twinkling lamps.

"I could not have had a more painless death."

Miss Craig looked up. The man was gone; she was alone on the moor.

She ran to the house, her teeth chattering, ran to the solid shadow that crossed and recrossed the kitchen blind.

As she entered the hall, the clock on the stairs struck the hour.

It was nine o'clock.

The Adventure of the German Student

Washington Irving

On a stormy night, in the tempestuous times of the French revolution, a young German was returning to his lodgings, at a late hour, across the old part of Paris. The lightning gleamed, and the loud daps of thunder rattled through the lofty narrow streets—but I should first tell you something about this young German.

Gottfried Wolfgang was a young man of good family. He had studied for some time at Gottingen, but being of a visionary and enthusiastic character, he had wandered into those wild and speculative doctrines which have so often bewildered German students. His secluded life, his intense application, and the singular nature of his studies, had an effect on both mind and body. His health was impaired; his imagination diseased. He had been indulging in fanciful speculations on spiritual essences, until, like Swedenborg, he had an ideal world of his own around him. He took up a notion, I do not know from what cause, that there was an evil influence hanging over him; an evil genius or spirit seeking to ensnare him and ensure his perdition. Such an idea working on his melancholy temperament, produced the most gloomy effects. He became haggard and desponding. His friends discovered the mental malady preying upon him, and determined that the best cure was a change of scene; he was sent, therefore, to finish his studies amidst the splendors and gayeties of Paris.

Wolfgang arrived at Paris at the breaking out of the revolution. The popular delirium at first caught his enthusiastic mind, and he was captivated by the political and philosophical theories of the day: but the scenes of blood which followed shocked his sensitive nature; disgusted him with society and the world, and made him more than ever a recluse. He shut himself up in a solitary apartment in the *Pays Latin*, the quarter of students. There, in a gloomy street not far from the monastic walls of the Sorbonne, he pursued his favorite speculations. Sometimes he spent hours together in the great libraries of Paris, those catacombs of departed authors, rummaging among their hoards of dusty and obsolete works in quest of food for his unhealthy appetite. He was, in a manner, a literary ghoul, feeding in the charnel-house of decayed literature.

Wolfgang, though solitary and recluse, was of an ardent temperament, but for a time it operated merely upon his imagination. He was too shy and ignorant of the world to make any advances to the fair, but he was a passionate admirer of female beauty, and in his lonely chamber would often lose himself in reveries on forms and faces which he had seen, and his fancy would deck out images of loveliness far surpassing the reality.

While his mind was in this excited and sublimated state, a dream produced an extraordinary effect upon him. It was of a female face of transcendent beauty. So strong was the impression made, that he dreamt of it again and again. It haunted his thoughts by day, his slumbers by night; in fine, he became passionately enamoured of this shadow of a dream. This lasted so long that it became one of those fixed ideas which haunt the minds of melancholy men, and are at times mistaken for madness.

Such was Gottfried Wolfgang, and such his situation at the time I mentioned. He was retaining home late one stormy night, through some of the old and gloomy streets of the *Marais*, the ancient part of Paris. The loud claps of thunder rattled among the high houses of the narrow streets. He came to the Place de Grève, the square where public executions are performed. The lightning quivered about the pinnacles of the ancient Hôtel de Ville, and shed dickering gleams over the open space in front. As Wolfgang was crossing the square, he shrank back with horror at finding himself dose by the guillotine. It was the height of the reign of terror, when this dreadful instrument of death stood ever ready, and its scaffold was continually running with the blood of the virtuous and the brave. It had that very day been actively employed in the work of carnage, and there it stood in grim array, amidst a silent and sleeping city, waiting for fresh victims.

Wolfgang's heart sickened within him, and he was turning juddering from the horrible engine, when he beheld a shadowy form, cowering as it were at the foot of the steps which led up to the scaffold. A succession of vivid flashes of lightning revealed it more distinctly. It was a female figure, dressed in black. She was seated on one of the lower steps of the scaffold, leaning forward, her face hid in her lap; and her long dishevelled tresses hanging to the ground, streaming with the rain which fell in torrents. Wolfgang paused. There was something awful in this solitary monument of wo. The female had the appearance of being above the common order. He knew the times to be full of vicissitude, and that many a fair head, which had once been pillowed on down, now wandered houseless. Perhaps this was some poor mourner whom the dreadful axe had rendered desolate, and who sat here heart-broken on the strand of existence, from which all that was dear to her had been launched into eternity.

He approached, and addressed her in the accents of sympathy. She raised her head and gazed wildly at him. What was his astonishment at beholding, by the bright glare of the lightning, the very face which had haunted him in his dreams. It was pale and disconsolate, but ravishingly beautiful.

Trembling with violent and conflicting emotions, Wolfgang again accosted her. He spoke something of her being exposed at such an hour of the night, and to the fury of such a storm, and offered to conduct her to her friends. She pointed to the guillotine with a gesture of dreadful signification.

"I have no friend on earth!" said she.

"But you have a home," said Wolfgang.

"Yes—in the grave!"

The heart of the student melted at the words.

"If a stranger dare make an offer," said he, "without danger of being misunderstood, I would offer my humble dwelling as a shelter; myself as a devoted friend. I am friendless myself in Paris, and a stranger in the land; but if my life could be of service, it is at your disposal, and should be sacrificed before harm or indignity should come to you."

There was an honest earnestness in the young man's manner that had its effect His foreign accent, too, was in his favor; it showed him not to be a hackneyed inhabitant of Paris. Indeed, there is an eloquence in true enthusiasm that is not to be doubted. The homeless stranger confided herself implicitly to the protection of the student.

He supported her faltering steps across the Pont Neuf, and by the place where the statue of Henry the Fourth had been overthrown by the populace. The storm had abated, and the thunder rumbled at a distance. All Paris was quiet; that great volcano of human passion slumbered for a while, to gather fresh strength for the next day's eruption. The student conducted his charge through the ancient streets of the *Pays Latin*, and by the dusky walls of the Sorbonne, to the great dingy hotel which he inhabited. The old portress who admitted them stared with surprise at the unusual sight of the melancholy Wolfgang with a female companion.

On entering his apartment, the student, for the first time, blushed at the scantiness and indifference of his dwelling. He had but one chamber—an old-fashioned saloon—heavily carved, and fantastically furnished with the remains of former magnificence, for it was one of those hotels in the quarter of the Luxembourg palace which had once belonged to nobility. It was lumbered with books and papers, and all the usual apparatus of a student, and his bed stood in a recess at one end.

When lights were brought, and Wolfgang had a better opportunity of contemplating the stranger, he was more than ever intoxicated by her beauty. Her face was pale, but of a dazzling fairness, set off by a profusion of raven hair that hung clustering about it. Her eyes were large and brilliant, with a singular expression approaching almost to wildness. As far as her black dress permitted her shape to be seen, it was of perfect symmetry. Her whole appearance was highly striking, though she was dressed in the simplest style. The only thing approaching to an ornament which she wore, was a broad black band round her neck, clasped by diamonds.

The perplexity now commenced with the student how to dispose of the helpless being thus thrown upon his protection. He thought of abandoning his chamber to her, and seeking shelter for himself elsewhere. Still he was so fascinated by her charms, there seemed to be spell a spell upon his thoughts and senses, that he could not tear himself from her presence. Her manner, too, was singular and unaccountable. She spoke no more of the guillotine. Her grief had abated. The attentions of the student had first won her confidence, and then, apparently, her heart. She was evidently an enthusiast like himself, and enthusiasts soon understand each other.

In the infatuation of the moment, Wolfgang avowed his passion for her. He told her the story of his mysterious dream, and how she had possessed his heart before he had even seen her. She was strangely affected by his recital, and acknowledged to have felt an impulse towards him equally unaccountable. It was the time for wild theory and wild actions. Old prejudices and superstitions were done away; every thing was under the sway of the "Goddess of Reason." Among other rubbish of the old times, the forms and ceremonies of marriage began to be considered superfluous bonds for honorable minds. Social compacts were the vogue. Wolfgang was too much of a theorist not to be tainted by the liberal doctrines of the day.

"Why should we separate?" said he: "our hearts are united; in the eye of reason and honor we are as one. What need is there of sordid forms to bind high souls together?"

The stranger listened with emotion: she had evidently received illumination at the same school.

"You have no home nor family," continued he; "let me be every thing to you, or rather let us be every thing to one another. If form is necessary, form shall be observed—there is my hand. I pledge myself to you for ever."

"For ever?" said the stranger, solemnly.

"For ever!" repeated Wolfgang.

The stranger clasped the hand extended to her. "Then I am yours," murmured she, and sank upon his bosom.

The next morning the student left his bride sleeping, and sallied forth at an early hour to seek more spacious apartments, suitable to the change in his situation. When he returned, he found the stranger lying with her head hanging over the bed, and one arm thrown over it. He spoke to her, but received no reply. He advanced to awaken her from her uneasy posture. On taking her hand, it was cold—there was no pulsation—her face was pallid and ghastly.—In a word—she was a corpse.

Horrified and frantic, he alarmed the house. A scene of confusion ensued. The police was summoned. As the officer of police entered the room, he started back on beholding the corpse.

"Great heaven!" cried he, "how did this woman come here?"

"Do you know any thing about her?" said Wolfgang, eagerly.

"Do I?" exclaimed the police officer: "she was guillotined yesterday."

He stepped forward; undid the black collar round the neck of the corpse, and the head rolled on the floor!

The student burst into a frenzy. "The fiend! the fiend has gained possession of me!" shrieked he: "I am lost for ever."

They tried to soothe him, but in vain. He was possessed with the frightful belief that an evil spirit had reanimated the dead body to ensnare him. He went distracted, and died in a mad-house.

Here the old gentleman with the haunted head finished his narrative.

"And is this really a fact?" said the inquisitive gentleman.

"A fact not to be doubted," replied the other. "I had it from the best authority. The student told it me himself. I saw him in a mad-house at Paris."

All Souls' Day

D. K. Broster

THE SAINT'S BREVIARY, WE WERE TOLD AT THE CHURCH, WAS KEPT AT THE *presbytère*, but M. le Curé would be delighted to show it to us. So we went thither, and passing under an archway in the wall, and through a tiny garden-corner bright with flowers, found that M. le Curé was out but was expected back at any moment, and were requested to wait in the parlour. This we were glad enough to do, for Breton roads in August are hot and dusty, and we were somewhat weary with our long walk. The parlour was rather dark and very cool; it had straight-backed chairs arranged with extreme precision along the walls, a round table in the middle, and was hung with a few sacred prints. At either end of the mantelpiece, under a glass shade, was a little crucifix of extremely uncouth workmanship.

The Curé not appearing, I was wandering aimlessly round the room, when my eyes fell upon the book which we had come to see, in a roughly-made case on a table in the window.

"Here's our quarry," I exclaimed. "I wonder why the housekeeper did not tell us that it was in here." A card, neatly written, gave us information as to the date and authenticity of the breviary, but we did not like to take the volume from its case to examine it more closely until its guardian should arrive.

"Our host has one or two good bindings up there," remarked my friend, his eyes travelling to a little bookcase upon the wall. "Moreover, if that's not an English seventeenth century tooling I'll eat my hat." Moved by the sacred enthusiasm of the bibliophile he stretched up a hand and plucked the book forth. "Look," he said.

It was a Dutch-printed Latin copy of The Imitation Of Christ, of the year 1620, and though I know little of bindings I saw the significance of the faded inscription on the fly-leaf. *Mildmay Fane*, presumably the owner's name, was written high up in the right-hand corner, and then lower down, and evidently at a different time, *Hunc librum ad L.R.E. de V. dedit, anno MDCXXXI in memoriam misericordisæ non obliviscendæ*, and lower down again, *Ora pro anima N.C.*

"By Jove!" I said, "given by an Englishman to a Frenchman in 1631. I wonder what it is doing here, and who N.C. was."

But as I spoke the door opened, and the Curé hurried in, full of gentle apologies for keeping us waiting. He was the most beautiful and fragile old man that it has ever been my lot to meet, and he had spoken but a few words before we knew that he had a mind to match his person. In a minute or so the saint's breviary was out of its case, and we were examining it with attention, while the priest discoursed of it in a manner that showed he had no small knowledge of medieval manuscripts. It seemed to be all that was claimed for it, while its guardian's pride in it, and his manifest pleasure in showing it to foreigners (of whom one at least was a competent critic) were delightful to witness. But the discussion became at the end too technical for my attention, which wandered off to the Englishman's à Kempis, lying close to my hand, and I turned over its yellow pages musingly until I realised that the examination of the breviary was finished.

"You are very amiable, Messieurs, to have come so far to see this relic," remarked the Curé, pulling his spectacles lower on his nose, and looking at us over them, "Especially as you are, I suppose, Protestants?" he added.

My friend and I disclaimed the title so hastily as to cause the old priest some amusement. "Well, well," he said indulgently, "at any rate you cannot have known the same devotion for the blessed Hugues which has brought here most of those who come to see his book."

"But there is one saint and his book," I observed, rather sententiously, I fear, "for whom we all have a like devotion, whatever our country, creed, or age." And holding out the Imitation, I asked him if he would be good enough to satisfy our curiosity about it.

"Ah, there you have a great treasure of mine," he said smiling. "It has been as an heirloom in my family. Messieurs, a bargain,—if you will stay and take *déjeuner* with an old man who has not often the pleasure of meeting an Englishman, I will tell you the story of your countryman and the inscription in his à Kempis."

We were at heart only too pleased to stay, and though I fancied the housekeeper was not so pleased, and that I heard vociferations from the kitchen, we had an excellent little *déjeuner*. The old priest was so charming a mixture of shrewdness and naïveté, of humility and knowledge of the world, that his conversation was wholly delightful. After the meal we went into the little walled garden, and sat under a pear-tree, where our coffee was brought out to us, after we had assisted the Curé to hunt a fowl out of his bed of seedling wallflowers. "I think the blessed St. Francis must have omitted to preach to the *basse-cour*," he said ruefully, as we came back. "For my part I often feel most unchristian to my sister the hen."

When we had finished our coffee he drew the book out of the pocket of his cassock. "I must warn you that this is a story for the fireside in winter, and not for all this,"—he waved his hand to include the little green garden, the warm and fragrant air, the stocks and wallflowers, flagging a trifle in the sun, and the drowsy cooing from an unseen dovecot—"but it does not matter.

"This book, then, was given to a member of my family by its owner, Mr. Fane, an English gentleman of great gifts both of mind and body, a very noble person,—*une âme d'élite*, as we say—all whose qualities were like to suffer ruin through a disaster which befell him in early manhood. This calamity, brought about through no fault of his own, plunged him into circumstances which were leading him in a direction very different from the path wherein he had early set his steps, and to which, by the mercy of God, he afterwards returned, through what strange agency you shall hear.

"About the end of the year 1629 Mr. Fane, then a little more than thirty years of age, was visiting Paris on his return from a foreign tour, when he had the misfortune to incur the enmity of a certain Chevalier de Crussol, a man of notoriously evil life. They had met but a few times when a violent quarrel took place between them, in which Mr. Fane, so far as human judgment goes, had undoubted right upon his side. As a result of this disagreement Mr. Fane held himself in readiness to receive a challenge from the Chevalier. The expected cartel was never sent, but M. de Crussol took other means to avenge himself. As the Englishman was returning alone at night from a ball he was set upon by the Chevalier and several of his lackeys, who, after a brief struggle, left him for dead in the street.

"The door at which Mr. Fane fell, with half a score of wounds upon him, was that of the house which Carl' Egidio, the Grand Duke of P——, was making his residence during a private sojourn in Paris. By the Grand Duke's domestics, then, Mr. Fane was found in the early morning, and, being carried within, was there cared for during the space of two or three months. For many weeks of this time his life was despaired of, and he was unable to give any account of himself. However, the Grand Duke, seeing that he had to do with a gentleman of condition, whose appearance moreover had from the first attracted him, spared nothing of his hospitality and care. It so chanced that Mr. Fane had despatched his servant to England before he entered Paris, and that none of his acquaintance in the city was aware of his presence there, nor, in consequence, of the disaster which had befallen him. There was no person therefore to make enquiries concerning him, nor to reveal his identity, which he, lying for weeks unconscious, was equally unable to disclose. The result of this general ignorance, when he returned at last to sense and life, was not long in reaching Mr. Fane's ears. His friends, in England and abroad alike, believed him dead, slipt out of life by some such door, perhaps, as that through which he had so nearly passed; and in England the lady whom he had hopes of winning was married to another.

"Mr. Fane now fell into a great despair and blackness of soul. So much did he feel the faithlessness of her whom a few short months' silence could so alienate, that the idea of a return to England was abhorrent to him. Nor to his disordered mind did it appear to signify that he had, after all, escaped the sword of his enemy. He persuaded himself that his friends had forgotten him, and when the Grand Duke, who had conceived a violent attachment for his company, implored him to return with him to Italy, Mr. Fane consented with a sort of indifferent pleasure, saying bitterly that a dead man had no right to come to life again. He accordingly left Paris in the train of the Grand Duke.

"Dead he was, in another and a more real sense,—not, indeed, so dead as the majority of those with whom he now consorted, but with scarcely a trace remaining of that interior life which had once been to him the only existence worthy of the name. Carl' Egidio, a prince of cultured vices, called him saint and recluse, and strove to draw him more intimately into the circle of his own pleasures, but that Mr. Fane was of a different fashion from most of the grand-ducal associates did not, after all, confer on him any real title to those names. Yet the pleasures of the court held little savour for him, and sometimes, on his knees with the others at the sumptuous masses which they all attended (for Carl' Egidio was extremely orthodox) faint and bitter memories of better days broke into his soul. And the shy little Grand Duchess Maria Maddalena, the poor little bride who regretted her convent, talked to him at times on themes which had once been more than a name to him, and which these conversations, he could not but know it, were almost all she had to prevent their becoming names to her also. It was for her sake that he suffered the mention of things once dear, now inexpressibly alien to him, and perhaps a little for her sake too that he kept himself clean of the grosser forms of vice.

"But these could not fail, in time, to close upon him. The ladies of the court were none too difficult, and he had every gift to commend him to a woman. Before the winter was come Donna Flavia Ranuccini, a married kinswoman of the Duke's, had lured him along a perilous path of intimacy to a disastrous end. He did not love her, but she had wrested from him as much as he had in those days to give to any woman; and to an intimacy of such a kind, at that time and in such surroundings, there could be but one conclusion. Mr. Fane was only fulfilling, alas, what his world expected of a gentleman of fashion, when after a year's residence in P—— he made preparations for becoming Donna Flavia's acknowledged lover.

"It was ten o'clock on the second evening in November. October, so lately fled, had carried off few leaves from the trees in the Duke's beautiful gardens, into which Mr. Fane sat looking from a window-seat of his apartment in the palace. A half-moon, sometimes obscured by light fingers of cloud, shone on the statues among the trees, the dryads and fauns, and the Silenus in the middle of the nearest plot, and through the open casement came now and then the shiver of the leaves. Half lying on the deep seat the Englishman propped his chin on his hand and looked out. Something in the tall cypresses reminded him of a graveyard, and the white and silent statues of monuments,—or ghosts. Ghosts might well walk in the palace gardens, the ghosts of those who had played out their lives there, on the lawns and terraces in summer, or in winter in the apartments on the other side, now alight with revelry from which he had withdrawn himself,—for what? Donna Flavia's letter was in his pocket,—in a few years she too would be a ghost of the garden,—and he? But he was already dead, and had a right to walk already. And then he remembered,—what indeed he had forgotten merely for an hour or two—that it was All Souls' Day.

"Even as he remembered it the heavy window-curtain swayed slowly out from its place, as a curtain by an open window will do either with a gust of wind or with the opening of a door. But the wind was nothing save an occasional light shudder in the garden, and the door at the end of the long dimly-lit room had in truth been opened, for, turning his head on the instant, Mr. Fane heard it softly closed. Looking down the room he discerned the figure of a man coming towards him, and with some vexation wondered who entered unannounced at such an hour. But as the intruder came nearer he started from the window with his hand on his sword. It was the Chevalier de Crussol.

"He was dressed, as always, with some elaboration, in rich and pale satins, with his dark lovelocks falling over Venice point, a jewel in his ear, and a medal, or an order, on a broad ribbon about his neck. Bareheaded, with his left hand, sparkling with rings, resting lightly on his sword-hilt, he came slowly down the room towards his foe, and his short velvet cloak swung from his shoulder as he walked. But when he was within a couple of yards from Mr. Fane he suddenly halted, and stood looking at him with an air of extraordinary seriousness. Mr. Fane's last recollection of him was very different, and of the wild passions and vindictive triumph which had then been imprinted on his countenance there was now no trace, nor indeed of any other emotion. All expression seemed to have been wiped, as with a sponge, from his face, which yet bore everything by which a man may recognise one whom he has loved, or hated.

"'What do you want here?' asked Mr. Fane, finding his voice at last under his amazement.

"The Chevalier made no answer, nor moved, but continued to look at him with eyes of a strange flickering greyness.

"'Speak, in God's name!' cried Fane. 'What are you here for? Are you mad?' And indeed there could scarcely be any other explanation of his audacity.

"'Do you not know,' said the Chevalier in a low tone, speaking French, 'that it is the *jour des Morts*?'

"The sound of his voice carried Mr. Fane back in an instant to the dark street in Paris, the torches, and the swords. 'I know it,' he returned in the same tongue. 'And you have, perhaps, a fancy to join them?'

"His visitor paid no heed, but continuing to look at Mr. Fane with the same indescribable calm, said gravely: 'I am come to warn you of peril.'

"'Another assassination!' exclaimed the Englishman bitterly.

"'Rather self-murder,' replied the Chevalier, with not the faintest sign of blenching at the taunt.

"His composure, but still more the reference to his own private affairs, was too much for Mr. Fane. 'Now, by Him that made me,' he began, springing towards him. The Chevalier retreated a step and put a hand to stay him; but Mr. Fane never touched him. In after years, I believe, he could never satisfactorily account for the reason of sudden enlightment; the figure, even in the subdued light, was so distinct, so real, with all the visible attributes of breathing humanity about it. But on his closer advance he knew.

"He recoiled very slowly, crossing himself almost mechanically, and the dead murderer and his living victim stood looking at each other across the riven veil. There was no fear in Mr. Fane's heart, but awe certainly, and a great wonder. Why had the creature come,—to ask his forgiveness? No, for as the thought shot through his mind (he forgetting for the moment what had already passed between them) the apparition answered it. 'I am beyond the reach of human pardon, Mr. Fane; but I entreat you, by Him you named just now, not to do this thing.'

"The strange dead eyes were full upon him, passionless and yet compelling. Fane was shaken, but to be brought to book by one whom he could not but know to be infinitely worse than himself touched his sore and haughty soul too sharply. The human passion swept away with it the sense (which one might have supposed overpowering) that he was speaking to no living man. 'Enough,' he said shortly, and added, ' you find yourself, surely, on a strange errand, M. le Chevalier.'

"'The messenger,' returned his visitor almostly inaudibly, 'is not accounted of,—and you will not listen, nor stay your steps before it be too late?'

"Mr. Fane, without replying in words, made a gesture of negation, and a clock in some recess of the room struck the quarter. It was the hour at which he had ordered his chair to await him. The figure of his visitant stood between him and the door through which he must pass to gain the courtyard, not that door at the end of the room by which the Chevalier had entered, but a *porte de dégagement* on the left of the window. He looked towards it impatiently, in a way that would have been plain to an earthly guest.

"'Mr. Fane,' said the figure, holding up his hand, while for the first time a trace of emotion thrilled in his low and even voice, 'Mr. Fane, I will call another to stay you. You shall not dare to pass that door.'

"And with that he turned on his heel, as naturally as a living man might turn. On the wall, not far from the door, there hung a beautifully carved crucifix of ivory and silver, Carl' Egidio's gift to his favourite. Before Fane had time to interpose the spirit of his enemy had it in his left hand, and in his right, the light glinting dully upon it, a little dagger which he drew from his breast. Now he was at the door, and put the crucifix high up against the central panel, and, holding it thus, drove the stiletto through the ring deep into the wood. Then he half turned, looked round at Fane, and—was gone.

"Mildmay Fane wiped the sweat from his forehead. The room was empty, just as it had been a few minutes ago, save for the white Christ hanging over against him, nailed to the oak by an assassin's dagger. The sense of having dealt with the unseen was a thousandfold more potent now than when he had spoken with the phantom. Great God! what did it mean?—and yet he knew.

"Then he told himself that he was dreaming. But the crucifix upon the door,—was it real, or was it not? He went slowly up to it, not daring to touch it. Yes, surely, it was as real as sight could prove it, and the little dagger, with the ruby in the hilt,— the dagger which he knew, which had once had his own blood upon it—was fast in the panel. He put out his hand and drew it back again. 'I will leave the Christ there until I return, and if it be there still I shall know that I am not dreaming. I am not afraid of ghosts,' he thought to himself. But he stood for a moment looking fixedly at the Figure so strangely suspended in his path.

"The clock struck the half-hour, and he turned away to get his cloak from the window-seat. When he had his back to the barred door he thought with a smile of his visitor's defiance, 'You shall not dare to pass that door!' He put the cloak about him and walked steadily to it again.

"Ah, God! how the Christ looked at him, under the thorn-crowned brows! And as Mildmay Fane stood with his hand upon the handle, in the act to turn the latch, he suddenly drew back trembling. Not knowing why, but as one dreaming, he put out his hand instead to the Chevalier's poignard. His fingers encountered nothing but the panel of the door, but the crucifix, as though its support were removed, slipped instantly down the polished oak. He caught it as it fell, and, as his fingers closed on the symbol which an incredible act of divine mercy had placed to bar his way, the temptation dropped dead in his breast like a shot bird, and with an overmastering sense of awe and gratitude he sank upon his knees with the crucifix pressed to his lips.

"A week later he had left P—— for ever. Of all the Grand Duke's gifts he carried away with him but one, and left nothing behind of permanency but his memory to the little Grand Duchess.

"So you see, my children," said the old priest, smiling upon us, "that even if on All Souls' Day you met the ghost of one who had been your enemy,—though I hope that neither of you has such a thing—you would not need to think he came to do you harm."

"But, Father," said I, infinitely touched by the sweetness of his tone, "why should it have been his enemy that was sent to Mr. Fane? Do you think it was in expiation of his crime?"

The priest shook his head. "That is not for me to say. Let us hope so. I think that when Mr. Fane prayed before the altar for the repose of the Chevalier's soul, as he did to the end of his life,—as he here asked his friend to pray—" he lifted the book—"that must have been a hope with him . . . when he prayed also (as I am sure he did) that he himself, to whom so great a mercy had been given,—*misericordiæ non obliviscendæ*—might not be found wanting in the day of the Lord."

At Ravenholme Junction

Mary E. Penn

Were you ever out in a more wretched night in your life?" asked Harry Luscombe in a tone of disgust, as we were trudging wearily along after a full half-hour of absolute silence.

The rain was certainly coming down "with a vengeance," as people say. We had been out all day fishing in some private waters about ten miles from home. A friend had given us a lift in his trap the greater part of the way in going, and we had arranged to walk back, never dreaming that the sunny day would resolve itself into so wet an evening. Fortunately, each of us had taken a light mackintosh, and we had on our thick fishing-boots, otherwise our plight would have been much worse than it was.

"Wretched night!" again ejaculated Harry, whose pipe the rain would persist in putting out.

"But surely we cannot be far from the Grange now?" I groaned.

"A good four miles yet, old fellow," answered my friend. "We must grin and bear it."

For ten more minutes we paced the slushy road in moist silence.

"I wouldn't have cared so much," growled Harry at last, "if we had only a decent lot of fish to take home. Won't Gerty and the governor chaff us in the morning!"

I winced. Harry had touched a sore point. I rather prided myself on my prowess with rod and line; yet here was I, after eight hours' patient flogging of the water, going back to the Grange with a creel that I should blush to open when I got there. It was most annoying.

By-and-by we came to a stile, crossing which we found a footpath through the meadows, just faintly visible in the dark. The footpath, in time, brought us to a level crossing over the railway. But instead of crossing the iron road to the fields beyond, as I expected he would do, Harry turned half round and began to walk along the line. "Where on earth are you leading me to?" I asked, as I stumbled and barked my shins over a heap of loose sleepers by the side of the rails, "Seest thou not yonder planets that flame so brightly in the midnight sky?" he exclaimed, pointing to two railway signals clearly visible some quarter of a mile away. "Thither are we bound. Disturb not the meditations of a great mind by further foolish questionings."

I was too damp to retort as I might otherwise have done, so I held my peace and stumbled quietly after him. Little by little we drew nearer to the signal lamps, till at last we stood close under them. They shone far and high above our heads, being, in fact, the crowning-points of two tall semaphore posts. But we were not going quite so far skyward as the lamps, our destination being the signalman's wooden hut from which the semaphores were worked. This of itself stood some distance above the ground, being built on substantial posts driven firmly into the embankment. It was reached by a flight of wooden steps, steep and narrow. We saw by the light shining from its windows that it was not without an occupant. Harry put a couple of fingers to his mouth and whistled shrilly. "Jim Crump," he shouted, "Jim Crump—hi! Where are you?"

"Is that you, Mr. Harry?" said a voice, and then the door above us was opened. "Wait a moment, sir, till I get my lantern. The steps are slippery with the rain, and one of them is broken."

"You see, my governor is one of the managing directors of this line," said Harry, in explanation, while we were waiting for the lantern, "so that I can come and go, and do pretty much as I like about here."

"But why have you come here at all?" I asked.

"For the sake of a rest and a smoke, and a talk with Jim Crump about his dogs."

Two minutes later and we had mounted the steps, and for the first time in my life I found myself in a signalman's box.

It was a snug little place enough, but there was not much room to spare. There were windows on three sides it, so that the man on duty might have a clear view both up and down the line. Five or six long iron levers were fixed in a row below the front window. The due and proper manipulation of these levers, which were connected by means of rods and chains with the points and signals outside, and the working of the simple telegraphic apparatus which placed him en rapport with the stations nearest to him, up and down, were the signalman's sole but onerous duties. Both the box and the lamps overhead were lighted with gas brought from the town, two miles away.

"I have been wanting to see you for the last two or three weeks, Mr. Harry," said Crump, a well-built man of thirty, with clear resolute eyes and a firm-set mouth.

"Ay, ay. What's the game now, Crump? Got some more of that famous tobacco?"

"Something better than the tobacco, Mr. Harry. I've got a bull terrier pup for you. Such a beauty!"

"The dickens you have!" cried Harry, his eyes all a-sparkle with delight. "Crump, you are a brick. A bull terrier pup is the very thing I've been hankering after for the last three months. Have you got it here?"

"No, it's at home. You see, I didn't know that you were coming to-night."

Harry's countenance fell. "That's a pity now, isn't it?"

"It don't rain near so fast as it did," said Crump, "and if you would like to take the pup with you, I'll just run home and fetch it. I can go there and back in twenty minutes. It's agen the rules to leave my box, I know, and I wouldn't leave it for anybody but you; and not even for you, Mr. Harry, if I didn't know that you knew how to work the levers and the telly a'most as well as I do myself. Besides all that, there will be nothing either up or down till twelve thirty. What say you, sir?"

"I say go by all means, Crump. You may depend on my looking well after the signals while you are away."

"Right you are, sir." And Crump proceeded to pull on his overcoat.

"I wish I could make you more comfortable, sir," said Crump to me. "But this is only a roughish place."

Harry and I sat down on a sort of bunk or locker at the back of the box. Harry produced his flask, which he had filled with brandy before leaving the hotel. Crump declined any of the proffered spirit, but accepted a cigar. Then he pulled up the collar of his coat and went. In the pauses of our talk we could hear the moaning of the telegraph wires outside as the invisible fingers of the wind touched them in passing.

"This is Ravenholme Junction," said Harry to me.

"Is it, indeed? Much obliged for the information," I answered drily.

"About two years ago a terrible accident happened close to this spot. No doubt you read about it at the time."

"Possibly so. But if I did, the facts have escaped my memory."

"The news was brought to the Grange, and I was on the spot in less than three hours after the smash. I shall never forget what I saw that night." He smoked in grave silence for a little while, and then he spoke again. "I don't know whether you are acquainted with the railway geography of this district, but Ravenholme—I am speaking of the village, which is nearly two miles away—is on a branch line, which diverges from the main line some six miles north of this box, and after zigzagging among various busy townships and hamlets, joins the main line again about a dozen miles south of the point where it diverged; thus forming what is known as the Ravenholme Loop Line. None of the main line trains run over the loop: Passengers from it going to any place on the main line have to change from the local trains at either the north or south junction, according to the direction they intend to travel."

I wondered why he was telling this.

"You will understand from this that the junction where we are now is rather an out-of-the-way spot—out of the way, that is, of any great bustle of railway traffic. It forms, in fact, the point of connection between the Ravenholme Loop and a single line of rails which turns off to the left about a hundred yards from here, and gives access to a cluster of important collieries belonging to Lord Exbrooke; and the duty of Crump is, by means of his signals, to guard against the possibility of a collision between the coal trains coming off the colliery line and the ordinary trains passing up and down the loop. You will readily comprehend that, at a quiet place like this, a signalman has not half the work to do, nor half the responsibility to labour under, of a man in a similar position at some busy junction on the main line. In fact, a signalman at Ravenholme Junction may emphatically be said to have an easy time of it."

I nodded.

"Some two years ago, however, it so fell out that an abutment of one of the bridges on the main line was so undermined by heavy floods that instructions had to be given for no more trains to pass over it till it had been thoroughly repaired. In order to prevent any interruption of traffic, it was decided that till the necessary repairs could be effected all main line trains should work, for the time being, over the Ravenholme Loop. As it was arranged so it was carried out."

"Well?"

"The signalman at that time in charge of this box was named Dazeley—a shy, nervous sort of man, as I have been told, lacking in self-confidence, and not to be depended upon in any unforeseen emergency. Such as he was, however, he had been at Ravenholme for three years, and had always performed the duties of his situation faithfully and well. As soon as the main line trains began to travel by the new route, another man was sent from head-quarters to assist Dazeley—there had been no night-work previously. The men came on duty turn and turn about, twelve hours on and twelve hours oft, the man who was on by day one week being on by night the following week."

"Go on."

"It is said that Dazeley soon began to look worn and depressed, and that he became more nervous and wanting in self-confidence than ever. Be that as it may, he never spoke a complaining word to anyone, but went on doing his duty in the silent depressed way habitual with him. One morning when he was coming off duty—it was his turn for night-work that week—his mate was taken suddenly ill and was obliged to go home again. There was no help for it: Dazeley was obliged to take the sick man's place for the day. When evening came round, his mate sent word that he was somewhat better, but not well enough to resume work before morning; so Dazeley had to take his third consecutive 'spell' of twelve hours in the box. You see, Ravenholme is a long way from head-quarters, and in any case it would have taken some time to get assistance; besides which, Dazeley expected that a few hours at the very most would see his mate thoroughly recovered. So nothing was said or done."

I was growing interested.

"The night mail from south to north was timed to pass Ravenholme Junction, without stopping, at 11:40. On the particular night to which we now come—the night of the accident—it is supposed that poor Dazeley, utterly worn out for want of rest, had lain down for a minute or two on this very bunk, and had there dropped off to sleep, his signals, as was usual at that hour, standing at 'all clear.' Had he remained asleep till after the mail had passed all would have been well, everything being clear for its safe transit past the junction; but unfortunately the night was somewhat foggy, and the engine-driver, not being able to see the lamps at the usual distance, blew his whistle loudly. Roused by the shrill summons, Dazeley, as it is supposed, started suddenly to his feet, and his brain being still muddled with sleep, he grasped one of the familiar levers, and all unconscious of what he was doing, he turned the mail train on to the single line that led to the collieries."

"Oh!"

"The consequences were terrible. Some two or three hundred yards down the colliery line a long coal train was waiting for the mail to pass before proceeding on its journey. Into this train the mail dashed at headlong speed. Two people were killed on the spot, and twenty or thirty more or less hurt."

"How dreadful!"

"When they came to look for Dazeley he was not to be found. Horror-stricken at the terrible consequences of his act, he had fled. A warrant for his arrest was obtained. He was found four days afterwards in a wood, hanging to the bough of a tree, dead. One of his hands clasped a scrap of paper on which a few half-illegible words had been scrawled, the purport of which was that after what had happened he could no longer bear to live."

"A sad story, truly," I said, as Harry finished. "It seems to me that the poor fellow was to be pitied more than blamed."

"Crump's twenty minutes are rather long ones," said Harry, as he looked at his watch. "It is now thirty-eight minutes past eleven. No chance of getting home till long after midnight."

The rain was over and the wind had gone with it. Not a sound was audible save now and again the faint moaning of the telegraph wires overhead. Harry crossed to the window and opened one of the three casements. "A breath of fresh air will be welcome," he said. "The gas makes this little place unbearable." Having opened the window he came back again and sat down beside me on the bunk.

Hardly had Harry resumed his seat, when all at once the gas sank down as though it were going out, but next moment it was burning as brightly as before. An icy shiver ran through me from head to foot. I turned my head to glance at Harry, and as I did so I saw, to my horror, that we were no longer alone. There had been but two of us only a moment before: the door had not been opened, yet now we were three. Sitting on a low wooden chair close to the levers, and with his head resting on them, was a stranger, to all appearance fast asleep!

I never before experienced the feeling of awful dread that crept over me at that moment, and I hope never to do so again. I knew instinctively that the figure before me was no corporeal being, no creature of flesh and blood like ourselves. My heart seemed to contract, my blood to congeal: my hands and feet turned cold as ice: the roots of my hair were stirred with a creeping horror that I had no power to control. I could not move my eyes from that sleeping figure. It was Dazeley come back again: a worn, haggard-looking man, restless, and full of nervous twitchings even in his sleep.

"Listen!" said Harry, almost inaudibly, to me. I wanted to look at him, I wanted to see whether he was affected in the same way that I was, but for the life of me I could not turn my eyes away from that sleeping phantom.

Listening as he bade me, I could just distinguish the first low dull murmur made by an on-coming train while it is still a mile or more away. It was a murmur that grew and deepened with every second, swelling gradually into the hoarse inarticulate roar of an express train coming towards us at full speed. Suddenly the whistle sounded its loud, shrill, imperative summons. For one moment I tore my eyes away from the sleeping figure. Yonder, a quarter, or it might be half a mile away, but being borne towards us in a wild rush of headlong fury, was plainly visible the glowing Cyclopean eye of the coming train. Still the whistle sounded, painful, intense—agonised, one might almost fancy.

Louder and louder grew the heavy thunderous beat of the train. It was close upon us now. Suddenly the sleeping figure started to its feet—pressed its hands to its head for a moment as though lost in doubt—gave one wild, frenzied glance round—and then seizing one of the levers with both hands, pulled it back and there held it.

A sudden flash—a louder roar—and the phantom train had passed us and was plunging headlong into the darkness beyond. The figure let go its hold of the lever, which fell back to its original position. As it did so, a dreadful knowledge seemed all at once to dawn on its face. Surprise, horror, anguish unspeakable—all were plainly depicted on the white, drawn features of the phantom before me. Suddenly it flung up its arms as if in wild appeal to Heaven, then sank coweringly on its knees, and buried its face in both its hands with an expression of misery the most profound.

Next moment the gas gave a flicker as though it were going out, and when I looked again Harry and I were alone. The phantom of the unhappy signalman had vanished: the noise of the phantom train had faded into silence. No sound was audible save the unceasing monotone of the electric wires above us. Harry was the first to break the spell.

"To-day is the eighth of September," he said, "and it was on the eighth of September, two years ago, that the accident happened. I had forgotten the date till this moment."

At this instant the door opened, and in came Jim Crump with the puppy under his arm. Struck with something in our faces he looked from one to the other of us, and did not speak for a few seconds. "Here be the pup, sir," he said at last, "and a reg'lar little beauty I call her."

"Was it not two years ago this very night that the accident took place?" asked Harry, as he took the puppy out of Crump's arms into his own.

Crump reflected for a few moments. "Yes, sir, that it was, though I'd forgotten it. It was on the eighth of September. I ought to know, because it was on that very night my youngster was born."

"Were you signalman here on the eighth of September last year—the year after the accident?"

"No, sir, a man of the name of Moffat was here then. I came on the twentieth of September. Moffat was ordered to be moved. They said he had gone a little bit queer in his head. He went about saying that Dazeley's ghost had shown itself to him in this very box, and that he saw and heard a train come past that wasn't a train, and I don't know what bosh; so it was thought best to remove him."

"We thought just now—my friend and I—that we heard a train coming," said Harry as he gently stroked the puppy. "Did you hear anything as you came along?"

"Nothing whatever, sir. Had a train been coming I must have heard it, because I walked from my house up the line. Besides, there's no train due yet for some time."

Harry glanced at me. He was evidently not minded to enlighten Crump as to anything we had seen or heard.

Five minutes later we left, carrying the dog with us. Whether or not Harry said anything to his father I don't know. This, however, I do know, that within six months from that time certain alterations were made on the line which necessitated the removal of the signalman's box at Ravenholme Junction to a point half a mile further south. But I have never visited it since that memorable night.

At the Dip of the Road

Mrs. Molesworth

Have I ever seen a ghost? I do not know.

That is the only reply I can truthfully make to the question nowadays so often asked. And sometimes, if inquirers care to hear more, I go on to tell them the one experience which makes it impossible for me to reply positively either in the affirmative or negative, and restricts me to "I do not know."

This was the story.

I was staying with relations in the country. Not a very isolated or out-of-the-way part of the world, and yet rather inconvenient of access by the railway. For the nearest station was six miles off. Though the family I was visiting were nearly connected with me I did not know much of their home or its neighbourhood, as the head of the house, an uncle of mine by marriage, had only come into the property a year or two previously to the date of which I am writing, through the death of an elder brother.

It was a nice place. A good comfortable old house, a prosperous, satisfactory estate. Everything about it was in good order, from the farmers—who always paid their rents—to the shooting—which was always good—and from the vineries—which were noted—to the woods, where the earliest primroses in all the countryside were yearly to be found.

And my uncle and aunt and their family deserved these pleasant things and made a good use of them.

But there was a touch of the commonplace about it all. There was nothing picturesque or romantic. The country was flat though fertile, the house, though old, was conveniently modern in its arrangements, airy, cheery, and bright.

"Not even a ghost, or the shadow of one," I remember saying one day with a faint grumble.

"Ah, well—as to that," said my uncle, "perhaps we—" but just then something interrupted him, and I forgot his unfinished speech.

Into the happy party of which for the time being I was one, there fell one morning a sudden thunderbolt of calamity. The post brought news of the alarming illness of the eldest daughter, Frances, married a year or two ago and living—as the crow flies—at no very great distance. But as the crow flies is not always as the railroad runs, and to reach the Aldoyns' home from Fawne Court, my uncle's place, was a complicated business—it was scarcely possible to go and return in a day.

"Can one of you come over?" wrote the young husband. "She is already out of danger, but longing to see her mother or one of you. She is worrying about the baby"—a child of a few months old—"and wishing for nurse."

We looked at each other.

"Nurse must go at once," said my uncle to me, as the eldest of the party.

Perhaps I should here say that I am a widow, though not old, and with no close ties or responsibilities. "But for your aunt it is impossible."

"Quite so," I agreed. For she was at the moment painfully lamed by rheumatism.

"And the other girls are almost too young at such a crisis," my uncle continued. "Would you, Charlotte—" and he hesitated. "It would be such a comfort to have personal news of her."

"Of course I will go," I said. "Nurse and I can start at once. I will leave her there, and return alone, to give you, I have no doubt, better news of poor Francie."

He was full of gratitude. So were they all.

"Don't hurry back to-night," said my uncle. "Stay till—till Monday if you like." But I could not promise. I knew they would be glad of news at once, and in a small house like my cousin's, at such a time, an inmate the more might be inconvenient.

"I will try to return to-night," I said. And as I sprang into the carriage I added: "Send to Moore to meet the last train, unless I telegraph to the contrary."

My uncle nodded; the boys called after me, "All right"; the old butler bowed assent, and I was satisfied.

Nurse and I reached our journey's end promptly, considering the four or five junctions at which we had to change carriages. But on the whole "going," the trains fitted astonishingly.

We found Frances better, delighted to see us, eager for news of her mother, and, finally, disposed to sleep peacefully now that she knew that there was an experienced person in charge. And both she and her husband thanked me so much that I felt ashamed of the little I had done. Mr. Aldoyn begged me to stay till Monday; but the house was upset, and I was eager to carry back my good tidings.

"They are meeting me at Moore by the last train," I said. "No, thank you, I think it is best to go."

"You will have an uncomfortable journey," he replied. "It is Saturday, and the trains will be late, and the stations crowded with the market people. It will be horrid for you, Charlotte."

But I persisted.

It *was* rather horrid. And it was queer. There was a sort of uncanny eeriness about that Saturday evening's journey that I have never forgotten. The season was very early spring. It was not very cold, but chilly and ungenial. And there were such odd sorts of people about. I travelled second-class; for I am not rich, and I am very independent. I did not want my uncle to pay my fare, for I liked the feeling of rendering him some small service in return for his steady kindness to me. The first stage of my journey was performed in the company of two old naturalists travelling to Scotland to look for some small plant which was to be found only in one spot in the Highlands. This I gathered from their talk to each other. You never saw two such extraordinary creatures as they were. They both wore black kid gloves much too large for them, and the ends of the fingers waved about like feathers.

Then followed two or three short transits, interspersed with weary waitings at stations. The last of these was the worst, and tantalising, too, for by this time I was within a few miles of Moore. The station was crowded with rough folk, all, it seemed to me, more or less tipsy. So I took refuge in a dark waiting-room on the small side line by which I was to proceed, where I felt I might have been robbed and murdered and no one the wiser.

But at last came my slow little train, and in I jumped, to jump out again still more joyfully some fifteen minutes later when we drew up.

I peered about for the carriage. It was not to be seen; only two or three tax-carts or dog-carts, farmers' vehicles, standing about, while their owners, it was easy to hear, were drinking far more than was good for them in the taproom of the Unicorn. Thence, never the less—not to the taproom, but to the front of the inn—I made my way, though not undismayed by the shouts and roars breaking the stillness of the quiet night.

"Was the Fawne Court carriage not here?" I asked.

The landlady was a good-natured woman, especially civil to any member of the "Court" family. But she shook her head.

"No, no carriage had been down to-day. There must have been some mistake."

There was nothing for it but to wait till she could somehow or other disinter a fly and a horse, and, worst of all a driver. For the "men" she had to call were all rather—"well, ma'am, you see it's Saturday night. We weren't expecting any one."

And when, after waiting half an hour, the fly at last emerged, my heart almost failed me. Even before he drove out of the yard, it was very plain that if ever we reached Fawne Court alive, it would certainly be more thanks to good luck than to the driver's management.

But the horse was old and the man had a sort of instinct about him. We got on all right till we were more than half way to our journey's end. The road was straight and the moonlight bright, especially after we had passed a certain corner, and got well out of the shade of the trees which skirted the first part of the way.

Just past this turn there came a dip in the road. It went down, down gradually, for a quarter of a mile or more, and I looked up anxiously, fearful of the horse taking advantage of the slope. But no, he jogged on, if possible more slowly than before, though new terrors assailed me when I saw that the driver was now fast asleep, his head swaying from side to side with extraordinary regularity. After a bit I grew easier again; he seemed to keep his equilibrium, and I looked out at the side window on the moon-flooded landscape, with some interest. I had never seen brighter moonlight.

Suddenly from out of the intense stillness and loneliness a figure, a human figure, became visible. It was that of a man, a young and active man, running along the footpath a few feet to our left, apparently from some whim, keeping pace with the fly. My first feeling was of satisfaction that I was no longer alone, at the tender mercies of my stupefied charioteer. But, as I gazed, a slight misgiving came over me. Who could it be running along this lonely road so late, and what was his motive in keeping up with us so steadily. It almost seemed as if he had been waiting for us, yet that, of course, was impossible. He was not very highwayman-like certainly; he was well dressed—neatly dressed that is to say, like a superior gamekeeper—his figure was remarkably good, tall and slight, and he ran gracefully.

But there was something queer about him, and suddenly the curiosity that had mingled in my observation of him was entirely submerged in alarm, when I saw that, as he ran, he was slowly but steadily drawing nearer and nearer to the fly.

"In another moment he will be opening the door and jumping in," I thought, and I glanced before me only to see that the driver was more hopelessly asleep than before; there was no chance of his hearing if I called out. And get out I could not without attracting the strange runner's attention, for as ill-luck would have it, the window was drawn up on the right side and I could not open the door without rattling the glass. While, worse and worse, the left hand window was down! Even that slight protection wanting!

I looked out once more. By this time the figure was close—very close to the fly. Then an arm was stretched out and laid along the edge of the door, as if preparatory to opening it, and then, for the first time I saw his face.

It was a young face, but terribly, horribly pale and ghastly, and the eyes—all was so visible in the moonlight—had an expression such as I had never seen before or since. It terrified me, though afterwards on recalling it, it seemed to me that it might have been more a look of agonised appeal than of menace of any kind.

I cowered back into my corner and shut my eyes, feigning sleep. It was the only idea that occurred to me. My heart was beating like a sledge hammer. All sorts of thoughts rushed through me; among them I remember saying to myself: "He must be an escaped lunatic—his eyes are so awfully wild".

How long I sat thus I don't know—whenever I dared to glance out furtively he was still there. But all at once a strange feeling of relief came over me. I sat up—yes, he was gone! And though, as I took courage, I leant out and looked round in every direction, not a trace of him was to be seen, though the road and the fields were bare and clear for a long distance round.

When I got to Fawne Court I had to wake the lodge-keeper—every one was asleep. But my uncle was still up, though not expecting me, and very distressed he was at the mistake about the carriage.

"However," he concluded, "all's well that ends well. It's delightful to have your good news. But you look sadly pale and tired, Charlotte."

Then I told him of my fright—it seemed now so foolish of me, I said. But my uncle did not smile—on the contrary.

"My dear," he said. "It sounds very like our ghost, though, of course, it may have been only one of the keepers."

He told me the story. Many years ago in his grandfather's time, a young and favourite gamekeeper had been found dead in a field skirting the road down there. There was no sign of violence upon the body; it was never explained what had killed him. But he had had in his charge a watch—a very valuable one—which his master for some reason or other had handed to him to take home to the house, not wishing to keep it on him. And when the body was found late that night, the watch was not on it. Since then, so the story goes, on a moonlight night the spirit of the poor fellow haunts the spot. It is supposed that he wants to tell what had become of his master's watch, which was never found. But no one has ever had courage to address him.

"He never comes farther than the dip in the road," said my uncle. "If you had spoken to him, Charlotte, I wonder if he would have told you his secret?"

He spoke half laughingly, but I have never quite forgiven myself for my cowardice. It was the look in those terrible eyes!

At the Gate

Myla Jo Closser

A shaggy Airedale scented his way along the highroad. He had not been there before, but he was guided by the trail of his brethren who had preceded him. He had gone unwillingly upon this journey, yet with the perfect training of dogs he had accepted it without complaint. The path had been lonely, and his heart would have failed him, traveling as he must without his people, had not these traces of countless dogs before him promised companionship of a sort at the end of the road.

The landscape had appeared arid at first, for the translation from recent agony into freedom from pain had been so numbing in its swiftness that it was some time before he could fully appreciate the pleasant dog-country through which he was passing. There were woods with leaves upon the ground through which to scurry, long grassy slopes for extended runs, and lakes into which he might plunge for sticks and bring them back to— But he did not complete his thought, for the boy was not with him. A little wave of homesickness possessed him.

It made his mind easier to see far ahead a great gate as high as the heavens, wide enough for all. He understood that only man built such barriers and by straining his eyes he fancied he could discern humans passing through to whatever lay beyond. He broke into a run that he might the more quickly gain this inclosure made beautiful by men and women; but his thoughts outran his pace, and he remembered that he had left the family behind, and again this lovely new compound became not perfect, since it would lack the family.

The scent of the dogs grew very strong now, and coming nearer, he discovered, to his astonishment that of the myriads of those who had arrived ahead of him thousands were still gathered on the outside of the portal. They sat in a wide circle spreading out on each side of the entrance, big, little, curly, handsome, mongrel, thoroughbred dogs of every age, complexion, and personality. All were apparently waiting for something, someone, and at the pad of the Airedale's feet on the hard road they arose and looked in his direction.

That the interest passed as soon as they discovered the new-comer to be a dog puzzled him. In his former dwelling-place a four-footed brother was greeted with enthusiasm when he was a friend, with suspicious diplomacy when a stranger, and with sharp reproof when an enemy; but never had he been utterly ignored.

He remembered something that he had read many times on great buildings with lofty entrances. "Dogs not admitted," the signs had said, and he feared this might be the reason for the waiting circle outside the gate. It might be that this noble portal stood as the dividing-line between mere dogs and humans. But he had been a member of the family, romping with them in the living-room, sitting at meals with them in the dining-room, going upstairs at night with them, and the thought that he was to be "kept out" would be unendurable.

He despised the passive dogs. They should be treating a barrier after the fashion of their old country, leaping against it, barking, and scratching the nicely painted door. He bounded up the last little hill to set them an example, for he was still full of the rebellion of the world; but he found no door to leap against. He could see beyond the entrance dear masses of people, yet no dog crossed the threshold. They continued in their patient ring, their gaze upon the winding road.

He now advanced cautiously to examine the gate. It occurred to him that it must be fly-time in this region, and he did not wish to make himself ridiculous before all these strangers by trying to bolt through an invisible mesh like the one that had baffled him when he was a little chap. Yet there were no screens, and despair entered his soul. What bitter punishment these poor beasts must have suffered before they learned to stay on this side the arch that led to human beings! What had they done on earth to merit this? Stolen bones troubled his conscience, runaway days, sleeping in the best chair until the key clicked in the lock. These were sins.

At that moment an English bull-terrier, white, with liver-colored spots and a jaunty manner, approached him, snuffling in a friendly way. No sooner had the bull-terrier smelt his collar than he fell to expressing his joy at meeting him. The Airedale's reserve was quite thawed by this welcome, though he did not know just what to make of it.

"I know you! I know you!" exclaimed the bull-terrier, adding inconsequently, "What's your name?"

"Tam o'Shanter. They call me Tammy," was the answer, with a pardonable break in the voice.

"I know them," said the bull-terrier. "Nice folks."

"Best ever," said the Airedale, trying to be nonchalant, and scratching a flea which was not there. "I don't remember you. When did you know them?"

"About fourteen tags ago, when they were first married. We keep track of time here by the license-tags. I had four."

"This is my first and only one. You were before my time, I guess." He felt young and shy.

"Come for a walk, and tell me all about them," was his new friend's invitation.

"Aren't we allowed in there?" asked Tam, looking toward the gate.

"Sure. You can go in whenever you want to. Some of us do at first, but we don't stay."

"Like it better outside?"

"No, no; it isn't that."

"Then why are all you fellows hanging around here? Any old dog can see it's better beyond the arch."

"You see, we're waiting for our folks to come."

The Airedale grasped it at once, and nodded understandingly.

"I felt that way when I came along the road. It wouldn't be what it's supposed to be without them. It wouldn't be the perfect place."

"Not to us," said the bull-terrier.

"Fine! I've stolen bones, but it must be that I have been forgiven, if I'm to see them here again. It's the great good place all right. But look here," he added as a new thought struck him, "do they wait for us?"

The older inhabitant coughed in slight embarrassment.

"The humans couldn't do that very well. It wouldn't be the thing to have them hang around outside for just a dog—not dignified."

"Quite right," agreed Tam. "I'm glad they go straight to their mansions. I'd—I'd hate to have them missing me as I am missing them." He sighed. "But, then, they wouldn't have to wait so long."

"Oh, well, they're getting on. Don't be discouraged," comforted the terrier. "And in the meantime it's like a big hotel in summer—watching the new arrivals. See, there is something doing now."

All the dogs were aroused to excitement by a little figure making its way uncertainly up the last slope. Half of them started to meet it, crowding about in a loving, eager pack.

"Look out; don't scare it," cautioned the older animals, while word was passed to those farthest from the gate: "Quick! Quick! A baby's come!"

Before they had entirely assembled, however, a gaunt yellow hound pushed through the crowd, gave one sniff at the small child, and with a yelp of joy crouched at its feet. The baby embraced the hound in recognition, and the two moved toward the gate. Just outside the hound stopped to speak to an aristocratic St. Bernard who had been friendly:

"Sorry to leave you, old fellow," he said, "but I'm going in to watch over the kid. You see, I'm all she has up here."

The bull-terrier looked at the Airedale for appreciation.

"That's the way we do it," he said proudly.

"Yes, but—" the Airedale put his head on one side in perplexity.

"Yes, but what?" asked the guide.

"The dogs that don't have any people—the nobodies' dogs?"

"That's the best of all. Oh, everything is thought out here. Crouch down,—you must be tired,—and watch," said the bull-terrier.

Soon they spied another small form making the turn in the road. He wore a Boy Scout's uniform, but he was a little fearful, for all that, so new was this adventure. The dogs rose again and snuffled, but the better groomed of the circle held back, and in their place a pack of odds and ends of the company ran down to meet him. The Boy Scout was reassured by their friendly attitude, and after petting them impartially, he chose an old-fashioned black and tan, and the two passed in.

Tam looked questioningly.

"They didn't know each other!" he exclaimed.

"But they've always wanted to. That's one of the boys who used to beg for a dog, but his father wouldn't let him have one. So all our strays wait for just such little fellows to come along. Every boy gets a dog, and every dog gets a master."

"I expect the boy's father would like to know that now," commented the Airedale. "No doubt he thinks quite often, 'I wish I'd let him have a dog.'"

The bull-terrier laughed.

"You're pretty near the earth yet, aren't you?"

Tam admitted it.

"I've a lot of sympathy with fathers and with boys, having them both in the family, and a mother as well."

The bull-terrier leaped up in astonishment.

"You don't mean to say they keep a boy?"

"Sure; greatest boy on earth. Ten this year."

"Well, well, this is news! I wish they'd kept a boy when I was there."

The Airedale looked at his new friend intently.

"See here, who are you?" he demanded.

But the other hurried on:

"I used to run away from them just to play with a boy. They'd punish me, and I always wanted to tell them it was their fault for not getting one."

"Who are you, anyway?" repeated Tam. "Talking all this interest in me, too. Whose dog *were* you?"

"You've already guessed. I see it in your quivering snout. I'm the old dog that had to leave them about ten years ago."

"Their old dog Bully?"

"Yes, I'm Bully." They nosed each other with deeper affection, then strolled about the glades shoulder to shoulder. Bully the more eagerly pressed for news. "Tell me, how are they getting along?"

"Very well indeed; they've paid for the house."

"I—I suppose you occupy the kennel?"

"No. They said they couldn't stand it to see another dog in your old place."

Bully stopped to howl gently.

"That touches me. It's generous in you to tell it. To think they missed me!"

For a little while they went on in silence, but as evening fell, and the light from the golden streets inside of the city gave the only glow to the scene, Bully grew nervous and suggested that they go back.

"We can't see so well at night, and I like to be pretty close to the path, especially toward morning."

Tam assented.

"And I will point them out. You might not know them just at first."

"Oh, we know them. Sometimes the babies have so grown up they're rather hazy in their recollection of how we look. They think we're bigger than we are; but you can't fool us dogs."

"It's understood," Tam cunningly arranged, "that when he or she arrives you'll sort of make them feel at home while I wait for the boy?"

"That's the best plan," assented Bully, kindly. "And if by any chance the little fellow should come first,—there's been a lot of them this summer—of course you'll introduce me?"

"I shall be proud to do it."

And so with muzzles sunk between their paws, and with their eyes straining down the pilgrims' road, they wait outside the gate.

Bone to His Bone

E. G. Swain

William Whitehead, Fellow of Emmanuel College, in the University of Cambridge, became Vicar of Stoneground in the year 1731. The annals of his incumbency were doubtless short and simple: they have not survived. In his day were no newspapers to collect gossip, no Parish Magazines to record the simple events of parochial life. One event, however, of greater moment then than now, is recorded in two places. Vicar Whitehead failed in health after 23 years of work, and journeyed to Bath in what his monument calls "the vain hope of being restored." The duration of his visit is unknown; it is reasonable to suppose that he made his journey in the summer, it is certain that by the month of November his physician told him to lay aside all hope of recovery.

Then it was that the thoughts of the patient turned to the comfortable straggling vicarage he had left at Stoneground, in which he had hoped to end his days. He prayed that his successor might be as happy there as he had been himself. Setting his affairs in order, as became one who had but a short time to live, he executed a will, bequeathing to the Vicars of Stoneground, for ever, the close of ground he had recently purchased because it lay next the vicarage garden. And by a codicil, he added to the bequest his library of books. Within a few days, William Whitehead was gathered to his fathers.

A mural tablet in the north aisle of the church, records, in Latin, his services and his bequests, his two marriages, and his fruitless journey to Bath. The house he loved, but never again saw, was taken down 40 years later, and re-built by Vicar James Devie. The garden, with Vicar Whitehead's "close of ground" and other adjacent lands, was opened out and planted, somewhat before 1850, by Vicar Robert Towerson. The aspect of everything has changed. But in a convenient chamber on the first floor of the present vicarage the library of Vicar Whitehead stands very much as he used it and loved it, and as he bequeathed it to his successors "for ever."

The books there are arranged as he arranged and ticketed them. Little slips of paper, sometimes bearing interesting fragments of writing, still mark his places. His marginal comments still give life to pages from which all other interest has faded, and he would have but a dull imagination who could sit in the chamber amidst these books without ever being carried back 180 years into the past, to the time when the newest of them left the printer's hands.

Of those into whose possession the books have come, some have doubtless loved them more, and some less; some, perhaps, have left them severely alone. But neither those who loved them, nor those who loved them not, have lost them, and they passed, some century and a half after William Whitehead's death, into the hands of Mr. Batchel, who loved them as a father loves his children. He lived alone, and had few domestic cares to distract his mind. He was able, therefore, to enjoy to the full what Vicar Whitehead had enjoyed so long before him. During many a long summer evening would he sit poring over long-forgotten books; and since the chamber, otherwise called the library, faced the south, he could also spend sunny winter mornings there without discomfort. Writing at a small table, or reading as he stood at a tall desk, he would browse amongst the books like an ox in a pleasant pasture.

There were other times also, at which Mr. Batchel would use the books. Not being a sound sleeper (for book-loving men seldom are), he elected to use as a bedroom one of the two chambers which opened at either side into the library. The arrangement enabled him to beguile many a sleepless hour amongst the books, and in view of these nocturnal visits he kept a candle standing in a sconce above the desk, and matches always ready to his hand.

There was one disadvantage in this close proximity of his bed to the library. Owing, apparently, to some defect in the fittings of the room, which, having no mechanical tastes, Mr. Batchel had never investigated, there could be heard, in the stillness of the night, exactly such sounds as might arise from a person moving about amongst the books. Visitors using the other adjacent room would often remark at breakfast, that they had heard their host in the library at one or two o'clock in the morning, when, in fact, he had not left his bed. Invariably Mr. Batchel allowed them to suppose that he had been where they thought him. He disliked idle controversy, and was unwilling to afford an opening for supernatural talk. Knowing well enough the sounds by which his guests had been deceived, he wanted no other explanation of them than his own, though it was of too vague a character to count as an explanation. He conjectured that the window-sashes, or the doors, or "something," were defective, and was too phlegmatic and too unpractical to make any investigation. The matter gave him no concern.

Persons whose sleep is uncertain are apt to have their worst nights when they would like their best. The consciousness of a special need for rest seems to bring enough mental disturbance to forbid it. So on Christmas Eve, in the year 1907,

Mr. Batchel, who would have liked to sleep well, in view of the labours of Christmas Day, lay hopelessly wide awake. He exhausted all the known devices for courting sleep, and, at the end, found himself wider awake than ever. A brilliant moon shone into his room, for he hated window-blinds. There was a light wind blowing, and the sounds in the library were more than usually suggestive of a person moving about. He almost determined to have the sashes "seen to," although he could seldom be induced to have anything "seen to," He disliked changes, even for the better, and would submit to great inconvenience rather than have things altered with which he had become familiar.

As he revolved these matters in his mind, he heard the clocks strike the hour of midnight, and having now lost all hope of falling asleep, he rose from his bed, got into a large dressing gown which hung in readiness for such occasions, and passed into the library, with the intention of reading himself sleepy, if he could.

The moon, by this time, had passed out of the south, and the library seemed all the darker by contrast with the moonlit chamber he had left. He could see nothing but two blue-grey rectangles formed by the windows against the sky, the furniture of the room being altogether invisible. Groping along to where the table stood, Mr. Batchel felt over its surface for the matches which usually lay there; he found, however, that the table was cleared of everything. He raised his right hand, therefore, in order to feel his way to a shelf where the matches were sometimes mislaid, and at that moment, whilst his hand was in mid-air, the matchbox was gently put into it!

Such an incident could hardly fail to disturb even a phlegmatic person, and Mr. Batchel cried "Who's this?" somewhat nervously. There was no answer. He struck a match, looked hastily round the room, and found it empty, as usual. There was everything, that is to say, that he was accustomed to see, but no other person than himself.

It is not quite accurate, however, to say that everything was in its usual state. Upon the tall desk lay a quarto volume that he had certainly not placed there. It was his quite invariable practice to replace his books upon the shelves after using them, and what we may call his library habits were precise and methodical. A book out of place like this, was not only an offence against good order, but a sign that his privacy had been intruded upon. With some surprise, therefore, he lit the candle standing ready in the sconce, and proceeded to examine the book, not sorry, in the disturbed condition in which he was, to have an occupation found for him.

The book proved to be one with which he was unfamiliar, and this made it certain that some other hand than his had removed it from its place. Its title was *The Compleat Gard'ner* of M. de la Quintinye made English by John Evelyn Esquire. It was not a work in which Mr. Batchel felt any great interest. It consisted of divers reflections on various parts of husbandry, doubtless entertaining enough, but too deliberate and discursive for practical purposes. He had certainly never used the book, and growing restless now in mind, said to himself that some boy having the freedom of the house, had taken it down from its place in the hope of finding pictures.

But even whilst he made this explanation he felt its weakness. To begin with, the desk was too high for a boy. The improbability that any boy would place a book there was equalled by the improbability that he would leave it there. To discover its uninviting character would be the work only of a moment, and no boy would have brought it so far from its shelf.

Mr. Batchel had, however, come to read, and habit was too strong with him to be wholly set aside. Leaving *The Compleat Gard'ner* on the desk, he turned round to the shelves to find some more congenial reading.

Hardly had he done this when he was startled by a sharp rap upon the desk behind him, followed by a rustling of paper. He turned quickly about and saw the quarto lying open. In obedience to the instinct of the moment, he at once sought a natural cause for what he saw. Only a wind, and that of the strongest, could have opened the book, and laid back its heavy cover; and though he accepted, for a brief moment, that explanation, he was too candid to retain it longer. The wind out of doors was very light. The window sash was closed and latched, and, to decide the matter finally, the book had its back, and not its edges, turned towards the only quarter from which a wind could strike.

Mr. Batchel approached the desk again and stood over the book. With increasing perturbation of mind (for he still thought of the matchbox) he looked upon the open page. Without much reason beyond that he felt constrained to do something, he read the words of the half completed sentence at the turn of the page—

at dead of night he left the house and passed into the solitude of the garden.

But he read no more, nor did he give himself the trouble of discovering whose midnight wandering was being described, although the habit was singularly like one of his own. He was in no condition for reading, and turning his back upon the volume he slowly paced the length of the chamber, "wondering at that which had come to pass."

He reached the opposite end of the chamber and was in the act of turning, when again he heard the rustling of paper, and by the time he had faced round, saw the leaves of the book again turning over. In a moment the volume lay at rest, open in another place, and there was no further movement as he approached it. To make sure that he had not been deceived, he read again the words as they entered the page. The author was following a not uncommon practice of the time, and throwing common speech into forms suggested by Holy Writ: "So dig," it said, "that ye may obtain."

This passage, which to Mr. Batchel seemed reprehensible in its levity, excited at once his interest and his disapproval. He was prepared to read more, but this time was not allowed. Before his eye could pass beyond the passage already cited, the leaves of the book slowly turned again, and presented but a termination of five words and a colophon.

The words were, "to the North, an Ilex." These three passages, in which he saw no meaning and no connection, began to entangle themselves together in Mr. Batchel's mind. He found himself repeating them in different orders, now beginning with one, and now with another. Any further attempt at reading he felt to be impossible, and he was in no mind for any more experiences of the unaccountable. Sleep was, of course, further from him than ever, if that were conceivable. What he did, therefore, was to blow out the candle, to return to his moonlit bedroom, and put on more clothing, and then to pass downstairs with the object of going out of doors.

It was not unusual with Mr. Batchel to walk about his garden at nighttime. This form of exercise had often, after a wakeful hour, sent him back to his bed refreshed and ready for sleep. The convenient access to the garden at such times lay through his study, whose French windows opened on to a short flight of steps, and upon these he now paused for a moment to admire the snow-like appearance of the lawns, bathed as they were in the moonlight. As he paused, he heard the city clocks strike the half-hour after midnight, and he could not forbear repeating aloud

"At dead of night he left the house, and passed into the solitude of the garden."

It was solitary enough. At intervals the screech of an owl, and now and then the noise of a train, seemed to emphasise the solitude by drawing attention to it and then leaving it in possession of the night. Mr. Batchel found himself wondering and conjecturing what Vicar Whitehead, who had acquired the close of land to secure quiet and privacy for a garden, would have thought of the railways to the west and north. He turned his face northwards, whence a whistle had just sounded, and saw a tree beautifully outlined against the sky. His breath caught at the sight. Not because the tree was unfamiliar. Mr. Batchel knew all his trees. But what he had seen was "to the north, an Ilex."

Mr. Batchel knew not what to make of it all. He had walked into the garden hundreds of times and as often seen the Ilex, but the words out of *The Compleat Gard'ner* seemed to be pursuing him in a way that made him almost afraid. His temperament, however, as has been said already, was phlegmatic. It was commonly said, and Mr. Batchel approved the verdict, whilst he condemned its inexactness, that "his nerves were made of fiddle-string," so he braced himself afresh and set upon his walk round the silent garden, which he was accustomed to begin in a northerly direction, and was now too proud to change. He usually passed the Ilex at the beginning of his perambulation, and so would pass it now.

He did not pass it. A small discovery, as he reached it, annoyed and disturbed him. His gardener, as careful and punctilious as himself, never failed to house all his tools at the end of a day's work. Yet there, under the Ilex, standing upright in moonlight brilliant enough to cast a shadow of it, was a spade.

Mr. Batchel's second thought was one of relief. After his extraordinary experiences in the library (he hardly knew now whether they had been real or not) something quite commonplace would act sedatively, and he determined to carry the spade to the tool-house.

The soil was quite dry, and the surface even a little frozen, so Mr. Batchel left the path, walked up to the spade, and would have drawn it towards him. But it was as if he had made the attempt upon the trunk of the Ilex itself. The spade would not be moved. Then, first with one hand, and then with both, he tried to raise it, and still it stood firm. Mr. Batchel, of course, attributed this to the frost, slight as it was. Wondering at the spade's being there, and annoyed at its being frozen, he was about to leave it and continue his walk, when the remaining works of *The Compleat Gard'ner* seemed rather to utter themselves, than to await his will—

"So dig, that ye may obtain"

Mr. Batchel's power of independent action now deserted him. He took the spade, which no longer resisted, and began to dig. "Five spadefuls and no more," he said aloud. "This is all foolishness."

Four spadefuls of earth he then raised and spread out before him in the moonlight. There was nothing unusual to be seen. Nor did Mr. Batchel decide what he would look for, whether coins, jewels, documents in canisters, or weapons. In point of fact, he dug against what he deemed his better judgment, and expected nothing. He spread before him the fifth and last spadeful of earth, not quite without result, but with no result that was at all sensational. The earth contained a bone. Mr. Batchel's knowledge of anatomy was sufficient to show him that it was a human bone. He identified it, even by moonlight, as the *radius*, a bone of the forearm, as he removed the earth from it, with his thumb.

Such a discovery might be thought worthy of more than the very ordinary interest Mr. Batchel showed. As a matter of fact, the presence of a human bone was easily to be accounted for. Recent excavations within the church had caused the upturning of numberless bones, which had been collected and reverently buried. But an earth-stained bone is also easily overlooked, and this *radius* had obviously found its way into the garden with some of the earth brought out of the church.

Mr. Batchel was glad, rather than regretful at this termination to his adventure. He was once more provided with something to do. The re-interment of such bones as this had been his constant care, and he decided at once to restore the bone to consecrated earth. The time seemed opportune. The eyes of the curious were closed in sleep, he himself was still alert and wakeful. The spade remained by his side and the bone in his hand. So he betook himself, there and then, to the churchyard. By the still generous light of the moon, he found a place where the earth yielded to his spade, and within a few minutes the bone was laid decently to earth, some 18 inches deep.

The city clocks struck one as he finished. The whole world seemed asleep, and Mr. Batchel slowly returned to the garden with his spade. As he hung it in its accustomed place he felt stealing over him the welcome desire to sleep. He walked quietly on to the house and ascended to his room. It was now dark: the moon had passed on and left the room in shadow. He lit a candle, and before undressing passed into the library. He had an irresistible curiosity to see the passages in John Evelyn's book which had so strangely adapted themselves to the events of the past hour.

In the library a last surprise awaited him. The desk upon which the book had lain was empty. *The Compleat Gard'ner* stood in its place on the shelf. And then Mr. Batchel knew that he had handled a bone of William Whitehead, and that in response to his own entreaty.

The Botathen Ghost

R. S. Hawker

There was something very painful and peculiar in the position of the clergy in the west of England throughout the seventeenth century. The Church of those days was in a transitory state, and her ministers, like her formularies, embodied a strange mixture of the old belief with the new interpretation. Their wide severance also from the great metropolis of life and manners, the city of London (which in those times was civilised England, much as the Paris of our own day is France), divested the Cornish clergy in particular of all personal access to the master-minds of their age and body. Then, too, the barrier interposed by the rude rough roads of their country, and by their abode in wilds that were almost inaccessible, rendered the existence of a bishop rather a doctrine suggested to their belief than a fact revealed to the actual vision of each in his generation. Hence it came to pass that the Cornish clergyman, insulated within his own limited sphere, often without even the presence of a country squire (and unchecked by the influence of the Fourth Estate—for until the beginning of this nineteenth century, *Flindell's Weekly Miscellany*, distributed from house to house from the pannier of a mule, was the only light of the West), became developed about middle life into an original mind and man, sole and absolute within his parish boundary, eccentric when compared with his brethren in civilised regions, and yet, in German phrase, "a whole and seldom man" in his dominion of souls. He was "the parson," in canonical phrase—that is to say, The Person, the somebody of consequence among his own people. These men were not, however, smoothed down into a monotonous aspect of life and manners by this remote and secluded existence. They imbibed, each in his own peculiar circle, the hue of surrounding objects, and were tinged into distinctive colouring and character by many a contrast of scenery and people. There was "the light of other days," the curate by the sea-shore, who professed to check the turbulence of the "smugglers' landing" by his presence on the sands, and who "held the lantern" for the guidance of his flock when the nights were dark, as the only proper ecclesiastical part he could take in the proceedings. He was soothed and silenced by the gift of a keg of hollands or a chest of tea. There was the merry minister of the mines, whose cure was honeycombed by the underground men. He must needs have been artist and poet in his way, for he had to enliven his people three or four times a-year by mastering the arrangements of a "guary," or religious mystery, which was duly performed in the topmost hollow of a green barrow or hill, of which many survive, scooped out into vast amphitheatres and surrounded by benches of turf, which held two thousand spectators. Such were the historic plays, "The Creation" and "Noe's Flood," which still exist in the original Celtic as well as the English text, and suggest what critics and antiquaries Cornish curates, masters of such revels, must have been,—for the native language of Cornwall did not lapse into silence until the end of the seventeenth century. Then, moreover, here and there would be one parson more learned than his kind in the mysteries of a deep and thrilling lore of peculiar fascination. He was a man so highly honoured at college for natural gifts and knowledge of learned books which nobody else could read, that when he "took his second orders" the bishop gave him a mantle of scarlet silk to wear upon his shoulders in church, and his lordship had put such power into it that when the parson had it rightly on, he could "govern any ghost or evil spirit," and even "stop an earthquake."

Such a powerful minister, in combat with supernatural visitations, was one Parson Rudall, of Launceston, whose existence and exploits we gather from the local tradition of his time, from surviving letters and other memoranda, and indeed from his own "Diurnal," which fell by chance into the hands of the present writer. Indeed the legend of Parson Rudall and the Botathen Ghost will be recognised by many Cornish people as a local remembrance of their boyhood.

It appears, then, from the diary of this learned master of the grammar-school—for such was his office as well as perpetual curate of the parish—"that a pestilential disease did break forth in our town in the beginning of the year A.D. 1665; yea, and it likewise invaded my school, insomuch that therewithal certain of the chief scholars sickened and died." "Among others who yielded to the malign influence was Master John Eliot, the eldest son and the worshipful heir of Edward Eliot, Esquire of Trebursey, a stripling of sixteen years of age, but of uncommon parts and hopeful ingenuity. At his own especial motion and earnest desire I did consent to preach his funeral sermon." It should be remembered here that, howsoever strange and singular it may sound to us that a mere lad should formally solicit such a performance at the hands of his master, it was in consonance with the habitual usage of those times. The old services for the dead had been abolished by law, and in the stead of sacrament and ceremony, month's mind and year's mind, the sole substitute which survived was the general desire "to partake," as they called it, of a posthumous discourse, replete with lofty eulogy and nattering remembrance of the living and the dead. The diary proceeds:—

"I fulfilled my undertaking, and preached over the coffin in the presence of a full assemblage of mourners and lachrymose friends. An ancient gentleman, who was then and there in the church, a Mr. Bligh of Botathen, was much affected with my discourse, and he was heard to repeat to himself certain parentheses therefrom, especially a phrase from Maro Virgilius, which I had applied to the deceased youth, '*Et puer ipse fuit cantari dignus*.'

"The cause wherefore this old gentleman was thus moved by my applications was this: He had a firstborn and only son—a child who, but a very few months before, had been not unworthy the character I drew of young Master Eliot, but who, by some strange accident, had of late quite fallen away from his parent's hopes, and become moody, and sullen, and distraught. When the funeral obsequies were over, I had no sooner come out of church than I was accosted by this aged parent, and he besought me incontinently, with a singular energy, that I would resort with him forthwith to his abode at Botathen that very night; nor could I have delivered myself from his importunity, had not Mr. Eliot urged his claim to enjoy my company at his own house. Hereupon I got loose, but not until I had pledged a fast assurance that I would pay him, faithfully, an early visit the next day."

"The Place," as it was called, of Botathen, where old Mr. Bligh resided, was a low-roofed gabled manor-house of the fifteenth century, walled and mullioned, and with clustered chimneys of dark-grey stone from the neighbouring quarries of Ventorgan. The mansion was flanked by a pleasaunce or enclosure in one space, of garden and lawn, and it was surrounded by a solemn grove of stag-horned trees. It had the sombre aspect of age and of solitude, and looked the very scene of strange and supernatural events. A legend might well belong to every gloomy glade around, and there must surely be a haunted room somewhere within its walls. Hither, according to his appointment, on the morrow, Parson Rudall betook himself. Another clergyman, as it appeared, had been invited to meet him, who, very soon after his arrival, proposed a walk together in the pleasaunce, on the pretext of showing him, as a stranger, the walks and trees, until the dinner-bell should strike. There, with much prolixity, and with many a solemn pause, his brother minister proceeded to "unfold the mystery."

"A singular infelicity," he declared, "had befallen young Master Bligh, once the hopeful heir of his parents and of the lands of Botathen. Whereas he had been from childhood a blithe and merry boy, 'the gladness,' like Isaac of old, of his father's age, he had suddenly, and of late, become morose and silent—nay, even austere and stern—dwelling apart, always solemn, often in tears. The lad had at first repulsed all questions as to the origin of this great change, but of late he had yielded to the importunate researches of his parents, and had disclosed the secret cause. It appeared that he resorted, every day, by a pathway across the fields, to this very clergyman's house, who had charge of his education, and grounded him in the studies suitable to his age. In the course of his daily walk he had to pass a certain heath or down where the road wound along through tall blocks of granite with open spaces of grassy sward between. There in a certain spot, and always in one and the same place, the lad declared that he encountered, every day, a woman with a pale and troubled face, clothed in a long loose garment of frieze, with one hand always stretched forth, and the other pressed against her side. Her name, he said, was Dorothy Dinglet, for he had known her well from his childhood, and she often used to come to his parents' house; but that which troubled him was, that she had now been dead three years, and he himself had been with the neighbours at her burial; so that, as the youth alleged, with great simplicity, since he had seen her body laid in the grave, this that he saw every day must needs be her soul or ghost. 'Questioned again and again,' said the clergyman, 'he never contradicts himself; but he relates the same and the simple tale as a thing that cannot be gainsaid. Indeed the lad's observance is keen and calm for a boy of his age. The hair of the appearance, sayeth he, is not like anything alive, but it is so soft and light that it seemeth to melt away while you look; but her eyes are set, and never blink—no, not when the sun shineth full upon her face. She maketh no steps, but seemeth to swim along the top of the grass; and her hand, which is stretched out alway, seemeth to point at something far away, out of sight. It is her continual coming; for she never faileth to meet him, and to pass on, that hath quenched his spirits; and although he never seeth her by night, yet cannot he get his natural rest.'

"Thus far the clergyman; whereupon the dinner clock did sound, and we went into the house. After dinner, when young Master Bligh had withdrawn with his tutor, under excuse of their books, the parents did forthwith beset me as to my thoughts about their son. Said I, warily, 'The case is strange, but by no means impossible. It is one that I will study, and fear not to handle, if the lad will be free with me, and fulfil all that I desire.' The mother was overjoyed, but I perceived that old Mr. Bligh turned pale, and was downcast with some thought which, however, he did not express. Then they bade that Master Bligh should be called to meet me in the pleasaunce forthwith. The boy came, and he rehearsed to me his tale with an open countenance, and, withal, a modesty of speech. Verily he seemed '*ingenui vultus puer ingenuique pudoris.*' Then I signified to him my purpose. 'To-morrow,' said I, 'we will go together to the place; and if, as I doubt not, the woman shall appear, it will be for me to proceed according to knowledge, and by rules laid down in my books.'"

The unaltered scenery of the legend still survives, and, like the field of the forty footsteps in another history, the place is still visited by those who take interest in the supernatural tales of old. The pathway leads along a moorland waste, where large masses of rock stand up here and there from the grassy turf, and clumps of heath and gorse weave their tapestry of golden and purple garniture on every side. Amidst all these, and winding along between the rocks, is a natural footway worn by the scant, rare tread of the village traveller. Just midway, a somewhat larger stretch than usual of green sod expands, which is skirted by the path, and which is still identified as the legendary haunt of the phantom, by the name of Parson Rudall's Ghost.

But we must draw the record of the first interview between the minister and Dorothy from his own words. "We met," thus he writes, "in the pleasaunce very early, and before any others in the house were awake; and together the lad and myself proceeded towards the field. The youth was quite composed, and carried his Bible under his arm, from whence he read to me verses, which he said he had lately picked out, to have always in his mind. These were Job vii. 14, 'Thou scarest me with dreams, and terrifiest me through visions'; and Deuteronomy xxviii. 67,' In the morning thou shalt say, Would to God it were evening, and in the evening thou shalt say, Would to God it were morning; for the fear of thine heart wherewith thou shalt fear, and for the sight of thine eyes which thou shalt see.'

"I was much pleased with the lad's ingenuity in these pious applications, but for mine own part I was somewhat anxious and out of cheer. For aught I knew this might be a *dæmonium meridianum*, the most stubborn spirit to govern and guide that any man can meet, and the most perilous withal. We had hardly reached the accustomed spot, when we both saw her at once gliding towards us; punctually as the ancient writers describe the motion of their 'lemures, which swoon along the ground, neither marking the sand nor bending the herbage.' The aspect of the woman was exactly that which had been related by the lad. There was the pale and stony face, the strange and misty hair, the eyes firm and fixed, that gazed, yet not on us, but on something that they saw far, far away; one hand and arm stretched out, and the other grasping the girdle of her waist. She floated along the field like a sail upon a stream, and glided past the spot where we stood, pausingly. But so deep was the awe that overcame me, as I stood there in the light of day, face to face with a human soul separate from her bones and flesh, that my heart and purpose both failed me. I had resolved to speak to the spectre in the appointed form of words, but I did not. I stood like one amazed and speechless, until she had passed clean out of sight. One thing remarkable came to pass. A spaniel dog, the favourite of young Master Bligh, had followed us, and lo! when the woman drew nigh, the poor creature began to yell and bark piteously, and ran backward and away, like a thing dismayed and appalled. We returned to the house, and after I had said all that I could to pacify the lad, and to soothe the aged people, I took my leave for that time, with a promise that when I had fulfilled certain business elsewhere, which I then alleged, I would return and take orders to assuage these disturbances and their cause.

"*January 7, 1665.*—At my own house, I find, by my books, what is expedient to be done; and then, Apage, Sathanas!

"*January 9, 1665.*—This day I took leave of my wife and family, under pretext of engagements elsewhere, and made my secret journey to our diocesan city, wherein the good and venerable bishop then abode.

"*January 10.*—*Deo gratias*, in safe arrival at Exeter; craved and obtained immediate audience of his lordship; pleading it was for counsel and admonition on a weighty and pressing cause; called to the presence; made obeisance; and then by command stated my case—the Botathen perplexity—which I moved with strong and earnest instances and solemn asseverations of that which I had myself seen and heard. Demanded by his lordship, what was the succour that I had come to entreat at his hands? Replied, licence for my exorcism, that so I might, ministerially, allay this spiritual visitant, and thus render to the living and the dead release from this surprise. 'But,' said our bishop, 'on what authority do you allege that I am intrusted with faculty so to do? Our Church, as is well known, hath abjured certain branches of her ancient power, on grounds of perversion and abuse.' 'Nay, my lord,' I humbly answered, 'under favour, the seventy-second of the canons ratified and enjoined on us, the clergy, anno Domino 1604, doth expressly provide, that "no minister, *unless he hath* the licence of his diocesan bishop, shall essay to exorcise a spirit, evil or good." Therefore it was,' I did here mildly allege, 'that I did not presume to enter on such a work without lawful privilege under your lordship's hand and seal.' Hereupon did our wise and learned bishop, sitting in his chair, condescend upon the theme at some length with many gracious interpretations from ancient writers and from Holy Scripture, and I did humbly rejoin and reply, till the upshot was that he did call in his secretary and command him to draw the aforesaid faculty, forthwith and without further delay, assigning him a form, insomuch that the matter was incontinently done; and after I had disbursed into the secretary's hands certain moneys for signitary purposes, as the manner of such officers hath always been, the bishop did himself affix his signature under the *sigillum* of his see, and deliver the document into my hands. When I knelt down to receive his benediction, he softly said, 'Let it be secret, Mr. R. Weak brethren! weak brethren!'"

This interview with the bishop, and the success with which he vanquished his lordship's scruples, would seem to have confirmed Parson Rudall very strongly in his own esteem, and to have invested him with that courage which he evidently lacked at his first encounter with the ghost.

The entries proceed: "*January 11, 1665.*—Therewithal did I hasten home and prepare my instruments, and cast my figures for the onset of the next day. Took out my ring of brass, and put it on the index-finger of my right hand, with the *scutum Davidis* traced thereon.

"*January 12, 1665.*—Rode into the gateway at Botathen, armed at all points, but not with Saul's armour, and ready. There is danger from the demons, but so there is in the surrounding air every day. At early morning then, and alone,—for so the usage ordains,—I betook me towards the field. It was void, and I had thereby due time to prepare. First, I paced and measured out my circle on the grass. Then did I mark my pentacle in the very midst, and at the intersection of the five angles I did set up and fix my crutch of *raun* [rowan]. Lastly, I took my station south, at the true line of the meridian, and stood facing due north. I waited and watched for a long time. At last there was a kind of trouble in the air, a soft and rippling sound, and all at once the shape appeared, and came on towards me gradually. I opened my parchment scroll, and read aloud the command. She paused, and seemed to waver and doubt; stood still; then I rehearsed the sentence again, sounding out every syllable like a chant. She drew near my ring, but halted at first outside, on the brink. I sounded again, and now at the third time I gave the signal in Syriac—the speech which is used, they say, where such ones dwell and converse in thoughts that glide.

"She was at last obedient, and swam into the midst of the circle, and there stood still, suddenly. I saw, moreover, that she drew back her pointing hand. All this while I do confess that my knees shook under me, and the drops of sweat ran down my flesh like rain. But now, although face to face with the spirit, my heart grew calm, and my mind was composed. I knew that the pentacle would govern her, and the ring must bind, until I gave the word. Then I called to mind the rule laid down of old, that no angel or fiend, no spirit, good or evil, will ever speak until they have been first spoken to. *N.B.*—This is the great law of prayer. God Himself will not yield reply until man hath made vocal entreaty, once and again. So I went on to demand, as the books advise; and the phantom made answer, willingly. Questioned wherefore not at rest? Unquiet, because of a certain sin. Asked what, and by whom? Revealed it; but it is *sub sigillo*, and therefore *nefas dictu*; more anon. Inquired, what sign she could give that she was a true spirit and not a false fiend? Stated, before next Yule-tide a fearful pestilence would lay waste the land and myriads of souls would be loosened from their flesh, until, as she piteously said, 'our valleys will be full.' Asked again, why she so terrified the lad? Replied: 'It is the law: we must seek a youth or a maiden of clean life, and under age, to receive messages and admonitions.' We conversed with many more words, but it is not lawful for me to set them down. Pen and ink would degrade and defile the thoughts she uttered, and which my mind received that day. I broke the ring, and she passed, but to return once more next day. At even-song, a long discourse with that ancient transgressor, Mr. B. Great horror and remorse; entire atonement and penance; whatsoever I enjoin; full acknowledgment before pardon.

"*January 13, 1665.*—At sunrise I was again in the field. She came in at once, and, as it seemed, with freedom. Inquired if she knew my thoughts, and what I was going to relate? Answered, 'Nay, we only know what we perceive and hear; we cannot see the heart.' Then I rehearsed the penitent words of the man she had come up to denounce, and the satisfaction he would perform. Then said she, 'Peace in our midst.' I went through the proper forms of dismissal, and fulfilled all as it was set down and written in my memoranda; and then, with certain fixed rites, I did dismiss that troubled ghost, until she peacefully withdrew, gliding towards the west. Neither did she ever afterward appear, but was allayed until she shall come in her second flesh to the valley of Armageddon on the last day."

These quaint and curious details from the "diurnal" of a simple-hearted clergyman of the seventeenth century appear to betoken his personal persuasion of the truth of what he saw and said, although the statements are strongly tinged with what some may term the superstition, and others the excessive belief, of those times. It is a singular fact, however, that the canon which authorises exorcism under episcopal licence, is still a part of the ecclesiastical law of the Anglican Church, although it might have a singular effect on the nerves of certain of our bishops if their clergy were to resort to them for the faculty which Parson Rudall obtained. The general facts stated in his diary are to this day matters of belief in that neighbourhood; and it has been always accounted a strong proof of the veracity of the Parson and the Ghost, that the plague, fatal to so many thousands, did break out in London at the close of that very year. We may well excuse a triumphant entry, on a subsequent page of the "diurnal," with the date of July 10, 1665: "How sorely must the infidels and heretics of this generation be dismayed when they know that this black death, which is now swallowing its thousands in the streets of the great city, was foretold six months agone, under the exorcisms of a country minister, by a visible and suppliant ghost! And what pleasures and improvements do such deny themselves who scorn and avoid all opportunity of intercourse with souls separate, and the spirits, glad and sorrowful, which inhabit the unseen world!"

Buggam Grange: A Good Old Ghost Story

Stephen Leacock

The evening was already falling as the vehicle in which I was contained entered upon the long and gloomy avenue that leads to Buggam Grange.

A resounding shriek echoed through the wood as I entered the avenue. I paid no attention to it at the moment, judging it to be merely one of those resounding shrieks which one might expect to hear in such a place at such a time. As my drive continued, however I found myself wondering in spite of myself why such a shriek should have been uttered at the very moment of my approach.

I am not by temperament in any degree a nervous man, and yet there was much in my surroundings to justify a certain feeling of apprehension. The Grange is situated in the loneliest part of England, the marsh country of the fens to which civilization has still hardly penetrated. The inhabitants, of whom there are only one and a half to the square mile, live here and there among the fens and eke out a miserable existence by frog fishing and catching flies. They speak a dialect so broken as to be practically unintelligible, while the perpetual rain which falls upon them renders speech itself almost superfluous.

Here and there where the ground rises slightly above the level of the fens there are dense woods tangled with parasitic creepers and filled with owls. Bats fly from wood to wood. The air on the lower ground is charged with the poisonous gases which exude from the marsh, while in the woods it is heavy with the dank odours of deadly nightshade and poison ivy.

It had been raining in the afternoon, and as I drove up the avenue the mournful dripping of the rain from the dark trees accentuated the cheerlessness of the gloom. The vehicle in which I rode was a fly on three wheels, the fourth having apparently been broken and taken off, causing the fly to sag on one side and drag on its axle over the muddy ground, the fly thus moving only at a foot's pace in a way calculated to enhance the dreariness of the occasion. The driver on the box in front of me was so thickly muffled up as to be indistinguishable, while the horse which drew us was so thickly coated with mist as to be practically invisible. Seldom, I may say, have I had a drive of so mournful a character.

The avenue presently opened out upon a lawn with overgrown shrubberies, and in the half darkness I could see the outline of the Grange itself, a rambling, dilapidated building. A dim light struggled through the casement of a window in a tower room. Save for the melancholy cry of a row of owls sitting on the roof, and croaking of the frogs in the moat which ran around the grounds, the place was soundless. My driver halted his horse at the hither side of the moat. I tried in vain to urge him, by signs, to go further. I could see by the fellow's face that he was in a paroxysm of fear, and indeed nothing but the extra sixpence which I had added to his fare would have made him undertake the drive up the avenue. I had no sooner alighted than he wheeled his cab about and made off.

Laughing heartily at the fellow's trepidation (I have a way of laughing heartily in the dark), I made my way to the door and pulled the bell-handle. I could hear the muffled reverberations of the bell far within the building. Then all was silent. I bent my ear to listen, but could hear nothing except, perhaps, the sound of a low moaning as of a person in pain or in great mental distress. Convinced, however, from what my friend Sir Jeremy Buggam had told me, that the Grange was not empty, I raised the ponderous knocker and beat with it loudly against the door.

But perhaps at this point I may do well to explain to my readers (before they are too frightened to listen to me) how I came to be beating on the door of Buggam Grange at nightfall on a gloomy November evening.

A year before I had been sitting with Sir Jeremy Buggam, the present baronet, on the verandah of his ranch in California.

"So you don't believe in the supernatural?" he was saying.

"Not in the slightest," I answered, lighting a cigar as I spoke. When I want to speak very positively, I generally light a cigar as I speak.

"Well, at any rate, Digby," said Sir Jeremy, "Buggam Grange is haunted. If you want to be assured of it go down there any time and spend the night and you'll see for yourself."

"My dear fellow," I replied, "nothing will give me greater pleasure. I shall be back in England in six weeks, and I shall be delighted to put your ideas to the test. Now tell me," I added somewhat cynically, "is there any particular season or day when your Grange is supposed to be specially terrible?"

Sir Jeremy looked at me strangely. "Why do you ask that?" he said. "Have you heard the story of the Grange?"

"Never heard of the place in my life," I answered cheerily. "Till you mentioned it to-night, my dear fellow, I hadn't the remotest idea that you still owned property in England."

"The Grange is shut up," said Sir Jeremy, "and has been for twenty years. But I keep a man there—Horrod—he was butler in my father's time and before. If you care to go, I'll write him that you're coming. And, since you are taking your own fate in your hands, the fifteenth of November is the day."

At that moment Lady Buggam and Clara and the other girls came trooping out on the verandah, and the whole thing passed clean out of my mind. Nor did I think of it again until I was back in London. Then, by one of those strange coincidences or premonitions—call it what you will—it suddenly occurred to me one morning that it was the fifteenth of November. Whether Sir Jeremy had written to Horrod or not, I did not know. But none the less nightfall found me, as I have described, knocking at the door of Buggam Grange.

The sound of the knocker had scarcely ceased to echo when I heard the shuffling of feet within, and the sound of chains and bolts being withdrawn. The door opened. A man stood before me holding a lighted candle which he shaded with his hand. His faded black clothes, once apparently a butler's dress, his white hair and advanced age left me in no doubt that he was Horrod of whom Sir Jeremy had spoken.

Without a word he motioned me to come in, and, still without speech, he helped me to remove my wet outer garments, and then beckoned me into a great room, evidently the dining room of the Grange.

I am not in any degree a nervous man by temperament, as I think I remarked before, and yet there was something in the vastness of the wainscoted room, lighted only by a single candle, and in the silence of the empty house, and still more in the appearance of my speechless attendant, which gave me a feeling of distinct uneasiness. As Horrod moved to and fro I took occasion to scrutinize his face more narrowly. I have seldom seen features more calculated to inspire a nervous dread. The pallor of his face and the whiteness of his hair (the man was at least seventy), and still more the peculiar furtiveness of his eyes, seemed to mark him as one who lived under a great terror. He moved with a noiseless step and at times he turned his head to glance in the dark corners of the room.

"Sir Jeremy told me," I said, speaking as loudly and as heartily as I could, "that he would apprise you of my coming."

I was looking into his face as I spoke.

In answer Horrod laid his finger across his lips and I knew that he was deaf and dumb. I am not nervous (I think I said that), but the realization that my sole companion in the empty house was a deaf mute struck a cold chill to my heart.

Horrod laid in front of me a cold meat pie, a cold goose, a cheese, and a tall flagon of cider. But my appetite was gone. I ate the goose, but found that after I had finished the pie I had but little zest for the cheese, which I finished without enjoyment. The cider had a sour taste, and after having permitted Horrod to refill the flagon twice I found that it induced a sense of melancholy and decided to drink no more.

My meal finished, the butler picked up the candle and beckoned me to follow him. We passed through the empty corridors of the house, a long line of pictured Buggams looking upon us as we passed, their portraits in the flickering light of the taper assuming a strange and life-like appearance as if leaning forward from their frames to gaze upon the intruder.

Horrod led me upstairs and I realized that he was taking me to the tower in the east wing, in which I had observed a light.

The rooms to which the butler conducted me consisted of a sitting room with an adjoining bedroom, both of them fitted with antique wainscoting against which a faded tapestry fluttered. There was a candle burning on the table in the sitting room but its insufficient light only rendered the surroundings the more dismal. Horrod bent down in front of the fireplace and endeavoured to light a fire there. But the wood was evidently damp, and the fire flickered feebly on the hearth.

The butler left me, and in the stillness of the house I could hear his shuffling step echo down the corridor. It may have been fancy, but it seemed to me that his departure was the signal for a low moan that came from somewhere behind the wainscot. There was a narrow cupboard door at one side of the room, and for the moment I wondered whether the moaning came from within. I am not as a rule lacking in courage (I am sure my reader will be decent enough to believe this), yet I found myself entirely unwilling to open the cupboard door and look within. In place of doing so I seated myself in a great chair in front of the feeble fire. I must have been seated there for some time when I happened to lift my eyes to the mantel above and saw, standing upon it, a letter addressed to myself. I knew the handwriting at once to be that of Sir Jeremy Buggam.

I opened it, and spreading it out within reach of the feeble candlelight, I read as follows:

My dear Digby,

In our talk that you will remember, I had no time to finish telling you about the mystery of Buggam Grange. I take for granted, however, that you will go there and that Horrod will put you in the tower rooms, which are the only ones that make any pretense of being habitable. I have, therefore, sent him this letter to deliver at the Grange itself.

The story is this:

On the night of the fifteenth of November, fifty years ago, my grandfather was murdered in the room in which you are sitting, by his cousin, Sir Duggam Buggam. He was stabbed from behind while seated at the little table at which you are probably reading this letter. The two had been playing cards at the table and my grandfather's body was found lying in a litter of cards and gold sovereigns on the floor. Sir Duggam Buggam, insensible from drink, lay beside him, the fatal knife at his hand, his fingers smeared with blood. My grandfather, though of the younger branch, possessed a part of the estates which were to revert to Sir Duggam on his death. Sir Duggam Buggam was tried at the Assizes and was hanged. On the day of his execution he was permitted by the authorities, out of respect for his rank, to wear a mask to the scaffold. The clothes in which he was executed are hanging at full length in the little cupboard to your right, and the mask is above them. It is said that on every fifteenth of November at midnight the cupboard door opens and Sir Duggam Buggam walks out into the room. It has been found impossible to get servants to remain at the Grange, and the place—except for the presence of Horrod—has been unoccupied for a generation. At the time of the murder Horrod was a young man of twenty-two, newly entered into the service of the family. It was he who entered the room and discovered the crime. On the day of the execution he was stricken with paralysis and has never spoken since. From that time to this he has never consented to leave the Grange, where he lives in isolation.

Wishing you a pleasant night after your tiring journey,

I remain,
Very faithfully,
Jeremy Buggam

I leave my reader to imagine my state of mind when I completed the perusal of the letter.

I have as little belief in the supernatural as anyone, yet I must confess that there was something in the surroundings in which I now found myself which rendered me at least uncomfortable. My reader may smile if he will, but I assure him that it was with a very distinct feeling of uneasiness that I at length managed to rise to my feet, and, grasping my candle in my hand, to move backward into the bedroom. As I backed into it something so like a moan seemed to proceed from the closed cupboard that I accelerated my backward movement to a considerable degree. I hastily blew out the candle, threw myself upon the bed and drew the bed clothes over my head, keeping, however, one eye and one ear still out and available.

How long I lay thus listening to every sound, I cannot tell. The stillness had become absolute. From time to time I could dimly hear the distant cry of an owl, and once far away in the building below a sound as of some one dragging a chain along a floor. More than once I was certain that I heard the sound of moaning behind the wainscot. Meantime I realized that the hour must now be drawing close upon the fatal moment of midnight. My watch I could not see in the darkness, but by reckoning the time that must have elapsed I knew that midnight could not be far away. Then presently my ear, alert to every sound, could just distinguish far away across the fens the striking of a church bell, in the clock tower of Buggam village church, no doubt, tolling the hour of twelve.

On the last stroke of twelve, the cupboard door in the next room opened. There is no need to ask me how I knew it. I couldn't, of course, see it, but I could hear, or sense in some way, the sound of it. I could feel my hair, all of it, rising upon my head. I was aware that there was a *presence* in the adjoining room, I will not say a person, a living soul, but a *presence*. Anyone who has been in the next room to a presence will know just how I felt. I could hear a sound as of some one groping on the floor and the faint rattle as of coins.

My hair was now perpendicular. My reader can blame it or not, but it was.

Then at this very moment from somewhere below in the building there came the sound of a prolonged and piercing cry, a cry as of a soul passing in agony. My reader may censure me or not, but right at this moment I decided to beat it. Whether I should have remained to see what was happening is a question that I will not discuss. My one idea was to get out, and to get out quickly. The window of the tower room was some twenty-five feet above the ground. I sprang out through the casement in one leap and landed on the grass below. I jumped over the shrubbery in one bound and cleared the moat in one jump. I went down the avenue in about six strides and ran five miles along the road through the fens in three minutes. This at least is an accurate transcription of my sensations. It may have taken longer. I never stopped till I found myself on the threshold of the Buggam Arms in Little Buggam, beating on the door for the landlord.

I returned to Buggam Grange on the next day in the bright sunlight of a frosty November morning, in a seven cylinder motor car with six local constables and a physician. It makes all the difference. We carried revolvers, spades, pickaxes, shotguns and an ouija board.

What we found cleared up forever the mystery of the Grange. We discovered Horrod the butler lying on the dining room floor quite dead. The physician said that he had died from heart failure. There was evidence from the marks of his shoes in the dust that he had come in the night to the tower room. On the table he had placed a paper which contained a full confession of his having murdered Jeremy Buggam fifty years before. The circumstances of the murder had rendered it easy for him to fasten the crime upon Sir Duggam, already insensible from drink. A few minutes with the ouija board enabled us to get a full corroboration from Sir Duggam. He promised, moreover, now that his name was cleared, to go away from the premises forever.

My friend, the present Sir Jeremy, has rehabilitated Buggam Grange. The place is rebuilt. The moat is drained. The whole house is lit with electricity. There are beautiful motor drives in all directions in the woods. He has had the bats shot and the owls stuffed. His daughter, Clara Buggam, became my wife. She is looking over my shoulder as I write. What more do you want?

The Burned House

Vincent O'Sullivan

One night at the end of dinner, the last time I crossed the Atlantic, somebody in our group remarked that we were just passing over the spot where the Lusitania had gone down. Whether this was the case or not, the thought of it was enough to make us rather grave, and we dropped into some more or less serious discussion about the emotions of men and women who see all hope gone, and realize that they are going to sink with the vessel. From that the talk wandered to the fate of the drowned: was not theirs, after all, a fortunate end? Somebody related details from the narratives of those who had been all but drowned in the accidents of the war. A Scotch lady inquired fancifully if the ghosts of those who are lost at sea ever appear above the waters and come aboard ships. Would there be danger of seeing one when the light was turned out in her cabin? This put an end to all seriousness, and most of us laughed. But a little tight-faced man from Fall River, bleak and iron-gray, who had been listening attentively, did not laugh. The lady noticed his decorum and appealed to him for support.

"You are like me—you believe in ghosts?" she asked lightly.

He hesitated, thinking it over. "In ghosts?" he repeated slowly. "N-no; I don't know as I do. I've never had any personal experience that way. I've never seen the ghost of any one I knew. Has anybody here?"

No one replied. Instead, most of us laughed again, a little uneasily, perhaps.

"Well, I guess not," resumed the man from Fall River. "All the same, strange-enough things happen in life, even if you cut out ghosts, that you can't clear up by laughing. You laugh till you've had some experience big enough to shock you, and then you don't laugh any more. It's like being thrown out of a car—"

At this moment there was a blast on the whistle, and everybody rushed up on deck. As it turned out, we had only entered into a belt of fog. On the upper deck I fell in again with the New-Englander, smoking a cigar and walking up and down. We took a few turns together, and he referred to the conversation at dinner. Our laughter evidently rankled in his mind.

"So many damn' strange things happen in life that you can't account for," he protested. "You go on laughing at faith-healing and at dreams and this and that, and then something comes along that you just can't explain. You have got to throw up your hands and allow that it doesn't answer to any tests our experience has provided us with. Now, I guess I'm as matter of fact a man as any of those folks down there. I'm in the outfitting business. My favorite author is Ingersoll; whenever I go on a journey like this I carry one of his books. If you read Ingersoll and *think* Ingersoll year in, year out, you don't have much use for woolgathering. But once I had an experience which I had to conclude was out of the ordinary. Whether other people believe it or not, or whether they think they can explain it, don't matter; it happened to me, and I could no more doubt it than I could doubt having had a tooth pulled after the dentist had done it. I only wish Ingersoll was still alive; I'd like to put it up to him. If you will sit down here with me in this corner out of the wind, I'll tell you how it was.

"Some years ago I had to be for several months in New York. I was before the courts; it does not signify now what for, and it is all forgotten by this time. But it was a long and worrying case, and it aged me by twenty years. Well, sir, all through the trial, in, that grimy courtroom, I kept thinking and thinking of a fresh little place I knew in the Vermont hills; and I helped to get through the hours by thinking that if things went well with me I'd go there at once. And so it was that on the very next morning after I was acquitted I stepped on the cars at the Grand Central station.

"It was the early fall; the days were closing in, and it was night and cold when I arrived. The village was very dark and deserted; they don't go out much after dark in those parts, anyhow, and the keen mountain wind was enough to quell any lingering desire. The hotel was not one of those modern places called inns from sentiment in America, which are equipped and upholstered like the great city hotels; it was one of the real old-fashioned New England taverns, about as uncomfortable places as there are on earth, where the idea is to show the traveler that traveling is a penitential state, and that morally and physically the best place for him is home. The landlord brought me a kind of supper, with his hat on and a pipe in his mouth. The room was chilly; but when I asked for a fire, he said he guessed he couldn't go out to the wood-pile till morning. There was nothing else to do when I had eaten my supper but to go outside, both to get the smell of the lamp out of my nose and to warm myself by a short walk.

"As I did not know the country well, I did not mean to go far. But although it was an overcast night, with a high northeast wind and an occasional flurry of rain, the moon was up, and even concealed by clouds as it was, it yet lit the night with a kind of twilight gray, not vivid, like the open moonlight, but good enough to see some distance. On account of this I prolonged my stroll, and kept walking on and on till I was a considerable way from the village, and in a region as lonely as anywhere in the State. Great trees and shrubs bordered the road, and many feet below was a mountain stream. What with the passion of the wind pouring through the high trees and the shout of the water racing among the boulders, it seemed to me sometimes like the noise of a crowd of people, and two or three times I turned to see if a crowd might be out after me, well as I knew that no crowd could be there. Sometimes the branches of the trees became so thick that I was walking as if in a black pit, unable to see my hand close to my face. Then, coming out from the tunnel of branches, I would step once more into a gray clearness which opened the road and surrounding country a good way on all sides.

"I suppose it might be some three quarters of an hour I had been walking when I came to a fork of the road. One branch ran downward, getting almost on a level with the bed of the torrent. The other mounted in a steep hill, and this, after a little idle debating, I decided to follow. After I had climbed for more than half a mile, thinking that if I should happen to lose track of one of the landmarks I should be very badly lost, the path—for it was now no more than that—curved, and I came out on a broad plateau. There, to my astonishment, I saw a house. It was a good-sized wooden house, three stories high, with a piazza round two sides of it, and from the elevation on which it stood it commanded a far stretch of country. There were a few great trees at a little distance from the house, and behind it, a stone's-throw away, was a clump of bushes. Still, it looked lonely and stark, offering its four sides unprotected to the winds. For all that, I was very glad to see it. 'It does not matter now,' I thought, 'whether I have lost my way or not. The house people will set me right.'

"But when I came up to it, I found that it was, to all appearance, uninhabited. The shutters were closed on all the windows; there was not a spark of light anywhere. There was something about it, something sinister and barren, that gave me the kind of shiver you have at the door of a room where you know that a dead man lies inside, or if you get thinking hard about dropping over the rail into that black waste of waters out there. This feeling, you know, isn't altogether unpleasant; you relish all the better your present security. It was the same with me standing before that house. I was not *really* scared. I was alone up here, miles from any kind of help, at the mercy of whoever might be lurking behind the shutters of that sullen house; but I felt that by all the chances I was perfectly alone and safe. My sensation of the uncanny was due to the effect on the nerves produced by wild scenery and the unexpected sight of a house in such a very lonely situation. Thus I reasoned, and instead of following the road farther, I walked over the grass till I came to a stone wall perhaps two hundred and fifty yards in front of the house, and rested my arms on it, looking forth at the scene.

"On the crests of the hills far away a strange light lingered, like the first touch of dawn in the sky on a rainy morning or the last glimpse of twilight before night comes. Between me and the hills was a wide stretch of open country. On my right hand was an apple-orchard, and I observed that a stile had been made in the wall of piled stones to enable the house people to go back and forth.

"Now, after I had been there leaning on the wall some considerable time, I saw a man coming toward me through the orchard. He was walking with a good, free stride, and as he drew nearer I could see that he was a tall, sinewy fellow between twenty-five and thirty, with a shaven face, wearing the slouch-hat of that country, a dark woolen shirt, and high boots. When he reached the stile and began climbing over it, I bade him good night in neighborly fashion. He made no reply, but he looked me straight in the face, and the look gave me a qualm. Not that it was an evil face, mind you,—it was a handsome, serious face,—but it was ravaged by some terrible passion: stealth was on it, ruthlessness, and a deadly resolution, and at the same time such a look as a man driven by some uncontrollable power might throw on surrounding things, asking for comprehension and mercy. It was impossible for me to resent his churlishness, his thoughts were so certainly elsewhere. I doubt if he even saw me.

"He could not have gone by more than a quarter of a minute when I turned to look after him. He had disappeared. The plateau lay bare before me, and it seemed impossible that even if he had sprinted like an athlete he could have got inside the house in so little time. But I have always made it a rule to attribute what I cannot understand to natural causes that I have failed to observe. I said to myself that no doubt the man had gone back into the orchard by some other opening in the wall lower down, or there might be some flaw in my vision owing to the uncertain and distorting light.

"But even as I continued to look toward the house, leaning my back now against the wall, I noticed that there were lights springing up in the windows behind the shutters. They were flickering lights, now bright, now dim, and had a ruddy glow like firelight. Before I had looked long, I became convinced that it was indeed firelight: the house was on fire. Black smoke began to pour from the roof: the red sparks flew in the wind. Then at a window above the roof of the piazza the shutters were thrown open, and I heard a woman shriek. I ran toward the house as hard as I could, and when I drew near I could see her plainly.

"She was a young woman; her hair fell in disorder over her white nightgown. She stretched out her bare arms, screaming. I saw a man come behind and seize her. But they were caught in a trap. The flames were licking round the windows, and the smoke was killing them. Even now the part of the house where they stood was caving in.

"Appalled by this horrible tragedy, which had thus suddenly risen before me, I made my way still nearer the house, thinking that if the two could struggle to the side of the house not bounded by the piazza they might jump, and I might break the fall. I was shouting this at them; I was right up close to the fire; and then I was struck by—I noticed for the first time an astonishing thing—the flames had no heat in them!

"I was standing near enough to the fire to be singed by it, and yet I felt no heat. The sparks were flying about my head; some fell on my hands, and they did not burn. And now I perceived that although the smoke was rolling in columns, I was not choked by the smoke, and that there had been no smell of smoke since the fire broke out. Neither was there any glare against the sky.

"As I stood there stupefied, wondering how these things could be, the whole house was swept by a very tornado of flame, and crashed down in a red ruin.

"Stricken to the heart by this abominable catastrophe, I made my way uncertainly down the hill, shouting for help. As I came to a little wooden bridge spanning the torrent, just beyond where the roads forked, I saw what appeared to be a rope in loose coils lying there. I saw that part of it was fastened to the railing of the bridge and hung outside, and I looked over. There was a man's body swinging by the neck between the road and the stream. I leaned over still farther, and then I recognized him as the man I had seen coming out of the orchard. His hat had fallen off, and the toes of his boots just touched the water.

"It seemed hardly possible, and yet it was certain. That was the man, and he was hanging there. I scrambled down at the side of the bridge, and put out my hand to seize the body, so that I might lift it up and relieve the weight on the rope. I succeeded in clutching hold of his loose shirt, and for a second I thought that it had come away in my hand. Then I found that my hand had closed on nothing; I had clutched nothing but air. And yet the figure swung by the neck before my eyes!

"I was suffocated with such horror that I feared for a moment I must lose consciousness. The next minute I was running and stumbling along that dark road in mortal anxiety, my one idea being to rouse the town and bring men to the bridge. That,

I say, was my intention; but the fact is that when I came at last in sight of the village, I slowed down instinctively and began to reflect. After all, I was unknown there; I had just gone through a disagreeable trial in New York, and rural people were notoriously given to groundless suspicion. I had had enough of the law and of arrests without sufficient evidence. The wisest thing would be to drop a hint or two before the landlord and judge by his demeanor whether to proceed.

"I found him sitting where I had left him, smoking, in his shirt-sleeves, with his hat on.

"'Well,' he said slowly, 'I didn't know where the gosh-blamed blazes you had got to. Been to see the folks?'

"I told him I had been taking a walk. I went on to mention casually the fork in the road, the hill, and the plateau.

"'And who lives in that house,' I asked with a good show of indifference, 'on top of the hill?'

"He stared.

"'House? There ain't no house up there,' he said positively. 'Old Joe Snedeker, who owns the land, says he's going to build a house up there for his son to live in when he gets married; but he ain't begun yet, and some folks reckon he never will.'

"'I feel sure I saw a house,' I protested feebly. But I was thinking—no heat in the fire, no substance in the body. I had not the courage to dispute.

"The landlord looked at me not unkindly. 'You seem sort of sick,' he remarked. 'Guess you been doin' too much down in the city. What you want is to go to bed.'"

The man from Fall River paused, and for a moment we sat silent, listening to the pant of the machinery, the thrumming of the wind in the wire stays, and the lash of the sea. Some voices were singing on the deck below. I considered him with the shade of contemptuous superiority we feel, as a rule, toward those who tell us their dreams or what some fortune-teller has predicted.

"Hallucinations," I said at last, with reassuring indulgence. "Trick of the vision, toxic ophthalmia. After the long strain of your trial your nerves were shattered."

"That's what I thought myself," he replied shortly, "especially after I had been out to the plateau the next morning and saw no sign that a house had ever stood there."

"And no corpse at the bridge?" I said, and laughed.

"And no corpse at the bridge."

He tried to get a light for another cigar. This took him some little time, and when at last he managed it, he got out of his chair and stood looking down at me.

"Now listen here. I told you that the thing happened several years ago. I'd got almost to forget it; if you can only persuade yourself that a thing is a freak of imagination, it pretty soon gets dim inside your head. Delusions have no staying power once it is realized that they are delusions. Whenever it did come back to me I used to think how near I had once been to going out of my mind. That was all.

"Well, last year I went up to that village again from Boston. I went to the same hotel and found the same landlord. He remembered me at once as 'The feller who come up from the city and thought he see a house. I believe you had the jimjams,' he said.

"We laughed, and the landlord spat.

"'There's been a house there since, though.'

"'Has there?'

"'Why, yes; an' it ha' been as well if there never had been. Old man Snedeker built it for his son, a fine big house with a piazza on two sides. The son, young Joe, got courting Mamie Elting from here around. She'd gone down to work in a store somewhere in Connecticut—darned if I can remember where. New Haven or Danbury, maybe. Well, sir, she used to get carrying on with another young feller 'bout here, Jim Travers, and Jim was sure wild about her; used to save up his quarters to go down State to see her. But she turned him down in the end, and married Joe; I guess because Joe had the house, and the old man's money to expect. Well, poor Jim must ha' gone plumb crazy. What do you think he did? The very first night the new-wed pair spent in that house he burned it down. Burned the two of them in their bed, and he was as nice and quiet a feller as you want to see. He may ha' been full of whisky at the time.'

"'No, he wasn't,' I said.

"The landlord looked surprised.

"'I guess you've heard some about it?'

"'No; go on.'

"'Yes, sir, he burned them in their bed. And then what do you think he did? He hung himself at the little bridge half a mile below. Do you remember where the road divides? Well, it was there. I saw his body hanging there myself the next morning. The toes of his boots were just touching the water.'"

Cara

Georgia Wood Pangborn

It was when Martha was four and a half and Tommy three, that I first began to hear them talking about "Cara." That was a very busy year; my maids were troublesome and there were other anxieties, so I was unable to watch my children as I had supposed I always should. If any one had told me when they were at the creeping and staggering stage that by the time they were running I should let days go by without knowing what their minds were doing! Probably all mothers go through this surprise sooner or later.

At first I thought they had named one of their dolls "Cara." Then, as they still used the word when no dolls were about, I finally bent from my grown-up concerns to ask what it meant. They answered, readily enough, that she was their sister. Remembering the highly colored and solid imaginings of my own childhood, I took the announcement without great surprise, and forgot about it until one night when Martha insisted on having an extra pillow in her crib. As Martha was already somewhat of a crowd for her crib, this seemed rather a pity, but when I took away the pillow she turned belligerent, after her own singular methods.

"I'll *frown* at you," said she, and did so forthwith.

"But tell me why you want it, dear?" I entreated. Such strange things they think of every minute!

"*You* know!" she said, with a naughty thrust of her foot, an airy kick at me through the bars.

"But I don't know, dear," I wearily insisted. She wriggled away, stuck her fingers in her mouth, and said with a sidelong shadow of a smile, very low, "Cara!"

"Oh—the little sister?"

She nodded. So at that, of course, there was nothing for it but to restore the pillow. And there had to be a toy under that pillow as well as under Martha's. When I went in after she was asleep her arm was cuddled over the pillow exactly as if it lay about a child's neck. After this I watched their "Cara" play a little, as I had time, and was amazed at the roots it had struck in their fancy, and at the vivid flowering of it.

Once I asked, doubtfully, whether they didn't mean Clara instead of Cara, but they were very emphatic about that. Cara, no other, was the name, and Cara it stayed.

Of course, one gets used to having invisible creatures about whenever children play, yet I confess that to see Martha coming down-stairs, one hand out as though grasping another child's hand, and talking, talking, talking to the little invisibility, it seemed carrying it rather far, and I wondered whether it were really wholesome, and if, after all, I ought to send them to a kindergarten. Yet they seemed so happy. There was never any quarreling in the "Cara" play, and before it began—well, I *had* been worried. I suppose it's always so when one child is just enough older and stronger than the other to hurt without meaning it.

Tommy was even more ingenuously brazen in his claims for Cara than Martha. She would never have done anything so inartistic as an assertion of his that Cara had made the circles with arms and legs over which I had seen him toiling. When he asked me, holding up the sheet, "Doesn't Cara make nice pictures?" Martha said, with contemptuous iconoclasm, "You made those yourself," whereat he sunk into puzzled silence, and turning his fat little back toward me, lifted his elbows, as a sign that he wanted to be taken into my lap and be comforted. At that elevation he drew me an engine, and successfully put Cara from his mind. In fact, he never seemed to understand her so well as Martha did, or to master the delicate rules of the game. Perhaps it was a masculine clumsiness and directness applied to a situation calling for endless feminine *finesse*. It seemed to be really Martha's game. I made many concessions: the extra pillow in the crib became a fixture, a third box of toys was added to the nursery and filled by contributions from Martha's and Tommy's, but at last I rebelled, on the day when they demanded that a new high-chair be purchased for Cara, so that she might sit with them at the table. They had a very poor opinion of the substitute which I offered of a dictionary in a grown-up chair, but when I had made it clear that Cara could expect nothing better, Martha sweetly abdicated her own chair and sat upon the dictionary.

"It's politer," she said, "because she's newer than I am."

But though they made no further reference to it, I fancy that either the refusal of their request, or—alas!—the manner of its refusal, had dampened their joy in the game; as if my lack of belief were a cold wind blowing through the airy fabric of their dream. At any rate, after this they repressed all mention of Cara when I was about, until, if I had not heard them talking about her, I should have thought her put by with other forgotten plays.

She had appeared on Christmas week along with the toys. When spring came she was still about the place, helping the babies to keep my borders quite free of crocusses and jonquils.

On the very day that Tommy was taken sick I saw—the three of them, I started to say—I saw Tommy and Martha running over the short spring grass, their arms stretched out toward each other as if each held the hand of a third child who ran between them. The pretense was wonderful; the way they turned their faces, laughing, not at each other, but at her.

Then came Tommy's sickness. We sent Martha to her grandmother's. There wasn't so very much to be done for him. I couldn't bear to have any one else take care of him. They kept telling me he would be better off with a trained nurse, but I didn't believe it. *No!* Until—after several nights—when I knew I was giving out, I began to be afraid I might make mistakes.

It was on the fifth night that I cried. That was after the nurse came. So I went away and cried all I needed to.

I must have fallen asleep so, for I thought that Martha was in the room; that she touched my wet cheek with the tip of her finger, curiously, as if to see what made it so. Then I remembered that Martha was at her grandmother's, and woke. No child was in the room, yet in the instant of my eyelids lifting (or was it before they lifted?) I had surely seen a little face—not Martha's! A surprised, lovely little face, sweet, grave;—and a tiny, upraised finger glistened with the wetness from my eyes.

My first thought was of shame that I had been crying in the presence of a little child. That is something one should never, never do, no matter what the pain! And then I realized with relief that it had only been a dream. What else? And yet . . .

I was singularly calm and rested; reassured about Tommy without any reason that I knew for being so; and yet, though I did not dare acknowledge it to myself, I did know the reason, trembling at its little worth. For though there remained no more of the dream than the half-seen face of a strange child, and the flower-like touch of its hand, I knew that there had been more to it than that. What I was able to remember was only the dear conclusion of some wonderful thing that had gone before. And the touch upon my cheek persisted so! The dream of something felt is rare. Dreams are chiefly made up of vague reminiscences of sight and hearing, but this memory of the investigating little finger was as real as the stains of my dried tears.

I suppose mothers have been comforted by dreams since brains began to be human at all. Perhaps before—who knows? Who knows anything at all? Not scientific men with microscopes, nor magicians, nor the founders of great philosophies. No. There is just one little path that really leads between the living and the dead. Dreams walk there, and sometimes—not dreams.

If the learned men ever begin to question the mothers upon this subject, and the mothers are able to answer intelligibly, something of value will turn up, I'm sure, in the way of "data." For in time, I suppose, they will call them "data"—these matters now known only to mothers and those to whom the path leads with such dear secrecy—no more than where a child's feet have pressed down the meadow-grass on its way to the woods. But mothers are oddly reticent upon these matters. There is a precedent. "And she hid these things in her heart."

At Tommy's door the sleepy nurse, with that fine, ironic edge upon her good-nature which meets over-anxious mothers at every turn of their anguished journey through the small, terrible years, told me, yawning, that my son's temperature was normal, and as I stood dumb and waiting, irritating her, no doubt, by the same look in my eyes that you can see any day in those of a cat or dog mother, she went on impressively: "And his pulse—*and* his respiration. He's perfectly all right, and he's a dear. I don't wonder you're crazy about him."

She went to her room, wiping her eyes, while I took my place as day nurse.

The children's pet play-place that spring was in the thick lilac hedges bordering the farther side of the curving drive that led up from the street. They were old bushes, making even at their base a six-foot-wide jungle within which were spaces too small for a grown-up's entrance; but the children moved about in it easily, even making small clearings and bowers by pressing down the young growth, and hovered there with their toys, mysteriously, like birds upon the nest. I looked in upon them occasionally, but with an awkward and intrusive feeling, for the most part contenting myself with the near exile of my window, whence I could follow in a clumsy way the swift veering of their fancy, and watch like any jungle creature when its young are at play. For there is something feral about even a human mother, something dangerous that has never answered to the taming forces of civilization. Old Puss, the other day, flung herself with valiant hopelessness into the jaws of a bull-dog, and afterward we found her kitten untouched but for a splash of its mother's blood upon its white fur. Curious instinct! I don't know just how the philosophers of the microscope account for it—but Puss and I, we understand!

So as I sat at the window with my embroidery not much escaped me. And yet I continually felt that there was something in their play that was strange, as if, when my eyes were wholly upon my work, I half saw something among the bushes that did not appear when leaned back and stared with full attention. But I realized that I had not yet recovered fully from Tommy's illness. Those things drain you of blood and of years and leave a strangeness. He was recovering finely, but I still felt the need of rest.

We had received word that an old school friend of mine would visit us hurriedly on her way to a long stay abroad. I pondered this with a kind of terror, looking at my own children with a feeling almost of guilt. Almost I wondered whether she could have forgotten, in the confusion of her own enormous trouble, that I had children—that my Martha was of the same age her own little girl had been. Examining my own endurance shudderingly, I seemed to see that in her place I should flee from children's voices as from arrows; then, remembering nature's processes, I considered that perhaps there might be some anodyne of which I was ignorant, some merciful dulling of the senses. For women are always being surprised by themselves, by some store of strength, just when they think they are failing, some lightning knowledge, some unsuspected capacity. So I waited, dreading and wondering.

My husband was to meet her at the station. The odor of the lilacs was almost overpowering. It was their best day. But I dropped my sewing and clenched my hands while I felt the carriage coming nearer through the village street, and the children, among the lilacs, grew wilder and wilder, pulling down the flowers in wanton heaps and throwing them about with frantic laughter. I was just condemning myself bitterly for not having sent them away for the day when the carriage turned into the drive.

It stopped suddenly opposite where the children were at play, and I saw her get out—so quickly that Henry could not help her—run toward them with her arms out—then stop short, her hands clasped to her heart. I was afraid that she might frighten them in some way. That was my first thought—not for her. And, weak as I was, I ran out.

Henry, scared and wretched, was looking at me over her head. Then she turned toward me, and in her pitiful, careless black (she who had used to be so gay in color and expression) her face was as if dead, only or the eyes; they were terrible and burning.

"What child was that playing with yours?" she asked.

She spoke at first in a whisper, as though afraid some one might overhear. Then, as I hesitated, she caught me by the arm, crying out the question in a dreadful way: "*What* child? She ran away! Where did she go?"

I put my arm about her. "Hush!" I said. "You mustn't frighten the babies. There wasn't any one with them. I've been watching them all the afternoon; they've been playing just with each other." I turned to Martha. "There wasn't anybody with you and Tommy, was there, dear?" I asked.

But the unsatisfactory little thin only ducked her head into my gown and looked up sidewise at my poor friend with a funny, confidential smile, as though in some odd way the had an understanding in common. The children seemed to have no perception whatever of any tragedy.

Tommy stood with his thin little legs apart, his hands behind him, and his head judicially on one side. Plainly, he approved of her.

She knelt at his baby feet. "Who was it?" she pleaded, and she got hold of her voice so that it was as soft as if she were speaking to her own child. "Who was that with you, dear?"

And he piped up—that clear, thrilly little voice—"Jes' on'y Cara."

She rose to her feet then, crushing her arms over her breast as women do when they are feeling the emptiness where once there was so much. Her face! She seemed to be looking through—beyond—and the terribleness fell away like a mask.

"Cara!" she whispered, "Beloved!" Then she fell, stretched out right at my children's feet.

They weren't frightened. They just went back to their jungle and calmly watched us while we got her to the house. I heard Martha say, "That's Cara's mother," as they began to be busy with the lilacs again. What did they know? What *did* they know?

They never spoke of Cara again in their play. I kept listening and expecting. Weeks afterward I screwed up my courage to a question, but was met by a sweet, blank stare. Tommy said nothing at all, but met my eyes very steadily. But Martha, after what seemed an obliging effort to remember, patronizingly explained that they hadn't played *that* for ever so long. They were building fairy cities now, and although much, very much, had been accomplished, there was still so much to do that they wouldn't be able to think of anything else for a long time—maybe a million years.

My friend made a slow convalescence with us that summer instead of keeping on with that wild flight from her sorrow. She believed that she had seen. But it was all so inchoate—such a jumble of children's pretense mixed inextricably with what we tremblingly believed we had seen for ourselves. We did not dare accept it—yet we did!

We agreed that they might have chanced upon her child's quaint pet name in the course of their constant manufacture of queer words. Then, too, there was the possibility that the third in the lilac-bush that day had, after all, been a neighbor's child: some little creature that I should not have cared to have jostling unsanitary elbows against my own children's protected cleanliness. Tommy's clear-eyed truthfulness—"Jes' on'y Cara," precluded that. Of course, too, the children were perfectly able to run about so fast that only a practised eye could be sure whether there were three or two of them. But neither of us convinced herself or the other by these explanations. We went through them for form's sake and out of respect to the logic in which we had been trained. *She* had seen—as briefly as by lightning, but as clearly—that which she had seen. And I had had my dream.

The Clock

William Fryer Harvey

I LIKED YOUR DESCRIPTION OF THE PEOPLE AT THE PENSION. I CAN SEE JUST THE PICTURE of the rather sinister Miss Cornelius, with her toupee and clinking bangles. I don't wonder you felt frightened that night when you found her sleep-walking in the corridor. But after all, why shouldn't she sleep-walk? As to the movements of the furniture in the lounge on the Sunday, you are, I suppose, in an earthquake zone, though an earthquake seems too big an explanation for the ringing of that little handbell on the mantelpiece. It's rather as if our parlourmaid—another new one!—were to call a stray elephant to account for the teapot we found broke yesterday. You have at least escaped the eternal problem of the maids in Italy.

Yes, my dear, I most certainly believe you. I have never had experiences quite like yours, but your mention of Miss Cornelius has reminded me of something rather similar that happened nearly twenty years ago, soon after I left school. I was staying with my aunt in Hempstead. You remember her, I expect; or, if not her, the poodle, Monsieur, that she used to make perform such pathetic tricks. There was another guest, whom I never met before, a Mrs. Caleb. She lived in Lewes and had been staying with my aunt for about a fortnight, recuperating after a series of domestic upheavals, which had culminated in her two servants leaving her at an hour's notice, without any reason, according to Mrs. Caleb; but I wondered. I had never seen the maids; I had seen Mrs. Caleb and, frankly, I disliked her. She left the same sort of impression on me as I gather your secretive Miss Cornelius leaves on you—something queer and secretive; underground, if you can use the expression, rather than underhand. And I could feel in my body that she did not like me.

It was summer. Joan Denton—you remember her; her husband was killed in Gallipoli—had suggested that I should go down to spend the day with her. Her people had rented a little cottage some three miles out of Lewes. We arranged a day. It was gloriously fine for a wonder, and I had planned to leave that stuffy old Hampstead house before the old ladies were astir. But Mrs. Caleb waylaid me in the hall, just as I was going out.

"I wonder," she said, "I wonder if you could do me a small favour. If you do have any time to spare in Lewes—only if you do—would you be so kind as to call at my house? I left a little traveling-clock there in the hurry of the parting. If it's not in the drawing-room, it will be in my bedroom or in one of the maid's bedrooms. I know I lent it to the cook, who was a poor riser, but I can't remember if she returned it. Would it be too much to ask? The house has been locked up for twelve days, but everything is in order. I have the keys here; the large one is for the garden gate, the small one for the front door."

I could only accept, and she proceeded to tell me how I could find Ash Grove House.

"You will feel quite like a burglar," she said. "But mind, it's only if you have time to spare."

As a matter of fact I found myself glad of any excuse to kill time. Poor old Joan had been taken suddenly ill in the night—they feared appendicitis—and though her people were very kind and asked me to stay to lunch, I could see that I should only be in the way, and made Mrs. Caleb's commission an excuse for an early departure.

I found Ash Grove without difficulty. It was a medium-sized red-brick house, standing by itself in a high-walled garden that bounded a narrow lane. A flagged path led from the gate to the front door, in front of which grew, not an ash, but a monkey-puzzle, that must have made the room unnecessarily gloomy. The side door, as I expected, was locked. The dining room and drawing-room lay on either side of the hall and, as the windows of both were shuttered, I left the hall door open, and in the dim light looked around hurriedly for the clock, which, from what Mrs. Caleb had said, I hardly expected to find in either of the downstairs rooms: It was neither on the table nor mantelpiece. The rest of the furniture was carefully covered over with white dust-sheets. Then I went upstairs. But before doing so, I closed the front door. I did in fact feel rather like a burglar, and I thought that if any one did happen to see the front door open, I might have difficulty in explaining things. Happily the upstairs windows were not shuttered. I made a hurried search of the principal bedrooms. They had been left in apple-pie order; nothing was out of place; but there was no sign of Mrs. Caleb's clock. The impression the house gave me—you know the sense of personality that a house conveys—was neither pleasing nor displeasing, but it was stuffy, stuffy from the absence of fresh air, with an additional stuffiness added, that seemed to come from the hangings and quilts and antimacassars. The corridor, on to which the bedrooms I had examined opened, communicated with a smaller wing, an older part of the house, I imagined, which contained a box-room and the maids' sleeping quarters. The last door I unlocked—(I should say that the doors of all the rooms were locked, and relocked by me after I had glanced inside them)—contained the object of my search. Mrs. Caleb's travelling-clock was on the mantelpiece, ticking away merrily.

That was how I thought of it at first. And then for the first time I realized that there was something wrong. The clock had no business to be ticking. The house had been shut up for twelve days. No one had come in to air it or to light fires. I remembered how Mrs. Caleb had told my aunt that if she left the keys with a neighbour, she was never sure who might get hold of them. And yet the clock was going. I wondered if some vibration had set the mechanism in motion, and pulled out my watch to see the time. It was five minutes to one. The clock on the mantelpiece said four minutes to the hour. Then, without quite knowing why, I shut the door on the landing, locked myself in, and again looked around the room. Nothing was out of place. The only thing that might have called for remark was that there appeared to be a slight indentation on the pillow and the bed; but the mattress was a feather mattress, and you know how difficult it is to make them perfectly smooth. You won't need to be told that I gave a hurried glance under the bed—do you remember your supposed burglar in Number Six at St. Ursula's—and then, and much more reluctantly, opened the doors of two horribly capacious cupboards, both happily empty, except for a framed text with its face to the wall. By this time I really was frightened. The clock went ticking on. I had a horrible feeling that an alarm might go off at any moment, and the thought of being in that empty house was almost too much for me. However, I made an attempt to pull myself together. It might after all be a fourteen-day clock. If it were, then it would be almost run down. I could roughly find out how long the clock had been going by winding it up. I hesitated to put the matter to the test; but the uncertainty was too much for me. I took it out of its case and began to wind. I had scarcely turned the winding screw twice when it stopped. The clock clearly was not running down; the hands had been set in motion probably only an hour or two before. I felt cold and faint, going to the window, threw up the sash, letting in the sweet, live air of the garden. I knew now that the house was queer, horribly queer. Could someone be living in the house? Was someone else in the house now? I thought that I had been in all the rooms, but had I? I had only just opened the bath-room door, and I had certainly not opened any cupboards, except those in the room in which I was. Then, as I stood by an open window, wondering what I should do next and feeling that I just couldn't go down that corridor into the darkened hall to fumble the latch at the front door with I don't know what behind me,

I heard a noise. It was very faint at first, and seemed to be coming from the stairs. It was a curious noise—not the noise of anyone climbing up the stairs, but—you will laugh if this letter reaches you by a morning post—of something hopping up the stairs, like a very big bird would hop. I heard it on the landing; it stopped. Then there was a curious scratching noise against one of the bedroom doors, the sort of noise you can make with the nail of your little finger scratching polished wood. Whatever it was, was coming slowly down the corridor, scratching at the doors as it went. I could stand it no longer. Nightmare pictures of locked doors opening filled my brain. I took up the clock, wrapped it in my mackintosh, and dropped it out of the window on to a flower-bed. Then I managed to crawl out of the window and, getting a grip on the sill, "successfully negotiated," as the journalists would say, "a twelve-foot drop." So much for our abused gym at St. Ursula's. Picking up the mackintosh, I ran round to the front door and locked it. Then I felt I could breathe, but not until I was on the far side of the gate in the garden wall did I feel I was safe.

Then I remembered that the bedroom window was open. What was I to do? Wild horses wouldn't have dragged me into the house again unaccompanied. I made up my mind to go to the police-station and tell them everything. I should be laughed at, of course, and they might easily refuse to believe my story of Mrs. Caleb's commission. I had actually begun to walk down the lane in the direction of the town, when I chanced to look back at the house. The window that I had left open was shut.

No, my dear, I didn't see any face or anything dreadful like that. . . and, of course, it may have shut by itself. It was an ordinary sash-window, and you know they are often difficult to keep open.

And the rest? Why, there's really nothing more to tell. I didn't even see Mrs. Caleb again. She had some sort of fainting fit just before lunch-time, my aunt informed me on my return, and had to go to bed. Next morning I traveled down to Cornwall to join mother and the children. I thought I had forgotten all about it, but when three years later Uncle Charles suggested giving me the traveling-clock for a twenty-first birthday present, I was foolish enough to prefer the alternative that he offered, a collected edition of the works of Thomas Carlyle.

The Closed Window

A. C. Benson

The Tower of Nort stood in a deep angle of the downs; formerly an old road led over the hill, but it is now a green track covered with turf; the later highway choosing rather to cross a low saddle of the ridge, for the sake of the beasts of burden. The tower, originally built to guard the great road, was a plain, strong, thick-walled fortress. To the tower had been added a plain and seemly house, where the young Sir Mark de Nort lived very easily and plentifully. To the south stretched the great wood of Nort, but the Tower stood high on an elbow of the down, sheltered from the north by the great green hills. The villagers had an odd ugly name for the Tower, which they called the Tower of Fear; but the name was falling into disuse, and was only spoken, and that heedlessly, by ancient men, because Sir Mark was vexed to hear it so called. Sir Mark was not yet thirty, and had begun to say that he must marry a wife; but he seemed in no great haste to do so, and loved his easy, lonely life, with plenty of hunting and hawking on the down. With him lived his cousin and heir, Roland Ellice, a heedless good-tempered man, a few years older than Sir Mark; he had come on a visit to Sir Mark, when he first took possession of the Tower; and there had seemed no reason why he should go away; the two suited each other; Sir Mark was sparing of speech, fond of books and of rhymes. Roland was different, loving ease and wine and talk, and finding in Mark a good listener. Mark loved his cousin, and thought it praiseworthy of him to stay and help to cheer so sequestered a house, since there were few neighbours within reach.

And yet Mark was not wholly content with his easy life; there were many days when he asked himself why he should go thus quietly on, day by day, like a stalled ox; still, there appeared no reason why he should do otherwise; there were but few folk on his land, and they were content; yet he sometimes envied them their bondage and their round of daily duties. The only place where he could else have been was with the army, or even with the Court; but Sir Mark was no soldier, and even less of a courtier; he hated tedious gaiety, and it was a time of peace. So because he loved solitude and quiet he lived at home, and sometimes thought himself but half a man; yet was he happy after a sort, but for a kind of little hunger of the heart.

What gave the Tower so dark a name was the memory of old Sir James de Nort, Mark's grandfather, an evil and secret man, who had dwelt at Nort under some strange shadow; he had driven his son from his doors, and lived at the end of his life with his books and his own close thoughts, spying upon the stars and tracing strange figures in books; since his death the old room in the turret top, where he came by his end in a dreadful way, had been closed; it was entered by a turret-door, with a flight of steps from the chamber below. It had four windows, one to each of the winds; but the window which looked upon the down was fastened up, and secured with a great shutter of oak.

One day of heavy rain, Roland, being wearied of doing nothing, and vexed because Mark sat so still in a great chair, reading in a book, said to his cousin at last that he must go and visit the old room, in which he had never set foot. Mark closed his book, and smiling indulgently at Roland's restlessness, rose, stretching himself, and got the key; and together they went up the turret stairs. The key groaned loudly in the lock, and, when the door was thrown back, there appeared a high faded room, with a timbered roof, and with a close, dull smell. Round the walls were presses, with the doors fast; a large oak table, with a chair beside it, stood in the middle. The walls were otherwise bare and rough; the spiders had spun busily over the windows and in the angles. Roland was full of questions, and Mark told him all he had heard of old Sir James and his silent ways, but said that he knew nothing of the disgrace that had seemed to envelop him, or of the reasons why he had so evil a name. Roland said that he thought it a shame that so fair a room should lie so nastily, and pulled one of the casements open, when a sharp gust broke into the room, with so angry a burst of rain, that he closed it again in haste; little by little, as they talked, a shadow began to fall upon their spirits, till Roland declared that there was still a blight upon the place; and Mark told him of the death of old Sir James, who had been found after a day of silence, when he had not set foot outside his chamber, lying on the floor of the room, strangely bedabbled with wet and mud, as though he had come off a difficult journey, speechless, and with a look of anguish on his face; and that he had died soon after they had found him, muttering words that no one understood. Then the two young men drew near to the closed window; the shutters were tightly barred, and across the panels was scrawled in red, in an uncertain hand, the words CLAUDIT ET NEMO APERIT, which Mark explained was the Latin for the text, *He shutteth and none openeth*. And then Mark said that the story went that it was ill for the man that opened the window, and that shut it should remain, for him. But Roland girded at him for his want of curiosity, and had laid a hand upon the bar as though to open it, but Mark forbade him urgently. "Nay," said he, "let it remain so—we must not meddle with the will of the dead!" and as he said the word, there came so furious a gust upon the windows that it seemed as though some stormy thing would beat them open; so they left the room together, and presently descending, found the sun struggling through the rain.

But both Mark and Roland were sad and silent all that day; for though they spake not of it, there was a desire in their minds to open the closed window, and to see what would befall; in Roland's mind it was like the desire of a child to peep into what is forbidden; but in Mark's mind a sort of shame to be so bound by an old and weak tale of superstition.

Now it seemed to Mark, for many days, that the visit to the turret-room had brought a kind of shadow down between them. Roland was peevish and ill-at-ease; and ever the longing grew upon Mark, so strongly that it seemed to him that something drew him to the room, some beckoning of a hand or calling of a voice.

Now one bright and sunshiny morning it happened that Mark was left alone within the house. Roland had ridden out early, not saying where he was bound. And Mark sat, more listlessly than was his wont, and played with the ears of his great dog, that sat with his head upon his master's knee, looking at him with liquid eyes, and doubtless wondering why Mark went not abroad.

Suddenly Sir Mark's eye fell upon the key of the upper room, which lay on the window-ledge where he had thrown it; and the desire to go up and pluck the heart from the little mystery came upon him with a strength that he could not resist; he rose twice and took up the key, and fingering it doubtfully, laid it down again; then suddenly he took it up, and went swiftly into the turret-stair, and up, turning, turning, till his head was dizzy with the bright peeps of the world through the loophole windows. Now all was green, where a window gave on the down; and now it was all clear air and sun, the warm breeze coming pleasantly into the cold stairway; presently Mark heard the pattering of feet on the stair below, and knew that the old hound had determined to follow him; and he waited a moment at the door, half pleased, in his strange mood, to have the company of a living thing. So when the dog was at his side, he stayed no longer, but opened the door and stepped within the room.

The room, for all its faded look, had a strange air about it, and though he could not say why, Mark felt that he was surely expected. He did not hesitate, but walked to the shutter and considered it for a moment; he heard a sound behind him. It was the old hound who sat with his head aloft, sniffing the air uneasily; Mark called him and held out his hand, but the hound would not move; he wagged his tail as though to acknowledge that he was called, and then he returned to his uneasy quest. Mark watched him for a moment, and saw that the old dog had made up his mind that all was not well in the room, for he lay down, gathering his legs under him, on the threshold, and watched his master with frightened eyes, quivering visibly. Mark, no lighter of heart, and in a kind of fearful haste, pulled the great staple off the shutter and set it on the ground, and then wrenched the shutters back; the space revealed was largely filled by old and dusty webs of spiders, which Mark lightly tore down, using the staple of the shutters to do this; it was with a strange shock of surprise that he saw that the window was dark, or nearly so; it seemed as though there were some further obstacle outside; yet Mark knew that from below the leaded panes of the window were visible. He drew back for a moment, but, unable to restrain his curiosity, wrenched the rusted casement open. But still all was dark without; and there came in a gust of icy wind from outside; it was as though something had passed him swiftly, and he heard the old hound utter a strangled howl; then turning, he saw him spring to his feet with his hair bristling and his teeth bare, and next moment the dog turned and leapt out of the room.

Mark, left alone, tried to curb a tide of horror that swept through his veins; he looked round at the room, flooded with the southerly sunlight, and then he turned again to the dark window, and putting a strong constraint upon himself, leaned out, and saw a thing which bewildered him so strangely that he thought for a moment his senses had deserted him. He looked out on a lonely dim hillside, covered with rocks and stones; the hill came up close to the window, so that he could have jumped down upon it, the wall below seeming to be built into the rocks. It was all dark and silent, like a clouded night, with a faint light coming from whence he could not see. The hill sloped away very steeply from the tower, and he seemed to see a plain beyond, where at the same time he knew that the down ought to lie. In the plain there was a light, like the firelit window of a house; a little below him some shape like a crouching man seemed to run and slip among the stones, as though suddenly surprised, and seeking to escape. Side by side with a deadly fear which began to invade his heart, came an uncontrollable desire to leap down among the rocks; and then it seemed to him that the figure below stood upright, and began to beckon him. There came over him a sense that he was in deadly peril; and, like a man on the edge of a precipice, who has just enough will left to try to escape, he drew himself by main force away from the window, closed it, put the shutters back, replaced the staple, and, his limbs all trembling, crept out of the room, feeling along the walls like a palsied man. He locked the door, and then, his terror overpowering him, he fled down the turret-stairs. Hardly thinking what he did, he came out on the court, and going to the great well that stood in the centre of the yard, he went to it and flung the key down, hearing it clink on the sides as it fell. Even then he dared not re-enter the house, but glanced up and down, gazing about him, while the cloud of fear and horror by insensible degrees dispersed, leaving him weak and melancholy.

Presently Roland returned, full of talk, but broke off to ask if Mark were ill. Mark, with a kind of surliness, an unusual mood for him, denied it somewhat sharply. Roland raised his eyebrows, and said no more, but prattled on. Presently after a silence he said to Mark, "What did you do all the morning?" and it seemed to Mark as though this were accompanied with a spying look. An unreasonable anger seized him. "What does it matter to you what I did?" he said. "May not I do what I like in my own house?"

"Doubtless," said Roland, and sate silent with uplifted brows; then he hummed a tune, and presently went out.

They sate at dinner that evening with long silences, contrary to their wont, though Mark bestirred himself to ask questions. When they were left alone, Mark stretched out his hand to Roland, saying, "Roland, forgive me! I spoke to you this morning in a way of which I am ashamed; we have lived so long together—and yet we came nearer to quarelling to-day than we have ever done before; it was my fault."

Roland smiled, and held Mark's hand for a moment. "Oh, I had not given it another thought," he said; "The wonder is that you can bear to be with an idle fellow as you do." Then they talked for a while with the pleasant glow of friendliness that two god comrades feel when they have been reconciled. But late in the evening Roland said, "Was there any story, Mark, about your grandfather's leaving any treasure of money behind him?"

The question grated somewhat unpleasantly upon Mark's mood; but he controlled himself and said, "No, none that I know of—except that he found the estate rich and left it poor—and what he did with his revenues no one knows—you have better ask the old men of the village; they know more about the house than I do. But, Roland, forgive me once more if I say that I do not desire Sir James's name to be mentioned between us. I wish he had not entered this room; I do not know how to express it, but it seems to me as though we had troubled him, and—as though he had joined us. I think he was an evil man, close and evil. And there hangs in my mind a verse of Scripture, where Samuel said to the witch, 'Why hast thou disquieted me to bring me up?' Oh," he went on, "I do not know why I talk wildly thus"; for he saw that Roland was looking at him with astonishment, with parted lips; "but a shadow has fallen upon me, and there seems evil abroad."

From that day forward a heaviness lay on the spirit of Mark that could not be scattered. He felt, he said to himself, as though he had meddled light-heartedly with something far deeper and more dangerous than he had supposed—like a child that has aroused some evil beast that slept. He had dark dreams too. The figure that he had seen among the rocks seemed to peep and beckon him, with a mocking smile, over perilous places, where he followed unwilling. But the heavier he grew the lighter-hearted Roland became; he seemed to walk in some bright vision of his own, intent upon a large and gracious design.

One day he came into the hall in the morning, looking so radiant that Mark asked him half enviously what he had to make him so glad. "Glad," said Roland, "oh, I know it! Merry dreams, perhaps. What do you think of a good grave fellow who beckons me on with a brisk smile, and shows me places, wonderful places, under banks and in woodland pits, where riches lie piled together? I am sure that some good fortune is preparing for me, Mark—but you shall share it." Then Mark, seeing in his words a certain likeness, with a difference, to his own dark visions, pressed his lips together and sate looking stonily before him.

At last, one still evening of spring, when the air was intolerably languid and heavy for mankind, but full of sweet promises for trees and hidden peeping things, though a lurid redness of secret thunder had lain all day among the heavy clouds in the plain, the two dined together. Mark had walked alone that day, and had lain upon the turf of the down, fighting against a weariness that seemed to be poisoning the very springs of life within him. But Roland had been brisk and alert, coming and going upon some secret and busy errand, with a fragment of a song upon his lips, like a man preparing to set off for a far country, who is glad to be gone. In the evening, after they had dined, Roland had let his fancy rove in talk. "If we were rich," he said, "how we would transform this old place!"

"It is fair enough for me," said Mark heavily; and Roland had chidden him lightly for his sombre ways, and sketched new plans of life.

Mark, wearied and yet excited, with an intolerable heaviness of spirit, went early to bed, leaving Roland in the hall. After a short and broken sleep, he awoke, and lighting a candle, read idly and gloomily to pass the heavy hours. The house seemed full of strange noises that night. Once or twice came a scraping and a faint hammering in the wall; light footsteps seemed to pass in the turret—but the tower was always full of noises, and Mark heeded them not; at last he fell asleep again, to be suddenly awakened by a strange and desolate crying, that came he knew not whence, but seemed to wail upon the air. The old dog, who slept in Mark's room, heard it too; he was sitting up in a fearful expectancy. Mark rose in haste, and taking the candle, went into the passage that led to Roland's room. It was empty, but a light burned there and showed that the room had not been slept in. Full of a horrible fear, Mark returned, and went in hot haste up the turret steps, fear and anxiety struggling together in his mind. When he reached the top, he found the little door broken forcibly open, and a light within. He cast a haggard look round the room, and then the crying came again, this time very faint and desolate.

Mark cast a shuddering glance at the window; it was wide open and showed a horrible liquid blackness; round the bar in the centre that divided the casements, there was something knotted. He hastened to the window, and saw that it was a rope, which hung heavily. Leaning out he saw that something dangled from the rope below him—and then came the crying again out of the darkness, like the crying of a lost spirit.

He could see as in a bitter dream the outline of the hateful hillside; but there seemed to his disordered fancy to be a tumult of some kind below; pale lights moved about, and he saw a group of forms which scattered like a shoal of fish when he leaned out. He knew that he was looking upon a scene that no mortal eye ought to behold, and it seemed to him at the moment as though he was staring straight into hell.

The rope went down among the rocks and disappeared; but Mark clenched it firmly and using all his strength, which was great, drew it up hand over hand; as he drew it up he secured it in loops round the great oak table; he began to be afraid that his strength would not hold out, and once when he returned to the window after securing a loop, a great hooded thing like a bird flew noiselessly at the window and beat its wings.

Presently he saw that the form which dangled on the rope was clear of the rocks below; it had come up through them, as though they were but smoke; and then his task seemed to him more sore than ever. Inch by painful inch he drew it up, working fiercely and silently; his muscles were tense, and drops stood on his brow, and the veins hammered in his ears; his breath came and went in sharp sobs. At last the form was near enough for him to seize it; he grasped it by the middle and drew Roland, for it was Roland, over the window-sill. His head dangled and drooped from side to side; his face was dark with strangled blood and his limbs hung helpless. Mark drew his knife and cut the rope that was tied under his arms; the helpless limbs sank huddling on the floor; then Mark looked up; at the window a few feet from him was a face, more horrible than he had supposed a human face, if it was human indeed, could be. It was deadly white, and hatred, baffled rage, and a sort of devilish malignity glared from the white set eyes, and the drawn mouth. There was a rush from behind him; the old hound, who had crept up unawares into the room, with a fierce outcry of rage sprang on to the window-sill; Mark heard the scraping of his claws upon the stone. Then the hound leapt through the window, and in a moment there was the sound of a heavy fall outside. At the same instant the darkness seemed to lift and draw up like a cloud; a bank of blackness rose past the window, and left the dark outline of the down, with a sky sown with tranquil stars.

The cloud of fear and horror that hung over Mark lifted too; he felt in some dim way that his adversary was vanquished; he carried Roland down the stairs and laid him on his bed; he roused the household, who looked fearfully at him, and then his own strength failed; he sank upon the floor of his room, and the dark tide of unconsciousness closed over him.

Mark's return to health was slow. One who has looked into the Unknown finds it hard to believe again in the outward shows of life. His first conscious speech was to ask for his hound; they told him that the body of the dog had been found, horribly mangled as though by the teeth of some fierce animal, at the foot of the tower. The dog was buried in the garden, with a slab above him, on which are the words:—

EUGE SERVE BOE ET FIDELIS

A silly priest once said to Mark that it was not meet to write Scripture over the grave of a beast. But Mark said warily that an inscription was for those who read it, to make them humble, and not to increase the pride of what lay below.

When Mark could leave his bed, his first care was to send for builders, and the old tower of Nort was taken down, stone by stone, to the ground, and a fair chapel built on the site; in the wall there was a secret stairway, which led from the top chamber, and came out among the elder-bushes that grew below the tower, and here was found a coffer of gold, which paid for the church; because, until it was found, it was Mark's design to leave the place desolate. Mark is wedded since, and has his children about his knee; those who come to the house see a strange and wan man, who sits at Mark's board, and whom he uses very tenderly; sometimes this man is merry, and tells a long tale of his being beckoned and led by a tall and handsome person, smiling, down a hillside to fetch gold; though he can never remember the end of the matter; but about the springtime he is silent or mutters to himself: and this is Roland; his spirit seems shut up within him in some close cell, and Mark prays for his release, but till God call him, he treats him like a dear brother, and with the reverence due to one who has looked out on the other side of Death, and who may not say what his eyes beheld.

The Cold Embrace

Mary Elizabeth Braddon

He was a student—such things as happened to him, happen sometimes to students.

He was a German—such things as happened to him, happen sometimes to Germans.

He was young, handsome, studious, enthusiastic, metaphysical, reckless, unbelieving, heartless.

And being young, handsome, and eloquent, he was beloved.

He was an orphan, under the guardianship of his dead father's brother, his uncle Wilhelm, in whose house he had been brought up from a little child; and she who loved him was his cousin—his cousin Gertrude, whom he swore he loved in return.

Did he love her? Yes, when he first swore it. But it soon wore out—this passionate love; how threadbare and wretched a sentiment it grew to be at last in the selfish heart of the student! But in its first golden dawn, when he was only nineteen, and had just returned from the university, and they wandered together in the most romantic outskirts of the city, at rosy sunset, by holy moonlight, or bright and joyous morning, how beautiful a dream!

They keep it a secret from Wilhelm, as he has the father's ambition of a wealthy suitor for his only child—a cold and dreary vision beside the lover's dream.

So they are betrothed and standing side by side when the dying sun and the pale rising moon divide the heavens. He puts the betrothal ring upon her finger, the white and taper finger whose slender shape he knows so well. This ring is a peculiar one, a massive golden serpent, its tail in its mouth, the symbol of eternity; it had been his mother's, and he would know it amongst a thousand. If he were to become blind to-morrow, he could select it from amongst a thousand by the touch alone.

He places it on her finger, and they swear to be true to each other for ever and ever—through trouble and danger—in sorrow and change—in wealth or poverty. Her father would be won to consent to their union by-and-by, for they were now betrothed, and death alone could part them.

But the young student, the scoffer at revelation, yet the enthusiastic adorer of the mystical, asks—

"Can death part us? I would return to you from the grave, Gertrude. My soul would come back to be near my love. And you—you, if you died before me, the cold earth would not hold you from me; if you loved me, you would return, and again these fair arms would be clasped round my neck as they are now."

But she told him, with a holier light in her deep blue eyes than had ever shone in his—she told him, that the dead who die at peace with God are happy in heaven, and cannot return to the troubled earth; and that it is only the suicide—the lost wretch on whom sorrowful angels shut the door of Paradise—whose unholy spirit haunts the footsteps of the living.

The first year of their betrothal is passed; and she is alone; for he has gone to Italy, on a commission for some rich man, to copy a Raphael, or a Titian, or a Guido, in a gallery at Florence. He has gone to win fame, perhaps; but it is not the less bitter—he is gone!

Of course her father misses his young nephew, who has been as a son to him; and he thinks his daughter's sadness no more than a cousin should feel for a cousin's absence.

In the meantime, the weeks and months pass. The lover writes—often at first, then seldom—at last, not at all.

How many excuses she invents for him. How many times she goes to the distant little post-office, to which he is to address his letters. How many times she hopes, only to be disappointed. How many times she despairs, only to hope again.

But real despair comes at last, and will not be put off any more. The rich suitor appears on the scene, and her father is determined. She is to marry at once. The wedding-day is fixed—the fifteenth of June.

The date seems burnt into her brain.

The date, written in fire, dances for ever before her eyes.

The date, shrieked by the Furies, sounds continually in her ears.

But there is time yet—it is the middle of May—there is time for a letter to reach him at Florence; there is time for him to come to Brunswick, to take her away and marry her in spite of her father—in spite of the whole world.

But the days and weeks fly by, and he does not write—he does not come. This is, indeed, despair which usurps her heart, and will not be put away.

It is the fourteenth of June. For the last time to the little post-office; for the last time she asks the old question, and they give her for the last time he dreary answer "No! no letter."

For the last time—for to-morrow is the day appointed for her bridal. Her father will hear no entreaties; her rich suitor will not listen to her prayers. They will not be put off a day—an hour; to-night alone is hers—this night, which she may employ as she will.

She takes another path than that which leads home; she hurries through some by-streets of the city, out on to a lonely bridge, where he and she had stood so often in the sunset, watching the rose-coloured light glow, fade, and die upon the river.

He returns from Florence. He had received her letter. That letter, blotted with tears, entreating, despairing—he had received it, but he loved her no longer. A young Florentine, who had sat to him for a model, had bewitched his fancy—that fancy which with him stood in place of a heart—and Gertrude had been half forgotten. If she had a richer suitor, good! let her marry him; better for her, better far for himself. He had no wish to fetter himself with a wife. Had he not his art always?—his eternal bride, his unchanging mistress.

Thus he thought it wiser to delay his journey to Brunswick, so that he should arrive when the wedding was over—arrive in time to salute the bride!

And the vows—the mystical fancies—the belief in his return, even after death, to the embrace of his beloved? Oh, gone out of his life; melted away for ever, those foolish dreams of his boyhood!

So, on the fifteenth of June he enters Brunswick, by that very bridge on which she stood, the stars looking down on her, the night before. He strolls across the bridge and down by the water's edge, a great rough dog at his heels, and the smoke from his short meerschaum pipe curling in blue wreaths fantastically in the pure morning air. He has his sketch-book under his arm, and, attracted now and then by some object that catches his artist's eye, stops to draw. A few weeds and pebbles on the river's brink—a crag on the opposite shore—a group of pollard willows in the distance. When he has done, he admires his drawing, shuts his sketch-book, empties the ashes from his pipe, refills from his tobacco-pouch, sings the refrain of a gay drinking song, calls to his dog, smokes again, and walks on. Suddenly he opens his sketch-book again; this time that which attracts him is a group of figures—but what is it?

It is not a funeral, for there are no mourners.

It is not a funeral, but it is a corpse lying on a rude bier covered with an old sail, carried between two bearers.

It is not a funeral, for the bearers are fishermen—fishermen in their every-day garb.

About a hundred yards from him they rest their burden on a bank—one stands at the head of the bier, the other throws himself down at the foot of it.

And thus they form a perfect group; he walks back two or three paces, selects his point of sight, and begins to sketch a hurried outline. He has finished it before they move; he hears their voices, though he cannot hear their words, and wonders what they can be talking of. Presently he walks on, and joins them.

"You have a corpse there, my friends?" he says.

"Yes; a corpse washed ashore an hour ago."

"Drowned?"

"Yes, drowned;—a young girl, very handsome."

"Suicides are always handsome," he says; and then he stands for a little while idly smoking and meditating, looking at the sharp outline of the corpse and the stiff folds of the rough canvas covering.

Life is such a golden holiday to him—young, ambitious, clever—that it seems as though sorrow and death could have no part in his destiny.

At last he says, that as this poor suicide is so handsome, he should like to make a sketch of her.

He gives the fishermen some money, and they offer to remove the sailcloth that covers her features.

No; he will do it himself. He lifts the rough, coarse, wet canvas from her face. What face?

The face that shone on the dreams of his foolish boyhood. The face which once was the light of his uncle's home. His cousin Gertrude—his betrothed!

He sees, as in one glance, while he draws one breath, the rigid features—the marble arms—the hands crossed on the cold bosom; and, on the third finger of the left hand, the ring which had been his mother's—the golden serpent; the ring which, if he were to become blind, he could select from a thousand others by the touch alone.

But he is a genius and a metaphysician—grief, true grief, is not for such as he. His first thought is flight—flight anywhere out of that accursed city— anywhere far from the brink of that hideous river—anywhere away from memory, away from remorse—anywhere to forget.

* * * * *

He is miles on the road that leads away from Brunswick before he knows that he has walked a step.

It is only when his dog lies down panting at his feet, that he feels how exhausted he is himself, and sits down upon a bank to rest. How the landscape spins round and round before his dazzled eyes, while his morning's sketch of the two fishermen and the canvas-covered bier glares redly at him out of the twilight.

At last, after sitting a long time by the roadside, idly playing with his dog, idly smoking, idly lounging, looking as any insouciant light-hearted travelling student might look, yet all the while acting over that morning's scene in his burning brain a hundred times a minute,—at last he grows a little more composed, and tries presently to think of himself as he is, apart from his cousin's suicide. Apart from that, he was no worse off than he was yesterday. His genius was not gone; the money he had earned at Florence still lined his pocket-book; he was his own master, free to go whither he would.

And while he sits on the roadside, trying to separate himself from the scene of that morning—trying to put away the image of the corpse covered with the damp canvas sail—trying to think of what he should do next, where he should go, to be furthest away from Brunswick and remorse, the old Diligence comes rumbling and jingling along. He remembers it; it goes from Brunswick to Aix-la-Chapelle.

He whistles to his dog, shouts to the postillion to stop, and springs into the coupé.

During the whole evening, through the long night, though he does not once close his eyes, he never speaks a word; but when morning dawns, and the other passengers awake and begin to talk to each other, he joins in the conversation. He tells them that he is an artist, that he is going to Cologne and to Antwerp to copy the Rubens. He remembered afterwards that he talked and laughed boisterously, and that when he was talking and laughing loudest, a passenger, older and graver than the rest, opened the window near him, and told him to put his head out. He remembered the fresh air blowing in his face, the singing of the birds in his ears, and the flat fields and roadside reeling before his eyes. He remembered this, and then falling in a heap on the floor of the Diligence.

It is a fever that keeps him for six long weeks laid on a bed at an hotel in Aix-la-Chapelle.

He gets well, and, accompanied by his dog, start on foot for Cologne. By this time he is his former self once more. Again the blue smoke from his short meerschaum curls upwards in the morning air—again he sings some old university drinking song—again stops here and there, meditating and sketching.

He is happy, and has forgotten his cousin—and so, on to Cologne.

It is by the great Cathedral he is standing, with his dog at his side. It is night, the bells have just chimed the hour, and the clocks are striking eleven; the moonlight shines full upon the magnificent pile, over which the artist's eye wanders, absorbed in the beauty of form.

He is not thinking of his drowned cousin, for he has forgotten her and is happy.

Suddenly some one—something from behind him, puts two cold arms round his neck, and clasps its hands on his breast.

And yet there is no one behind him, for on the flags bathed in the broad moonlight there are only two shadows, his own and his dog's. He turns quickly round—there is no one—nothing to be seen in the broad square but himself and his dog; and though he feels, he cannot see the cold arms clasped round his neck.

It is not ghostly, this embrace, for it is palpable to the touch—it cannot be real, for it is impalpable to the sight.

He tries to throw off the cold caress. He clasps the hands in his own to tear them asunder, and to cast them off his neck. He can feel the long delicate finger cold and wet beneath his touch, and on the third finger of the left hand he can feel the ring which was his mother's—the golden serpent—the ring which he has always said he would know among a thousand by the touch alone. He knows it now!

His dead cousin's cold arms are round his neck—his dead cousin's wet hands are clasped upon his breast. He will die! He will go mad! "Up Leo!" he shouts. "Up, up, boy!" and the Newfoundland leaps to his shoulders—the dog's paws are on the dead hands, and the animal utters a terrific howl, and springs away from his master.

The student stands in the moonlight, the dead arms round his neck, and the dog at a little distance, moaning piteously.

Presently a watchman, alarmed by the howling of the dog, comes into the square to see what is wrong.

In a breath the cold arms are gone.

He takes the watchman home to the hotel with him and gives him money; in his gratitude he could have given that man half his little fortune.

Will it ever come to him again, this embrace of the dead?

He tries never to be alone; he makes a hundred acquaintances, and shares the chamber of another student. He starts up if he is left by himself in the public room at the inn where he is staying, and runs into the street. People notice his strange actions, and begin to think that he is mad.

But, in spite of all, he is alone once more, for one night the public room being empty for a moment, when on some idle pretence he strolls into the street, the street is empty too, and for the second time he feels the cold arms round his neck, and for the second time, when he calls his dog, the animal slinks away from him with a piteous howl.

After this he leaves Cologne, still travelling on foot—for economy now, as his money is getting low. He joins travelling hawkers, he walks side by side with labourers, he talks to every foot-passenger he falls in with, and tries from morning till night to get company on the road.

At night he sleeps by the fire in the kitchen of the inn at which he stops, but do what he will, he is often alone, and it is now an old thing for him to feel the cold arms around his neck.

Many months have passed since his cousin's death,—autumn, winter, early spring. His money is nearly gone, his health is utterly broken, he is the shadow of hi former self, and he is getting near Paris. He will reach that city at the time of the Carnival. To this he looks forward. In Paris, in Carnival time, he need never, surely, be alone, never feel that deadly caress; he might even recover his lost gaiety, his lost health, once more resume his profession, once more earn fame and money by his art.

How hard he tries to get over the distance that divides him from Paris, while day by day he grows weaker and weaker, and his step more slow and heavy.

But there is an end at last; the long and dreary roads are passed. This is Paris, which he enters for the first time—Paris, of which he has dreamed so much—Paris, whose million voices are to exorcise his phantom.

To him, to-night, Paris seems one vast chaos of lights, music, and confusion—lights which dance before his eyes and will not be still—music that rings in his ears and deafens him—confusion which makes his head whirl round and round.

But in spite of all, he finds the opera-house, where there is a masked ball. He has enough money left to buy a ticket of admission, and to hire a domino to throw over his shabby dress. It seems only a moment after his entering the gates of Paris, that he is in the very midst of the wild gaiety of the opera-house ball.

No more darkness, no more loneliness, but a mad crowd, shouting and dancing, and a lovely Débardeur hanging on his arm.

The boisterous gaiety he feels surely is his old light-heartedness come back. He hears the people round him talking of the outrageous conduct of some drunken student, and it is to him they point when they say this—to him, who has not moistened his lips since yesterday at noon—for even now he will not drink; though his lips are parched, and his throat burning, he cannot drink. His voice is thick and hoarse, and his utterance indistinct, but still this must be his old light-heartedness come back that makes him so wildly gay.

The little Débardeur is wearied out—her arm rests on his shoulder heavier than lead—the other dancers one by one drop off.

The lights in the chandeliers one by one die out.

The decorations look pale and shadowy in that dim light that is neither night nor day.

A faint glimmer from the dying lamps, a pale streak through the half-open shutters of cold grey light from the new-born day.

And by this light the bright-eyed Débardeur fades sadly. He looks her in the face. How the brightness of her eyes dies out. Again he looks her in the face. How white that face has grown. Again—and now it is the shadow of a face alone that looks in his.

Again—and they are gone—the bright eyes—the face—the shadow of the face. He is alone, alone in that vast saloon.

Alone, and in the terrible silence, he hears the echoes of his own footsteps in that dismal dance which has no music.

No music, but the beating of his heart against his breast. For the cold arms are round his neck—they whirl him round, they will not be flung off, or cast away; he can no more escape from their icy grasp than he can escape from death. He looks behind him—there is nothing but himself in the great empty ball; but he can feel—cold, deathlike, but oh, how palpable—the long slender fingers, and the ring which was his mother's.

He tries to shout, but he has no power in his burning throat. The silence of the place is only broken by the echoes of his own footsteps in the dance from which he cannot extricate himself. Who says he has no partner? The cold hands are clasped on his breast, and now he does not shun their caress. No! One more polka, if he drops down dead.

The lights are all out, and half-an-hour after, the *gendarmes* come in with a lantern to see that the house is empty; they are followed by a great dog that they have found seated howling on the steps of the theatre. Near the principal entrance they stumble over—

The body of a student, who has died from want of food, exhaustion, and the breaking of a bloodvessel.

Colonel Halifax's Ghost Story

Sabine Baring-Gould

I had just come back to England, after having been some years in India, and was looking forward to meet my friends, among whom there was none I was more anxious to see than Sir Francis Lynton. We had been at Eton together, and for the short time I had been at Oxford before entering the Army we had been at the same college. Then we had been parted. He came into the title and estates of the family in Yorkshire on the death of his grandfather—his father had predeceased—and I had been over a good part of the world. One visit, indeed, I had made him in his Yorkshire home, before leaving for India, of but a few days.

It will easily be imagined how pleasant it was, two or three days after my arrival in London, to receive a letter from Lynton saying he had just seen in the papers that I had arrived, and begging me to come down at once to Byfield, his place in Yorkshire.

"You are not to tell me," he said, "that you cannot come. I allow you a week in which to order and try on your clothes, to report yourself at the War Office, to pay your respects to the Duke, and to see your sister at Hampton Court; but after that I shall expect you. In fact, you are to come on Monday. I have a couple of horses which will just suit you; the carriage shall meet you at Packham, and all you have got to do is to put yourself in the train which leaves King's Cross at twelve o'clock."

Accordingly, on the day appointed I started; in due time reached Packham, losing much time on a detestable branch line, and there found the dogcart of Sir Francis awaiting me. I drove at once to Byfield.

The house I remembered. It was a low, gabled structure of no great size, with old-fashioned lattice windows, separated from the park, where were deer, by a charming terraced garden.

No sooner did the wheels crunch the gravel by the principal entrance, than, almost before the bell was rung, the porch door opened, and there stood Lynton himself, whom I had not seen for so many years, hardly altered, and with all the joy of welcome beaming in his face. Taking me by both hands, he drew me into the house, got rid of my hat and wraps, looked me all over, and then, in a breath, began to say how glad he was to see me, what a real delight it was to have got me at last under his roof, and what a good time we would have together, like the old days over again.

He had sent my luggage up to my room, which was ready for me, and he bade me make haste and dress for dinner.

So saying, he took me through a panelled hall up an oak staircase, and showed me my room, which, hurried as I was, I observed was hung with tapestry, and had a large fourpost bed, with velvet curtains, opposite the window.

They had gone into dinner when I came down, despite all the haste I made in dressing; but a place had been kept for me next Lady Lynton.

Besides my hosts, there were their two daughters, Colonel Lynton, a brother of Sir Francis, the chaplain, and some others whom I do not remember distinctly.

After dinner there was some music in the hall, and a game of whist in the drawing-room, and after the ladies had gone upstairs, Lynton and I retired to the smoking-room, where we sat up talking the best part of the night. I think it must have been near three when I retired. Once in bed, I slept so soundly that my servant's entrance the next morning failed to arouse me, and it was past nine when I awoke.

After breakfast and the disposal of the newspapers, Lynton retired to his letters, and I asked Lady Lynton if one of her daughters might show me the house. Elizabeth, the eldest, was summoned, and seemed in no way to dislike the task.

The house was, as already intimated, by no means large; it occupied three sides of a square, the entrance and one end of the stables making the fourth side. The interior was full of interest—passages, rooms, galleries, as well as hall, were panelled in dark wood and hung with pictures. I was shown everything on the ground floor, and then on the first floor. Then my guide proposed that we should ascend a narrow twisting staircase that led to a gallery. We did as proposed, and entered a handsome long room or passage, leading to a small chamber at one end, in which my guide told me her father kept books and papers.

I asked if anyone slept in this gallery, as I noticed a bed, and fireplace, and rods, by means of which curtains might be drawn, enclosing one portion where were bed and fireplace, so as to convert it into a very cosy chamber.

She answered "No," the place was not really used except as a playroom, though sometimes, if the house happened to be very full, in her great-grandfather's time, she had heard that it had been occupied.

By the time we had been over the house, and I had also been shown the garden and the stables, and introduced to the dogs, it was nearly one o'clock. We were to have an early luncheon, and to drive afterwards to see the ruins of one of the grand old Yorkshire abbeys.

This was a pleasant expedition, and we got back just in time for tea, after which there was some reading aloud. The evening passed much in the same way as the preceding one, except that Lynton, who had some business, did not go down to the smoking-room, and I took the opportunity of retiring early in order to write a letter for the Indian mail, something having been said as to the prospect of hunting the next day.

I had finished my letter, which was a long one, together with two or three others, and had just got into bed when I heard a step overhead as of someone walking along the gallery, which I now knew ran immediately above my room. It was a slow, heavy, measured tread which I could hear getting gradually louder and nearer, and then as gradually fading away as it retreated into the distance.

I was startled for a moment, having been informed that the gallery was unused; but the next instant it occurred to me that I had been told it communicated with a chamber where Sir Francis kept books and papers. I knew he had some writing to do, and I thought no more on the matter.

I was down the next morning at breakfast in good time. "How late you were last night!" I said to Lynton, in the middle of breakfast. "I heard you overhead after one o'clock."

Lynton replied rather shortly, "Indeed you did not, for I was in bed last night before twelve."

"There was someone certainly moving overhead last night," I answered, "for I heard his steps as distinctly as I ever heard anything in my life, going down the gallery."

Upon which Colonel Lynton remarked that he had often fancied he had heard steps on his staircase, when he knew that no one was about. He was apparently disposed to say more, when his brother interrupted him somewhat curtly, as I fancied, and asked me if I should feel inclined after breakfast to have a horse and go out and look for the hounds. They met a considerable way off, but if they did not find in the coverts they should first draw, a thing not improbable, they would come our way, and we might fall in with them about one o'clock and have a run. I said there was nothing I should like better. Lynton mounted me on a very nice chestnut, and the rest of the party having gone out shooting, and the young ladies being otherwise engaged, he and I started about eleven o'clock for our ride.

The day was beautiful, soft, with a bright sun, one of those delightful days which so frequently occur in the early part of November.

On reaching the hilltop where Lynton had expected to meet the hounds no trace of them was to be discovered. They must have found at once, and run in a different direction. At three o'clock, after we had eaten our sandwiches, Lynton reluctantly abandoned all hopes of falling in with the hounds, and said we would return home by a slightly different route.

We had not descended the hill before we came on an old chalk quarry and the remains of a disused kiln.

I recollected the spot at once. I had been here with Sir Francis on my former visit, many years ago. "Why—bless me!" said I. "Do you remember, Lynton, what happened here when I was with you before? There had been men engaged removing chalk, and they came on a skeleton under some depth of rubble. We went together to see it removed, and you said you would have it preserved till it could be examined by some ethnologist or anthropologist, one or other of those dry-as-dusts, to decide whether the remains are dolichocephalous or brachycephalous, whether British, Danish, or—modern. What was the result?"

Sir Francis hesitated for a moment, and then answered: "It is true, I had the remains removed."

"Was there an inquest?"

"No. I had been opening some of the tumuli on the Wolds. I had sent a crouched skeleton and some skulls to the Scarborough Museum. This I was doubtful about, whether it was a prehistoric interment—in fact, to what date it belonged. No one thought of an inquest."

On reaching the house, one of the grooms who took the horses, in answer to a question from Lynton, said that Colonel and Mrs. Hampshire had arrived about an hour ago, and that, one of the horses being lame, the carriage in which they had driven over from Castle Frampton was to put up for the night. In the drawing-room we found Lady Lynton pouring out tea for her husband's youngest sister and her husband, who, as we came in, exclaimed: "We have come to beg a night's lodging."

It appeared that they had been on a visit in the neighbourhood, and had been obliged to leave at a moment's notice in consequence of a sudden death in the house where they were staying, and that, in the impossibility of getting a fly, their hosts had sent them over to Byfield.

"We thought," Mrs. Hampshire went on to say, "that as we were coming here the end of next week, you would not mind having us a little sooner; or that, if the house were quite full, you would be willing to put us up anywhere till Monday, and let us come back later."

Lady Lynton interposed with the remark that it was all settled; and then, turning to her husband, added: "But I want to speak to you for a moment."

They both left the room together.

Lynton came back almost immediately, and, making an excuse to show me on a map in the hall the point to which we had ridden, said as soon as we were alone, with a look of considerable annoyance: "I am afraid we must ask you to change your room. Shall you mind very much? I think we can make you quite comfortable upstairs in the gallery, which is the only room available. Lady Lynton has had a good fire lit; the place is really not cold, and it will be for only a night or two. Your servant has been told to put your things together, but Lady Lynton did not like to give orders to have them actually moved before my speaking to you."

I assured him that I did not mind in the very least, that I should be quite as comfortable upstairs, but that I did mind very much their making such a fuss about a matter of that sort with an old friend like myself.

Certainly nothing could look more comfortable than my new lodging when I went upstairs to dress. There was a bright fire in the large grate, an armchair had been drawn up beside it, and all my books and writing things had been put in, with a reading-lamp in the central position, and the heavy tapestry curtains were drawn, converting this part of the gallery into a room to itself. Indeed, I felt somewhat inclined to congratulate myself on the change. The spiral staircase had been one reason against this place having been given to the Hampshires. No lady's long dress trunk could have mounted it.

Sir Francis was necessarily a good deal occupied in the evening with his sister and her husband, whom he had not seen for some time. Colonel Hampshire had also just heard that he was likely to be ordered to Egypt, and when Lynton and he retired to the smoking-room, instead of going there I went upstairs to my own room to finish a book in which I was interested. I did not, however, sit up long, and very soon went to bed.

Before doing so, I drew back the curtains on the rod, partly because I like plenty of air where I sleep, and partly also because I thought I might like to see the play of the moonlight on the floor in the portion of the gallery beyond where I lay, and where the blinds had not been drawn.

I must have been asleep for some time, for the fire, which I had left in full blaze, was gone to a few sparks wandering among the ashes, when I suddenly awoke with the impression of having heard a latch click at the further extremity of the gallery, where was the chamber containing books and papers.

I had always been a light sleeper, but on the present occasion I woke at once to complete and acute consciousness, and with a sense of stretched attention which seemed to intensify all my faculties. The wind had risen, and was blowing in fitful gusts round the house.

A minute or two passed, and I began almost to fancy I must have been mistaken, when I distinctly heard the creak of the door, and then the click of the latch falling back into its place. Then I heard a sound on the boards as of one moving in the gallery. I sat up to listen, and as I did so I distinctly heard steps coming down the gallery. I heard them approach and pass my bed. I could see nothing, all was dark; but I heard the tread proceeding towards the further portion of the gallery where were the uncurtained and unshuttered windows, two in number; but the moon shone through only one of these, the nearer; the other was dark, shadowed by the chapel or some other building at right angles. The tread seemed to me to pause now and again, and then continue as before.

I now fixed my eyes intently on the one illumined window, and it appeared to me as if some dark body passed across it: but what? I listened intently, and heard the step proceed to the end of the gallery and then return.

I again watched the lighted window, and immediately that the sound reached that portion of the long passage it ceased momentarily, and I saw, as distinctly as I ever saw anything in my life, by moonlight, a figure of a man with marked features, in what appeared to be a fur cap drawn over the brows.

It stood in the embrasure of the window, and the outline of the face was in silhouette; then it moved on, and as it moved I again heard the tread. I was as certain as I could be that the thing, whatever it was, or the person, whoever he was, was approaching my bed.

I threw myself back in the bed, and as I did so a mass of charred wood on the hearth fell down and sent up a flash of—I fancy sparks, that gave out a glare in the darkness, and by that—red as blood—I saw a face near me.

With a cry, over which I had as little control as the scream uttered by a sleeper in the agony of a nightmare, I called: "Who are you?"

The next instant there was a rush on the stairs and Lynton burst into the room, just as he had sprung out of bed, crying: "For God's sake, what is the matter? Are you ill?"

I could not answer. Lynton struck a light and leant over the bed. Then I seized him by the arm, and said without moving: "There has been something in this room—gone in thither."

The words were hardly out of my mouth when Lynton, following the direction of my eyes, had sprung to the end of the corridor and thrown open the door there.

He went into the room beyond, looked round it, returned, and said: "You must have been dreaming."

By this time I was out of bed.

"Look for yourself," said he, and he led me into the little room. It was bare, with cupboards and boxes, a sort of lumber-place. "There is nothing beyond this," said he, "no door, no staircase. It is a *cul-de-sac*." Then he added: "Now pull on your dressing-gown and come downstairs to my sanctum."

I followed him, and after he had spoken to Lady Lynton, who was standing with the door of her room ajar in a state of great agitation, he turned to me and said: "No one can have been in your room. You see my and my wife's apartments are close below, and no one could come up the spiral staircase without passing my door. You must have had a nightmare. Directly you screamed I rushed up the steps, and met no one descending; and there is no place of concealment in the lumber-room at the end of the gallery."

Then he took me into his private snuggery, blew up the fire, lighted a lamp, and said: "I shall be really grateful if you will say nothing about this. There are some in the house and neighbourhood who are silly enough as it is. You stay here, and if you do not feel inclined to go to bed, read—here are books. I must go to Lady Lynton, who is a good deal frightened, and does not like to be left alone."

He then went to his bedroom.

Sleep, as far as I was concerned, was out of the question, nor do I think that Sir Francis or his wife slept much either.

I made up the fire, and after a time took up a book, and tried to read, but it was useless.

I sat absorbed in thoughts and questionings till I heard the servants stirring in the morning. I then went to my own room, left the candle burning, and got into bed. I had just fallen asleep when my servant brought me a cup of tea at eight o'clock.

At breakfast Colonel Hampshire and his wife asked if anything had happened in the night, as they had been much disturbed by noises overhead, to which Lynton replied that I had not been very well, and had an attack of cramp, and that he had been upstairs to look after me. From his manner I could see that he wished me to be silent, and I said nothing accordingly.

In the afternoon, when everyone had gone out, Sir Francis took me into his snuggery and said: "Halifax, I am very sorry about that matter last night. It is quite true, as my brother said, that steps have been heard about this house, but I never gave heed to such things, putting all noises down to rats. But after your experiences I feel that it is due to you to tell you something, and also to make to you an explanation. There is—there was—no one in the room at the end of the corridor, except the skeleton that was discovered in the chalk-pit when you were here many years ago. I confess I had not paid much heed to it. My archaeological fancies passed; I had no visits from anthropologists; the bones and skull were never shown to experts, but remained packed in a chest in that lumber-room. I confess I ought to have buried them, having no more scientific use for them, but I did not—on my word, I forgot all about them, or, at least, gave no heed to them. However, what you have gone through, and have described to me, has made me uneasy, and has also given me a suspicion that I can account for that body in a manner that had never occurred to me before."

After a pause, he added: "What I am going to tell you is known to no one else, and must not be mentioned by you—anyhow, in my lifetime, You know now that, owing to the death of my father when quite young, I and my brother and sister were brought up here with our grandfather, Sir Richard. He was an old, imperious, short-tempered man. I will tell you what I have made out of a matter that was a mystery for long, and I will tell you afterwards how I came to unravel it. My grandfather was in the habit of going out at night with a young underkeeper, of whom he was very fond, to look after the game and see if any poachers, whom he regarded as his natural enemies, were about.

"One night, as I suppose, my grandfather had been out with the young man in question, and, returning by the plantations, where the hill is steepest, and not far from that chalk-pit you remarked on yesterday, they came upon a man, who, though not actually belonging to the country, was well known in it as a sort of travelling tinker of indifferent character, and a notorious poacher. Mind this, I am not sure it was at the place I mention; I only now surmise it. On the particular night in question, my grandfather and the keeper must have caught this man setting snares; there must have been a tussle, in the course of which, as subsequent circumstances have led me to imagine, the man showed fight and was knocked down by one or other of the two—my grandfather or the keeper. I believe that after having made various attempts to restore him, they found that the man was actually dead.

"They were both in great alarm and concern—my grandfather especially. He had been prominent in putting down some factory riots, and had acted as magistrate with promptitude, and had given orders to the military to fire, whereby a couple of lives had been lost. There was a vast outcry against him, and a certain political party had denounced him as an assassin. No man was more vituperated; yet, in my conscience, I believe that he acted with both discretion and pluck, and arrested a mischievous movement that might have led to much bloodshed. Be that as it may, my impression is that he lost his head over this fatal affair with the tinker, and that he and the keeper together buried the body secretly, not far from the place where he was killed. I now think it was in the chalk-pit, and that the skeleton found years after there belonged to this man."

"Good heavens!" I exclaimed, as at once my mind rushed back to the figure with the fur cap that I had seen against the window.

Sir Francis went on: "The sudden disappearance of the tramp, in view of his well-known habits and wandering mode of life, did not for some time excite surprise; but, later on, one or two circumstances having led to suspicion, an inquiry was set on foot, and among others, my grandfather's keepers were examined before the magistrates. It was remembered afterwards that the under-keeper in question was absent at the time of the inquiry, my grandfather having sent him with some dogs to a brother-in-law of his who lived upon the moors; but whether no one noticed the fact, or if they did, preferred to be silent, I know not, no observations were made. Nothing came of the investigation, and the whole subject would have dropped if it had not been that two years later, for some reasons I do not understand, but at the instigation of a magistrate recently imported into the division, whom my grandfather greatly disliked, and who was opposed to him in politics, a fresh inquiry was instituted. In the course of that inquiry it transpired that, owing to some unguarded words dropped by the under-keeper, a warrant was about to be issued for his arrest. My grandfather, who had had a fit of the gout, was away from home at the time, but on hearing the news he came home at once. The evening he returned he had a long interview with the young man, who left the house after he had supped in the servants' hall. It was observed that he looked much depressed. The warrant was issued the next day, but in the meantime the keeper had disappeared. My grandfather gave orders to all his own people to do everything in their power to assist the authorities in the search that was at once set on foot, but was unable himself to take any share in it.

"No trace of the keeper was found, although at a subsequent period rumours circulated that he had been heard of in America. But the man having been unmarried, he gradually dropped out of remembrance, and as my grandfather never allowed the subject to be mentioned in his presence, I should probably never have known anything about it but for the vague tradition which always attaches to such events, and for this fact: that after my grandfather's death a letter came addressed to him from somewhere in the United States from someone—the name different from that of the keeper—but alluding to the past, and implying the presence of a common secret, and, of course, with it came a request for money. I replied, mentioning the death of Sir Richard, and asking for an explanation. I did get an answer, and it is from that that I am able to fill in so much of the story. But I never learned *where* the man had been killed and buried, and my next letter to the fellow was returned with 'Deceased' written across it. Somehow, it never occurred to me till I heard your story that possibly the skeleton in the chalk-pit might be that of the poaching tinker. I will now most assuredly have it buried in the churchyard."

"That certainly ought to be done," said I.

"And—" said Sir Francis, after a pause, "I give you my word. After the burial of the bones, and you are gone, I will sleep for a week in the bed in the gallery, and report to you if I see or hear anything. If all be quiet, then—well, you form your own conclusions."

I left a day after. Before long I got a letter from my friend, brief but to the point: "All quiet, old boy; come again."

The Conquering Will

Harriet Prescott Spofford

There was no doubt that he was a masterful man. He ruled everyone on shore as he had ruled everyone at sea. His wife had never meant to marry him; but she did. When the fleet went into Asiatic waters she had declared she would not follow; but she did. When the child died she had wished to clothe herself in black; but she didn't. Wherever he was Captain Gilbert's will was the only will. Whenever she resisted him she felt like a wave shattering itself to foam against a rock in the mid-seas.

Sometimes she wondered if there were any hypnotic quality about him. Her mother had said she was possessed. But she really knew better. So far as she was concerned, she knew that the reason the Captain had his own way was simply because she loved him. And so far as everyone else was concerned, she was glad he did have his own way.

She had at first admired Captain Gilbert more than she loved him—admired his superb and stalwart figure of the large, heroic type; his Greek head, ringed over with short, yellow curls; his bold features, his eyes, that had in them the blue of the skies but also the glance of the eagle; his commanding air. And moreover, his manner, when he chose, had an inexpressible charm that carried all before it. No one dared contend with him—and then no one wished to do so. No wonder he was a masterful man. He was never resisted; and the habit had become nature.

Indeed, his wife hardly knew, after a while, when she had a wish other than her husband's. It is true she thought blue more becoming, but he liked to see her in pink, and she always went about like a lovely blush rose. It was also true that there had been a time when she cared for dancing; but Captain Gilbert would not endure the familiarity of the waltz, and so she never waltzed—when Captain Gilbert was looking. It is true she enjoyed the theatre; but Captain Gilbert prepared to go to church, and she went to church, and felt afterward very righteous and content.

But on the other hand, she loved riding; and the Captain kept her provided with a mount that was the envy of all the other women in the field. He himself rode like a centaur, and she never admired him more than in the saddle. She was fond of sea bathing, and he took for her every Summer a little place by the seaside, and none of the merpeople ever disported themselves with more sense of possession of the deep sea caves than they did. She would have enjoyed land travel; but Captain Gilbert preferred seafaring, so that she never saw any other world than the world of waters. She recovered from her seasickness after a few days, and then took keenest pleasure in the bounding and soaring from billow to billow, as if she were a seagull sitting on the wave or flying over it. Alone, too, in the vast region of sunlit sky and sea, or when night carried space into dark infinity, or when they rode triumphant over storm, and every man on the yacht was a machine moved by the Captain's will, he seemed to her each time a more positive potency than before.

But if the Captain had his own way in the outside things of life his way was usually right. It was because he said that it simply should be done that the salary of Dr. Saintly was raised to living limit. It was he who, when the rest of the town where he lived when off duty frowned down an embezzling bank officer who had served his term in prison, insisted that the man should be helped to work and to respect again. It was he who brought home a forsaken woman of the place, and required civility for her so long as she did right. "If there is one thing certain," said the Captain, "it is that love is the best thing in the world. And I mean, Fanny, that you and I shall be as much at one with this great spirit filling the universe as holding the helpful hand to all can make us."

Perhaps, however, the Captain would not have carried things so before him if all his little world had not known of certain splendid achievements in the sea fights, giving him, in a measure, the right to his own way, giving him also the wounds that enforced his retirement and shortened his life. Wherever they were, people turned to look at him and to approve, and it gratified Mrs. Gilbert as much as when they turned to look at her—she was the woman whom this wonder among men had chosen out of all the women on the earth. But they always found it well worth their while to look at her. "The Lord may have thought He made the most beautiful thing possible when He made this rose," the Captain said to her once, stooping to a wayside bramble, "but I think He made the most beautiful thing when He made a woman. And you are a woman and a rose, too!"

"You make me blush," said Mrs. Gilbert; "and here, on the street!" They were going home from church across the fields. "Yes, I should wonder why I was given such a wife if it were not that she has such a husband," he added, laughing. And when Captain Gilbert laughed Mrs. Gilbert felt that the world went well, and she laughed, too. And she never looked prettier than when her red lips curved apart over the rice-pearl teeth, and disclosed ravishing little dimples in either velvet cheek.

But possibly Captain Gilbert could not have so completely dominated his wife if she had not felt in him a fine superiority to the small things of life and had not had a fearsome joy in sometimes following his thought out into what he called the Fourth Dimension. "This earth and its envelopings are beautiful," he said, "but when I remember that there are colors we cannot see, sounds too fine for our ears, I know we are only spelling the alphabet of all we shall find—out there. Nights when I have walked the deck, virtually alone, and have seen the stars sentineling the great courts of space beyond space, I have felt sure they were made for no idleness—that there were reasons for their being; and in some form or other we shall tread their mazes and come out upon the reason for all things." She did not entirely understand him; but it may be that she admired him all the more on that account.

But there was one thing in which Captain Gilbert failed to have his own way. One thing?—two things! He could not hinder men from staring at Mrs. Gilbert, and he could not hinder Mrs. Gilbert from showing—in the mildest mannered way—that she was conscious of the gaze and possibly not unpleased. "I am sure I can't help their looking at me," she pouted, turning away from the window.

"You can help making eyes at them!" he replied.

"Captain Gilbert! What language!"

"Suiting the word to the action."

"And as if I could help my eyes!" the tears making them like live jewels.

"I know they're beautiful eyes!" said the Captain, remorsefully. "But they're my eyes! They don't belong to every fool going by."

"I never knew such a tyrant! You're like the man in the 'Morte d'Arthur' who wanted his wife hideous before the court, but beautiful when alone with him."

"Precisely," said Captain Gilbert, laughing. "And I wish we had those days back—days when a man owned his wife, like any other precious thing, till a stronger took her——"

"It's always a stronger that takes her, one way or another."

"He'll be stronger than the laws of the universe if he takes you, that's all," said the Captain, lifting her in his arms and walking down the room with her as if she had been a child; "for by all the laws of the universe you are mine! And mine you will be forever, alive or dead!" And, to her troubled amazement, he was sobbing. "Fanny," he cried, "if you married another man after I died—after I died—if I were in the farthest star of the farthest heavens I should come back and punish him!"

"Oh!" cried Mrs. Gilbert. Then, through her own tears: "Why not leave that to me?"

Mrs. Gilbert was one of the women with whom this brigand-like way of making love is effective. And when, shortly afterward, Captain Gilbert betook himself to the farthest star and left her widowed, she missed the excitations and the raptures and the sense of being adored, even if tyrannized over; and she was not at all consoled by the fact that she looked charming in black, which there was no one now to forbid her.

But a little time works wonders. Mrs. Gilbert one day woke to the fact that she was free, with no one to say her nay; free as a bird in the air. At least, she would have been free if she had had any money to be free with. But Captain Gilbert's half-pay had stopped with his breath, and there was a delay about pension business and about other money, during which Mrs. Gilbert found herself so hard pressed as to be almost in despair about ways and means. And when Mr. Mercer proposed that she share a million with him, she was in more minds than one about accepting the idea, and she actually asked for time. Captain Gilbert, she reasoned, would never want her to be put about this way for money—her mourning was positively shabby. And she thought of it very seriously—it might do—Mr. Mercer was a gentleman. But when he called for his reply she came down, white to her lips, so white that she was ghastly, and said it was impossible.

It was the same way with Dr. Vaughn. It seemed so eminently respectable, so altogether what the gossips would have called too good a chance to lose, she would be so well cared for—and she was just on the point of yielding. But after a night's reflection she wrote that it was out of the question, her hand shaking so that her script looked like a field of wheat bowed in the wind.

And after that she went for a while so sedately, so demurely, so entirely as the fond and faithful widow should, that who but the rector should be acknowledging her fascination? And she knew in her heart that she would be a capital wife for a clergyman, that she might have the parish under her little thumb—she, a helpmeet better than the best! She said to herself it was a pity if she could not do as she pleased; she smiled on him; she came near giving him her hand to kiss in token of the ring it might wear presently. And then she sent him in his turn the hurried note that laid all hope low.

Captain Gilbert had been lost to the breathing world almost half a dozen years, and his wife was as much like a lovely blooming rose as ever, when John Mowbray crossed her path. And he not only crossed it, but he obstructed it. The years had passed quietly; her affairs had adjusted themselves; although she could have spent more, she was no longer in need of money. She had almost forgotten Mr. Mercer and his successors in misfortune. And John Mowbray was a man of an unfamiliar and engaging type. He loved music, the opera, Wagner; she had never had enough of music in her life. He was more or less of a student, acquainted with books, a haunter of libraries; it seemed to her that he held the gates open to a fair and inviting plaisance. Well born and well bred, he had the air, without having traveled much, of knowing men and manners and the world; but to travel was his intention—and she saw the gates open to a life of infinitely wider interest than this small daily round. He was on the sunny side, as she was; with a most agreeable personality, with a delightful courtesy, and as she began to suspect, with a sincere affection for herself.

He had come to see her, that snowy night, through all the storm, bringing her an armful of great red roses. There was something very pleasant about his coming in; it gave her a feeling of protection, emphasized the idea of shelter. She heaped the fire and presently the ruddy flames danced over the room and the flowers, and over the pretty woman disposing them in their bowls and jars, till it all seemed to John Mowbray, still warming his hands at the blaze, the ideal of a home. What a place to come to every night! What a place never to go away from! What a dream!

She knew what was coming very well. Some subtle instinct made her try to fortify herself against it. She sat down behind a table and leaned forward, rearranging with twinkling fingers the roses in the vase that nearly hid her face. And then in another moment he was half-kneeling beside her, and he was murmuring, "Fanny, Fanny! let it be real—this dream. I am dreaming! Tell me not to wake! Say, dear, say that you love me!" And before she knew it the strong arms were about her, and she was hiding her face on his shoulder.

What an evening of deep, serene happiness it was! Side by side they looked into the future, and its glow shed a light over them. "It is too much, too much happiness," she said, as they parted. "Something will hinder. I—I shall not be allowed—" And she grew very pale.

"Thank heaven, there is no one to allow or to disallow," said John Mowbray. "You are not now the young girl to be dominated, but the woman whose beautiful nature has developed the power to choose, and I am crowned and blessed by your choice!"

"I am afraid—I am afraid—" she said, as he bade her good-night.

"Of what, my love?" he asked her.

"Oh, of nothing, of nothing, so long as you are here!" she said, clinging to him more closely.

And "I am afraid!" she repeated again, as she went up stairs, though trembling with joy.

She had half a mind to sit up that night and not go to sleep at all. She dropped the curtain quickly as she saw the stars sparkling in the sky from which the snow clouds were already blowing away. The thought of that farthest star would come back and make her shiver. But she was tired out with emotion—with hope and joy and fear—and she fell asleep in the big armchair just as Captain Gilbert came into the room, strong, stalwart, mighty, and looking like the hero of some Viking legend.

The wind had blown a fine color into his face; his curls were sprayed with the melted snow, his eyes were as dazzlingly blue as a noonday sky. "I have come a long way to see you, my wife," he said, and the old familiar tone rang sweetly through all the chambers of her heart. "And I never saw you lovelier. How dear, how beautiful you are! How long we have belonged to each other! Do you remember the night by the gate under the honeysuckles, when you reached out your hand in the dark, uncertain if I was there, and suddenly I clasped it? Dear hand! I have never, never let it go! I never will! I saw a sapphire as blue as Lyra on my way here. I will have it for this little hand—only the hand is so slight, the sapphire is so heavy. How quiet it is here—it is always quiet about you, my wife—you are so serene, and your husband is so stormy! Here is the smell of roses that always hovers about you—oh, how sweet, how sweet you are! Up, and let me sit down and hold you in my arms, you featherweight! There, rest the dear head. What makes you shiver so? It is warm. I am here—your husband. Warm? I am warm to my marrow, being with you, holding you, living again the delicious life we used to live. Oh, what life will be again with you, most perfect of women, most faithful of wives! I have been so cold, so far off, so longing for you! What ways I have traversed, what have I encountered, just for this hour! And it is worth it all. There are great things in store for us, little woman. Lean your cheek on mine—how velvet soft, how warm—you are mine, mine, mine—"

She heard, she remembered no more, but woke with the sun pouring into the window and streaming over her through the crimson warmth of the geraniums, and all her heart expanded with the old affection.

Suffused still with the mood of the night, she made her toilette and went down, thoughtless, reckless, almost gay—and met John Mowbray coming through the door, his sleighbells still jangling at the gate—he had come to take her sleighing. But at the first sight of his eager, expectant face she stopped. All her bloom fell away, she shook like a leaf; and he sprang forward, thinking she was about to fall. "No, no, no!" she cried. "Forget last night! Forget everything! It is impossible! It is out of the question. I am Captain Gilbert's wife still. Captain Gilbert—will not—will not allow it."

And then she dropped fainting into his arms.

She did not, however, lose consciousness entirely. She knew very well that John Mowbray was covering her face with kisses while carrying her to the sofa. The blood surged over her forehead in a conviction of guilt, and then she turned her face to the wall.

"What does this mean?" cried John Mowbray.

"He—he has been here," she faltered.

"Who has been here?" he demanded.

"Captain Gilbert."

"What—what is it you say?" he exclaimed, springing to his feet.

"He was here last night—I am not out of my head. Oh, no, I am not beside myself! He has been here before—the same way—whenever—Oh, see how unworthy I am!"

And she covered her face with her hands.

He seated himself on the edge of the sofa and took down the two hands, holding them in his own.

"You mean you dreamed last night," he said.

"Oh, no, no! Dreamed? Oh, it was too real! Dreamed? I don't know— Do you suppose it could be just a dream? Always the same dream, only with differences? And he so all he used to be when he was best and tenderest, making me feel that he was my husband forever and ever, that I— Oh, you see I love him still!"

"I should be ashamed of you if you didn't!" said John Mowbray, sternly. "But you love me, too! You know you do!"

"How can I love two men at once?" cried Fanny.

"You don't. One of us is an angel in heaven. I shall never have the least jealousy of your affection for him. You and I are on the earth. And when we are as the angels in heaven we shall never marry or be given in marriage. Come, you need the air. Where is your thick cloak, your furs, a hood? Here is the sleigh at the gate. We will drive up the river. On the way we will stop at the rectory—"

"But—but—"

"Not a but about it. I shall have the right then to shield my wife in her dreams and from her dreams. And I don't believe anyone will come where I am to challenge him!"

And Fanny Gilbert had found again the power that surrounded her like a fortress and the will that was perhaps as strong as Captain Gilbert's will.

It seemed that John Mowbray must have been right. After the sleigh ride and the brief ceremony at the rector's he took his wife away and into a round of gaieties that gave her no time to reflect. And then came the voyage overseas and the travel that should so fill thought and memory as to leave no room for the past. Under all the novelty and pleasure and excitement, and Mr. Mowbray's constant presence and care, she became a new creature. Blooming with fresh being, enlarged to the larger life, her prettiness became beauty, her liveliness sparkling, and her sweetness, to John Mowbray, enchanting. His pride in her was equal to his passion. It was with pleasure that he saw men's eyes follow her, and women's, too. When she rode, her trim grace and dauntless spirit hung afterward before his own eyes, as if he had seen Dian and her train pass by. At the opera, as she stood a moment, easy, gracious, dropping off her cloak and revealing a dazzle of jewels and gleaming tissues, of eyes like jewels, too, of roses, cream and blush, and of smiles, and when he saw her breathless, rapt in the music and the play, he felt a joy of possession that was like a pain; but with the emotion came a vague fear of its evanescence.

The premonition was not felt at once, however. There was a season of unassailed rapture before he noticed that Mrs. Mowbray had become very restless, seeking perpetually some new object, and so absent-minded that he sometimes spoke twice or thrice before she heard him. Glowing with color and life and happiness in the evening, in the morning she would be as pale and sad and languid as if she had danced all night with witches, so that he wondered if she slept at all. She ate almost nothing, started at every sound, laughed nervously at nothing, and her eyes filled with tears likewise at nothing. She began to grow very thin. Suddenly he perceived that she was wasting away before his eyes.

Like Asa of old, Mr. Mowbray had recourse to the physicians, and that without loss of time. But as she persisted that nothing ailed her, and had no symptoms to present other than those they saw, they could do little beyond administering tonics, which were as idle as spring water.

"My dear one," he said to her at last, "tell me—what is it? There is something you hide from me. My precious one, my wife, tell me; are you unhappy?"

"Oh, yes, yes, yes!" she cried, lifting her hands passionately. "I am wretched! I am wretched!"

He turned as white as she. “Fanny!” he cried.

“Oh, not the way you think!” she cried. “But, oh! I cannot tell you!”

He sat down beside her and took her in his arms. “Whatever it is, you must tell me,” he said, gently. “You are my one thought in life. I can do nothing to serve you if I am in the dark.”

“It is I!—It is I who am in the dark!” she wept.

“Tell me what you mean, my darling,” he urged her.

“I—I don’t know if I am your darling!” she exclaimed. “I don’t know who I am!”

“Fanny, dearest, I don’t understand. Be reasonable, my little wife, let me know.”

“Am I your wife? or am I his?”

“Dearest!”

“I don’t know. He comes—he has come every night—”

He clasped her convulsively in his arms. “I live a double life,” she said, moving herself feebly yet resistingly. “All day I am yours. All night I am his!”

“Dear child! dear little one! You are ill. You are letting a dream—”

“It is not like any dream—”

“But, dream or not, it is when all your powers are submerged in sleep, when you are not fully yourself—”

“Oh, but in the daylight—”

“Yes, in the daylight, when you are you, then—then you are only mine!”

“I am afraid—I am afraid,” she sighed. “Every night when I go to sleep—I don’t know what may happen. Some night, some night, he will take me!” And her voice died to a whisper.

“Never!” he cried. “Never while I am beside you.”

At that moment, as she lay in his arms, they were both possessed by a great shuddering and fear. It was dark all about them, as if it were already night. A wind seemed to fill the room and then to hold its breath, a wind that might have been blowing from nowhere to nowhere, but hanging now still and chill.

“Hold me, hold me fast, John!” she murmured. “He has come for me!” Her arms fell, her head drooped nerveless over his arm. “Oh, John, I love—”

The lips, wide open, said no more. And in the instant of that last sigh John Mowbray knew, by some other than the sense of sight, that Captain Gilbert, masterful, laughing, debonair, towered like a shaft of sunlight before him.

“You are wrong of nothing,” a voice that had no sound was ringing in his ears. “The bindweed falls that leans upon a straw. You would have made her happy if you might. But you could not conquer the unconquerable will. And I have come for my own!"

"As a destroying force—destroying joy, destroying life!" cried John Mowbray. "And I defy you! For though you carry her beyond your farthest star, she loves me best, and I will follow you!"

"Spirit to spirit, flesh to flesh, John Mowbray. She is mine!"

There was a flutter of the purple-veined eyelids in the face that had fallen from his arm, a tremor of the lips, a long, slow, bubbling sigh. Slipping, slipping from his grasp, a lifeless heap lay on the floor—and by all the avenues through which the viewless thing may reach the soul, John Mowbray saw Captain Gilbert fading into an intenser light, his wife held close beside him. And then, though it was broad noonday, the world was black and still.

The Damned Spot

Violet M. Methley

I am not quite sure whether this occurrence can be classed as tragedy or farce. It was a mixture of both, at the time, and it still remains in my mind as a mixture—like most things in life.

There is really no need for preliminary explanations. You don't want to know exactly who and what I am, and I don't want to tell you. Moreover, it does not affect the story in the least. It is quite enough to say that on a certain day in November last year I was staying at a hotel in a certain town in Midlands. My name is of no importance, and the name of the town had better remain unknown, so I won't mention either.

I got up at seven o'clock that morning, in an extremely bad temper, since it was necessary for me to keep an early and unpleasant appointment.

It was a day of yellowish fog, and the air of the corridor felt clammy and unclean, as I passed along it towards the bathroom. The bathroom was a good-sized apartment at the end of the passage. The bath was in a kind of recess, and on the opposite side of the room, near the door, was a fixed basin. A faint glimmer of daylight came through the frosted-glass window. I switched on the electric light—or tried to—but nothing happened, and the fact that the lamp was out of order did not improve my temper.

However, the water was hot, and that comforted me considerably. I had been pessimistically prepared for the worst in that respect. I got into the bath and stretched myself out luxuriously, my back being turned towards the door and the fixed basin. This last fact is important.

Then, all of a sudden, I became aware that someone else had come into the room. Not only that; that someone was a woman. . . .

I didn't hear the door open, but I heard her dress rustling over the oil-clothed floor, and the soft thud-thud of slippered feet padding along. Her breathing was hurried, quick, and short, as though she had been running.

Evidently the lock of the bathroom door did not work, and this female had entered, not knowing I was there. In order to apprise her of the fact, I splashed about in the bath and coughed. I imagined that, realizing my presence, she would scream, or apologise, or merely decamp, in dumb and horrible confusion, according to her nature, but, anyway, depart at once.

She didn't. She showed no sign whatever of being aware of my presence. The faint rustle of her gown, the quickened breathing, continued, and, in addition, the tap was now turned on, and water began to gurgle in the basin.

The only explanation was that the woman was deaf, stone-deaf, and with that realisation an idea came to me. If her back was turned and she could not hear, it was just possible that I might be able to slip out of the room, or, at any rate, snatch my bath-robe from its peg on the door, before she saw me. If luck was on my side, I might even reach my bedroom unseen.

I must make a bold dash for it. I rose quietly, faced towards the bathroom door—and stood staring in amazement.

No one was there!

The door was still shut. My bath-robe hung dejectedly on its peg. A chair and a mat constituted the entire movable furniture in the bathroom. In the ugly, yellow light everything was perfectly distinct and unmistakable. And yet, from the basin, there still came the sound of splashing, the panting breaths, the little rustling movements, as of a female washing her hands.

Someone was there in the room, close to me, not two yards away—but I could not see her.

The quick breathing was interrupted by a sound which was something between a sigh and a sob—almost a moan. It was a sound infinitely pitiful; it seemed to come from someone in desperate distress. Then followed a renewal of the splashing—another pause—another heartbroken sob—a tearing, desolate sound, which made me forget my own absurd and undignified position.

"I say—what is it? What's the matter? Can't I do anything?" I asked.

There was no answer. Only the sounds from the direction of the basin continued uninterruptedly. And there I stood in the bath, staring at nothing visible, the steam rising about me, the water dripping from my body, a ridiculous sight enough—if there had been anyone to see. But I had forgotten that. I was only conscious of someone very near at hand, apparently in desperate misery.

The splashing ceased. Again came the long-drawn sound like a groan. The rustling of the skirt, the padding steps passed towards the door. Then silence.

I shivered in the cold, dank air, got out of the bath, rubbed myself into dryness and comparative warmth, slipped into my bathrobe, and returned hurriedly to my bedroom.

I thought of nothing else while I dressed. The thing haunted me and would not be shaken off. But I did not go downstairs with a haggard face and whitened hair. The hotel manager did not say: "Good God!" and stand horrified at the sight of me and afterwards whisper, in tense accents: "Have you *seen* anything?"

No, nothing of that sort happened. The manager encountered me in the hall and merely said: "Good morning, sir," whilst I went on to seek for breakfast, which had to be despatched hurriedly in order that I might keep my appointment.

But I was not quite so hungry as usual, and I thought a good deal during that solitary and rather cheerless meal—thought to such purpose that I found something stowed away in a dusty corner of my memory, something almost entirely forgotten, a vague memory of a name—a place—of things printed, under big headlines, in the newspapers.

Those memories drifted together—dropped into shape—formed themselves into something more or less tangible, as I walked to my appointment, as I transacted my business, as I lunched and talked.

And at lunch I questioned, carelessly, my business friend, a resident in the town.

"Oh, by the way, I can't remember exactly what happened," I said, "but wasn't there a lot in the papers about this place a few years ago—a suicide, or murder, or something beastly in that hotel I've been staying at?"

"Yes, yes, you're right!" My friend leant forward over the table, with a healthy enjoyment of horror.

"Murder it was—the murder of Mr. Burton, who was staying with his wife at the hotel. It was a terrible business. I can tell you, it made a tremendous sensation here. They found Burton in bed one morning with his throat cut, d'you remember? And his wife, poor little woman, was crouched in a corner of the room simply out of her senses with terror. She could not give any intelligible account of what had happened. She must have actually seen the crime committed, and, although I don't think Burton was much of a chap, still, after all, he was her husband."

"Did they ever catch the murderer?"

"No—or, at least, not then. But the police knew well enough who it was. A desperate sort of fellow had been about, robbing and assaulting people. You remember the case, I expect. He shot himself, a few weeks later, after murdering a taxi-driver.

More or less mad, I believe. So far as could be guessed, he must have got into the bedroom through the window—there was a fire escape just outside—and cut Burton's throat. After that he had gone out by the door, for he had actually washed his hands in the bathroom. They found the basin full of blood-stained water. As no one had seen him in the hotel, it was concluded that he escaped through the bathroom window. It's only a short drop to the garage roof."

"What became of the wife?"

"She never recovered sufficiently to give any coherent evidence. She had to be shut up. I wonder if she's dead now—poor soul!"

I wondered, too. And I wondered something else.

For the person whom I had heard washing her hands in the bathroom that morning was, most certainly, a woman.

Dark Dignum

Bernard Capes

"I'd not go nigher, sir," said my landlady's father.

I made out his warning through the shrill piping of the wind; and stopped and took in the plunging seascape from where I stood. The boom of the waves came up from a vast distance beneath; sky and the horizon of running water seemed hurrying upon us over the lip of the rearing cliff.

"It crumbles!" he cried. "It crumbles near the edge like as frosted mortar. I've seen a noble sheep, sir, eighty pound of mutton, browsing here one moment, and seen it go down the next in a puff of white dust. Hark to that! Do you hear it?"

Through the tumult of the wind in that high place came a liquid vibrant sound, like the muffled stroke of iron on an anvil. I thought it the gobble of water in clanging caves deep down below.

"It might be a bell," I said.

The old man chuckled joyously. He was my cicerone for the nonce; had come out of his chair by the ingle-nook to taste a little the salt of life. The north-easter flashed in the white cataracts of his eyes and woke a feeble activity in his scrannel limbs. When the wind blew loud, his daughter had told me, he was always restless, like an imprisoned sea-gull. He would be up and out. He would rise and flap his old draggled pinions, as if the great air fanned an expiring spark into flame.

"It *is* a bell!" he cried—"the bell of old St. Dunstan's, that was swallowed by the waters in the dark times."

"Ah," I said. "That is the legend hereabouts."

"No legend, sir—no legend. Where be the tombstones of drownded mariners to prove it such? Not one to forty that they has in other sea-board parishes. For why? Dunstan bell sounds its warning, and not a craft will put out."

"There is the storm cone," I suggested.

He did not hear me. He was punching with his staff at one of a number of little green mounds that lay about us.

"I could tell you a story of these," he said. "Do you know where we stand?"

"On the site of the old churchyard?"

"Ay, sir; though it still bore the name of the *new* yard in my first memory of it."

"Is that so? And what is the story?"

He dwelt a minute, dense with introspection. Suddenly he sat himself down upon a mossy bulge in the turf, and waved me imperiously to a place beside him.

"The old order changeth," he said. "The only lasting, foundations of men's works shall be godliness and law-biding. Long ago they builded a new church—here, high up on the cliffs, where the waters could not reach; and, lo! the waters wrought beneath and sapped the foundations, and the church fell into the sea."

"So I understand," I said.

"The godless are fools," he chattered knowingly. "Look here at these bents—thirty of 'em, may be. Tombstones, sir; perished like man his works, and the decayed stumps of them coated with salt grass."

He pointed to the ragged edge of the cliff a score paces away.

"They raised it out there," he said, "and further—a temple of bonded stone. They thought to bribe the Lord to a partnership in their corruption, and He answered by casting down the fair mansion into the waves."

I said, "Who—who, my friend?"

"They that builded the church," he answered.

"Well," I said. "It seems a certain foolishness to set the edifice so close to the margin."

Again he chuckled.

"It was close, close, as you say; yet none so close as you might think nowadays. Time hath gnawed here like a rat on a cheese. But the foolishness appeared in setting the brave mansion between the winds and its own graveyard. Let the dead lie seawards, one had thought, and the church inland where we stand. So had the bell rung to this day; and only the charnel bones flaked piecemeal into the sea."

"Certainly, to have done so would show the better providence."

"Sir, I said the foolishness *appeared*. But, I tell you, there was foresight in the disposition—in neighbouring the building to the cliff path. *For so they could the easier enter unobserved, and store their kegs of Nantes brandy in the belly of the organ.*"

"They? Who were they?"

"Why, who—but two-thirds of all Dunburgh?"

"Smugglers?"

"It was a nest of 'em—traffickers in the eternal fire o' weekdays, and on the Sabbath, who so sanctimonious? But honesty comes not from the washing, like a clean shirt, nor can the piety of one day purge the evil of six. They built their church anigh the margin, forasmuch as it was handy, and that they thought, 'Surely the Lord will not undermine His own?' A rare community o' blasphemers, fro' the parson that took his regular toll of the organ-loft, to him that sounded the keys and pulled out the joyous stops as if they was so many spigots to what lay behind."

"Of when do you speak?"

"I speak of nigh a century and a half ago. I speak of the time o' the Seven Years' War and of Exciseman Jones, that, twenty year after he were buried, took his revenge on the cliff side of the man that done him to death."

"And who was that?"

"They called him Dark Dignum, sir—a great feat smuggler, and as wicked as he was bold."

"Is your story about him?"

"Ay, it is; and of my grandfather, that were a boy when they laid, and was glad to lay, the exciseman deep as they could dig; for the sight of his sooty face in his coffin was worse than a bad dream."

"Why was that?"

The old man edged closer to me, and spoke in a sibilant voice.

"He were murdered, sir, foully and horribly, for all they could never bring it home to the culprit."

"Will you tell me about it?"

He was nothing loth. The wind, the place of perished tombs, the very wild-blown locks of this 'withered apple-john,' were eerie accompaniments to the tale he piped in my ear:—

"When my grandfather were a boy," he said, "there lighted in Dunburgh Exciseman Jones. P'r'aps the village had gained an ill reputation. P'r'aps Exciseman Jones's predecessor had failed to secure the confidence o' the exekitive. At any rate, the new man was little to the fancy of the village. He was a grim, sour-looking, brass-bound galloot; and incorruptible—which was the worst. The keg o' brandy left on his doorstep o' New Year's Eve had been better unspiled and run into the gutter; for it led him somehow to the identification of the innocent that done it, and he had him by the heels in a twinkling. The squire snorted at the man, and the parson looked askance; but Dark Dignum, he swore he'd be even with him, if he swung for it. They was hurt and surprised, that was the truth, over the scrupulosity of certain people; and feelin' ran high against Exciseman Jones.

"At that time Dark Dignum was a young man with a reputation above his years for profaneness and audacity. Ugly things there were said about him; and amongst many wicked he was feared for his wickedness. Exciseman Jones had his eye on him; and that was bad for Exciseman Jones.

"Now one murk December night Exciseman Jones staggered home with a bloody long slice down his scalp, and the red drip from it spotting the cobble-stones.

"'Summut fell on him from a winder,' said Dark Dignum, a little later, as he were drinkin' hisself hoarse in the Black Boy. 'Summut fell on him retributive, as you might call it. For, would you believe it, the man had at the moment been threatenin' me? He did. He said, "I know damn well about you, Dignum; and for all your damn ingenuity, I'll bring you with a crack to the ground yet." '

"What had happened? Nobody knew, sir. But Exciseman Jones was in his bed for a fortnight; and when he got on his legs again, it was pretty evident there was a hate between the two men that only blood-spillin' could satisfy.

"So far as is known, they never spoke to one another again. They played their game of death in silence—the lawful, cold and unfathomable; the unlawful, swaggerin' and crool—and twenty year separated the first move and the last.

"This were the first, sir—as Dark Dignum leaked it out long after in his cups. This were the first; and it brought Exciseman Jones to his grave on the cliff here.

"It were a deep soft summer night; and the young smuggler sat by hisself in the long room of the Black Boy. Now, I tell you he were a fox-ship intriguer—grand, I should call him, in the aloneness of his villainy. He would play his dark games out of his own hand; and sure, of all his wickedness, this game must have seemed the sum.

"I say he sat by hisself; and I hear the listening ghost of him call me a liar. For there were another body present, though invisible to mortal eye; and that second party were Exciseman Jones, who was hidden up the chimney.

"How had he inveigled him there? Ah, they've met and worried that point out since. No other will ever know the truth this side the grave. But reports come to be whispered; and reports said as how Dignum had made an appointment with a bodiless master of a smack as never floated, to meet him in the Black Boy and arrange for to run a cargo as would never be shipped; and that somehow he managed to acquent Exciseman Jones o' this dissembling appointment, and to secure his presence in hidin' to witness it.

"That's conjecture; for Dignum never let on so far. But what *is* known for certain is that Exciseman Jones, who were as daring and determined as his enemy—p'r'aps more so—for some reason was in the chimney, on to a grating in which he had managed to lower hisself from the roof; and that he could, if given time, have scrambled up again with difficulty, but was debarred from going lower. And, further, this is known—that, as Dignum sat on, pretendin' to yawn and huggin' his black intent, a little sut plopped down the chimney and scattered on the coals of the laid fire beneath.

"At that—'Curse this waitin'!' said he. 'The room's as chill as a belfry'; and he got to his feet, with a secret grin, and strolled to the hearth-stone.

"'I wonder,' said he, 'will the landlord object if I ventur' upon a glint of fire for comfort's sake?' and he pulled out his flint and steel, struck a spark, and with no more feelin' than he'd express in lighting a pipe, set the flame to the sticks.

"The trapt rat above never stirred or give tongue. My God! what a man! Sich a nature could afford to bide and bide—ay, for twenty year, if need be.

"Dignum would have enjoyed the sound of a cry; but he never got it. He listened with the grin fixed on his face; and of a sudden he heard a scrambling struggle, like as a dog with the colic jumping at a wall; and presently, as the sticks blazed and the smoke rose denser, a thick coughin', as of a consumptive man under bed-clothes. Still no cry, nor any appeal for mercy; no, not from the time he lit the fire till a horrible rattle come down, which was the last twitches of somethin' that choked and died on the sooty gratin' above.

"When all was quiet, Dignum he knocks with his foot on the floor and sits hisself down before the hearth, with a face like a pillow for innocence.

"'I were chilled and lit it,' says he to the landlord. 'You don't mind?'

"Mind? Who would have ventur'd to cross Dark Dignum's fancies?

"He give a boisterous laugh, and ordered in a double noggin of humming stuff.

"'Here,' he says, when it comes, 'is to the health of Exciseman Jones, that swore to bring me to the ground.'

"'To the ground,' mutters a thick voice from the chimney.

"'My God!' says the landlord—'there's something up there!'

"Something there was; and terrible to look upon when they brought it to light. The creature's struggles had ground the sut into its face, and its nails were black below the quick.

"Were those words the last of its death-throe, or an echo from beyond? Ah! we may question; but they were heard by two men.

"Dignum went free. What could they prove agen him? Not that he knew there was aught in the chimney when he lit the fire. The other would scarcely have acquent him of his plans. And Exciseman Jones was hurried into his grave alongside the church up here.

"And therein he lay for twenty year, despite that, not a twelvemonth after his coming, the sacrilegious house itself sunk roaring into the waters. For the Lord would have none of it, and, biding His time, struck through a fortnight of deluge, and hurled church and cliff into ruin. But the yard remained, and, nighest the seaward edge of it, Exciseman Jones slept in his fearful winding sheet and bided *his* time.

"It came when my grandfather were a young man of thirty, and mighty close and confidential with Dark Dignum. God forgive him! Doubtless he were led away by the older smuggler, that had a grace of villainy about him, 'tis said, and used Lord Chesterfield's printed letters for wadding to his bullets.

"By then he was a ramping, roaring devil; but, for all his bold hands were stained with crime, the memory of Exciseman Jones and of his promise dwelled with him and darkened him ever more and more, and never left him. So those that knew him said.

"Now all these years the cliff edge agen the graveyard, where it was broke off, was scabbing into the sea below. But still they used this way of ascent for their ungodly traffic; and over the ruin of the cliff they had drove a new path for to carry up their kegs.

"It was a cloudy night in March, with scud and a fitful moon, and there was a sloop in the offing, and under the shore a loaded boat that had just pulled in with muffled rowlocks. Out of this Dark Dignum was the first to sling hisself a brace of rundlets; and my grandfather followed with two more. They made softly for the cliff path—began the ascent—was half-way up.

"Whiz!—a stone of chalk went by them with a skirl, and slapped into the rubble below.

"'Some more of St. Dunstan's gravel!' cried Dignum, pantin' out a reckless laugh under his load; and on they went again.

"Hwish!—a bigger lump came like a thunder-bolt, and the wind of it took the bloody smuggler's hat and sent it swooping into the darkness like a bird.

"'Thunder!' said Dignum; 'the cliffs breaking away!'

"The words was hardly out of his mouth, when there flew such a volley of chalk stones as made my grandfather, though none had touched him, fall upon the path where he stood, and begin to gabble out what he could call to mind of the prayers for the dying. He was in the midst of it, when he heard a scream come from his companion as froze the very marrow in his bones. He looked up, thinkin' his hour had come.

"My God! What a sight he saw! The moon had shone out of a sudden, and the light of it struck down on Dignum's face, and that was the colour of dirty parchment. And he looked higher, and give a sort of sob.

"For there, stickin' out of the cliff side, was half the body of Exciseman Jones, with its arms stretched abroad, *and it was clawin' out lumps of chalk and hurling them down at Dignum!*

"And even as he took this in through his terror, a great ball of white came hurtling, and went full on to the man's face with a splash—and he were spun down into the deep night below, a nameless thing."

The old creature came to a stop, his eyes glinting with a febrile excitement.

"And so," I said, " Exciseman Jones was true to his word?"

The tension of memory was giving—the spring slowly uncoiling itself.

"Ay," he said doubtfully. "The cliff had flaked away by degrees to his very grave. They found his skelington stickin' out of the chalk."

"His *skeleton*?" said I, with the emphasis of disappointment.

"The first, sir, the first. Ay, his was the first. There've been a many exposed since. The work of decay goes on, and the bones they fall into the sea. Sometimes, sailing off shore, you may see a shank or an arm protrudin' like a pigeon's leg from a pie. But the wind or the weather takes it and it goes. There's more to follow yet. Look at 'em! look at these bents! Every one a grave, with a skelington in it. The wear and tear from the edge will reach each one in turn, and then the last of the ungodly will have ceased from the earth."

"And what became of your grandfather?"

"My grandfather? There were something happened made him renounce the devil. He died one of the elect. His youth were heedless and unregenerate; but, 'tis said, after he were turned thirty he never smiled agen. There was a reason. Did I ever tell you the story of Dark Dignum and Exciseman Jones?"

The Delusion of Ralph Penwyn

Julian Hawthorne

Ten years ago Ralph Penwyn was still a very handsome man. For that matter, he was a little past thirty, but looked forty; his dark hair had begun to turn gray on the front part of his head, and there were lines of maturity in his face. His ancestors were black Celts of Cornwall, and he had their tall, athletic frame, black, kindling eyes, and passionate, artistic temperament.

He had studied art, and after visiting Europe had painted some good pictures. One of them, "The Profanation," had been commended by the great Watts. "About as compelling an imaginative thing," he said of it, "as ever I saw." I had not at that time seen it myself; but had been told that the composition centered about a female figure, beautiful and tragic.

It was the last thing Ralph painted. "What we call a work of art," said he, "is but a by-product. Art is a spiritual culture whose best conceptions are never brought down to the physical plane." This may have been esoteric philosophy, or it may have been an excuse for indolence—of that intellectual kind that often accompanies great powers.

Ralph had money and did not have to work. He got a volunteer commission and went through the Spanish War, performing conspicuous exploits; in all he did he was conspicuous, though indifferent. Instead of accepting promotion he resigned and went to India, and was not heard from for some years. He never told what he did there or what happened to him.

Is there really a school or brotherhood of adepts in India? Is Yoga and all that sort of thing truth or a fairy-tale?

He returned unannounced to New York and took up his abode in one of the family heirlooms, an old brownstone house on Second Avenue. He refitted and furnished it in accordance with his taste, and gave a few informal receptions, attended by a score of his friends—all men. He entertained us with some curious "border-land" scientific experiments which would have been called magic a few years ago. For my own part, I thought I saw something in a crystal sphere which was not to be explained upon any scientific basis that I know of. But what is the use of being surprised at anything nowadays? Hypnotism, incarnate or disincarnate, accounts for everything.

For the rest, we had good punch and cigars and very fetching music, coming and going like a breeze from another world; the musicians were behind a screen—if there were any musicians! Ralph, as host, was genial but quieter than of old, and personally quite matter of fact—perhaps from a motive of artistic contrast to the entertainment. He told us interesting but credible things about his adventures abroad, and discussed art, literature, politics, every-day matters. All the time I was thinking of the woman's face I had imagined I saw in the crystal sphere. Had I met its possessor somewhere? Who? and where?

I walked home that night with a famous sculptor (now dead) who knew Ralph more intimately than I did. "Did Ralph ever have a romance—anything with a woman in it?" I asked him.

"A fellow of his strong masculine fiber naturally would have—and probably not more than one."

"Which would make up by its intensity for its uniqueness?"

"And by the tragedy of it—unless it happened just right."

"His wasn't just right?"

"I could give you no more than a guess; and I suppose it isn't a thing one has any right to guess about."

That was all I got from the man of bronze and marble.

Next evening I made my regular weekly call on old Mrs. Montrose Capet. She was a patrician of Virginia, rich, exclusive, fastidious, and, at seventy, a bit eccentric; to persons she liked, the best and kindest of women. One thing about her I had never quite approved—that sixth sense which she possessed in addition to the ordinary five; for I am not fond of the occult. Few persons then living, however, knew that she had the "faculty," and our own intercourse had never looked in that direction. I sought her for her normal and unusual gifts of conversation and human nature.

I found her alone; the former queen of society had few familiars left now. Teapot and cups were ready on the Oriental stand in the little gold-room, as she called her boudoir. We were happy and cozy for ten minutes; then I noticed signs of uneasiness in her. She kept putting her hand to her forehead.

"Headache?"

"Not exactly," she replied; "but you've been up to something. And you've brought it with-you, the—what do you call it ?—the aura, you know. Mercy, how strong!"

She brushed her fingers across her eyes once or twice.

"H'm—yes—oh, yes! My dear boy, I really beg your pardon! Do you want me to go on? or shall I switch it off?"

I was polite enough to beg her not to switch it off, whatever it was.

She brought the fingers of her right hand close together and pressed them to the center of her forehead; then she began a muttering, half to herself, half to me. "It's really so exceptional I must have a look at it. A handsome boy that! Oh, a studio, of course, and she's his model. Well, he can certainly paint! But what a theme! Terrible! In earnest about it, too! Ah—h'm! What I expected. This will end badly. All his fault, but he'll regret it. And she—oh, my heart! Oh!"

Mrs. Capet's hand dropped to her lap, and she leaned back in her chair.

I felt rather embarrassed. "So it will end badly?" I murmured.

"Eh? No, say no more about it. I've had quite enough. Mercy, what people! I advise you to cut his acquaintance. Ended? No, but it's coming, and all India can't prevent it. Have some more tea, my dear. What's that?"

It was something on me, apparently, for her eyes—and especially her left eye, suddenly grown preternaturally bright—were fixed upon a point just above my heart. I glanced down in that direction.

I had gone to Ralph's reception the night before in a Prince Albert coat—the thing being informal—and had on the same garment now. He had presented to each if us a little memento; mine was a silver medallion with some Oriental device figured upon it in relief. I had stuck it in my left lapel buttonhole, hardly examining it at the time, and forgetting all about it afterward.

"The button? Anything wrong with it?" I queried.

My admirable friend pointed at it with a finger that trembled a little. "The whole story is right there," she said. "No; I've had enough for to-day, I tell you! But if anything queer about that person turns up—and it will before long, too—you'll find the explanation in that button, as you call it. And now," she added, changing her tone, "please, like a good boy, take the thing out of your buttonhole and put it where I can't see it; and then we'll have one more cup of tea."

I may remark that my subsequent investigation of the physical attributes of my button did not supply me with grounds for supposing that it had any other significance, as accounting for Mrs. Capet's manifestations, than the fact of its having belonged to Ralph Penwyn; in other words, I had witnessed an illustration by her of what occultists call psychometrizing. The "aura" of his personal equation, or of his character and adventures, had become attached to the material object, and had in some way revealed to her sixth sense this equation or what these adventures were. At all events, the button turned out to be nothing more than a silver disk of antique design and workmanship, decorated with the effigy of some heathen deity squatting in the midst of an inscription in some Oriental language. I leave the further interpretation of the incident to those whose philosophical erudition qualifies them for the task. So far as I understood then, or have learned since, an ordinary bone shirt-stud, if it had previously belonged to Penwyn, would have served the purpose just as well.

I cannot deny, though, that my spontaneous speculativeness concerning Penwyn was a good deal stimulated by Mrs. Capet's little séance. Her utterances, Orphic though they had been, served to confirm my suspicion that he had been involved in some romance, and indicated that it had been of a sinister sort. A studio, a beautiful model, a catastrophe—it was not difficult to fill in the gaps. He had used the model, doubtless, for the chief figure in his "Profanation" picture of some years before. This inference prompted in me a strong desire to see the picture, and my eagerness was inflamed by a very fantastic notion; to wit, that the face in the picture would turn out to be identical with the one which I had imagined I saw in the crystal sphere. Fantastic, indeed, nay, irrational and ridiculous, such a notion was, and I was ashamed of it, but could not banish it. I was additionally preoccupied by the impression (already mentioned) that I had met somewhere the original of the specter of the sphere. For if the model for the picture and the original of the specter should prove to be one and the same, not only would Penwyn's romance become extremely interesting, but I should feel that I was, in a manner, mixed up with it myself.

A few days later I happened into the sculptor's studio. He had discerned an idea buried in a great mass of clay, and was digging it out with his customary quiet energy.

"Glad you came in," he said, continuing his work. "What do you think of this Penwyn business?"

"I haven't seen or heard of him since the other evening."

"He was in here yesterday. I feel uneasy about him. His experience in India did him no good. He talked of going back there. A man of his imagination and temperament can't dabble in that sort of thing with impunity. Between you and me, I think it's affecting his mind. He spoke of being 'obsessed by devils' quite in a matter-of-course way, as I might of dyspepsia. He asked me to take charge of one of his pictures, and, if I did not hear from him to the contrary within a given time, to destroy it. It's the finest painting he ever did. He seemed to fancy he was pursued by a fatal destiny—in some peril or other, physical or spiritual. And all the while he was as quiet as possible, outwardly. I don't like it at all. I shall get Harkness to look him over—without letting him suspect it, of course. Poor old Ralph!"

After expressing my surprise, sympathy, and concern, I said: "What picture do you refer to? Has he taken up painting again?"

"No; this is an old one. 'Profanation,' he calls it. I remember it made a sensation in Paris six or seven years back. Did you never see it? That's it, in the corner, with the sheet over it."

I moved the sheet aside, and for the first time saw "The Profanation."

It was a remarkable work, more, however, as regards design than technical execution. A beautiful young woman, in nuns' garb, on the arm of a man in evening dress, stands at the entrance to a masked ball, and proffers to the gate-keeper a goblet of emerald, richly carved, from which emanates a celestial luster. The Holy Grail in exchange for an evening's pleasure! The expression in the three faces, and especially in hers, is wonderfully impressive. The smile on her lips has the pathos of innocent childhood in it, but the sparkle in her eyes carries a hideous significance.

The influence of the picture was so strong that it was some moments before I realized that the nun's face was entirely different from that of the specter of the sphere.

Just then I heard the sculptor say something, and, supposing he had addressed me, I turned round. A lady had entered the studio; she was well known in New York society, and I was myself slightly acquainted with her. In fact, she was Mrs. Benton-Howard. As I turned toward them she greeted me by name, but I stared at her without responding.

"He looks as if he'd seen a ghost," said the sculptor, laughing.

"Something very like one," I replied, pulling myself together. "Isn't there a book called 'Phantasms of the Living'? I saw your face the other night in one of those Japanese crystal balls, Mrs. Howard, but until this instant I hadn't identified it."

"I'm living, I suppose," said she.

"Do you know Ralph Penwyn?" the sculptor asked her.

"Yes—at least, long ago I did. I haven't seen him since before the war."

She spoke without self-consciousness, but it must have been a matter of course to her that men should adore her; she was irresistibly lovely and, for a wonder, as good and wise as she was adorable to the senses. No portrait of her exists because, though every artist who saw her wanted to paint her, and several had induced her to sit, the results of the efforts even of the best of them were such ridiculous caricatures that they were always rubbed out. "Nobody can paint her," declared incomparable John, shaking his head over his own hopeless failure. "She's a spirit; I don't half believe she has a body!"

I took my leave—the lady and the sculptor had business together—but before I went I gave another long look at "The Profanation." There was certainly not the slightest similarity between the nun on the canvas and the exquisite being known as Edith Benton-Howard. But Penwyn had known both women; one of them had met a tragic fate, and the other—well, her countenance had been conjured into Penwyn's crystal.

The more I mulled over it the keener grew my antipathy to the occult.

About the middle of the winter season the Cadwaladers gave a masked ball at that immense palace of theirs on the upper avenue. The rooms were crowded, for the palace was new, and there was curiosity to see what it looked like. All the persons mentioned in this narrative were there, including even Mrs. Montrose Capet, looking surprisingly well and animated. It was her first social outing for ten years, and I wondered what had induced her to come. When Ralph Penwyn appeared I wondered more than ever.

Except for his greetings to our hosts and nods of recognition to his acquaintances, Penwyn devoted himself almost exclusively to lovely Mrs. Benton-Howard; so pointedly, indeed, that it was generally noticed. It so happened that he wore a Faust costume, and she was Marguerite; so they paired off suitably. There was another Marguerite among the guests, but she kept on her mask and was not identified. The circumstance, however, led to some misapprehensions characteristic of a masked ball.

"They seem to be making up for the time lost in their acquaintance," said I to the sculptor. "I've never seen Mrs. Howard more gracious."

"I've told her about him; she understands," he replied.

"She understands what?"

"Harkness contrived to examine him without his suspecting it," said the sculptor, in my ear. "He admits that the man is insane. He has delusions—there's no doubt about it. There's no great danger at present, but sooner or later he will have to be taken care of. Edith is humoring him, that's all. He imagines they're in love with each other, poor chap! I tried to prevent his coming here, but it was no use."

"A man needn't be insane to imagine he's in love with Mrs. Howard," I suggested.

But the artist—a very serious-minded man—only shook his head and scratched his beard.

Later in the evening I saw Faust and Marguerite pass toward the conservatory. He was talking to her with deep earnestness; she was listening with her head bent, and fingering the beautiful pearl necklace that she wore. He appeared in love, certainly, but otherwise sane enough. And if she were humoring him it seemed to me she was doing it very well.

I strolled about till I found a place beside Mrs. Capet. "You have made everybody else jealous of the Cadwaladers," I said.

"They needn't be," she replied, with a smile. "I came to see the last scene of the romance. But the very last will not be here."

"I'm told Doctor Harkness regards the case as pathological; Penwyn is of unsound mind."

"It will be so given out at the inquest," returned this appalling old lady. "But we know better. I do, at any rate."

"The inquest?"

"Wait till to-morrow," she said, fixing that wonderful eye upon me.

"You don't mean that Mrs. Howard is in any danger, I hope?"

"People of her sort are never in danger, but—well, you'll see."

Penwyn and Mrs. Howard are not known to have been seen again at the ball, after passing into the conservatory together. It was said, however, that she and her husband (who had spent most of the evening playing cards with three other prosperous merchants in an up-stairs room of the palace) had gone home together about one o'clock. There was another rumor to the effect that a man in the costume of Faust, accompanied by a lady dressed as Marguerite, had entered Penwyn's carriage nearly at the same hour, and been driven south. There was still another report that Penwyn had gone away alone. All that we can be certain of, however, is the fact that Edith Howard was in her own house the next morning and that she appeared much shocked at the news that was brought to her there.

The questionable period is that which intervened between the moment Edith and Ralph disappeared in the conservatory and that when his carriage arrived at his house on Second Avenue. There is only one person who professes to know what took place during that interval. I am now to tell the story that came to me from that source. I do not vouch for its truth, nor shall I attempt to reproduce the exact words of the narrator. Take it, if you please, as a chapter from an ordinary tale of romance, in which the writer claims the conventional omniscience of the fiction-monger; and judge as to its verity according to your own attitude toward the facts and the mysteries of human life.

As Ralph turned, just within the threshold of the conservatory, he observed that his companion had resumed her white-silk mask, with its veil falling below her chin.

"Darling, why do you cover your face? We are alone here."

"Let it be so," she whispered in reply. "There will be time enough afterward. No, you must not kiss me yet. Be patient a little longer."

"You love me, Edith?"

"I love you. I have always loved you. I have never loved any other man. Can you say as much, Ralph?"

"Until we met I never believed love possible for me. But why should we talk like children?" he exclaimed passionately. "A man is not a boy—he has put away boyish things. I knew a woman long ago; she is dead. I have been a student, since then, in the school of the masters, and have created a new being in myself. The laws of darkness are abrogated in the kingdom of light. You and I are free; we make our own world."

"Have you no fear of that dead woman—no regret for her, even?"

"No, neither regret nor fear. I should have done her worse wrong in staying with her than I did in leaving her. It was better for her that her body should die than that our souls should destroy each other. What we called our love would have turned out to be the deadliest enmity."

"If she could speak now, do you think she would confirm your words?" whispered the other after a pause.

"Let her speak, if she will—and can. I would agree to be bound by her verdict. But neither she nor anyone can come between us, beloved. She has long since taken up her new life and forgotten me as I had forgotten her."

"Can a woman who has died for love of a man ever forget him?"

"It was her error killed her, not her love. Oh, let us be done with this! It is our privilege and duty to live in the present, and the future. I have made everything ready. Tomorrow we shall be on our way. There is a heaven on earth, and we will live in it."

She laid her hand over his heart, and her eyes met his through the holes of her mask. "Heaven or hell, I will follow you everywhere," she said. There was a strangeness in her voice, and the hand that rested on him seemed to strike coldness through him. But he was too deeply impassioned to heed it. He led her to the rear entrance of the conservatory, and down a flight of stairs to a door on the side street. There he wrapped round her the domino that he carried on his arm, and they entered his carriage and were driven away.

"At last!" he exclaimed, with passionate exultation.

"Never to be parted again!" she murmured, still with that strangeness in her tones.

For a time they sat silent, her cold hand in his hot one. But as they approached the neighborhood of his home he turned to her.

"Off with the mask now—with all masks!" said he. "Give me the kiss that is my life—and my life to come!"

"You will never forget me?" she said, holding him back for a moment.

"Never, never, never!"

"Take me, then!"

He raised his hands to remove the silken vizard, but it seemed to crumble away at his first contact; and, as he bent forward, his warm lover's breath touched, not the soft pure cheeks of Edith Howard, but—to his madman's stare—the grisly surface of a naked skull. That, too, disintegrated before his eyes, the domino fell together, and a necklace of pearls dropped with a soft rattle to the floor of the carriage.

Such is my rendering, derived from information communicated to me by Mrs. Capet several days after the catastrophe, of what took place in Penwyn's carriage in the small hours of that winter morning; but inasmuch as its credibility depends solely upon our belief in the integrity of the old lady's clairvoyant powers we need lose no time in pronouncing it apocryphal and absurd. A few facts, however, remain to be recorded.

When the carriage arrived at Penwyn's door he failed to alight; upon which, after a few minutes, the coachman got down from his box and opened the door. He saw the figure of his master seated within; but examination showed that he was dead, and that the hilt of a small dagger was sticking out of his breast. The blade had been driven through his heart. No one else was in the carriage, and the only rational inference was the one which was made at the coroner's inquest (additionally confirmed by the testimony of Doctor Harkness as to the dead man's insanity), that he had committed suicide while in a state of unsound mind.

It was also mentioned in the evidence (though no significance could be attached to it) that a woman's domino was found on the seat of the carriage, beside the body; and that a valuable pearl necklace lay on the floor. Moreover—and this was really odd—on the forehead of Penwyn's body was branded or impressed a small circular mark or stamp, representing—so far as could be discerned—the effigy of an Oriental deity, surrounded by what seemed to be a sentence in an unknown language.

When I told Mrs. Capet about this she nodded, and muttered to herself something that sounded like "The seal of the brotherhood."

A few weeks later I got a note from the sculptor, asking me to come to the studio. "I wanted you to be a witness of my discharge of an obligation imposed upon me by our poor friend Penwyn," he said, when I arrived. "This is the day which be appointed for the destruction of his 'Profanation.' It seems a pity to annihilate so fine a work, but I have it on my conscience, as it were, you know."

The picture had been taken out of its frame, and stood near a large brazier filled with glowing coals.

I scrutinized for the last time, with a very eager interest, I must confess, the face of the nun in the picture. The mingling, in her smile, of the angel and the demon was still perceptible, but I fancied that the former had gained a little upon the latter since I saw the painting last.

"Do you suppose the woman who posed for that figure could have had any connection with Ralph's insanity and death?" I asked.

"My dear fellow! A model? What a wild idea!" he laughed.

"Did you notice the second Marguerite at the Cadwaladers' ball?"

"I believe there were two, now you mention it," said he. "Yes, Mrs. Howard and the other. A masquerade mystification, probably. Well, here goes for the burnt offering."

He cut the canvas from the stretcher, folded it up, and laid it upon the red-hot coals. In a minute it was in flames. And just then Mrs. Howard came hastily into the studio.

After a few commonplaces, her errand came out. "I know Mr. Penwyn had left his picture of 'The Profanation' with you. I want to know whether it can be bought. I would like to have it."

"My dear lady, you are too late," replied the sculptor, waving a hand toward the brazier. "'The Profanation,' at Ralph's request, has become fire and air, like the genius that produced it."

Her face was pale and her eyes dark as she watched the leaping and gradual subsidence of the flames. She twisted her flexible hands together. "It is gone, it is no more!" she murmured at last, as the canvas sank into ashes and became gray. "After all, perhaps that is best. There was something noble in his soul."

She bowed to us and went out. The sculptor glanced at me, elevated his eyebrows, scratched his beard, and ordered his servant to remove the brazier.

The Demon Spell

Hume Nisbet

It was about the time when spiritualism was all the craze in England, and no party was reckoned complete without a spirit-rapping séance being included amongst the other entertainments.

One night I had been invited to the house of a friend, who was a great believer in the manifestations from the unseen world, and who had asked for my special edification a well-known trance medium. "A pretty as well as heaven-gifted girl, whom you will be sure to like, I know," he said as he asked me.

I did not believe in the return of spirits, yet, thinking to be amused, consented to attend at the hour appointed. At that time I had just returned from a long sojourn abroad, and was in a very delicate state of health, easily impressed by outward influences, and nervous to a most extraordinary extent.

To the hour appointed I found myself at my friend's house, and was then introduced to the sitters who had assembled to witness the phenomena. Some were strangers like myself to the rules of the table, others who were adepts took their places at once in the order to which they had in former meetings attended. The trance medium had not yet arrived, and while waiting upon her coming we sat down and opened the séance with a hymn.

We had just furnished the second verse when the door opened and the medium glided in, and took her place on a vacant set by my side, joining in with the others in the last verse, after which we all sat motionless with our hands resting upon the table, waiting upon the first manifestation from the unseen world.

Now, although I thought all this performance very ridiculous, there was something in the silence and the dim light, for the gas had been turned low down, and the room seemed filled with shadows; something about the fragile figure at my side, with her drooping head, which thrilled me with a curious sense of fear and icy horror such as I had never felt before.

I am not by nature imaginative or inclined to superstition, but, from the moment that young girl had entered the room, I felt as if a hand had been laid upon my heart, a cold iron hand, that was compressing it, and causing it to stop throbbing. My sense of hearing also had grown more acute and sensitive, so that the beating of the watch in my vest pocket sounded like the thumping of a quartz-crushing machine, and the measured breathing of those about me as loud and nerve-disturbing as the snorting of a steam engine.

Only when I turned to look upon the trance medium did I become soothed; then it seemed as if a cold-air wave had passed through my brain, subduing, for the time-being, those awful sounds.

"She is possessed," whispered my host on the other side of me. "Wait, and she will speak presently, and tell us whom we have got beside us."

As we sat and waited the table moved several times under our hands, while knockings at intervals took place in the table and all round the room, a most weird and blood-curdling, yet ridiculous performance, which made me feel half inclined to run out with fear, and half inclined to sit still and laugh; on the whole, I think, however, that horror had the more complete possession of me.

Presently she raised her head and laid her hand upon mine, beginning to speak in a strange monotonous, far away voice, "This is my first visit since I passed from earth-life, and you have called me here."

I shivered as her hand touched mine, but had not strength to withdraw it from her light, soft grasp.

"I am what you would call a lost soul; that is, I am in the lowest sphere. Last week I was in the body, but met my death down Whitechapel way. I was what you call an unfortunate, aye, unfortunate enough. Shall I tell you how it happened?"

The medium's eyes were closed, and whether it was my distorted imagination or not, she appeared to have grown older and decidedly debauched-looking since she sat down, or rather as if a light, filmy mask of degrading and soddened vice had replaced the former delicate features.

No one spoke, and the trance medium continued: "I had been out all that day and without any luck or food, so that I was dragging my wearied body along through the slush and mud for it had been wet all day, and I was drenched to the skin, and miserable, ah, ten thousand times more wretched than I am now, for the earth is a far worse hell for such as I than our hell here.

"I had importuned several passers by as I went along that night, but none of them spoke to me, for work had been scarce all this winter, and I suppose I did not look so tempting as I have been; only once a man answered me, a dark-faced, middle-sized man, with a soft voice, and much better dressed than my usual companions.

"He asked me where I was going, and then left me, putting a coin into my hand, for which I thanked him. Being just in time for the last public-house, I hurried up, but on going to the bar and looking at my hand, I found it to be a curious foreign coin, with outlandish figures on it, which the landlord would not take, so I went out again to the dark fog and rain without my drink after all.

"There was no use going any further that night. I turned up the court where my lodgings were, intending to go home and get a sleep, since I could get no food, when I felt something touch me softly from behind like as if someone had caught hold of my shawl; then I stopped and turned about to see who it was.

"I was alone, and with no one near me, nothing but fog and the half light from the court lamp. Yet I felt as if something had got hold of me, though I could not see what it was, and that it was gathering about me.

"I tried to scream out, but could not, as this unseen grasp closed upon my throat and choked me, and then I fell down and for a moment forgot everything.

"Next moment I woke up, outside my own poor mutilated body, and stood watching the fell work going on—as you see it now."

Yes I saw it all as the medium ceased speaking, a mangled corpse lying on a muddy pavement, and a demoniac, dark, pock-marked face bending over it, with the lean claws outspread, and the dense fog instead of a body, like the half formed incarnation of muscles.

"That is what did it, and you will know it again," she said. "I have come for you to find it."

"Is he an Englishman?" I gasped, as the vision faded away and the room once more became definite.

"It is neither man nor woman, but it lives as I do, it is with me now and may be with you to-night, still if you will have me instead of it, I can keep it back, only you must wish for me with all your might."

The séance was now becoming too horrible, and by general consent our host turned up the gas, and then I saw for the first time the medium, now relieved from her evil possession, a beautiful girl of about nineteen, with I think the most glorious brown eyes I had ever before looked into.

"Do you believe what you have been speaking about?" I asked her as we were sitting talking together.

"What was that?"

"About the murdered woman."

"I don't know anything at all. Only that I have been sitting at the table. I never know what my trances are." Was she speaking the truth? Her dark eyes looked truth, so that I could not doubt her. That night when I went to my lodgings I must confess that it was some time before I could make up my mind to go to bed. I was decidedly upset and nervous, and wished that I had never gone to this spirit meeting, making a mental vow, as I threw off my clothes and hastily got into bed, that it was the last unholy gathering I would ever attend.

For the first time in my life I could not put out the gas, I felt as if the room was filled with ghosts, as if this pair of ghastly spectres, the murderer and his victim, had accompanied me home, and were at that moment disputing the possession of me, so instead, I pulled the bedclothes over my head, it being a cold night, and went that fashion off to sleep.

Twelve o'clock! and the anniversary of the day that Christ was born. Yes, I heard it striking from the street spire and counted the strokes, slowly tolled out, listening to the echoes from other steeples, after this one had ceased, as I lay awake in that gas-lit room, feeling as if I was not alone this Christmas morn.

Thus, while I was trying to think what had made me wake so suddenly, I seemed to hear a far off echo cry "Come to me." At the same time the bedclothes were slowly pulled from the bed, and left in a confused mass on the floor.

"Is that you, Polly?" I cried, remembering the spirit séance, and the name by which the spirit had announced herself when she took possession.

Three distinct knocks resounded on the bedpost at my ear, the signal for "Yes."

"Can you speak to me?"

"Yes," an echo rather than a voice replied, while I felt my flesh creeping, yet strove to be brave.

"Can I see you?"

"No!"

"Feel you?"

Instantly the feeling of a light cold hand touched my brow and passed over my face.

"In God's name what do you want?"

"To save the girl I was in tonight. It is after her and will kill her if you do not come quickly."

In an instant I was out of the bed, and tumbling my clothes on any way, horrified through it all, yet feeling as if Polly were helping me to dress. There was a

Kandian dagger on my table which I had brought from Ceylon, an old dagger which I had bought for its antiquity and design, and this I snatched up as I left the room, with that light unseen hand leading me out of the house and along the deserted snow-covered streets.

I did not know where the trance medium lived, but I followed where that light grasp led me through the wild, blinding snow-drift, round corners and through short cuts, with my head down and the flakes falling thickly about me, until at last I arrived at a silent square and in front of a house which by some instinct, I knew that I must enter.

Over by the other side of the street I saw a man standing looking up to a dimly-lighted window, but I could not see him very distinctly and I did not pay much attention to him at the time, but rushed instead up the front steps and into the house, that unseen hand still pulling me forward.

How that door opened, or if it did open I could not say, I only know that I got in, as we get into places in a dream, and up the inner stairs, I passed into a bedroom where the light was burning dimly.

It was her bedroom, and she was struggling in the thug-like grasp of those same demon claws, and the rest of it drifting away to nothingness.

I saw it all at a glance, her half-naked form, with the disarranged bedclothes, as the unformed demon of muscles clutched that delicate throat, and then I was at it like a fury with my Kandian dagger, slashing crossways at those cruel claws and that evil face, while blood streaks followed the course of my knife, making ugly stains, until at last it ceased struggling and disappeared like a horrid nightmare, as the half-strangled girl, now released from that fell grip, woke up the house with her screams, while from her releasing hand dropped a strange coin, which I took possession of.

Thus I left her, feeling that my work was done, going downstairs as I had come up, without impediment or even seemingly, in the slightest degree, attracting the attention of the other inmates of the house, who rushed in their nightdresses towards the bedroom from whence the screams were issuing.

Into the street again, with that coin in one hand and my dagger in the other I rushed, and then I remembered the man whom I had seen looking up at the window. Was he there still? Yes, but on the ground in a confused black mass amongst the white snow as if he had been struck down.

I went over to where he lay and looked at him. Was he dead? Yes. I turned him round and saw that his throat was gashed from ear to ear, and all over his face—the same dark, pallid, pock-marked evil face, and claw-like hands, I saw the dark slashes of my Kandian dagger, while the soft white snow around him was stained with crimson life pools, and as I looked I heard the clock strike one, while from the distance sounded the chant of the coming waits, then I turned and fled blindly into the darkness.

The Diary of Mr. Poynter

M. R. James

The sale-room of an old and famous firm of book auctioneers in London is, of course, a great meeting-place for collectors, librarians, dealers: not only when an auction is in progress, but perhaps even more notably when books that are coming on for sale are upon view. It was in such a sale-room that the remarkable series of events began which were detailed to me not many months ago by the person whom they principally affected, namely, Mr. James Denton, M. A., F. S. A., etc., etc., some time of Trinity Hall, now, or lately, of Rendcomb Manor in the county of Warwick.

He, on a certain spring day not many years since, was in London for a few days upon business connected principally with the furnishing of the house which he had just finished building at Rendcomb. It may be a disappointment to you to learn that Rendcomb Manor was new; that I cannot help. There had, no doubt, been an old house; but it was not remarkable for beauty or interest. Even had it been, neither beauty nor interest would have enabled it to resist the disastrous fire which about a couple of years before the date of my story had razed it to the ground. I am glad to say that all that was most valuable in it had been saved, and that it was fully insured. So that it was with a comparatively light heart that Mr. Denton was able to face the task of building a new and considerably more convenient dwelling for himself and his aunt who constituted his whole *ménage*.

Being in London, with time on his hands, and not far from the sale-room at which I have obscurely hinted, Mr. Denton thought that he would spend an hour there upon the chance of finding, among that portion of the famous Thomas collection of MSS., which he knew to be then on view, something bearing upon the history or topography of his part of Warwickshire.

He turned in accordingly, purchased a catalogue and ascended to the sale-room, where, as usual, the books were disposed in cases and some laid out upon the long tables. At the shelves, or sitting about at the tables, were figures, many of whom were familiar to him. He exchanged nods and greetings with several, and then settled down to examine his catalogue and note likely items. He had made good progress through about two hundred of the five hundred lots—every now and then rising to take a volume from the shelf and give it a cursory glance—when a hand was laid on his shoulder, and he looked up. His interrupter was one of those intelligent men with a pointed beard and a flannel shirt, of whom the last quarter of the nineteenth century was, it seems to me, very prolific.

It is no part of my plan to repeat the whole conversation which ensued between the two. I must content myself with stating that it largely referred to common acquaintances, e.g., to the nephew of Mr. Denton's friend who had recently married and settled in Chelsea, to the sister-in-law of Mr. Denton's friend who had been seriously indisposed, but was now better, and to a piece of china which Mr. Denton's friend had purchased some months before at a price much below its true value. From which you will rightly infer that the conversation was rather in the nature of a monologue. In due time, however, the friend bethought himself that Mr. Denton was there for a purpose, and said he, "What are you looking out for in particular? I don't think there's much in this lot." "Why, I thought there might be some Warwickshire collections, but I don't see anything under Warwick in the catalogue." "No, apparently not," said the friend. "All the same, I believe I noticed something like a Warwickshire diary. What was the name again? Drayton? Potter? Painter—either a P or a D, I feel sure." He turned over the leaves quickly. "Yes, here it is. Poynter. Lot 486. That might interest you. There are the books, I think: out on the table. Some one has been looking at them. Well, I must be getting on. Good-bye, you'll look us up, won't you? Couldn't you come this afternoon? We've got a little music about four. Well, then, when you're next in town." He went off. Mr. Denton looked at his watch and found to his confusion that he could spare no more than a moment before retrieving his luggage and going for the train. The moment was just enough to show him that there were four largish volumes of the diary—that it concerned the years about 1710, and that there seemed to be a good many insertions in it of various kinds. It seemed quite worth while to leave a commission of five and twenty pounds for it, and this he was able to do, for his usual agent entered the room as he was on the point of leaving it.

That evening he rejoined his aunt at their temporary abode, which was a small dower-house not many hundred yards from the Manor. On the following morning the two resumed a discussion that had now lasted for some weeks as to the equipment of the new house. Mr. Denton laid before his relative a statement of the results of his visit to town—particulars of carpets, of chairs, of wardrobes, and of bedroom china. "Yes, dear," said his aunt, "but I don't see any chintzes here. Did you go to ——?"

Mr. Denton stamped on the floor (where else, indeed, could he have stamped?). "Oh dear, oh dear," he said, "the one thing I missed. I *am* sorry. The fact is I was on my way there and I happened to be passing Robins's." His aunt threw up her hands. "Robins's! Then the next thing will be another parcel of horrible old books at some outrageous price. I do think, James, when I am taking all this trouble for you, you might contrive to remember the one or two things which I specially begged you to see after. It's not as if I was asking it for myself. I don't know whether you think I get any pleasure out of it, but if so I can assure you it's very much the reverse. The thought and worry and trouble I have over it you have no idea of, and *you* have simply to go to the shops and order the things." Mr. Denton interposed a moan of penitence. "Oh, aunt—" "Yes, that's all very well, dear, and I don't want to speak sharply, but you *must* know how very annoying it is: particularly as it delays the whole of our business for I can't tell how long: here is Wednesday—the Simpsons come to-morrow, and you can't leave them. Then on Saturday we have friends, as you know, coming for tennis. Yes, indeed, you spoke of asking them yourself, but, of course, I had to write the notes, and it is ridiculous, James, to look like that. We must occasionally be civil to our neighbours: you wouldn't like to have it said we were perfect bears. What was I saying? Well, anyhow it comes to this, that it must be Thursday in next week at least, before you can go to town again, and until we have decided upon the chintzes it is impossible to settle upon one single other thing."

Mr. Denton ventured to suggest that as the paint and wallpapers had been dealt with, this was too severe a view: but this his aunt was not prepared to admit at the moment. Nor, indeed, was there any proposition he could have advanced which she would have found herself able to accept. However, as the day went on, she receded a little from this position: examined with lessening disfavour the samples and price lists submitted by her nephew, and even in some cases gave a qualified approval to his choice.

As for him, he was naturally somewhat dashed by the consciousness of duty unfulfilled, but more so by the prospect of a lawn-tennis party, which, though an inevitable evil in August, he had thought there was no occasion to fear in May. But he was to some extent cheered by the arrival on the Friday morning of an intimation that he had secured at the price of £12 10s. the four volumes of Poynter's manuscript diary, and still more by the arrival on the next morning of the diary itself.

The necessity of taking Mr. and Mrs. Simpson for a drive in the car on Saturday morning and of attending to his neighbours and guests that afternoon prevented him from doing more than open the parcel until the party had retired to bed on the Saturday night. It was then that he made certain of the fact, which he had before only suspected, that he had indeed acquired the diary of Mr. William Poynter, Squire of Acrington (about four miles from his own parish)—that same Poynter who was for a time a member of the circle of Oxford antiquaries, the centre of which was Thomas Hearne, and with whom Hearne seems ultimately to have quarrelled—a not uncommon episode in the career of that excellent man. As is the case with Hearne's own collections, the diary of Poynter contained a good many notes from printed books, descriptions of coins and other antiquities that had been brought to his notice, and drafts of letters on these subjects, besides the chronicle of everyday events. The description in the sale-catalogue had given Mr. Denton no idea of the amount of interest which seemed to lie in the book, and he sat up reading in the first of the four volumes until a reprehensibly late hour.

On the Sunday morning, after church, his aunt came into the study and was diverted from what she had been going to say to him by the sight of the four brown leather quartos on the table. "What are these?" she said suspiciously. "New, aren't they? Oh! Are these the things that made you forget my chintzes? I thought so. Disgusting. What did you give for them, I should like to know? Over Ten Pounds? James, it is really sinful. Well, if you have money to throw away on this kind of thing, there *can* be no reason why you should not subscribe—and subscribe handsomely—to my anti-Vivisection League. There is not, indeed, James, and I shall be very seriously annoyed if—. Who did you say wrote them? Old Mr. Poynter, of Acrington? Well, of course, there is some interest in getting together old papers about this neighbourhood. But Ten Pounds!" She picked up one of the volumes—not that which her nephew had been reading—and opened it at random, dashing it to the floor the next instant with a cry of disgust as a earwig fell from between the pages. Mr. Denton picked it up with a smothered expletive and said, "Poor book! I think you're rather hard on Mr. Poynter." "Was I, my dear? I beg his pardon, but you know I cannot abide those horrid creatures. Let me see if I've done any mischief." "No, I think all's well: but look here what you've opened him on." "Dear me, yes, to be sure! how very interesting. Do unpin it, James, and let me look at it."

It was a piece of patterned stuff about the size of the quarto page, to which it was fastened by an old-fashioned pin. James detached it and handed it to his aunt, carefully replacing the pin in the paper.

Now, I do not know exactly what the fabric was; but it had a design printed upon it, which completely fascinated Miss Denton. She went into raptures over it, held it against the wall, made James do the same, that she might retire to contemplate it from a distance: then pored over it at close quarters, and ended her examination by expressing in the warmest terms her appreciation of the taste of the ancient Mr. Poynter who had had the happy idea of preserving this sample in his diary. "It is a most charming pattern," she said, "and remarkable too. Look, James, how delightfully the lines ripple. It reminds one of hair, very much, doesn't it. And then these knots of ribbon at intervals. They give just the relief of colour that is wanted. I wonder—" "I was going to say," said James with deference, "I wonder if it would cost much to have it copied for our curtains." "Copied? how could you have it copied, James?" "Well, I don't know the details, but I suppose that is a printed pattern, and that you could have a block cut from it in wood or metal." "Now, really, that is a capital idea, James. I am almost inclined to be glad that you were so—that you forgot the chintzes on Monday. At any rate, I'll promise to forgive and forget if you get this *lovely* old thing copied. No one will have anything in the least like it, and mind, James, we won't allow it to be sold. Now I *must* go, and I've totally forgotten what it was I came in to say: never mind, it'll keep."

After his aunt had gone James Denton devoted a few minutes to examining the pattern more closely than he had yet had a chance of doing. He was puzzled to think why it should have struck Miss Benton so forcibly. It seemed to him not specially remarkable or pretty. No doubt it was suitable enough for a curtain pattern: it ran in vertical bands, and there was some indication that these were intended to converge at the top. She was right, too, in thinking that these main bands resembled rippling—almost curling—tresses of hair. Well, the main thing was to find out by means of trade directories, or otherwise, what firm would undertake the reproduction of an old pattern of this kind. Not to delay the reader over this portion of the story, a list of likely names was made out, and Mr. Denton fixed a day for calling on them, or some of them, with his sample.

The first two visits which he paid were unsuccessful: but there is luck in odd numbers. The firm in Bermondsey which was third on his list was accustomed to handling this line. The evidence they were able to produce justified their being entrusted with the job. "Our Mr. Cattell" took a fervent personal interest in it. "It's 'eartrending, isn't it, sir," he said, "to picture the quantity of reelly lovely medeevial stuff of this kind that lays well-nigh unnoticed in many of our residential country 'ouses: much of it in peril, I take it, of being cast aside as so much rubbish. What is it Shakespeare says—unconsidered trifles. Ah, I often say he 'as a word for us all, sir. I say Shakespeare, but I'm well aware all don't 'old with me there—I 'ad something of an upset the other day when a gentleman came in—a titled man, too, he was, and I think he told me he'd wrote on the topic, and I 'appened to cite out something about 'Ercules and the painted cloth. Dear me, you never see such a pother. But as to this, what you've kindly confided to us, it's a piece of work we shall take a reel enthusiasm in achieving it out to the very best of our ability. What man 'as done, as I was observing only a few weeks back to another esteemed client, man can do, and in three to four weeks' time, all being well, we shall 'ope to lay before you evidence to that effect, sir. Take the address, Mr. 'Iggins, if you please."

Such was the general drift of Mr. Cattell's observations on the occasion of his first interview with Mr. Denton. About a month later, being advised that some samples were ready for his inspection, Mr. Denton met him again, and had, it seems, reason to be satisfied with the faithfulness of the reproduction of the design. It had been finished off at the top in accordance with the indication I mentioned, so that the vertical bands joined. But something still needed to be done in the way of matching the colour of the original. Mr. Cattell had suggestions of a technical kind to offer, with which I need not trouble you. He had also views as to the general desirability of the pattern which were vaguely adverse. "You say you don't wish this to be supplied excepting to personal friends equipped with a authorization from yourself, sir. It shall be done. I quite understand your wish to keep it exclusive: lends it a catchit, does it not, to the suite? What's every man's, it's been said, is no man's."

"Do you think it would be popular if it were generally obtainable?" asked Mr. Denton.

"I 'ardly think it, sir," said Cattell, pensively clasping his beard. "I 'ardly think it. Not popular: it wasn't popular with the man that cut the block, was it, Mr. 'Iggins?"

"Did he find it a difficult job?"

"He'd no call to do so, sir; but the fact is that the artistic temperament—and our men are artists, sir, every man of them—true artists as much as many that the world styles by that term—it's apt to take some strange 'ardly accountable likes or dislikes, and here was an example. The twice or thrice that I went to inspect his progress: language I could understand, for that's 'abitual to him, but reel distaste for what I should call a dainty enough thing, I did not, nor am I now able to fathom. It seemed," said Mr. Cattell, looking narrowly upon Mr. Denton, "as if the man scented something almost Hevil in the design."

"Indeed? did he tell you so? I can't say I see anything sinister in it myself."

"Neether can I, sir. In fact I said as much. 'Come, Gatwick,' I said, 'what's to do here? What's the reason of your prejudice—for I can call it no more than that?' But, no! no explanation was forthcoming. And I was merely reduced, as I am now, to a shrug of the shoulders, and a *cui bono*. However, here it is," and with that the technical side of the question came to the front again.

The matching of the colours for the background, the hem, and the knots of ribbon was by far the longest part of the business, and necessitated many sendings to and fro of the original pattern and of new samples. During part of August and September, too, the Dentons were away from the Manor. So that it was not until October was well in that a sufficient quantity of the stuff had been manufactured to furnish curtains for the three or four bedrooms which were to be fitted up with it.

On the feast of Simon and Jude the aunt and nephew returned from a short visit to find all completed, and their satisfaction at the general effect was great. The new curtains, in particular, agreed to admiration with their surroundings. When Mr. Denton was dressing for dinner, and took stock of his room, in which there was a large amount of the chintz displayed, he congratulated himself over and over again on the luck which had first made him forget his aunt's commission and had then put into his hands this extremely effective means of remedying his mistake. The pattern was, as he said at dinner, so restful and yet so far from being dull. And Miss Denton—who, by the way, had none of the stuff in her own room—was much disposed to agree with him.

At breakfast next morning he was induced to qualify his satisfaction to some extent—but very slightly. "There is one thing I rather regret," he said, "that we allowed them to join up the vertical bands of the pattern at the top. I think it would have been better to leave that alone."

"Oh?" said his aunt interrogatively.

"Yes: as I was reading in bed last night they kept catching my eye rather. That is, I found myself looking across at them every now and then. There was an effect as if some one kept peeping out between the curtains in one place or another, where there was no edge, and I think that was due to the joining up of the bands at the top. The only other thing that troubled me was the wind."

"Why, I thought it was a perfectly still night."

"Perhaps it was only on my side of the house, but there was enough to sway my curtains and rustle them more than I wanted."

That night a bachelor friend of James Denton's came to stay, and was lodged in a room on the same floor as his host, but at the end of a long passage, halfway down which was a red baize door, put there to cut off the draught and intercept noise.

The party of three had separated. Miss Denton a good first, the two men at about eleven. James Denton, not yet inclined for bed, sat him down in an arm-chair and read for a time. Then he dozed, and then he woke, and bethought himself that his brown spaniel, which ordinarily slept in his room, had not come upstairs with him. Then he thought he was mistaken: for happening to move his hand which hung down over the arm of the chair within a few inches of the floor, he felt on the back of it just the slightest touch of a surface of hair, and stretching it out in that direction he stroked and patted a rounded something. But the feel of it, and still more the fact that instead of a responsive movement, absolute stillness greeted his touch, made him look over the arm. What he had been touching rose to meet him. It was in the attitude of one that had crept along the floor on its belly, and it was, so far as could be collected, a human figure. But of the face which was now rising to within a few inches of his own no feature was discernible, only hair. Shapeless as it was, there was about it so horrible an air of menace that as he bounded from his chair and rushed from the room he heard himself moaning with fear: and doubtless he did right to fly. As he dashed into the baize door that cut the passage in two, and—forgetting that it opened towards him—beat against it with all the force in him, he felt a soft ineffectual tearing at his back which, all the same, seemed to be growing in power, as if the hand, or whatever worse than a hand was there, were becoming more material as the pursuer's rage was more concentrated. Then he remembered the trick of the door—he got it open—he shut it behind him—he gained his friend's room, and that is all we need know.

It seems curious that, during all the time that had elapsed since the purchase of Poynter's diary, James Denton should not have sought an explanation of the presence of the pattern that had been pinned into it. Well, he had read the diary through without finding it mentioned, and had concluded that there was nothing to be said. But, on leaving Rendcomb Manor (he did not know whether for good), as he naturally insisted upon doing on the day after experiencing the horror I have tried to put into words, he took the diary with him. And at his seaside lodgings he examined more narrowly the portion whence the pattern had been taken. What he remembered having suspected about it turned out to be correct. Two or three leaves were pasted together, but written upon, as was patent when they were held up to the light. They yielded easily to steaming, for the paste had lost much of its strength, and they contained something relevant to the pattern.

The entry was made in 1707.

Old Mr. Casbury, of Acrington, told me this day much of young Sir Everard Charlett, whom he remember'd Commoner of University College, and thought was of the same Family as Dr. Arthur Charlett, now master of ye Coll. This Charlett was a personable young gent., but a loose atheistical companion, and a great Lifter, as they then call'd the hard drinkers, and for what I know do so now. He was noted, and subject to severall censures at different times for his extravagancies: and if the full history of his debaucheries had bin known, no doubt would have been expell'd ye Coll., supposing that no interest had been imploy'd on his behalf, of which Mr. Casbury had some suspicion. He was a very beautiful person, and constantly wore his own Hair, which was very abundant, from which, and his loose way of living, the cant name for him was Absalom, and he was accustom'd to say that indeed he believ'd he had shortened old David's days, meaning his father, Sir Job Charlett, an old worthy cavalier.

Note that Mr. Casbury said that he remembers not the year of Sir Everard Charlett's death, but it was 1692 or 3. He died suddenly in October. [Several lines describing his unpleasant habits and reputed delinquencies are omitted.] Having seen him in such topping spirits the night before, Mr. Casbury was amaz'd when he learn'd the death. He was found in the town ditch, the hair as was said pluck'd clean off his head. Most bells in Oxford rung out for him, being a nobleman, and he was buried next night in St. Peter's in the East. But two years after, being to be moved to his country estate by his successor, it was said the coffin, breaking by mischance, proved quite full of Hair: which sounds fabulous, but yet I believe precedents are upon record, as in Dr. Plot's *History of Staffordshire*.

His chambers being afterwards stripp'd, Mr. Casbury came by part of the hangings of it, which 'twas said this Charlett had design'd expressly for a memorial of his Hair, giving the Fellow that drew it a lock to work by, and the piece which I have fasten'd in here was parcel of the same, which Mr. Casbury gave to me. He said he believ'd there was a subtlety in the drawing, but had never discover'd it himself, nor much liked to pore upon it.

The money spent upon the curtains might as well have been thrown into the fire, as they were. Mr. Cattell's comment upon what he heard of the story took the form of a quotation from Shakespeare. You may guess it without difficulty. It began with the words "There are more things."

The Door

Henry S. Whitehead

Those in the motor-car hardly felt the slight, though sickening impact. It was rather, indeed, because of the instinct for something gone wrong, than because of a conviction that he had struck anything more important than a roll of tangled burlap from some passing moving-van, that the driver brought his heavy car to a stop with a grinding of brakes strenuously applied, and went back to see what he had struck.

He had turned the corner almost incidentally; but when he alighted and went back, when the thin gleam of his flashlight revealed to him the heap of huddled pulp which lay there, the driver realized in the throes of a hideous nausea what it was his heavy machine had spurned and crushed. . . .

Roger Phillips, intent upon the first really decent act of his whole life, hardly noticed what was forward. He had been crossing the street. He continued to be intent on his own concerns. Interrupted only by a kind of cold shudder to which he gave only passing thought as if with the very outer edge of his mind, he did not stop, but crossed the sidewalk, looking up as he had done many times before to reassure himself that the lights were out in the living room of the apartment up there on the third floor of the apartment house.

They were out, as he had confidently anticipated, and, reassured, he quickly mounted the steps to the front entrance. Someone came out, hurriedly, and passed him as he entered, the rush taking him by surprise. He turned his head as quickly as he could, to avoid recognition. It was old Mr. Osler, his father's neighbour, who had rushed out. The elderly man was in his shirt sleeves, and appeared greatly agitated, so much that young Phillips was certain he had not been recognised, had hardly even been noticed. He breathed an audible sigh of relief. He did not want old Osler to mention this chance meeting to his father the next time he should see him, and he knew Osler to be garrulous.

The young man mounted lightly and hurriedly the two flights of steps that led to the door of his father's apartment. He thrust his key into the patent lock of the apartment door confidently, almost without thought—a mechanical motion. As mechanically, he turned the key to the right. It was an old key, and it fitted the keyhole easily. He knew that his father and mother were at the symphony concert. They had not missed one for years during the season for symphony concerts, and this was their regular night. He had chosen this night for that reason. He knew that the coloured maid was out, too. He had seen her, not five minutes earlier, getting on a car for Boston. "The coast," as he phrased the thought to himself, somewhat melodramatically, "was clear!" He was certain of security from interruption. Only let him get safely into the apartment, do what he had to do, and as quietly and unobtrusively depart, and he would be satisfied, quite satisfied.

But the lock offered unexpected resistance. It was inexplicable, irritating. His overtense nerves revolted abruptly at this check. The key had slipped into the slot, as always, without difficulty—but it would not turn! Furiously he twisted it this way and that. At last he removed it and stared at it curiously. There was nothing amiss with the key. Could his father have had the lock changed?

Anger and quick shame smote him, suddenly. He looked closely at the lock. No, it was unchanged. There were the numberless tiny scratch-marks of innumerable insertions. It was the same.

Gingerly, carefully, he inserted the key again. He turned it to the right. Of course it turned to the right; he remembered that clearly. He had so turned it countless times.

It would not move. He put out all his puny strength, and still it would not turn. Hot exasperation shook him.

As he swore under his breath in his irritation at this bar to the fulfillment of his purpose, he became for the first time conscious of a rising commotion in the street below, and he paused, irresolutely, and listened, his nerves suddenly strung taut. Many voices seemed to be mingled in the excited hum that came to his ears. Bits of phrases, even, could be distinguished. Something had happened down there, it seemed. As he listened, the commotion of spoken sound resolved into a tone which, upon his subconscious effort to analyze it, seemed to express horror and commiseration, with an overtone of fear. The fear communicated itself to him. He shook, as the voice of the growing throng came up to him in sickening waves of apprehension.

What if this should mean an interruption? Impatiently wrenching himself away from his preoccupation and back to his more immediate concern with the door, he thrust the key into the lock a third time, this time aggressively, violently. Again he tried to snap the lock. Again it resisted him, unaccountably, devilishly, as it seemed to him.

Then, in his pause of desperation, he thought he heard his own name spoken. He could feel his face go white, the roots of his hair prickle. He listened, intently, crouching cat-like on the empty landing, before the door of his father's apartment, and as he listened, every nerve intent, he heard the entrance-door below flung open, and the corporate voice of the throng outside, hitherto muffled and faint, came to him suddenly with a wave of sound, jumbled and obscure as a whole, but with certain strident voices strangely clear and distinct.

A shuffle of heavy feet came to his ears, as if several persons were entering the lower hallway, their footsteps falling heavily on the tiled flooring. They would be coming upstairs!

He shrank back against the door—that devilish door! If only he could get it open!

Something like this, he told himself, in a wave of self-pity that swept him—something like this, unexpected, unforeseen, unreasonable—something like this was always happening to him!

The door! It was an epitome of his futile, worthless life. That had happened to him, just the same kind of thing, a month ago when he had been turned out of his home. The events of the intervening weeks rushed, galloping, through his overtensed mind. And now, as ever since that debacle, there was present with him a kind of unforgettable vision of his mother—his poor mother, her face covered with the tears which she had made no effort to wipe away—his poor mother, looking at him, stricken, through those tears which blurred her face; and there was his father, the kindly face now set in a stern mask, pale and deep with lines—his father telling him that this was the end. There would be no public prosecution. Was he not their son? But he must go! His home would be no longer his home.

He recalled the dazed days that followed; the mechanical activities of his daily employment; his search, half-hearted, for a furnished room. He recalled, shuddering, the several time when, moved by the mechanism of long-established usage, he had nearly taken an Allston car for "home," which was to be no longer his home. . . .

He had not sent back the key. He could not tell why he had kept it. He had forgotten to hand it back to his father when he had left, and his father, doubtless unthinkingly, had not suggested its return. That was why he still had it, and here he stood, now, on the very threshold of that place which had been "home" to him for so many years, about to make the restitution that would do something to remove the saddest of all the blots on his conscience—and he could not get in!

The men, talking with hushed voices, had reached the first landing. Young Phillips, caught by a sudden gust of abject terror, shrank against the stubborn door, the door which unaccountably he could not open. Then, his mind readjusting itself, he remembered that he had no reason for concealment, for fear. Even though he might be seen here, even though these people should be coming all the way up the stairs, it could not matter. Let him be seen; what of it? He was supposed to live here, of course. It was only a short time since he had actually ceased to live here, and his father said nothing. No public charge had been made against him. How one's conscience could make one a coward!

Under the invigorating stress of this reaction, he straightened himself, stood up boldly. Realizing that it might appear odd for him to be discovered standing here aimlessly on the landing, he started to go downstairs. By now the narrow staircase was completely blocked by the ascending group. He stopped, halfway from that flight. The men were carrying something, something heavy, and of considerable bulk, it would seem. He could not see clearly in the dim light just what it was. He stopped, halfway down, but none of the men carrying the awkward bundle, covered with what looked like an automobile curtain, looked up, or appeared to notice him. Neither did the straggling group of men, and a woman or two, who were following them.

Fascinated he gazed at what they were carrying. As they approached and took the turn in the stairs, so that the electric light shone more directly upon it, he looked closer. It was the body of a man! It hung limp, and ungainly, in their somewhat awkward grasp as they shoulder up towards him.

Something about it seemed vaguely familiar, the details presenting themselves to his fascinated gaze in rapid succession: the trouser-ends, the shoes. . . .

The men turned the last corner in the winding stairway and came into full view. As they turned the corner, the leather curtain slipped and the face of the dead man was for a moment exposed to view. Roger Phillips looked at it fascinated, horrified. Then one of the men, halting for an instant, drew the corner of the curtain over the face again, and he could no longer see it. The head rolled. The broken body had been grievously crushed.

Roger Phillips, utterly distraught, cowered, a limp heap again, against the unyielding door of his father's apartment. He had looked for one horrific instant into his own distorted, dead face!

The men, breathing hard, reached the landing. One of them, gingerly shifting his portion of the burden upon the shoulder of another, stepped forward to ring the bell of the Phillips apartment. No one answered the ring, and the man rang again, impatiently, insistently. The bell trilled inside the empty apartment. The men stood, silently, shifting uneasily from one foot to another. Behind them, a thin mutter came from the waiting stragglers who had followed them, moved by an inordinate curiosity.

"Here's a key sticking in the door," said the man who had rung the bell. "Guess we'd be all right if we opened the door and took the young fellow in. There doesn't seem to be any one home."

A murmur of assent came from the other men.

He turned the key to the left, then to the right, and the door opened. They carried the broken body inside and carefully laid it on the sofa in the living room.

Dr. Trifulgas

Jules Verne

I

Swish! It is the wind, let loose.

Swash! It is the rain, falling in torrents.

This shrieking squall bends down the trees of the Volsinian coast, and hurries on, flinging itself against the sides of the mountains of Crimma. Along the whole length of the littoral are high rocks, gnawed by the billows of the vast Sea of Megalocrida.

Swish! swash!

Down by the harbour nestles the little town of Luktrop; perhaps a hundred houses, with green palings, which defend them indifferently from the wild wind; four or five hilly streets—ravines rather than streets—paved with pebbles and strewn with ashes thrown from the active cones in the background. The volcano is not far distant; it is called the Vauglor. During the day it sends forth sulphurous vapours; at night, from time to time, great outpourings of flame. Like a lighthouse carrying a hundred and fifty kertzes, the Vauglor indicates the port of Luktrop to the coasters, felzans, verliches, and balanzes, whose keels furrow the waters of Megalocrida.

On the other side of the town are ruins dating from the Crimmarian era. Then a suburb, Arab in appearance, much like a casbah, with white walls, domed roofs, and sun-scorched terraces, which are all nothing but accumulations of square stones thrown together at random. Veritable dice are these, whose numbers will never be effaced by the rust of Time.

Among others we notice the Six-four, a name given to a curious erection, having six openings on one side and four on the other.

A belfry overlooks the town, the square belfry of Saint Philfilena, with bells hung in the thickness of the walls, which sometimes a hurricane will set in motion. That is a bad sign; the people tremble when they hear it.

Such is Luktrop. Then come the scattered habitations in the country, set amid heath and broom, as in Brittany. But this is not Brittany. Is it in France? I do not know. Is it in Europe? I cannot tell. At all events, do not look for Luktrop on any map.

II

Rat-tat! A discreet knock is struck upon the narrow door of Six-four, at the left corner of the Rue Messaglière. This is one of the most *comfortable* houses in Luktrop—if such a word is known there—one of the richest, if gaining some millions of fretzers, by hook or by crook, constitutes riches.

The rat-tat is answered by a savage bark, in which is much a lupine howl, as if a wolf should bark. Then a window is opened above the door of Six-four, and an ill-tempered voice says, "Deuce take people who come bothering here!"

A young girl, shivering in the rain wrapped in a thin cloak, asks if Dr. Trifulgas is at home.

"He is, or he is not, according to circumstances."

"I want him to come to my father, who is dying."

"Where is he dying?"

"At Val Karnion, four kertzes from here."

"And his name?"

"Vort Kartif."

"Vort Kartif, the herring-salter?"

"Yes; and if Dr. Trifulgas—"

"Dr. Trifulgas is not at home."

And the window is closed with a slam, while the swishes of the wind and the swashes of the rain mingle in a deafening uproar.

III

A hard man, this Dr. Trifulgas, with little compassion, and attending no one unless paid cash in advance. His old Hurzof, a mongrel of bulldog and spaniel, would have had more feeling than he. The house called Six-four admitted no poor, and opened only to the rich. Further, it had a regular tariff: so much for a typhoid fever, so much for a fit, so much for a pericarditis, and for other complaints which doctors invent by the dozen. Now, Vort Kartif, the herring-salter, was a poor man, and of low degree. Why should Dr. Trifulgas have taken any trouble, and on such a night?

"Is it nothing that I should have had to get up?" he murmured, as he went back to bed; "that alone is worth ten fretzers."

Hardly twenty minutes had passed, when the iron hammer was again struck on the door of Six-four.

Much against his inclination the doctor left his bed, and leaned out of his window.

"Who is there?" he cried.

"I am the wife of Vort Kartif."

"The herring-salter of Val Karnion?"

"Yes; and if you refuse to come, he will die."

"All right; you will be a widow."

"Here are twenty fretzers."

"Twenty fretzers for going to Val Karnion, four kertzes from here! Thank you! Be off with you!"

And the window was closed again. Twenty fretzers! A grand fee! Risk a cold or lumbago for twenty fretzers, especially when to-morrow one has to go to Kiltreno to visit the rich Edzingov, laid up with gout, which is valued at fifty fretzers the visit! With this agreeable prospect before him, Dr. Trifulgas slept more soundly than before.

Swish! Swash! and then rat-tat! rat-tat! rat-tat! To the noises of the squall were now added three blows of the knocker, struck by a more decided hand. The doctor slept. He woke, but in a fearful humour. When he opened the window the storm came in like a charge of shot.

"I am come about the herring-salter."

"That wretched herring-salter again!"

"I am his mother."

"May his mother, his wife, and his daughter perish with him!"

"He has had an attack——"

"Let him defend himself."

"Some money has been paid us," continued the old woman, "an instalment on the house sold to the camondeur Doutrup, of the Rue Messaglière. If you do not come, my granddaughter will no longer have a father, my daughter-in-law a husband, myself a son."

It was piteous and terrible to hear the old woman's voice—to know that the wind was freezing the blood in her veins, that the rain was soaking her very bones beneath her thin flesh.

"A fit! why, that would be two hundred fretzers!" replied the heartless Trifulgas.

"We have only a hundred and twenty."

"Good-night," and the window was again closed. But, after due reflection, it appeared that a hundred and twenty fretzers for an hour and a half on the road, *plus* half an hour of visit, made a fretzer a minute. A small profit, but still, not to be despised.

Instead of going to bed again, the doctor slipped into his coat of valveter, went down in his wading boots, stowed himself away in his great coat of lurtaine, with his *sourouët* on his head, and his mufflers on his hands. He left his lamp lighted close to the pharmacopœia, open at page 197. Then, pulling the door of Six-four, he paused on the threshold. The old woman was there, leaning on her stick, bowed down by her eighty years of misery.

"The hundred and twenty fretzers."

"Here is the money; and may God multiply it for you a hundredfold!"

"God! Who ever saw the colour of *His* money?"

The doctor whistled for Hurzof, gave him a small lantern to carry, and took the road towards the sea. The old woman followed.

IV

What swishy-swashy weather! The bells of St. Philfilena are all swinging by reason of the gale. A bad sign! But Dr. Trifulgas is not superstitious. He believes in nothing—not even in his own science, except for what it brings him in. What weather, and also what a road! Pebbles and ashes; the pebbles slippery with seaweed, the ashes crackling with iron refuse. No other light than that from Hurzof's lantern, vague and uncertain. At times jets of flame from Vauglor uprear themselves, and in the midst of them appear great comical silhouettes. In truth no one knows what is in the depths of those unfathomable craters. Perhaps spirits of the other world, which volatilise themselves as they come forth.

The doctor and the old woman follow the curves of the little bays of the littoral. The sea is white with livid whiteness—a mourning white. It sparkles as it throws off the crests of the surf, which seem like outpourings of glow-worms.

These two persons go on thus as far as the turn in the road between sand-hills, where the brooms and the reeds clash together with a shock like that of bayonets.

The dog had drawn near to his master, and seemed to say to him, "Come, come! a hundred and twenty fretzers for the strong box! That is the way to make a fortune.

Another rood added to the vineyard; another dish added to our supper; another meat pie for the faithful Hurzof. Let us look after the rich invalids, and look after them—according to their purses!"

At that spot the old woman pauses. With her trembling finger she points out among the shadows a reddish light. There is the house of Vort Kartif, the herring-salter.

"There?" said the doctor.

"Yes," said the old woman.

"Hurrah!" cries the dog Hurzof.

A sudden explosion from the Vauglor, shaken to its very base. A sheaf of lurid flame springs up to the zenith, forcing its way through the clouds. Dr. Trifulgas is hurled to the ground. He swears roundly, picks himself up, and looks about him.

The old woman is no longer there. Has she disappeared through some fissure of the earth, or has she flown away on the wings of the mist? As for the dog, he is there still, standing on his hind legs, his jaws apart, his lantern extinguished.

"Nevertheless, we will go on," mutters Dr. Trifulgas. The honest man has been paid his hundred and twenty fretzers, and he must earn them.

V

Only a luminous speck at the distance of half a kertz. It is the lamp of the dying—perhaps the dead. Of course, it is the herring-salter's house; the old woman pointed to it with her finger; no mistake is possible. Through the whistling swishes and the dashing swashes, through the uproar of the tempest, Dr. Trifulgas tramps on with hurried steps. As he advances, the house becomes more distinct, being isolated in the midst of the landscape.

It is very remarkable how much it resembles that of Dr. Trifulgas, the Six-four of Luktrop. The same arrangement of windows, the same little arched door. Dr. Trifulgas hastens on as fast as the gale allows him. The door is ajar; he has but to push it. He pushes it, he enters, and the wind roughly closes it behind him. The dog Hurzof, left outside, howls, with intervals of silence.

Strange! One would have said that Dr. Trifulgas had come back to his own house. And yet he has not wandered; he has not even taken a turning. He is at Val Karnion, not at Luktrop. And yet, here is the same low, vaulted passage, the same wooden staircase, with high banisters, worn away by the constant rubbing of hands.

He ascends. He reaches the landing. Beneath the door a faint light filters through, as in Six-four. Is it a delusion? In the dimness he recognises his room—the yellow sofa, on the right the old chest of pearwood, on the left the brass-bound strong box, in which he intended to deposit his hundred and twenty fretzers. There is his armchair, with the leathern cushions; there is his table, with its twisted legs, and on it, close to the expiring lamp, his pharmacopœia, open at page 197.

"What is the matter with me?" he murmurs.

What is the matter with him? Fear! His pupils are dilated; his body is contracted, shrivelled; an icy perspiration freezes his skin—every hair stands on end.

But hasten! For want of oil, the lamp expires; and also the dying man! Yes, there is the bed—his own bed—with posts and canopy; as wide as it is long, shut in by heavy curtains. Is it possible that this is the pallet of a wretched herring-salter? With a quaking hand Dr. Trifulgas seizes the curtains; he opens them; he looks in.

The dying man, his head uncovered, is motionless, as if at his last breath. The doctor leans over him——

Ah! what a cry, to which, outside, responds an unearthly howl from the dog.

The dying man is not the herring-salter, Vort Kartif—it is Dr. Trifulgas; it is *he*, whom congestion has attacked—he himself! Cerebral apoplexy, with sudden accumulation of serosity on the cavities of the brain, with paralysis of the body on the side opposite that of the seat of the lesion.

Yes, it is *he*, who was sent for, and for whom a hundred and twenty fretzers have been paid. *He* who, from hardness of heart, refused to attend the herring-salter—*he* who was dying.

Dr. Trifulgas is like a madman, he knows himself lost. At each moment the symptoms increase. Not only all the functions of the organs slacken, but the lungs and the heart cease to act. And yet he has not quite lost consciousness. What can be done? Bleed! If he hesitates, Dr. Trifulgas is dead. In those days they still bled; and then, as now, medical men cured all those apoplectic patients who were not going to die.

Dr. Trifulgas seizes his case, takes out his lancet, opens a vein in the arm of his double. The blood does not flow. He rubs his chest violently—his own breathing grows slower. He warms his feet with hot bricks—his own grow cold.

Then his double lifts himself, falls back, and draws one last breath. Dr. Trifulgas, notwithstanding all that his science has taught him to do, *dies beneath his own hands.*

VI

In the morning a corpse was found in the house Six-four—that of Dr. Trifulgas. They put him in a coffin, and carried him with much pomp to the cemetery of Luktrop, wither he had sent so many others—in a professional manner.

As to old Hurzof, it is said that, to this day, he haunts the country with his lantern alight, and howling like a lost dog. I do not know if that be true; but strange things happen in Volsinia, especially in the neighbourhood of Luktrop.

And, again, I warn you not to hunt for that town on the map. The best geographers have not yet agreed as to its latitude—nor even as to its longitude.

The Dream Giver

Chris Sewell

I respected Dr. Widgery because of his wide margins and unclosed avenues. When a case puzzled him, he said so bluntly, with his big shoulders raised.

He was a mental specialist—neither of the old school nor the new, but a school of his own.

"We are at the beginning of things, Dale," he said to me one day. "What are Freud and Jung? Infants crying in the night. Look here! What d'you make of *this*? and he plunged headlong into the history of one of his own cases.

"She had been married just a year," he began; "lets call her Mrs. Loveday. One of her friends brought her to me on the strict Q.T., because she was sure there was something badly wrong. Mrs. Loveday had 'gone off queer and depressed and got so terribly thin.'

"Then followed the usual inch-by-inch examination—you know my old-maidish ways. Physically there was nothing amiss with the girl, save a certain amount of general debility; but mentally"—he threw out both hands—"Armageddon! I made further tests. What do I discover? No scandals, no secret grief—no lawless passion on either side. The little lady was martially as happy as a singing lark. *But* she was an Italian from Baveno. Her husband had met her on a Cook's tour to the Lakes, and married her out of hand—one of the absurd, feckless affairs—love at first sight and all that. He was a City clerk on nothing a year, and had brought her from the bosom of Maggiore to Hammersmith. You know Maggiore? Exactly! And you know Hammersmith? Very well—think it out."

He crossed his arms and leant back, but I did not need to think it out. "Nostalgia," I diagnosed.

"Of course, but a nostalgia that you and cannot dimly comprehend. People go mad of it, die of it—rot under it. You see, she had spent her whole life with mountains which poke their noses slap into the face of Heaven. And cypresses—a cypress draws one—perhaps you noticed it?"

I nodded. "Most things in Italy draw," I sighed. "Take the greens alone! from the emerald of infant olives to the savage black of firs."

"Quite so. And then substitute a patch of grass the size of a first-aid sling—a border of nasturtiums generally dusty, and houses in endless rows which rub shoulders and goggle down at trams, and the band and reek of it all! Of *course*, she was losing her reason. So would you or I if we knew the language imperfectly, and the *femme à tout faire* (as I interpreted in our London suburbs) not at all. *He* was away all day, I remember."

I nodded again.

"When she found I spoke Italian at least passably she came out of her flutter, and told me a great deal. It seemed that the prize horror of all was that, though she slept fully in fits and starts, she 'couldn't dream properly.'"

"Couldn't dream properly?" I repeated.

"That was her own expression. She *did* dream after a fashion, but her dreams were the fleeting, grotesque visions of the neurasthenic. It came out that she had been from babyhood a peculiarly vivid dreamer. She gave me one or two instances of set dreams recurring which were quite interesting, though not unique. For obvious reasons I led her away from the subject, and asked her if an occasional holiday to the old home was within the range of possibility. But her eyes said 'no.'

"'We are very poor,' she told me. 'With good luck and very hard work on my husband's part we may get to Baveno by the summer after next—we are saving for *that*; but oh! *doctor*—the summer after next—two years—it's a lifetime—how *can* I wait? . . . I am being stifled. . . .'"

Dr. Widgery stopped, and his two middle fingers slid slowly down the wood which bounded the leather of his desk; and his eyes watched their progress.

"Now, quite frankly," he went on, "she was perfectly right. She couldn't wait. The girl looked deadly frightened—*was* deadly frightened in point of fact. Polyphobia would be as good a name for her complaint as any other. I had a short chat with the friend who brought her; she confirmed one or two of my impressions. Perhaps I ought to have insisted on seeing the husband—I don't know. When I made the suggestion, they told me he was a Christian Scientist, and repudiated doctors. They had seized the opportunity of his being away for a fortnight on business to come to me—so I counted him out. But the thing was urgent. Not for a single instant since the morning she left for England had Mrs. Loveday been able to recapture the land she loved, in any sense whatever. Her only sister, who was married and lived in Baveno, wrote letters, it is true; but I do not think they were very graphic ones. 'If only I could sleep, doctor,' she wailed, 'I believe it would all come back.

That is why I consented to consult you—they promised me that you could give sleep. *Can't* you?'"

Again his fingers made that thoughtful glissade of the desk, and I gathered that his next move, whatever it was, had not been enterprised lightly.

"It came to this," he said. "The presumption manifestly was a few doses of her old home. In actuality, impossible—but in another sense—well, why should I not be able to restore to her the power of vivid dreaming? It seemed worth trying. Oh! I grant you that it was an experiment, and I grant you that experiments fascinate me; but reason as I would I could not see why this one should gang agley.

"So I tried hypnosis, in which, as you know, I am pretty skillful. She was eminently hypnotisable, as I had guessed she would be; and when she was under, I informed her—very slowly and insistently—that she would slumber soundly that night and for many nights to come, and that her dreams would be of Baveno—always of Baveno. This I repeated two or three times in a level, clear voice with added insistence. 'You will find yourself there,' I told her, 'directly you are asleep—by the lake opposite the tea-shop of Signora Ruffoni. You will hear the click of the small *zoccoli*, and see the women washing at the water edge. The *Isola Madre* will be before you, and the high hills round you, and you may wander where you please.' Then I woke her.

"She was to come to me again in a fortnight's time to report progress. I noted the case down, and, as one always does, put it as far as possible out of my mind."

"And she came?" I asked.

"Came?" He smiled most radiantly. "Dale, it was my *pièce de résistance*. Never in my thirty years of practice have I seen such a complete metamorphosis. On the occasion of her first visit she had been a scarecrow with haunted eyes; she returned a beautiful woman, he whole face ashine with *joie de vivre*. Man, she was *cured*!"

"By your suggestions alone?"

Widgery twisted in his chair and winced, as though a sudden spasm of pain had passed through him.

"There you are. How do *I* know? What means have I of telling? That's just where it is!"

"But what did *she* say?"

"She was emotional and un-English, and wanted to kiss my hands—would have knelt, but that I pulled her up in time."

"Then she believed it. She got her dreams back all right, if that is what you mean; only——"

He paused so long that I ventured an "Only what?"

"They were far more than dreams, it appears. Look here, Dale, it sounds stark rot put into cold words, but she solemnly swore that night after night she was *in* Baveno—literally there, in her own body, though it appeared to be invisible to every one. She was free to do what she pleased, as I had told her she should be—to boat on the lake—to scale the hills—to cuddle up on the grass listening to the bees—to sit with her sister or watch her friends at work or play. She gave minute descriptions of all she had done; and when she only succeeded in convincing me that she had a profitable imagination, actual tears of mortification stood in her eyes. 'But, doctor, I assure you on my oath—they are *not* dreams. If they had been, how should I know that this season the big round flower bed outside the Bellevue Hotel had cineraries planted in it, and that they are *lapis lazuli* in colour with a border of white marguerites, or that Alietti the carpenter was making a coffin for old Signor Brentano last Monday week—working outside his shop, as he always does? I heard him tell the proprietor of the *albergo* near the bridge over the torrent that Signor Brentano had died suddenly of a blood-vessel on the brain. . . . Read what my sister says.'

"She snatched open a fancy bag, and produced a letter. The paragraph to which she pointed me ran something like this:

> You are perfectly correct: there *are* cinerarias in the middle bed of Hotel Bellevue—*such* blue ones! and bordered by marguerites, as you say. As for Signor Brentano, he died in a minute last Monday of an apoplexy; so again you are right. I wish I could see you when you flit about, *Carissima mia*. No, I felt no kiss upon my brow on my birthday morning, though I was, true to your description, busy arranging a cluster of Marécho-Niel roses in the great majolica vase our grandmother left me. . . .

"Dale, what was I to think. The girl was as sane as a Royal Commission—saner. Her idea was that the power—this power of projection, as the Extremists call it—must have always been latent in her, but that I had developed an intensified it, till it became a normal faculty. In the end I am bund t confess that she convinced me that she was getting super-normal information about her old surroundings somehow, though I should hesitate to say what part I played in it. At any rate, one fact emerged—my treatment, such as it was, had resulted in a perfect resurrection.

There was now nothing or almost nothing to cause me anxiety. I might cross her off my books without a qualm."

"You say," I remarked, "that there was 'almost' nothing to cause you anxiety. What do you mean by 'almost'?"

"Ah, that's it—that's just it. I was coming to that. Mrs. Loveday declared that her visions were perfectly straightforward except in one respect—a curious one. Any attempt to enter the church—and she made several, being a devout Catholic apparently—was met by what she described as a 'thought barrier.' 'Something *always* pushes me back when I try to go in,' she told me—'something stronger than I. It does not use words, but it impresses me, exactly as if it did, that there is danger inside, and that I must not step over the threshold, or I should never return. When I ask why, there is no answer.' D'you remember the Baveno church, Dale?"

"More or less. It's in the middle of town, isn't it?—with a paved courtyard in front and a baptistery or something at the left. A very dim religious interior, if I recollect rightly."

"Yes—it's not striking—just typical of most Italian churches; but she loved it. She had been christened and confirmed there—had taken her *prima communione* there. She was sentimental about it. 'I simply long to go in,' she said, 'but I mustn't. You think I mustn't, don't you? If I did——'

"She left the sentence unfinished, and I switched off the subject. Finally I told her I could take no more fees for giving advice to a patient who was in better health than her doctor. So I dismissed her. 'If anything noteworthy should occur in the future, just write to me,' I suggested; and we parted."

"And did she write?"

"She did—about three months later—a smudged, incoherent letter. Her sister had died quite unexpectedly from some form of food poisoning. She—Mrs. Loveday—had been present—shall I say in spirit?—at the end, and was evidently inmost frantic grief. 'Her body will be taken into the church tonight,' she wrote. 'She always wished it, and I must go keep watch beside her. I tell you this, doctor, that you may understand—whatever happens, but please realise, *I must go*.' The three last words were heavily underscored. Can you fancy my not sleeping that night and demonstrating to myself that I needed a change to get my work off my nerves!"

"I can quite believe you were uneasy."

"I was so uneasy," he continued, "that when morning came I positively posted off to Hammersmith to breakfast to reassure myself by looking at the house."

"And did it reassure you?"

He looked at me sombrely.

"No. The blinds were all down. Still the Continent mourns more ostentatiously than our island, so I didn't let that altogether discourage me. What do you think I had the effrontery to do? I knocked at the door and asked for her—for Mrs. Loveday——"

"Yes?"

"*Then* I got it full in the neck. She was dead—had been found dead in bed that morning beside her husband."

THE ELEVENTH OF MARCH

AMELIA B. EDWARDS

FORTY YEARS AGO!

An old pocket-book lies before me, bound in scarlet morocco, and fastened with a silver clasp. The leather is mildewed; the silver tarnished; the paper yellow; the ink faded. It has been hidden away at the back of an antique oaken bureau since the last day of the year during which I had it in use; and that was forty years ago. Ay, here is a page turned down—turned down at Wednesday, March the eleventh, eighteen hundred and twenty-six. The entry against that date is brief and obscure enough.

> Wednesday, March 11th.—Walked from Frascati to Palazzuola, the ancient site of Alba Longa, on the Alban lake. Lodged at Franciscan convent. Brother Geronimo. Dare one rely on the testimony of the senses? *Dieu sait tout.*

Brief as it is, however, that memorandum tires a train of long-dormant memories, and brings back with painful vividness all the circumstances to which it bears reference. I will endeavour to relate them as calmly and succinctly as possible.

I started on foot from Frascati immediately after breakfast, and rested midway in the shade of a wooded ravine between Marino and the heights of Alba Longa. I seem to remember every trivial incident of that morning walk. I remember how the last year's leaves crackled under my feet, and how the green lizards darted to and fro in the sunlight. I fancy I still hear the slow drip of the waters that trickled down the cavernous rocks on either hand. I fancy I still smell the heavy perfume of the violets among the ferns. It was not yet noon when I emerged upon the upper ridge, and took the path that leads to Monte Cavo. The woodcutters were busy among the chestnut slopes of Palazzuola. They paused in their work, and stared at me sullenly as I passed by. Presently a little turn in the footway brought the whole lake of Albano before my eyes. Blue, silent, solitary, set round with overhanging woods, it lay in the sunshine, four hundred feet below, like a sapphire at the bottom of a malachite vase. Now and then, a soft breath from the west ruffled the placid mirror, and blurred the pictured landscape on its surface. Now and then, a file of mules, passing unseen among the forest-paths, sent a faint sound of tinkling bells across the lake. I sat down in the shade of a clump of cork-trees, and contemplated the panorama. To my left, on a precipitous platform at the verge of the basin, with Monte Cavo towering up behind, stretched the long white façade of the Convent of Palazzuola; on the opposite height, standing clear against the sky, rose the domes and pines of Castel Gondolfo; to the far right, in the blinding sunshine of the Campagna, lay Rome and the Etruscan hills.

In this spot I established myself for the day's sketching. Of so vast a scene, I could, necessarily, only select a portion. I chose the Convent, with its background of mountain, and its foreground of precipice and lake; and proceeded patiently to work out, first the leading features, and next the minuter details of the subject. Thus occupied (with an occasional pause to watch the passing of a cloud-shadow, or listen to the chiming of a distant chapel-bell), I lingered on, hour after hour, till the sun hung low in the west, and the woodcutters were all gone to their homes. I was now at least three miles from either the town of Albano or the village of Castel Gondolfo, and was, moreover, a stranger to the neighbourhood. I looked at my watch. There remained but one half hour of good daylight, and it was important that I should find my way before the dusk closed in. I rose reluctantly, and, promising myself to return to the same spot on the morrow, packed away my sketch, and prepared for the road.

At this moment, I saw a monk standing in an attitude of meditation upon a little knoll of rising ground some fifty yards ahead. His back was turned towards me; his cowl was up, his arms were folded across his breast. Neither the splendour of the heavens, nor the tender beauty of the earth, was anything to him. He seemed unconscious even of the sunset.

I hurried forward, eager to inquire my nearest path along the woods that skirt the lake; and my shadow lengthened out fantastically before me as I ran. The monk turned abruptly. His cowl fell. He looked at me, face to face. There were not more than eighteen yards between us. I saw him as plainly as I now see the page on which I write. Our eyes met . . . My God! shall I ever forget those eyes?

He was still young, still handsome, but so lividly pale, so emaciated, so worn with passion, and penance, and remorse, that I stopped involuntarily, like one who finds himself on the brink of a chasm. We stood thus for a few seconds—both silent, both motionless. I could not have uttered a syllable, had my life depended on it. Then, as abruptly as he had turned towards me, he turned away, and disappeared among the trees. I remained for some minutes gazing after him. My heart throbbed painfully. I shuddered, I knew not why. The very air seemed to have grown thick and oppressive; the very sunset, so golden a moment since, had turned suddenly to blood.

I went on my way, disturbed and thoughtful. The livid face and lurid eyes of the monk haunted me. I dreaded every turn of the path, lest I should again encounter them. I started when a twig fell, or a dead leaf fluttered down beside me. I was almost ashamed of the sense of relief with which I heard the sound of voices some few yards in advance, and, emerging upon an open space close against the convent, saw some half dozen friars strolling to and fro in the sunset. I inquired my way to Albano, and learned that I was still more than two miles distant.

"It will be quite dark before the Signore arrives," said one, courteously. "The Signore would do well to accept a cell at Palazzuola for the night."

I remembered the monk, and hesitated.

"There is no moon now," suggested another; "and the paths are unsafe for those who do not know them."

While I was yet undecided, a bell rang, and three or four of the loiterers went in.

"It is our supper hour," said the first speaker. "The Signore will at least condescend to share our simple fare; and afterwards, if he still decides to sleep at Albano, one of our younger brethren shall accompany him as far as the Cappucini, at the entrance to the town."

I accepted this proposition gratefully, followed my entertainers through the convent gates, and was ushered into a stone hall, furnished with a long dining table, a pulpit, a clock, a double row of deal benches, and an indifferent copy of the Last Supper of Leonardo da Vinci. The Superior advanced to welcome me.

"You have come among us, Signore," he said, "on an evening when our table is but poorly provided. Although this is not one of the appointed fast-days of the Church, we have been abstaining at Palazzuola in memory of certain circumstances connected with our own brotherhood. I hope, however, that our larder may be found to contain something better suited to a traveller's appetite than the fare you now see before you."

Saying thus, he placed me at his right hand at the upper end of the board, and there stood till the monks were all in their places. He then repeated a Latin grace; after which each brother took his seat and began. They were twenty-three in number, twelve on one side, and eleven on the other; but I observed that a place was left vacant near the foot of the table, as if the twelfth man were yet to come. The twelfth, I felt sure, was he whom I had encountered on the way. Once possessed with this conviction, I could not keep from watching the door. Strange! I so dreaded and loathed his coming, that I almost felt as if his presence would be less intolerable than the suspense in which I awaited it!

In the meantime the monks ate in silence; and even the Superior, whose language and address were those of a well-informed man, seemed constrained and thoughtful. Their supper was of the most frugal description, and consisted of only bread, salad, grapes, and maccaroni. Mine was before long reinforced with a broiled pigeon and a flask of excellent Orvieto. I enjoyed my fare, however, as little as they seemed to enjoy theirs. Fasting as I was, I had no appetite. Weary as I was, I only longed to push my plate aside, and resume my journey.

"The Signore will not think of going farther to-night," said the Superior, after an interval of prolonged silence.

I muttered something about being expected at Albano.

"Nay, but it is already dusk, and the sky hath clouded over suddenly within the last fifteen minutes," urged he. "I fear much that we have a storm approaching. What sayest thou, Brother Antonio?"

"It will be a wild night," replied the brother with whom I had first spoken.

"Ay, a wild night," repeated an old monk, lower down the table; "like this night last year—like this night two years ago!"

The Superior struck the table angrily with his open hand.

"Silence!" he exclaimed authoritatively. "Silence there; and let Brother Anselmo bring lights."

It was now so dark that I could scarcely distinguish the features of the last speaker, or those of the monk who rose and left the room. Again the profoundest silence fell upon all present. I could hear the footsteps of Brother Anselmo echo down the passage, till they died away; and I remember listening vaguely to the ticking of the clock at the farther end the refectory, and comparing it in my own mind to the horrible beating of an iron heart. Just at that moment a sharp gust of wind moaned past the windows, bearing with it a prolonged reverberation of distant thunder.

"Our storms up here in the mountain are severe and sudden," said the Prior, resuming our conversation at the point where it had been interrupted; "and even the waters of yonder placid lake are sometimes so tempestuous that no boat dare venture across. I fear, Signore, that you will find it impossible to proceed to Albano."

"Should the tempest come up, reverend father," I replied, "I will undoubtedly accept your hospitality, and be grateful for it; but if. . . ."

I broke off abruptly. The words failed on my lips, and I pushed away the flask from which I was about to fill my glass.

Brother Anselmo had brought in the lamps, and there, in the twelfth seat at the opposite side of the table, sat the monk. I had not seen him take his place. I had not heard him enter. Yet there he sat, pale and deathlike, with his burning eyes fixed full upon me! No one noticed him. No one spoke to him. No one helped him to the dishes on the table. He neither ate, nor drank, nor held companionship with any of his fellows; but sat among them like an excommunicated wretch, whose penance was silence and fasting.

"You do not eat, Signore," said the prior.

"I—I thank you, reverend father," I faltered. "I have dined."

"I fear, indifferently. Would you like some other wine? Our cellar is not so ill-furnished as our larder."

I declined by a gesture.

"Then we will retire to my room, and take coffee."

And the Superior rose, repeated a brief Latin thanksgiving, and ushered me into a small well-lighted parlour, opening off a passage at the upper end of the hall, where there were some half-dozen shelves of books, a couple of easy chairs, a bright wood fire, and a little table laden with coffee and cakes. We had scarcely seated ourselves when a tremendous peal of thunder seemed to break immediately over the convent, and was followed by a cataract of rain.

"The Signore is safer here than on the paths between Palazzuola and Albano," said the Superior, sipping his coffee.

"I am, indeed," I replied. "Do I understand that you had a storm here on the same night last year, and the year before?"

The Prior's face darkened.

"I cannot deny the coincidence," he said, reluctantly; "but it is a mere coincidence, after all. The—the fact is that a very grievous and terrible catastrophe happened to our community on this day two years ago; and the brethren believe that heaven sends the tempest in memory of that event. Monks, Signore, are superstitious; and if we consider their isolated lives, it is not surprising that they should be so."

I bowed assent. The Prior was evidently a man of the world.

"Now, with regard to Palazzuola," continued he, disregarding the storm, and chatting on quite leisurely, "here are twenty-three brethren, most of them natives of the small towns among the mountains hereabout; and of that twenty-three, not ten have even been so far as Home in their lives."

"Twenty-three," I repeated. "Twenty-four, surely, *mio padre*!"

"I did not include myself," said the Prior, stiffly.

"Neither did I include you," I replied; "but I counted twenty-four of the order at table just now."

The Prior shook his head.

"No, no, Signore," said he. "Twenty-three only."

"But I am positive," said I.

"And so am I," rejoined he, politely but firmly.

I paused. I was certain. I could not be mistaken.

"Nay, *mio padre*," I said; "they were twenty-three at first; but the brother who came in afterwards made the twenty-fourth."

"Afterwards!" echoed the Prior. "I am not aware that any brother came in afterwards."

"A sickly, haggard-looking monk," pursued I, "with singularly bright eyes—eyes which, I confess, produced on me a very unpleasant impression. He came in just before the lights were brought."

The Prior moved uneasily in his chair, and poured out another cup of coffee.

"Where did you say he sat, Signore?" said he.

"In the vacant seat at the lower end of the table, on the opposite side to myself."

The Prior set down his coffee untasted, and rose in great agitation.

"For God's sake, Signore," stammered he, "be careful what you say! Did you—did you see this? Is this true?"

"True?" I repeated, trembling I knew not why, and turning cold from head to foot. "As true as that I live and breathe! Why do you ask?"

"Sickly and haggard-looking, with singularly bright eyes," said the Prior, looking very pale himself. "Had it—had it the appearance of a young man?"

"Of a young man worn with suffering and remorse," I replied. "But—but it was not the first time, *mio padre*! I saw him before—this afternoon—down near the chestnut woods, on a knoll of rising ground, overlooking the lake. He was standing with his back to the sunset."

The Prior fell on his knees before a little carved crucifix that hung beside the fireplace.

"*Requiem æternam dona eis, Domine; et lux perpetua luceat eis*," said he, brokenly.

The rest of his prayer was inaudible, and he remained for some minutes with his face buried in his hands.

"I implore you to tell me the meaning of this," I said, when he at length rose, and sank, still pale and agitated, into his chair.

"I will tell what I may, Signore," he replied; "but I must not tell you all. It is a secret that belongs to our community, and none of us are at liberty to repeat it. Two years ago, one of our brethren was detected in the commission of a great crime. He had suffered, struggled against it, and at last, urged by a terrible opportunity, committed it. His life paid for the offence. One who was deeply wronged by the deed, met him as he was flying from the spot, and slew him as he fled. Signore, the name of that monk was the Fra Geronimo. We buried him where he fell, on a knoll of rising ground close against the chestnut woods that border the path to Marino. We had no right to lay his remains in consecrated ground; but we fast, and say masses for his soul, on each anniversary of that fearful day."

The Prior paused and wiped his brow.

"But, *mio padre*. . ." I began.

"This day last year," interrupted he, "one of the woodcutters yonder took a solemn oath that he met the Fra Geronimo on that very knoll at sunset. Our brethren believed the man—but I, heaven forgive me! was incredulous. Now, however. . ."

"Then—then you believe," faltered I, "you believe that I have seen. . ."

"Brother Geronimo," said the Prior, solemnly.

And I believe it too. I am told, perhaps, that it was an illusion of the senses. Granted; but is not such an illusion, in itself, a phenomenon as appalling as the veriest legend that superstition evokes from the world beyond the grave? How shall we explain the nature of the impression? Whence comes it? By what material agency is it impressed upon the brain? These are questions leading to abysses of speculation before which the sceptic and the philosopher alike recoil—questions which I am unable to answer. I only know that these things came within the narrow radius of my own experience; that I saw them with my own eyes; and that they happened just forty years ago, on the eleventh of March, anno Domini eighteen hundred and twenty-six.

Eveline's Visitant

Mary Elizabeth Braddon

It was at a masked ball at the Palais Royal that my fatal quarrel with my first cousin André de Brissac began. The quarrel was about a woman. The women who followed the footsteps of Philip of Orleans were the causes of many such disputes; and there was scarcely one fair head in all that glittering throng which, to a man versed in social histories and mysteries, might not have seemed bedabbled with blood.

I shall not record the name of her for love of whom André de Brissac and I crossed one of the bridges, in the dim August dawn, on our way to the waste ground beyond the church of Saint-Germain des Près.

There were many beautiful vipers in those days, and she was one of them. I can feel the chill breath of that August morning blowing in my face, as I sit in my dismal chamber at my château of Puy Verdun to-night, alone in the stillness, writing the strange story of my life. I can see the white mist rising from the river, the grim outline of the Châtelet, and the square towers of Notre Dame black against the pale-gray sky. Even more vividly can I recall André's fair young face, as he stood opposite to me with his two friends—scoundrels both, and alike eager for that unnatural fray. We were a strange group to be seen in a summer sunrise, all of us fresh from the heat and clamour of the Regent's saloons—André in a quaint hunting-dress copied from a family portrait at Puy Verdun, I costumed as one of Law's Mississippi Indians; the other men in like garish frippery, adorned with broideries and jewels that looked wan in the pale light of dawn.

Our quarrel had been a fierce one—a quarrel which could have but one result, and that the direst. I had struck him; and the welt raised by my open hand was crimson upon his fair womanish face as he stood opposite to me. The eastern sun shone on the face presently, and dyed the cruel mark with a deeper red; but the sting of my own wrongs was fresh, and I had not yet learned to despise myself for that brutal outrage.

To André de Brissac such an insult was most terrible. He was the favourite of Fortune, the favourite of women; and I was nothing,—a rough soldier who had done my country good service, but in the boudoir of a Parabère a mannerless boor.

We fought, and I wounded him mortally. Life had been very sweet for him; and I think that a frenzy of despair took possession of him when he felt the life-blood ebbing away. He beckoned me to him as he lay on the ground. I went, and knelt at his side.

"Forgive me, André!" I murmured.

He took no more heed of my words than if that piteous entreaty had been the idle ripple of the river near at hand.

"Listen to me, Hector de Brissac," he said. "I am not one who believes that a man has done with earth because his eyes glaze and his jaw stiffens. They will bury me in the old vault at Puy Verdun; and you will be master of the château. Ah, I know how lightly they take things in these days, and how Dubois will laugh when he hears that *Ça* has been killed in a duel. They will bury me, and sing masses for my soul; but you and I have not finished our affair yet, my cousin. I will be with you when you least look to see me,—I, with this ugly scar upon the face that women have praised and loved. I will come to you when your life seems brightest I will come between you and all that you hold fairest and dearest. My ghostly hand shall drop a poison in your cup of joy. My shadowy form shall shut the sunlight from your life. Men with such iron will as mine can do what they please, Hector de Brissac. It is my will to haunt you when I am dead."

All this in short broken sentences he whispered into my ear. I had need to bend my ear close to his dying lips; but the iron will of André de Brissac was strong enough to do battle with Death, and I believe he said all he wished to say before his head fell back upon the velvet cloak they had spread beneath him, never to be lifted again.

As he lay there, you would have fancied him a fragile stripling, too fair and frail for the struggle called life; but there are those who remember the brief manhood of André de Brissac, and who can bear witness to the terrible force of that proud nature.

I stood looking down at the young face with that foul mark upon it; and God knows I was sorry for what I had done.

Of those blasphemous threats which he had whispered in my ear I took no heed. I was a soldier, and a believer. There was nothing absolutely dreadful to me in the thought that I had killed this man. I had killed many men on the battlefield; and this one had done me cruel wrong.

My friends would have had me cross the frontier to escape the consequences of my act; but I was ready to face those consequences, and I remained in France. I kept aloof from the court, and received a hint that I had best confine myself to my own province. Many masses were chanted in the little chapel of Puy Verdun for the soul of my dead cousin, and his coffin filled a niche in the vault of our ancestors.

His death had made me a rich man; and the thought that it was so made my newly-acquired wealth very hateful to me. I lived a lonely existence in the old château, where I rarely held converse with any but the servants of the household, all of whom had served my cousin, and none of whom liked me.

It was a hard and bitter life. It galled me, when I rode through the village, to see the peasant-children shrink away from me. I have seen old women cross themselves stealthily as I passed them by. Strange reports had gone forth about me; and there were those who whispered that I had given my soul to the Evil One as the price of my cousin's heritage. From my boyhood I had been dark of visage and stern of manner; and hence, perhaps, no woman's love had ever been mine. I remember my mother's face in all its changes of expression; but I can remember no look of affection that ever shone on me. That other woman, beneath whose feet I laid my heart, was pleased to accept my homage, but she never loved me; and the end was treachery.

I had grown hateful to myself, and had well-nigh begun to hate my fellow-creatures, when a feverish desire seized upon me, and I pined to be back in the press and throng of the busy world once again. I went back to Paris, where I kept myself aloof from the court, and where an angel took compassion upon me.

She was the daughter of an old comrade, a man whose merits had been neglected, whose achievements had been ignored, and who sulked in his shabby lodging like a rat in a hole, while all Paris went mad with the Scotch Financier, and gentlemen and lacqueys were trampling one another to death in the Rue Quincampoix. The only child of this little cross-grained old captain of dragoons was an incarnate sunbeam, whose mortal name was Eveline Duchalet.

She loved me. The richest blessings of our lives are often those which cost us least. I wasted the best years of my youth in the worship of a wicked woman, who jilted and cheated me at last. I gave this meek angel but a few courteous words—a little fraternal tenderness—and lo, she loved me. The life which had been so dark and desolate grew bright beneath her influence; and I went back to Puy Verdun with a fair young bride for my companion.

Ah, how sweet a change there was in my life and in my home! The village children no longer shrank appalled as the dark horseman rode by, the village crones no longer crossed themselves; for a woman rode by his side—a woman whose charities had won the love of all those ignorant creatures, and whose companionship had transformed the gloomy lord of the château into a loving husband and a gentle master. The old retainers forgot the untimely fate of my cousin, and served me with cordial willingness, for love of their young mistress.

There are no words which can tell the pure and perfect happiness of that time. I felt like a traveller who had traversed the frozen seas of an arctic region, remote from human love or human companionship, to find himself on a sudden in the bosom of a verdant valley, in the sweet atmosphere of home. The change seemed too bright to be real; and I strove in vain to put away from my mind the vague suspicion that my new life was but some fantastic dream.

So brief were those halcyon hours, that, looking back on them now, it is scarcely strange if I am still half inclined to fancy the first days of my married life could have been no more than a dream.

Neither in my days of gloom nor in my days of happiness had I been troubled by the recollection of André's blasphemous oath. The words which with his last breath he had whispered in my ear were vain and meaningless to me. He had vented his rage in those idle threats, as he might have vented it in idle execrations. That he will haunt the footsteps of his enemy after death is the one revenge which a dying man can promise himself; and if men had power thus to avenge themselves, the earth would be peopled with phantoms.

I had lived for three years at Puy Verdun; sitting alone in the solemn midnight by the hearth where he had sat, pacing the corridors that had echoed his footfall; and in all that time my fancy had never so played me false as to shape the shadow of the dead. Is it strange, then, if I had forgotten André's horrible promise?

There was no portrait of my cousin at Puy Verdun. It was the age of boudoir art, and a miniature set in the lid of a gold bonbonnière, or hidden artfully in a massive bracelet, was more fashionable than a clumsy life-size image, fit only to hang on the gloomy walls of a provincial château rarely visited by its owner. My cousin's fair face had adorned more than one bonbonnière, and had been concealed in more than one bracelet; but it was not among the faces that looked down from the paneled walls of Puy Verdun.

In the library I found a picture which awoke painful associations. It was the portrait of a De Brissac, who had flourished in the time of Francis the First; and it was from this picture that my cousin André had copied the quaint hunting-dress he wore at the Regent's ball. The library was a room in which I spent a good deal of my life; and I ordered a curtain to be hung before this picture.

* * * * *

We had been married three months, when Eveline one day asked, "Who is the lord of the château nearest to this?"

I looked at her with astonishment.

"My dearest," I answered, "do you not know that there is no other château within forty miles of Puy Verdun?"

"Indeed!" she said; "that is strange."

I asked her why the fact seemed strange to her; and after much entreaty I obtained from her the reason of her surprise.

In her walks about the park and woods during the last month, she had met a man who, by his dress and bearing, was obviously of noble rank. She had imagined that he occupied some château near at hand, and that his estate adjoined ours. I was at a loss to imagine who this stranger could be; for my estate of Puy Verdun lay in the heart of a desolate region, and unless when some traveller's coach went lumbering and jingling through the village, one had little more chance of encountering a gentleman than of meeting a demigod.

"Have you seen this man often, Eveline?" I asked.

She answered, in a tone which had a touch of sadness, "I see him every day."

"Where, dearest?"

"Sometimes in the park, sometimes in the wood. You know the little cascade, Hector, where there is some old neglected rock-work that forms a kind of cavern. I have taken a fancy to that spot, and have spent many mornings there reading. Of late I have seen the stranger there every morning."

"He has never dared to address you?"

"Never. I have looked up from my book, and have seen him standing at a little distance, watching me silently. I have continued reading; and when I have raised my eyes again I have found him gone. He must approach and depart with a stealthy tread, for I never hear his footfall. Sometimes I have almost wished that he would speak to me. It is so terrible to see him standing silently there."

"He is some insolent peasant who seeks to frighten you."

My wife shook her head.

"He is no peasant," she answered. "It is not by his dress alone I judge, for that is strange to me. He has an air of nobility which it is impossible to mistake."

"Is he young or old?"

"He is young and handsome."

I was much disturbed by the idea of this stranger's intrusion on my wife's solitude; and I went straight to the village to inquire if any stranger had been seen there. I could hear of no one. I questioned the servants closely, but without result. Then I determined to accompany my wife in her walks, and to judge for myself of the rank of the stranger.

For a week I devoted all my mornings to rustic rambles with Eveline in the park and woods; and in all that week we saw no one but an occasional peasant in *sabots*, or one of our own household returning from a neighbouring farm.

I was a man of studious habits, and those summer rambles disturbed the even current of my life. My wife perceived this, and entreated me to trouble myself no further.

"I will spend my mornings in the pleasaunce, Hector," she said; "the stranger cannot intrude upon me there."

"I begin to think the stranger is only a phantasm of your own romantic brain," I replied, smiling at the earnest face lifted to mine. "A châtelaine who is always reading romances may well meet handsome cavaliers in the woodlands. I daresay I have Mdlle. Scuderi to thank for this noble stranger, and that he is only the great Cyrus in modern costume."

"Ah, that is the point which mystifies me, Hector," she said. "The stranger's costume is not modern. He looks as an old picture might look if it could descend from its frame."

Her words pained me, for they reminded me of that hidden picture in the library, and the quaint hunting costume of orange and purple which André de Brissac wore at the Regent's ball.

After this my wife confined her walks to the pleasaunce; and for many weeks I heard no more of the nameless stranger. I dismissed all thought of him from my mind, for a graver and heavier care had come upon me. My wife's health began to droop. The change in her was so gradual as to be almost imperceptible to those who watched her day by day. It was only when she put on a rich gala dress which she had not worn for months that I saw how wasted the form must be on which the embroidered bodice hung so loosely, and how wan and dim were the eyes which had once been brilliant as the jewels she wore in her hair.

I sent a messenger to Paris to summon one of the court physicians; but I knew that many days must needs elapse before he could arrive at Puy Verdun.

In the interval I watched my wife with unutterable fear.

It was not her health only that had declined. The change was more painful to behold than any physical alteration. The bright and sunny spirit had vanished, and in the place of my joyous young bride I beheld a woman weighed down by rooted melancholy. In vain I sought to fathom the cause of my darling's sadness. She assured me that she had no reason for sorrow or discontent, and that if she seemed sad without a motive, I must forgive her sadness, and consider it as a misfortune rather than a fault.

I told her that the court physician would speedily find some cure for her despondency, which must needs arise from physical causes, since she had no real ground for sorrow. But although she said nothing, I could see she had no hope or belief in the healing powers of medicine.

One day, when I wished to beguile her from that pensive silence in which she was wont to sit an hour at a time, I told her, laughing, that she appeared to have forgotten her mysterious cavalier of the wood, and it seemed also as if he had forgotten her.

To my wonderment, her pale face became of a sudden crimson; and from crimson changed to pale again in a breath.

"Yon have never seen him since you deserted your woodland grotto?" I said.

She turned to me with a heart-rending look.

"Hector," she cried, "I see him every day; and it is that which is killing me."

She burst into a passion of tears when she had said this. I took her in my arms as if she had been a frightened child, and tried to comfort her.

"My darling, this is madness," I said. "You know that no stranger can come to you in the pleasaunce. The moat is ten feet wide and always full of water, and the gates are kept locked day and night by old Massou. The châtelaine of a mediæval fortress need fear no intruder in her antique garden."

My wife shook her head sadly.

"I see him every day," she said.

On this I believed that my wife was mad. I shrank from questioning her more closely concerning her mysterious visitant. It would be ill, I thought, to give a form and substance to the shadow that tormented her by too close inquiry about its look and manner, its coming and going.

I took care to assure myself that no stranger to the household could by any possibility penetrate to the pleasaunce. Having done this, I was fain to await the coming of the physician.

He came at last. I revealed to him the conviction which was my misery. I told him that I believed my wife to be mad. He saw her—spent an hour alone with her, and then came to me. To my unspeakable relief he assured me of her sanity.

"It is just possible that she may be affected by one delusion," he said; "but she is so reasonable upon all other points, that I can scarcely bring myself to believe her the subject of a monomania. I am rather inclined to think that she really sees the person of whom she speaks. She described him to me with a perfect minuteness. The descriptions of scenes or individuals given by patients afflicted with monomania are always more or less disjointed; but your wife spoke to me as clearly and calmly as I am now speaking to you. Are you sure there is no one who can approach her in that garden where she walks?"

"I am quite sure."

"Is there any kinsman of your steward, or hanger-on of your household,—a young man with a fair womanish face, very pale, and rendered remarkable by a crimson scar, which looks like the mark of a blow?"

"My God!" I cried, as the light broke in upon me all at once. "And the dress—the strange old-fashioned dress?"

"The man wears a hunting costume of purple and orange," answered the doctor.

I knew then that André de Brissac had kept his word, and that in the hour when my life was brightest his shadow had come between me and happiness.

I showed my wife the picture in the library, for I would fain assure myself that there was some error in my fancy about my cousin. She shook like a leaf when she beheld it, and clung to me convulsively.

"This is witchcraft, Hector," she said. "The dress in that picture is the dress of the man I see in the pleasaunce; but the face is not his."

Then she described to me the face of the stranger; and it was my cousin's face line for line—André de Brissac, whom she had never seen in the flesh. Most vividly of all did she describe the cruel mark upon his face, the trace of a fierce blow from an open hand.

After this I carried my wife away from Puy Verdun. We wandered far—through the southern provinces, and into the very heart of Switzerland. I thought to distance the ghastly phantom, and I fondly hoped that change of scene would bring peace to my wife.

It was not so. Go where we would, the ghost of André de Brissac followed us. To my eyes that fatal shadow never revealed itself. *That* would have been too poor a vengeance. It was my wife's innocent heart which André made the instrument of his revenge. The unholy presence destroyed her life. My constant companionship could not shield her from the horrible intruder. In vain did I watch her; in vain did I strive to comfort her.

"He will not let me be at peace," she said; "he comes between us, Hector. He is standing between us now. I can see his face with the red mark upon it plainer than I see yours."

One fair moonlight night, when we were together in a mountain village in the Tyrol, my wife cast herself at my feet, and told me she was the worst and vilest of women. "I have confessed all to my director," she said; "from the first I have not hidden my sin from Heaven. But I feel that death is near me; and before I die I would fain reveal my sin to you."

"What sin, my sweet one?"

"When first the stranger came to me in the forest, his presence bewildered and distressed me, and I shrank from him as from something strange and terrible. He came again and again; by and by I found myself thinking of him, and watching for his coming. His image haunted me perpetually; I strove in vain to shut his face out of my mind. Then followed an interval in which I did not see him; and, to my shame and anguish, I found that life seemed dreary and desolate without him. After that came the time in which he haunted the pleasaunce; and—O, Hector, kill me if you will, for I deserve no mercy at your hands!—I grew in those days to count the hours that must elapse before his coming, to take no pleasure save in the sight of that pale face with the red brand upon it. He plucked all old familiar joys out of my heart, and left in it but one weird unholy pleasure—the delight of his presence. For a year I have lived but to see him. And now curse me, Hector; for this is my sin. Whether it comes of the baseness of my own heart, or is the work of witchcraft, I know not; but I know that I have striven against this wickedness in vain."

I took my wife to my breast, and forgave her. In sooth, what had I to forgive? Was the fatality that overshadowed us any work of hers? On the next night she died, with her hand in mine; and at the very last she told me, sobbing and affrighted, that *he* was by her side.

A Far-Away Melody

Mary E. Wilkins Freeman

The clothes-line was wound securely around the trunks of four gnarled, crooked old apple-trees, which stood promiscuously about the yard back of the cottage. It was tree-blossoming time, but these were too aged and sapless to blossom freely, and there was only a white bough here and there shaking itself triumphantly from among the rest, which had only their new green leaves. There was a branch occasionally which had not even these, but pierced the tender green and the flossy white in hard, grey nakedness. All over the yard, the grass was young and green and short, and had not yet gotten any feathery heads. Once in a while there was a dandelion set closely down among it.

The cottage was low, of a dark-red colour, with white facings around the windows, which had no blinds, only green paper curtains.

The back door was in the centre of the house, and opened directly into the green yard, with hardly a pretence of a step, only a flat oval stone before it.

Through this door, stepping cautiously on the stone, came presently two tall, lank women in chocolate-coloured calico gowns, with a basket of clothes between them. They set the basket underneath the line on the grass, with a little clothes-pin bag beside it, and then proceeded methodically to hang out the clothes. Everything of a kind went together, and the best things on the outside line, which could be seen from the street in front of the cottage.

The two women were curiously alike. They were about the same height, and moved in the same way. Even their faces were so similar in feature and expression that it might have been a difficult matter to distinguish between them. All the difference, and that would have been scarcely apparent to an ordinary observer, was a difference of degree, if it might be so expressed. In one face the features were both bolder and sharper in outline, the eyes were a trifle larger and brighter, and the whole expression more animated and decided than in the other.

One woman's scanty drab hair was a shade darker than the other's, and the negative fairness of complexion, which generally accompanies drab hair, was in one relieved by a slight tinge of warm red on the cheeks.

This slightly intensified woman had been commonly considered the more attractive of the two, though in reality there was very little to choose between the personal appearance of these twin sisters, Priscilla and Mary Brown. They moved about the clothes-line, pinning the sweet white linen on securely, their thick, white-stockinged ankles showing beneath their limp calicoes as they stepped, and their large feet in cloth slippers flattening down the short, green grass. Their sleeves were rolled up, displaying their long, thin, muscular arms, which were sharply pointed at the elbows.

They were homely women; they were fifty and over now, but they never could have been pretty in their 'teens, their features were too irredeemably irregular for that. No youthful freshness of complexion or expression could have possibly done away with the impression that they gave. Their plainness had probably only been enhanced by the contrast, and these women, to people generally, seemed better-looking than when they were young. There was an honesty and patience in both faces that showed all the plainer for their homeliness.

One, the sister with the darker hair, moved a little quicker than the other, and lifted the wet clothes from the basket to the line more frequently. She was the first to speak, too, after they had been hanging out the clothes for some little time in silence. She stopped as she did so, with a wet pillow-case in her hand, and looked up reflectively at the flowering apple-boughs overhead, and the blue sky showing between, while the sweet spring wind ruffled her scanty hair a little.

"I wonder, Mary," said she, "if it would seem so very queer to die a mornin' like this, say. Don't you believe there's apple branches a-hangin' over them walls made out of precious stones, like these, only there ain't any dead limbs among 'em, an' they're all covered thick with flowers? An' I wonder if it would seem such an awful change to go from this air into the air of the New Jerusalem." Just then a robin hidden somewhere in the trees began to sing. "I s'pose," she went on, " that there's angels instead of robins, though, and they don't roost up in the trees to sing, but stand on the ground, with lilies growin' round their feet, may be, up to their knees, or on the gold stones in the street, an' play on their harps to go with the singin'."

The other sister gave a scared, awed look at her. "Lor, don't talk that way, sister," said she. "What has got into you lately? You make me crawl all over, talkin' so much about dyin'. You feel well, don't you?"

"Lor, yes," replied the other, laughing, and picking up a clothes-pin for her pillow-case; "I feel well enough, an' I don't know what has got me to talkin' so much about dyin' lately, or thinkin' about it. I guess it's the spring weather. P'r'aps flowers growin' make anybody think of wings sproutin' kinder naterally. I won't talk so much about it if it bothers you, an' I don't know but it's sorter nateral it should. Did you get the potatoes before we came out, sister?"—with an awkward and kindly effort to change the subject.

"No," replied the other, stooping over the clothes-basket. There was such a film of tears in her dull blue eyes that she could not distinguish one article from another.

"Well, I guess you had better go in an' get 'em, then; they ain't worth anything, this time of year, unless they soak a while, an' I'll finish hangin' out the clothes while you do it."

"Well, p'r'aps I'd better," the other woman replied, straightening herself up from the clothes-basket. Then she went into the house without another word; but down in the damp cellar, a minute later, she sobbed over the potato barrel as if her heart would break. Her sister's remarks had filled her with a vague apprehension and grief which she could not throw off. And there was something a little singular about it. Both these women had always been of a deeply religious cast of mind. They had studied the Bible faithfully, if not understandingly, and their religion had strongly tinctured their daily life. They knew almost as much about the Old Testament prophets as they did about their neighbours; and that was saying a good deal of two single women in a New England country town. Still this religious element in their natures could hardly have been termed spirituality. It deviated from that as much as anything of religion—which is in one way spirituality itself—could.

Both sisters were eminently practical in all affairs of life, down to their very dreams, and Priscilla especially so. She had dealt in religion with the bare facts of sin and repentance, future punishment and reward. She had dwelt very little, probably, upon the poetic splendours of the Eternal City, and talked about them still less. Indeed, she had always been reticent about her religious convictions, and had said very little about them even to her sister.

The two women, with God in their thoughts every moment, seldom had spoken His Name to each other. For Priscilla to talk in the strain that she had to-day, and for a week or two previous, off and on, was, from its extreme deviation from her usual custom, certainly startling.

Poor Mary, sobbing over the potato barrel, thought it was a sign of approaching death. She had a few superstitious-like grafts upon her practical, commonplace character.

She wiped her eyes finally, and went upstairs with her tin basin of potatoes, which were carefully washed and put to soak by the time her sister came in with the empty basket.

At twelve exactly the two sat down to dinner in the clean kitchen, which was one of the two rooms the cottage boasted. The narrow entry ran from the front door to the back. On one side was the kitchen and living-room; on the other, the room where the sisters slept. There were two small unfinished lofts overhead, reached by a step-ladder through a little scuttle in the entry ceiling; and that was all. The sisters had earned the cottage and paid for it years before, by working as tailoresses. They had, besides, quite a snug little sum in the bank, which they had saved out of their hard earnings. There was no need for Priscilla and Mary to work so hard, people said; but work hard they did, and work hard they would as long as they lived. The mere habit of work had become as necessary to them as breathing.

Just as soon as they had finished their meal and cleared away the dishes, they put on some clean starched purple prints, which were their afternoon dresses, and seated themselves with their work at the two front windows; the house faced south-west, so the sunlight streamed through both. It was a very warm day for the season, and the windows were open. Close to them in the yard outside stood great clumps of lilac bushes. They grew on the other side of the front door too; a little later the low cottage would look half-buried in them. The shadows of their leaves made a dancing network over the freshly washed yellow floor.

The two sisters sat there and sewed on some coarse vests all the afternoon. Neither made a remark often. The room, with its glossy little cooking-stove, its eight-day clock on the mantel, its chintz-cushioned rocking chairs, and the dancing shadows of the lilac leaves on its yellow floor, looked pleasant and peaceful.

Just before six o'clock a neighbour dropped in with her cream pitcher to borrow some milk for tea, and she sat down for a minute's chat after she had got it filled. They had been talking a few moments on neighbourhood topics, when all of a sudden Priscilla let her work fall and raised her hand. "Hush!" whispered she.

The other two stopped talking, and listened, staring at her wonderingly, but they could hear nothing.

"What is it, Miss Priscilla?" asked the neighbour, with round blue eyes. She was a pretty young thing, who had not been married long.

"Hush! Don't speak. Don't you hear that beautiful music?" Her ear was inclined towards the open window, her hand still raised warningly, and her eyes fixed on the opposite wall beyond them.

Mary turned visibly paler than her usual dull paleness, and shuddered. "I don't hear any music," she said. "Do you, Miss Moore?"

"No-o," replied the caller, her simple little face beginning to put on a scared look, from a vague sense of a mystery she could not fathom. Mary Brown rose and went to the door, and looked eagerly up and down the street. "There ain't no organ-man in sight anywhere," said she, returning, "an' I can't hear any music, an' Miss Moore can't, an' we're both sharp enough o' hearin'. You're jest imaginin' it, sister."

"I never imagined anything in my life," returned the other, "an' it ain't likely I'm goin' to begin now. It's the beautifulest music. It comes from over the orchard there. Can't you hear it? But it seems to me it's growin' a little fainter like now. I guess it's movin' off perhaps."

Mary Brown set her lips hard. The grief and anxiety she had felt lately turned suddenly to unreasoning anger against the cause of it; through her very love she fired with quick wrath at the beloved object. Still she did not say much, only, "I guess it must be movin' off," with a laugh, which had an unpleasant ring in it.

After the neighbour had gone, however, she said more, standing before her sister with her arms folded squarely across her bosom. "Now, Priscilla Brown," she exclaimed, "I think it's about time to put a stop to this. I've heard about enough of it. What do you s'pose Miss Moore thought of you? Next thing it'll be all over town that you're gettin' spiritual notions. To-day it's music that nobody else can hear, an' yesterday you smelled roses, and there ain't one in blossom this time o' year, and all the time you're talkin' about dyin'. For my part, I don't see why you ain't as likely to live as I am. You're uncommon hearty on vittles. You ate a pretty good dinner to-day for a dyin' person."

"I didn't say I was goin' to die," replied Priscilla meekly: the two sisters seemed suddenly to have changed natures. "An' I'll try not to talk so, if it plagues you. I told you I wouldn't this mornin', but the music kinder took me by surprise like, an' I thought may be you an' Miss Moore could hear it. I can jest hear it a little bit now, like the dyin' away of a bell."

"There you go agin!" cried the other sharply. "Do, for mercy's sake, stop, Priscilla. There ain't no music."

"Well, I won't talk any more about it," she answered patiently; and she rose and began setting the table for tea, while Mary sat down and resumed her sewing, drawing the thread through the cloth with quick, uneven jerks.

That night the pretty girl neighbour was aroused from her first sleep by a distressed voice at her bedroom window, crying, "Miss Moore! Miss Moore!"

She spoke to her husband, who opened the window. "What's wanted?" he asked, peering out into the darkness.

"Priscilla's sick," moaned the distressed voice; "awful sick. She's fainted, an' I can't bring her to. Go for the doctor— quick! quick! *quick*!" The voice ended in a shriek on the last word, and the speaker turned and ran back to the cottage, where, on the bed, lay a pale, gaunt woman, who had not stirred since she left it. Immovable through all her sister's agony, she lay there, her features shaping themselves out more and more from the shadows, the bed-clothes that covered her limbs taking on an awful rigidity.

"She must have died in her sleep," the doctor said, when he came, "without a struggle."

When Mary Brown really understood that her sister was dead, she left her to the kindly ministrations of the good women who are always ready at such times in a country place, and went and sat by the kitchen window in the chair which her sister had occupied that afternoon.

There the women found her when the last offices had been done for the dead.

"Come home with me tonight," one said; "Miss Green will stay with *her*," with a turn of her head towards the opposite room, and an emphasis on the pronoun which distinguished it at once from one applied to a living person.

"No," said Mary Brown; "I'm a-goin' to set here an' listen." She had the window wide open, leaning her head out into the chilly night air.

The women looked at each other; one tapped her head, another nodded hers. "Poor thing!" said a third.

"You see," went on Mary Brown, still speaking with her head leaned out of the window, "I was cross with her this afternoon because she talked about hearin' music. I was cross, an' spoke up sharp to her, because I loved her, but I don't think she knew. I didn't want to think she was goin' to die, but she was. An' she heard the music. It was true. An' now I'm a-goin' to set here an' listen till I hear it too, an' then I'll know she ain't laid up what I said agin me, an' that I'm a-goin' to die too."

They found it impossible to reason with her; there she sat till morning, with a pitying woman beside her, listening all in vain for unearthly melody.

Next day they sent for a widowed niece of the sisters, who came at once, bringing her little boy with her. She was a kindly young woman, and took up her abode in the little cottage, and did the best she could for her poor aunt, who, it soon became evident, would never be quite herself again. There she would sit at the kitchen window and listen day after day. She took a great fancy to her niece's little boy, and used often to hold him in her lap as she sat there. Once in a while she would ask him if he heard any music. "An innocent little thing like him might hear quicker than a hard, unbelievin' old woman like me," she told his mother once.

She lived so for nearly a year after her sister died. It was evident that she failed gradually and surely, though there was no apparent disease. It seemed to trouble her exceedingly that she never heard the music she listened for. She had an idea that she could not die unless she did, and her whole soul seemed filled with longing to join her beloved twin sister, and be assured of her forgiveness. This sister-love was all she had ever felt, besides her love of God, in any strong degree; all the passion of devotion of which this homely, commonplace woman was capable was centred in that, and the unsatisfied strength of it was killing her. The weaker she grew, the more earnestly she listened. She was too feeble to sit up, but she would not consent to lie in bed, and made them bolster her up with pillows in a rocking-chair by the window. At last she died, in the spring, a week or two before her sister had the preceding year. The season was a little more advanced this year, and the apple-trees were blossomed out further than they were then. She died about ten o'clock in the morning. The day before her niece had been called into the room by a shrill cry of rapture from her: "I've heard it! I've heard it!" she cried. "A faint sound o' music, like the dyin' away of a bell."

Father Macclesfield's Tale

R. H. Benson

Father Macclesfield arrived at supper.

He was a little, unimposing, dry man, with a hooked nose and gray hair. He was rather silent at supper, but there was no trace of shyness in his manner as he took his seat upstairs, and without glancing round once began in an even and dispassionate voice:

"I once knew a Catholic girl that married an old Protestant three times her own age. I entreated her not to do so, but it was useless. And when the disillusionment came she used to write to me piteous letters, telling me that her husband had in reality no religion at all. He was a convinced infidel, and scouted even the idea of the soul's immortality.

"After two years of married life the old man died. He was about sixty years old, but very hale and hearty till the end.

"Well, when he took to his bed the wife sent for me, and I had half a dozen interviews with him, but it was useless. He told me plainly that he wanted to believe—in fact, he said that the thought of annihilation was intolerable to him. If he had had a child he would not have hated death so much; if his flesh and blood in any manner survived him he could have fancied that he had a sort of vicarious life left; but as it was, there was no kith or kin of his alive, and he could not bear that."

Father Macclesfield sniffed cynically and folded his hands.

"I may say that his deathbed was extremely unpleasant. He was a coarse old fellow, with plenty of strength in him, and he used to make remarks about the churchyard and—and, in fact, the worms, that used to send his poor child of a wife half fainting out of the room. He had lived an immoral life, too, I gathered.

"Just at the last it was—well, disgusting. He had no consideration. God knows why she married him! The agony was a very long one; he caught at the curtains round the bed, calling out, and all his words were about death and the dark. It seemed to me that he caught hold of the curtains as if to hold himself into this world. And at the very end he raised himself clean up in bed and stared horribly out of the window that was open just opposite.

"I must tell you that straight away beneath the window lay a long walk between sheets of dead leaves with laurels on either side and the branches meeting overhead, so that it was very dark there even in summer, and at the end of the walk away from the house was the churchyard gate."

Father Macclesfield paused and blew his nose. Then he went on, still without looking at us.

"Well, the old man died, and he was carried along this laurel path and buried.

"His wife was in such a state that I simply dared not go away. She was frightened to death; and, indeed, the whole affair of her husband's dying was horrible. But she would not leave the house. She had a fancy that it would be cruel to him. She used to go down twice a day to pray at the grave; but she never went along the laurel walk. She would go round by the garden and in at a lower gate and come back the same way, or by the upper garden.

"This went on for three or four days. The man had died on a Saturday and was buried on Monday; it was in July, and he had died about eight o'clock.

"I made up my mind to go on the Saturday after the funeral. My curate had managed alone very well for a few days, but I did not like to leave him for a second Sunday.

"Then on the Friday at lunch—her sister had come down, by the way, and was still in the house—on the Friday the widow said something about never daring to sleep in the room where the old man had died. I told her it was nonsense, and so on; but you must remember she was in a dreadful state of nerves, and she persisted. So I said I would sleep in the room myself. I had no patience with such ideas then.

"Of course she said all sorts of things, but I had my way and my things were moved in on Friday evening.

"I went to my new room about a quarter before eight to put on my cassock for dinner. The room was very much as it had been—rather dark because of the trees at the end of the walk outside. There was the four-poster, there with the damask curtains, the table and chairs, the cupboard where his clothes were kept, and so on.

"When I went to put my cassock on I went to the window to look out. To the right and left were the gardens, with the sunlight just off them, but still very bright and gay with the geraniums, and exactly opposite was the laurel walk, like a long, green shady tunnel, dividing the upper and lower lawns.

"I could see straight down it to the churchyard gate, which was about a hundred yards away, I suppose. There were limes overhead and laurels, as I said, on each side.

"Well, I saw some one coming up the walk, but it seemed to me at first that he was drunk. He staggered several times as I watched— I suppose he would be fifty yards away—and once I saw him catch hold of one of the trees and cling to it as if he were afraid of falling. Then he left it and came on again slowly, going from side to side, with his hands out. He seemed desperately keen to get to the house.

"I could see his dress, and it astonished me that a man dressed so should be drunk, for he was quite plainly a gentleman. He wore a white top hat and a gray cutaway coat and gray trousers, and I could make out his white spats.

"Then it struck me he might be ill, and I looked harder than ever, wondering whether I ought to go down.

"When he was about twenty yards away he lifted his face, and it struck me as very odd; but it seemed to me he was extraordinarily like the old man we had buried on Monday; but it was darkish where he was, and the next moment he dropped his face, threw up his hands, and fell flat on his back.

"Well, of course I was startled at that, and I leaned out of the window and called out something. He was moving his hands, I could see, as if he were in convulsions, and I could hear the dry leaves rustling.

"Well, then I turned and ran out and downstairs."

Father Macclesfield stopped a moment.

"Gentlemen," he said abruptly, "when I got there there was not a sign of the old man. I could see that the leaves had been disturbed, but that was all."

There was an odd silence in the room as he paused, but before any of us had time to speak he went on.

"Of course, I did not say a word of what I had seen. We dined as usual. I smoked for an hour or so by myself after prayers and then I went up to bed. I cannot say I was perfectly comfortable, for I was not, but neither was I frightened.

"When I got to my room I lit all my candles and then went to a big cupboard I had noticed and pulled out some of the drawers. In the bottom of the third drawer I found a gray cutaway coat and gray trousers; I found several pairs of white spats in the top drawer and a white hat on the shelf above. That is the first incident."

"Did you sleep there, Father?" said a voice softly.

"I did," said the priest; "there was no reason why I should not. I did not fall asleep for two or three hours, but I was not disturbed in any way and came to breakfast as usual.

"Well, I thought about it all a bit, and finally I sent a wire to my curate telling him I was detained. I did not like to leave the house just then."

Father Macclesfield settled himself again in his chair and went on in the same dry, uninterested voice.

"On Sunday we drove over to the Catholic church, six miles off, and I said mass. Nothing more happened till the Monday evening.

"That evening I went to the window again about a quarter before eight, as I had done both on the Saturday and Sunday. Everything was perfectly quiet till I heard the churchyard gate unlatch and I saw a man come through.

"But I saw almost at once that it was not the same man I had seen before; it looked to me like a keeper, for he had a gun across his arm; then I saw him hold the gate open an instant, and a dog came through and began to trot up the path toward the house with his master following.

"When the dog was about fifty yards away he stopped dead and pointed.

"I saw the keeper throw his gun forward and come up softly, and as he came the dog began to slink backward. I watched very closely, clean forgetting why I was there, and the next instant something—it was too shadowy under the trees to see exactly what it was—but something about the size of a hare burst out of the laurels and made straight up the path, dodging from side to side, but coming like the wind.

"The beast could not have been more than twenty yards from me when the keeper fired, and the creature went over and over in the dry leaves and lay struggling and screaming. It was horrible! But what astonished me was that the dog did not come up. I heard the keeper snap out something, and then I saw the dog making off down the avenue in the direction of the churchyard as hard as he could go.

"The keeper was running now toward me, but the screaming of the hare, or of whatever it was, had stopped, and I was astonished to see the man come right up to where the beast was struggling and kicking and then stop as if he were puzzled.

"I leaned out of the window and called to him.

"'Right in front of you, man,' I said; 'for God's sake kill the brute.'

"He looked up at me and then down again.

"'Where is it, sir?' he said; 'I can't see it anywhere.'

"And there lay the beast clear before him all the while not a yard away, still kicking.

"Well, I went out of the room and downstairs and out to the avenue.

"The man was standing there still, looking terribly puzzled, but the hare was gone. There was not a sign of it. Only the leaves were disturbed, and the wet earth showed beneath.

"The keeper said that it had been a great hare; he could have sworn to it, and that he had orders to kill all hares and rabbits in the garden enclosure. Then he looked rather odd.

"'Did you see it plainly, sir,' he asked.

"I told him not very plainly; but I thought it a hare, too.

"'Yes, sir,' he said; 'it was a hare, sure enough; but do you know, sir, I thought it to be a kind of silver-gray, with white feet. I never saw one like that before!'

"The odd thing was that not a dog would come near. His own dog was gone, but I fetched the yard dog, a retriever, out of his kennel in the kitchen yard, and if ever I saw a frightened dog it was this one. When we dragged him up at last, all whining and pulling back, he began to snap at us so fiercely that we let go, and he went back like the wind to his kennel. It was the same with the terrier.

"Well, the bell had gone, and I had to go in and explain why I was late; but I didn't say anything about the color of the hare. That was the second incident."

Father Macclesfield stopped again, smiling reminiscently to himself. I was very much impressed by his quiet air and composure. I think it helped his story a good deal.

Again, before we had time to comment or question, he went on.

"The third incident was so slight that I should not have mentioned it, or thought anything of it, if it had not been for the others; but it seemed to me there was a kind of diminishing gradation of energy which explained. Well, now you shall hear.

"On the other nights of that week I was at my window again, but nothing happened till the Friday. I had arranged to go for certain next day; the widow was much better and more reasonable, and even talked of going abroad herself in the following week.

"On that Friday evening I dressed a little earlier and went down to the avenue this time, instead of staying at my window, at about twenty minutes to eight.

"It was rather a heavy, depressing evening, without a breath of wind, and it was darker than it had been for some days.

"I walked slowly down the avenue to the gate and back again; and I suppose it was fancy, but I felt more uncomfortable than I had felt at all up to then. I was rather relieved to see the widow come out of the house and stand looking down the avenue. I came out myself then and went toward her. She started rather when she saw me and then smiled.

"'I thought it was some one else,' she said. 'Father, I have made up my mind to go. I shall go to town to-morrow, and start on Monday. My sister will come with me.'

"I congratulated her, and then we turned and began to walk back to the lime avenue. She stopped at the entrance, and seemed unwilling to come any further.

"'Come down to the end,' I said, 'and back again. There will be time before dinner.'

"She said nothing, but came with me, and we went straight down to the gate and then turned to come back.

"I don't think either of us spoke a word; I was very uncomfortable indeed by now, and yet I had to go on.

"We were half way back, I suppose, when I heard a sound like a gate rattling; and I whisked round in an instant, expecting to see some one at the gate. But there was no one.

"Then there came a rustling overhead in the leaves; it had been dead still before. Then, I don't know why, but I took my friend suddenly by the arm and drew her to one side out of the path, so that we stood on the right hand, not a foot from the laurels.

"She said nothing, and I said nothing; but I think we were both looking this way and that, as if we expected to see something.

"The breeze died, and then sprang up again, but it was only a breath. I could hear the living leaves rustling overhead, and the dead leaves underfoot, and it was blowing gently from the churchyard.

"Then I saw a thing that one often sees; but I could not take my eyes off it, nor could she. It was a little column of leaves, twisting and turning and dropping and picking up again in the wind, coming slowly up the path. It was a capricious sort of draught, for the little scurry of leaves went this way and that, to and fro across the path. It came up to us, and I could feel the breeze on my hands and face. One leaf struck me softly on the cheek, and I can only say that I shuddered as if it had been a toad. Then it passed on.

"You understand, gentlemen, it was pretty dark; but it seemed to me that the breeze died and the column of leaves—it was no more than a little twist of them—sank down at the end of the avenue.

"We stood there perfectly still for a moment or two, and when I turned she was staring straight at me, but neither of us said one word.

"We did not go up the avenue to the house. We pushed our way through the laurels and came back by the upper garden.

"Nothing else happened; and the next morning we all went off by the eleven o'clock train.

"That is all, gentlemen."

The Fifteenth Man

Richard Marsh

It was not until we were actually in the field, and were about to begin to play, that I learnt that the Brixham men had come one short. It seemed that one of their men had been playing in a match the week before—in a hard frost, if you please! and, getting pitched on to his head, had broken his skull nearly into two clean halves. That is the worst of playing in a frost; you are nearly sure to come to grief. Not to ordinary grief, either, but a regular cracker. It was hard lines on the Brixham team. Some men always are getting themselves smashed to pieces just as a big match is due! The man's name was Joyce, Frank Joyce. He played halfback for Brixham, and for the county too—so you may be sure Lance didn't care to lose him. Still, they couldn't go and drag the man out of the hospital with a hole in his head big enough to put your fist into. They had tried to get a man to take his place, but at the last moment the substitute had failed to show.

"If we can't beat them—fifteen to their fourteen!—I think we'd better go in for challenging girl schools. Last year they beat us, but this year, as we've one man to the good, perhaps we might manage to pull it off."

That's how Mason talked to us, as if *we* wanted them to win! Although they were only fourteen men, they could play. I don't think I ever saw a team who were stronger in their forwards. Lance, their captain, kicked off; Mason, our chief, returned. Then one of their men, getting the leather, tried a run. We downed him, a scrimmage was formed, then, before we knew it, they were rushing the ball across the field. When it did show, I was on it like a flash. I passed to Mason. But he was collared almost before he had a chance to start. There was another turn at scrimmaging, and lively work it was, especially for us who had the pleasure of looking on. So, when again I got a sight of it, I didn't lose much time. I had it up, and I was off. I didn't pass; I tried a run upon my own account. I thought that I was clear away. I had passed the forwards; I thought that I had passed the field, when, suddenly, someone sprang at me, out of the fog—it was a little thick, you know—caught me round the waist, lifted me off my feet, and dropped me on my back. That spoilt it! Before I had a chance of passing they were all on top of me. And again the ball was in the scrimmage.

When I returned to my place behind I looked to see who it was had collared me. The fellow, I told myself, was one of their half-backs. Yet, when I looked at their halves, I couldn't make up my mind which of them it was.

Try how we could—although we had the best of the play—we couldn't get across their line. Although I say it, we all put in some first-rate work. We never played better in our lives. We all had run after run, the passing was as accurate as if it had been mechanical, and yet we could not do the trick. Time after time, just as we were almost in, one of their men put a stop to our little game, and spoilt us. The funny part of the business was that, either owing to the fog, or to our stupidity, we could not make up our minds which of their men it was.

At last I spotted him. Mason had been held nearly on their goal line. They were playing their usual game of driving us back in the scrimmage, when the ball broke through. I took it. I passed to Mason. I thought he was behind, when—he was collared and thrown.

"Joyce!" I cried. "Why, I thought that you weren't playing."

"What are you talking about?" asked one of their men. "Joyce isn't playing."

I stared.

"Not playing! Why, it was he who collared Mason."

"Stuff!"

I did not think the man was particularly civil. It was certainly an odd mistake which I had made. I was just behind Mason when he was collared, and I saw the face of the man who collared him. I could have sworn it was Frank Joyce!

"Who was that who downed you just now?" I asked of Mason, directly I had the chance.

"Their half-back."

Their half-back! Their halves were Tom Wilson and Granger. How could I have mistaken either of them for Joyce?

A little later Giffard was puzzled.

"One of their fellows plays a thundering good game, but, do you know, I can't make out which one of them it is."

"Do you mean the fellow who keeps collaring."

"That's the man!"

The curious part of it was that I never saw the man except when he was collaring.

"The next time," said Giffard, when, for about the sixth time, he had been on the point of scoring, "if I don't get in, I'll know the reason why. I'll kill that man."

It was all very well to talk about our killing him. It looked very much more like his killing us. Mason passed the word that if there was anything like a chance we were to drop. The chance came immediately afterwards. They muffed somehow in trying to pass. Blaine got the leather. He started to run.

"Drop," yelled Mason.

In that fog, and from where Blaine was, dropping a goal was out of the question. He tried the next best thing—he tried to drop into touch. But the attempt was a failure. The kick was a bad one—the ball was as heavy as lead, so that there was not much kick in it—and as it was coming down one of their men, appearing right on the spot, caught it, dropped a drop which was a drop, sent the ball right over our heads, and as near as a toucher over the bar.

Just then the whistle sounded.

"Do you know," declared Ingall, as we were crossing over, "I believe they're playing fifteen men." Mason scoffed.

"Do you think, without giving us notice, they would play fifteen when they told us they were only playing fourteen?"

"Hanged if I don't count them!" persisted Ingall.

He did, and we all did. We faced round and reckoned them up. There were only fourteen, unless one was slinking out of sight somewhere in the dim recesses of the fog, which seemed scarcely probable. Still Ingall seemed dissatisfied.

"They're playing four three-quarters," whispered Giffard, when the game restarted.

So they were—Wheeler, Pendleton, Marshall, and another. Who the fourth man was I couldn't make out. He was a big, strapping fellow, I could see that; but the play was so fast that more than that I couldn't see.

"Who is the fourth man?"

"Don't know; can't see his face. It's so confoundedly foggy!"

It was foggy; but still, of course, it was not foggy enough to render a man's features indistinguishable at the distance of only a few feet. All the same, somehow or other he managed to keep his face concealed from us. While Giffard and I had been whispering they had been packing in. The ball broke out our side. I had it. I tried to run. Instantly I saw that fourth three-quarter rush at me. As he came I saw his face. I was so amazed that I stopped dead. Putting his arms about me he held me as in a vice.

"Joyce!" I cried.

Before the word was out of my mouth half a dozen of their men had hold of the ball. "Held! held!" they screamed.

"Down!" I gasped.

And it was down, with two or three of their men on top of me. They were packing the scrimmage before I had time to get fairly on my feet again.

"That was Joyce who collared me!" I exclaimed.

"Pack in! pack in!" shouted Mason from behind.

And they did pack in with a vengeance. Giffard had the ball. They were down on him; it was hammer and tongs. But through it all we stuck to the leather. They downed us, but not before we had passed it to a friend. Out of it came Giffard, sailing along as though he had not been swallowing mud in pailfuls. I thought he was clear—but no! He stopped short, and dropped the ball!—dropped it, as he stood there, from his two hands as though he were a baby! They asked no questions. They had it up; they were off with it, as though they meant to carry it home. They carried it, too, all the way—almost! It was in disagreeable propinquity to our goal by the time that it was held.

"Now then, Brixham, you've got it!"

That was what they cried.

"Steyning! Steyning! All together!"

That was what we answered. But though we did work all together, it was as much as we could manage.

"Where's Giffard?" bellowed Mason.

My impression was that he had remained like a sign-post rooted to the ground. I had seen him standing motionless after he had dropped the ball, and even as the Brixham men rushed past him. But just then he put in an appearance.

"I protest!" he cried.

"What about?" asked Mason.

"What do they mean by pretending they're not playing Frank Joyce when all the time they are?"

"Oh, confound Frank Joyce! Play up, do. You've done your best to give them the game already. Steady, Steyning, steady. Left, there, left Centre, steady!"

We were steady. We were more than steady. Steadiness alone would not have saved us. We all played forward. At last, somehow, we got the ball back into something like the middle of the field. Giffard kept whispering to me all the time, even in the hottest of the rush.

"What lies, pretending that they're not playing Joyce!" Here he had a discussion with the ball, mostly on his knees. "Humbug about his being in the hospital!"

We had another chance. Out of the turmoil, Mason was flying off with a lead. It was the first clear start he had that day. When he has got that it is catch him who catch can!

As he pelted off the fog, which kept coming and going, all at once grew thicker. He had passed all their men. Of ours, I was the nearest to him. It looked all the world to a china orange that we were going to score at last, when, to my disgust, he reeled, seemed to give a sort of spring, and then fell right over on to his back! I did not understand how he had managed to do it, but I supposed that he had slipped in the mud. Before I could get within passing distance the Brixham men were on us, and the ball was down.

"I thought you'd done it that time."

I said this to him as the scrimmage was being formed. He did not answer. He stood looking about him in a hazy sort of way, as though the further proceedings had no interest for him.

"What's the matter? Are you hurt?"

He turned to me.

"Where is he?" he asked.

"Where's who?"

I couldn't make him out. There was quite a curious look upon his face. "Joyce!"

Somehow, as he said this, I felt a trifle queer. It was his face, or his tone, or something. "Didn't you see him throw me?"

I didn't know what he meant. But before I could say so we had another little rough and tumble—one go up and the other go down. A hubbub arose. There was Ingall shouting.

"I protest! I don't think this sort of thing's fair play."

"What sort of thing?"

"You said you weren't playing Joyce."

"Said we weren't! We aren't."

"Why, he just took the ball out of my hands! Joyce, where are you?"

"Yes, where is he?"

Then they laughed. Mason intervened.

"Excuse me, Lance; we've no objection to your playing Joyce, but why do you say you aren't?"

"I don't think you're well. I tell you that Frank Joyce is at this moment lying in Brixham hospital."

"He just now collared me."

I confess that when Mason said that I was a trifle staggered. I had distinctly seen that he had slipped and fallen. No one had been within a dozen yards of him at the time. Those Brixham men told him so—not too civilly.

"Do you fellows mean to say," he roared, "that Frank Joyce didn't just now pick me up and throw me?"

I struck in.

"I mean to say so. You slipped and fell. My dear fellow, no one was near you at the time." He sprang round at me. "Well, that beats anything!"

"At the same time," I added, "it's all nonsense to talk about Joyce being in Brixham hospital, because, since half-time at any rate, he's been playing three-quarter."

"Of course he has," cried Ingall. "Didn't I see him?"

"And didn't he collar me?" asked Giffard.

The Brixham men were silent. We looked at them, and they at us.

"You fellows are dreaming," said Lance. "It strikes me that you don't know Joyce when you see him."

"That's good," I cried, "considering that he and I were five years at school together."

"Suppose you point him out then?"

"Joyce!" I shouted. "You aren't ashamed to show your face, I hope?"

"Joyce!" they replied, in mockery. "You aren't bashful, Joyce?"

He was not there. Or we couldn't find him, at any rate. We scrutinised each member of the team; it was really absurd to suppose that I could mistake any of them for Joyce. There was not the slightest likeness.

Dryall appealed to the referee.

"Are you sure nobody's sneaked off the field?"

"Stuff!" he said. "I've been following the game all the time, and know every man who's playing, and Joyce hasn't been upon the ground."

"As for his playing three-quarter, Pendleton, Marshall, and I have been playing three-quarter all the afternoon, and I don't think that either of us is very much like Joyce."

This was Tom Wilson.

"You've been playing four three-quarters since we crossed over."

"Bosh!" said Wilson.

That was good, as though I hadn't seen the four with my own eyes.

"Play!" sang out the referee. "Don't waste any more time."

We were at it again. We might be mystified. There was something about the whole affair which was certainly mysterious to me. But we did not intend to be beaten.

"They're only playing three three-quarters now," said Giffard.

So they were. That was plain enough. I wondered if the fourth man had joined the forwards. But why should they conceal the fact that they had been playing four?

One of their men tried a drop. Mason caught it, ran, was collared, passed—wide to the left—and I was off. The whole crowd was in the centre of the field. I put on the steam. Lance came at me. I dodged, he missed. Pendleton was bearing down upon me from the right. I outpaced him. I got a lead. Only Rivers, their back, was between the Brixham goal and me. He slipped just as he made his effort. I was past. It was only a dozen yards to the goal. Nothing would stop me now. I was telling myself that the only thing left was the shouting, when, right in front of me, stood—Joyce! Where he came from I have not the least idea. Out of nothing, it seemed to me. He stood there, cool as a cucumber, waiting—as it appeared—until I came within his reach. His sudden appearance baulked me. I stumbled. The ball slipped from beneath my arm. I saw him smile. Forgetting all about the ball, I made a dash at him. The instant I did so he was gone!

I felt a trifle mixed. I heard behind me the roar of voices. I knew that I had lost my chance. But, at the moment, that was not the trouble. Where had Joyce come from? Where had he gone?

"Now then, Steyning! All together, and you'll do it!"

I heard Mason's voice ring out above the hubbub.

"Brixham, Brixham!" shouted Lance. "Play up!"

"Joyce or no Joyce," I told myself, "hang me if I won't do it yet!"

I got on side. Blaine had hold of the leather. They were on him like a cartload of bricks. He passed to Giffard.

"Don't run back!" I screamed.

They drove him back. He passed to me. They were on the ball as soon as I was. They sent me spinning. Somebody got hold of it. Just as he was off I made a grab at his leg. He went down on his face. The ball broke loose. I got on to my feet. They were indulging in what looked to me very much like hacking. We sent the leather through, and Lance was off! Their fellows backed him up in style. They kept us off until he had a start. He bore off to the right. Already he had shaken off our forwards. I saw Mason charge him. I saw that he sent Mason flying. I made for him. I caught him round the waist. He passed to Pendleton. Pendleton was downed. He lost the ball. Back it came to me, and I was off!

I was away before most of them knew what had become of the leather. Again there was only Rivers between the goal and me. He soon was out of the reckoning. The mud beat him. As he was making for me down he came upon his hands and knees. I had been running wide till then. When he came to grief I centred. Should I take the leather in, or drop?

"Drop!" shouted a voice behind.

That settled me. I was within easy range of the goal. I ought to manage the kick. I dropped—at least, I tried to. It was only a try, because, just as I had my toe against the ball, and was in the very act of kicking, Joyce stood right in front of me! He stood so close that, so to speak, he stood right on the ball. It fell dead, it didn't travel an inch. As I made my fruitless effort, and was still poised upon one leg, placing his hand against my chest, he pushed me over backwards. As I fell I saw him smile—just as I had seen him smile when he had baulked me just before.

I didn't feel like smiling. I felt still less like smiling when, as I yet lay sprawling, Rivers, pouncing on the ball, dropped it back into the centre of the field. He was still standing by me when I regained my feet. He volunteered an observation.

"Lucky for us you muffed that kick."

"Where's Joyce?" I asked.

"Where's who?"

"Joyce."

He stared at me.

"I don't know what you're driving at. I think you fellows must have got Joyce on the brain."

He returned to his place in the field. I returned to mine. I had an affectionate greeting from Giffard.

"That's the second chance you've thrown away. Whatever made you muff that kick?"

"Giffard," I asked, "do you think I'm going mad?"

"I should think you've gone."

I could not—it seems ridiculous, but I could not ask if he had seen Joyce. It was so evident that he had not. And yet, if I had seen him, he must have seen him too. As he suggested—I must have gone mad!

The play was getting pretty rough, the ground was getting pretty heavy. We had churned it into a regular quagmire. Sometimes we went above the ankle in liquid mud. As for the state that we were in!

One of theirs had the ball. Half a dozen of ours had hold of him.

"Held! held!" they yelled. "It's not held," he gasped.

They had him down, and sat on him. Then he owned that it was held.

"Let it through," cried Mason, when the leather was in scrimmage.

Before our forwards had a chance they rushed it through. We picked it up; we carried it back. They rushed it through again. The tide of battle swayed, now to this side, now to that. Still we gained. Two or three short runs bore the ball within punting distance of their goal. We more than retained the advantage. Yard by yard we drove them back. It was a match against time. We looked like winning if there was only time enough. At last it seemed as though matters had approached something very like a settlement. Pendleton had the ball. Our men were on to him. To avoid being held he punted. But he was charged before he really had a chance. The punt was muddled. It was a catch for Mason. He made his mark—within twenty yards of their goal! There is no better drop-kick in England than Alec Mason. If from a free kick at that distance he couldn't top their bar, we might as well go home to bed.

Mason took his time. He judged the distance with his eye. Then, paying no attention to the Brixham forward, who had stood up to his mark, he dropped a good six feet on his own side of it.

There was an instant's silence. Then they raised a yell; for as the ball left Mason's foot one of their men sprang at him, and, leaping upwards, caught the ball in the air. It was wonderfully done! Quick as lightning, before we had recovered from our surprise, he had dropped the ball back into the centre of the field.

"Now then, Brixham," bellowed Lance.

And they came rushing on. They came on too! We were so disconcerted by Mason's total failure that they got the drop on us. They reached the leather before our back had time to return. It was all we could do to get upon the scene of action quickly enough to prevent their having the scrimmage all to themselves. Mason's collapse had put life into them as much as, for the moment, it had taken it out of us. They carried the ball through the scrimmage as though our forwards were not there.

"Now then, Steyning, you're not going to let them beat us!"

As Mason held his peace I took his place as fugleman.

But we could not stand against them—we could not—in scrimmage or out of it. All at once they seemed to be possessed. In an instant their back play improved a hundred per cent. One of their men, in particular, played like Old Nick himself. In the excitement—and they were an exciting sixty seconds—I could not make out which one of them it was; but he made things lively. He as good as played us single-handed; he was always on the ball; he seemed to lend their forwards irresistible impetus when it was in the scrimmage. And when it was out of it, wasn't he just upon the spot. He was ubiquitous—here, there, and everywhere. And at last he was off. Exactly how it happened is more than I can say, but I saw that he had the ball. I saw him dash away with it. I made for him. He brushed me aside as though I were a fly. I was about to start in hot pursuit when someone caught me by the arm. I turned—in a trifle of a rage. There was Mason at my side.

"Never mind that fellow. Listen to me." These were funny words to come from the captain of one's team at the very crisis of the game. I both listened and looked. Something in the expression of his face quite startled me. "Do you know who it was who spoilt my kick? It was either Joyce or—Joyce's ghost."

Before I was able to ask him what it was he meant there arose a hullaballoo of shouting. I turned, just in time to see the fellow, who had run away with the leather, drop it, as sweetly as you please, just over our goal. They had won! And at that moment the whistle sounded—they had done it just on time!

The man who had done the trick turned round and faced us. He was wearing a worsted cap, such as brewers wear. Taking it off, he waved it over his head. As he did so there was not a man upon the field who did not see him clearly, who did not know who he was. He was Frank Joyce! He stood there for a moment before us all, and then was gone.

"Lance," shouted the referee, "here's a telegram for you."

Lance was standing close to Mason and to me. A telegraph boy came pelting up. Lance took the yellow envelope which the boy held out to him. He opened it.

"Why! what!" Through the mud upon his face he went white, up to the roots of his hair. He turned to us with startled eyes. "Joyce died in Brixham Hospital nearly an hour ago. The hospital people have telegraphed to say so."

Fingers of a Hand

H. D. Everett

> In the same hour came forth the fingers of a man's hand and wrote . . . and the king saw the part of the hand that wrote.

The children were supposed to need a seaside change, and I daresay they did, poor wee things, as they had had whooping-cough in the spring, and measles to follow. As you know, we are taking care of them for Bernard, who is in India with his wife, and so we are even more anxious about them than if they were our own. That is one great use of unmarried aunts—to shoulder other people's responsibilities; and I, for one, think the world would be a poorer place if the "million of unwanted women" were, by some convulsion of nature, to be swept away. I only mention the children's measles as the reason why we took those lodgings at Cove at the beginning of July, for, now one has to economise, we should not have gone in for a seaside change as a luxury for ourselves.

The lodgings were clean and fairly comfortable, and we took them for two months certain, letting our own pretty cottage in the midlands for a similar term. And that was why we had no home of our own to retreat to when— But I am telling my story upside down, as Sara says I always do. You would not be likely to understand, if I did not begin in the right place, with what went before.

The house was Number Seven, Cliff Terrace, a row of detached villas above the road, on the other side of which was the esplanade and the sea. There were no other lodgers, as we took both Mrs. Mills's "sets"; nobody in the house but ourselves and the bairns, and that important person Nurse, except Mrs. Mills herself, and her daughter who waited on us. So you see there was no one who could have played tricks— But again I am getting on too fast.

We had never been to Cove before, or to St. Eanswyth either, the larger watering-place which lies to the east of Cove; but we thought our choice of place for a summer holiday was amply justified by the pretty inland neighbourhood and the sweet air, and a safe beach close at hand, where the children could be out playing early and late under the guardian wing of Nurse. For the first fortnight we were all satisfied and happy, and, both in metaphor and actually, there was not a cloud in the sky.

Then the rain began, not brief summer showers and sunshine in between, but the worst weather of a wet July—a continuous downpour with hardly ten minutes intermission, and going on for days: such rain as Noah must have witnessed before the beginning of the Flood.

Of course the poor children had to keep the house, and, though they and Nurse had the dining-room set to themselves, there was but little space for them to play about. Sara and I occupied the drawing-room, and she had been sketching from the window—not that there was much visible to make into a picture: a leaden sea and slanting lines of rain, and boats drawn up on the beach. At last she pushed away colour-box and pencils.

"I can't stand this any longer," she said. "Rain or no rain, I am going out. It will be a good opportunity to test the resisting powers of my new cloak. You must stay in to-day, as I believe you have caught cold."

I did not dispute her fiat. Sara always decides what is, or what is not to be done, and I, who am a biddable person, submit to be ruled. And, to say the truth, I was not particularly anxious to get wet. I went on with my sewing till it was nearly time for Miss Mills to appear with the luncheon-tray, and then I began to clear the table of Sara's scattered possessions.

Some blank sheets of paper were lying about, besides the one pinned to her board with the half-finished sketch; and on one of these I noticed some large scrawled writing. Not Sara's writing, which is particularly small and neat; not the writing of any one I knew. The words were quite legible, but they were very odd. GO—by itself at the top of the sheet; and the same word repeated twice below, followed by GET OUT AT ONCE.

Of course I showed Sara this when she came in to luncheon, and she could not account for it any more than I. The sheets were unmarked when she took them out of her portfolio; of that she seemed to be certain.

"Some one has been playing a trick on us," she said. "If it is Mrs. Mills, it is an odd sort of notice"; and at this very mild witticism both of us laughed.

But the idea of a trick being played was absurd: I had been in the room the whole time, as I said.

"Unless you think I dozed off while you were out, and did it in my sleep!"

Sara laughed again, and began to sort the loose papers back into place.

"Why, here is more of it," she exclaimed; and I saw on the sheet she held out, in the same large scrawl, a repetition of the words—GET OUT—GET OUT AT ONCE.

Now I could have sworn—had swearing been of any use—that I had looked those papers over on both sides after finding the first writing, and with that sole exception they bore no mark whatever. So these last words must have been written after my discovery and before Sara's return, and while I was beside them in the room. Surely they had been traced by no mortal hand!

You will not wonder that such a curious happening was the subject of discussion between us during the rest of that wet day. "I'd give anything to know who did it," Sara was saying, while I added: "I should like better still to know what it means." I am more credulous than Sara, and it seemed to me there must be some meaning in anything so unaccountable. I had this feeling from the very first, and, as you will see, both the conviction and the reason for it grew.

I pass on to the following Sunday. The weather was still wet, and the children were kept mainly to the house. For the sake of variety for them, Sara had little Dick and Nancy upstairs in our sitting-room for their Sunday lessons, which as a rule devolve on her to give, as she is a cleverer teacher than I. Lessons of the simplest, as they generally consist of showing pictures and giving explanations; and to be allowed to look at Sara's illustrated Bible is a frequent Sabbath treat. The children had gone down again to Nurse, and Sara was about to tidy the book away, when she gave a sharp exclamation.

"Grace, look here. Who can have done this?"

The volume was lying open at the nineteenth chapter of Genesis, and these words in the twenty-second verse were scored under blackly in pencil—*Haste thee: escape*.

Now Sara, who is particular in everything, is especially so about her books. She hates any soil or mark upon them, and nothing irritates her more than to have a lent volume returned with "purple passages" scored beside in the margin, whether in approval or otherwise. "Tut-tut," she was saying, at the usual pitch of exasperation. "It is really unpardonable. *Where* is my india-rubber? I must see if I can take it out. It could not have been the children. And the Millses would never——! But there is nobody else."

"You would have seen, had it been the children. They are good little things, and would not: besides, they had not a pencil"—(thus I weakened an argument based on their righteousness). "And what odd words to have chosen to mark, when you think of the other scrawls. I wonder if this is all. It is possible there may be more."

"I shall look the book right through and see, and then I shall lock it in my box."

Sara sat down to her task armed with the piece of rubber, and by no means in a Sabbath spirit of peace and good-will. She did find two other texts scored under, and these were the marked words:

2 Kings, ninth chapter and third verse. *Open the door and flee and tarry not.*

St. Matthew, seventh chapter and twenty-seventh verse. *The . . . house . . . fell, and great was the fall thereof.*

I was superstitious, because disturbed by these happenings. So I was told, yet who would not have been affected in my place? I believe Sara too was disquieted in her secret mind, though she would not allow it. But then she was used to pride herself on being an *esprit fort*.

I kept saying to myself. What next?—and the next came quickly. I did not tell Sara what I purposed doing, but I left a couple of sheets of paper and a freshly-cut pencil displayed on the table when we were going out. More writing might be done with the opportunity given, and "it" might vouchsafe to make clear "its" meaning. I could not then have analysed what I meant by the convenient impersonal pronoun, nor am I clear of the exact meaning now.

We were about to do some shopping in the town, and I had stupidly left my purse on the mantel-shelf in the sitting-room, so I was obliged to turn back to get it. As I opened the door, my eyes fell at once upon the papers, and I saw some dark object moving across the white surface, and then quickly disappearing over the table edge. It was too big for a mouse; could it have been a rat? The thought of a rat gave me a nervous shiver; I think I would have a greater terror of rats than of ghosts. I looked at the papers though I did not touch them; yes, a vague scrawl was begun upon the upper one, not developed into legible words. I had disturbed the writer too soon. But what could the writer be, coming in the form of a rat, or the shadow of a rat, and yet able to write words which appeared to convey a message? I left the papers as they were, but the scrawl was not continued; no doubt that unexpected first return had scared away the writer.

I said nothing to Sara of my failed experiment; but next day about the same time I laid my trap again, this time staying in the room, but retired into a distant corner, where I set myself to watch.

For a long while there was nothing. Then an object ill-defined and shadowy crept across the paper, stealing towards the pencil as it lay. I hardly dared breathe, the excitement was so tense. Over the pencil this shadow paused, and now became denser, taking solid form. It was not the whole of a hand, but a thumb and two fingers, forming something like a claw. But, if you consider, a thumb and two fingers are all a hand needs to manipulate a pencil, and "it" may not have cared to materialise anything superfluous. The pencil now slanted upwards between these fingers and the thumb, and—yes, no doubt remained—the claw was writing. Now we would know all, such was my sanguine thought, not forecasting how deep the mystery would remain.

It was Sara this time who interrupted, coming in. The pencil dropped, the claw from a solid form became a shadow, and slipped away over the edge of the table, as I had seen it vanish before. Sara noticed nothing; she was too full of her news, and of the letter open in her hand.

"Look at this. We ought to have had it two days ago, but there was a mistake in the address. It is from Mrs. Bernard's mother" (Mrs. Bernard is our brother's wife). "She is at Diplake for ten days before they go to Scotland, and she wants one of us to bring the children there just for the time they stay. She says she is sorry she cannot have us both, but it is a case of single room, as the house is full. She is expecting us to-morrow, so I shall have to wire, and tell Nurse to get ready. Will you go, Grace, or shall I?"

"Of course you must be the one. I should never get on at Diplake, and with a large, gay party. You must go, Sara, and put your best foot foremost, for Bernard's sake. And—I'm glad you have to take the children. For look what is written here!"

I showed her the paper on which the claw had scrawled. Over and over again the word DANGER, as if it could not be too often insisted on. Then, also repeated: GO. GET OUT. Then an attempt at *children*, afterwards clearly written: DANGER. CHILDREN MUST GO.

I think Sara was impressed at last, though she hardly believed in the claw I had seen writing. As to that, I must—she said—have been hallucinated, or else slept and dreamed. But little time remained for argument, as all was in a hurry of preparation—boxes to be packed, and the children to be consoled, for their enjoyment of the seaside pleasures was very keen, and the attraction small of going to stay with an almost unknown grandmother. "But we are coming back?" said little Nancy. "We are coming back again here?" I believe I told her yes, but as to what will happen in the future, who can say?

They set out early next morning, Sara and the three children and Nurse, and I saw them off at the station. Sara said almost at the last:

"I don't half like leaving you alone here, Grace. If you find the lodgings too solitary, why not take a room at the hotel for the days I am away?"

I said I would think of it, but in truth I felt no special nervousness or concern, only an intense curiosity to see what would happen now we had (by pure accident) obeyed the dictation of the writing, and sent the children away.

The lonely evening passed for me without disturbance; Miss Mills came at the usual time to carry down my supper tray, and wished me good-night, and shortly after this I went to bed.

I slept, and do not remember any warning dreams. But in the very early daylight I was suddenly startled broad awake—not I think by any noise, but by an alteration in the level of my bed. My head was low, almost on the floor, and my feet were high in air. Everything in the room was sliding and altering; basin and ewer slipped from the washstand, crashed and broke, and pictures flapped from the wall. Then came a greater crash like the jolting of a thunder-clap, and it was close at hand; chimney-pots falling, walls and roofs collapsing: was it an earthquake that had happened? I heard screams and shouts, but the sliding movement had stopped.

I struggled up and to my feet, for I had been half buried by the bedclothes falling back upon me; and there opposite was a great crack or rent in the outer wall, wide enough to admit my arm, with the new morning looking through, and a waft of air blowing in keenly from the sea. It was as if the house had broken in two. What but an earthquake could have caused such a disaster?—and again I heard people screaming. The often repeated warning, the scored words in the Bible ran in my head. I could be thankful indeed that Sara and the children were safe at Diplake out of the way: what an agony had they been still here, and those screams possibly theirs!

I do not know how long it took me to scramble up the slanting floor, to find my clothes, my shoes, where all was confusion, so that if it were possible to get out of the house I might go forth clad. Then I tried the door.

It was in some way jammed, and it seemed as if ages passed before I could wrench it open. When at last it gave way, the wreck revealed without was worse than the wreck within. The staircase was a heap of broken wood, and the back wall had fallen inwards; there was no getting down that way. What had become, I wondered, of Mrs. Mills and her daughter, and was it their screams that I heard? I called to them by name, but there was no answer.

Baffled so, I looked from the window, which had hardly a whole pane left. It was as if the terrace had disappeared: the road was broken up, and the house had been carried down with the sliding earth, many yards nearer the sea. A crowd had assembled, staring at this phenomenon, but at a safe distance. I shouted to them, and a man called up to me instructions to stay where I was, as a ladder would presently be brought.

I knew later that they feared at first to touch the house, lest it should collapse in total ruin like the one next on the terrace, where, alas! two people had been killed, overwhelmed and buried in their sleep.

This was a danger indeed, about which that warning came. The part of our house which fell, was where the children would have been sleeping. I was told that tons and tons of masonry had crushed in their little beds; even now it makes me sick to think of what we so narrowly escaped. The Millses, mother and daughter, were dug out of the basement quite unharmed, but I am afraid, poor people, they are heavy losers. I myself had not a scratch.

The great landslip at Cove, with all its damage and disaster, will surely pass into history: the slide of the undercliff down into the sea, the gaping fissure torn above, hundreds of feet in length—the alteration of the ground below, heaped into mounds and billows like the waves of the sea, while the buildings in the course of the slide are broken up and displaced like a set of children's toys, playthings in the hands of a giant. People who are wise about the geological formation, talk of a bed of slippery clay underlying the upper strata, and say water had percolated down to it owing to the wet spring, and, following upon that, the heavy rains of that dismal week in July. But they are wise after the event and did not forecast it: indeed it was anticipated by no one other than the writer of those mysterious words.

The Footsteps in the Dust

Alice Perrin

Here and there, mysteriously, in India exist Englishmen who seem to have been left behind on the strenuous march of British administration; who, from instability, misfortune, or wickedness, have sunk down, not entirely to the level of the loafer, but to a stage where they remain rooted in exile, apparently without home connections, correspondents, or interests, and who live and die in apathetic obscurity, while their histories, curious, pitiful, or unworthy, remain unrecorded and forgotten.

Captain Bogle was one of these derelicts. Being the oldest European inhabitant of Mynapur, he was accepted by the ever-changing officials of the district, who played cards and billiards with him in the little club, and whose wives occasionally asked him to dinner. He was an elderly man, and lived in a miserable little two-roomed bungalow opposite the great white stuccoed mansion owned by Gunga Pershad, the rich Hindoo "buniah," or merchant; but no one could say how long he had lived there, who he was, whence came his means of living, what had been his regiment, or why he voluntarily buried himself in a small civil station in Northern India. There had been rumours; of course: he had eloped with his Colonel's wife and been ruined over the damages; he had been dismissed from the army for embezzling mess funds; he was a Russian spy, a suspected murderer, the rightful heir to a great title, &c. &c. But nothing was ever proved, and Captain Bogle saw Collector, Joint Magistrate, Civil Surgeon, Police Officer, and Engineer, come and go, while his bungalow, and that of Gunga Pershad, remained the only dwellings in the station that still held their original occupants.

Captain Bogle and the buniah were apparently close friends, that is to say, the Englishman had the use of the native's horses, baskets of vegetables and fruit from the rambling garden, and they occasionally attended a race meeting down country together, when it was popularly supposed that if Captain Bogle lost, Gunga Pershad paid up—but not *vice versa*. In the evenings the couple were frequently to be seen driving in Gunga Pershad's roomy old-fashioned landau drawn by a pair of big Australian horses, with a fat coachman in purple livery, and a tatterdemalion outrider clattering behind on a white stallion. Gunga Pershad, clad in a plum-coloured satin coat, with a yellow turban, his loose lips stained red with betel-nut juice, would loll in his seat deep in conversation with his companion whose appearance resembled that of a decayed Mephistopheles.

"It's a queer alliance," said the Civil Surgeon, who had lately been transferred to Mynapur, and had not yet assimilated the accepted customs of the place. "And it's my belief that Bogle gets far more out of Gunga Pershad than meets the naked eye."

"I have sometimes thought so myself lately," replied Petersham, the police officer, with whom the doctor had been dining, and the two were now seated in the veranda smoking their Bahadur cheroots. "And yet the fellow lives on like a half-caste in that little pig-sty of a bungalow, and his clothes would disgrace a rag-and-bone shop."

"You see he drinks," said the doctor.

"I've never seen him drunk, and I've been here six months—worse luck!"

"No, and I don't suppose you ever would. That chap's pickled with spirit from head to foot. He can stand any amount, I should say; but it must come to an end sooner or later. It's my belief that he's taught Gunga Pershad the same game—half brandy, half champagne is probably their usual drink. A native does that kind of thing pretty thoroughly when he once takes to it."

The police officer grew thoughtful. "I was here some years ago as assistant," he said recollectively, "and now I come to think of it, Gunga Pershad was then a very different being from what he is at present. He was a smart, healthy-looking fellow, always riding about, and ready for a chat whenever one met him, and now he's fat and bloated and never stirs out except in that old shandridan of his; and he can't look one in the face or answer civilly when he's spoken to. I see a great change in him for the worse."

"Natives go down hill fast when they start, and I fancy our friend the Captain gave him the first shove and keeps him going. My bearer declares that the pair of them sit up till four o'clock every morning drinking and gambling in Gunga Pershad's bungalow."

Then, since the hour was late, and he had to be up early on duty, the doctor said good-night, and started home on foot, carrying his own lantern, for all the bungalows in Mynapur were fairly close together. His route led him past the large untidy compound, in the centre of which stood Gunga Pershad's mansion with the deep verandas, pucca roof, and imposing porch. The long doors, reaching almost from ceiling to floor, stood wide open, for the night was hot and airless, and the lofty room facing the road was brightly illuminated with rows of wall lamps, while a great white punkah waved to and fro. Under the punkah stood a card table, and at it sat Gunga Pershad and the Captain, absorbed in their game, with long tumblers full of liquid at their elbows.

The doctor, fascinated by the curious picture, stood and gazed, and presently the native threw down his cards, and stood up gesticulating wildly. Captain Bogle leaned back in his chair, and proceeded to light a cheroot. Then the voice of Gunga Pershad rose in angry remonstrance, though to the watcher outside the words were not distinguishable; but they sounded threatening, beseeching, despairing by turns. The man dragged off his turban, tore his clothes, and beat his breast; he knelt in front of the Englishman, and laid his forehead on the stone floor, and throughout this piteous scene the Captain sat apparently unmoved, blowing clouds of smoke through his nostrils. The doctor turned away in disgust. The sight sickened him, it was sordid and revolting, and made him ashamed of his countryman. What did it all mean? That Bogle had been compassing the ruin of Gunga Pershad for some years past he felt convinced, and it now seemed as though a crisis had arrived. Something was going to happen.

And next morning came the news that Gunga Pershad had committed suicide by taking poison; moreover, it eventually transpired that the once rich merchant had died penniless, and that the big bungalow, the landau and horses, the mirrors, chandeliers, marble-topped tables, and all the rest of the garish possessions so dear to the heart of a native, together with savings, and investments, and valuable house property in the bazaar, had all been gambled away to Captain Bogle.

The question most discussed in the station was what the man would do with his evilly won fortune? That he was legally entitled to it all there was no disputing, but public opinion rose high against him, and though curiosity raged in every breast, Captain Bogle found himself ignored when he entered the little club, and apparently invisible when he met any one on the road.

This treatment at last caused him to avoid the club and his English neighbours, but he remained on in the shabby bungalow, and only took long solitary drives in the landau so lately the property of his victim. People wondered why he did not occupy the big white house now it was his own, or why he stayed on in Mynapur instead of going home, and old gossip and conjectures concerning him revived with additions and improvements.

Still he continued his curious existence, driving out in the evenings along the hard, dusty roads; and the doctor who met him often on his way back from the Government dispensary, expressed his opinion that the man was on the verge of delirium tremens.

"I saw him yesterday afternoon," he said to Petersham, "driving along jabbering like a monkey, just for all the world as if he had some one beside him! He seemed to be arguing and explaining till I felt quite uncanny. I could have sworn that old Gunga Pershad was sitting next him if I hadn't seen for myself that the seat was empty!"

"He was going on anyhow last night too," said Petersham. "I heard him when I was coming home from dining with the Dunnes. You know how close that little hovel of his is to the road; he was standing outside waving his hands and shouting in Hindustani. I pulled up and asked him what was the matter, and he solemnly implored me to go over and tell Gunga Pershad to stop calling him, because nothing would induce him to go over to the bungalow and give the native his revenge at cards. I said, 'My dear chap, Gunga Pershad's dead, how *can* he call you, or play cards, or do anything else?' But he only looked at me like a screwed owl and said he knew Gunga Pershad was dead, well enough, and that was just why he didn't want to go over and play cards with him! We shall have trouble with that fellow, sooner or later."

"I think I'd better go and look him up to-day," said the doctor, who was a kind-hearted individual. But, owing to an unexpected press of work, it was not until after a late and hurried tiffin at a patient's house that he found himself free to visit Captain Bogle.

The little bungalow looked deserted when he drove up to the veranda, and it was some minutes before his shouts attracted the attention of the servants. He could hear them laughing, coughing, gossiping in the cook-house. At length a disreputable creature appeared who pronounced himself to be the Captain-sahib's bearer, as he hastily wound a dirty turban about his greasy black head.

"Where is the sahib?" inquired the doctor.

"Huzoor! He commanded the carriage but two hours since, and drove forth to eat the air. Whither he went thy slave knoweth not."

Rather relieved than otherwise the doctor turned his trap round; but as he drove down the road past the opposite compound he caught sight of the well-known landau standing under the porch of the big bungalow, and he drove in through the white gate-posts and up the ill-kept drive. The place had not been touched since Gunga Pershad's death, and the house had stood unlived in and neglected.

When he reached the porch he found the pair of horses standing in easy attitudes with drooping heads, while the coachman and groom were seated on the ground sharing a hookah and conversing in low tones. They had the patient apathetic air of natives, to whom time is no object, and one spot quite as satisfactory as another in which to smoke and discuss the price of food. They rose when they saw the doctor, and the fat coachman explained that the Captain-sahib was within the bungalow, and had been there for nearly two hours.

"It be the first time he hath entered the building since the death of Gunga Pershad," he added, as though to account for the length of the visit.

The utter silence of the neglected house struck the doctor with an odd sense of uneasiness. He descended from his trap and looked into the entrance hall. The dust lay thick on the matting, and in the dust, sharply imprinted, were the marks of Captain Bogle's boots. The doctor followed the footsteps, and they led him into the principal room where the dust covered everything. It soiled the satin upholstered chairs and couches, dimmed the mirrors, clung to the dingy punkah frill, and was deep on the floor. In the middle of the vast room was a little green-covered card table with two chairs, one of which had been pushed aside as though the occupant had risen abruptly. Cards were scattered over the table and a few lay on the floor with the remains of a broken tumbler. Evidently, thought the doctor, the room had never been touched since Gunga Pershad had played his last disastrous game.

He followed the fresh footmarks up to the table, noticed that the Captain must have first sat down in the chair that was turned aside, for it had been pushed back quite recently, and the footmarks about it were a little confused. He was vaguely conscious of something unnatural, and then realised suddenly that though the steps had led up to the table they were neither continued nor retraced. The dust lay undisturbed everywhere else—the fine grey Indian dust that gathers thickly even in a few hours if unopposed; and yet Captain Bogle was not present.

The doctor stood completely puzzled, gazing with attention at the tracks that were unmistakably in one direction only. Then he lifted up his voice and called the Captain by name again and again. His voice echoed through the lofty rooms; but there was no reply, except the scream of a frightened starling that had built its nest in a ventilator in the ceiling. He picked his way carefully back, stepping as far as possible in his own footmarks, and looked into the other rooms that led from the entrance hall. There was nothing but silence, emptiness, undisturbed dust.

Captain Bogle was not in the bungalow, and with a feeling of resentful bewilderment the doctor drove off to fetch Petersham, after giving the waiting servants orders that no one was to enter the house until his return. He brought the police officer back with him, and together they surveyed the single line of footsteps terminating at the table, the chair's position, the evidence of its occupant having sat down and risen hurriedly.

"The other chair hasn't been sat in," said Petersham, peering at it closely; "it's covered with dust, but those cards have only lately been dropped on the floor. Bogle came in here right enough, but how the devil did he get out again—unless he flew!"

Together the two men went over every room and every corner. They searched the roof, the garden, the stables, the outhouses; but Captain Bogle was nowhere to be found. He had disappeared completely and unaccountably, and the very last traces of him ever discovered were the footsteps in the dust that led up to the card table in the middle of the big room of Gunga Pershad's bungalow—and no farther.

The Former Passengers

B. M. Croker

Who is whispering and calling through the rain?
    Far above the tempest crashing,
    And the torrent's ceaseless dashing,
I hear a weary calling, as of pain.

"If any one can help you, it will be Captain Blane."

This sentence was uttered by a smart young clerk, in a shipping office in Rangoon, who, clothed in cool white drill, leant his elbows confidentially on the desk, and concluded his speech with a reassuring nod.

I was *en route* from Upper Burmah to Singapore, in order to attend my sister's wedding. Our flat river-boat was late, and when I presented myself at the booking-office of the P. and O., I found to my dismay that the steamer for the Straits had sailed at dawn, and that there would not be another for a week! I was therefore bound to miss the wedding, and waste my precious leave in Rangoon, thanks to the leisurely old tub that had dawdled down from Mandalay.

I turned my eyes expectantly on Captain Blane, a short-necked, weather-beaten sailor, in a blue serge coat with gilt buttons, and a peaked cap. He surveyed me steadily, with a pair of small keen eyes, and evidently did not receive the suggestion with enthusiasm.

"We don't carry passengers," he announced in a gruff voice. "My ship is only a cargo-boat, a tramp; and we have no accommodation whatsoever."

"No accommodation!" echoed the clerk, incredulously. "Oh, I say, come!"

"Why, you know very well that all the cabins are chock-full of cargo; and we have never carried a passenger since I took command."

"If there was any hole or corner where you could stow me, I don't mind how I rough it," I urged; "and I'll pay full first-class fare."

"Oh, there's lots of holes and corners," admitted the captain. "And you'd just get the ship's rations, same as the officers and myself; no soups and *entrées*—plain roast and boiled."

"I'm not particular; I'm ready to eat salt junk and sea biscuit. I'll do anything, short of swimming, to get to Singapore by next Wednesday."

"Is it so *very* important?" demanded Captain Blane.

"A wedding. No—no," in answer to his commiserating stare, "not my own—but I've to give away the bride."

"Well, well, I suppose I must try and stretch a point. Mind! I'll take you at your word about the passage money. 'Never refuse a good offer,' is my motto; so, Mr. ——?" and he paused interrogatively.

"Lawrence is my name."

"Mr. Lawrence, if you'll be down at Godwin's Wharf to-morrow, at nine o'clock, with your baggage and bedding and servant, we will lie off' a bit, and any sampan will put you aboard in five minutes. Ask for the *Wandering Star*;" and with a nod between the clerk and myself, he turned his back and stumped out.

"He is not very keen about passengers, eh?" remarked the clerk with a laugh. "I wonder why?"

"I suppose because she is a dirty old cargo-boat. But any port in a storm, or rather, any ship, in this crisis, for me!"

"Ah," said the clerk, rubbing his chin reflectively, "I've a sort of idea—though perhaps I dreamt it—that there is something rum, or out of the way, about this *Wandering Star*."

"Well, whatever it is, I'll risk it," I answered with a laugh, as I followed the captain's example, and took my departure.

Punctually at nine o'clock next morning I embarked in a sampan, and was rowed down the swift Irrawaddy.

"That cannot be my steamer," I protested, as the boatman made for a long, low, raking craft, a craft of considerable pretensions! She looked like one of the smaller vessels of the P. and O. fleet.

But sure enough the boatman was right, for as we passed under her stern, I read in yellow letters the name—*Wandering Star*.

A closer inspection showed her to be simply what her commander had stated—a tramp; she was dirty, rusty, and travel-stained. When I clambered aboard, I found no snowy decks, or shining brasses, but piles of cargo, bustling coolies, and busy blue-clad lascars. I was immediately accosted by the captain, who presented me to the chief officer, and to a fellow-traveller, a sallow, lanky youth of nineteen, going to join his friends in the Straits.

"I thought he would be company for you," explained the sailor. "We are off in half an hour," pointing to the Blue Peter at the fore. "And we're loaded to the hatches. Mr. Kelly here will show you your quarters."

As I followed the chief officer, I was astonished at the dimensions of the *Star*; it was a considerable distance from the captain's snug cabin, near the bridge, to the poop. We made our way below, into a long saloon with tables and seats intact, but the aft part piled high with bales. There was a strange, musty, mouldy smell; it felt damp and vault-like, and afforded a sharp contrast to the blazing sun and cobalt sky on deck.

As my eye became used to the gloom, I noticed the lavish carving, the handsome mahogany and brass fittings, the maple-wood doors and panels—the remains of better days!

My cabin contained two bunks, and in one of these my servant, a Madras butler, called "Sawmy," had already arranged my bedding.

"I wonder you don't carry passengers?" I remarked to Mr. Kelly. "What a fine saloon! I should have thought it would have paid well."

"She carried hundreds in her day," he said complacently. "You see there is where the piano was hitched, and there the swinging lamps, and bookcase; but, all the same, it would never pay us to take passengers"; and he laughed—an odd sort of laugh. "We are not a regular liner, you know, trading between two ports. Regular liners look on us as dirt; but lots of 'em would give a good deal for our lines, and our engines. There's some of them I would not send my old boots home in! We pick up cargo as we find it; one time we run to Zanzibar, another to Hong Kong, another to the Cape, or maybe Sydney. I've not been home this three years. I hope you'll find your bunk comfortable; the youngster is opposite, just across the saloon—you know your way back!" and having done the honours, he left me.

Certainly, the *Star* was much above her present business, and bore the remains of having seen better days. Even my marble washstand was not in keeping with a cargo-steamer. I opened the next cabin; it was crammed to the door with freight—bird-cages in this instance. Every cabin was no doubt similarly packed. I was not sorry to exchange the earthy, chill atmosphere below for the bright sunshine on deck. Soon we had weighed anchor, and were moving smoothly down the rapid Irrawaddy, between high banks of tawny grass, gradually losing sight of the shipping, then of the golden Pagoda, then of Elephant Point; finally the *Star* put her nose straight out, to cross the Gulf of Martaban. The sea was calm, we were well fed and found, and made a pleasant party of six; the captain, first and second officers, the chief engineer, and two passengers. I slept like a top that night, and awoke next morning, and found we were anchored off Moulmein, with its hills covered with pagodas and palms. From Moulmein we put to sea, and still the weather once more favoured us. The captain was a capital companion, full of anecdotes and sea-stories; the chief engineer was a first-rate chess-player, and I began to think I had done rather a smart thing in securing a passage in this stray steamer. As the captain concluded a thrilling yarn apropos of a former ship, in which he had been third officer, I suddenly recalled the shipping clerk's hint, and asked—

"Are there no stories about this one? has she no history?" Captain Blane looked at the chief officer with a knowing grin, and then replied—

"History?—of course she has. What do you call the log-book? That's her history. I suppose that chap at the office told you she was considered an unlucky ship? Eh? Come, now, own up!"

"No; but he said he had an idea that there was something queer about her—he could not remember what it was."

"Well, I've been in command of her now four years, and I've seen nothing to complain of. What do you say, Kelly?" appealing to the first officer.

"I say that I never wish to put foot on a better sea-boat, and there's nothing wrong with her, as far as *I* know."

But Sawmy, my Madras boy, entertained a totally different opinion of the *Star*. When I asked him why he did not sleep outside my door in the saloon, he frankly replied—

"Because plenty devil in this ship; the chief Serang" (head of the Lascars) "telling me that saloon plenty bad place."

We were now within forty-eight hours of Singapore, when the weather suddenly changed, as it frequently does in those treacherous seas. The awning was taken down—sure presage of a bad time coming. The ports were closed, and all was made ready for a blow; and we were not disappointed—it came. We had a rough night, but I was not in the least inconvenienced; I slept like a dormouse rocked in the cradle of the deep.

In the morning my fellow-passenger (whose name, by the way, was Mellish, and who had evidently "suffered," to judge by his ghastly appearance) accosted me timidly and said—

"Did you get up and walk about last night?"

"No."

"Do you ever walk in your sleep?" he continued.

"Not to my knowledge—why?"

"Because last night some one came and hammered on my cabin door, and shouted, 'The ship's aground.' What do you think it can have been?" he asked with a frightful face.

"I think there is no doubt that it was the hot tinned lobster you had for supper," I answered promptly.

"No, no, no, it was not a dream—it woke me," he returned. "I thought it was *you*. Then I tried to think it was a nightmare, and had almost brought myself to believe it, and was dropping off to sleep, when a cold, cold wet hand was passed slowly across my face"; and he shuddered violently.

"Lobster!" I repeated emphatically. "No, no. Oh, Mr. Lawrence, I heard moaning and whispering and praying. I'm afraid to sleep in that cabin alone; may I come and share yours?"

"There is no room," I answered, rather shortly. "The top berth is crammed full of my things."

At breakfast there was a good deal of movement, and now and then a loud splash upon the deck. The captain, who had been tapping the barometer, looked unusually solemn, and said—

"We are in for a bit of dirty weather; unless I'm mistaken, there's a cyclone somewhere about. I don't think we shall do more than touch the edge of it, and this is a stout craft, so you need not be uneasy."

This was vastly reassuring, when the sky to the west changed from a lowering grey to an inky black. The wind rose with a whimper, that increased to a shriek; it lashed the sea with fury, lashed it into enormous waves, and, laden as we were, we began to roll, at first majestically, then heavily, then helplessly. We took in great green seas over the bows, tons of water discharged themselves amidships, and made us stagger and groan, but still through it all the engines thumped doggedly on.

We seized our dinner anyhow; sitting, standing, kneeling, adapting ourselves to the momentary angle of the vessel. It was a miserable evening, wet and cold, and Mellish and I went to bed early. The dead-lights were down, the hatchway closed behind us; we were entirely cut off from the rest of our shipmates for the night, and the saloon smelt more vault-like than ever. I turned away from Mellish's grey frightened face, and stammering, piteous importunities, shut myself into my cabin, bolted the door, went to bed, and fell asleep. Meanwhile the storm increased to a hurricane, the motion was tremendous. I was flung violently out on the floor, as the *Star* made one awful plunge, and then righted herself. I was, needless to state, now thoroughly awake, and scrambling back into my berth, and clinging to the woodwork with both hands, lay listening to the roaring of the tempest, which rose now and then to a shrill shriek, that had a terribly human sound; my heart beat fast, as my ears assured it that I was not merely listening to the raving of the gale, but actually to the piercing screams of women, and the hoarse shouts of men! Just as I had arrived at this amazing conclusion, the door of the cabin was burst open, and an elderly man, in his shirt-sleeves, was hurled in.

"She's going down," he bawled excitedly, "and the hatches are fast."

I sprang up, and the next lurch shot us both out into the saloon. And what a scene did I behold by three lamps that swung violently to and fro! Their fitful light showed me a large number of half-dressed strangers, in the last extremity of mortal fear; there was the horrible, selfish pushing and struggling of a panic-stricken crowd, fighting their way towards the companion-ladder; the wild frenzied distraction people exhibit when striving to escape from some deadly peril; the tumult, the cries and shrieks of frightened women making frantic appeals for rescue—cries heart-rending to hear.

Besides the dense struggling block at one end of the cabin, battling fiercely for escape, there were various groups, apparently resigned to their impending fate. A family at prayer; two men drinking raw brandy out of tumblers; an ayah beating her head upon the floor, and calling on "Ramasawmy"; an old lady, with a shawl over her head, and a Bible on her knee; a young man and a girl, hand locked in hand, whispering last words; a pale woman, with a sleeping child in her arms. I saw them all. I saw Mellish clinging to the saloon hand-rail, his eyes glazed with horror, and gibbering like an idiot.

The crash of broken crockery, the shrieks of despair, the roaring of the wind, the sullen thundering of the seas overhead, combined to make up the most frightful scene that could possibly be imagined.

Then all at once, a beautiful girl, with long dark hair, streaming over a white gown, rushed out of a cabin, and threw herself upon me, flinging her arms round my neck; she sobbed—

"Oh, save me—save me! Don't let me die—don't let me die!"

Her wild agonized face was pressed closely to mine; her frantic clasp round my neck tightened like a band of steel—closer, closer, *closer*. I was choking. I could not move or breathe. She was strangling me, as she shrieked in my ear—

"It is coming now! *This is death!*"

There was one awful lurch, a grinding crash, a sinking sensation, a vice-like grip about my throat—and outer darkness.

* * * * *

I was aroused in broad daylight by Sawmy, who had brought my tea and shaving-water. I was lying on the floor of the saloon, and he was stooping over me, with a frightened expression on his broad, brown countenance.

"At first I thinking master dead!" was his candid announcement. "Me plenty fraiding. Why master lying here and no in bed?" Why indeed!

A plunge of my head into cool water, and a cup of tea, brought me to myself, and then I flung on my dressing-gown, and hurried across the saloon to see what had become of the miserable Mellish.

He was stretched in his berth, with a life-belt beside him, rigid and cold, and in a sort of fit.

With brandy, burnt brown paper, and great difficulty, Sawmy and I brought him round. As soon as he had come to his senses, and realized that he was still in the land of the living, he sat up and turned on me quite ferociously, and said—

"And that's what you call lobster!"

The weather had moderated considerably, and though I had no great appetite, I was able to appear at breakfast. Mellish was too shattered to join us, and lay in a long chair in the deckhouse, sipping beef-tea, and hysterically assuring all inquirers that "he would never again set foot in the saloon—no, he would *much* rather die!"

"I suppose you got knocked about a bit last night?" inquired the captain, with a searching glance.

"Not exactly knocked about; I did not mind *that* so much, but—" and I hesitated.

"But you were disturbed?" he added significantly.

"Yes, very much so; I hope I shall never be disturbed in such a way again."

"Then I take it you've seen them—the former passengers? They are generally aboard, they say, in dirty weather."

"Whatever they were, I trust in God I may never witness such another scene."

"You don't wonder now that we are not free of offering cabin accommodation, eh? Not that I ever saw anything myself."

"But you admit that there is something."

"So they say"—nodding his head with a jaunty air.

"And what is the explanation? *What* do they say?" I asked impatiently.

"Just this. *The Wandering Star* was once the *Atalanta*, a fine passenger steamer, and, coming out her last trip, she fell in for the tail of a cyclone, and came to grief off the Laccadives; blown out of her course, engine-fires put out, went on a rock, and sank in ten fathoms; every soul on board went down, except a steward and a fireman, who got off on a hen-coop. It was an awful business—sixty-nine passengers, besides officers and crew. She sank like a stone, no time to get battered to pieces, and so she was right well worth her salvage. A company bought her cheap; she was but little damaged—they raised and sold her. She was intended for the pilgrim traffic, from Bombay to Mecca, and in fact she did make a couple of trips; but somehow she got a bad name; the pilgrims said she was possessed of devils—ha! ha!—and so the owners put her into the wheat and rice and general cargo trade, and we have no complaints. She has been at it these five years, and is, as I take you to witness, a grand sea-boat, and has fine accommodation betweendecks as well as aft; it's only in real dirty weather that there is anything amiss, and that in the saloon. They say," lowering his voice to a hoarse whisper, "they kept the passengers below, battened down; they got no chance for their lives. It was a mistake; they were all drowned like rats in their holes. Mind you, *I*'ve seen nothing, and I'm not a superstitious man."

"Would you sleep in the saloon?" I sternly demanded.

"No; for in a blow *my* place is on the bridge. But I'll not deny that a second officer, who has left us, tried a bunk down there once, out of curiosity, and did not repeat the experiment; he was properly scared"; and the captain chuckled at the recollection.

"I suppose we shall get in to-night?" I remarked, as we paced the deck together.

"Yes, about eleven o'clock. We are doing our twelve knots, dirty-looking old hooker as we are!"

"So much the better," I answered, "for you will not be surprised to hear that I'm not anxious to occupy my berth again."

I am thankful to relate that I slept on land that same night, and was not "disturbed."

I often glance at the shipping lists, to see if there is any news of the *Wandering Star*. I note that she is still tramping the ocean from China to Peru, and I have not the smallest doubt but that, on stormy nights, the saloon is still crowded with the distracted spectres of her former passengers.

The Furnished Room

O. Henry

Restless, shifting, fugacious as time itself is a certain vast bulk of the population of the red brick district of the lower West Side. Homeless, they have a hundred homes. They flit from furnished room to furnished room, transients forever—transients in abode, transients in heart and mind. They sing "Home, Sweet Home" in ragtime; they carry their *lares et penates* in a bandbox; their vine is entwined about a picture hat; a rubber plant is their fig tree.

Hence the houses of this district, having had a thousand dwellers, should have a thousand tales to tell, mostly dull ones, no doubt; but it would be strange if there could not be found a ghost or two in the wake of all these vagrant guests.

One evening after dark a young man prowled among these crumbling red mansions, ringing their bells. At the twelfth he rested his lean hand-baggage upon the step and wiped the dust from his hatband and forehead. The bell sounded faint and far away in some remote, hollow depths.

To the door of this, the twelfth house whose bell he had rung, came a housekeeper who made him think of an unwholesome, surfeited worm that had eaten its nut to a hollow shell and now sought to fill the vacancy with edible lodgers.

He asked if there was a room to let.

"Come in," said the housekeeper. Her voice came from her throat; her throat seemed lined with fur. "I have the third floor back, vacant since a week back. Should you wish to look at it?"

The young man followed her up the stairs. A faint light from no particular source mitigated the shadows of the halls. They trod noiselessly upon a stair carpet that its own loom would have forsworn. It seemed to have become vegetable; to have degenerated in that rank, sunless air to lush lichen or spreading moss that grew in patches to the staircase and was viscid under the foot like organic matter. At each turn of the stairs were vacant niches in the wall. Perhaps plants had once been set within them. If so they had died in that foul and tainted air. It may be that statues of the saints had stood there, but it was not difficult to conceive that imps and devils had dragged them forth in the darkness and down to the unholy depths of some furnished pit below.

"This is the room," said the housekeeper, from her furry throat. "It's a nice room. It ain't often vacant. I had some most elegant people in it last summer—no trouble at all, and paid in advance to the minute. The water's at the end of the hall. Sprowls and Mooney kept it three months. They done a vaudeville sketch. Miss B'retta Sprowls—you may have heard of her—Oh, that was just the stage names—right there over the dresser is where the marriage certificate hung, framed. The gas is here, and you see there is plenty of closet room. It's a room everybody likes. It never stays idle long."

"Do you have many theatrical people rooming here?" asked the young man.

"They comes and goes. A good proportion of my lodgers is connected with the theatres. Yes, sir, this is the theatrical district. Actor people never stays long anywhere. I get my share. Yes, they comes and they goes."

He engaged the room, paying for a week in advance. He was tired, he said, and would take possession at once. He counted out the money. The room had been made ready, she said, even to towels and water. As the housekeeper moved away he put, for the thousandth time, the question that he carried at the end of his tongue.

"A young girl—Miss Vashner—Miss Eloise Vashner—do you remember such a one among your lodgers? She would be singing on the stage, most likely. A fair girl, of medium height and slender, with reddish, gold hair and a dark mole near her left eyebrow."

"No, I don't remember the name. Them stage people has names they change as often as their rooms. They comes and they goes. No, I don't call that one to mind."

No. Always no. Five months of ceaseless interrogation and the inevitable negative. So much time spent by day in questioning managers, agents, schools and choruses; by night among the audiences of theatres from all-star casts down to music halls so low that he dreaded to find what he most hoped for. He who had loved her best had tried to find her. He was sure that since her disappearance from home this great, water-girt city held her somewhere, but it was like a monstrous quicksand, shifting its particles constantly, with no foundation, its upper granules of to-day buried to-morrow in ooze and slime.

The furnished room received its latest guest with a first glow of pseudo-hospitality, a hectic, haggard, perfunctory welcome like the specious smile of a demirep. The sophistical comfort came in reflected gleams from the decayed furniture, the ragged brocade upholstery of a couch and two chairs, a foot-wide cheap pier glass between the two windows, from one or two gilt picture frames and a brass bedstead in a corner.

The guest reclined, inert, upon a chair, while the room, confused in speech as though it were an apartment in Babel, tried to discourse to him of its divers tenantry.

A polychromatic rug like some brilliant-flowered rectangular, tropical islet lay surrounded by a billowy sea of soiled matting. Upon the gay-papered wall were those pictures that pursue the homeless one from house to house—The Huguenot Lovers, The First Quarrel, The Wedding Breakfast, Psyche at the Fountain. The mantel's chastely severe outline was ingloriously veiled behind some pert drapery drawn rakishly askew like the sashes of the Amazonian ballet. Upon it was some desolate flotsam cast aside by the room's marooned when a lucky sail had borne them to a fresh port—a trifling vase or two, pictures of actresses, a medicine bottle, some stray cards out of a deck.

One by one, as the characters of a cryptograph become explicit, the little signs left by the furnished room's procession of guests developed a significance. The threadbare space in the rug in front of the dresser told that lovely woman had marched in the throng. Tiny finger prints on the wall spoke of little prisoners trying to feel their way to sun and air. A splattered stain, raying like the shadow of a bursting bomb, witnessed where a hurled glass or bottle had splintered with its contents against the wall. Across the pier glass had been scrawled with a diamond in staggering letters the name "Marie." It seemed that the succession of dwellers in the furnished room had turned in fury—perhaps tempted beyond forbearance by its garish coldness—and wreaked upon it their passions. The furniture was chipped and bruised; the couch, distorted by bursting springs, seemed a horrible monster that had been slain during the stress of some grotesque convulsion. Some more potent upheaval had cloven a great slice from the marble mantel. Each plank in the floor owned its particular cant and shriek as from a separate and individual agony. It seemed incredible that all this malice and injury had been wrought upon the room by those who had called it for a time their home; and yet it may have been the cheated home instinct surviving blindly, the resentful rage at false household gods that had kindled their wrath. A hut that is our own we can sweep and adorn and cherish.

The young tenant in the chair allowed these thoughts to file, soft-shod, through his mind, while there drifted into the room furnished sounds and furnished scents. He heard in one room a tittering and incontinent, slack laughter; in others the monologue of a scold, the rattling of dice, a lullaby, and one crying dully; above him a banjo tinkled with spirit. Doors banged somewhere; the elevated trains roared intermittently; a cat yowled miserably upon a back fence. And he breathed the breath of the house—a dank savour rather than a smell—a cold, musty effluvium as from underground vaults mingled with the reeking exhalations of linoleum and mildewed and rotten woodwork.

Then, suddenly, as he rested there, the room was filled with the strong, sweet odour of mignonette. It came as upon a single buffet of wind with such sureness and fragrance and emphasis that it almost seemed a living visitant. And the man cried aloud: "What, dear?" as if he had been called, and sprang up and faced about. The rich odour clung to him and wrapped him around. He reached out his arms for it, all his senses for the time confused and commingled. How could one be peremptorily called by an odour? Surely it must have been a sound. But, was it not the sound that had touched, that had caressed him?

"She has been in this room," he cried, and he sprang to wrest from it a token, for he knew he would recognise the smallest thing that had belonged to her or that she had touched. This enveloping scent of mignonette, the odour that she had loved and made her own—whence came it?

The room had been but carelessly set in order. Scattered upon the flimsy dresser scarf were half a dozen hairpins—those discreet, indistinguishable friends of womankind, feminine of gender, infinite of mood and uncommunicative of tense. These he ignored, conscious of their triumphant lack of identity. Ransacking the drawers of the dresser he came upon a discarded, tiny, ragged handkerchief. He pressed it to his face. It was racy and insolent with heliotrope; he hurled it to the floor. In another drawer he found odd buttons, a theatre programme, a pawnbroker's card, two lost marshmallows, a book on the divination of dreams. In the last was a woman's black satin hair bow, which halted him, poised between ice and fire. But the black satin hair-bow also is femininity's demure, impersonal, common ornament, and tells no tales.

And then he traversed the room like a hound on the scent, skimming the walls, considering the corners of the bulging matting on his hands and knees, rummaging mantel and tables, the curtains and hangings, the drunken cabinet in the corner, for a visible sign, unable to perceive that she was there beside, around, against, within, above him, clinging to him, wooing him, calling him so poignantly through the finer senses that even his grosser ones became cognisant of the call. Once again he answered loudly: "Yes, dear!" and turned, wild-eyed, to gaze on vacancy, for he could not yet discern form and colour and love and outstretched arms in the odour of mignonette. Oh, God! whence that odour, and since when have odours had a voice to call? Thus he groped.

He burrowed in crevices and corners, and found corks and cigarettes. These he passed in passive contempt. But once he found in a fold of the matting a half-smoked cigar, and this he ground beneath his heel with a green and trenchant oath. He sifted the room from end to end. He found dreary and ignoble small records of many a peripatetic tenant; but of her whom he sought, and who may have lodged there, and whose spirit seemed to hover there, he found no trace.

And then he thought of the housekeeper.

He ran from the haunted room downstairs and to a door that showed a crack of light. She came out to his knock. He smothered his excitement as best he could.

"Will you tell me, madam," he besought her, "who occupied the room I have before I came?"

"Yes, sir. I can tell you again. 'Twas Sprowls and Mooney, as I said. Miss B'retta Sprowls it was in the theatres, but Missis Mooney she was. My house is well known for respectability. The marriage certificate hung, framed, on a nail over—"

"What kind of a lady was Miss Sprowls—in looks, I mean?"

"Why, black-haired, sir, short, and stout, with a comical face. They left a week ago Tuesday."

"And before they occupied it?"

"Why, there was a single gentleman connected with the draying business. He left owing me a week. Before him was Missis Crowder and her two children, that stayed four months; and back of them was old Mr. Doyle, whose sons paid for him. He kept the room six months. That goes back a year, sir, and further I do not remember."

He thanked her and crept back to his room. The room was dead. The essence that had vivified it was gone. The perfume of mignonette had departed. In its place was the old, stale odour of mouldy house furniture, of atmosphere in storage.

The ebbing of his hope drained his faith. He sat staring at the yellow, singing gaslight. Soon he walked to the bed and began to tear the sheets into strips. With the blade of his knife he drove them tightly into every crevice around windows and door. When all was snug and taut he turned out the light, turned the gas full on again and laid himself gratefully upon the bed.

It was Mrs. McCool's night to go with the can for beer. So she fetched it and sat with Mrs. Purdy in one of those subterranean retreats where house-keepers foregather and the worm dieth seldom.

"I rented out my third floor, back, this evening," said Mrs. Purdy, across a fine circle of foam. "A young man took it. He went up to bed two hours ago."

"Now, did ye, Mrs. Purdy, ma'am?" said Mrs. McCool, with intense admiration. "You do be a wonder for rentin' rooms of that kind. And did ye tell him, then?" she concluded in a husky whisper, laden with mystery.

"Rooms," said Mrs. Purdy, in her furriest tones, "are furnished for to rent. I did not tell him, Mrs. McCool."

"'Tis right ye are, ma'am; 'tis by renting rooms we kape alive. Ye have the rale sense for business, ma'am. There be many people will rayjict the rentin' of a room if they be tould a suicide has been after dyin' in the bed of it."

"As you say, we has our living to be making," remarked Mrs. Purdy.

"Yis, ma'am; 'tis true. 'Tis just one wake ago this day I helped ye lay out the third floor, back. A pretty slip of a colleen she was to be killin' herself wid the gas—a swate little face she had, Mrs. Purdy, ma'am."

"She'd a-been called handsome, as you say," said Mrs. Purdy, assenting but critical, "but for that mole she had a-growin' by her left eyebrow. Do fill up your glass again, Mrs. McCool."

The Ghost and the Bone-Setter

J. Sheridan Le Fanu

In looking over the papers of my late valued and respected friend, Francis Purcell, who for nearly fifty years discharged the arduous duties of a parish priest in the south of Ireland, I met with the following document. It is one of many such, for he was a curious and industrious collector of old local traditions—a commodity in which the quarter where he resided mightily abounded. The collection and arrangement of such legends was, as long as I can remember him, his *hobby*; but I had never learned that his love of the marvellous and whimsical had carried him so far as to prompt him to commit the results of his enquiries to writing, until, in the character of *residuary legatee*, his will put me in possession of all his manuscript papers. To such as may think the composing of such productions as these inconsistent with the character and habits of a country priest, it is necessary to observe, that there did exist a race of priests—those of the old school, a race now nearly extinct—whose habits were from many causes more refined, and whose tastes more literary than are those of the alumni of Maynooth.

It is perhaps necessary to add that the superstition illustrated by the following story, namely, that the corpse last buried is obliged, during his juniority of interment, to supply his brother tenants of the church-yard in which he lies, with fresh water to allay the burning thirst of purgatory, is prevalent throughout the south of Ireland. The writer can vouch for a case in which a respectable and wealthy farmer, on the borders of Tipperary, in tenderness to the corns of his departed helpmate, enclosed in her coffin two pair of brogues, a light and a heavy, the one for dry, the other for sloppy weather; seeking thus to mitigate the fatigues of her inevitable perambulations in procuring water, and administering it to the thirsty souls of purgatory. Fierce and desperate conflicts nave ensued in the case of two funeral parties approaching the same church-yard together, each endeavouring to secure to his own dead priority of sepulture, and a consequent immunity from the tax levied upon the pedestrian powers of the last comer. An instance not long since occurred, in which one of two such parties, through fear of losing to their deceased friend this inestimable advantage, made their way to the churchyard by a *short cut*, and in violation of one of their strongest prejudices, actually threw the coffin over the wall, lest time should be lost in making their entrance through the gate. Innumerable instances of the same kind might be quoted, all tending to shew how strongly, among the peasantry of the south, this superstition is entertained. However, I shall not detain the reader further, by any prefatory remarks, but shall proceed to lay before him the following:—

EXTRACT FROM THE MS. PAPERS OF THE LATE REV. FRANCIS PURCELL, OF DRUMCOOLAGH

"I tell the following particulars, as nearly as I can recollect them, in the words of the narrator. It may be necessary to observe that he was what is termed a *well-spoken* man, having for a considerable time instructed the ingenious youth of his native parish in such of the liberal arts and sciences as he found it convenient to profess—a circumstance which may account for the occurrence of several big words, in the course of this narrative, more distinguished for euphonious effect, than for correctness of application. I proceed then, without further preface, to lay before you the wonderful adventures of Terry Neil."

"Why, thin, 'tis a quare story, an as thrue as you're sittin' there; and I'd make bould to say there isn't a boy in the seven parishes could tell it better nor crickther than myself, for 'twas my father himself it happened to, an' manys the time I heerd it out iv his own mouth; an' I can say, an' I'm proud av that same, my father's word was as incredible as any squire's oath in the counthry; and so signs an' if a poor man got into any unlucky throuble, he was the boy id go into the court an' prove; but that dosen't signify—he was as honest and as sober a man, barrin' he was a little bit too partial to the glass, as you'd find in a day's walk; an' there wasn't the likes of him in the counthry round for nate labourin' an' *baan* diggin'; and he was mighty handy entirely for carpenther's work, and mendin' ould spudethrees, an' the likes i' that. An' so he tuck up with bone-setting, as was most nathural, for none of them could come up to him in mendin' the leg iv a stool or a table; an' sure, there never was a bone-setter got so much custom—man an' child, young an' ould—there never was such breakin' and mendin' of bones known in the memory of man. Well, Terry Neil, for that was my father's name, began to feel his heart growin' light, and his purse heavy; an' he took a hit iv a farm in Squire Phalim's ground, just undher the ould castle, an' a pleasant little spot it was; an' day an' mornin', poor crathurs not able to put a foot to the ground, with broken arms and broken legs, id be comin' ramblin' in from all quarters to have their bones spliced up. Well, yer honour, all this was as well as well could be; but it was customary when Sir Phelim id go any where out iv the country, for some iv the tinants to sit up to watch in the ould castle, just for a kind of a compliment to the ould family—an' a mighty unpleasant compliment it was for the tinants, for there wasn't a man of them but knew there was some thing quare about the ould castle. The neighbours had it, that the squire's ould grandfather, as good a gintleman, God be with him, as I heer'd, as ever stood in shoe leather, used to keep walkin' about in the middle iv the night, ever sinst he bursted a blood vessel pullin' out a cork out iv a bottle, as you or I might be doin', and will too, plase God; but that dosen't signify. So, as I was sayin', the ould squire used to come down out of the frame, where his picthur was hung up, and to brake the bottles and glasses, God be marciful to us all, an' dhrink all he could come at—an' small blame to him for that same; and then if any of the family id be comin' in, he id be up again in his place, looking as quite an' innocent as if he didn't know any thing about it—the mischievous ould chap.

"Well, your honour, as I was sayin', one time the family up at the castle was stayin' in Dublin for a week or two; and so as usual, some of the tenants had to sit up in the castle, and the third night it kem to my father's turn. 'Oh, tare an ouns,' says he unto himself, 'an' must I sit up all night, and that ould vagabond of a sperit, glory be to God,' says he, 'serenading through the house, an doin' all sorts iv mischief.' Howover, there was no getting' aff, and so he put a bould face on it, an' he went up at night-fall with a bottle of pottieen, and another of holy wather.

"It was rainin' smart enough, an' the evenin' was darksome and gloomy, when my father got in; and what with the rain he got, and the holy wather he sprinkled on himself, it wasn't long till he had to swallee a cup iv the pottieen, to keep the cowld out iv his heart. It was the ould steward, Lawrence Connor, that opened the door—and he an' my father wor always very great. So when he seen who it was, an' my father tould him how it was his turn to watch in the castle, he offered to sit up along with him; and you may be sure my father wasn't sorry for that same. So says Larry,

"'We'll have a hit iv fire in the parlour,' says he.

"'An' why not in the hall?' says my father, for he knew that the squire's picthur was hung in the parlour.

"'No fire can be lit in the hall,' says Lawrence, 'for there's an ould jackdaw's nest in the chimney.'

"'Oh thin,' says my father, 'let us stop in the kitchen, for it's very umproper for the likes iv me to be sittin' in the parlour,' says he.

"'Oh, Terry, that can't be,' says Lawrence; 'if we keep up the ould custom at all, we may as well keep it up properly,' says he.

"'Divil sweep the ould custom,' says my father—to himself, do ye mind, for he didn't like to let Lawrence see that he was more afeard himself.

"'Oh, very well,' says he. 'I'm agreeable, Lawrence,' says he; and so down they both went to the kitchen, until the fire id be lit in the parlour—an' that same wasn't long doin'.

"Well, your honour, they soon wint up again, an' sat down mighty comfortable by the parlour fire, and they beginn'd to talk, an' to smoke, an' to dhrink a small taste iv the pottieen; and, moreover, they had a good rousing fire of bogwood and turf, to warm their shins over.

"Well, sir, as I was sayin' they kep convarsin' and smokin' together most agreeable, until Lawrence beginn'd to get sleepy, as was but nathural for him, for he was an ould sarvint man, and was used to a great dale iv sleep.

"'Sure it's impossible,' says my father, 'it's gettin' sleepy you are?'

"'Oh, divil a taste,' says Larry, 'I'm only shuttin' my eyes,' says he, 'to keep out the parfume of the tibacky smoke, that's makin' them wather,' says he. So don't you mind other people's business,' says he stiff enough, (for he had a mighty high stomach av his own, (rest his sowl,) and go on,' says he, 'with your story, for I'm listenin',' says he, shuttin' down his eyes.

"Well, when my father seen spakin' was no use, he went on with his story.—By the same token, it was the story of Jim Soolivan and his ould goat he was tellin'—an' a pleasant story it is—an' there was so much divarsion in it, that it was enough to waken a dor mouse, let alone to pervint a Christian goin' asleep. But, faix, the way my father tould it, I believe there never was the likes heerd sinst nor before, for he bawled out every word av it, as if the life was fairly leavin' him, thrying to keep ould Larry awake; but, faix, it was no use, for the hoorsness came an him, an' before he kem to the end of his story, Larry O'Connor beginned to snore like a bagpipes.

"'Oh, blur an' agres,' says my father, 'isn't this a hard case,' says he, 'that ould villain, lettin' on to be my friend, and to go asleep this way, an' us both in the very room with a sperit,' says he. 'The crass o' Christ about us,' says he; and with that he was goin' to shake Lawrence to waken him, but he just remimbered if he roused him, that he'd surely go off to his bed, an' lave him complately alone, an' that id be by far worse.

"'Oh thin,' says my father,' I'll not disturb the poor boy. It id be neither friendly nor good-nathured,' says he, 'to tormint him while he is asleep,' says he; 'only I wish I was the same way, myself,' says he.

"An' with that he beginned to walk' up an' down, an' savin' his prayers, until he worked himself into a sweat, savin' your presence. But it was all no good; so he dhrunk about a pint of sperits, to compose his mind.

"'Oh,' says he,' I wish to the Lord I was as asy in my mind us Larry there. Maybe,' says he, 'if I thried I could go asleep'; an' with that he pulled a big arm-chair close beside Lawrence, an' settled himself in it as well as he could.

"But there was one quare thing I forgot to tell you. He couldn't help, in spite av himself, lookin' now an' thin at the picthur, an' he immediately obsarved that the eyes av it was follyin' him about, an' starin' at him, an' winkin' at him, wherever he wint. 'Oh,' says he, when he seen that, 'it's a poor chance I have,' says he; 'an' bad luck was with me the day I kem into this unforthunate place,' says he; 'but any way there's no use in bein' freckened now,' says he; 'for if I am to die, I may as well parspire undaunted,' says he.

"Well, your honour, he thried to keep himself quite an' asy, an' he thought two or three times he might have wint asleep, but for the way the storm was groanin' and creekin' through the great heavy branches outside, an' whistlin' through the ould chimnies iv the castle. Well, afther one great roarin' blast iv the wind, you'd think the walls iv the castle was just goin' to fall, quite an' clane, with the shakin' iv it. All av a suddint the storm stopt, as silent an' as quite as if it was a July evenin.' Well, your honour, it wasn't stopped blowin' for three minnites, before he thought he hard a sort iv a noise over the chimney-piece; an' with that my father just opened his eyes the smallest taste in life, an' sure enough he seen the ould squire gettin' out iv the picthur, for all the world as if he was throwin' aff his ridin' coat, until he stept out clane an' complate, out av the chimly-piece, an' thrun himself down an the floor. Well, the slieveen ould chap—an' my father thought it was the dirtiest turn iv all—before he beginned to do anything out iv the way, he stopped, for a while, to listen wor they both asleep; an' as soon as he thought all was quite, he put out his hand, and tuck hould iv the whiskey bottle, an' dhrank at laste a pint iv it. Well, your honour, when he tuck his turn out iv it, he settled it back mighty cute intirely, in the very same spot it was in before. An' he beginn'd to walk up an' down the room, lookin' as sober an as solid as if he never done the likes at all. An' whinever he went apast my father, he thought he felt a great scent of brimstone, an' it was that that freckened him entirely; for he knew it was brimstone that was burned in hell, savin' your presence. At any rate, he often heer'd it from Father Murphy, an' he had a right to know what belonged to it—he's dead since, God rest him. Well, your honour, my father was asy enough until the sperit kem past him; so close, God be marciful to us all, that the smell iv the sulphur tuek the breath clane out iv him: an' with that he tuck such a fit iv coughin', that it al-a-most shuck him out iv the chair he was sittin' in.

"'Ho, ho!' says the squire, stoppin' short about two steps atti and turnin' round facin' my father, 'is it you that's in it?—an' how's all with you, Terry Neil?'

"'At your honour's sarvice,' says my father (as well as the fright id let him, for he was more dead than alive), 'an' it's proud I am to see your honour tonight,' says he.

"'Terence,' says the squire, 'you're a respectable man (an' it was thrue for him), an industhrious, sober man, an' an example of inebriety to the whole parish,' says he.

"'Thank your honour,' says my father, gettin' courage, 'you were always a civil spoken gintleman, God rest your honour.'

"'Rest my honour,' says the sperit (fairly gettin' red in the face with the madness), 'Rest my honour?' says he. 'Why, you ignorant spalpeen,' says he, 'you mane, niggarly ignoramush,' says he, 'where did you lave your manners?' says he. 'If I *am* dead, it's no fault iv mine,' says he; 'an' it's not to be thrun in my teeth at every hand's turn, by the likes iv you,' says he, stampin' his foot an the flure, that you'd think the boords id smash undher him.

"'Oh,' says my father, 'I'm only a foolish, ignorant, poor man,' says he.

"'You're nothing else,' says the squire; 'but any way,' says he, 'it's not to be listenin' to your gosther, nor convarsin' with the likes iv you, that I came *up*—down I mane,' says he,—(an' as little as the mistake was, my father tuck notice iv it). 'Listen to me now, Terence Neil,' says he, 'I was always a good masther to Pathrick Neil, your grandfather,' says he.

"''Tis thrue for your honour,' says my father.

"'And, moreover, I think I was always a sober, riglar gintleman,' says the squire.

"'That's your name, sure enough,' says my father (though it was a big lie for him, but he could not help it).

"'Well,' says the sperit, 'although I was as sober as most men—at laste as most gintlemen'—says he; 'an' though I was at different pariods a most extempory Christian, and most charitable and inhuman to the poor,' says he; 'for all that I'm not as asy where I am now,' says he, 'as I had a right to expect,' says he.

"'An more's the pity,'" says my father; 'maybe yeour honour id wish to have a word with Father Murphy?'

"'Hould your tongue, you misherable bliggard,' says the squire; 'it's not ivmy sowl I'm thinkin'—an' I wondher you have the impotence to talk to a gintleman consarnin' his sowl;—and when I want *that* fixed,' says he, slappin' his thigh, 'I'll go to them that knows what belongs to the likes,' says he. 'It's not my sowl,' says he, sittin' down opposite my father; 'it's not my sowl that's annoyin' me most—I'm unasy on my right leg,' says he, 'that I bruck at Glenvarloch cover the day I killed black Barney.'

"(My father found out afther, it was a favourite horse that fell undher him, afther leapin' the big fince that runs along by the glen.)

"'I hope,' says my father, 'your honour's not unasy about the killin' iv him?

"'Hould your tongue, ye fool,' said the squire, 'an' I'll tell you why I'm anasy an my leg,' says he. 'In the place, where I spend most iv my time,' says he, 'except the little leisure I have for lookin' about me here,' says he, 'I have to walk a great dale more than I was ever used to,' says he, 'and by far more than is good for me either,' says he; 'for I must tell you,' says he, 'the people where I am is ancommonly fond iv could wather, for there is nothin' betther to be had; an', moreover, the weather is hotter than is altogether plisint,' says he; 'and I'm appinted,' says he, 'to assist in carryin' the wather, an' gets a mighty poor share iv it myself,' says he, 'an' a mighty throublesome, warin' job it is, I can tell you,' says he; 'for they're all of them surprisingly dhry, and dhrinks it as fast as my legs can carry it,' says he; 'but what kills me entirely,' says he, 'is the wakeness in my leg,' says he, 'an' I want you to give it a pull or two to bring it to shape,' says he, 'and that's the long an' the short iv it,' says he.

"'Oh, plase your honour,' says my father (for he didn't like to handle the sperit at all), 'I wouldn't have the impitence to do the likes to your honour,' says he; 'it's only to poor crathurs like myself I'd do it to,' says he.

"'None iv your blarney,' says the squire, 'here's my leg,' says he, cockin' it up to him, 'pull it fur the bare life,' says he; an' if you don't, by the immortal powers I'll not lave a bone in your carcish I'll not powdher,' says he.

"When my father heerd that, he seen there was no use in purtendin', so he tuck hould iv the leg, an' he kep pullin' an' pullin', till the sweat, God less us, beginned to pour down his face."

"'Pull, you divil,' says the squire.

"'At your sarvice, your honour,' says my father.

"'Pull harder,' says the squire.

"My father pulled like the divil.

"'I'll take a little sup,' says the squire, rachin' over his hand to the bottle, 'to keep up my courage,' says he, lettin' an to be very wake in himself intirely. But, as cute as he was, he was out here, for he tuck the wrong one. 'Here's to your good health, Terence,' says he, 'an' now pull like the very divil,' an' with that he lifted the bottle of holy wather, but it was hardly to his mouth, whin he let a screech out, you'd think the room id fairly split with it, an' made one chuck that sent the leg clane aff his body in my father's hands; down wint the squire over the table, an' bang wint my father half way across the room on his back, upon the flure. Whin he kem to himself the cheerful mornin' sun was shinin' through the windy shutthers, an' he was lying flat an his back, with the leg iv one of the great ould chairs pulled clane out iv the socket an' tight in his hand, pintin' up to the ceilin', an' ould Larry fast asleep, an' snorin' as loud as ever. My father wint that mornin' to Father Murphy, an' from that to the day of his death, he never neglected confission nor mass, an' what he tould was betther believed that he spake av it but Seldom. An', as for the squire, that is the sperit, whether it was that he did not like his liquor, or by rason iv the loss iv his leg, he was never known to walk again."

A Ghost from the Sea

J. E. Muddock

Towards the latter half of the fifties, Melbourne, in Australia, was startled by an extraordinary and terrible crime. It was at the very height of what was known as the "gold fever." A year or two before, news had spread like wildfire that gold had been discovered in enormous quantities in various parts of the country. That news literally seemed to turn people mad, and young and old, the halt, the lame, and even the blind, rushed away for the fabled regions of El Dorado. Whole families, who had been content to jog on quietly year after year, earning fair wages, and getting all the necessaries of life, were seized with the fever, and, selling up their belongings rump and stump, invested in billies, tomahawks, spades, pickaxes, washing-pans, and other etceteras, and shouldering their swags set off for the mysterious regions, where it was rumoured gold was lying on the surface of the ground in big nuggets. Fortunate, indeed, were those who had any belongings to sell in order to provide themselves with the plant required for roughing it in the bush; for many had nothing at all, save what they stood upright in, but, imagining that they were going to gather in the precious metal in sackfulls, they started off with the rest, only to perish, it may be, miserably of starvation, disappointment, and broken hearts. This period in the history of our Australian colonies is a startling record of human credulity, human folly, wickedness, despair and death. The fever was confined to no particular class of people. Clergymen, bankers, landowners, shipowners, merchants, shopkeepers, sailors, labourers, classical scholars and ignoramuses alike fell under the fascination. The worst passions of our nature manifested themselves; hatred, envy, jealousy, greed, uncharitableness. The parsons were no better than the paupers; the classical scholars than the ignoramuses. The thin veneering of so-called civilisation was rubbed off, and the savage appeared in all his fierceness at the cry of "Gold! gold!"

It is at such periods as these that the moralist finds his pabulum, and those good but weak-minded people who think that human nature has improved with the advance of time have only to get on the house-tops and utter the cry of "Gold!" again, to prove that we are not a whit better than our ancestors were three thousand years ago. This may not be very flattering to us, but alas! it is true. In those days of Australian gold rushes the bush was a veritable *terra incognita*. Explorers had attempted to penetrate into the mystic interior, but many never came back again, and to this day it is not known where their bones moulder. Those who did return were gaunt, famine-stricken, hollow-eyed, for they had looked upon death, and the stories they told were calculated to appal everyone but the most daring and reckless. But the report of the gold finds so turned the heads of people that, forgetting all about the dangers and privations they would have to endure, they started off into those unknown regions, and thousands literally perished by the way. The experiences of some of these unfortunate people are in themselves amongst the most pathetic and moving of human stories.

Melbourne at the time of this narrative was not the Melbourne of to-day. It was then simply a collection of canvas and wooden huts and houses, with a few buildings of a more substantial character. One of the most imposing houses in the place was that known as "Jackson's Boarding-house." It was built partly of wood and partly of stone, and was kept by a man and his wife named Jackson. Very little, if anything, was known of the Jacksons' history, beyond that they had come to the colony a few years previously. Jackson was a nautical man, and had purchased a schooner with which he traded up and down the coast, though with indifferent success.

At last his schooner was wrecked, and Jackson and his wife, who had always sailed with him, built a wooden shanty, in what was then known as Canvas Town—now Melbourne—where they sold liquors and provisions. They seemed to have done fairly well, for very soon they erected what was then quite an imposing building, and they called it "Jackson's Boarding-house."

Jackson was remarkable for an extraordinarily powerful physique. He stood about six feet high, and his muscular development was so great that it was said he could lift a cask of split peas, weighing nearly three hundredweight, from the ground, and raise it at arm's length above his head. He was an ill-favoured man, however, for he had a low brow, small, cunning sort of eyes, and was exceedingly passionate in his temper. But it was notable that he seemed to be strongly attached to his wife, and they were never known to disagree.

Mrs. Jackson was a striking contrast to her husband, for she was a slightly built little woman, with a pink and white face, sickly blue eyes, and a mass of tow-like hair that was almost the colour of flax, whereas her husband was as dark as a raven.

Soon after these people had opened their boarding-house, there came to lodge with them a Mr. and Mrs. Harvey, who had recently arrived from England. They had, like many others, come out to try and improve their fortunes. A warm intimacy seemed to spring up between the two couples, and they lived apparently in the greatest harmony. It was understood that Mr. Harvey was a mechanic by trade. He was a strong, healthy man, very handy and useful, and did odd jobs for the community. His wife was a pretty, agreeable woman, and soon became a great favourite, for she played the piano and sang well, and was always ready to afford amusement or render assistance to anyone needing it, where it lay in her power. Her husband acquired the character of a rather indolent, good-natured sort of fellow, whose aim seemed to be to suddenly accumulate wealth without doing much labour for it.

At length the gold fever set in, and amongst those who started off in the first rush for the regions of fabulous wealth was Harvey, his wife remaining behind at Jackson's boardinghouse. Some eight months later Harvey returned, and soon the report spread that he had brought thousands of pounds' worth of nuggets and gold dust. He remained in the town for four weeks, during which he and his wife denied themselves nothing, and it was evident that the report about his wealth was in the main true. Then, having furnished himself with an extensive outfit in the shape of tent, cooking-stove, digging and washing utensils, he started up the country again, Mrs. Harvey still remaining at the boarding-house. She purchased a horse and buggy, provided herself with fine clothes and jewellery, and common gossip had it that this little, blue-eyed, flaxen-haired woman was the richest person in Melbourne. Two months later, her husband still being absent at the diggings, the community was startled one morning by a report that Mrs. Harvey had been murdered. The report proved to be only too true, and the story told by a female servant in the boarding-house was this. She went to the lady's room to see why she had not appeared, it being an hour and a half after her usual time of rising. She found the door locked, and, repeated knocking having failed to elicit a response, she informed her master, and expressed fears that something was wrong. Jackson at once went upstairs with some of the lodgers, and, failing to get any answer, he at once broke open the door, and then a terrible sight revealed itself.

Lying across the bed was the body of Mrs. Harvey. She was dressed only in her night-dress, which was disarranged and torn as if she had struggled desperately, as in fact she had, for further evidence of this was forthcoming. She was on her back, her head hanging over the farthest side of the bed. Twisted tightly round her neck until it had cut into the flesh was a crimson cord sash or belt, such as in those days was common—these sashes, or, more correctly speaking, scarves, being worn by men round their waists to keep their trousers up, instead of braces. The horribly distorted features showed that the poor woman had been strangled, and subsequent medical examination brought to light that her head had been forced back with such tremendous force that the neck was absolutely broken. Discolorations about the mouth indicated that a heavy hand had been pressed there to keep her from screaming. There were also deep indents and bruises on the wrists, which proved that she had struggled and been firmly grasped there by the murderer. Other parts of the body were also terribly bruised, as if in the struggle she had been banged repeatedly against the massive wooden bedstead.

Murder had been done, that was certain. That the murderer was a man was equally certain, for no female could have exerted such tremendous force as had evidently been used. It was no less certain that robbery had been the motive, for a very large travelling trunk or box had been forced open, in spite of an unusually strong lock, and two iron bands round it which were secured with padlocks. All the poor creature's clothes had been turned out of the box, and were scattered about the floor, as well as her jewellery, nothing in that way being taken. Now what did that prove? It proved this: the murderer, with the cunning of a devil, knew that in such a place to possess himself of her jewellery, valuable as it was, would almost certainly lead to his detection. No, it was neither her jewellery nor her clothes he wanted, but the nuggets and gold dust her husband had brought from the diggings. No one could swear to gold dust or nuggets, and both were plentiful, for diggers, especially sailors, were constantly arriving from the diggings with hoards of gold, which they sold for ready cash for below their value; for at this early period there was no regular exchange or agency for the purchase of the precious metal.

The next question was: How did the murderer get into the room? Not by the door, for a dozen witnesses vowed that it was locked on the inside, the key still in the lock, when Jackson broke open the door. The only other entrance, then, was by the window, twenty-five feet from the ground. There was no indication that a ladder had been used, and so the theory was that the murderer had secreted himself under the bed, and when his fiendish work was completed he had gone out by the window, climbed up by means of an iron gutter pipe to the roof, and had then descended into the house through a skylight.

Now came the most important question of all: Who was the murderer? At the time of the crime there were nearly forty people staying in the boarding-house, mostly men, a good many of them being sailors. The police arrangements of the town were very primitive, and by no means equal to coping with such a mysterious tragedy, and unfortunately not an atom of evidence could be got that would have justified the arrest of any individual. The result was the mystery was destined to remain a mystery for ever; and the times were too exciting and too changing for such a crime even as that to long occupy the public mind, and so, almost with the burying of the flaxen-haired woman who had been so cruelly done to death, the tragedy was forgotten for a time. Three months later, however, its memory was revived by the arrival of Mr. Harvey. He had written two or three times to his wife, had received no answer, had got alarmed, and had come to see what was the matter. The news almost drove him off his mind, for he had been passionately attached to his wife. He stated that he had left her with about ten thousand pounds' worth of gold; and he now offered to give anyone five thousand pounds' worth of gold who would bring the murderer to justice. The offer, however, proved of no avail; not the faintest clue could be obtained. Jackson had taken charge of the murdered woman's effects, and these he handed to the husband, who certified his belief that they were all correct except the gold, which was in nuggets and dust, one nugget alone being valued at between two and three thousand pounds. And so the poor husband departed, an utterly changed and broken man.

Another person in the community had also changed considerably. This was Jackson, the boarding-house keeper. He generally bore the character of being a steady, industrious man, but he suddenly developed a craving for drink, and as a consequence neglected his business, which, of course, declined, the result being an opposition house was started, and Jackson's once nourishing boarding establishment lost all its custom. Jackson drank harder than ever then, and even his wife gave way to the vice. At length, a year after the murder, Jackson sold off his effects, and he and his wife took their passage for England, in a ship called the *Gloriana*.

This ends the first part of the record, but the sequel—startling and inexplicable—has yet to be told.

The *Gloriana* was a large, full-rigged, clipper ship, one of a line trading between the mother country and the colonies. She was commanded by a hard-headed Scotchman, Captain Norman Douglas, who was well known in the trade, and, in fact, was one of the most popular skippers on that route. He bore the reputation of being a singularly conscientious and truthful man, and utterly without sentiment or superstition. There are no doubt plenty of people still living who were acquainted with him, who would unhesitatingly endorse this statement.

The *Gloriana* had a fair complement of passengers, first and second class. Amongst the first class were Jackson and his wife. It is necessary, in order to make what follows more clearly intelligible, to describe one portion of the ship. She was fitted with what was known in the old days as a "monkey poop," with an alloway or passage running on each side. This passage was reached from the main deck by three or four wooden steps. Eight aft a short flight of steps led to the poop, on which was a hurricane house, with a companion way going down to the cuddy, or, as it is now called, the saloon. In the break of the poop, flush with the main deck, so that his window and door faced the bows of the vessel, was the captain's state-room, and alongside of his door was the entrance to the cuddy from the main deck. The Jacksons' cabin was the first in the cuddy on the left-hand side on entering, and next to the captain's, though it must be remembered that the captain had to come out of the cuddy to get into his room. That is, his door opened from the main deck, whereas the Jacksons' opened from the cuddy, and consequently at right angles with the captain's.

The vessel made a splendid passage through Bass's Straits, the weather being magnificent, but it was noted with some astonishment that the Jacksons rarely appeared on deck, but remained in their cabin, and it was whispered about that Mr. Jackson was almost constantly muddled more or less with drink. He and his wife kept to themselves, and seemed to carefully avoid their fellow passengers. One night, when the ship was well out in the South Pacific, and bowling along under double-reefed top-sails, Captain Douglas was sleeping soundly in the middle watch, when his door was suddenly opened, and Jackson precipitated himself into his room, dressed only in his night shirt. He was ghastly pale, was trembling like an aspen leaf, and seemed to be suffering from the effects of a terrible fright.

Naturally thinking that something was the matter, the captain sprang from his bed, and was surprised to find Jackson on his knees, his lips blanched, his face streaming with a cold perspiration.

"What is the meaning of this?" the captain demanded.

"For God's sake save me!" Jackson moaned in terror.

"Save you from what and whom?" asked the captain, thinking that his passenger was suffering from delirium tremens.

"From her," groaned the man. "She all but lured me into the sea, but I broke the spell in time, and rushed in here."

This extraordinary remark naturally tended to confirm the captain's idea about the delirium, and so he soothed his passenger as well as he could, and then led him back to his cabin, where he noted that Mrs. Jackson was soundly asleep in her bunk. He helped Jackson into his bunk, tucked him well up with the clothes, and left him; and as he came out of the cuddy on to the deck to reach his own room again, he started back until he all but fell, for it seemed to him that a flash of brilliant light had almost blinded him, while something soft touched his face. He thought that this might be a sea-bird, but what was the light?

It was the second mate's watch, and that officer was walking the poop, while the portion of the crew on duty were lying or sitting about in the waist of the vessel.

"Mr. Harrington," sang out the captain to the second mate, "what was that light?"

"What light, sir?" asked the officer in astonishment.

"Why, didn't you see a brilliant flash of light?"

"No, sir," answered the officer, thinking the captain must have been indulging in a little too much grog.

"Ahoy, there, you fellows," roared the skipper to the watch on deck, "where did that light come from?"

"What light, sir?" asked several voices.

"Good heavens! did you not see a flash of bright light?" exclaimed the captain angrily, for he thought he was being made a fool of.

"No, sir, we saw no light," answered the crew unanimously.

Captain Douglas was mystified. What did this mean? Was it a delusion? Had he been made a fool of by his senses, or what?

He went into his cabin again with his mind strangely disturbed. The ship was sailing splendidly, a heavy sea running after her, a gale was blowing, the sky was clear, the stars shining brightly, and neither in sea nor sky was there anything to account for that flash of light, or that *something* that had touched him. His officer and his men could not have been in collusion, and therefore Captain Douglas came to the conclusion that he had been made a fool of by his own senses, though, taken in connection with Jackson's strange remarks, Captain Douglas was affected as he had never been affected before.

Next day the crew told one another that "the old man" had been "soaking himself."

Captain Douglas was unusually thoughtful. He invited Jackson into his cabin and asked him what had been the matter with him during the night. Jackson appeared to be very ill, with a scared, cowed expression in his face.

"I don't know," he replied a little sullenly, "I think I must have been dreaming."

"Well, I hope you won't dream again like that," remarked the captain, and then he told his own experience. As he heard this Jackson seemed to grow terrified again, and he groaned between chattering teeth:

"Heaven pity me then, it's a reality!"

"What is?" asked the astonished captain.

Jackson covered his face with his hands as he answered:

"Three times since we left Melbourne I have seen the vision of a woman, and she tries to lure me into the sea." He shuddered like one who was seized with palsy.

A few hours before this Captain Douglas would have roared with incredulous laughter had he been told such a thing. Now he was solemnly silent, for his own experience—the touch and the flash of light—permitted of no explanation that he could furnish. And so this tough old sailor, who had sailed the salt seas from his youth, and braved the perils of the deep in all parts of the world, was seized with a nameless fear that he could not allay.

The good ship continued to bowl along before favouring gales until she drew into the stormy ocean that roars around Cape Horn. During this time Jackson was seldom seen except for an hour or two in the early part of the day, when he and his wife would promenade the poop. He seemed to have changed very much. Everyone on board said that he looked ten years older since leaving Melbourne. His hair had blanched, his face was pallid and wrinkled, his eyes were restless as if from fear.

The vessel fell in with terrific weather off the Horn. Monstrous icebergs and field ice made navigation perilous, while the hurricane's wrath lashed the ice-strewn ocean into mountainous waves. The ship could only pursue her course under storm sails, and only then by ceaseless vigilance being exercised on the part of all the crew. For nearly a week the captain was on deck, snatching an hour or two's sleep as best he could during the twenty-four.

One night, when the *Gloriana* had nearly doubled the Horn, the weather seemed to grow worse, so that it became necessary to heave the ship to under a close-reefed main topsail. The sky was inky in its blackness. Not a star shone out from the ebony vault; but over the sea were vast flashing fields of phosphorescent foam as the giant waves broke with an awful roar; while looming in the blackness were ponderous icebergs in whose hollows the sea thundered. Now and again unusually terrific squalls came howling up from the south, bringing showers of jagged ice and hailstones as big as marbles. It was a night of horror and danger such as those who have never sailed in that stormy southern ocean can form but a faint conception of.

Vigilant and anxious, and clad in heavy sea-boots and oilskins, Captain Douglas stood on the poop with the chief mate; the second mate and several of the crew being on the forecastle straining their eyes on the look-out for the ice, while both in the main and foretop a man was lashed also on the look-out. Suddenly as the captain and chief officer stood together at the break of the poop sheltering themselves under the lee of a tarpaulin lashed in the rigging, the captain staggered, and seizing the officer's arm exclaimed hoarsely:

"My God! what is that?"

And well might he so exclaim, for to his horrified gaze there appeared on the main deck a mass of trembling light that in an instant seemed to change into a woman's figure, a woman with long, streaming fair hair, while round her white neck a scarf was twisted. The captain and his mate were transfixed with horror, for they both saw it. But they were to see even a more fearsome sight yet. The apparition rose, waving her arms the while, and floating out over the howling waste of black, writhing waters; and as she rose there suddenly darted from the cabin doorway the half-naked Jackson, his hair streaming in the wind. The apparition still waved her arm, still floated out away from the ship, and then, before the terror-stricken men who witnessed the awful sight could move to stop him, the wretched man uttered a scream of despair and fear that froze the blood of those who heard it, and with one bound he leapt into the boiling waters, and at that instant the apparition disappeared like a flash of lightning.

It was some moments before either of the two men had sufficiently recovered to speak. Then they asked each other if their senses had fooled them. But the captain, remembering his former experience, rushed to Jackson's cabin. Mrs. Jackson alone was in it, and she was sleeping. It was no delusion then. Jackson had jumped overboard, lured by that ghost from the sea. It was impossible to make the slightest attempt to save him; he had gone down into the black and boiling waters never to rise again.

Mrs. Jackson was not informed of her husband's suicide until the following day, and when she heard of it she fell down in a swoon; and, on recovering, it was found that she had lost her reason, so that it was necessary to watch and guard her for the rest of the voyage. On arrival in England it was deemed prudent to place her in an asylum, where she died six months later. No word ever escaped her lips that would have tended to elucidate the awful mystery. She seemed to be tortured with some indescribable anguish, and from morning till night she paced to and fro, wringing her hands and moaning piteously. But to those who witnessed that appalling scene off Cape Horn when Jackson went to his doom, the mystery required no explanation, for it explained itself: and that explanation was that it was he who had murdered poor Mrs. Harvey, and the phantom of his victim had lured him to a terrible death.

The Ghost in the Chair

Lettice Galbraith

This story requires explanation. The explanation will never be given, because no one of the theories of cerebral pressure, spectral illusion, or hypnotic influence, by which people try to explain away the inexplicable, can get rid of the single fact that, shortly after three o'clock on a certain Friday afternoon, one hundred and fifty sane and sober men saw, or thought they saw, Curtis Yorke take the chair at a general meeting of the San Sacrada Mining Company, Limited, at which time, according to subsequent medical evidence, he must have been dead for several hours.

For some time his friends had known that Yorke was going a little bit too fast. While hardly more than a boy, on brilliant hit had gained him a reputation in the City far beyond his years, and at an age when most men are expending their superfluous energy on the tennis-court or river, he was finding brains for the working out of several big undertakings.

Six years of unbroken success taught him to believe his luck infallible. When that changed, as sooner or later it was bound to do, he began to lose confidence in himself. Like many men, who keep a level head in prosperity, he could not play a losing game, and for months past anxiety and overwork had been telling steadily on his nerves.

Moreover he was superstitious, and though he made no profession of religion, he retained an odd belief in the Puritanical dogmas of hell-fire and a personal devil. This in some measure accounts for what he said to Fielden four days before his tragic end.

The directorate of the San Sacrada Mining Company had been holding an extraordinary meeting. A crisis was impending, and things looked black for the company, which was no "bubble speculation," but a sound and solid concern, suffering from the effects of a persistent run of bad luck.

Now, luck has more to do with the making or marring of mines and than the moralists would have us believe, and the luck of the San Sacrada Mining Company had all along been execrable.

Unexpected hitches had occurred in securing the title to the property. The contractors had seen fit to export the machinery reversely to the order in which it was required. Delays had been caused by scarcity of water, and when at last the returns promised to justify the small fortune sunk in the shaft, the Yankee manager, whose appointment had been backed by flaming testimonials, demonstrated his native 'cuteness by "skipping out" with twenty-five thousand dollars of the company's money. His place was filled by an Englishman in every way qualified for the post; but before the good effects of this change of administration could become apparent the mine was flooded, and all operations for the time being perforce suspended. Nor was this all.

Unpleasant rumours began to circulate as to the stability of the concern. It was said that money had been borrowed at a ruinous rate of interest; that the company was insolvent; that the plant had already been seized by the creditors.

One of the financial journals got hold of the story, and treated it after its own inimitable fashion. The company brought an action against the paper, and won their case, thereby incurring heavy law expenses and advertising the scandal, for the public to a man read the offending article, while only a very small section took the trouble to acquaint themselves with the proofs of its inaccuracy.

The shareholders grew restive, and it became known that the forthcoming general meeting was likely to be stormy. It was then that the board held their extraordinary council. There was much discussion, and many futile suggestions, but no resolution was passed, because, if the situation were to be saved, it would be the work of one man, and he hadn't had time to think out a plan of action. This was the chairman, Curtis Yorke, who, having nothing to say, had said it exceedingly well, and was now aimlessly scribbling on the back of some papers lying before him on the table.

The board-room was almost deserted. Four of the five directors had gone home; the fifth remained at the special request of the chairman, who had relapsed into silence and hieroglyphs.

A casual observer might have judged his occupation mere idling, and interrupted him without hesitation. Fielden knew better.

He not infrequently annoyed his own clients during important interviews by adorning his blotting-pad with minutely detailed presentments of cutters and yawls, and he understood that miscellaneous sketching may be on occasion the outcome of deep thought.

Therefore he waited, leisurely drawing on his gloves, until at the end of twenty minutes Yorke, without lifting his head from the paper, began to speak.

He said in a low, even voice that the company was going to the devil; that there was only one man who might be induced to see them through, and he was on the Continent, and his exact address uncertain.

That the most important thing now was to gain time, and for that purpose they must find a smart junior, a man who could talk and wasn't too well known; give him five shares and a cheque for fifty guineas, and put him on at the general meeting to impress the shareholders with the necessity for keeping quiet.

He went on to say that the San Sacrada Mine was the third venture that had gone wrong within six months, and that he, Yorke, regarded it as an omen. That if it came to grief he should never do another stroke of business; that he would be down and done for.

But that it should *not* come to grief, because he intended to pull it through at the price of his own soul. That he was prepared to sell his soul for that end, and he believed the sale would shortly be concluded.

At that moment the first crackled, and Yorke jumped as if he had been shot. Then he laughed rather awkwardly, and explained that he had not slept for a fortnight, and his nerves were all to pieces.

"I believe," he said apologetically, "that I've been talking damn rot. To tell the truth, I don't know all the time what I'm saying. It's this beastly insomnia. But you understand what I want for Friday. I made that clear. We must have someone to tackle this Simpson brute, or he'll carry the whole meeting with him. Nothing the Board can say will weigh with the shareholders; but a split among themselves may gain time, and time is money to us just now."

Fielden thought he knew a man who would do, and he asked who Simpson was.

"A dirty little outside broker. The miserable beast hasn't more than a hundred shares in all; but he's quite capable of upsetting our cart as things are at present."

"It is always the small holders who give the most trouble," said Fielden, preparing to go. "I'll see my man tonight, and send you a wire in the morning. If I were you, Yorke, I'd look in at my doctor's on the way home, and get him to give me some bromide or something. You're running under too big a strain. It isn't nice to hear a sensible man talking nonsense about his soul. If you came out with that sort of thing at a meeting the reporters would say you were drunk. Besides there's no demand for the article nowadays. They are altogether too cheap. Goodnight.

Yorke went with him to the door.

It was raining hard, and the evening air felt raw and chilly. He shivered as he returned to the empty board-room. His head felt heavy, and there were two pink spots on the green cloth which worried him.

He sat down again at the table and began to play with his pen, writing odd words on the blank sheet of paper.

He certainly had been a fool to let himself go in that way before Fielden. He must have been a bit off his head. And yet it was true. He would sell his soul if that would ensure his coming safely through this business.

His soul! Fielden had said souls were cheap. If City men had souls, what mean, shabby things some of them would be. Yorke tried to imagine what one would look like and laughed. His laugh was not good to hear.

And yet it was a big price to offer, for it was the last possession of the human being—the only thing he has to carry out of this world into the blank Beyond. And it could burn!

He remembered a picture he had seen as child in an old Bible, of souls burning in hell. Souls with human faces horribly distorted by pain. Yes, that was the end of lost souls—hot fire.

The rain swirled against the long windows, and Yorke's teeth chattered. He was cold now, and the company was going to smash. He had said all along, if this venture went down he should go with it. It had come to mean everything or nothing to him, and to know for certain that he was going to pull it through he *would* sell his soul.

He began writing again, the words forming themselves automatically beneath his fingers—

> I, the undersigned, hereby covenant and agree to guarantee the loan of such moneys as shall cover the working expenses of the San Sacrada Gold Mine for the space of six calendar months, and further to insure the complete success of the company, in consideration of the surrender of Curtis Yorke, chairman at such time and for such purpose as I may hereafter determine.
>
> (Signed)
>
> X his mark.

It was the merest vagary of a disordered brain, but Yorke's heart gave a great bound as he read and re-read the words.

Then his jaw fell, and his face grew set and rigid with terror, the terror that wipes out all manly strength and courage, and leaves room for nothing but an abject shaking cowardice. The perspiration stood out in great drops on his forehead, and his eyes were bolting out of his head as he gazed at the paper before him.

On the blank space left for the signature five letters had come out in characters that shimmered and glowed as if they were traced in flame.

Every drop of blood in Yorke's body went to his heart. For one awful moment he remained paralysed and immovable. The next, with a desperate effort, he had seized the sheet of foolscap, and, staggering across the room, flung it into the fire.

The thick paper shriveled, curled, and broke into a blaze. Yorke snatched up the paper and stirred the coals to a fiercer heat, crushing the charred fragments into the glowing embers.

Then the poker fell from his hand with a crash, and he sank into the nearest chair, shaking and sweating like a scared pony.

The clock on the mantelpiece struck six, and the sound recalled him to a sense of mundane things. He stood up and passed his hand across his damp forehead.

"Good God!" he muttered, "my head must be going. It wasn't real. It couldn't be real. Fielden's right. I'm running under too big a strain. I'll see Jones at once, and get something to pull me together."

He put on his overcoat and went downstairs.

A clerk was coming up the passage with a telegram in his hand.

Yorke stopped under the gas-burner to open the yellow envelope, and his face turned a shade paler as he read the contents.

It was the message for which he had been waiting all day. The address of the one man who could save the company.

This happened on Monday. By Wednesday afternoon Yorke had reached Paris, seen Van Hooten, and brought their conference to a successful issue.

His conduct of the transaction was throughout masterly, and aroused the great financier to an almost paternal expression of admiration.

"You are von ver' clever young man," he said to Yorke at the close for the interview. "I haf watched you for three, four, five years, and I say to myself, 'He does go far, zat boy; but he will arrive.' What! you made von leetle mistake last Spring about those 'Guatemalas,' Zat is nothing. I myself haf also made mistakes. You are young; you buy your experience. So! But, in ze end, you will succeed, for you haf a head. Mein Gott! What a head for a man so young. You see, I haf belief in you. I lend you my influence. I trust you with money, because I look for you one day to do great things. There is no fear. You will succeed."

"I shall succeed this time," said Yorke.

He took leave of the big man gratefully, for Van Hooten had been a good friend to him.

When he got back to his hotel he locked himself into his room and drew a paper out of his pocket-book. It was an exact duplicate of the weird bond he had burned in the board-room on the Monday evening. Impelled by an insane desire to see if the horrible delusion would repeat itself, he had three times re-written the document, watching with a painful admixture of interest and dismay the ghastly signature come out on the white paper. Then, in an access of terror, he would destroy the evidence of his unholy compact, only to reproduce it on the first occasion he found himself alone.

Meanwhile, the treatment prescribed by his doctor exercised a slightly beneficial effect. He did not sleep, but his brain, on the single point in which he was vitally interested, became phenomenally clear, and his powers of endurance appeared to be practically unlimited.

In the three days intervening between the board and general meetings Yorke did the work of ten men. On the Thursday night he devoted himself to the preparation of his speech. He told his servant, who left him in his own room at eleven o'clock, to put a glass of milk and syphon of soda beside the bed, and on no account to disturb him in the morning until he rang for his shaving-water.

He was then writing. The man went to bed. Yorke must have worked late into the night, for he had made a fair copy of the rough draft of his speech and added several sheets of notes.

When the speech was delivered, it was noticed that, contrary to custom, the chairman used no notes at all. He brought with him no papers whatever, and he arrived very late.

The room was packed, and the general temper of the meeting so manifestly turbulent that Fielden's neighbour had given it as his opinion that if Yorke did not turn up soon, neither he nor any one else would be able to obtain a hearing.

The words were scarcely past his lips before the tall figure of the chairman became visible amidst the crowd surging about the door. He wore a heavily-furred overcoat, which he did not attempt to remove, though the atmosphere was oppressively close.

As he made his way up the room and took his place at the table, a peculiar stillness became apparent. It originated with those in the immediate neighbourhood of the chair, and passed like a magnetic wave over the entire audience. Gradually the indeterminate hum of voices dropped, wavered and died away. When Curtis Yorke rose to address the meeting, he was received in absolute silence.

The speech which followed was the most remarkable piece of oratory ever delivered at a company's meeting. It comprised the entire history of the San Sacrada Gold Mine, with details and statistics, several of which, unknown at the time even to the directors, were subsequently verified by telegram and proved to be absolutely exact.

Yorke's manner created a profound impression. He spoke for an hour without a single hesitation, and he held his hearers spell-bound. Not an argument was wasted, not a point lost, not a possible objection left unanswered. The man was transfigured by his intense earnestness. His face was inspired, his whole person dilated. He predicted the future success of the company with the authority of one who *knew*. Every word he uttered carried conviction, and when at last a vote of confidence in the Board was put to the meeting, it was carried without a single dissentient.

Then an odd thing happened.

Without a word the chairman rose and left the room. The crowd fell back, making a way for him to the door. His disappearance was succeeded by a second of dead silence. Then Fielden, acting on an impulse, for which he could never afterwards account, sprang up and followed.

He wasn't more than a minute in gaining the stairs, but when he reached the passage Yorke was nowhere to be seen.

He hurried out to the pavement.

A brougham had just pulled up at the kerb, and someone called him by name.

It was the doctor whom Yorke was in the habit of consulting.

He said something, the drift of which Fielden did not catch, for he was looking up and down the street, and answered by the question uppermost in his mind—

"Have you seen Yorke?"

The reply was startling.

"Yes, poor fellow, but there was nothing to be done. He must have been dead for hours. His servant begged me to come to you. He says there are some important papers which you—"

"What the deuce are you talking about?" Fielden interrupted impatiently. "Yorke's no more dead than I am. He has been at the meeting since three o'clock. He has only just this minute left. I followed him downstairs."

Then, catching the peculiar expression of the medical man's face, he added warmly—

"I'm neither mad nor drunk, Dr. Jones. If you don't believe me, go upstairs. The whole meeting's there, reporters and all. Ask them who took the chair this afternoon. Dead men don't make such speeches as Yorke has just given us."

There was no doubting the sincerity of his tones.

Dr. Jones considered a moment; then he asked a rather singular question—

"Did you," he said, "speak to Mr. Yorke yourself?"

"No; he left the room suddenly, without addressing any one individually. I thought the strain had been too much for him—he had spoken really magnificently—and I followed, but—"

"Ah!" interjected the other softly; "I think, Mr. Fielden, I must ask you to come back with me. There are papers of which you, as the intimate personal friend of Mr. Yorke's and a representative of the company, had better take charge. Besides, you may be able to elucidate—"

"Do you," said Fielden, "seriously expect me to believe in the death of a man whom I have seen within the last five minutes?"

"I expect nothing. I merely tell you that Mr. Yorke was found dead in his room at half-past two this afternoon. He had given orders overnight that he was not to be disturbed until he rang; but his servant, knowing he was to attend an important meeting at three o'clock, became uneasy, and, after repeated attempts to obtain admission, broke open the door and found his master as I have said. The man at once sent for me, also for Dr. Lewis of Harley Street; but of course there was nothing to be done. Mr. Yorke must have been dead for at least five hours. The body was quite cold. The cause of death was cerebral apoplexy, brought on by nervous pressure and prolonged mental strain. I have known for some days that he was in a serious condition of health."

The brougham rolled noiselessly on its way. Fielden was staggered. His mind refused to take full meaning of the doctor's words. Neither man spoke again until the carriage drew up at the chambers which Yorke occupied. His servant was waiting for them in the hall and led the way upstairs. The bedroom was in disorder; the candles had burned down in their sockets; papers were scattered over the writing-table and floor.

On the bed, which had not been occupied during the night, lay the dead body of Curtis Yorke.

"He was found here," said the doctor, indicating the writing-table. "Evidently he was working up to—the end."

Fielden had been standing by the bed, reverently looking down at the still face on the pillow. The door of a wardrobe opposite had swung back. As he raised his head his eyes fell upon Yorke's fur-lined overcoat, and the events of the afternoon came back upon him in all their weird improbability. He crossed the room and laid a shaking hand on the doctor's arm.

"What does it mean?" he asked hoarsely. "What does it mean? I saw him, I tell you, not half an hour ago. I heard him speak, and yet—he is dead. For God's sake, what *does* it mean?"

"I don't know," the other answered, simply. 'There are some things that won't bear explanation. The affairs of the company were very much on his mind"; and, turning over the papers lying on the table, he added: "He was preparing his speech when the end came. Look here; is this anything like what you heard?"

Fielden looked, and a smothered exclamation escaped his lips as he looked down the closely-written pages. He was reading, word for word, the speech to which he had listened barely an hour before.

The eyes of the two men met, and Fielden nodded. There was a pause, broken only by the rattle of a passing cab. A corner of the hearthrug was turned up, and the doctor stooped mechanically to straighten it. Under the fold lay a piece of paper. It had dropped from the dead man's hand and remained there unnoticed since the removal of the body.

Fielden heard his companion draw in his breath with a soft, sibilant sound, and looked up.

"What is it?" he asked.

"Convincing proof, if any were needed, of that poor fellow's mental condition. Good God! What a strain he must have been running under before things got to this pass. Read it for yourself. What do you make of it?"

Fielden read, and there came back to his mind the words Yorke had spoken in the board-room four days before—

"I am prepared to sell my soul for that end, and I believe the sale will be shortly concluded."

It was the last copy of that extraordinary document by which the unhappy man believed he had saved the San Sacrada Mining Company and lost his own soul.

On the back of the paper Yorke had written:—

"My friend Fielden has said that there is no demand for souls nowadays—that they are altogether too cheap—but he is wrong. The devil is never weary of bringing men to destruction, as I am proving at what cost is known only to myself. Though I am now past hope in this world or the next, I solemnly swear that I did not seriously intend to register this shameful bargain what the powers of darkness.

"In a moment of abstraction, hardly know what I did, I wrote out the original of this agreement. Three minutes later it was *signed*, and I knew that I was lost.

"I saw the vile name come out in letters of fire—the fire of hell, in which my soul, that I have bartered away, must burn hereafter.

"Six times I have destroyed the outward evidence of this cursed bond, only to be compelled, by a power stronger than myself, to reproduce it, and watch the awful signature again affixed. *His* share of the compact will soon be completed. My part is yet to come. The surrender of my soul 'at such time and for such purpose.' The purpose I know only too well. The time is yet uncertain, but I feel that it will not be long. I am now tormented by one terrible fear; that the call may come before I have seen the success of the company assured; that after all I may be cheated out of my dearly-bought triumph. But that I am not resolved to suffer. Surely my body will have strength to resist; my will-power suffice to claim that last privilege. Come what may, I *will not* yield up my immortal self before Friday's meeting. After that I care little how soon the summons comes. This hourly suspense is torture, worse than any actual suffering. My brain is burning already. My mind is already in hell. But—"

Here the writing ceased, with a faint downward stroke of the en, as it had slipped through the nerveless fingers.

It was Curtis Yorke's last word.

The summons had come.

Fielden's eyes were wet as he finished reading.

"Poor fellow," he said under his breath. "Poor Yorke. My God! What he must have gone through!"

He turned the paper over, and looked at the strangely worded agreement.

The space left for the signature was blank.

This is the truth of a story to which no one will give credence, least of all the hundred and fifty odd men who heard Yorke's speech at the general meeting of the San Sacrada Mining Company. They will prefer to believe that two competent medical authorities made a mistake of five hours in assigning the time of his death. For there is nothing to which human nature objects so strongly as contact with the supernatural, and no credulity equal to the credulity of the incredulous.

A Grammatical Ghost

Elia W. Peattie

There was only one possible objection to the drawing-room, and that was the occasional presence of Miss Carew; and only one possible objection to Miss Carew. And that was, that she was dead.

She had been dead twenty years, as a matter of fact and record, and to the last of her life sacredly preserved the treasures and traditions of her family, a family bound up—as it is quite unnecessary to explain to any one in good society—with all that is most venerable and heroic in the history of the Republic. Miss Carew never relaxed the proverbial hospitality of her house, even when she remained its sole representative. She continued to preside at her table with dignity and state, and to set an example of excessive modesty and gentle decorum to a generation of restless young women.

It is not likely that having lived a life of such irreproachable gentility as this, Miss Carew would have the bad taste to die in any way not pleasant to mention in fastidious society. She could be trusted to the last, not to outrage those friends who quoted her as an exemplar of propriety. She died very unobtrusively of an affection of the heart, one June morning, while trimming her rose trellis, and her lavender-colored print was not even rumpled when she fell, nor were more than the tips of her little bronze slippers visible.

"Isn't it dreadful," said the Philadelphians, "that the property should go to a very, very distant cousin in Iowa or somewhere else on the frontier, about whom nobody knows anything at all?"

The Carew treasures were packed in boxes and sent away into the Iowa wilderness; the Carew traditions were preserved by the Historical Society; the Carew property, standing in one of the most umbrageous and aristocratic suburbs of Philadelphia, was rented to all manner of folk—anybody who had money enough to pay the rental—and society entered its doors no more.

But at last, after twenty years, and when all save the oldest Philadelphians had forgotten Miss Lydia Carew, the very, very distant cousin appeared. He was quite in the prime of life, and so agreeable and unassuming that nothing could be urged against him save his patronymic, which, being Boggs, did not commend itself to the euphemists. With him were two maiden sisters, ladies of excellent taste and manners, who restored the Carew china to its ancient cabinets, and replaced the Carew pictures upon the walls, with additions not out of keeping with the elegance of these heirlooms. Society, with a magnanimity almost dramatic, overlooked the name of Boggs—and called.

All was well. At least, to an outsider all seemed to be well. But, in truth, there was a certain distress in the old mansion, and in the hearts of the well-behaved Misses Boggs. It came about most unexpectedly. The sisters had been sitting upstairs, looking out at the beautiful grounds of the old place, and marvelling at the violets, which lifted their heads from every possible cranny about the house, and talking over the cordiality which they had been receiving by those upon whom they had no claim, and they were filled with amiable satisfaction. Life looked attractive. They had often been grateful to Miss Lydia Carew for leaving their brother her fortune. Now they felt even more grateful to her. She had left them a Social Position—one, which even after twenty years of desuetude, was fit for use.

They descended the stairs together, with arms clasped about each other's waists, and as they did so presented a placid and pleasing sight. They entered their drawing-room with the intention of brewing a cup of tea, and drinking it in calm sociability in the twilight. But as they entered the room they became aware of the presence of a lady, who was already seated at their tea-table, regarding their old Wedgwood with the air of a connoisseur.

There were a number of peculiarities about this intruder. To begin with, she was hatless, quite as if she were a habitué of the house, and was costumed in a prim lilac-colored lawn of the style of two decades past. But a greater peculiarity was the resemblance this lady bore to a faded daguerrotype. If looked at one way, she was perfectly discernible; if looked at another, she went out in a sort of blur. Notwithstanding this comparative invisibility, she exhaled a delicate perfume of sweet lavender, very pleasing to the nostrils of the Misses Boggs, who stood looking at her in gentle and unprotesting surprise.

"I beg your pardon," began Miss Prudence, the younger of the Misses Boggs, "but—"

But at this moment the Daguerrotype became a blur, and Miss Prudence found herself addressing space. The Misses Boggs were irritated. They had never encountered any mysteries in Iowa. They began an impatient search behind doors and portières, and even under sofas, though it was quite absurd to suppose that a lady recognizing the merits of the Carew Wedgwood would so far forget herself as to crawl under a sofa.

When they had given up all hope of discovering the intruder, they saw her standing at the far end of the drawing-room critically examining a water-color marine. The elder Miss Boggs started toward her with stern decision, but the little Daguerrotype turned with a shadowy smile, became a blur and an imperceptibility.

Miss Boggs looked at Miss Prudence Boggs.

"If there were ghosts," she said, "this would be one."

"If there were ghosts," said Miss Prudence Boggs, "this would be the ghost of Lydia Carew."

The twilight was settling into blackness, and Miss Boggs nervously lit the gas while Miss Prudence ran for other tea-cups, preferring, for reasons superfluous to mention, not to drink out of the Carew china that evening.

The next day, on taking up her embroidery frame, Miss Boggs found a number of old-fashioned cross-stitches added to her Kensington. Prudence, she knew, would never have degraded herself by taking a cross-stitch, and the parlor-maid was above taking such a liberty. Miss Boggs mentioned the incident that night at a dinner given by an ancient friend of the Carews.

"Oh, that's the work of Lydia Carew, without a doubt!" cried the hostess. "She visits every new family that moves to the house, but she never remains more than a week or two with any one."

"It must be that she disapproves of them," suggested Miss Boggs.

"I think that's it," said the hostess. "She doesn't like their china, or their fiction."

"I hope she'll disapprove of us," added Miss Prudence.

The hostess belonged to a very old Philadelphian family, and she shook her head.

"I should say it was a compliment for even the ghost of Miss Lydia Carew to approve of one," she said severely.

The next morning, when the sisters entered their drawing-room there were numerous evidences of an occupant during their absence. The sofa pillows had been rearranged so that the effect of their grouping was less bizarre than that favored by the Western women; a horrid little Buddhist idol with its eyes fixed on its abdomen, had been chastely hidden behind a Dresden shepherdess, as unfit for the scrutiny of polite eyes; and on the table where Miss Prudence did work in water colors, after the fashion of the impressionists, lay a prim and impossible composition representing a moss-rose and a number of heartsease, colored with that caution which modest spinster artists instinctively exercise.

"Oh, there's no doubt it's the work of Miss Lydia Carew," said Miss Prudence, contemptuously. "There's no mistaking the drawing of that rigid little rose. Don't you remember those wreaths and bouquets framed, among the pictures we got when the Carew pictures were sent to us? I gave some of them to an orphan asylum and burned up the rest."

"Hush!" cried Miss Boggs, involuntarily. "If she heard you, it would hurt her feelings terribly. Of course, I mean—" and she blushed. "It might hurt her feelings—but how perfectly ridiculous! It's impossible!"

Miss Prudence held up the sketch of the moss-rose.

"*That* may be impossible in an artistic sense, but it is a palpable thing."

"Bosh!" cried Miss Boggs.

"But," protested Miss Prudence, "how do you explain it?"

"I don't," said Miss Boggs, and left the room.

That evening the sisters made a point of being in the drawing-room before the dusk came on, and of lighting the gas at the first hint of twilight. They didn't believe in Miss Lydia Carew—but still they meant to be beforehand with her. They talked with unwonted vivacity and in a louder tone than was their custom. But as they drank their tea even their utmost verbosity could not make them oblivious to the fact that the perfume of sweet lavender was stealing insidiously through the room. They tacitly refused to recognize this odor and all that it indicated, when suddenly, with a sharp crash, one of the old Carew tea-cups fell from the tea-table to the floor and was broken. The disaster was followed by what sounded like a sigh of pain and dismay.

"I didn't suppose Miss Lydia Carew would ever be as awkward as that," cried the younger Miss Boggs, petulantly.

"Prudence," said her sister with a stern accent, "please try not to be a fool. You brushed the cup off with the sleeve of your dress."

"Your theory wouldn't be so bad," said Miss Prudence, half laughing and half crying, "if there were any sleeves to my dress, but, as you see, there aren't," and then Miss Prudence had something as near hysterics as a healthy young woman from the West can have.

"I wouldn't think such a perfect lady as Lydia Carew," she ejaculated between her sobs, "would make herself so disagreeable! You may talk about good-breeding all you please, but I call such intrusion exceedingly bad taste. I have a horrible idea that she likes us and means to stay with us. She left those other people because she did not approve of their habits or their grammar. It would be just our luck to please her."

"Well, I like your egotism," said Miss Boggs.

However, the view Miss Prudence took of the case appeared to be the right one. Time went by and Miss Lydia Carew still remained. When the ladies entered their drawing-room they would see the little lady-like Daguerrotype revolving itself into a blur before one of the family portraits. Or they noticed that the yellow sofa cushion, toward which she appeared to feel a peculiar antipathy, had been dropped behind the sofa upon the floor, or that one of Jane Austen's novels, which none of the family ever read, had been removed from the book shelves and left open upon the table.

"I cannot become reconciled to it," complained Miss Boggs to Miss Prudence. "I wish we had remained in Iowa where we belong. Of course I don't believe in the thing! No sensible person would. But still I cannot become reconciled."

But their liberation was to come, and in a most unexpected manner.

A relative by marriage visited them from the West. He was a friendly man and had much to say, so he talked all through dinner, and afterward followed the ladies to the drawing-room to finish his gossip. The gas in the room was turned very low, and as they entered Miss Prudence caught sight of Miss Carew, in company attire, sitting in upright propriety in a stiff-backed chair at the extremity of the apartment.

Miss Prudence had a sudden idea.

"We will not turn up the gas," she said, with an emphasis intended to convey private information to her sister. "It will be more agreeable to sit here and talk in this soft light."

Neither her brother nor the man from the West made any objection. Miss Boggs and Miss Prudence, clasping each other's hands, divided their attention between their corporeal and their incorporeal guests. Miss Boggs was confident that her sister had an idea, and was willing to await its development. As the guest from Iowa spoke, Miss Carew bent a politely attentive ear to what he said.

"Ever since Richards took sick that time," he said briskly, "it seemed like he shed all responsibility." (The Misses Boggs saw the Daguerrotype put up her shadowy head with a movement of doubt and apprehension.) "The fact of the matter was, Richards didn't seem to scarcely get on the way he might have been expected to."

(At this conscienceless split to the infinitive and misplacing of the preposition, Miss Carew arose trembling perceptibly.) "I saw it wasn't no use for him to count on a quick recovery—"

The Misses Boggs lost the rest of the sentence, for at the utterance of the double negative Miss Lydia Carew had flashed out, not in a blur, but with mortal haste, as when life goes out at a pistol shot!

The man from the West wondered why Miss Prudence should have cried at so pathetic a part of his story:

"Thank Goodness!"

And their brother was amazed to see Miss Boggs kiss Miss Prudence with passion and energy.

It was the end. Miss Carew returned no more.

The Halfway House

Mary Heaton Vorse

David Ellison agreed with towns so little that he escaped from them early. Towns, he said, made him think of worms' nests, a writhing, weaving horror, the members bound together by a common rapacity. Though what he said was not just to the coast villages. These towns cannot escape the imminent tragedy of the sea nor the splendid austerity of the unconquerable seacoast which, in some parts, has not given man a foothold since the Pilgrims first made their adventurous landing.

These towns breed brave men and women, and occasionally a lad like David Ellison grows up, who seems to be kin to the sea and to the lonely and savage coast.

He escaped to the coast guards. He could not take the outward-bound course like his forefathers on the open sea, on account of his mother. The sea had claimed already too many of the Ellisons. Up over Town Hill in the old cemetery there was a lot where one after another the Ellisons' tombstones were marked with the words, "Lost at Sea."

The men of the coast guards are an odd people, when you come to think of it, and a queer kind of life they live; their thoughts are forever concentrated on the sea and on the vessels moving over the surface of the sea. The men who have grown old in the service are both grave and friendly; they sense things other people do not perceive; they have a knowledge of storms and a way of being able to know the shapes of vessels which to common eyes are only undistinguishable spots on the horizon.

All night long the men guard the coast and inform the stations of the fates of vessels. By day the men sit looking out to sea; they are isolated as though they were on board ship. Sand, sky, sea, and the vessels sailing the sea bound their lives. Many stations are in distant places, hard to get at; they are joined to the life of the towns only by a narrow road running through soft marsh and wind-swept forest and moorland.

These are the shores haunted by ghosts of dead ships and the dead men who sailed in them. There is the legend of a white stallion, sole survivor of a wrecked vessel, that ran wild for years on the dunes, and that, after he was trapped, freed himself and ran back into the sea whence he came. There are legends of wrecks and stories of wreckers and smugglers to be heard at the life-saving stations; stories of miraculous escapes and of mysterious vessels sailing along safely, but with no hand at the rudder.

Nor are all these stories of yesterday. The mystery of the rose is a story of this generation; everyone has heard David Ellison's story and that of Assunta Flores. The rose is still blooming in the sparse earth on Spinet Rock Light, where Mary Angus was raised.

David's station was in Gurnet Reef Hollow, a part of the coast known as the Graveyard of the Atlantic. This coast is strewn with bones of dead ships; a sand cliff borders the ocean, and every now and then, at some great storm, the sea breaks in through the sand barrier and hurls inland the wreck of a vessel, and in time the shifting sand buries it and perhaps uncovers it again before the eyes of some other generation.

The towns of this wild country border the bay. The back country comes to their very gardens—an impenetrable tract of marsh, heath, and woodland, after that the cruel and encroaching dunes. Back country, dunes, and sea are all of them untamed; all of them exist to-day as in the beginning.

David grew up with them, knowing which dune had shifted under the fury of the winter's winds and which hollow was filling, and where the forests were being eaten by the sinister sands. He loved the savage coast that was forever untamable by man's hand.

Nothing broke the harmonious procession of his days, not even love. For love didn't come to David in a scorching flame. He fell in love as one breathes. He was so long Mary Angus's friend that he didn't know he had love in his heart for her until it blossomed between them.

Mary Angus was the only girl David had ever known well, and to others she was as inaccessible as a princess in a fairy tale. Spinet Rock was her father's Light, a second-class Light, a white light of a thirty-two flash, own cousin to great Highhead Light, except in magnitude. She was born in the Light, and she tended the Light from the time she was a baby.

If there was a girl that seemed predestined to be a mate to David it was Mary, with her smooth hair so blond that it seemed almost silver in the sun, and a flush of honey-colored tan across her face, and her swift ways like a bird, and her capable hands.

It wasn't but a few weeks after they had found out they cared for each other and decided to marry that David was coming along from Spinet Rock Light to the station; his time off just took him there and back easily, and gave him an hour with Mary.

All the afternoon the sea had been an almost intolerable blue and the horizon cut by a low fog bank—there it had stayed and had not moved; light clouds scurried overhead on some upper strata of wind, scurried and flowed as though afraid of a coming storm, and after it had passed over the face of the dune it had stained it with scudding lavender shadows. The sun plunged down red behind the cloud bank. By the time David passed Dead Man's Bar station it had set. The sea was lavender and the sky through the scudding clouds looked pale and high.

David got to the halfway house when a torn fog wraith tore past him; it enveloped him and the world and sped on, as though some one had torn a cloud with hands and cast it from him; little clouds of fog flew through the bayberry bushes and over sad-colored Mary's-flower that at this place clothed the face of the sand in sparse patches. He could see the fog advancing in a barrier, preceded by the wind-blown fog wraiths; he could see the fog wraiths racing inland like frightened creatures, shutting out the dunes. He walked along rapidly. All the world now shut away from him and now opened up before him. The fog had come on in a strange fashion, not stealthily like a mist that was cousin to a rain, but violently, as though horrified at a coming disaster—a cold fog, a fog that smelled of storm; and now it had cut off David from all the World, infolding him in its moist gray blanket.

Down below, at the foot of the sand hill, he could hear the lap-lapping of waves; out from behind the fog the frightened voices of vessels; below the Spinet he could hear two large vessels talking to each other. Spinet, Dead Man's Bar, and the Gurnet Reef Hollow gave warning by horn and bell, and all the time the world was full of whispering, as though the voices of storm conversed together; this was broken only by the insistent lisping of the waves on the beach. The surface of the sea had begun to heave uneasily, and far off? David could hear the whistling of the buoy on the shoals.

There was something cold and secretive in this fog and in the wind that followed at its heels and tore it along—a wind that had not yet ruffled the face of the sea. Something exciting made his blood run faster.

Suddenly he stood still, as though at the command of an unheard voice, and then, drawn as by a magnet, he turned inland and made toward the old halfway house. An encroaching dune had swallowed it; its roof was covered with sand, only the door remained; one still could go in, and one half of a window high up let in at noon an uncertain ray of light. David walked without hesitation and without argument with himself toward the halfway house, as though to keep an appointment made with death itself. Then there came a sound that made his heart stop for a beat, as though from the fog some one had whispered his name.

"Hello!" he cried, and then again, "Hello!" There was no answer. His voice sounded shockingly loud in the moist, enveloping fog. He stood still, and then the world was silent, except for the whispering of the voices of the storm.

It had got dark swiftly; unseen clouds blanketed the face of the evening sky. Suddenly a whirl of wind parted the fog and David saw for a moment some one sitting near the halfway house, bowed over. He saw that this was a girl and that she was crying. He hurried forward, and then the fog cut him off, and it was not until he was close upon her that he saw her again.

She seemed very young to David, and lonely and helpless in the immensity of the sand and the fog. She was dressed in black, as though in mourning, which was relieved only by a soft white band around her throat; her hair was dark and was pulled straight back from her forehead and done in an elaborate foreign-looking knot; her dark eyes were frightened and swimming in tears.

"Oh!" she said. "You have come." She spoke as though she had expected him and as though he were late.

"Didn't you hear me calling?" said David.

She shook her head, looking at him in a dumb, frightened sort of way.

"What are you doing so far away?" David asked.

She was so little and soft that a surge of pity engulfed him. Then with her puzzled air she said, very distinctly, always looking straight at him, as though he might unravel the mystery for her:

"I do not understand at all why I am here or why I have come." Then she added, "I only knew that I must."

At these words a sensation, almost of fear, ran over David, as though a keen wind had hit him at the roots of his hair.

"Did you get lost?"

"The fog cut me off," she answered.

"Do you often come here?"

There were a few summer cottages not far from Dead Man's Bar. Here the coast rises up sheerly and there is a far view of the sea; a few daring people who can bear isolation have built cottages near the neighboring farms. David assumed that she must have walked from there.

She didn't answer, and he repeated what he had said. She looked away from him, as though trying to see through the fog.

"I like it here," she said. "There is peace here."

She seemed so tired as she spoke that again a surge of pity carried David along like a wave on its crest.

Then for a while she sat there looking at David and he stood looking at her. It seemed to him, as he thought of it afterward, that they had been cut off from time and space—it was like meeting some one in eternity without any of the things of life to divert them from the thought of each other—as though a fog had cut them off from the world and that there remained only their two souls which had met face to face.

He had no more fear of her than if she had been a little girl, though in the presence of all women except Mary Angus he had been dumb, and he feared them all and disliked many, for they lived herded in towns. He was drawn close to this child by an intolerable pity.

"Your trail isn't far from here," he told her. "I'll take you to it."

He walked beside her, always feeling as though he were alone in the world with her, and that because of this he was closer to her than he had ever been to any other human being.

He found the coast road which winds along the shore, uniting one station with the other; the road was covered with grass; the wagon ruts showed dimly. By this time the bay, the elder and wild rose bordering it, were dripping with the fog.

He noticed that she was dressed in black and that she wore a wedding ring, and he found himself asking, "Are you married?" It hurt him to ask this, but he couldn't have told why.

She looked up at him with an expression of dumb suffering.

"I was married. He died—not long ago," she answered.

David wanted to take her in his arms and hush her on his shoulder as though she were a child. He wanted to cry out: "Oh, don't! Oh, don't!" by which he meant, "Oh, don't suffer so!" But he said nothing. It was as if she had told him all the story of her life.

Then she added, "I have a little girl."

David felt glad of that.

They got to the path which led to Dead Man's Bar station to join the road—a quicker path than the one by the beach—leading directly to the little settlement.

"You go here," he said. "Shall I go with you?" As he looked at her he saw she was afraid, but not afraid of the lonely path. What she was afraid of he couldn't tell.

They stood looking at each other questioningly, and there wrapped itself around David the feeling of being in a dream—this wasn't life; this was something else. Then he found himself saying:

"You are coming back again, aren't you?"

"Oh yes!" she said.

"Soon?" David asked.

"Very soon I shall come. Good-by, David."

Again, David had the light sensation of cold on his back. He knew she had never seen him before and she had not known his name, and he knew that this was the voice he had heard whispering to him when she had called "Hello!" into the smothering silence of the fog.

He could not forget her. The feeling of pity which she had aroused invaded him and shut away from him the realities of life.

"What has come to me," he thought, "and what is the matter with me?" In all his life he had never seen anything so lonely as that little girl in black sitting beside the smothered halfway house, and the thought of her loneliness was a shadow to all his thoughts; he could not escape it, and he did not want to escape it.

He saw her again three afternoons later on his way to Mary Angus. Instead of taking the beach, he walked along the wagon road. This grown-over track seemed more remote than the dunes themselves. He walked along this track because he had a certainty that she would be there; he had the security as one has that the sun will rise, that somewhere near the halfway house he would find her, and yet, when he saw her walking slowly toward him, again his heart missed a beat. A sense of strangeness enveloped him, as though he were moving in a fatal dream, and again the pity for her tore at his heart. She looked so little, she looked so lonely, it hurt him to see her in this wild place. He wanted to shelter her and defend her.

She came toward him smiling. She carried in her hand some roses; they were strange roses, single, and looking like tropical butterflies with crimson petals and yellow centers, the foliage around was exotic and thick and glossy, and they had a perfume as penetrating strong as attar of roses.

"You didn't find these here?" asked David.

"I brought them from home," she answered.

He held out his hand for a rose and she gave one to him. Later he could not remember what they had said. They spoke the fragmentary words of friends, the kind of words one throws into a silence so that it may not become too full of meaning.

They sat down on the crest of a dune on which some green things were growing—bayberry, Mary's flower, and beach grass. One could look at the sea.

"I wonder if these roses would grow if I put them in the sand?" she asked.

"Wild roses grow well out here," he answered. "I have heard my mother say you could slip roses in sand."

She planted them gravely, one after another.

"If it rains they may grow," she said. Then she rose and they walked in silence the short distance that had separated them from the trail leading to Dead Man's Bar.

"I leave you here," she said, and in a moment a clump of elders had hidden her from him.

He went on his way toward Mary's, a confusion in his heart. He felt as though life was asking him something, as though this meeting was a shadow of some portentous thing.

"That's a queer rose you have," said Mary. She took it from him. "I never saw one on the Cape before like it. Where did you find it, David?"

"Out on the dunes."

"Out on the dunes? Do such roses grow on the dunes?"

"A girl on the dunes gave it to me. I don't know who she is." It hurt him intolerably to say that he did not know who she was; it seemed preposterous that he shouldn't know her when she had so impressed herself upon his heart.

Mary's mother came into the room. She had been an inland woman and had made flowers bloom in the little garden around the Light.

"There are no roses like this one in all the Cape," she said. "That's a rose from a foreign country. I saw one like that one time up in Maine, brought by a man who had been in the China trade." He wanted to talk about the girl to Mary. He wanted to say he found her lost in the fog and to-day she came to meet him with the rose. But when he came to put it into words, it sound foolish and he could say nothing; so he sat there still, feeling as though he were under the enchantment of a dream.

During the next few days David consciously tried to put the girl from his mind. There was no reason why he should think of her, and yet she was there, forever a background of his thoughts. He turned to Mary for comfort; he clung to her as a child clings to its mother in the dark.

A few days after this as he sat in the Light it seemed to Mary as though he were listening to something outside, as one might listen for a voice calling. He got up.

"Well, I must be going," he said.

"You must be going? Why is that?" asked Mary's mother, for David always stayed until the last moment, giving himself just time to get back to his station. He looked at the two women, dazed.

Mary put her hand on his shoulder. "What is it, David?" she asked. And it seemed to him that the kindness she had in her heart streamed out of her.

"I don't rightly know," he answered. "But I must be off."

Mary's mother looked at them fixedly a moment, and left them standing together.

"David," said Mary, "can't you tell me your trouble? Can't you tell me what's been in your heart, David, and what it is that's been coming between us?"

A longing for his untroubled days and his undivided life surged up around him. He struggled for words. None came to him. What could he tell her? That he loved some one else—a strange girl whose name he did not know? Words seemed to rob the whole thing of meaning; and yet there it was, some unspoken obligation, something he could not escape, something he had to see through.

Mary bent over and kissed his forehead. "David," she said, "I know one thing. I know I love you forever. And I know your face is turned away from me and you can't tell me why. But I know when you turn your face back to me you'll find me here waiting for you. But, oh, my dear, it's hard that I can't help the trouble that's in your heart." With that she kissed him again.

And with his heart breaking he strode off, not looking behind him. It was as though he had been sucked out of the house on a tide of longing that was neither love nor desire, but which was stronger than either. A desperate homesickness had seized him, the nostalgia of which men die in foreign countries,

He went to the halfway house as a magnet to the pole, secure and content in his knowledge that she would be there waiting for him, a little, lonely, bowed figure who had put on him some mysterious claim. And as he went a fog came up and walked along with him as though it were the inevitable accompaniment of his meeting with her, as though the fog knew his purpose and intended to shut him off from the world with its impenetrable intimacy.

She was sitting as though waiting for him, and for a while they sat near each other, not speaking. David was rocked in his own contentment, His conflict was over; he had no longer feeling of any betrayal. It was as though the door of his heart was opened that led into a secret place which he had never known existed. For a moment he did not struggle with life.

Then, as they sat there, suddenly the fog parted, baring the cold, bright glitter of innumerable stars, infinitely remote. David looked up at them with awe. It seemed as though he had shrunk into nothingness in the presence of the still splendor of the heavens. He needed the touch of a human being, and he heard himself imploring this unknown girl:

"Let me hold you in my arms for a moment."

"Not now," she whispered to him, putting her hand up in a faint, protesting gesture. She looked at him with a trust. "Not now, but the next time I come." And then she walked away from him slowly. It was as though she stepped off the edge of the world; the fog had blotted her out, and David was left alone.

How long he sat there he could not have told. The immense importance of what had just happened beat on him like an insistent, drenching rain. He was under some enchantment which cut him off from the life he had known. This strange and lonely child needed him, and he had pledged himself to her service.

He got up and went back to the station. Throughout the long walk his thoughts went around in the treadmill.

His life had been unified, complete, and now he had been invaded by this strange love from the outside; it assailed him like an outside force, asking something of him. So his undivided life was now divided. His heart lay torn in two before him. It was as though he were divided into two persons, one plunged deep into the inexplicable thing which had befallen him, and the other his usual self, alive to every whisper of the wind. He sensed storm in the air; everything spoke of storm. Disaster was brewing, disaster was coming upon the breath of the lifting wind. There were vessels behind the blanket of fog, vessels below the brim of the horizon fated to destruction.

All through his sleep he felt the storm rising. By morning the breakers were thundering on the beach, driven by the wind that has no check to it; it sweeps clear across the ocean from Spain to America. And yet the fog persisted; the wind drove the fog before it and there was more fog; it could not drive it clear. Behind the fog came the tumultuous talking of frightened vessels.

Mixed in David's mind was the thought of Mary and the thought of the girl in the halfway house. It was so inexplicable that it would not give him rest, a mystery clamoring to be solved, while always below the surface of his thoughts there was the homesickness which she had aroused in him.

This became so unbearable that late in the afternoon he got into his oilskins and went to the halfway house, knowing beforehand that it was impossible she should be there. It looked more lonely than ever, smothered over with sand.

He went within to shelter himself from the smiting rain and from the howling cruelty of the wind. It was like a tomb, a grave of hope. There was the place where the stove had been, and still a bench and a locker for coal and wood. The place stifled him and he plowed back to the station again. His thoughts whirled through his mind like leaves before a storm.

By nightfall the storm had become a tempest, and he went to bed with the captain's voice in his ears:

"Better get what sleep we can; like as not we'll be turned out before morning."

He sank instantly into profound sleep, and it seemed that no time had passed before he heard the alarm. With the sleep still heavy upon him he struggled into his clothes and out with the lifeboat. A vessel had gone ashore on the bar. The fog was still drifting in; one could barely make out the distress signal. A sense of apprehension gripped him. He heard them discuss whether it would be possible to launch the boat. He said, aloud:

"We'll be too late if we don't hurry! We'll be too late!"

Then he heard the captain call out, "We'll have to try the lifeboat!" But the fog had shut down again, and they launched the boat as if by a miracle. They struggled outward over the cruel mountains of dark water.

A torch like a red eye was flaring from the deck of the vessel. The lifeboat toiled up the steep, glassy side of a wave. Then he thought he heard his name, "David!" and then again, "David!" He felt the familiar sensation of cold, as though a wind had been blowing at the roots of his hair. Again he fought doggedly with the cruel fury of the waves, toiling toward the torch's red eye. A whirl of wind parted the fog and on the deck of the reeling vessel he thought he saw a frightened figure of a girl dressed in black.

A terror gripped him, for it was the little bowed figure he knew so well, frightened and lonely, but no more frightened and no more lonely than he had seen her at the halfway house. She stood there with her puzzled air, as if waiting for the next move of fate, as though she dumbly expected some new disaster which never failed her. In her arms she held a little girl.

With a baby in her arms she should be the first to enter the boat. They made alongside of the vessel's lee and held themselves there with difficulty, the boat rising and falling on the crest of the greedy waves. She handed the child to David, and her lips formed some word inaudible to him in the storm. He saw plainly her face lit up by the torch, plainly he saw a flaming, startled recognition in her eyes, a glad recognition. Then the word was given her to jump, and she jumped and missed and the water closed over her head. Then David saw a glimpse of her white face as she was swept down by the onrushing seas—and in a moment he was after her. He had her in his arms; then darkness enshrouded him as he battled toward the lifeboat.

The next hour was blank to David. He retained consciousness and nothing more. How they got ashore he could not remember. He had only a vague memory of a limp figure at the bottom of the boat, his own exhaustion, and of a child's voice amid the storm.

His next memory was the life-saving station. She lay there less lonely now than she had seemed to him when he had first seen her there sitting with bowed head in the smothering immensity of the fog. The men and women grouped themselves around her pityingly; they were foreigners; some spoke English. The wrecked vessel was a bark twenty days from Fayal.

Then a woman spoke to the captain of the station:

"She was always worrying about her baby. She used to sit and look out to sea, as if wondering what would happen to her. She seemed to know—"

"Who are her relatives?" the captain asked. "Who knows about her?"

"She had none. Her husband was dead. She was coming here to join her brother; just before she sailed she heard that he, also, had died—so, not knowing what to do, she came anyway."

There was silence. Then one of the women asked, "What will become of the child?"

David had stood there listening to them, as though from a great distance, and then suddenly the amazing meaning of it swept over him. He went forward and picked the baby up.

"It is mine," he said. She clung to him and put her face close to his, as though she knew him. "I'll take it to Mary Angus."

You may say such things can't happen. But there are stranger legends than these that come from the Graveyard of the Atlantic; and if you don't believe this you may go to Gurnet Reef station and they will tell you about it, and you can see Assunta Flores with her foreign eyes and her heavy dark hair, and you can see Mary Angus, whom she calls mother. And then if you go up to the old halfway house by the wagon track and climb the dune above you will find growing there clumps of rose bushes which in their season bloom with strange, exotic flowers. You can go, if you like, and see at Spinet Rock the same flower that Mary's mother slipped into the sand and which has flourished.

Then, if you like, you can explain it all by coincidence—that some lonely girl strayed from the cottages to talk to David on the dunes, and that she brought him the roses. But if you have been much on the outside shore you will not make your explanation chime with reason, because you will know that the reason of man is but a puny measure for creation's immensity.

The Haunted Burglar

W. C. Morrow

Anthony Ross doubtless had the oddest and most complex temperament that ever assured the success of burglary as a business. This fact is mentioned in order that those who choose may employ it as an explanation of the extraordinary ideas that entered his head and gave a strangely tragic character to his career.

Though ignorant, the man had an uncommonly fine mind in certain aspects. Thus it happened that, while lacking moral perception, he cherished an artistic pride in the smooth, elegant, and finished conduct of his work. Hence a blunder on his part invariably filled him with grief and humiliation; and it was the steadily increasing recurrence of these errors that finally impelled him to make a deliberate analysis of his case. Among the stupid acts with which he charged himself was the murder of the banker Uriah Mattson, a feeble old man whom a simple choking or a sufficient tap on the skull would have rendered helpless. Instead of that, he had choked his victim to death in the most brutal and unnecessary manner, and in doing so had used the fingers of his left hand in a singularly sprawled and awkward fashion. The whole act was utterly unlike him; it appalled and horrified him,—not for the sin of taking human life, but because it was unnecessary, dangerous, subversive of the principles of skilled burglary, and monstrously inartistic. A similar mishap had occurred in the case of Miss Jellison, a wealthy spinster, merely because she was in the act of waking, which meant an ensuing scream. In this case, as in the other, he was unspeakably shocked to discover that the fatal choking had been done by the left hand, with sprawled and awkward fingers, and with a savage ferocity entirely uncalled for by his peril.

In setting himself to analyze these incongruous and revolting things he dragged forth from his memory numerous other acts, unlike those two in detail, but similar to them in spirit. Thus, in a fit of passionate anger at the whimpering of an infant, he had flung it brutally against the wall. Another time he was nearly discovered through the needless torturing of a cat, whose cries set pursuers at his heels. These and other insane, inartistic, and ferocious acts he arrayed for serious analysis.

Finally the realization burst upon him that all his aberrations of conduct had proceeded from his left hand and arm. Search his recollection ever so diligently, he could not recall a single instance wherein his right hand had failed to proceed on perfectly fine, sure, and artistic lines. When he made this discovery he realized that he had brought himself face to face with a terrifying mystery; and its horrors were increased when he reflected that while his left hand had committed acts of stupid atrocity in the pursuit of his burglarious enterprises, on many occasions when he was not so engaged it had acted with a less harmful but none the less coarse, irrational, and inartistic purpose.

It was not difficult for such a man to arrive at strange conclusions. The explanation that promptly suggested itself, and that his coolest and shrewdest wisdom could not shake, was that his left arm was under the dominion of a perverse and malicious spirit, that it was an entity apart from his own spirit, and that it had fastened itself upon that part of his body to produce his ruin. It were useless, however inviting, to speculate upon the order of mind capable of arriving at such a conclusion; it is more to the point to narrate the terrible happenings to which it gave rise.

About a month after the burglar's mental struggle a strange-looking man applied for a situation at a saw-mill a hundred miles away. His appearance was exceedingly distressing. Either a grievous bodily illness or fearful mental anguish had made his face wan and haggard and filled his eyes with the light of a hard desperation that gave promise of dire results. There were no marks of a vagabond on his clothing or in his manner. He did not see to be suffering for physical necessities. He held his head aloft and walked like a man, and an understanding glance would have seen that his look of determination meant something profounder and more far-reaching than the ordinary business concerns of life.

He gave the name of Hope. His manner was so engaging, yet withal so firm and abstracted, that he secured a position without difficulty; and so faithfully did he work, and so quick was his intelligence, that in good time his request to be given the management of a saw was granted. It might have been noticed that his face thereupon wore a deeper and more haggard look, but that its rigors were softened by a light of happy expectancy. As he cultivated no friendships among the men, he had no confidants; he went his dark way alone to the end.

He seemed to take more than the pleasure of an efficient workman in observing the products of his skill. He would stealthily hug the big brown logs as they approached the saw, and his eyes would blaze when the great tool went singing and roaring at its work. The foreman, mistaking this eagerness for carelessness, quietly cautioned him to beware; but when the next log was mounted for the saw the stranger appeared to slip and fall. He clasped the moving log in his arms, and the next moment the insatiable teeth had severed his left arm near the shoulder, and the stranger sank with a groan into the soft sawdust that filled the pit.

There was the usual commotion attending such accidents, for the faces of workmen turn white when they see one of their number thus maimed for life. But Hope received good surgical care, and in due time was able to be abroad. Then the men observed that a remarkable change had come over him. His moroseness had disappeared, and in its stead was a hearty cheer of manner that amazed them. Was the losing of a precious arm a thing to make a wretched man happy? Hope was given light work in the office, and might have remained to the end of his days a competent and prosperous man; but one day he left, and was never seen thereabout again.

Then Anthony Ross, the burglar, reappeared upon the scenes of his former exploits. The police were dismayed to note the arrival of a man whom all their skill had been unable to convict of terrible crimes which they were certain he had committed, and they questioned him about the loss of his arm; but he laughed them away with the fine old *sang-froid* with which they were familiar, and soon his handiwork appeared in reports of daring burglaries.

A watch of extraordinary care and minuteness was set upon him, but that availed nothing until a singular thing occurred to baffle the officers beyond measure: Ross had suddenly become wildly reckless and walked red-handed into the mouth of the law. By evidence that seemed irrefragable a burglary and atrocious murder were traced to him. Stranger than all else, he made no effort to escape, though heaving a hanging trail behind him. When the officers overhauled him, they found him in a state of utter dejection, wholly different from the light-hearted bearing that had characterized him ever since he had returned without his left arm. Neither admitting nor denying his guilt, he bore himself with the hopelessness of a man already condemned to the gallows.

Even when he was brought before a jury and placed on trial, he made no fight for his life. Although possessed of abundant means, he refused to employ an attorney, and treated with scant courtesy the one assigned him by the judge. He betrayed irritation at the slow dragging of the case as the prosecution piled up its evidence against him. His whole manner indicated that he wished the trial to end as soon as possible and hoped for a verdict of guilty.

This incomprehensible behavior placed the young and ambitious attorney on his mettle. He realized that some inexplicable mystery lay behind the matter, and this sharpened his zeal to find it. He plied his client with all manner of questions, and tried in all ways to secure his confidence: Ross remained sullen, morose, and wholly given over to despairing resignation. The young lawyer had made a wonderful discovery, which he at first felt confident would clear the prisoner, but any mention of it to Ross would only throw him into a violent passion and cause him to tremble as with a palsy. His conduct on such occasions was terrible beyond measure. He seemed utterly beside himself, and thus his attorney had become convinced of the man's insanity. The trouble in proving it was that he dared not mention his discovery to others, and that Ross exhibited no signs of mania unless that one object was broached.

The prosecution made out a case that looked impregnable, and this fact seemed to fill the prisoner with peace. The young lawyer for the defense had summoned a number of witnesses, but in the end he used only one. His opening statement to the jury was merely that it was a physical impossibility for the prisoner to have committed the murder,—which was done by choking. Ross made a frantic attempt to stop him from putting forth that defense, and from the dock wildly denounced it as a lie.

The young lawyer nevertheless proceeded with what he deemed his duty to his unwilling client. He called a photographer and had him produce a large picture of the murdered man's face and neck. He proved that the portrait was that of the person whom Ross was charged with having killed. As he approached the climax of the scene, Ross became entirely ungovernable in his frantic efforts to stop the introduction of the evidence, and so it became necessary to bind and gag him and strap him to the chair.

When quiet was restored, the lawyer handed the photograph to the jury and quietly remarked,—

"You may see for yourselves that the choking was done with the left hand, and you have observed that my client has no such member."

He was unmistakably right. The imprint of the thumb and fingers, forced into the flesh in a singularly ferocious, sprawling, and awkward manner, was shown in the photograph with absolute clearness. The prosecution, taken wholly by surprise, blustered and made attempts to assail the evidence, but without success. The jury returned a verdict of not guilty.

Meanwhile the prisoner had fainted, and his gag and bonds had been removed; but he recovered at the moment when the verdict was announced. He staggered to his feet, and his eyes rolled; then with a thick tongue he exclaimed,—

"It was the left arm that did it! This one"—holding his right arm as high as he could reach—"never made a mistake. It was always the left one. A spirit of mischief and murder was in it. I cut it off in a saw-mill, but the spirit stayed where the arm used to be, and it choked this man to death. I didn't want you to acquit me. I wanted you to hang me. I can't go through life having this thing haunting me and spoiling my business and making a murderer of me. It tries to choke me while I sleep. There it is! Can't you see it?" And he looked with wide-staring eyes at his left side.

"Mr. Sheriff," gravely said the judge, "take this man before the Commissioners of Lunacy to-morrow."

The Haunted Mill; or, The Ruined Home

Jerome K. Jerome

Well, you all know my brother-in-law, Mr. Parkins (began Mr. Coombes, taking the long clay pipe from his mouth, and putting it behind his ear: we did not know his brother-in-law, but we said we did, so as to save time), and you know of course that he once took a lease of an old mill in Surrey, and went to live there.

Now you must know that, years ago, this very mill had been occupied by a wicked old miser, who died there, leaving—so it was rumored—all his money hidden somewhere about the place. Naturally enough, every one who had since come to live at the mill had tried to find the treasure; but none had ever succeeded, and the local wiseacres said that nobody ever would, unless the ghost of the miserly miller should, one day, take a fancy to one of the tenants, and disclose to him the secret of the hiding-place.

My brother-in-law did not attach much importance to the story, regarding it as an old woman's tale, and, unlike his predecessors, made no attempt whatever to discover the hidden gold.

"Unless business was very different then from what it is now," said my brother-in-law, "I don't see how a miller could very well have saved anything, however much of a miser he might have been: at all events, not enough to make it worth the trouble of looking for it."

Still, he could not altogether get rid of the idea of that treasure.

One night he went to bed. There was nothing very extraordinary about that, I admit. He often did go to bed of a night. What *was* remarkable, however, was that exactly as the clock of the village church chimed the last stroke of twelve, my brother-in-law woke up with a start, and felt himself quite unable to go to sleep again.

Joe (his Christian name was Joe) sat up in bed, and looked around.

At the foot of the bed something stood very still, wrapped in shadow.

It moved into the moonlight, and then my brother-in-law saw that it was the figure of a wizened little old man, in knee-breeches and a pig-tail.

In an instant the story of the hidden treasure and the old miser flashed across his mind.

"He's come to show me where it's hid," thought my brother-in-law; and he resolved that he would not spend all this money on himself. But would devote a small percentage of it towards doing good to others.

The apparition moved towards the door: my brother-in-law put on his trousers and followed it. The ghost went downstairs into the kitchen, glided over and stood in front of the hearth, sighed and disappeared.

Next morning, Joe had a couple of bricklayers in, and made them haul out the stove and pull down the chimney, while he stood behind with a potato-sack in which to put the gold.

They knocked down half the wall, and never found as much as a four-penny bit. My brother-in law did not know what to think.

The next night the old man appeared again, and again led the way into the kitchen. This time, however, instead of going to the fireplace, it stood more in the middle of the room, and sighed there.

"Oh, I see what he means now," said my brother-in-law to himself; "it's under the floor. Why did the old idiot go and stand up against the stove, so as to make me think it was up the chimney?"

They spent the next day in taking up the kitchen floor, but the only thing they found was a three-pronged fork, and the handle of that was broken.

On the third night, the ghost reappeared, quite unabashed, and for a third time made for the kitchen. Arrived there, it looked up at the ceiling and vanished.

"Umph! he don't seem to have learned much sense where he's been to," muttered Joe, as he trotted back to bed; "I should have thought he might have done that at first."

Still, there seemed no doubt now where the treasure lay, and the first thing after breakfast they started pulling down the ceiling. They got every inch of the ceiling down, and they took up the boards of the room above.

They discovered about as much treasure as you would expect to find in an empty quart-pot.

On the fourth night, when the ghost appeared, as usual, my brother-in-law was so wild that he threw his boots at it; and the boots passed through the body, and broke a looking-glass.

On the fifth night, when Joe awoke, as he always did now at twelve, the ghost was standing in a dejected attitude, looking very miserable. There was an appealing look in its large sad eyes that quite touched my brother-in-law.

"After all," he thought, "perhaps the silly chap's doing his best. Maybe he has forgotten where he really did put it, and is trying to remember. I'll give him another chance."

The ghost appeared grateful and delighted at seeing Joe prepare to follow him, and led the way into the attic, pointed to the ceiling, and vanished.

"Well, he's hit it this time, I do hope," said my brother-in-law; and next day they set to work to take the roof off the place.

It took them three days to get the roof thoroughly off, and all they found was a bird's nest; after securing which they covered up the house with tarpaulins, to keep it dry.

You might have thought that would have cured the poor fellow of looking for treasure. But it didn't.

He said there must be something in it all, or the ghost would never keep on coming as it did; and that, having gone so far, he would go on to the end, and solve the mystery, cost what it might.

Night after night, he would get out of his bed and follow that spectral old fraud about the house. Each night, the old man would indicate a different place; and, on each following day, my brother-in-law would proceed to break up the mill at the point indicated, and look for the treasure. At the end of three weeks, there was not a room in the mill fit to live in. Every wall had been pulled down, every floor had been taken up, every ceiling had had a hole knocked in it. And then, as suddenly as they had begun, the ghost's visits ceased; and my brother-in-law was left in peace, to rebuild the place at his leisure.

"What induced the old image to play such a silly trick upon a family man and a ratepayer?" Ah! that's just what I cannot tell you.

Some said that the ghost of the wicked old man had done it to punish my brother-in-law for not believing in him at first; while others held that the apparition was probably that of some deceased local plumber and glazier, who would naturally take an interest in seeing a house knocked about and spoilt. But nobody knew anything for certain.

The Haunted Orchard

Richard Le Gallienne

Spring was once more in the world. As she sang to herself in the faraway woodlands her voice reached even the ears of the city, weary with the long winter. Daffodils flowered at the entrances to the Subway, furniture removing vans blocked the side streets, children clustered like blossoms on the doorsteps, the open cars were running, and the cry of the "cash clo'" man was once more heard in the land.

Yes, it was the spring, and the city dreamed wistfully of lilacs and the dewy piping of birds in gnarled old apple-trees, of dogwood lighting up with sudden silver the thickening woods, of water-plants unfolding their glossy scrolls in pools of morning freshness.

On Sunday mornings, the outbound trains were thronged with eager pilgrims, hastening out of the city, to behold once more the ancient marvel of the spring; and, on Sunday evenings, the railway termini were aflower with banners of blossom from rifled woodland and orchard carried in the hands of the returning pilgrims, whose eyes still shone with the spring magic, in whose ears still sang the fairy music.

And as I beheld these signs of the vernal equinox I knew that I, too, must follow the music, forsake awhile the beautiful siren we call the city, and in the green silences meet once more my sweetheart Solitude.

As the train drew out of the Grand Central, I hummed to myself,

"I've a neater, sweeter maiden, in a greener, cleaner land"—

and so I said good-by to the city, and went forth with beating heart to meet the spring.

I had been told of an almost forgotten corner on the south coast of Connecticut, where the spring and I could live in an inviolate loneliness—a place uninhabited save by birds and blossoms, woods and thick grass, and an occasional silent farmer, and pervaded by the breath and shimmer of the Sound.

Nor had rumor lied, for when the train set me down at my destination I stepped out into the most wonderful green hush, a leafy Sabbath silence through which the very train, as it went farther on its way, seemed to steal as noiselessly as possible for fear of breaking the spell.

After a winter in the town, to be dropped thus suddenly into the intense quiet of the country-side makes an almost ghostly impression upon one, as of an enchanted silence, a silence that listens and watches but never speaks, finger on lip. There is a spectral quality about everything upon which the eye falls: the woods, like great green clouds, the wayside flowers, the still farm-houses half lost in orchard bloom—all seem to exist in a dream. Everything is so still, everything so supernaturally green. Nothing moves or talks, except the gentle susurrus of the spring wind swaying the young buds high up in the quiet sky, or a bird now and again, or a little brook singing softly to itself among the crowding rushes.

Though from the houses one notes here and there, there are evidently human inhabitants of this green silence, none are to be seen. I have often wondered where the countryfolk hide themselves, as I have walked hour after hour, past farm and croft and lonely door-yards, and never caught sight of a human face. If you should want to ask the way, a farmer is as shy as a squirrel, and if you knock at a farm-house door, all is as silent as a rabbit-warren.

As I walked along in the enchanted stillness, I came at length to a quaint old farm-house—"old Colonial" in its architecture—embowered in white lilacs, and surrounded by an orchard of ancient apple-trees which cast a rich shade on the deep spring grass. The orchard had the impressiveness of those old religious groves, dedicated to the strange worship of sylvan gods, gods to be found now only in Horace or Catullus, and in the hearts of young poets to whom the beautiful antique Latin is still dear.

The old house seemed already the abode of Solitude. As I lifted the latch of the white gate and walked across the forgotten grass, and up on to the veranda already festooned with wistaria, and looked into the window, I saw Solitude sitting by an old piano, on which no composer later than Bach had ever been played.

In other words, the house was empty; and going round to the back, where old barns and stables leaned together as if falling asleep, I found a broken pane, and so climbed in and walked through the echoing rooms. The house was very lonely. Evidently no one had lived in it for a long time. Yet it was all ready for some occupant, for whom it seemed to be waiting. Quaint old four-poster bedsteads stood in three rooms—dimity curtains and spotless linen—old oak chests and mahogany presses;

and, opening drawers in Chippendale sideboards, I came upon beautiful frail old silver and exquisite china that set me thinking of a beautiful grandmother of mine, made out of old lace and laughing wrinkles and mischievous old blue eyes.

There was one little room that particularly interested me, a tiny bedroom all white, and at the window the red roses were already in bud. But what caught my eye with peculiar sympathy was a small bookcase, in which were some twenty or thirty volumes, wearing the same forgotten expression—forgotten and yet cared for—which lay like a kind of memorial charm upon everything in the old house. Yes, everything seemed forgotten and yet everything, curiously—even religiously—remembered. I took out book after book from the shelves, once or twice flowers fell out from the pages—and I caught sight of a delicate handwriting here and there and frail markings. It was evidently the little intimate library of a young girl. What surprised me most was to find that quite half the books were in French—French poets and French romancers: a charming, very rare edition of Ronsard, a beautifully printed edition of Alfred de Musset, and a copy of Théophile Gautier's *Mademoiselle de Maupin*. How did these exotic books come to be there alone in a deserted New England farm-house?

This question was to be answered later in a strange way. Meanwhile I had fallen in love with the sad, old, silent place, and as I closed the white gate and was once more on the road, I looked about for someone who could tell me whether or not this house of ghosts might be rented for the summer by a comparatively living man.

I was referred to a fine old New England farm-house shining white through the trees a quarter of a mile away. There I met an ancient couple, a typical New England farmer and his wife; the old man, lean, chin-bearded, with keen gray eyes flickering occasionally with a shrewd humor, the old lady with a kindly old face of the withered-apple type and ruddy. They were evidently prosperous people, but their minds—for some reason I could not at the moment divine—seemed to be divided between their New England desire to drive a hard bargain and their disinclination to let the house at all.

Over and over again they spoke of the loneliness of the place. They feared I would find it very lonely. No one had lived in it for a long time, and so on. It seemed to me that afterwards I understood their curious hesitation, but at the moment only regarded it as a part of the circuitous New England method of bargaining. At all events, the rent I offered finally overcame their disinclination, whatever its cause, and so I came into possession—for four months—of that silent old house, with the white lilacs, and the drowsy barns, and the old piano, and the strange orchard; and, as the summer came on, and the year changed its name from May to June, I used to lie under the apple-trees in the afternoons, dreamily reading some old book, and through half-sleepy eyelids watching the silken shimmer of the Sound.

I had lived in the old house for about a month, when one afternoon a strange thing happened to me. I remember the date well. It was the afternoon of Tuesday, June 13th. I was reading, or rather dipping here and there, in Burton's *Anatomy of Melancholy*. As I read, I remember that a little unripe apple, with a petal or two of blossom still clinging to it, fell upon the old yellow page. Then I suppose I must have fallen into a dream, though it seemed to me that both my eyes and my ears were wide open, for I suddenly became aware of a beautiful young voice singing very softly somewhere among the leaves. The singing was very frail, almost imperceptible, as though it came out of the air. It came and went fitfully, like the elusive fragrance of sweetbrier—as though a girl was walking to and fro, dreamily humming to herself in the still afternoon. Yet there was no one to be seen. The orchard had never seemed more lonely. And another fact that struck me as strange was that the words that floated to me out of the aerial music were French, half sad, half gay snatches of some long-dead singer of old France. I looked about for the origin of the sweet sounds, but in vain. Could it be the birds that were singing in French in this strange orchard? Presently the voice seemed to come quite close to me, so near that it might have been the voice of a dryad singing to me out of the tree against which I was leaning. And this time I distinctly caught the words of the sad little song:

> "Chante, rossignol, chante,
> Toi qui as le cœur gai;
> Tu as le cœur à rire,
> Moi, je l'ai-t-à pleurer."

But, though the voice was at my shoulder, I could see no one, and then the singing stopped with what sounded like a sob; and a moment or two later I seemed to hear a sound of sobbing far down the orchard. Then there followed silence, and I was left to ponder on the strange occurrence. Naturally, I decided that it was just a day-dream between sleeping and waking over the pages of an old book; yet when next day and the day after the invisible singer was in the orchard again, I could not be satisfied with such mere matter-of-fact explanation.

"A la claire fontaine,"

went the voice to and fro through the thick orchard boughs,

"M'en allant promener,
J'ai trouvé l'eau si belle
Que je m'y suis baigné,
Lui y a longtemps que je t'aime,
Jamais je ne t'oubliai."

It was certainly uncanny to hear that voice going to and fro the orchard, there somewhere amid the bright sun-dazzled boughs—yet not a human creature to be seen—not another house even within half a mile. The most materialistic mind could hardly but conclude that here was something "not dreamed of in our philosophy." It seemed to me that the only reasonable explanation was the entirely irrational one—that my orchard was haunted: haunted by some beautiful young spirit, with some sorrow of lost joy that would not let her sleep quietly in her grave.

And next day I had a curious confirmation of my theory. Once more I was lying under my favorite apple-tree, half reading and half watching the Sound, lulled into a dream by the whir of insects and the spices called up from the earth by the hot sun. As I bent over the page, I suddenly had the startling impression that some one was leaning over my shoulder and reading with me, and that a girl's long hair was falling over me down on to the page. The book was the Ronsard I had found in the little bedroom. I turned, but again there was nothing there. Yet this time I knew that I had not been dreaming, and I cried out:

"Poor child! tell me of your grief—that I may help your sorrowing heart to rest."

But, of course, there was no answer; yet that night I dreamed a strange dream. I thought I was in the orchard again in the afternoon and once again heard the strange singing—but this time, as I looked up, the singer was no longer invisible. Coming toward me was a young girl with wonderful blue eyes filled with tears and gold hair that fell to her waist. She wore a straight, white robe that might have been a shroud or a bridal dress. She appeared not to see me, though she came directly to the tree where I was sitting. And there she knelt and buried her face in the grass and sobbed as if her heart would break. Her long hair fell over her like a mantle, and in my dream I stroked it pityingly and murmured words of comfort for a sorrow I did not understand. . . .

Then I woke suddenly as one does from dreams. The moon was shining brightly into the room. Rising from my bed, I looked out into the orchard. It was almost as bright as day. I could plainly see the tree of which I had been dreaming, and then a fantastic notion possessed me. Slipping on my clothes, I went out into one of the old barns and found a spade. Then I went to the tree where I had seen the girl weeping in my dream and dug down at its foot.

I had dug little more than a foot when my spade struck upon some hard substance, and in a few more moments I had uncovered and exhumed a small box, which, on examination, proved to be one of those pretty old-fashioned Chippendale work-boxes used by our grandmothers to keep their thimbles and needles in, their reels of cotton and skeins of silk. After smoothing down the little grave in which I had found it, I carried the box into the house, and under the lamplight examined its contents.

Then at once I understood why that sad young spirit went to and fro the orchard singing those little French songs—for the treasure-trove I had found under the apple-tree, the buried treasure of an unquiet, suffering soul, proved to be a number of love-letters written mostly in French in a very picturesque hand—letters, too, written but some five or six years before. Perhaps I should not have read them—yet I read them with such reverence for the beautiful, impassioned love that animated them, and literally made them "smell sweet and blossom in the dust," that I felt I had the sanction of the dead to make myself the confidant of their story. Among the letters were little songs, two of which I had heard the strange young voice singing in the orchard, and, of course, there were many withered flowers and such like remembrances of bygone rapture.

Not that night could I make out all the story, though it was not difficult to define its essential tragedy, and later on a gossip in the neighborhood and a headstone in the churchyard told me the rest.

The unquiet young soul that had sung so wistfully to and fro the orchard was my landlord's daughter. She was the only child of her parents, a beautiful, willful girl, exotically unlike those from whom she was sprung and among whom she lived with a disdainful air of exile. She was, as a child, a little creature of fairy fancies, and as she grew up it was plain to her father and mother that she had come from another world than theirs. To them she seemed like a child in an old fairy-tale strangely found on his hearth by some shepherd as he returns from the fields at evening—a little fairy girl swaddled in fine linen, and dowered with a mysterious bag of gold.

Soon she developed delicate spiritual needs to which her simple parents were strangers. From long truancies in the woods she would come home laden with mysterious flowers, and soon she came to ask for books and pictures and music, of which the poor souls that had given her birth had never heard. Finally she had her way, and went to study at a certain fashionable college; and there the brief romance of her life began. There she met a romantic young Frenchman who had read Ronsard to her and written her those picturesque letters I had found in the old mahogany work-box. And after a while the young Frenchman had gone back to France, and the letters had ceased. Month by month went by, and at length one day, as she sat wistful at the window, looking out at the foolish sunlit road, a message came. He was dead. That headstone in the village churchyard tells the rest. She was very young to die—scarcely nineteen years; and the dead who have died young, with all their hopes and dreams still like unfolded buds within their hearts, do not rest so quietly in the grave as those who have gone through the long day from morning until evening and are only too glad to sleep.

Next day I took the little box to a quiet corner of the orchard, and made a little pyre of fragrant boughs—for so I interpreted the wish of that young, unquiet spirit—and the beautiful words are now safe, taken up again into the aerial spaces from which they came.

But since then the birds sing no more little French songs in my old orchard.

He?

Guy de Maupassant

My dear friend, you cannot understand it by any possible means, you say, and I perfectly believe you. You think I am going mad? It may be so, but not for the reasons which you suppose.

Yes, I am going to get married, and I will tell you what has led me to take that step.

My ideas and my convictions have not changed at all. I look upon all legalized cohabitation as utterly stupid, for I am certain that nine husbands out of ten are cuckolds; and they get no more than their deserts for having been idiotic enough to fetter their lives and renounce their freedom in love, the only happy and good thing in the world, and for having clipped the wings of fancy which continually drives us on toward all women. You know what I mean. More than ever I feel that I am incapable of loving one woman alone, because I shall always adore all the others too much. I should like to have a thousand arms, a thousand mouths, and a thousand—*temperaments*, to be able to strain an army of these charming creatures in my embrace at the same moment.

And yet I am going to get married!

I may add that I know very little of the girl who is going to become my wife to-morrow; I have only seen her four or five times. I know that there is nothing unpleasant about her, and that is enough for my purpose. She is small, fair, and stout; so of course the day after to-morrow I shall ardently wish for a tall, dark, thin woman.

She is not rich, and belongs to the middle classes. She is a girl such as you may find by the gross, well adapted for matrimony, without any apparent faults, and with no particularly striking qualities. People say of her: "Mlle. Lajolle is a very nice girl," and to-morrow they will say: "What a very nice woman Madame Raymon is." She belongs, in a word, to that immense number of girls who make very good wives for us till the moment comes when we discover that we happen to prefer all other women to that particular woman we married.

"Well," you will say to me, "what on earth do you get married for?"

I hardly like to tell you the strange and seemingly improbable reason that urged me on to this senseless act; the fact, however, is that I am frightened of being alone!

I don't know how to tell you or to make you understand me, but my state of mind is so wretched that you will pity and despise me.

I do not want to be alone any longer at night; I want to feel that there is some one close to me touching me, a being who can speak and say something, no matter what it be.

I wish to be able to awaken somebody by my side, so that I may be able to ask some sudden question even, if I feel inclined, so that I may hear a human voice, and feel that there is some waking soul close to me, some one whose reason is at work—so that when I hastily light the candle I may see some human face by my side—because—because—I am ashamed to confess it—because I am afraid of being alone.

Oh! you don't understand me yet.

I am not afraid of any danger; if a man were to come into the room I should kill him without trembling. I am not afraid of ghosts, nor do I believe in the supernatural. I am not afraid of dead people, for I believe in the total annihilation of every being that disappears from the face of this earth.

Well,—yes, well, it must be told; I am afraid of myself, afraid of that horrible sensation of incomprehensible fear.

You may laugh, if you like. It is terrible and I cannot get over it. I am afraid of the walls, of the furniture, of the familiar objects, which are animated, as far as I am concerned, by a kind of animal life. Above all, I am afraid of my own dreadful thoughts, of my reason, which seems as if it were about to leave me, driven away by a mysterious and invisible agony.

At first I feel a vague uneasiness in my mind which causes a cold shiver to run all over me. I look round, and of course nothing is to be seen, and I wish there were something there, no matter what, as long as it were something tangible: I am frightened, merely because I cannot understand my own terror.

If I speak, I am afraid of my own voice. If I walk, I am afraid of I know not what, behind the door, behind the curtains, in the cupboard, or under my bed, and yet all the time I know there is nothing anywhere, and I turn round suddenly because I am afraid of what is behind me, although there is nothing there, and I know it.

I get agitated; I feel that my fear increases, and so I shut myself up in my own room, get into bed, and hide under the clothes, and there, cowering down rolled into a ball, I close my eyes in despair and remain thus for an indefinite time, remembering that my candle is alight on the table by my bedside, and that I ought to put it out, and yet—I dare not do it!

It is very terrible, is it not, to be like that?

Formerly I felt nothing of all that; I came home quite comfortably, and went up and down in my rooms without anything disturbing my calmness of mind. Had anyone told me that I should be attacked by a malady—for I can call it nothing else—of most improbable fear, such a stupid and terrible malady as it is, I should have laughed outright. I was certainly never afraid of opening the door in the dark; I used to go to bed slowly without locking it, and never got up in the middle of the night to make sure that everything was firmly closed.

It began last year in a very strange manner, on a damp autumn evening. When my servant had left the room, after I had dined, I asked myself what I was going to do. I walked up and down my room for some time, feeling tired without any reason for it, unable to work, and without enough energy to read. A fine rain was falling, and I felt unhappy, a prey to one of those fits of casual despondency which make us feel inclined to cry, or to talk, no matter to whom, so as to shake off our depressing thoughts.

I felt that I was alone and that my rooms seemed to me to be more empty than they had ever been before. I was surrounded by a sensation of infinite and overwhelming solitude. What was I to do? I sat down, but then a kind of nervous impatience agitated my legs, so that I got up and began to walk about again. I was feverish, for my hands, which I had clasped behind me, as one often does when walking slowly, almost seemed to burn one another. Then suddenly a cold shiver ran down my back, and I thought the damp air might have penetrated into my room, so I lit the fire for the first time that year, and sat down again and looked at the flames. But soon I felt that I could not possibly remain quiet. So I got up again and determined to go out, to pull myself together, and to seek a friend to bear me company.

I could not find anyone, so I went on to the boulevards to try and meet some acquaintance or other there.

I was wretched everywhere, and the wet pavement glistened in the gaslight, while the oppressive mist of the almost impalpable rain lay heavily over the streets and seemed to obscure the light from the lamps.

I went on slowly, saying to myself, "I shall not find a soul to talk to."

I glanced into several *cafés*, from the Madeleine as far as the Faubourg Poissonière, and saw many unhappy-looking individuals sitting at the tables, who did not seem even to have enough energy left to finish the refreshments they had ordered.

For a long time I wandered aimlessly up and down, and about midnight I started off for home; I was very calm and very tired. My *concierge* opened the door at once, which was quite unusual for him, and I thought that another lodger had no doubt just come in.

When I go out I always double-lock the door of my room. Now I found it merely closed, which surprised me; but I supposed that some letters had been brought up for me in the course of the evening.

I went in, and found my fire still burning so that it lighted up the room a little. In the act of taking up a candle, I noticed somebody sitting in my armchair by the fire, warming his feet, with his neck toward me.

I was not in the slightest degree frightened. I thought very naturally that some friend or other had come to see me. No doubt the porter, whom I had told when I went out, had lent him his own key. In a moment I remembered all the circumstances of my return, how the street door had been opened immediately, and that my own door was only latched, and not locked.

I could see nothing of my friend but his head. He had evidently gone to sleep while waiting for me, so I went up to him to rouse him. I saw him quite clearly; his right arm was hanging down and his legs were crossed, while his head, which was somewhat inclined to the left of the armchair, seemed to indicate that he was asleep. "Who can it be?" I asked myself. I could not see clearly, as the room was rather dark, so I put out my hand to touch him on the shoulder, and it came in contact with the back of the chair. There was nobody there; the seat was empty.

I fairly jumped with fright. For a moment I drew back as if some terrible danger had suddenly appeared in my way; then I turned round again, impelled by some imperious desire to look at the armchair again. I remained standing upright, panting with fear, so upset that I could not collect my thoughts, and ready to drop.

But I am naturally a cool man, and soon recovered myself. I thought: "It is a mere hallucination, that is all," and I immediately began to reflect about this phenomenon. Thoughts fly very quickly at such moments.

I had been suffering from a hallucination, that was an incontestable fact. My mind had been perfectly lucid and had acted regularly and logically, so there was nothing the matter with the brain. It was only my eyes that had been deceived; they had had a vision, one of those visions which lead simple folk to believe in miracles. It was a nervous accident to the optical apparatus, nothing more; the eyes were rather overwrought, perhaps.

I lit my candle, and when I stooped down to the fire in so doing, I noticed that I was trembling, and I raised myself up with a jump, as if somebody had touched me from behind.

I was certainly not by any means reassured.

I walked up and down a little, and hummed a tune or two. Then I double-locked my door, and felt rather reassured; now, at any rate, nobody could come in.

I sat down again, and thought over my adventure for a long time; then I went to bed, and put out my light.

For some minutes all went well; I lay quietly on my back. Then an irresistible desire seized me to look round the room, and I turned on to my side.

My fire was nearly out and the few glowing embers threw a faint light on to the floor by the chair, where I fancied I saw the man sitting again.

I quickly struck a match, but I had been mistaken, for there was nothing there; I got up, however, and hid the chair behind my bed, and tried to get to sleep as the room was now dark. But I had not forgotten myself for more than five minutes when in my dream I saw all the scene which I had witnessed as clearly as if it were reality. I woke up with a start, and, having lit the candle, sat up in bed, without venturing even to try and go to sleep again.

Twice, however, sleep overcame me for a few moments in spite of myself, and twice I saw the same thing again, till I fancied I was going mad. When day broke, however, I thought that I was cured, and slept peacefully till noon.

It was all past and over. I had been feverish, had had the nightmare; I don't know what. I had been ill, in a word, but yet I thought that I was a great fool.

I enjoyed myself thoroughly that evening; I went and dined at a restaurant; afterward I went to the theater, and then started home. But as I got near the house I was seized by a strange feeling of uneasiness once more; I was afraid of *seeing* him again. I was not afraid of him, not afraid of his presence, in which I did not believe; but I was afraid of being deceived again; I was afraid of some fresh hallucination, afraid lest fear should take possession of me.

For more than an hour I wandered up and down the pavement; then I thought that I was really too foolish, and returned home. I panted so that I could scarcely get upstairs, and remained standing outside my door for more than ten minutes; then suddenly I took courage and pulled myself together. I inserted my key into the lock, and went in with a candle in my hand. I kicked open my half-open bedroom door, and gave a frightened look toward the fireplace; there was nothing there. A—h!

What a relief and what a delight! What a deliverance: I walked up and down briskly and boldly, but I was not altogether reassured, and kept turning round with a jump; the very shadows in the corners disquieted me.

I slept badly, and was constantly disturbed by imaginary noises, but I did not see *him*; no, that was all over.

Since that time I have been afraid of being alone at night. I feel that the specter is there, close to me, around me; but it has not appeared to me again. And supposing it did, what would it matter, since I do not believe in it and know that it is nothing?

It still worries me, however, because I am constantly thinking of it: *his right arm hanging down and his head inclined to the left like a man who was asleep*—Enough of that, in Heaven's name! I don't want to think about it!

Why, however, am I so persistently possessed with this idea? His feet were close to the fire!

He haunts me; it is very stupid, but so it is. Who and what is HE? I know that he does not exist except in my cowardly imagination, in my fears, and in my agony! There—enough of that!

Yes, it is all very well for me to reason with myself, *to stiffen myself*, so to say; but I cannot remain at home, because I know he is there. I know I shall not see him again; he will not show himself again; that is all over. But he is there all the same in my thoughts. He remains invisible, but that does not prevent his being there. He is behind the doors, in the closed cupboards, in the wardrobe, under the bed, in every dark corner. If I open the door or the cupboard, if I take the candle to look under the bed and throw a light on to the dark places, he is there no longer, but I feel that he is behind me. I turn round, certain that I shall not see him, that I shall never see him again; but he is, none the less, behind me.

It is very stupid, it is dreadful; but what am I to do? I cannot help it.

But if there were two of us in the place, I feel certain that he would not be there any longer, for he is there just because I am alone, simply and solely because I am alone!

The House of the Nightmare

Edward Lucas White

I first caught sight of the house from the brow of the mountain as I cleared the woods and looked across the broad valley several hundred feet below me, to the low sun sinking toward the far blue hills. From that momentary viewpoint I had an exaggerated sense of looking almost vertically down. I seemed to be hanging over the checkerboard of roads and fields, dotted with farm buildings, and felt the familiar deception that I could almost throw a stone upon the house. I barely glimpsed its slate roof.

What caught my eyes was the bit of road in front of it, between the mass of dark-green shade trees about the house and the orchard opposite. Perfectly straight it was, bordered by an even row of trees, through which I made out a cinder side path and a low stone wall.

Conspicuous on the orchard side between two of the flanking trees was a white object, which I took to be a tall stone, a vertical splinter of one of the tilted limestone reefs with which the fields of the region are scarred.

The road itself I saw plain as a box-wood ruler on a green baize table. It gave me a pleasurable anticipation of a chance for a burst of speed. I had been painfully traversing closely forested, semi-mountainous hills. Not a farmhouse had I passed, only wretched cabins by the road, more than twenty miles of which I had found very bad and hindering. Now, when I was not many miles from my expected stopping-place, I looked forward to better going, and to that straight, level bit in particular.

As I sped cautiously down the sharp beginning of the long descent the trees engulfed me again, and I lost sight of the valley. I dipped into a hollow, rose on the crest of the next hill, and again saw the house, nearer, and not so far below.

The tall stone caught my eye with a shock of surprise. Had I not thought it was opposite the house next the orchard? Clearly it was on the left-hand side of the road toward the house. My self-questioning lasted only the moment as I passed the crest. Then the outlook was cut off again; but I found myself gazing ahead, watching for the next chance at the same view.

At the end of the second hill I only saw the bit of road obliquely and could not be sure, but, as at first, the tall stone seemed on the right of the road.

At the top of the third and last hill I looked down the stretch of road under the overarching trees, almost as one would look through a tube. There was a line of whiteness which I took for the tall stone. It was on the right.

I dipped into the last hollow. As I mounted the farther slope I kept my eyes on the top of the road ahead of me. When my line of sight surmounted the rise I marked the tall stone on my right hand among the serried maples. I leaned over, first on one side, then on the other, to inspect my tires, then I threw the lever.

As I flew forward I looked ahead. There was the tall stone—on the left of the road! I was really scared and almost dazed. I meant to stop dead, take a good look at the stone, and make up my mind beyond peradventure whether it was on the right or the left—if not, indeed, in the middle of the road.

In my bewilderment I put on the highest speed. The machine leaped forward; everything I touched went wrong; I steered wildly, slewed to the left, and crashed into a big maple.

When I came to my senses I was flat on my back in the dry ditch. The last rays of the sun sent shafts of golden green light through the maple boughs overhead. My first thought was an odd mixture of appreciation of the beauties of nature and disapproval of my own conduct in touring without a companion—a fad I had regretted more than once. Then my mind cleared and I sat up. I felt myself from the head down. I was not bleeding; no bones were broken; and, while much shaken, I had suffered no serious bruises.

Then I saw the boy. He was standing at the edge of the cinder-path, near the ditch. He was stocky and solidly built; barefoot, with his trousers rolled up to his knees; wore a sort of butternut shirt, open at the throat; and was coatless and hatless. He was tow-headed, with a shock of tousled hair; was much freckled, and had a hideous harelip. He shifted from one foot to the other, twiddled his toes, and said nothing whatever, though he stared at me intently.

I scrambled to my feet and proceeded to survey the wreck. It seemed distressingly complete. It had not blown up, nor even caught fire; but otherwise the ruin appeared hopelessly thorough. Everything I examined seemed worse smashed than the rest. My two hampers alone, by one of those cynical jokes of chance, had escaped—both had pitched clear of the wreckage and were unhurt, not even a bottle broken.

During my investigations the boy's faded eyes followed me continuously, but he uttered no word. When I had convinced myself of my helplessness I straightened up and addressed him:

"How far is it to a blacksmith shop?"

"Eight mile," he answered. He had a distressing case of cleft palate and was scarcely intelligible.

"Can you drive me there?" I inquired.

"Nary team on the place," he replied; "*nary* horse, nary cow."

"How far to the next house?" I continued.

"Six mile," he responded.

I glanced at the sky. The sun had set already. I looked at my watch: it was going seven thirty-six.

"May I sleep in your house to-night?" I asked.

"You can come in if you want to," he said, "and sleep if you can. House all messy; ma's been dead three year, and dad's away. Nothin' to eat but buckwheat flour and rusty bacon."

"I've plenty to eat," I answered, picking up a hamper. "Just take that hamper, will you?"

"You can come in if you're a mind to," he said, "but you got to carry your own stuff." He did not speak gruffly or rudely, but appeared mildly stating an inoffensive fact.

"All right," I said, picking up the other hamper; "lead the way."

The yard in front of the house was dark under a dozen or more immense ailanthus trees. Below them many smaller trees had grown up, and beneath these a dank underwood of tall, rank suckers out of the deep, shaggy, matted grass. What had once been, apparently, a carriage-drive left a narrow, curved track, disused and grass-grown, leading to the house. Even here were some shoots of the ailanthus, and the air was unpleasant with the vile smell of the roots and suckers and the insistent odor of their flowers.

The house was of gray stone, with green shutters faded almost as gray as the stone. Along its front was a veranda, not much raised from the ground, and with no balustrade or railing. On it were several hickory splint rockers. There were eight shuttered windows toward the porch, and midway of them a wide door, with small violet panes on either side of it and a fanlight above.

"Open the door," I said to the boy.

"Open it yourself," he replied, not unpleasantly nor disagreeably, but in such a tone that one could not but take the suggestion as a matter of course.

I put down the two hampers and tried the door. It was latched, but not locked, and opened with a rusty grind of its hinges, on which it sagged crazily, scraping the floor as it turned. The passage smelt moldy and damp. There were several doors on either side; the boy pointed to the first on the right.

"You can have that room," he said.

I opened the door. What with the dusk, the interlacing trees outside, the piazza roof, and the closed shutters, I could make out little.

"Better get a lamp," I said to the boy.

"Nary lamp," he declared cheerfully. "Nary candle. Mostly I get abed before dark."

I returned to the remains of my conveyance. All four of my lamps were merely scrap metal and splintered glass. My lantern was mashed flat. I always, however, carried candles in my valise. This I found split and crushed, but still holding together. I carried it to the porch, opened it, and took out three candles.

Entering the room, where I found the boy standing just where I had left him, I lit the candle. The walls were whitewashed, the floor bare. There was a mildewed, chilly smell, but the bed looked freshly made up and clean, although it felt clammy.

With a few drops of its own grease I stuck the candle on the corner of a mean, rickety little bureau. There was nothing else in the room save two rush-bottomed chairs and a small table. I went out on the porch, brought in my valise, and put it on the bed. I raised the sash of each window and pushed open the shutters. Then I asked the boy, who had not moved or spoken, to show me the way to the kitchen. He led me straight through the hall to the back of the house. The kitchen was large, and had no furniture save some pine chairs, a pine bench, and a pine table.

I stuck two candles on opposite corners of the table. There was no stove or range in the kitchen, only a big hearth, the ashes in which smelt and looked a month old. The wood in the wood-shed was dry enough, but even it had a cellary, stale smell. The ax and hatchet were both rusty and dull, but usable, and I quickly made a big fire. To my amazement, for the mid-June evening was hot and still, the boy, a wry smile on his ugly face, almost leaned over the flame, hands and arms spread out, and fairly roasted himself.

"Are you cold?" I inquired.

"I'm allus cold," he replied, hugging the fire closer than ever, till I thought he must scorch.

I left him toasting himself while I went in search of water. I discovered the pump, which was in working order and not dry on the valves; but I had a furious struggle to fill the two leaky pails I had found. When I had put water to boil I fetched my hampers from the porch.

I brushed the table and set out my meal—cold fowl, cold ham, white and brown bread, olives, jam, and cake. When the can of soup was hot and the coffee made I drew up two chairs to the table and invited the boy to join me.

"I ain't hungry," he said; "I've had supper."

He was a new sort of boy to me; all the boys I knew were hearty eaters and always ready. I had felt hungry myself, but somehow when I came to eat I had little appetite and hardly relished the food. I soon made an end of my meal, covered the fire, blew out the candles, and returned to the porch, where I dropped into one of the hickory rockers to smoke. The boy followed me silently and seated himself on the porch floor, leaning against a pillar, his feet on the grass outside.

"What do you do," I asked, "when your father is away?"

"Just loaf 'round," he said. "Just fool 'round."

"How far off are your nearest neighbors?" I asked.

"Don't no neighbors never come here," he stated. "Say they're afeared of the ghosts."

I was not at all startled; the place had all those aspects which lead to a house being called haunted. I was struck by his odd matter-of-fact way of speaking—it was as if he had said they were afraid of a cross dog.

"Do you ever see any ghosts around here?" I continued.

"Never see 'em," he answered, as if I had mentioned tramps or partridges. "Never hear 'em. Sort o' feel 'em 'round sometimes."

"Are you afraid of them?" I asked.

"Nope," he declared. "I ain't skeered o' ghosts; I'm skeered o' nightmares. Ever have nightmares?"

"Very seldom," I replied.

"I do," he returned. "Allus have the same nightmare—big sow, big as a steer, trying to eat me up. Wake up so skeered I could run to never. Nowheres to run to. Go to sleep, and have it again. Wake up worse skeered than ever. Dad says it's buckwheat cakes in summer."

"You must have teased a sow some time," I said.

"Yep," he answered. "Teased a big sow wunst, holding up one of her pigs by the hind leg. Teased her too long. Fell in the pen and got bit up some. Wisht I hadn't 'a' teased her. Have that nightmare three times a week sometimes. Worse 'n being burnt out. Worse 'n ghosts. Say, I sorter feel ghosts around now."

He was not trying to frighten me. He was as simply stating an opinion as if he had spoken of bats or mosquitoes. I made no reply, and found myself listening involuntarily. My pipe went out. I did not really want another, but felt disinclined for bed as yet, and was comfortable where I was, while the smell of the ailanthus blossoms was very disagreeable. I filled my pipe again, lit it, and then, as I puffed, somehow dozed off for a moment.

I awoke with a sensation of some light fabric trailed across my face. The boy's position was unchanged.

"Did you do that?" I asked sharply.

"Ain't done nary thing," he rejoined. "What was it?"

"It was like a piece of mosquito-netting brushed over my face."

"That ain't netting," he asserted; "that's a veil. That's one of the ghosts. Some blow on you; some touch you with their long, cold fingers. That one with the veil she drags acrost your face—well, mostly I think it's ma."

He spoke with the unassailable conviction of the child in "We Are Seven." I found no words to reply, and rose to go to bed.

"Good night," I said.

"Good night," he echoed. "I'll set out here a spell yet."

I lit a match, found the candle I had stuck on the corner of the shabby little bureau, and undressed. The bed had a comfortable husk mattress, and I was soon asleep.

I had the sensation of having slept some time when I had a nightmare—the very nightmare the boy had described. A huge sow, big as a dray horse, was reared up on her forelegs over the foot-board of the bed, trying to scramble over to me. She grunted and puffed, and I felt I was the food she craved. I knew in the dream that it was only a dream, and strove to wake up. Then the gigantic dream-beast floundered over the foot-board, fell across my shins, and I awoke.

I was in darkness as absolute as if I were sealed in a jet vault, yet the shudder of the nightmare instantly subsided, my nerves quieted; I realized where I was, and felt not the least panic. I turned over and was asleep again almost at once. Then I had a real nightmare, not recognizable as a dream, but appallingly real—an unutterable agony of reasonless horror.

There was a Thing in the room; not a sow, nor any other namable creature, but a Thing. It was as big as an elephant, filled the room to the ceiling, was shaped like a wild boar, seated on its haunches, with its forelegs braced stiffly in front of it. It had a hot, slobbering, red mouth, full of big tusks, and its jaws worked hungrily. It shuffled and hunched itself forward, inch by inch, till its vast forelegs straddled the bed.

The bed crushed up like wet blotting-paper, and I felt the weight of the Thing on my feet, on my legs, on my body, on my chest. It was hungry, and I was what it was hungry for, and it meant to begin on my face. Its dripping mouth was nearer and nearer.

Then the dream-helplessness that made me unable to call or move suddenly gave way, and I yelled and awoke. This time my terror was positive and not to be shaken off.

It was near dawn: I could descry dimly the cracked, dirty window-panes. I got up, lit the stump of my candle and two fresh ones, dressed hastily, strapped my ruined valise, and put it on the porch against the wall near the door. Then I called the boy. I realized quite suddenly that I had not told him my name or asked his.

I shouted "Hello!" a few times, but won no answer. I had had enough of that house. I was still permeated with the panic of the nightmare. I desisted from shouting, made no search, but with two candles went out to the kitchen. I took a swallow of cold coffee and munched a biscuit as I hustled my belongings into my hampers. Then, leaving a silver dollar on the table, I carried the hampers out on the porch and dumped them by my valise.

It was now light enough to see to walk, and I went out to the road. Already the night-dew had rusted much of the wreck, making it look more hopeless than before. It was, however, entirely undisturbed. There was not so much as a wheel-track or a hoofprint on the road. The tall, white stone, uncertainty about which had caused my disaster, stood like a sentinel opposite where I had upset.

I set out to find that blacksmith shop. Before I had gone far the sun rose clear from the horizon, and almost at once scorching. As I footed it along I grew very much heated, and it seemed more like ten miles than six before I reached the first house. It was a new frame house, neatly painted and close to the road, with a whitewashed fence along its garden front.

I was about to open the gate when a big black dog with a curly tail bounded out of the bushes. He did not bark, but stood inside the gate wagging his tail and regarding me with a friendly eye; yet I hesitated with my hand on the latch, and considered. The dog might not be as friendly as he looked, and the sight of him made me realize that except for the boy I had seen no creature about the house where I had spent the night; no dog or cat; not even a toad or bird. While I was ruminating upon this a man came from behind the house.

"Will your dog bite?" I asked.

"Naw," he answered; "he don't bite. Come in."

I told him I had had an accident to my automobile, and asked if he could drive me to the blacksmith shop and back to my wreckage.

"Cert," he said. "Happy to help you. I'll hitch up foreshortly. Where'd you smash?"

"In front of the gray house about six miles back," I answered.

"That big stone-built house?" he queried.

"The same," I assented.

"Did you go a-past here?" he inquired astonished. "I didn't hear ye."

"No," I said; "I came from the other direction."

"Why," he meditated, "you must 'a' smashed 'bout sunup. Did you come over them mountains in the dark?"

"No," I replied; "I came over them yesterday evening. I smashed up about sunset."

"Sundown!" he exclaimed. "Where in thunder've ye been all night?"

"I slept in the house where I broke down."

"In that there big stone-built house in the trees?" he demanded.

"Yes," I agreed.

"Why," he quavered excitedly, "that there house is haunted! They say if you have to drive past it after dark, you can't tell which side of the road the big white stone is on."

"I couldn't tell even before sunset," I said.

"There!" he exclaimed. "Look at that, now! And you slep' in that house! Did you sleep, honest?"

"I slept pretty well," I said. "Except for a nightmare, I slept all night."

"Well," he commented, "I wouldn't go in that there house for a farm, nor sleep in it for my salvation. And you slep'! How in thunder did you get in?"

"The boy took me in," I said.

"What sort of a boy?" he queried, his eyes fixed on me with a queer, countrified look of absorbed interest.

"A thick-set, freckle-faced boy with a harelip," I said.

"Talk like his mouth was full of mush?" he demanded.

"Yes," I said; "bad case of cleft palate."

"Well!" he exclaimed. "I never did believe in ghosts, and I never did half believe that house was haunted, but I know it now. And you slep'!"

"I didn't see any ghosts," I retorted irritably.

"You seen a ghost for sure," he rejoined solemnly. "That there harelip boy's been dead six months."

How He Left the Hotel

Louisa Baldwin

I used to work the passenger-lift in the Empire Hotel, that big block of building in lines of red and white brick like streaky bacon, that stands at the corner of —— Street. I'd served my time in the army, and got my discharge with good-conduct stripes; and how I got the job was in this way. The hotel was a big company affair with a managing committee of retired officers and such-like; gentlemen with a bit o' money in the concern, and nothing to do but fidget about it, and my late Colonel was one of 'em. He was as good-tempered a man as ever stepped when his will wasn't crossed, and when I asked him for a job, "Mole," says he, "you're the very man to work the lift at our big hotel. Soldiers are civil and businesslike, and the public like 'em only second best to sailors. We've had to give our last man the sack, and you can take his place."

I liked my work well enough and my pay, and kept my place a year, and I should have been there still if it hadn't been for a circumstance— But don't let me anticipate. Ours was a hydraulic lift. None o' them rickety things swung up like a poll parrot's cage in a well staircase that I shouldn't care to trust my neck to. It ran as smooth as oil, a child might have worked it, and safe as standing on the ground. Instead of being stuck full of advertisements like an omnibus, we'd mirrors in it, and the ladies would look at themselves, and pat their hair, and set their mouths when I was taking 'em downstairs dressed of an evening. It was a little sitting-room, with red velvet cushions to sit down on, and you'd nothing to do but get into it, and it 'ud float you up or float you down light as a bird.

All the visitors used the lift one time or another, going up or coming down. Some of them was French, and they called the lift the "*assenser*," and good enough for them in their language, no doubt; but why the Americans, that can speak English when they choose, and are always finding out ways of doing things quicker than other folks, should waste time and breath calling a lift an elevator, I can't make out.

I was in charge of the lift from noon till midnight. By that time the theatre and dining-out folks had come in, and anyone returning late walked upstairs, for my day's work was done. One of the porters worked the lift till I come on duty in the morning;

but before twelve there was nothing particular going on, and not much till after two o'clock. Then it was pretty hot work with visitors going up and down constant, and the electric bell ringing you from one floor to another like a house on fire. Then came a quiet spell while dinner was on, and I'd sit down comfortable in the lift and read my paper, only I mightn't smoke. But nobody else might neither, and I had to ask furren gentlemen to please not smoke in it, it was against the rule. I hadn't so often to tell English gentlemen, they're not like furreners that seem as if their cigars was glued to their lips.

I always noticed faces as folks got into the lift, for I've sharp sight and a good memory, and none of the visitors needed to tell me twice where to take them. I knew them and I knew their floor as well as they did themselves.

It was in November that Colonel Saxby came to the Empire Hotel. I noticed him particularly, because you could see at once that he was a soldier. He was a tall, thin man about fifty, with a hawk nose, keen eyes, and a grey moustache, and walked stiff from a gun-shot wound in the knee. But what I noticed most was the scar of a sabre-cut across the right side of the face. As he got into the lift to go to his room on the fourth floor, I thought what a difference there is among officers. Colonel Saxby put me in mind of a telegraph-post for height and thinness; and my old Colonel was like a barrel in uniform, but a brave soldier and a gentleman all the same. Colonel Saxby's room was number 210, just opposite the glass door leading to the lift, and every time I stopped on the fourth floor number 210 stared me in the face. The Colonel used to go up in the lift every day regular, though he never came down in it till— But I'm coming to that presently. Sometimes, when he was alone in the lift, he'd speak to me. He asked me in what regiment I'd served, and said he knew the officers in it. But I can't say he was comfortable to talk to. There was something stand-off about him, and he always seemed deep in his own thoughts. He never sat down in the lift. Whether it was empty or full he stood bolt upright under the lamp, where the light fell on his pale face and scarred cheek.

One day in February I didn't take the Colonel up in the lift, and as he was regular as clockwork I noticed it, but I supposed he'd gone away for a few days, and I thought no more about it. Whenever I stopped on the fourth floor the door of 210 was shut, and as he often left it open, I made sure the Colonel was away. At the end of a week I heard a chambermaid say that Colonel Saxby was ill; so, thinks I, that's why he hasn't been in the lift lately.

It was a Tuesday night, and I'd had an uncommonly busy time of it. It was one stream of traffic up and down, and so it went on the whole evening. It was on the strike of midnight, and I was about to put out the light in the lift, lock the door, and leave the key in the office for the man in the morning, when the electric bell rang out sharp; I looked at the dial, and saw I was wanted on the fourth floor. It struck twelve as I stepped into the lift. As I passed the second and third floors, I wondered who it was that had rung so late, and thought it must be a stranger that didn't know the rule of the house. But when I stopped at the fourth floor and flung open the door of the lift, Colonel Saxby was standing there wrapped in a military cloak. The door of his room was shut behind him, for I read the number on it. I thought he was ill in his bed, and ill enough he looked, but he had his hat on, and what could a man that had been in bed ten days want with going out on a winter midnight? I don't think he saw me, but when I'd set the lift in motion, I looked at him standing under the lamp, with the shadow of his hat hiding his eyes, and the light full on the lower part of his face, that was deadly pale, the scar on his cheek showing still paler.

"Glad to see you're better, sir," said I; but he said nothing, and I didn't like to look at him again. He stood like a statue with his cloak about him, and I was downright glad when I opened the door of the lift for him to step out in the hall. I saluted as he got out, and he went past me towards the front door.

"The Colonel wants to go out," I said to the porter who stood staring, and he opened the door and Colonel Saxby walked out into the snow.

"That's a queer go!" he said.

"It is," said I. "I don't like the Colonel's looks, he doesn't seem himself at all. He's ill enough to be in his bed, and there he is gone out on a night like this."

"Anyhow he's got a famous cloak to keep him warm. I say, supposing he's gone to a fancy ball, and got that cloak on to hide his dress," said the porter, laughing uneasily, for we both felt queerer than we cared to say, and as we spoke there came a loud ring at the door-bell.

"No more passengers for me!" I said; and I was really putting the light out this time, when Joe opened the door, and two gentlemen entered that I knew at a glance were doctors. One was tall, and the other was short and stout, and they both came to the lift.

"Sorry, gentlemen, but it's against the rule for the lift to go up after midnight."

"Nonsense!" said the stout gentleman; "it's only just past twelve, and a matter of life and death. Take us up at once to the fourth floor," and they were in the lift like a shot; so up we went, and when I opened the door, they walked straight to number 210. A nurse came out to meet them, and the stout doctor said: "No change for the worse, I hope?"

And I heard her reply: "The patient died five minutes ago, sir."

Though I'd no business to speak, that was more than I could stand. I followed the doctors to the door and said: "There's some mistake here, gentlemen, I took the Colonel down in the lift since the clock struck twelve, and he went out."

The stout doctor said sharply: "A case of mistaken identity. It was someone else you took for the Colonel."

"Begging your pardon, gentlemen, it was the Colonel himself, and the night porter that opened the front door for him knew him as well as me. He was dressed for a night like this, with his military cloak wrapped round him."

"Step in and see for yourself," said the nurse.

I followed the doctor into the room, and there lay Colonel Saxby looking just as I had seen him a few minutes before. There he lay, dead as his forefathers, and the great cloak spread over the bed to keep him warm that would feel heat and cold no more. I never slept that night. I sat up with Joe, expecting every minute to hear the Colonel ring the front door bell. Next day, every time the bell for the lift rang sharp and sudden, the sweat broke out on me and I shook again. I felt as bad as I did the first time I was in action. Me and Joe told the manager all about it, and he said we'd been dreaming; but, said he, "Mind you don't talk about it, or the house'll be empty in a week."

The Colonel's coffin was smuggled into the house the next night. Me and the manager and the undertaker's men took it up in the lift, and it lay right across it, and not an inch to spare. They carried it into number 210, and while I waited for them to come out again, a queer feeling came over me. Then the door opened softly, and four men carried out the long coffin straight across the passage, and set it down with its foot towards the door of the lift, and the manager looked round for me.

"I can't do it, sir," I said. "I can't take the Colonel down *again*. I took him down at midnight yesterday, and that was enough for me."

"Push it in," said the manager, speaking short and sharp, and they ran the coffin into the lift without a sound. The manager got in last, and before he closed the door he said, "Mole, you've worked this lift for the last time, it strikes me." And I had, for I wouldn't have stayed on at the Empire Hotel after what had happened, not if they'd doubled my wages; and me and the night porter left together.

"If You See Her Face"

B. M. Croker

I heard a voice across the press,
Of one who called in vain.
–Barrack Room Ballads

Daniel Gregson, Esq., B. S. C., political agent to the Rajah of Oonomore (a child of seven years of age), and Percy Goring, his junior assistant, were travelling from their own state to attend the great Delhi durbar. Mr. Gregson was a civilian of twenty-five years' standing, short of neck, short of stature, and short of temper. His red face, pale prominent eyes, and fierce bushy brows had gained for him the nickname of "The Prawn"; but he was also known as a marvellously clever financier, ambitious, shrewd, and prompt in action; and by those who were under him, he was less loved than feared. Young Goring was just twenty-six, and much more eager to discuss good shooting, or a good dance, than the assessment of land, the opium trade, or even acting allowances!

The pair journeyed with due ceremony on the native state line, and in the little Rajah's own gilt and royal carriage. *He* was laid up in the palace with chicken-pock, and had wept sorely because he had been unable to accompany his guide, philosopher, and friend to the grand "Tamasha," to wear his new velvet coat, and all his jewels, and to hear the guns, that would thunder in his honour. Child as he was, he was already keenly sensitive respecting his salute!

Meanwhile the agent and his subordinate got on capitally without him, travelling at the leisurely rate of ten miles an hour, that fine November afternoon, surrounded with tiffin-baskets, cigarettes, ice-boxes, and other luxurious accompaniments. About four o'clock the train came to a sudden standstill—there was no station to account for this, merely a country road, a white gate, and a mud hut. The halt resolved itself into a full step; Mr. Gregson thrust his red face out of the window, and angrily inquired the reason of the delay.

"Beg your pardon, sir," said the Eurasian guard, "there has been a break on the linebridge gone—and we can't get forward nohow."

Mr. Gregson glanced out on the prospect—the dusty cactus hedge, the white telegraph posts, the expanse of brownish grass, black goats, and jungle.

"Any village, any dâk bungalow?" demanded the political agent, who might have known better than to ask.

"I'm afraid not, your honour. If your honour will wait here, we will send a messenger to the next station on foot, and tell them to telegraph for another train from the junction. This will arrive at the other side of the break, and take you on about twelve o'clock to-morrow."

"And meanwhile we are to sit here!" cried Mr. Gregson, indignantly. "A pretty state of affairs! I'll send a memo to the railway engineer that will astonish him," he said, turning to Goring. "It's four now, and we shall be here till twelve o'clock to-morrow, if we don't mind. We shall be late for the durbar, and I shall have to wire, 'unavoidably absent.'"

"I wonder if there is any sport to be had?" said Goring, descending from the carriage, and stretching his long legs. "Any shooting, any black buck?" looking at the guard interrogatively.

"Ah, that reminds me!" exclaimed Mr. Gregson. "The Rajah has a hunting box somewhere in these parts—Kori; we can go there for the night."

"Yes, your honour," assented a listener, with profound respect; "but it is four koss from here—a 'Kutcha' road—and a very poor part of the state."

"I vote we stop here," said Goring. "We can shoot a bit, and come back and dine, and sleep in the train. We shall be all right and jolly; twice as comfortable as in some tumble-down old summer-house."

"I shall go to Kori, at any rate," rejoined his superior officer, who resented opposition. "The place is kept up, and I've never seen it. This will be a capital opportunity to inspect it."

"But it's four koss away; and how are we to get our baggage, and bedding, and grub over?"

"Coolies," was the laconic rejoinder. "Get them ready to start at once"—to his head servant, with an imperious wave of his hand.

"There is no way of transport for your majesty," said his obsequious bearer with a deep salaam. "No ponies, not even an ekka—unless the 'Protector of the Poor' would stoop to a country cart?" (Which same is a long rude open basket, between two round wooden wheels, and drawn by a pair of bullocks.)

"I really think it is hardly worth while to move," urged Goring, as he cast a greedy eye in the direction of a promising snipe jheel. "It will be an awful fag, and you know you hate walking!"

"You can please yourself, and stay here," said Mr. Gregson, with immense dignity, who, if he hated walking, liked his own way.

As the whole suite (not to mention the commissariat) were bound to accompany him, Goring was compelled to submit; he dared not run counter to his arbitrary companion, who, rejecting with scorn the lowly vehicle that had been suggested, set out for Kori on foot, whither a long string of coolies had already preceded him. The sandy country road wound over a barren, melancholy-looking tract, diversified with scanty pasture and marshy patches (or jheels), pools of water, tall reeds, and brown grasses. It was dotted with droves of lean cattle, paddy birds, milk-white herons, and cranes—especially the tall sirius family, who danced to one another in a stately, not to say solemn, fashion.

Truly a bleak, desolate-looking region, and, save one or two miserable huts and some thorn bushes, there was no sign of tree or human habitation. At last they came in sight of a wretched village—the once prosperous hanger-on of the now deserted hunting palace—that showed its delicate stone pinnacles behind a high wall; apparently it stood in an enclosure of vast extent, an enclosure that must have cost lakhs of rupees. Two sahibs were naturally an extraordinary sight in this out-of-the-way district; the fame and name of Mr. Gregson, a Burra-Burra sahib, had been spread before him by the coolies, therefore beggars and petitioners swarmed eagerly round this great and all-powerful personage.

Mr. Gregson liked to feel his own importance at a durbar, or an official dinner, but it was quite another matter to have it thrust upon him by a gang of clamouring paupers—the maimed, the halt, the blind—crying out against taxation, imploring alms, and mercy. He was a hard man, with a quick, impatient temper. An aged blind beldame got in his way, and he struck her savagely with his stick. She shrank back with a sharp cry, and Goring, who was ever known as "a sahib with a soft heart," spoke to her and gave her a rupee—a real rupee; it was years since she had felt one!

"Although she is blind, sahib, beware of her," said an officious youth, with his hair in a topknot. " She has the evil eye! "

"Peace, dog!" she screamed; then to Goring, "I am a lone old woman; my kindred are dead—I have lived too long. I remember the former days—rich days; but bad days. Sahib, if you would be wise, go not to the palace Khana."

Goring was moving on when the hag hastily clutched him by the sleeve, and added in a rasping whisper—

"If you see her face—you die!"

"She is mad," he said to himself, as he hastened to join Mr. Gregson, who had arrived at the great iron-studded gates in a state of crimson fury.

"You say we have land—true!" shouted a haggard, wild-eyed ryot; "but what is land without crops? What is a remission of five per cent to wretches like us? It is but as a carraway seed in a camel's mouth! The wild beasts take our cattle and destroy our grain, and yet we must work and pay you, and starve! Would that the Rajah was a man grown! Would that *you* were dead!"

Mr. Gregson' hurried inside, and banged the great gate violently in the face of the importunate crowd.

"It is a very poor district, and much too heavily assessed," said Goring to himself. "There is not even a pony in the place. The very Bunnia is in rags; the deer eat the crops, such as they are, since the deer are preserved, and there is no one now to shoot them. It is abominable!"

The palace was a pretty, light stone building, two stories in height, with a tower at either end, and a double verandah all the way round. In front of it a large space was paved with blocks of white marble, which ran the whole length of the building, and it was surrounded by the most exquisite gardens, kept up in perfect order—doubtless by the taxes wrung from the wretched creatures outside its gates—a garden that was never entered by its proprietor or enjoyed by any one from year's end to year's end, save the mallee's children and the monkeys. The monkeys ate the fruit, the roses and lilies bloomed unseen, the fountains dripped unheeded; it was a paradise for the doves and squirrels, like a garden in a fairy tale.

The chokedar and head mallee (*he* was a rich man) received their great guest with every expression of humble delight. Dinner was prepared with much bustle in the hall of audience, whilst Mr. Gregson and his junior explored. There were long shady walks paved with white marble, immense bushes of heliotrope and myrtle, delicate palms, fine mango trees, peach trees, and orange trees. It was truly an oasis in the desert when one contrasted it with the bare, desolate, barren country that lay outside its walls.

"I shall bring the little chap here," said Mr. Gregson, pompously. "We will have a camp here at Christmas." And then he strolled back to the palace, and made an excellent dinner of roast turkey, and asparagus, and champagne.

After this repast he got out his despatch-box and his cigarette-case, and set about writing an official, whilst Goring took a chair, and adjourned to the marble pavement outside the palace.

It was an exquisite night; a low moon was peering over the wall—the air was heavy with the scent of syringa and orange blossoms; there was not a sound, not a voice to be heard, not a soul in sight, save Mr. Gregson, who, illuminated by two wax candles, bent eagerly over his pen, as he sat in the open hall of audience.

Goring, as he smoked, thought of many things; of the half-famished villagers; of the splendid shooting that was going to waste; of the grand bag he could make, and would make, at Christmas. Then he began sleepily to recall some stories—half-told stories—about this very place; tales of hideous atrocities, and crimes that had been done here, in the days of the Tiger Rajah, the present ruler's grandfather. He was gradually dozing off, when he was aroused by the sounds of distant tom-toms, playing with extravagant spirit. The drumming came slowly nearer and nearer; it actually seemed to be in the garden—louder and louder—with a whispered murmuring and low applause, and as it were the footsteps of a great multitude. But there was nothing whatever to be seen, and it was as light as day. He moved uneasily in his chair, and gazed behind him; no! nothing to be seen but his senior steadily covering sheets of foolscap. He turned his head, and was aware of an unexpected sight—as startling as it was uncanny! Two twinkling little brown feet, dancing before him on the marble pavement! exquisite feet, that seemed scarcely to touch the ground, and that kept perfect time to the inspiriting sounds of the tom-toms; they were decked with massive golden anklets, which tinkled as they moved, and above them waved a few inches of the heavy yellow gold-embroidered skirt of the dancing-girl. No more was visible. Round and round the fairy feet flitted, in a very poetry of motion; faster and faster played the tom-toms. Such dancing, such nimble feet, it had never been young Goring's lot to behold! Yes—but where was the rest of the body?

As he gazed in half-stupefied amazement, he suddenly recalled the old hag's warning, with an unpleasant thrill——

"If you see her face—you *die*! "

At this instant there was a scraping sound, of the pushing back of a chair, of slow footsteps on the marble, of a loud cry, and a heavy fall.

Goring jumped up, and beheld Mr. Gregson lying prone on his face. He rushed to his assistance, and raised him with considerable difiiculty. His eyes were fixed with an expression of unutterable horror. He gave one or two shuddering gasps, his head drooped forward on his breast, and he expired.

Goring looked round apprehensively. The feet had disappeared; the tom-toms had ceased.

He shouted for help, and immediately a vast crowd of dismayed retainers assembled around him, and Babel ensued.

"The Burra sahib dead! Well, well, it was ever an evil place. Ah, bah! Ah, bah! It was the nautch-girl, without doubt."

They further informed Goring that the old Rajah had once tortured a dancing-girl on that very spot, and inhumanly disfigured her face. More than one had seen her since, and perished thus.

That morning, at sunrise, the dead body of Mr. Gregson was placed in a native cart, similar to the one he had so scornfully rejected, and taken by slow stages to the nearest station and back to the city, accompanied by Goring.

The doctors, European and native, declared with one consent that Mr. Gregson had died in a fit—an apoplectic seizure.

Goring—wise man—said nothing.

In Kropfsberg Keep

Ralph Adams Cram

To the traveller from Innsbrück to Munich, up the lovely valley of the silver Inn, many castles appear, one after another, each on its beetling cliff or gentle hill—appear and disappear, melting into the dark fir trees that grow so thickly on every side—Laneck, Lichtwer, Ratholtz, Tratzberg, Matzen, Kropfsberg, gathering close around the entrance to the dark and wonderful Zillerthal.

But to us—Tom Rendel and myself—there are two castles only: not the gorgeous and princely Ambras, nor the noble old Tratzberg, with its crowded treasures of solemn and splendid mediævalism; but little Matzen, where eager hospitality forms the new life of a never-dead chivalry, and Kropfsberg, ruined, tottering, blasted by fire and smitten with grievous years—a dead thing, and haunted—full of strange legends, and eloquent of mystery and tragedy.

We were visiting the von C——s at Matzen, and gaining our first wondering knowledge of the courtly, cordial castle life in the Tyrol—of the gentle and delicate hospitality of noble Austrians. Brixleg had ceased to be but a mark on a map, and had become a place of rest and delight, a home for homeless wanderers on the face of Europe, while Schloss Matzen was a synonym for all that was gracious and kindly and beautiful in life. The days moved on in a golden round of riding and driving and shooting: down to Landl and Thiersee for chamois, across the river to the magic Achensee, up the Zillerthal, across the Schmerner Joch, even to the railway station at Steinach. And in the evenings after the late dinners in the upper hall where the sleepy hounds leaned against our chairs looking at us with suppliant eyes, in the evenings when the fire was dying away in the hooded fireplace in the library, stories. Stories, and legends, and fairy tales, while the stiff old portraits changed countenance constantly under the flickering firelight, and the sound of the drifting Inn came softly across the meadows far below.

If ever I tell the Story of Schloss Matzen, then will be the time to paint the too inadequate picture of this fair oasis in the desert of travel and tourists and hotels; but just now it is Kropfsberg the Silent that is of greater importance, for it was only in Matzen that the story was told by Fräulein E——, the gold-haired niece of Frau von C——, one hot evening in July, when we were sitting in the great west window of the drawing-room after a long ride up the Stallenthal. All the windows were open to catch the faint wind, and we had sat for a long time watching the Otzethaler Alps turn rose-color over distant Innsbrück, then deepen to violet as the sun went down and the white mists rose slowly until Lichtwer and Laneck and Kropfsberg rose like craggy islands in a silver sea.

And this is the story as Fräulein E—— told it to us—the Story of Kropfsberg Keep.

A great many years ago, soon after my grandfather died, and Matzen came to us, when I was a little girl, and so young that I remember nothing of the affair except as something dreadful that frightened me very much, two young men who had studied painting with my grandfather came down to Brixleg from Munich, partly to paint, and partly to amuse themselves—"ghost-hunting" as they said, for they were very sensible young men and prided themselves on it, laughing at all kinds of "superstition," and particularly at that form which believed in ghosts and feared them. They had never seen a real ghost, you know, and they belonged to a certain set of people who believed nothing they had not seen themselves—which always seemed to me *very* conceited. Well, they knew that we had lots of beautiful castles here in the "lower valley," and they assumed, and rightly, that every castle has at least *one* ghost story connected with it, so they chose this as their hunting ground, only the game they sought was ghosts, not chamois. Their plan was to visit every place that was supposed to be haunted, and to meet every reputed ghost, and prove that it really was no ghost at all.

There was a little inn down in the village then, kept by an old man named Peter Rosskopf, and the two young men made this their headquarters. The very first night they began to draw from the old innkeeper all that he knew of legends and ghost stories connected with Brixleg and its castles, and as he was a most garrulous old gentleman he filled them with the wildest delight by his stories of the ghosts of the castles about the mouth of the Zillerthal. Of course the old man believed every word he said, and you can imagine his horror and amazement when, after telling his guests the particularly blood-curdling story of Kropfsberg and its haunted keep, the elder of the two boys, whose surname I have forgotten, but whose Christian name was Rupert, calmly said, "Your story is most satisfactory: we will sleep in Kropfsberg Keep to-morrow night, and you must provide us with all that we may need to make ourselves comfortable."

The old man nearly fell into the fire. "What for a blockhead are you?" he cried, with big eyes. "The keep is haunted by Count Albert's ghost, I tell you!"

"That is why we are going there to-morrow night; we wish to make the acquaintance of Count Albert."

"But there was a man stayed there once, and in the morning he was dead."

"Very silly of him; there are two of us, and we carry revolvers."

"But it's a *ghost*, I tell you," almost screamed the innkeeper; "are ghosts afraid of firearms?"

"Whether they are or not, we are *not* afraid of *them*."

Here the younger boy broke in—he was named Otto von Kleist. I remember the name, for I had a music teacher once by that name. He abused the poor old man shamefully; told him that they were going to spend the night in Kropfsberg in spite of Count Albert and Peter Rosskopf, and that he might as well make the most of it and earn his money with cheerfulness.

In a word, they finally bullied the old fellow into submission, and when the morning came he set about preparing for the suicide, as he considered it, with sighs and mutterings and ominous shakings of the head.

You know the condition of the castle now—nothing but scorched walls and crumbling piles of fallen masonry. Well, at the time I tell you of, the keep was still partially preserved. It was finally burned out only a few years ago by some wicked boys who came over from Jenbach to have a good time. But when the ghost hunters came, though the two lower floors had fallen into the crypt, the third floor remained. The peasants said it *could* not fall, but that it would stay until the Day of Judgment, because it was in the room above that the wicked Count Albert sat watching the flames destroy the great castle and his imprisoned guests, and where he finally hung himself in a suit of armor that had belonged to his mediæval ancestor, the first Count Kropfsberg.

No one dared touch him, and so he hung there for twelve years, and all the time venturesome boys and daring men used to creep up the turret steps and stare awfully through the chinks in the door at that ghostly mass of steel that held within itself the body of a murderer and suicide, slowly returning to the dust from which it was made. Finally it disappeared, none knew whither, and for another dozen years the room stood empty but for the old furniture and the rotting hangings.

So, when the two men climbed the stairway to the haunted room, they found a very different state of things from what exists now. The room was absolutely as it was left the night Count Albert burned the castle, except that all trace of the suspended suit of armor and its ghastly contents had vanished.

No one had dared to cross the threshold, and I suppose that for forty years no living thing had entered that dreadful room.

On one side stood a vast canopied bed of black wood, the damask hangings of which were covered with mould and mildew. All the clothing of the bed was in perfect order, and on it lay a book, open, and face downward. The only other furniture in the room consisted of several old chairs, a carved oak chest, and a big inlaid table covered with books and papers, and on one corner two or three bottles with dark solid sediment at the bottom, and a glass, also dark with the dregs of wine that had been poured out almost half a century before. The tapestry on the walls was green with mould, but hardly torn or otherwise defaced, for although the heavy dust of forty years lay on everything the room had been preserved from further harm. No spider web was to be seen, no trace of nibbling mice, not even a dead moth or fly on the sills of the diamond-paned windows; life seemed to have shunned the room utterly and finally.

The men looked at the room curiously, and, I am sure, not without some feelings of awe and unacknowledged fear; but, whatever they may have felt of instinctive shrinking, they said nothing, and quickly set to work to make the room passably inhabitable. They decided to touch nothing that had not absolutely to be changed, and therefore they made for themselves a bed in one corner with the mattress and linen from the inn. In the great fireplace they piled a lot of wood on the caked ashes of a fire dead for forty years, turned the old chest into a table, and laid out on it all their arrangements for the evening's amusement: food, two or three bottles of wine, pipes and tobacco, and the chess-board that was their inseparable travelling companion.

All this they did themselves: the innkeeper would not even come within the walls of the outer court; he insisted that he had washed his hands of the whole affair, the silly dunderheads might go to their death their own way. *He* would not aid and abet them. One of the stable boys brought the basket of food and the wood and the bed up the winding stone stairs, to be sure, but neither money nor prayers nor threats would bring him within the walls of the accursed place, and he stared fearfully at the harebrained boys as they worked around the dead old room preparing for the night that was coming so fast.

At length everything was in readiness, and after a final visit to the inn for dinner Rupert and Otto started at sunset for the Keep. Half the village went with them, for Peter Rosskopf had babbled the whole story to an open-mouthed crowd of wondering men and women, and as to an execution the awe-struck crowd followed the two boys dumbly, curious to see if they surely would put their plan into execution. But none went farther than the outer doorway of the stairs, for it was already growing twilight. In absolute silence they watched the two foolhardy youths with their lives in their hands enter the terrible Keep, standing like a tower in the midst of the piles of stones that had once formed walls joining it with the mass of the castle beyond. When a moment later a light showed itself in the high windows above, they sighed resignedly and went their ways, to wait stolidly until morning should come and prove the truth of their fears and warnings.

In the mean time the ghost hunters built a huge fire, lighted their many candles, and sat down to await developments. Rupert afterwards told my uncle that they really felt no fear whatever, only a contemptuous curiosity, and they ate their supper with good appetite and an unusual relish. It was a long evening. They played many games of chess, waiting for midnight. Hour passed after hour, and nothing occurred to interrupt the monotony of the evening. Ten, eleven, came and went—it was almost midnight. They piled more wood in the fireplace, lighted new candles, looked to their pistols—and waited. The clocks in the village struck twelve; the sound coming muffled through the high, deep-embrasured windows. Nothing happened, nothing to break the heavy silence; and with a feeling of disappointed relief they looked at each other and acknowledged that they had met another rebuff.

Finally they decided that there was no use in sitting up and boring themselves any longer, they had much better rest; so Otto threw himself down on the mattress, falling almost immediately asleep. Rupert sat a little longer, smoking, and watching the stars creep along behind the shattered glass and the bent leads of the lofty windows; watching the fire fall together, and the strange shadows move mysteriously on the mouldering walls. The iron hook in the oak beam, that crossed the ceiling midway, fascinated him, not with fear, but morbidly. So, it was from that hook that for twelve years, twelve long years of changing summer and winter, the body of Count Albert, murderer and suicide, hung in its strange casing of mediæval steel; moving a little at first, and turning gently while the fire died out on the hearth, while the ruins of the castle grew cold, and horrified peasants sought for the bodies of the score of gay, reckless, wicked guests whom Count Albert had gathered in Kropfsberg for a last debauch, gathered to their terrible and untimely death. What a strange and fiendish idea it was, the young, handsome noble who had ruined himself and his family in the society of the splendid debauchees, gathering them all together, men and women who had known only love and pleasure, for a glorious and awful riot of luxury, and then, when they were all dancing in the great ballroom, locking the doors and burning the whole castle about them, the while he sat in the great keep listening to their screams of agonized fear, watching the fire sweep from wing to wing until the whole mighty mass was one enormous and awful pyre, and then, clothing himself in his great-great-grandfather's armor, hanging himself in the midst of the ruins of what had been a proud and noble castle. So ended a great family, a great house.

But that was forty years ago.

He was growing drowsy; the light flickered and flared in the fireplace; one by one the candles went out; the shadows grew thick in the room. Why did that great iron hook stand out so plainly? why did that dark shadow dance and quiver so mockingly behind it?—why— But he ceased to wonder at anything. He was asleep.

It seemed to him that he woke almost immediately; the fire still burned, though low and fitfully on the hearth. Otto was sleeping, breathing quietly and regularly; the shadows had gathered close around him, thick and murky; with every passing moment the light died in the fireplace; he felt stiff with cold. In the utter silence he heard the clock in the village strike two. He shivered with a sudden and irresistible feeling of fear, and abruptly turned and looked towards the hook in the ceiling.

Yes, It was there. He knew that It would be. It seemed quite natural, he would have been disappointed had he seen nothing; but now he knew that the story was true, knew that he was wrong, and that the dead *do* sometimes return to earth, for there, in the fast-deepening shadow, hung the black mass of wrought steel, turning a little now and then, with the light flickering on the tarnished and rusty metal. He watched it quietly; he hardly felt afraid; it was rather a sentiment of sadness and fatality that filled him, of gloomy forebodings of something unknown, unimaginable. He sat and watched the thing disappear in the gathering dark, his hand on his pistol as it lay by him on the great chest. There was no sound but the regular breathing of the sleeping boy on the mattress.

It had grown absolutely dark; a bat fluttered against the broken glass of the window. He wondered if he was growing mad, for—he hesitated to acknowledge it to himself—he heard music; far, curious music, a strange and luxurious dance, very faint, very vague, but unmistakable.

Like a flash of lightning came a jagged line of fire down the blank wall opposite him, a line that remained, that grew wider, that let a pale cold light into the room, showing him now all its details—the empty fireplace, where a thin smoke rose in a spiral from a bit of charred wood, the mass of the great bed, and, in the very middle, black against the curious brightness, the armored man, or ghost, or devil, standing, not suspended, beneath the rusty hook. And with the rending of the wall the music grew more distinct, though sounding still very, very far away.

Count Albert raised his mailed hand and beckoned to him; then turned, and stood in the riven wall.

Without a word, Rupert rose and followed him, his pistol in hand. Count Albert passed through the mighty wall and disappeared in the unearthly light. Rupert followed mechanically. He felt the crushing of the mortar beneath his feet, the roughness of the jagged wall where he rested his hand to steady himself.

The keep rose absolutely isolated among the ruins, yet on passing through the wall Rupert found himself in a long, uneven corridor, the floor of which was warped and sagging, while the walls were covered on one side with big faded portraits of an inferior quality, like those in the corridor that connects the Pitti and Uffizzi in Florence. Before him moved the figure of Count Albert—a black silhouette in the ever-increasing light. And always the music grew stronger and stranger, a mad, evil, seductive dance that bewitched even while it disgusted.

In a final blaze of vivid, intolerable light, in a burst of hellish music that might have come from Bedlam, Rupert stepped from the corridor into a vast and curious room where at first he saw nothing, distinguished nothing but a mad, seething whirl of sweeping figures, white, in a white room, under white light, Count Albert standing before him, the only dark object to be seen. As his eyes grew accustomed to the fearful brightness, he knew that he was looking on a dance such as the damned might see in hell, but such as no living man had ever seen before.

Around the long, narrow hall, under the fearful light that came from nowhere, but was omnipresent, swept a rushing stream of unspeakable horrors, dancing insanely, laughing, gibbering hideously; the dead of forty years. White, polished skeletons, bare of flesh and vesture, skeletons clothed in the dreadful rags of dried and rattling sinews, the tags of tattering grave-clothes flaunting behind them. These were the dead of many years ago. Then the dead of more recent times, with yellow bones showing only here and there, the long and insecure hair of their hideous heads writhing in the beating air. Then green and gray horrors, bloated and shapeless, stained with earth or dripping with spattering water; and here and there white, beautiful things, like chiselled ivory, the dead of yesterday, locked it may be, in the mummy arms of rattling skeletons.

Round and round the cursed room, a swaying, swirling maelstrom of death, while the air grew thick with miasma, the floor foul with shreds of shrouds, and yellow parchment, clattering bones, and wisps of tangled hair.

And in the very midst of this ring of death, a sight not for words nor for thought, a sight to blast forever the mind of the man who looked upon it: a leaping, writhing dance of Count Albert's victims, the score of beautiful women and reckless men who danced to their awful death while the castle burned around them, charred and shapeless now, a living charnel-house of nameless horror.

Count Albert, who had stood silent and gloomy, watching the dance of the damned, turned to Rupert, and for the first time spoke.

"We are ready for you now; dance!"

A prancing horror, dead some dozen years, perhaps, flaunted from the rushing river of the dead, and leered at Rupert with eyeless skull.

"Dance!"

Rupert stood frozen, motionless.

"Dance!"

His hard lips moved. "Not if the devil came from hell to make me."

Count Albert swept his vast two-handed sword into the fœtid air while the tide of corruption paused in its swirling, and swept down on Rupert with gibbering grins.

The room, and the howling dead, and the black portent before him circled dizzily around, as with a last effort of departing consciousness he drew his pistol and fired full in the face of Count Albert.

Perfect silence, perfect darkness; not a breath, not a sound: the dead stillness of a long-sealed tomb. Rupert lay on his back, stunned, helpless, his pistol clenched in his frozen hand, a smell of powder in the black air. Where was he? Dead? In hell? He reached his hand out cautiously; it fell on dusty boards. Outside, far away, a clock struck three. Had he dreamed? Of course; but how ghastly a dream! With chattering teeth he called softly—

"Otto!"

There was no reply, and none when he called again and again. He staggered weakly to his feet, groping for matches and candles. A panic of abject terror came on him; the matches were gone! He turned towards the fireplace: a single coal glowed in the white ashes. He swept a mass of papers and dusty books from the table, and with trembling hands cowered over the embers, until he succeeded in lighting the dry tinder. Then he piled the old books on the blaze, and looked fearfully around.

No: It was gone—thank God for that; the hook was empty.

But why did Otto sleep so soundly; why did he not awake?

He stepped unsteadily across the room in the flaring light of the burning books, and knelt by the mattress.

So they found him in the morning, when no one came to the inn from Kropfsberg Keep, and the quaking Peter Rosskopf arranged a relief party—found him kneeling beside the mattress where Otto lay, shot in the throat and quite dead.

In the Dark

Mary E. Penn

"It is the strangest, most unaccountable thing I ever knew! I don't think I am superstitious, but I can't help fancying that——"

Ethel left the sentence unfinished, wrinkling her brows in a thoughtful frown as she gazed into the depths of her empty tea-cup.

"What has happened?" I enquired, glancing up from the Money Article of the *Times* at my daughter's pretty, puzzled face. "Nothing uncanny, I hope? You haven't discovered that a 'ghost' is included among the fixtures of our new house?"

This new house, The Cedars, was a pretty old-fashioned riverside villa between Richmond and Kew, which I had taken furnished, as a summer residence, and to which we had only just removed.

Let me state, in parenthesis, by way of introducing myself to the reader, that I, John Dysart, am a widower with one child: the blue-eyed, fair-haired young lady who sat opposite to me at the breakfast table that bright June morning: and that I have been for many years the manager of an old-established Life Insurance Company in the City.

"What is the mystery?" I repeated, as Ethel did not reply.

She came out of her brown study, and looked at me impressively.

"It really is a mystery, papa, and the more I think of it the more puzzled I am."

"I am in the dark at present as to what 'it' may be," I reminded her.

"Something that happened last night. You know that adjoining my bedroom there is a large, dark closet, which can be used as a box or store-room?"

"I had forgotten the fact, but I will take your word for it. Well, Ethel?"

"Well, last night I was restless, and it was some hours before I could sleep. When at last I did so, I had a strange dream about that closet. It seemed that as I lay in bed I heard a noise within, as if someone were knocking at the door, and a child's voice, broken by sobs, crying piteously 'Let me out, let me out!' I thought that I got out of bed and opened the door, and there, crouching all in a heap against the wall, was a little boy; a pretty, pale little fellow of six or seven, looking half wild with fright. At the same moment I woke."

"And lo, it was a dream!" I finished. "If that is all Ethel—"

"But it is not," she interposed. "The strangest part of the story has to come. The dream was so vivid that when I woke I sat up in bed, and looked towards the closet door, almost expecting to hear the sounds again. Papa, you may believe me or not, but it is a fact that I *did* hear them, the muffled knocking, and the pitiful cry. As I listened, it grew fainter and fainter and at length ceased altogether. Then I summoned courage to get out of bed and open the door. There was no living creature in the place. Was it not mysterious?" she concluded. "What can it mean?"

I glanced at her with a smile, as I refolded the paper and rose from my chair.

"It means, my dear, that you had night-mare last night. Let me recommend you for the future not to eat cucumber at dinner."

"No, papa," she interrupted. "I was broad awake, and I heard the child's voice as plainly as I ever heard a sound in my life."

"Why didn't you call me?"

"I was afraid to stir till the sound had ceased; but if I ever hear it again, I will let you know at once."

"Be sure you do. Meantime, suppose you come into the garden," I continued, throwing open the French windows; "the morning-air will blow all these cobwebs from your brain."

Ethel complied, and for the present I heard no more of the subject.

Some days passed away, and we began to feel quite at home in our new quarters.

A more delightful summer retreat than The Cedars could hardly be imagined, with its cool, dusky rooms, from which the sunlight was excluded by the screen of foliage outside; its trellised verandah, overgrown with creepers, and its smooth lawn, shaded by the rare old cedar-trees which gave the place its name.

Our friends soon discovered its attractions and took care that we should not stagnate for want of society. We kept open house; lawn-tennis, garden-parties, and boating excursions were the order of the day. It was glorious summer weather, the days warm and golden, the nights starlit and still.

One night, having important letters to finish, I sat up writing after all the household were in bed. The window was open, and at intervals I glanced up from my paper across the moonlit lawn, where the shadows of the cedars lay dark and motionless. Now and then a great downy moth would flutter in and hover round the shaded lamp; now and then the swallows under the eaves uttered a faint, sleepy chirp. For all other signs and sounds of life I might have been the only watcher in all the sleeping world.

I had finished my task and was just closing my writing-case when I heard a hurried movement in the room above—Ethel's. Footsteps descended the stairs, and the next moment the dining-room door opened, and Ethel appeared, in a long, white dressing-gown, with a small night-lamp in her hand.

There was a look on her face which made me start up and exclaim:

"What is the matter? What has happened?"

She set down the lamp and came towards me.

"I have heard it again," she breathed, laying her hand on my wrist.

"You have heard—what?"

"The noise in the box-room."

I stared at her a moment in bewilderment, and then half smiled.

"Oh, is that it?" I exclaimed, in a tone of relief. "You have been dreaming again, it seems."

"I have not been asleep at all," she replied. "The sounds have kept me awake. They are louder than the first time; the child seems to be sobbing and crying as if his heart would break. It is miserable to hear it."

"Have you looked inside?" I asked, impressed in spite of myself by her manner.

"No, I dared not to-night. I was afraid of seeing—something," she returned with a shiver.

"Come, we must get to the bottom of this mystery," I said cheerfully, and taking up the lamp I led the way upstairs to her room.

As the door of the mysterious closet was level with the wall, and papered like it, I did not perceive it till Ethel pointed it out. I listened with my ear close to it, but heard not the faintest sound, and after waiting a moment, threw it open and looked in, holding the lamp so that every corner was lighted. It was a cramped, close, airless place, the ceiling (which was immediately below the upper staircase) sloping at an acute angle to the floor. A glance showed me that it contained nothing but a broken chair and a couple of empty boxes.

Slightly shrugging my shoulders, I closed the door.

"Your ghost is 'vox et præterea nihil,' it seems," I remarked drily. "Don't you think, Ethel, you may have been———"

Ethel held up her hand, motioning me to silence.

"Hark," she whispered, "there it is again! But it is dying away now. Listen———"

I complied, half infected by her excitement, but within and without the house all was profoundly still.

"There—it has ceased," she said at length, drawing a deep breath. "You heard it, did you not?"

I shook my head. "My dear Ethel, there was nothing to hear."

She opened her blue eyes to their widest.

"Papa—am I not to believe the evidence of my own senses?"

"Not when they are affected by nervous excitement. If you give way to this fancy, you will certainly make yourself ill. See how you tremble! Come, lie down again, and try to sleep."

"Not here," she returned, glancing round with a shudder. "I shall go to the spare chamber. Nothing would induce me to spend another night in this room."

I said no more, but I felt perplexed and uneasy. It was so unlike Ethel to indulge in superstitious fancies that I began to fear she must be seriously out of health, and I resolved for my own satisfaction to have a doctor's opinion regarding her.

It happened that our nearest neighbour was a physician, whom I knew by repute, though not personally acquainted with him. After breakfast, without mentioning my intention to my daughter, I sent a note to Dr. Cameron, requesting him to call at his earliest convenience.

He came without delay: a tall, grey-bearded man of middle age, with a grave, intelligent face, observant eyes and sympathetic manner.

His patient received him with undisguised astonishment, and on learning that he had called at my request she gave me a look of mute reproach.

"I am sorry that papa troubled you, Dr. Cameron. There is really nothing whatever the matter with me," she said.

And indeed at that moment, with flushed cheeks, and eyes even brighter than usual, she looked as little like an invalid as could well be imagined.

"My dear Ethel," I interposed, "when people take to dreaming startling dreams, and hearing supernatural sounds, it is a sign of something wrong with either mind or body—as I am sure Dr. Cameron will tell you."

The doctor started perceptibly. "Ah—is that Miss Dysart's case?" he enquired, turning to her with a sudden look of interest.

She coloured and hesitated. "I have had a strange—experience, which papa considers a delusion. I daresay you will be of the same opinion."

"Suppose you tell me what it was?" he suggested.

She was silent, trifling with one of her silver bangles.

"Please excuse me," she said hurriedly, at length. "I don't care to speak of it; but papa will tell you." And before I could detain her, she had hurriedly left the room.

When we were alone he turned to me enquiringly, and in a few words I related to him what the reader already knows. He listened without interruption, and when I had finished, sat for some moments without speaking, thoughtfully stroking his beard.

He was evidently impressed by what he had heard, and I waited anxiously for his opinion. At length he looked up.

"Mr. Dysart," he said, gravely, "you will be surprised to learn that your daughter is not the first who has had this strange 'experience.' Previous tenants of The Cedars have heard exactly the sounds which she describes."

I pushed my chair back half-a-yard in my astonishment.

"Impossible!"

He nodded emphatically.

"It is a fact, though I don't pretend to explain it. These strange manifestations have been noticed at intervals for the last three or four years; ever since the house was occupied by a Captain Vandeleur, whose orphan nephew——"

"Vandeleur?" I interrupted; "why, he was a client of ours. He insured his nephew's life in our office for a large amount, and——"

"And a few months afterwards, the child suddenly and mysteriously died?" my companion put in. "A singular coincidence, to say the least of it."

"So singular," I acquiesced, "that we thought it a case for enquiry, particularly as the ex-captain did not bear the best of characters, and was known to be over head and ears in debt. But I am bound to say that after the closest investigation nothing was discovered to suggest a suspicion of foul play."

"Nevertheless there *had* been foul play," was the doctor's reply.

"You don't mean that he murdered the boy! that pretty, fragile-looking little fellow—"

"No, he did not murder him, but he let him die," Dr. Cameron rejoined. "Perhaps you were not aware," he continued, "that the little lad was somewhat feeble in mind as well as body? I attended him more than once, at Vandeleur's request, and found that among other strange fears and antipathies he had a morbid dread of darkness. To be left alone in a dark room for only a few minutes was enough to throw him into a paroxysm of nervous excitement. His uncle—who by the way, professed more affection for him than I could quite believe in, when I noticed how the child shrank from him—consulted me as to the best means of overcoming this weakness. I strongly advised him to humour it for the present, warning him that any mental shock might endanger the boy's reason, or even his life. I little thought those words of mine would prove his death warrant."

"What do you mean?"

"Only a few days afterwards, Vandeleur locked him up all night in a dark closet, where he was found the next morning, crouching against the wall; his hands clenched, his eyes fixed and staring—dead."

"Good heavens, how horrible! But no word of this was mentioned at the inquest?"

"No; and I did not hear of it myself till long afterwards, from a woman who had been Vandeleur's housekeeper, but was too much afraid of him to betray him at the time. From her, too, I learnt by what refined cruelty the poor little lad's nerves had been shaken and his health undermined. If 'the intention makes the deed,' James Vandeleur was a murderer."

I was silent a moment, thinking, with an uncomfortable thrill, of Ethel's dream. "I wish I had never entered this ill-omened house!" I exclaimed at length. "I dread the effect of this revelation on my daughter's mind."

"Why need you tell her?" he questioned. "My advice is to say nothing more about it. The sooner she forgets the subject the better. Send her away to the sea-side; change of air and scene will soon efface it from her memory."

He rose as he spoke, and took up his hat.

"What has become of Vandeleur?" I enquired. "I have heard nothing of him since we paid the policy."

"He has been living abroad, I believe—going to the dogs, no doubt. But he is in England now," the doctor added: "or else it was his 'fetch' which I saw at your gate the other night."

"At our gate!" I echoed in astonishment. "What the deuce was he doing there?"

"He seemed to be watching the house. It was last Sunday evening. I had been dining with friends at Richmond, and on my way back, between eleven and twelve o'clock, I noticed a man leaning over the gate of The Cedars. On hearing footsteps he turned and walked away, but not before I had caught a glimpse of his face in the moonlight."

"And you are sure it was he?"

"Almost certain—though he was greatly altered for the worse. I have a presentiment do you know, that you will see or hear of him yourself before long," he added thoughtfully, as he shook hands and went his way.

I lost no time in following his advice with regard to Ethel, whom I despatched to Scarborough, in charge of my married sister, a few days later.

I had taken a hearty dislike to The Cedars, and resolved to get it off my hands as soon as might be.

Until another tenant could be found however, I continued to occupy it, going to and from town as before.

One evening I was sitting on the lawn, smoking an after-dinner cigar, and re-reading Ethel's last letter, which quite reassured me as to her health and spirits, when our sedate old housekeeper presented herself with the information that "a party" had called to see the house.

"A gentleman or a lady?" I enquired.

"A gentleman, sir, but he didn't give his name."

I found the visitor standing near the open window of the drawing-room; a tall, gaunt man of thirty-five or thereabouts, with handsome but haggard features, and restless dark eyes. His lips were covered by a thick moustache, which he was nervously twisting as he stood looking out at the lawn.

"This house is to be let, I believe; will you allow me to look over it?" he asked, turning towards me as I entered.

His voice seemed familiar; I looked at him more closely, and then, in spite of the change in his appearance, I recognised Captain Vandeleur.

What could have brought him here, I wondered. Surely he would not care to return to the house, even if he were in a position to do so—which, judging from the shabbiness of his appearance, seemed very doubtful.

Half-a-dozen vague conjectures flashed through my mind, as I glanced at his face, and noticed the restless, "hunted" look which told of some wearing dread or anxiety.

After a moment's hesitation I assented to his request, and resolved to conduct him myself on his tour of inspection.

"I think I have met you before," I said, feeling curious to know whether he recollected me.

He glanced at me absently.

"Possibly—but not of late years; for I have been living abroad," was his reply.

Having shown him the apartments on the ground-floor, I led the way upstairs. He followed me from room to room in an absent, listless fashion, till we came to the chamber which Ethel had occupied. Then his interest seemed to revive all at once.

He glanced quickly round the walls, his eyes resting on the door of the box-closet.

"That is a bath or dressing-room, I suppose," he said, nodding towards it.

"No, only a place for lumber. Perhaps I ought to tell you that it is said to be haunted," I added, affecting to speak carelessly, while I kept my eyes on his face.

He started and turned towards me.

"Haunted—by what?" he enquired, with a faint sneer. "Nothing worse than rats or mice, I expect."

"There is a tragical story connected with that place," I answered, deliberately. "It is said that an unfortunate child was shut up there to die of fear, in the dark."

The colour rushed to his face, then retreated, leaving it deadly white.

"Indeed!" he faltered; "and do you mean to say that he—the child—has been seen?"

"No, but he has been heard, knocking within, and crying to be let out. The fact is confirmed by every tenant who has occupied the house since——"

I stopped short, startled by the effect of my revelation.

My companion was gazing at me with a blank stare of horror which banished all other expression from his face.

"Good heavens !" I heard him mutter; "can it be true? Can this be the reason why I was drawn back to the place in spite of myself?"

Recollecting himself, however, he turned to me, and forced his white lips into a smile.

"A mysterious story!" he commented, drily. "I don't believe a word of it, myself, but I should hardly care to take a house with such an uncanny reputation. I think I need not trouble you any further."

As he turned towards the door, I saw his figure sway as if he were falling. He put his hand to his side, with a gasp of pain, a bluish shade gathering over his face.

"Are you ill?" I exclaimed, in alarm.

"I—it is nothing. I have a weakness of the heart, and I am subject to these attacks. May I ask you for a glass of water?"

I left the room to procure it. When I returned I found that he had fallen upon the bed in a dead swoon.

I hastily despatched a servant for Dr. Cameron, who happened to be at home, and came immediately.

He recognised my visitor at once, and glanced at me significantly. I rapidly explained what had happened, while he bent over the unconscious man, and bared his chest to listen to the heart-beats.

When he raised himself his face was ominously grave.

"Is he in danger?" I asked, quickly.

"Not in immediate danger, but the next attack will probably be his last. His heart is mortally diseased."

It was nearly an hour before Vandeleur awoke, and then only to partial consciousness. He lay in a sort of stupor, his limbs nerveless, his hands damp and cold.

"It is impossible to remove him in this condition," the doctor remarked; "I fear he must stay here for the night. I will send you someone to watch him."

"Don't trouble—I intend to sit up with him myself," I replied, speaking on an impulse I could hardly explain.

He looked at me keenly over his spectacles.

"Should you like me to share your watch?" he enquired, after a moment.

"I shall be only too glad of your company, if you can come without inconvenience."

He nodded.

"I must leave you now, but I will return in an hour," he responded.

Three hours had passed away; it was nearly midnight. The night was oppressively close, and profoundly still. The bedroom window stood wide open, but not a breath of air stirred the curtains. Outside, all was vague and dark, for neither moon nor stars were visible.

Vandeleur still lay, half-dressed, on the bed, but now asleep. His deep, regular breathing sounded distinctly in the silence. Dr. Cameron sat near the dressing-table, reading by the light of a shaded lamp. I, too, had a book, but found it impossible to keep my attention fixed upon it. My mind was possessed by an uneasy feeling, half dread, half expectation. I found myself listening nervously to fancied sounds, and starting when the doctor turned a leaf.

At length, overcome by the heat and stillness, I closed my eyes, and unconsciously sank into a doze. How long it lasted I cannot tell, but I woke abruptly, and looked round with a sense of vague alarm. I glanced at the doctor. He had laid down his book, and was leaning forward with one arm on the dressing-table, looking intently towards the door of the box-room. Instinctively I held my breath and listened.

Never shall I forget the thrill that ran through my nerves when I heard from within a muffled knocking sound, and a child's voice, distinct, though faint, and broken by sobs, crying piteously: "Let me out—let me out!"

"Do you hear?" I whispered, bending forward to my companion.

He inclined his head in assent and motioned me to be silent, pointing towards the bed. Its occupant moved uneasily, as if disturbed, muttering some incoherent phrases. Suddenly he pushed back his covering and sat upright, gazing round with a wild, bewildered stare.

The pitiful entreaty was repeated more violently, more passionately than before. "Let me out, let me out!"

With a cry that rang through the room, Vandeleur sprang from the bed, reached the closet door in two strides and tore it open.

It was empty. Empty at least to our eyes, but it was evident that our companion beheld what we could not.

For a few breathless seconds he stood as if frozen, his eyes fixed with the fascination of terror on something just within the threshold; then, as if retreating before it, he recoiled step by step across the room till he was stopped by the opposite wall, where he crouched in an attitude of abject fear.

The sight was so horrible that I could bear it no longer.

"Are you dreaming? wake up!" I exclaimed, and shook his shoulder.

He raised his eyes, and looked at me vacantly. His lips moved, but no sound came from them. Suddenly a convulsive shudder ran through him and he fell heavily forward at my feet.

"He has swooned again," I said turning to my companion, who stooped and lifted the drooping head on to his knee.

After one glance, he laid it gently down again.

"He is dead," was his grave reply.

And with Vandeleur's death my story ends, for after that night the sounds were heard no more.

The forlorn little ghost was at rest.

The Interval

Vincent O'Sullivan

Mrs. Wilton passed through a little alley leading from one of the gates which are around Regent's Park, and came out on the wide and quiet street. She walked along slowly, peering anxiously from side to side so as not to overlook the number. She pulled her furs closer round her; after her years in India this London damp seemed very harsh. Still, it was not a fog to-day. A dense haze, gray and tinged ruddy, lay between the houses, sometimes blowing with a little wet kiss against the face. Mrs. Wilton's hair and eyelashes and her furs were powdered with tiny drops. But there was nothing in the weather to blur the sight; she could see the faces of people some distance off and read the signs on the shops.

Before the door of a dealer in antiques and second-hand furniture she paused and looked through the shabby uncleaned window at an unassorted heap of things, many of them of great value. She read the Polish name fastened on the pane in white letters.

"Yes; this is the place."

She opened the door, which met her entrance with an ill-tempered jangle. From somewhere in the black depths of the shop the dealer came forward. He had a clammy white face, with a sparse black beard, and wore a skull cap and spectacles. Mrs. Wilton spoke to him in a low voice.

A look of complicity, of cunning, perhaps of irony, passed through the dealer's cynical and sad eyes. But he bowed gravely and respectfully.

"Yes, she is here, madam. Whether she will see you or not I do not know. She is not always well; she has her moods. And then, we have to be so careful. The police— Not that they would touch a lady like you. But the poor alien has not much chance these days."

Mrs. Wilton followed him to the back of the shop, where there was a winding staircase. She knocked over a few things in her passage and stooped to pick them up, but the dealer kept muttering, "It does not matter—surely it does not matter." He lit a candle.

"You must go up these stairs. They are very dark; be careful. When you come to a door, open it and go straight in."

He stood at the foot of the stairs holding the light high above his head and she ascended.

The room was not very large, and it seemed very ordinary. There were some flimsy, uncomfortable chairs in gilt and red. Two large palms were in corners. Under a glass cover on the table was a view of Rome. The room had not a business-like look, thought Mrs. Wilton; there was no suggestion of the office or waiting-room where people came and went all day; yet you would not say that it was a private room which was lived in. There were no books or papers about; every chair was in the place it had been placed when the room was last swept; there was no fire and it was very cold.

To the right of the window was a door covered with a plush curtain. Mrs. Wilton sat down near the table and watched this door. She thought it must be through it that the soothsayer would come forth. She laid her hands listlessly one on top of the other on the table. This must be the tenth seer she had consulted since Hugh had been killed. She thought them over. No, this must be the eleventh. She had forgotten that frightening man in Paris who said he had been a priest. Yet of them all it was only he who had told her anything definite. But even he could do no more than tell the past. He told of her marriage; he even had the duration of it right—twenty-one months. He told too of their time in India—at least, knew that her husband had been a soldier, and said he had been on service in the "colonies." On the whole, though, he had been as unsatisfactory as the others. None of them had given her the consolation she sought. She did not want to be told of the past. If Hugh was gone forever, then with him had gone all her love of living, her courage, all her better self. She wanted to be lifted out of the despair, the dazed aimless drifting from day to day, longing at night for the morning, and in the morning for the fall of night, which had been her life since his death. If somebody could assure her that it was not all over, that he was somewhere, not too far away, unchanged from what he had been here, with his crisp hair and rather slow smile and lean brown face, that he saw her sometimes, that he had not forgotten her . . .

"Oh, Hugh, darling!"

When she looked up again the woman was sitting there before her. Mrs. Wilton had not heard her come in. With her experience, wide enough now, of seers and fortune-tellers of all kinds, she saw at once that this woman was different from the others. She was used to the quick appraising look, the attempts, sometimes clumsy, but often cleverly disguised, to collect some fragments of information whereupon to erect a plausible vision. But this woman looked as if she took it out of herself.

Not that her appearance suggested intercourse with the spiritual world more than the others had done; it suggested that, in fact, considerably less. Some of the others were frail, yearning, evaporated creatures, and the ex-priest in Paris had something terrible and condemned in his look. He might well sup with the devil, that man, and probably did in some way or other.

But this was a little fat, weary-faced woman about fifty, who only did not look like a cook because she looked more like a sempstress. Her black dress was all covered with white threads. Mrs. Wilton looked at her with some embarrassment. It seemed more reasonable to be asking a woman like this about altering a gown than about intercourse with the dead. That seemed even absurd in such a very commonplace presence. The woman seemed timid, and oppressed: she breathed heavily and kept rubbing her dingy hands, which looked moist, one over the other; she was always wetting her lips, and coughed with a little dry cough. But in her these signs of nervous exhaustion suggested overwork in a close atmosphere, bending too close over the sewing-machine. Her uninteresting hair, like a rat's pelt, was eked out with a false addition of another color. Some threads had got into her hair too.

Her harried, uneasy look caused Mrs. Wilton to ask compassionately: "Are you much worried by the police?"

"Oh, the police! Why don't they leave us alone? You never know who comes to see you. Why don't they leave me alone? I'm a good woman. I only think. What I do is no harm to any one."...

She continued in an uneven querulous voice, always rubbing her hands together nervously. She seemed to the visitor to be talking at random, just gabbling, like children do sometimes before they fall asleep.

"I wanted to explain—" hesitated Mrs. Wilton.

But the woman, with her head pressed close against the back of the chair, was staring beyond her at the wall. Her face had lost whatever little expression it had; it was blank and stupid. When she spoke it was very slowly and her voice was guttural.

"Can't you see him? It seems strange to me that you can't see him. He is so near you. He is passing his arm round your shoulders."

This was a frequent gesture of Hugh's. And indeed at that moment she felt that somebody was very near her, bending over her. She was enveloped in tenderness. Only a very thin veil, she felt, prevented her from seeing. But the woman saw. She was describing Hugh minutely, even the little things like the burn on his right hand.

"Is he happy? Oh, ask him does he love me?"

The result was so far beyond anything she had hoped for that she was stunned. She could only stammer the first thing that came into her head. "Does he love me?"

"He loves you. He won't answer, but he loves you. He wants me to make you see him; he is disappointed, I think, because I can't. But I can't unless you do it yourself."

After a while she said:

"I think you will see him again. You think of nothing else. He is very close to us now."

Then she collapsed, and fell into a heavy sleep and lay there motionless, hardly breathing. Mrs. Wilton put some notes on the table and stole out on tip-toe.

She seemed to remember that downstairs in the dark shop the dealer with the waxen face detained her to show some old silver and jewelry and such like. But she did not come to herself, she had no precise recollection of anything, till she found herself entering a church near Portland Place. It was an unlikely act in her normal moments. Why did she go in there? She acted like one walking in her sleep.

The church was old and dim, with high black pews. There was nobody there. Mrs. Wilton sat down in one of the pews and bent forward with her face in her hands.

After a few minutes she saw that a soldier had come in noiselessly and placed himself about half-a-dozen rows ahead of her. He never turned round; but presently she was struck by something familiar in the figure. First she thought vaguely that the soldier looked like her Hugh. Then, when he put up his hand, she saw who it was.

She hurried out of the pew and ran towards him. "Oh, Hugh, Hugh, have you come back?"

He looked round with a smile. He had not been killed. It was all a mistake. He was going to speak . . .

Footsteps sounded hollow in the empty church. She turned and glanced down the dim aisle.

It was an old sexton or verger who approached. "I thought I heard you call," he said.

"I was speaking to my husband." But Hugh was nowhere to be seen.

"He was here a moment ago." She looked about in anguish. "He must have gone to the door."

"There's nobody here," said the old man gently. "Only you and me. Ladies are often taken funny since the war. There was one in here yesterday afternoon said she was married in this church and her husband had promised to meet her here. Perhaps you were married here?"

"No," said Mrs. Wilton, desolately. "I was married in India."

It might have been two or three days after that, when she went into a small Italian restaurant in the Bayswater district. She often went out for her meals now: she had developed an exhausting cough, and she found that it somehow became less troublesome when she was in a public place looking at strange faces. In her flat there were all the things that Hugh had used; the trunks and bags still had his name on them with the labels of places where they had been together. They were like stabs. In the restaurant, people came and went, many soldiers too among them, just glancing at her in her corner.

This day, as it chanced, she was rather late and there was nobody there. She was very tired. She nibbled at the food they brought her. She could almost have cried from tiredness and loneliness and the ache in her heart.

Then suddenly he was before her, sitting there opposite at the table. It was as it was in the days of their engagement, when they used sometimes to lunch at restaurants. He was not in uniform. He smiled at her and urged her to eat, just as he used in those days. . . .

I met her that afternoon as she was crossing Kensington Gardens, and she told me about it.

"I have been with Hugh." She seemed most happy.

"Did he say anything?"

"N-no. Yes. I think he did, but I could not quite hear. My head was so very tired. The next time—"

I did not see her for some time after that. She found, I think, that by going to places where she had once seen him—the old church, the little restaurant—she was more certain to see him again. She never saw him at home. But in the street or the park he would often walk along beside her. Once he saved her from being run over. She said she actually felt his hand grabbing her arm, suddenly, when the car was nearly upon her.

She had given me the address of the clairvoyant: and it is through that strange woman that I know—or seem to know—what followed.

Mrs. Wilton was not exactly ill last winter, not so ill, at least, as to keep to her bedroom. But she was very thin, and her great handsome eyes always seemed to be staring at some point beyond, searching. There was a look in them that seamen's eyes sometimes have when they are drawing on a coast of which they are not very certain. She lived almost in solitude: she hardly ever saw anybody except when they sought her out. To those who were anxious about her she laughed and said she was very well.

One sunny morning she was lying awake, waiting for the maid to bring her tea. The shy London sunlight peeped through the blinds. The room had a fresh and happy look.

When she heard the door open she thought that the maid had come in. Then she saw that Hugh was standing at the foot of the bed. He was in uniform this time, and looked as he had looked the day he went away.

"Oh, Hugh, speak to me! Will you not say just one word?"

He smiled and threw back his head, just as he used to in the old days at her mother's house when he wanted to call her out of the room without attracting the attention of the others. He moved towards the door, still signing to her to follow him. He picked up her slippers on his way and held them out to her as if he wanted her to put them on. She slipped out of bed hastily. . . .

It is strange that when they came to look through her things after her death the slippers could never be found.

John Charrington's Wedding

Edith Nesbit

No one ever thought that May Forster would marry John Charrington; but he thought differently, and things which John Charrington intended had a queer way of coming to pass. He asked her to marry him before he went up to Oxford. She laughed and refused him. He asked her again next time he came home. Again she laughed, tossed her dainty blonde head, and again refused. A third time he asked her; she said it was becoming a confirmed bad habit, and laughed at him more than ever.

John was not the only man who wanted to marry her: she was the belle of our village coterie, and we were all in love with her more or less; it was a sort of fashion, like heliotrope ties or Inverness capes. Therefore we were as much annoyed as surprised when John Charrington walked into our little local Club—we held it in a loft over the saddler's, I remember—and invited us all to his wedding.

"Your wedding?"

"You don't mean it?"

"Who's the happy fair? When's it to be?"

John Charrington filled his pipe and lighted it before he replied. Then he said—

"I'm sorry to deprive you fellows of your only joke—but Miss Forster and I are to be married in September."

"You don't mean it?"

"He's got the mitten again, and it's turned his head."

"No," I said, rising, "I see it's true. Lend me a pistol some one—or a first-class fare to the other end of Nowhere. Charrington has bewitched the only pretty girl in our twenty-mile radius. Was it mesmerism, or a love-potion, Jack?"

"Neither, sir, but a gift you'll never have—perseverance—and the best luck a man ever had in this world."

There was something in his voice that silenced me, and all chaff of the other fellows failed to draw him further.

The queer thing about it was that when we congratulated Miss Forster, she blushed and smiled and dimpled, for all the world as though she were in love with him, and had been in love with him all the time. Upon my word, I think she had. Women are strange creatures.

We were all asked to the wedding. In Brixham every one who was anybody knew everybody else who was any one. My sisters were, I truly believe, more interested in the *trousseau* than the bride herself, and I was to be best man. The coming marriage was much canvassed at afternoon tea-tables, and at our little Club over the saddler's, and the question was always asked: "Does she care for him?"

I used to ask that question myself in the early days of their engagement, but after a certain evening in August I never asked it again. I was coming home from the Club through the churchyard. Our church is on a thyme-grown hill, and the turf about it is so thick and soft that one's footsteps are noiseless.

I made no sound as I vaulted the low lichened wall, and threaded my way between the tombstones. It was at the same instant that I heard John Charrington's voice, and saw her face. May was sitting on a low flat gravestone, her face turned towards the full splendour of the western sun upon her *mignonne* face. Its expression ended, at once and for ever, any question of love for him; it was transfigured to a beauty I should not have believed possible, even to that beautiful little face.

John lay at her feet, and it was his voice that broke the stillness of the golden August evening.

"My dear, my dear, I believe I should come back from the dead if you wanted me!"

I coughed at once to indicate my presence, and passed on into the shadow fully enlightened.

The wedding was to be early in September. Two days before I had to run up to town on business. The train was late, of course, for we are on the South-Eastern, and as I stood grumbling with my watch in my hand, whom should I see but John Charrington and May Forster. They were walking up and down the unfrequented end of the platform, arm in arm, looking into each other's eyes, careless of the sympathetic interest of the porters.

Of course I knew better than to hesitate a moment before burying myself in the booking-office, and it was not till the train drew up at the platform, that I obtrusively passed the pair with my Gladstone, and took the corner in a first-class smoking-carriage. I did this with as good an air of not seeing them as I could assume. I pride myself on my discretion, but if John were travelling alone I wanted his company. I had it.

"Hullo, old man," came his cheery voice as he swung his bag into my carriage; "here's luck; I was expecting a dull journey!"

"Where are you off to?" I asked, discretion still bidding me turn my eyes away, though I saw, without looking, that hers were red-rimmed.

"To old Branbridge's," he answered, shutting the door and leaning out for a last word with his sweetheart.

"Oh, I wish you wouldn't go, John," she was saying in a low, earnest voice. "I feel certain something will happen."

"Do you think I should let anything happen to keep me, and the day after to-morrow our wedding-day?"

"Don't go," she answered, with a pleading intensity which would have sent my Gladstone on to the platform and me after it. But she wasn't speaking to me. John Charrington was made differently; he rarely changed his opinions, never his resolutions.

He only stroked the little ungloved hands that lay on the carriage door.

"I must, May. The old boy's been awfully good to me, and now he's dying I must go and see him, but I shall come home in time for—" the rest of the parting was lost in a whisper and in the rattling lurch of the starting train.

"You're sure to come?" she spoke as the train moved.

"Nothing shall keep me," he answered; and we steamed out. After he had seen the last of the little figure on the platform he leaned back in his corner and kept silence for a minute.

When he spoke it was to explain to me that his godfather, whose heir he was, lay dying at Peasmarsh Place, some fifty miles away, and had sent for John, and John had felt bound to go.

"I shall be surely back to-morrow," he said, "or, if not, the day after, in heaps of time. Thank Heaven, one hasn't to get up in the middle of the night to get married nowadays!"

"And suppose Mr. Branbridge dies?"

"Alive or dead I mean to be married on Thursday!" John answered, lighting a cigar and unfolding the *Times*.

At Peasmarsh station we said "good-bye," and he got out, and I saw him ride off; I went on to London, where I stayed the night.

When I got home the next afternoon, a very wet one, by the way, my sister greeted me with—

"Where's Mr. Charrington?"

"Goodness knows," I answered testily. Every man, since Cain, has resented that kind of question.

"I thought you might have heard from him," she went on, "as you're to give him away to-morrow."

"Isn't he back?" I asked, for I had confidently expected to find him at home.

"No, Geoffrey,"—my sister Fanny always had a way of jumping to conclusions, especially such conclusions as were least favourable to her fellow-creatures—"he has not returned, and, what is more, you may depend upon it he won't. You mark my words, there'll be no wedding to-morrow."

My sister Fanny has a power of annoying me which no other human being possesses.

"You mark my words," I retorted with asperity, "you had better give up making such a thundering idiot of yourself. There'll be more wedding to-morrow than ever you'll take the first part in." A prophecy which, by the way, came true.

But though I could snarl confidently to my sister, I did not feel so comfortable when, late that night, I, standing on the doorstep of John's house, heard that he had not returned. I went home gloomily through the rain. Next morning brought a brilliant blue sky, gold sun, and all such softness of air and beauty of cloud as go to make up a perfect day. I woke with a vague feeling of having gone to bed anxious, and of being rather averse to facing that anxiety in the light of full wakefulness.

But with my shaving-water came a note from John which relieved my mind and sent me up to the Forsters' with a light heart.

May was in the garden. I saw her blue gown through the hollyhocks as the lodge gates swung to behind me. So I did not go up to the house, but turned aside down the turfed path.

"He's written to you too," she said, without preliminary greeting, when I reached her side.

"Yes, I'm to meet him at the station at three, and come straight on to the church."

Her face looked pale, but there was a brightness in her eyes, and a tender quiver about the mouth that spoke of renewed happiness.

"Mr. Branbridge begged him so to stay another night that he had not the heart to refuse," she went on. "He is so kind, but I wish he hadn't stayed."

I was at the station at half-past two. I felt rather annoyed with John. It seemed a sort of slight to the beautiful girl who loved him, that he should come as it were out of breath, and with the dust of travel upon him, to take her hand, which some of us would have given the best years of our lives to take.

But when the three o'clock train glided in, and glided out again having brought no passengers to our little station, I was more than annoyed. There was no other train for thirty-five minutes; I calculated that, with much hurry, we might just get to the church in time for the ceremony; but, oh, what a fool to miss that first train! What other man could have done it?

That thirty-five minutes seemed a year, as I wandered round the station reading the advertisements and the time-tables, and the company's bye-laws, and getting more and more angry with John Charrington. This confidence in his own power of getting everything he wanted the minute he wanted it was leading him too far. I hate waiting. Every one does, but I believe I hate it more than any one else. The three thirty-five was late, of course.

I ground my pipe between my teeth and stamped with impatience as I watched the signals. Click. The signal went down. Five minutes later I flung myself into the carriage that I had brought for John.

"Drive to the church!" I said, as some one shut the door. "Mr. Charrington hasn't come by this train."

Anxiety now replaced anger. What had become of the man? Could he have been taken suddenly ill? I had never known him have a day's illness in his life. And even so he might have telegraphed. Some awful accident must have happened to him. The thought that he had played her false never—no, not for a moment—entered my head. Yes, something terrible had happened to him, and on me lay the task of telling his bride. I almost wished the carriage would upset and break my head so that some one else might tell her, not I, who—but that's nothing to do with his story.

It was five minutes to four as we drew up at the churchyard gate. A double row of eager on-lookers lined the path from lychgate to porch. I sprang from the carriage and passed up between them. Our gardener had a good front place near the door. I stopped.

"Are they waiting still, Byles?" I asked, simply to gain time, for of course I knew they were by the waiting crowd's attentive attitude.

"Waiting, sir? No, no, sir; why, it must be over by now."

"Over! Then Mr. Charrington's come?"

"To the minute, sir; must have missed you somehow, and, I say, sir," lowering his voice, "I never see Mr. John the least bit so afore, but my opinion is he's been drinking pretty free. His clothes was all dusty and his face like a sheet. I tell you I didn't like the looks of him at all, and the folks inside are saying all sorts of things. You'll see, something's gone very wrong with Mr. John, and he's tried liquor. He looked like a ghost, and in he went with his eyes straight before him, with never a look or a word for none of us; him that was always such a gentleman!"

I had never heard Byles make so long a speech. The crowd in the churchyard were talking in whispers and getting ready rice and slippers to throw at the bride and bridegroom. The ringers were ready with their hands on the ropes to ring out the merry peal as the bride and bridegroom should come out.

A murmur from the church announced them; out they came. Byles was right. John Charrington did not look himself. There was dust on his coat, his hair was disarranged. He seemed to have been in some row, for there was a black mark above his eyebrow. He was deathly pale. But his pallor was not greater than that of the bride, who might have been carved in ivory—dress, veil, orange blossoms, face and all.

As they passed out the ringers stooped—there were six of them—and then, on the ears expecting the gay wedding peal, came the slow tolling of the passing bell.

A thrill of horror at so foolish a jest from the ringers passed through us all. But the ringers themselves dropped the ropes and fled like rabbits out into the sunlight. The bride shuddered, and grey shadows came about her mouth, but the bridegroom led her on down the path where the people stood with the handfuls of rice; but the handfuls were never thrown, and the wedding-bells never rang. In vain the ringers were urged to remedy their mistake: they protested with many whispered expletives that they would see themselves further first.

In a hush like the hush in the chamber of death the bridal pair passed into their carriage and its door slammed behind them.

Then the tongues were loosed. A babel of anger, wonder, conjecture from the guests and the spectators.

"If I'd seen his condition, sir," said old Forster to me as we drove off, "I would have stretched him on the floor of the church, sir, by Heaven I would, before I'd have let him marry my daughter!"

Then he put his head out of the window.

"Drive like hell," he cried to the coachman; "don't spare the horses."

He was obeyed. We passed the bride's carriage. I forebore to look at it, and old Forster turned his head away and swore. We reached home before it.

We stood in the hall doorway, in the blazing afternoon sun, and in about half a minute we heard wheels crunching the gravel. When the carriage stopped in front of the steps old Forster and I ran down.

"Great Heaven, the carriage is empty! And yet——"

I had the door open in a minute, and this is what I saw—

No sign of John Charrington; and of May, his wife, only a huddled heap of white satin lying half on the floor of the carriage and half on the seat.

"I drove straight here, sir," said the coachman, as the bride's father lifted her out; "and I'll swear no one got out of the carriage."

We carried her into the house in her bridal dress and drew back her veil. I saw her face. Shall I ever forget it? White, white and drawn with agony and horror, bearing such a look of terror as I have never seen since except in dreams. And her hair, her radiant blonde hair, I tell you it was white like snow.

As we stood, her father and I, half mad with the horror and mystery of it, a boy came up the avenue—a telegraph boy. They brought the orange envelope to me. I tore it open.

> Mr. Charrington was thrown from the dogcart on his way to the station at half-past one. Killed on the spot!

And he was married to May Forster in our parish church at half-past three, in presence of half the parish.

"I shall be married, dead or alive!"

What had passed in that carriage on the homeward drive? No one knows—no one will ever know. Oh, May! oh, my dear!

Before a week was over they laid her beside her husband in our little churchyard on the thyme-covered hill—the churchyard where they had kept their love-trysts.

Thus was accomplished John Charrington's wedding.

Joseph: A Story

Katherine Rickford

They were sitting round the fire after dinner—not an ordinary fire, one of those fires that has a little room all to itself with seats at each side of it to hold a couple of people or three.

The big dining-room was panelled with oak. At the far end was a handsome dresser that dated back for generations. One's imagination ran riot when one pictured the people who must have laid those pewter plates on the long, narrow, solid table. Massive, mediæval chests stood against the walls. Arms and parts of armour hung against the panelling; but one noticed few of these things, for there was no light in the room save what the fire gave.

It was Christmas Eve. Games had been played. The old had vied with the young at snatching raisins from the burning snapdragon. The children had long since gone to bed; it was time their elders followed them, but they lingered round the fire, taking turns at telling stories. Nothing very weird had been told; no one had felt any wish to peep over his shoulder or try to penetrate the darkness of the far end of the room; the omission caused a sensation of something wanting. From each one there this thought went out, and so a sudden silence fell upon the party. It was a girl who broke it—a mere child; she wore her hair up that night for the first time, and that seemed to give her the right to sit up so late.

"Mr. Grady is going to tell one," she said.

All eyes were turned to a middle-aged man in a deep armchair placed straight in front of the fire. He was short, inclined to be fat, with a bald head and a pointed beard like the beards that sailors wear. It was plain that he was deeply conscious of the sudden turning of so much strained yet forceful thought upon himself. He was restless in his chair as people are in a room that is overheated. He blinked his eyes as he looked round the company. His lips twitched in a nervous manner. One side of him seemed to be endeavouring to restrain another side of him from a feverish desire to speak.

"It was this room that made me think of him," he said thoughtfully.

There was a long silence, but it occurred to no one to prompt him. Everyone seemed to understand that he was going to speak, or rather that something inside him was going to speak, some force that craved expression and was using him as a medium.

The little old man's pink face grew strangely calm, the animation that usually lit it was gone. One would have said that the girl who had started him already regretted the impulse, and now wanted to stop him. She was breathing heavily, and once or twice made as though she would speak to him, but no words came. She must have abandoned the idea, for she fell to studying the company. She examined them carefully, one by one. "This one," she told herself, "is so-and-so, and that one there just another so-and-so." She stared at them, knowing that she could not turn them to herself with her stare. They were just bodies kept working, so to speak, by some subtle sort of sentry left behind by the real selves that streamed out in pent-up thought to the little old man in the chair in front of the fire.

"His name was Joseph: at least they called him Joseph. He dreamed, you understand—dreams. He was an extraordinary lad in many ways. His mother—I knew her very well—had three children in quick succession, soon after marriage; then ten years went by and Joseph was born. Quiet and reserved he always was, a self-contained child whose only friend was his mother. People said things about him, you know how people talk. Some said he was not Clara's child at all, but that she had adopted him; others, that her husband was not his father, and these put her change of manner down to a perpetual struggle to keep her husband comfortably in the dark. I always imagined that the boy was in some way aware of all this gossip, for I noticed that he took a dislike to the people who spread it most."

The little man rested his elbows on the arms of his chair and let the tips of his fingers meet in front of him. A smile played about his mouth. He seemed to be searching among his reminiscences for the one that would give the clearest portrait of Joseph.

"Well, anyway," he said at last, "the boy was odd, there is no gainsaying the fact. I suppose he was eleven when Clara came down here with her family for Christmas. The Coningtons owned the place then—Mrs. Conington was Clara's sister. It was Christmas Eve, as it is now, many years ago. We had spent a normal Christmas Eve; a little happier, perhaps, than usual by reason of the family reunion and because of the presence of so many children. We had eaten and drank, laughed and played and gone to bed.

"I woke in the middle of the night from sheer restlessness. Clara, knowing my weakness, had given me a fire in my room. I lit a cigarette, played with a book, and then, purely from curiosity, opened the door and looked down the passage. From my door I could see the head of the staircase in the distance; the opposite wing of the house, or the passage rather beyond the stairs, was in darkness. The reason I saw the staircase at all was that the window you pass coming downstairs allowed the moon to throw an uncertain light upon it, a weird light because of the stained glass. I was arrested by the curious effect of this patch of light in so much darkness when suddenly someone came into it, turned, and went downstairs. It was just like a scene in a theatre; something was about to happen that I was going to miss. I ran as I was, barefooted, to the head of the stairs and looked over the banister. I was excited, strung up, too strung up to feel the fright that I knew must be with me. I remember the sensation perfectly. I knew that I was afraid, yet I did not feel fright.

"On the stairs nothing moved. The little hall down here was lost in darkness. Looking over the banister I was facing the stained glass window. You know how the stairs run round three sides of the hall; well, it occurred to me that if I went half-way down and stood under the window I should be able to keep the top of the stairs in sight and see anything that might happen in the hall. I crept down very cautiously and waited under the window. First of all, I saw the suit of empty armour just outside the door here. You know how a thing like that, if you stare at it in a poor light, appears to move; well, it moved sure enough, and the illusion was enhanced by clouds being blown across the moon. By the fire like this one can talk of these things rationally, but in the dead of night it is a different matter, so I went down a few steps to make sure of that armour, when suddenly something passed me on the stairs. I did not hear it, I did not see it, I sensed it in no way, I just knew that something had passed me on its way upstairs. I realized that my retreat was cut off, and with the knowledge fear came upon me.

"I had seen someone come down the stairs; that, at any rate, was definite; now I wanted to see him again. Any ghost is bad enough, but a ghost that one can see is better than one that one can't. I managed to get past the suit of armour, but then I had to feel my way to these double doors here."

He indicated the direction of the doors by a curious wave of his hand. He did not look toward them nor did any of the party. Both men and women were completely absorbed in his story, they seemed to be mesmerized by the earnestness of his manner. Only the girl was restless, she gave an impression of impatience with the slowness with which he came to his point. One would have said that she was apart from her fellows, an alien among strangers.

"So dense was the darkness that I made sure of finding the first door closed, but it was not, it was wide open, and, standing between them, I could feel that the other was open, too. I was standing literally in the wall of the house, and as I peered into the room, trying to make out some familiar object, thoughts ran through my mind of people who had been bricked up in walls and left there to die. For a moment I caught the spirit of the inside of a thick wall. Then suddenly I felt the sensation I have often read about but never experienced before: I knew there was someone in the room. You are surprised, yes, but wait! I knew more: I knew that that someone was conscious of my presence. It occurred to me that whoever it was might want to get out of the door. I made room for him to pass. I waited for him, made sure of him, began to feel giddy, and then a man's voice, deep and clear:

"'There is someone there; who is it?'

"I answered mechanically: 'George Grady.'

"'I'm Joseph.'

"A match was drawn across a match-box, and I saw the boy bending over a candle waiting for the wick to catch. For a moment I thought he must be walking in his sleep, but he turned to me quite naturally and said in his own boyish voice:

"'Lost anything?'

"I was amazed at the lad's complete calm. I wanted to share my fright with someone, instead I had to hide it from this boy. I was conscious of a curious sense of shame. I had watched him grow, taught him, praised him, scolded him, and yet here he was waiting for an explanation of my presence in the dining-room at that odd hour of the night.

"Soon he repeated the question: 'Lost anything?'

"'No,' I said, and then I stammered: 'Have you?'

"'No,' he said with a little laugh. 'It's that room, I can't sleep in it.'

"'Oh,' I said. 'What's the matter with the room?'

"'It's the room I was killed in,' he said quite simply.

"Of course I had heard about his dreams, but I had had no direct experience of them; when, therefore, he said that he had been killed in his room I took it for granted that he had been dreaming again. I was at a loss to know quite how to tackle him; whether to treat the whole thing as absurd and laugh it off as such, or whether to humour him and hear his story. I got him upstairs to my room, sat him in a big armchair, and poked the fire into a blaze.

"'You've been dreaming again,' I said bluntly.

"'Oh, no I haven't. Don't you run away with that idea.'

"His whole manner was so grown up that it was quite unthinkable to treat him as the child he really was. In fact, it was a little uncanny, this man in a child's frame.

"'I was killed there,' he said again.

"'How do you mean killed?' I asked him.

"'Why, killed—murdered. Of course it was years and years ago, I can't say when; still I remember the room. I suppose it was the room that reminded me of the incident.'

"'Incident!' I exclaimed.

"'What else? Being killed is only an incident in the existence of anyone. One makes a fuss about it at the time, of course, but really when you come to think of it . . .'

"'Tell me about it,' I said, lighting a cigarette. He lit one too, that child, and began.

"'You know my room is the only modern one in this old house. Nobody knows why it is modern. The reason is obvious. Of course it was made modern after I was killed there. The funny thing is that I should have been put there. I suppose it was done for a purpose, because I—I—'

"He looked at me so fixedly I knew he would catch me if I lied.

"'What,' I asked.

"'Dream.'

"'Yes,' I said, 'that is why you were put there.'

"'I thought so, and yet of all the rooms—but then, of course, no one knew. Anyhow I did not recognize the room until after I was in bed. I had been asleep some time and then I woke suddenly. There is an old wheel-back chair there—the only old thing in the room. It is standing facing the fire as it must have stood the night I was killed. The fire was burning brightly, the pattern of the back of the chair was thrown in shadow across the ceiling. Now the night I was murdered the conditions were exactly the same, so directly I saw that pattern on the ceiling I remembered the whole thing. I was not dreaming, don't think it, I was not. What happened that night was this: I was lying in bed counting the parts of the back of that chair in shadow on the ceiling. I probably could not get to sleep: you know the sort of thing, count up to a thousand and remember in the morning where you got to. Well, I was counting those pieces when suddenly they were obliterated, the whole back became a shadow, someone was sitting in the chair. Now, surely you understand that directly I saw the shadow of that chair on the ceiling to-night I realized that I had not a moment to lose. At any moment that same person might come back to that same chair and escape would be impossible. I slipped from my bed as quickly as I could and ran downstairs.'

"'But were you not afraid,' I asked, 'downstairs?'

"'That she might follow me? It was a woman, you know. No, I don't think I was. She does not belong downstairs. Anyhow she didn't.'

"'No,' I said. 'No.'

"My voice must have been out of control, for he caught me up at once.

"'You don't mean to say you saw her?' he said vehemently.

"'Oh, no.'

"'You felt her?'

"'She passed me as I came downstairs,' I said.

"'What can I have done to her that she follows me so?' He buried his face in his hands as though searching for an answer to his thought. Suddenly he looked up and stared at me.

"'Where had I got to? Oh yes, the murder. I can remember it all distinctly.

"'You can imagine how startled I was to see that shadow in the chair—startled, you know, but not really frightened. I leaned up in bed and looked at the chair, and sure enough a woman was sitting in it—a young woman. I watched her with a profound interest until she began to turn in her chair, as I felt, to look at me; when she did that I shrank back in bed. I dared not meet her eyes. She might not have had eyes, she might not have had a face. You know the sort of pictures that one sees when one glances back at all one's soul has ever thought.

"'I got back in the bed as far as I could and peeped over the sheets at the shadow on the ceiling. I was tired; frightened to death; I grew weary of watching; I must have fallen asleep, for suddenly the fire was almost out, the pattern of the chair barely discernible, the shadow had gone. I raised myself with a sense of huge relief. Yes, the chair was empty, but, just think of it: the woman was on the floor, on her hands and knees, crawling toward the bed.

"'I fell back stricken with terror.

"'Very soon I felt a gentle pull at the counterpane. I thought I was in a nightmare but too lazy or too comfortable to try to wake myself from it. I waited in an agony of suspense, but nothing seemed to be happening, in fact I had just persuaded myself that the movement of the counterpane was fancy when a hand brushed softly over my knee. There was no mistaking it, I could feel the long, thin fingers. Now was the time to do something. I tried to rouse myself, but all my efforts were futile, I was stiff from head to foot.

"'Although the hand was lost to me, outwardly, it now came within my range of knowledge, if you know what I mean. I knew that it was groping its way along the bed, feeling for some other part of me. At any moment I could have said exactly where it had got to. When it was hovering just over my chest another hand knocked lightly against my shoulder. I fancied it lost, and wandering in search of its fellow.

"'I was lying on my back staring at the ceiling when the hands met; the weight of their presence brought a feeling of oppression to my chest. I seemed to be completely cut off from my body; I had no sort of connection with any part of it, nothing about me would respond to my will to make it move.

"'There was no sound at all anywhere.

"'I fell into a state of indifference, a sort of patient indifference that can wait for an appointed time to come. How long I waited I cannot say, but when the time came it found me ready. I was not taken by surprise.

"'There was a great upward rush of pent-up force released; it was like a mighty mass of men who have been lost in prayer rising to their feet. I can't remember clearly, but I think the woman must have got on to my bed. I could not follow her distinctly, my whole attention was concentrated on her hands. All the time I felt those fingers itching for my throat.

"'At last they moved; slowly at first, then quicker; and then a long-drawn swish like the sound of an overbold wave that has broken too far up the beach and is sweeping back to join the sea.'

"The boy was silent for a moment, then he stretched out his hand for the cigarettes.

"'You remember nothing else?' I asked him.

"'No,' he said. 'The next thing I remember clearly is deliberately breaking the nursery window because it was raining and mother would not let me go out.'"

There was a moment's tension, then the strain of listening passed and everyone seemed to be speaking at once. The Rector was taking the story seriously.

"Tell me, Grady," he said. "How long do you suppose elapsed between the boy's murder and his breaking the nursery window?"

But a young married woman in the first flush of her happiness broke in between them. She ridiculed the whole idea. Of course the boy was dreaming. She was drawing the majority to her way of thinking when, from the corner where the girl sat, a hollow-sounding voice:

"And the boy? Where is he?"

The tone of the girl's voice inspired horror, that fear that does not know what it is it fears; one could see it on every face; on every face, that is, but the face of the bald-headed little man; there was no horror on his face, he was smiling serenely as he looked the girl straight in the eyes.

"He's a man now," he said.

"Alive?" she cried.

"Why not?" said the little old man, rubbing his hands together.

She tried to rise, but her frock had got caught between the chairs and pulled her to her seat again. The man next her put out his hand to steady her, but she dashed it away roughly. She looked round the party for an instant for all the world like an animal at bay, then she sprang to her feet and charged blindly. They crowded round her to prevent her falling; at the touch of their hands she stopped. She was out of breath as though she had been running.

"All right," she said, pushing their hands from her. "All right. I'll come quietly. I did it."

They caught her as she fell and laid her on the sofa watching the colour fade from her face.

The hostess, an old woman with white hair and a kind face, approached the little old man; for once in her life she was roused to anger.

"I can't think how you could be so stupid," she said. "See what you have done."

"I did it for a purpose," he said.

"For a purpose?"

"I have always thought that girl was the culprit. I have to thank you for the opportunity you have given me of making sure."

The Journal of Edward Hargood

"D. N. J."

Several years ago I happened to be in the Library of Downing College for the purpose of consulting some Register, and in my wanderings in search of the catalogue of books, I came upon an old dirty, long-neglected volume, bound in cardboard and dingy yellow leather, stamped on the back with the title "Journal of Edward Hargood, Surgeon, of Cambridge." Inside the cover was an inscription to the effect that this book, with many others, had been left to the College by one John Hamilton Craik, at the time of his death in 1852, and to judge from its outward appearance it had never been touched since the first day of its sojourn in the College. On turning over the pages, I was surprised to find, not some hundred odd pages of dull print, as I had expected, but a long manuscript journal, written in a firm, clear hand, bound up with a few letters and papers. This was, in itself, surprising enough, but on reading some way into the book, my eye fell upon a sentence which effectually roused my interest. It ran as follows: "Jan. 18. To-day at work all day with Dr. Dunning who made a communication [to] me of greatest importance." A few pages further on I read again: "Dunning at work with me most of this day and a long conversation after."

I need hardly retail in full to Cambridge readers the strange story that centres round the name of Dunning, but in case there should be some who have not yet heard it, I will relate, without adornment, the main facts of his life. He was born in 1692 and came to Benét College, Cambridge, in 1710. From 1714 to 1720 he resided as a Fellow of his College, but in the last-mentioned year he seems to have inherited some considerable fortune, and for the next seventeen years he was never in Cambridge. But in 1737 he suddenly re-appeared, evidently a poor man once more, and for thirty years lived in his old rooms on the ground-floor of L staircase in Benét College, seeing hardly a soul outside his College, and devoting his energies to the translation of the works of several obscure German physicians. Towards the end of the year 1767 he disappeared as suddenly as he had re-appeared, and to this day, in spite of many theories, the mystery of his fate has never been solved.

Readers, therefore, will understand my excitement when I came across this name in the manuscript journal in Downing Library. I obtained leave to take it home with me, and at once looked up the dates of its commencement and ending; my interest was, if possible, redoubled on finding that the first entry was made on January 1st, 1761, and the last on November 9th, 1768, that is to say, about twelve months after Dunning's disappearance. At last, I thought, I shall find some clue to the Dunning Mystery. But on reading through the journal I was, at first, bitterly disappointed and then horribly fascinated. It is one of the most amazing productions that it has ever been my fate to read. Of life and thought in Cambridge in the eighteenth century it gives hardly a glimpse, and in all its three hundred and seventy-three pages there are only about twenty names mentioned, the most frequent of which is that of Dunning. The rest of the book is confined to a few domestic details of rather a sordid nature, a vast deal of outrageous and indecent blasphemy, and long-drawn descriptions of disease and of operations carried out with all the barbarity of surgery in the eighteenth century. These last descriptions fill nearly three-quarters of the book, and they shew a dark and perverted nature, absolutely heartless and devoid of any feeling for human weakness or human pain. Over all there reigns a spirit of grim and brutal humour that finds expression in comments that, at first, sound only naive and childish, until their lurking ferocity becomes manifest. For instance, in describing the death of some unhappy victim under his hands, he writes: "never did I hear a boy give so much outcry; he died after a vast deal of it, as I was scraping the bone, more of the pain than his injuries I suppose." This is one of the more tolerable incidents recorded; others are too repulsive for print, and the kindest interpretation to put upon them is that Edward Hargood had lost all semblance of humanity in his love of his profession.

But, as regards Dunning, the journal is, at first sight, disappointing. In the beginning there are several records of him, such as "at work with old Mr. Dunning again in Findsilver St.," "a long talk with old Dunning," and once or twice mention is made of "a conversation through his window with D. tonight till very late." But in the crucial year of 1767 Dunning is only mentioned by name five times, and at the supposed date of his disappearance from his rooms there is one of the frequent lacunae in the journal, of some seven weeks duration. Although all Cambridge was gossipping about the "strange story," Hargood, one of Dunning's few acquaintances outside his college, makes no mention of it until January 17th, 1768. On January 17th, he notes that "Mr. Cowper came to see [me] to-day from the Master and Fellows of his college, and asked me of this alledged disappearance of Mr. Dunning. I gave what information I could, and said I thought he was only gone from Cambridge a time." After this entry follows a diatribe against "Fellows and the like," with whom Hargood, to judge from one or two earlier passages, was not on good terms.

After this incursion of foreign interest, the journal continues on its bloodthirsty way, and the accounts of dissections and operations are given with greater regularity and almost more copiousness than usual, and Dunning's name is not mentioned again until November 7th. At this date the Diary assumes, of a sudden, a most dramatic form, which we must describe in detail.

On November 7th the entry is short and alarming, and runs as follows:

> Nov. 7. to-night had in Mr. Morden of Catherine Hall, who talk of publishing Dunning's old papers, which worthless, when a most surprising Occurence. I was standing talking to M. seated before me, when he goes into a Fit, becoming first much suffused with Blood in the Face, and very red, his eyes shooting out, as he saw something which frightened [him]. Then he became very pale, his mouth dropping down in a Grin, and he waves, half rising from the Chair, his Hand at the Mirrour behind me, as if he saw something, and falls in a Swoon upon the Floor. I have in help and he was carried to his Rooms. I am curious to know what gave him such Terrour and what he thought to see behind me.

Under this startling entry there comes a black line, evidently drawn with a quill pen in some impatience. On close inspection, under this line, can be descried some faded handwriting, extraordinarily minute and spider-like and quite illegible. Two days later, Hargood notes that Morden has died "of the Fit he had in my House," and then the entry goes on to say

> being ill with a putrid sore throat, little work to-day, and I am much provoked to find th—

The entry breaks off dramatically at this point, and then follows this strange exclamation, written in an agitated hand,

God whom I have denied help me.

and again underneath,

God whom I have denied help me.

But under this second wild appeal for help, once more there can be descried the faint, weird handwriting that appears under the black line on November 7th. After these two last entries there comes a sentence, written in quite a different hand.

I have guessed ....this is a terrible book,

and so the journal ends.

So far, it may be said that this Journal throws no new light on the Dunning mystery, but I now must quote two MSS I found incorporated with the Journal. The first is short and runs as follows:

> This book came into the possession of my friend Charles Morrison from the Library of his uncle, Archdeacon Morrison. I have often heard him tell how he found it in his uncle's hands at the time of his sudden death. (signed) J. H. Craik.

The other document is a letter from Charles Morrison to John Craik, Esq (dated March 2nd, 1851) and copied out in Craik's handwriting. It runs as follows:

> Dear Craik. I have found out the mystery of that abominable book and I wish to Heaven I had not. All my suspicions of H. were true.
>
> The truth suddenly flashed through my mind as I was sitting by myself after dinner with the book on my knees, and before I knew what I was about, I was round at the side-board and had flung the book upside down before the glass, open at the last page, where that horrible little impish handwriting comes. After a few minutes poring, I made out in the reflection of the page, that the first sentence after Hargood's remark "I am curious to know what he thought to see behind me," ran as follows, with no capitals and repeated twice:
>
> "it was i o mine enemy."
>
> I was hurrying on in wild agitation to the next sentence under H's appeal for help, when suddenly an overpowering thought seized me. I remembered

how my uncle had died with this book in his hand and *I felt I now knew why.* I did not dare to look up or take my eyes away from the reflected page, but stood staring at it stupidly. You may laugh at what I saw next, but I tell you in that moment I saw in the glass the hand of an old man, very thin and wrinkled and very cruel looking, with soiled ruffles at the wrist, glide over my sleeve and point with its fore-finger to the second sentence and slowly pass along the page. Fascinated I followed it and read "i come to-morrow the end of one year for mine enemy." At the end of the sentence the hand stopped. I did not dare to look up to see what might be at my back, but shut my eyes and turned round, opening them saw—nothing. I have not been able to abide the sight of a looking glass these last two days, and write to ask you to come quickly, yours, C. Morrison.

Postscript. My poor friend died before I came to him, on March 5th, 1851. J.H.C.

Inspired by my interest in this book, some years ago, I made enquiries into Hargood's life. I met with disappointingly little success. All I could find was that he lived in Cambridge from 1759 to 1768 in a large house on the High Street, next door to the Dolphin Inn, with a small garden at the back, going up to the walls of Benét College. This house (which was once occupied by the famous E. D. Clarke) was destroyed in 1817 to make room for the new buildings of Corpus Christi College. The other fact which I found of any interest is that he was buried in St Benét's Churchyard on November 12th, 1768.

Whether the terrible theory propounded in the letter I have quoted contains the right explanation of the story or whether it is a grim joke of Mr. Craik's conception, I have not presumed to find out. I returned the book to the Library the day after I had taken it out, and there it is lying probably at the present moment, unknown and untouched by any hand since the day I placed it once more upon its obscure and dusty shelf.

The Kirk Spook

E. G. Swain

Before many years have passed it will be hard to find a person who has ever seen a Parish Clerk. The Parish Clerk is all but extinct. Our grandfathers knew him well—an oldish, clean-shaven man, who looked as if he had never been young, who dressed in rusty black, bestowed upon him, as often as not, by the Rector, and who usually wore a white tie on Sundays, out of respect for the seriousness of his office. He it was who laid out the rector's robes, and helped him to put them on; who found the places in the large Bible and Prayer Book, and indicated them by means of decorous silken book-markers; who lighted and snuffed the candles in the pulpit and desk, and attended to the little stove in the squire's pew; who ran busily about, in short, during the quarter-hour which preceded Divine Service, doing a hundred little things, with all the activity, and much of the appearance, of a beetle.

Just such a one was Caleb Dean, who was Clerk of Stoneground in the days of William IV. Small in stature, he possessed a voice which Nature seemed to have meant for a giant, and in the discharge of his duties he had a dignity of manner disproportionate even to his voice. No one was afraid to sing when he led the Psalm, so certain was it that no other voice could be noticed, and the gracious condescension with which he received his meagre fees would have been ample acknowledgement of double their amount.

Man, however, cannot live by dignity alone, and Caleb was glad enough to be sexton as well as clerk, and to undertake any other duties by which he might add to his modest income. He kept the Churchyard tidy, trimmed the lamps, chimed the bells, taught the choir their simple tunes, turned the barrel of the organ, and managed the stoves.

It was this last duty in particular, which took him into Church "last thing," as he used to call it, on Saturday night. There were people in those days, and may be some in these, whom nothing would induce to enter a Church at midnight; Caleb, however, was so much at home there that all hours were alike to him. He was never an early man on Saturdays. His wife, who insisted upon sitting up for him, would often knit her way into Sunday before he appeared, and even then would find it hard to get him to bed. Caleb, in fact, when off duty, was a genial little fellow; he had many friends, and on Saturday evenings he knew where to find them.

It was not, therefore, until the evening was spent that he went to make up his fires; and his voice, which served for other singing than that of Psalms, could usually be heard, within a little of midnight, beguiling the way to Church with snatches of convivial songs. Many a belated traveller, homeward bound, would envy him his spirits, but no one envied him his duties. Even such as walked with him to the neighbourhood of the Churchyard would bid him 'Good-night' whilst still a long way from the gate. They would see him disappear into the gloom amongst the graves, and shudder as they turned homewards.

Caleb, meanwhile, was perfectly content. He knew every stone in the path; long practice enabled him, even on the darkest night, to thrust his huge key into the lock at the first attempt, and on the night we are about to describe—it had come to Mr. Batchel from an old man who heard it from Caleb's lips—he did it with a feeling of unusual cheerfulness and contentment.

Caleb always locked himself in. A prank had once been played upon him, which had greatly wounded his dignity; and though it had been no midnight prank, he had taken care, ever since, to have the Church to himself. He locked the door, therefore, as usual, on the night we speak of, and made his way to the stove. He used no candle. He opened the little iron door of the stove, and obtained sufficient light to show him the fuel he had laid in readiness; then, when he had made up his fire, he closed this door again, and left the church in darkness. He never could say what induced him upon this occasion to remain there after his task was done. He knew that his wife was sitting up, as usual, and that, as usual, he would have to hear what she had to say. Yet, instead of making his way home, he sat down in the corner of the nearest seat. He supposed that he must have felt tired, but had no distinct recollection of it.

The Church was not absolutely dark. Caleb remembered that he could make out the outlines of the windows, and that through the window nearest to him he saw a few stars. After his eyes had grown accustomed to the gloom he could see the lines of the seats taking shape in the darkness, and he had not long sat there before he could dimly see everything there was. At last he began to distinguish where books lay upon the shelf in front of him. And then he closed his eyes. He does not admit having fallen asleep, even for a moment. But the seat was restful, the neighbouring stove was growing warm, he had been through a long and joyous evening, and it was natural that he should at least close his eyes.

He insisted that it was only for a moment. Something, he could not say what, caused him to open his eyes again immediately. The closing of them seemed to have improved what may be called his dark sight. He saw everything in the Church quite distinctly, in a sort of grey light. The pulpit stood out, large and bulky, in front. Beyond that, he passed his eyes along the four windows on the north side of the Church. He looked again at the stars, still visible through the nearest window on his left hand as he was sitting. From that, his eyes fell to the further end of the seat in front of him, where he could even see a faint gleam of polished wood. He traced this gleam to the middle of the seat, until it disappeared in black shadow, and upon that his eye passed on to the seat he was in, and there he saw a man sitting beside him.

Caleb described the man very clearly. He was, he said, a pale, old-fashioned looking man, with something very churchy about him. Reasoning also with great clearness, he said that the stranger had not come into the Church either with him or after him, and that therefore he must have been there before him. And in that case, seeing that the Church had been locked since two in the afternoon, the stranger must have been there for a considerable time.

Caleb was puzzled; turning therefore, to the stranger, he asked "How long have you been here?"

The stranger answered at once "Six hundred years."

"Oh! come!" said Caleb.

"Come where?" said the stranger.

"Well, if you come to that, come out," said Caleb.

"I wish I could," said the stranger, and heaved a great sigh.

"What's to prevent you?" said Caleb. "There 's the door, and here 's the key."

"That's it," said the other.

"Of course it is," said Caleb. "Come along."

With that he proceeded to take the stranger by the sleeve, and then it was that he says you might have knocked him down with a feather. His hand went right into the place where the sleeve seemed to be, and Caleb distinctly saw two of the stranger's buttons on the top of his own knuckles.

He hastily withdrew his hand, which began to feel icy cold, and sat still, not knowing what to say next. He found that the stranger was gently chuckling with laughter, and this annoyed him.

"What are you laughing at?" he enquired peevishly. "It's not funny enough for two," answered the other.

"Who are you, anyhow?" said Caleb.

"I am the kirk spook," was the reply.

Now Caleb had not the least notion what a "kirk spook" was. He was not willing to admit his ignorance, but his curiosity was too much for his pride, and he asked for information.

"Every Church has a spook," said the stranger, "and I am the spook of this one."

"Oh," said Caleb, "I've been about this Church a many years, but I've never seen you before."

"That," said the spook, "is because you've always been moving about. I'm flimsy—very flimsy indeed—and I can only keep myself together when everything is quite still."

"Well," said Caleb, "you've got your chance now. What are you going to do with it?"

"I want to go out," said the spook, "I'm tired of this Church, and I've been alone for six hundred years. It's a long time."

"It does seem rather a long time," said Caleb, "but why don't you go if you want to? There's three doors."

"That's just it," said the spook. "They keep me in."

"What?" said Caleb, "when they're open."

"Open or shut," said the spook, "it's all one."

"Well, then," said Caleb, "what about the windows?"

"Every bit as bad," said the spook, "They're all pointed." Caleb felt out of his depth. Open doors and windows that kept a person in—if it was a person—seemed to want a little understanding. And the flimsier the person, too, the easier it ought to be for him to go where he wanted. Also, what could it matter whether they were pointed to not?

The latter question was the one which Caleb asked first.

"Six hundred years ago," said the Spook, "all arches were made round, and when these pointed things came in I cursed them. I hate new-fangled things."

"That wouldn't hurt them much," said Caleb.

"I said I would never go under one of them," said the spook.

"That would matter more to you than to them," said Caleb.

"It does," said the spook, with another great sigh.

"But you could easily change your mind," said Caleb.

"I was tied to it," said the spook, "I was told that I never more should go under one of them, whether I would or not."

"Some people will tell you anything," answered Caleb.

"It was a Bishop," explained the spook.

"Ah!" said Caleb, "that's different, of course."

The spook told Caleb how often he had tried to go under the pointed arches, sometimes of the doors, sometimes of the windows, and how a stream of wind always struck him from the point of the arch, and drifted him back into the Church. He had long given up trying.

"You should have been outside," said Caleb, "before they built the last door."

"It was my Church," said the spook, "and I was too proud to leave."

Caleb began to sympathize with the spook. He had a pride in the Church himself, and disliked even to hear another person say Amen before him. He also began to be a little jealous of this stranger who had been six hundred years in possession of the Church in which Caleb had believed himself, under the vicar, to be master. And he began to plot.

"Why do you want to get out?" he asked. "I'm no use here," was the reply, "I don't get enough to do to keep myself warm. And I know there are scores of Churches now without any kirk-spooks at all. I can hear their cheap little bells dinging every Sunday."

"There's very few bells hereabouts," said Caleb.

"There's no hereabouts for spooks," said the other. "We can hear any distance you like."

"But what good are you at all?" said Caleb.

"Good!" said the spook. "Don't we secure proper respect for Churches, especially after dark? A Church would be like any other place if it wasn't for us. You must know that."

"Well, then," said Caleb, "you're no good here. This Church is all right. What will you give me to let you out?"

"Can you do it?" asked the spook.

"What will you give me?" said Caleb.

"I'll say a good word for you amongst the spooks," said the other.

"What good will that do me?" said Caleb.

"A good word never did anybody any harm yet," answered the spook.

"Very well then, come along," said Caleb.

"Gently then," said the spook; "don't make a draught."

"Not yet," said Caleb, and he drew the spook very carefully (as one takes a vessel quite full of water) from the seat.

"I can't go under pointed arches," cried the spook, as Caleb moved off.

"Nobody wants you to," said Caleb. "Keep close to me."

He led the spook down the aisle to the angle of the wall where a small iron shutter covered an opening into the flue. It was used by the chimney sweep alone, but Caleb had another use for it now. Calling to the spook to keep close, he suddenly removed the shutter.

The fires were by this time burning briskly. There was a strong up-draught as the shutter was removed. Caleb felt something rush across his face, and heard a cheerful laugh away up in the chimney. Then he knew that he was alone. He replaced the shutter, gave another look at his stoves, took the keys, and made his way home.

He found his wife asleep in her chair, sat down and took off his boots, and awakened her by throwing them across the kitchen.

"I've been wondering when you'd wake," he said.

"What?" she said, "Have you been in long?"

"Look at the clock," said Caleb. "Half after twelve."

"My gracious," said his wife. "Let's be off to bed."

"Did you tell her about the spook?" he was naturally asked.

"Not I," said Caleb. "You knew what she'd say. Same as she always does of a Saturday night."

This fable Mr. Batchel related with reluctance. His attitude towards it was wholly deprecatory. Psychic phenomena, he said, lay outside the province of the mere humourist, and the levity with which they had been treated was largely responsible for the presumptuous materialism of the age.

He said more, as he warmed to the subject, than can here be repeated. The reader of the foregoing tales, however, will be interested to know that Mr. Batchel's own attitude was one of humble curiosity. He refused even to guess why the *revenant* was sometimes invisible, and at other times partly or wholly visible; sometimes capable of using physical force, and at other times powerless. He knew that they had their periods, and that was all.

There is room, he said, for the romancer in these matters; but for the humourist, none. Romance was the play of intelligence about the confines of truth. The invisible world, like the visible, must have its romancers, its explorers, and its interpreters; but the time of the last was not yet come.

Criticism, he observed in conclusion, was wholesome and necessary. But of the idle and mischievous remarks which were wont to pose as criticism, he held none in so much contempt as the cheap and irrational POOH-POOH.

THE LADY AND THE GHOST

ROSE CECIL O'NEILL

IT WAS SOME MOMENTS BEFORE THE LADY BECAME RATIONALLY CONVINCED THAT THERE was something occurring in the corner of the room, and then the actual nature of the thing was still far from clear.

"To put it as mildly as possible," she murmured, "the thing verges upon the uncanny"; and, leaning forward upon her silken knees, she attended upon the phenomenon.

At first it had seemed like some faint and unexplained atmospheric derangement, occasioned, apparently, neither by an opened window nor by a door. Some papers fluttered to the floor, the fringes of the hangings softly waved, and, indeed, it would still have been easy to dismiss the matter as the effect of a vagrant draft had not the state of things suddenly grown unmistakably unusual. All the air of the room, it then appeared, rushed even with violence to the point and there underwent what impressed her as an aerial convulsion, in the very midst and well-spring of which, so great was the confusion, there seemed to appear at intervals almost the semblance of a shape.

The silence of the room was disturbed by a book that flew open with fluttering leaves, the noise of a vase of violets blown over, from which the perfumed water dripped to the floor, and soft touchings all around as of a breeze passing through a chamber full of trifles.

The ringlets of the Lady's hair were swept forward toward the corner upon which her gaze was fixed, and in which the conditions had now grown so tense with imminent occurrence and so rent with some inconceivable throe that she involuntarily rose, and, stepping forward against the pressure of her petticoats which were blown about her ankles, she impatiently thrust her hand into the——

She was immediately aware that another hand had received it, though with a far from substantial envelopment, and for another moment what she saw before her trembled between something and nothing. Then from the precarious situation there slowly emerged into dubious view the shape of a young man dressed in evening clothes over which was flung a mantle of voluminous folds such as is worn by ghosts of fashion.

"The very deuce was in it!" he complained; "I thought I should never materialize."

She flung herself into her chair, confounded; yet, even in the shock of the emergency, true to herself, she did not fail to smooth her ruffled locks.

Her visitor had been scanning his person in a dissatisfied way, and with some vexation he now ejaculated: "Beg your pardon, my dear, but are my feet on the floor, or where in thunder are they?"

It was with a tone of reassurance that she confessed that his patent-leathers were the trivial matter of two or three inches from the rug. Whereupon, with still another effort, he brought himself down until his feet rested decently upon the floor. It was only when he walked about to examine the bric-à-brac that a suspicious lightness was discernible in his tread.

When he had composed himself by the survey, effecting it with an air of great insouciance, which, however, failed to conceal the fact that his heart was beating somewhat wildly, he approached the Lady.

"Well, here we are again, my love!" he cried, and devoured her hands with ghostly kisses. "It seems an eternity that I've been struggling back to you through the outer void and what-not. Sometimes, I confess I all but despaired. Life is not, I assure you, all beer and skittles for the disembodied."

He drew a long breath, and his gaze upon her and the entire chamber seemed to envelop all and cherish it.

"Little room, little room! And so you are thus! Do you know," he continued, with vivacity, "I have wondered about it in the grave, and I could hardly sleep for this place unpenetrated. Heigho! What a lot of things we leave undone! I dashed this off at the time, the literary passion strong in me, thus:

"Now, when all is done, and I lie so low,
   I cannot sleep for this, my only care;
For though of that dim place I could not know;
   That where my heart was fain I did not go,
Nor saw you musing there!

"Well, well, these things irk a ghost so. Naturally, as soon as possible I made my way back—to be satisfied—to be satisfied that you were still mine." He bent a piercing look upon her.

"I observe by the calendar on your writing-table that some years have elapsed since my—um—since I expired," he added, with a faint blush. It appears that the matter of their dissolution is, in conversation, rather kept in the background by well-bred ghosts.

"Heigho! How time does fly! You'll be joining me soon, my dear."

She drew herself splendidly up, and he was aware of her beauty in the full of its tenacious excellence—of the delicate insolence of Life looking upon Death—of the fact *that she had forgotten him.*

He rose, and confronted this, his trembling hands thrust into his pockets, then turned away to hide the dismay of his countenance. He was, however, a spook of considerable spirit, and in a jiffy he met the occasion. To her blank, indignant gaze he drew a card from his case, and, taking a pencil from the secretary, wrote, beneath the name:

Quiet to the breast
 Wheresoe'er it be,
That gave an hour's rest
 To the heart of me.
Quiet to the breast
 Till it lieth dead,
And the heart be clay
 Where I visited.
Quiet to the breast,
 Though forgetting quite
The guest it sheltered once;
 To the heart, good night!

Handing her the card he bowed, and, through force of habit, turned to the door, forgetting that his ghostly pressure would not turn the knob.

As the door did not open, with a sigh of recollection for his spiritual condition, he prepared to disappear, casting one last look at the faithless Lady. She was still looking at the card in her hand, and the tears ran down her face.

"She has remembered," he reflected; "how courteous!" For a moment it seemed he could contain his disappointment, discreetly removing himself now at what he felt was the vanishing-point, with the customary reticence of the dead, but feeling overcame him. In an instant he had her in his arms, and was pouring out his love, his reproaches, the story of his longing, his doubts, his discontent, and his desperate journey back to earth for a sight of her. "And, ah!" cried he, "picture my agony at finding that you had forgotten. And yet I surmised it in the gloom. I divined it by my restlessness and my despair. Perhaps some lines that occurred to me will suggest the thing to you—you recall my old knack for versification?

"Where the grasses weep
O'er his darkling bed,
And the glow-worms creep,
Lies the weary head
Of one laid deep, who cannot sleep:
The unremembered dead."

He took a chair beside her, and spoke of their old love for each other, of his fealty through all transmutations; incidentally of her beauty, of her cruelty, of the light of her face which had illumined his darksome way to her—and of a lot of other things—and the Lady bowed her head, and wept.

The hours of the night passed thus: the moon waned, and a pallor began to tinge the dusky cheek of the east, but the eloquence of the visitor still flowed on, and the Lady had his misty hands clasped to her reawakened bosom. At last a suspicion of rosiness touched the curtain. He abruptly rose.

"I cannot hold out against the morning," he said; "it is time all good ghosts were in bed."

But she threw herself on her knees before him, clasping his ethereal waist with a despairing embrace.

"Oh, do not leave me," she cried, "or my love will kill me!"

He bent eagerly above her. "Say it again—convince me!"

"I love you," she cried, again and again and again, with such an anguish of sincerity as would convince the most skeptical spook that ever revisited the glimpses of the moon.

"You will forget again," he said.

"I shall never forget!" she cried. "My life will henceforth be one continual remembrance of you, one long act of devotion to your memory, one oblation, one unceasing penitence, one agony of waiting!"

He lifted her face, and saw that it was true.

"Well," said he, gracefully wrapping his cloak about him, "well, now I shall have a little peace."

He kissed her, with a certain jaunty grace, upon her hair, and prepared to dissolve, while he lightly tapped a tattoo upon his leg with the dove-colored gloves he carried.

"Good-by, my dear!" he said; "henceforth I shall sleep o' nights; my heart is quite at rest."

"But mine is breaking," she wailed, madly trying once more to clasp his vanishing form.

He threw her a kiss from his misty finger-tips, and all that remained with her, besides her broken heart, was a faint disturbance of the air.

The Last Squire of Ennismore

Mrs. J. H. Riddell

"Did I see it myself? No, sir; I did not see it; and my father before me did not see it; nor his father before him, and he was Phil Regan, just the same as myself. But it is true, for all that; just as true as that you are looking at the very place where the whole thing happened. My great-grandfather (and he did not die till he was ninety-eight) used to tell, many and many's the time, how he met the stranger, night after night, walking lonesome-hike about the sands where most of the wreckage came ashore."

"And the old house, then, stood behind that belt of Scotch firs?"

"Yes; and a fine house it was, too. Hearing so much talk about it when a boy, my father said, made him often feel as if he knew every room in the building, though it had all fallen to ruin before he was born. None of the family ever lived in it after the squire went away. Nobody else could be got to stop in the place. There used to be awful noises, as if something was being pitched from the top of the great staircase down in to the hall; and then there would be a sound as if a hundred people were clinking glasses and talking all together at once. And then it seemed as if barrels were rolling in the cellars; and there would be screeches, and howls, and laughing, fit to make your blood run cold. They say there is gold hid away in the cellars; but not one has ever ventured to find it. The very children won't come here to play; and when the men are plowing the field behind, nothing will make them stay in it, once the day begins to change. When the night is coming on, and the tide creeps in on the sand, more than one thinks he has seen mighty queer things on the shore."

"But what is it really they think they see? When I asked my landlord to tell me the story from beginning to end, he said he could not remember it; and, at any rate, the whole rigmarole was nonsense, put together to please strangers."

"And what is he but a stranger himself? And how should he know the doings of real quality like the Ennismores? For they were gentry, every one of them—good old stock; and as for wickedness, you might have searched Ireland through and not found their match. It is a sure thing, though, that if Riley can't tell you the story, I can; for, as I said, my own people were in it, of a manner of speaking. So, if your honour will rest yourself off your feet, on that bit of a bank, I'll set down my creel and give you the whole pedigree of how Squire Ennismore went away from Ardwinsagh."

It was a lovely day, in the early part of June; and, as the Englishman cast himself on a low ridge of sand, he looked over Ardwinsagh Bay with a feeling of ineffable content. To his left lay the Purple Headland; to his right, a long range of breakers, that went straight out into the Atlantic till they were lost from sight; in front lay the Bay of Ardwinsagh, with its bluish-green water sparkling in the summer sunlight, and here and there breaking over some sunken rock, against which the waves spent themselves in foam.

"You see how the current's set, Sir? That is what makes it dangerous for them as doesn't know the coast, to bathe here at any time, or walk when the tide is flowing. Look how the sea is creeping in now, like a race-horse at the finish. It leaves that tongue of sand bars to the last, and then, before you could look round, it has you up to the middle. That is why I made bold to speak to you; for it is not alone on the account of Squire Ennismore the bay has a bad name. But it is about him and the old house you want to hear. The last mortal being that tried to live in it, my great-grandfather said, was a creature, by name Molly Leary; and she had neither kith nor kin, and begged for her bite and sup, sheltering herself at night in a turf cabin she had built at the back of a ditch. You may be sure she thought herself a made woman when the agent said, 'Yes: she might try if she could stop in the house; there was peat and bog-wood,' he told her, 'and half-a-crown a week for the winter, and a golden guinea once Easter came,' when the house was to be put in order for the family; and his wife gave Molly some warm clothes and a blanket or two; and she was well set up.

"You may be sure she didn't choose the worst room to sleep in; and for a while all went quiet, till one night she was wakened by feeling the bedstead lifted by the four corners and shaken like a carpet. It was a heavy four-post bedstead, with a solid top: and her life seemed to go out of her with the fear. If it had been a ship in a storm off the Headland, it couldn't have pitched worse and then, all of a sudden, it was dropped with such a bang as nearly drove the heart into her mouth.

"But that, she said, was nothing to the screaming and laughing, and hustling and rushing that filled the house. If a hundred people had been running hard along the passages and tumbling downstairs, they could not have made greater noise.

"Molly never was able to tell how she got clear of the place; but a man coming late home from Ballycloyne Fair found the creature crouched under the old thorn there, with very little on her—saving your honour's presence. She had a bad fever, and talked about strange things, and never was the same woman after."

"But what was the beginning of all this? When did the house first get the name of being haunted?"

"After the old Squire went away: that was what I purposed telling you. He did not come here to live regularly till he had got well on in years. He was near seventy at the time I am talking about; but he held himself as upright as ever, and rode as hard as the youngest; and could have drunk a whole roomful under the table, and walked up to bed as unconcerned as you please at the dead of the night.

"He was a terrible man. You couldn't lay your tongue to a wickedness he had not been in the forefront of—drinking, duelling, gambling,—all manner of sins had been meat and drink to him since he was a boy almost. But at last he did something in London so bad, so beyond the beyonds, that he thought he had best come home and live among people who did not know so much about his goings on as the English. It was said that he wanted to try and stay in this world for ever; and that he had got some secret drops that kept him well and hearty. There was something wonderful queer about him, anyhow.

"He could hold foot with the youngest; and he was strong, and had a fine fresh colour in his face; and his eyes were like a hawk's; and there was not a break in his voice—and him near upon threescore and ten!

"At last and at long last it came to be the March before he was seventy—the worst March ever known in all these parts—such blowing, sheeting, snowing, had not been experienced in the memory of man; when one blusterous night some foreign vessel went to bits on the Purple Headland. They say it was an awful sound to hear the deathcry that went up high above the noise of the wind; and it was as bad a sight to see the shore there strewed with corpses of all sorts and sizes, from the little cabin-boy to the grizzled seaman.

"They never knew who they were or where they came from, but some of the men had crosses, and beads, and such like, so the priest said they belonged to him, and they were all buried deeply and decently in the chapel graveyard.

"There was not much wreckage of value drifted on shore. Most of what is lost about the Head stays there; but one thing did come into the bay—a puncheon of brandy.

"The Squire claimed it; it was his right to have all that came on his land, and he owned this sea-shore from the Head to the breakers—every foot—so, in course, he had the brandy; and there was sore illwill because he gave his men nothing, not even a glass of whiskey.

"Well, to make a long story short, that was the most wonderful liquor anybody ever tasted. The gentry came from far and near to take share, and it was cards and dice, and drinking and story-telling night after night—week in, week out. Even on Sundays, God forgive them! The officers would drive over from Ballyclone, and sit emptying tumbler after tumbler till Monday morning came, for it made beautiful punch.

"But all at once people quit coming—a word went round that the liquor was not all it ought to be. Nobody could say what ailed it, but it got about that in some way men found it did not suit them.

"For one thing, they were losing money very fast.

"They could not make head against the Squire's luck, and a hint was dropped the puncheon ought to have been towed out to sea, and sunk in fifty fathoms of water.

"It was getting to the end of April, and fine, warm weather for the time of year, when first one and then another, and then another still, began to take notice of a stranger who walked the shore alone at night. He was a dark man, the same colour as the drowned crew lying in the chapel graveyard, and had rings in his ears, and wore a strange kind of hat, and cut wonderful antics as he walked, and had an ambling sort of gait, curious to look at. Many tried to talk to him, but he only shook his head; so, as nobody could make out where he came from or what he wanted, they made sure he was the spirit of some poor wretch who was tossing about the Head, longing for a snug corner in holy ground.

"The priest went and tried to get some sense out of him.

"'Is it Christian burial you're wanting?' asked his reverence; but the creature only shook his head.

"'Is it word sent to the wives and daughters you've left orphans and widows, you'd like?' But no; it wasn't that.

"'Is it for sin committed you're doomed to walk this way? Would masses comfort ye? There's a heathen,' said his reverence; 'Did you ever hear tell of a Christian that shook his head when masses were mentioned?'

"'Perhaps he doesn't understand English, Father,' says one of the officers who was there; 'Try him with Latin.'

"No sooner said than done. The priest started off with such a string of ayes and paters that the stranger fairly took to his heels and ran.

"'He is an evil spirit,' explained the priest, when he stopped, tired out, 'and I have exorcised him.'

"But next night my gentleman was back again, as unconcerned as ever.

"'And he'll just have to stay,' said his reverence, 'For I've got lumbago in the small of my back, and pains in all my joints—never to speak of a hoarseness with standing there shouting; and I don't believe he understood a sentence I said.'

"Well, this went on for a while, and people got that frightened of the man, or appearance of a man, they would not go near the sand; till in the end, Squire Ennismore, who had always scoffed at the talk, took it into his head he would go down one night, and see into the rights of the matter. He, maybe, was feeling lonesome, because, as I told your honour before, people had left off coming to the house, and there was nobody for him to drink with.

"Out he goes, then, bold as brass; and there were a few followed him. The man came forward at sight of the Squire and took off his hat with a foreign flourish. Not to be behind in civility, the Squire lifted his.

"'I have come, sir,' he said, speaking very loud, to try to make him understand, 'to know if you are looking for anything, and whether I can assist you to find it.'

"The man looked at the Squire as if he had taken the greatest liking to him, and took oft his hat again.

"'Is it the vessel that was wrecked you are distressed about?'

"There came no answer, only a mournful shake of the head.

"'Well, *I* haven't your ship, you know; it went all to bits months ago; and, as for the sailors, they are snug and sound enough in consecrated ground.'

"The man stood and looked at the Squire with a queer sort of smile on his face.

"'What *do* you want?' asked Mr. Ennismore in a bit of a passion. 'If anything belonging to you went down with the vessel, it's about the Head you ought to be looking for it, not here—unless, indeed, it's after the brandy you're fretting!'"

"Now, the Squire had tried him in English and French, and was now speaking a language you'd have thought nobody could understand; but, faith, it seemed natural as kissing to the stranger.

"'Oh! That's where you are from, is it?' said the Squire. 'Why couldn't you have told me so at once? I can't give you the brandy, because it mostly is drunk; but come along, and you shall have as stiff a glass of punch as ever crossed your lips.' And without more to-do off they went, as sociable as you please, jabbering together in some outlandish tongue that made moderate folks' jaws ache to hear it.

"That was the first night they conversed together, but it wasn't the last. The stranger must have been the height of good company, for the Squire never tired of him. Every evening, regularly, he came up to the house, always dressed the same, always smiling and polite, and then the Squire called for brandy and hot water, and they drank and played cards till cock-crow, talking and laughing into the small hours.

"This went on for weeks and weeks, nobody knowing where the man came from, or where he went; only two things the old housekeeper did know—that the puncheon was nearly empty, and that the Squire's flesh was wasting off him; and she felt so uneasy she went to the priest, but he could give her no manner of comfort.

"She got so concerned at last that she felt bound to listen at the dining-room door; but they always talked in that foreign gibberish, and whether it was blessing or cursing they were at she couldn't tell.

"Well, the upshot of it came one night in July—on the eve of the Squire's birthday—there wasn't a drop of spirit left in the puncheon—no, not as much as would drown a fly. They had drunk the whole lot clean up—and the old woman stood trembling, expecting every minute to hear the bell ring for more brandy, for where was she to get more if they wanted any?

"All at once the Squire and the stranger came out into the hall. It was a full moon, and light as day.

"'I'll go home with you to-night by way of a change,' says the Squire.

"'Will you so?' asked the other.

"'That I will,' answered the Squire.

"'It is your own choice, you know.'

"'Yes; it is my own choice; let us go.'

"So they went. And the housekeeper ran up to the window on the great staircase and watched the way they took. Her niece lived there as housemaid, and she came and watched, too; and, after a while, the butler as well. They all turned their faces this way, and looked after their master walking beside the strange man along these very sands. Well, they saw them walk on, and on, and on, and on, till the water took them to their knees, and then to their waists, and then to their arm-pits, and then to their throats and their heads; but long before that the women and the butler were running out on the shore as fast as they could, shouting for help."

"Well?" said the Englishman.

"Living or dead, Squire Ennismore never came back again. Next morning, when the tides ebbed again, one walking over the sand saw the print of a cloven foot—that he tracked to the water's edge. Then everybody knew where the Squire had gone, and with whom."

"And no more search was made?"

"Where would have been the use searching?"

"Not much, I suppose. It's a strange story, anyhow."

"But true, your honour—every word of it."

"Oh! I have no doubt of that," was the satisfactory reply.

The Lonely Road

H. D. Everett

"I am awfully sorry, Tom, I am indeed, and after all your kindness in coming down to see me about that tiresome business, but we can't drive you to the station this evening as I promised. The mare has been kicking in the stable again, and Summers has just discovered she is dead lame. You must really make up your mind to stay another night, and we will get a conveyance over from Ardkellar first thing to-morrow. If I write at once I shall catch the post: we haven't a telegraph office in the village, or I would wire. Summers has only just made the discovery, so he tells me. Now do be reasonable, and say you'll stay."

"That is kind of you, Margaret."

Tom Pulteney fixed again in his left eye the single eyeglass that was always dropping out. This so that he might look at his widowed cousin with the right expression, and she was good to look at, though no longer in her first youth.

"A few more hours here is a temptation; a greater one than I can say. But I'm positively bound to get back to Dublin to-night, and somehow or other I must contrive to catch the 8:50. I'm not such a weakling that I can't walk the distance. How far do you call it to the station?"

"It is eight miles good from here to Ardkellar. And it is a lonely road—"

"Well—I shan't need company for that short distance. I shall be too full of regrets after tearing myself away from you—to say nothing of Adelaide. Though you know very well that Adelaide does not count."

"I don't know anything of the sort. But I hate you going—all that way on foot, and at such an hour."

"Hate my going by all means—I'd wish nothing better. But for a different reason."

"Oh, Tom, do be serious: but if you must go, take care. The road has had a bad character of late; there have been assaults and robberies. Of course you don't go about with a revolver—here. But do you carry a heavy stick?"

"I didn't bring one. But I've got my fists, and I know how to use them."

"You must have a stick. I will lend you Laurence's; it is loaded at the head. I know you will sometime let me have it back."

"If it will make you easy about me——"

"It will make me easier. I am vexed about the mare—and not knowing till the last minute. I am afraid you will have to set off at once if that train is to be caught. And it is getting dusk even now."

The farewells followed, which Tom Pulteney made as affectionate as he dared. It was something of a triumph to him that Margaret was really concerned about the possible risk he was running, on a lonely stretch of road where there had been at least one attempted murder; and he set out with that conviction kept warm at heart.

To him an eight mile walk was truly a light matter, but he happened to be burdened carrying a suit-case made heavy by expensive fittings, and before the end of the first half mile he began to wish he had slipped his pet razors into his pocket, and asked his cousin to send the case after him, which without doubt she would have done. And for a reason other than the weight: if thieves were abroad, and he was attacked by two, it would be easily snatched by a confederate while one of them knocked him on the head. And a good sound leather suit-case, all but new, is worth stealing now-a-days apart from what it may contain. The contents of Tom's were also of value, things that he could ill spare—among other oddments a handsome finger-ring which he had brought from town, hoping he might find courage to offer it to Margaret as a *gage d' amour*. The parcel had not been opened: opportunity had not served, or else he had feared to damage his own cause by speaking too early in her widowhood. These articles would, he reflected, be safer if carried on his person, and then he could abandon the suit-case with less reluctance should there be need.

He was now far beyond Ballymacor, and the road before him was solitary. On a sudden impulse he deposited the case under the hedge, unsnapped the locks, and sought in the fast-fading light for his more treasured possessions. These he secured in innermost pockets, again shouldered his burden, and went on whistling under his breath, as might a man light-hearted and unafraid.

But was he unafraid? Was he not assuming the pretence of a boldness he did not possess? In the midst of that search into his luggage, a doubt beset him that the action there and then had been unwise; for at the same time he heard, or thought he heard, a rustle of movement behind the hedge. There was nothing for it then but to go on, and trust he had been mistaken, or the presence and movement wholly innocent. But presently he imagined—imagination first, but soon there was no doubt—that he heard footsteps following. He swung round twice and glanced behind him, but so far as he could see in the dusk the road was clear.

The sound went on, and now the footsteps approached nearer, quickening upon his, and he was already bracing every nerve, preparing for the encounter he expected.

At this critical moment a huge white dog leaped over the fence on the right.

"Why, Boris," he exclaimed unthinking, and the creature came beside him with wagging tail: surely in the event of attack, here would be a formidable ally.

The dog was friendly, and appeared to answer to the name called. Margaret had had such a dog in her husband's lifetime, a Russian wolf-hound of which she had been fond; Pulteney had often seen them together, the tall elegant woman followed by the noble hound. Surely this must be Boris; and yet he had a dim recollection of some mischance mentioned in a letter of Adelaide's, an accident in which the dog had been injured, and he thought killed. Certainly he had not seen Boris on any recent visit to Ballymacor. If only he could keep the dog beside him, he would, he thought, be safe. So he spoke to the creature by name, and spoke again; and each time Boris responded in dog fashion, pleased by the recognition, or so it seemed.

The footsteps still were following; and now, bolder because accompanied, he glanced over his shoulder. Yes, there were two men, and they were close behind, of villainous aspect in the dusk. The dog also looked round and growled, showing his teeth, formidable white fangs, set in a jaw like an alligator's: if the creature was strong enough and fierce enough to pull down a wolf, he would surely be a match for any man. But supposing the followers were armed, and their object murder and not mere robbery, what then?

The sky by this time was clearing, and behind the breaking clouds there came some shining of the moon, showing the way in front and the white hound beside him, and, as he remembered after, both their shadows. From time to time he spoke to his four-footed companion, and also put out his hand to pat the dog's neck; but somehow he never succeeded in touching him—the white rough coat seemed always just beyond reach, though there was no shrinking away to avoid contact.

Pulteney all the while was on the strain to listen, and though he still heard the following footsteps, double footsteps, it seemed to him that they were falling further behind. He could not now be far from Ardkellar, his destination; the railway-line here crossed the road high up on bridge and embankment, and a luggage train lumbered over before him, with gleaming lights and a long rattle of trucks. Not far beyond there was a cross-roads, and here the footsteps stopped. Pulteney glanced again over his shoulder, and saw that the two men had halted there, and seemed to be consulting together.

He turned and went on, and now he heard no more the pursuing feet. He was close to the outskirts of the country town, and, he concluded, in comparative safety. He could still see the dog beside him, and was beginning to wonder how he could best dispose of his companion in safety, and contrive to let Margaret know; as Boris who had befriended him, must certainly have strayed from Ballymacor. They had reached the first row of houses and the outpost of street lights, when he noticed that the form of the dog was altering, becoming shadowy in outline, instead of substantial as before. Still the creature kept step by step beside him, though a figure compacted of white mist growing more and more transparent, till at last, at the passing of the third lamp, this ghostly likeness of Boris faded into nothing and was gone. Tom Pulteney walked into the station of Ardkellar, grateful for his escape, but a bewildered man.

He wrote the history of that night's adventure to his cousin Margaret.

> Upon my word of honour, this is the literal truth, though you will find it difficult to believe. I made sure the dog was yours, as he seemed to know me, and evidently would have shown fight had I been attacked. And I believe the men saw him just as I did, and were deterred from carrying out their plan. It is true I could not touch him, though I tried; but no one could have been more astonished than I was when he dissolved into something like white smoke and then was gone. It was an experience I shall never forget.

To him, Margaret in reply.

> I do believe your story, and to me it is altogether convincing, though so strange. My dear Boris died two years ago: there was an accident I cannot bear to think of, even now. He was caught by a touring car going at speed, and caring nothing for the life or safety of a dog. I had him shot in mercy; I never say destroyed. And what you saw that night is witness that under other conditions he is in existence still. He was so good, so faithful: I never called on him in vain, and he knew almost my thought before I spoke. I was thinking of him that evening. I said to Adelaide—she will tell you—how I wished I had had Boris here, for I would have sent him with you on that lonely walk, and then you would have been safe. For I was very anxious. I believe my

thought, my wish, did send him, dear, dear fellow. But I cannot expect you to receive this as I do, or think that it explains.

Tom Pulteney to Margaret.

I am convinced, indeed. It was you who worked the miracle, and you worked it for me. Your letter, which explains so much, tells me one thing more: may I hope it is the one thing I would give the world to know? You were anxious—you cared what became of me. Could you care always—could you care enough? I pray that the post may bring me the answer I long for; but I am ever your devoted lover, however you reply.

Lost Hearts

M. R. James

It was, as far as I can ascertain, in September of the year 1811 that a postchaise drew up before the door of Aswarby Hall, in the heart of Lincolnshire. The little boy who was the only passenger in the chaise, and who jumped out as soon as it had stopped, looked about him with the keenest curiosity during the short interval that elapsed between the ringing of the bell and the opening of the hall door. He saw a tall, square, red-brick house, built in the reign of Anne; a stone-pillared porch had been added in the purer classical style of 1790; the windows of the house were many, tall and narrow, with small panes and thick white woodwork. A pediment, pierced with a round window, crowned the front. There were wings to right and left, connected by curious glazed galleries, supported by colonnades, with the central block. These wings plainly contained the stables and offices of the house. Each was surmounted by an ornamental cupola with a gilded vane.

An evening light shone on the building, making the window-panes glow like so many fires. Away from the Hall in front stretched a flat park studded with oaks and fringed with firs, which stood out against the sky. The clock in the church-tower, buried in trees on the edge of the park, only its golden weather-cock catching the light, was striking six, and the sound came gently beating down the wind. It was altogether a pleasant impression, though tinged with the sort of melancholy appropriate to an evening in early autumn, that was conveyed to the mind of the boy who was standing in the porch waiting for the door to open to him.

He had just come from Warwickshire, and some six months ago had been left an orphan. Now, owing to the generous and unexpected offer of his elderly cousin, Mr. Abney, he had come to live at Aswarby. The offer was unexpected, because all who knew anything of Mr. Abney looked upon him as a somewhat austere recluse, into whose steady-going household the advent of a small boy would import a new and, it seemed, incongruous element. The truth is that very little was known of Mr. Abney's pursuits or temper. The Professor of Greek at Cambridge had been heard to say that no one knew more of the religious beliefs of the later pagans than did the owner of Aswarby. Certainly his library contained all the then available books bearing on the Mysteries, the Orphic poems, the worship of Mithras, and the Neo-Platonists. In the marble-paved hall stood a fine group of Mithras slaying a bull, which had been imported from the Levant at great expense by the owner. He had contributed a description of it to the *Gentleman's Magazine,* and he had written a remarkable series of articles in the *Critical Museum* on the superstitions of the Romans of the Lower Empire. He was looked upon, in fine, as a man wrapped up in his books, and it was a matter of great surprise among his neighbours that he should ever have heard of his orphan cousin, Stephen Elliott, much more that he should have volunteered to make him an inmate of Aswarby Hall.

Whatever may have been expected by his neighbours, it is certain that Mr. Abney— the tall, the thin, the austere—seemed inclined to give his young cousin a kindly reception. The moment the front-door was opened he darted out of his study, rubbing his hands with delight.

"How are you, my boy?—how are you? How old are you?" said he—"that is, you are not too much tired, I hope, by your journey to eat your supper?"

"No, thank you, sir," said Master Elliott; "I am pretty well."

"That's a good lad," said Mr. Abney. "And how old are you, my boy?"

It seemed a little odd that he should have asked the question twice in the first two minutes of their acquaintance.

"I'm twelve years old next birthday, sir," said Stephen.

"And when is your birthday, my dear boy? Eleventh of September, eh? That's well—that's very well. Nearly a year hence, isn't it? I like—ha, ha!—I like to get these things down in my book. Sure it's twelve? Certain?"

"Yes, quite sure, sir."

"Well, well! Take him to Mrs. Bunch's room, Parkes, and let him have his tea—supper—whatever it is."

"Yes, sir," answered the staid Mr. Parkes; and conducted Stephen to the lower regions.

Mrs. Bunch was the most comfortable and human person whom Stephen had as yet met in Aswarby. She made him completely at home; they were great friends in a quarter of an hour: and great friends they remained. Mrs. Bunch had been born in the neighbourhood some fifty-five years before the date of Stephen's arrival, and her residence at the Hall was of twenty years' standing. Consequently, if anyone knew the ins and outs of the house and the district, Mrs. Bunch knew them; and she was by no means disinclined to communicate her information.

Certainly there were plenty of things about the Hall and the Hall gardens which Stephen, who was of an adventurous and inquiring turn, was anxious to have explained to him. Who built the temple at the end of the laurel walk? Who was the old man whose picture hung on the staircase, sitting at a table, with a skull under his hand? These arid many similar points were cleared up by the resources of Mrs. Bunch's powerful intellect. There were others, however, of which the explanations furnished were less satisfactory.

One November evening Stephen was sitting by the fire in the housekeeper's room reflecting on his surroundings.

"Is Mr. Abney a good man, and will he go to heaven?" he suddenly asked, with the peculiar confidence which children possess in the ability of their elders to settle these questions, the decision of which is believed to be reserved for other tribunals.

"Good?—bless the child!" said Mrs. Bunch. "Master's as kind a soul as ever I see! Didn't I never tell you of the little boy as he took in out of the street, as you may say, this seven years back? and the little girl, two years after I first come here?"

"No. Do tell me all about them, Mrs. Bunch—now this minute!"

"Well," said Mrs. Bunch, "the little girl I don't seem to recollect so much about. I know master brought her back with him from his walk one day, and give orders to Mrs. Ellis, as was housekeeper then, as she should be took every care with. And the pore child hadn't no one belonging to her—she telled me so her own self—and here she lived with us a matter of three weeks it might be; and then, whether she were somethink of a gipsy in her blood or what not, but one morning she out of her bed afore any of us had opened a eye and neither track nor yet trace of her have I set eyes on since. Master was wonderful put about, and had ail the ponds dragged; but it's my belief she was had away by them gipsies, for there was singing round the house for as much as an hour the night she went, and Parkes, he declare as he heard them a-calling in the woods all that afternoon. Dear, dear! a hodd child she was, so silent in her ways and all, but I was wonderful taken up with her, so domesticated she was—surprising."

"And what about the little boy?' said Stephen.

"Ah, that pore boy!" sighed Mrs. Bunch. "He were a foreigner—Jevanny he called hisself—and he come a-tweaking his 'urdy-gurdy round and about the drive one winter day, and master 'ad him in that minute, and ast all about where he came from, and how old he was, and how he made his way, and where was his relatives, and all as kind as heart could wish. But it went the same way with him. They're a hunruly lot, them foreign nations, I do suppose, and he was off one fine morning just the same as the girl. Why he went and what he done was our question for as much as a year after; for he never took his 'urdy-gurdy, and there it lays on the shelf."

The remainder of the evening was spent by Stephen in miscellaneous cross-examination of Mrs. Bunch and in efforts to extract a tune from the hurdy-gurdy.

That night he had a curious dream. At the end of the passage at the top of the house, in which his bedroom was situated, there was an old disused bathroom. It was kept locked, but the upper half of the door was glazed, and, since the muslin curtains which used to hang there had long been gone, you could look in and see the lead-lined bath affixed to the wall on the right hand, with its head towards the window.

On the night of which I am speaking, Stephen Elliott found himself, as he thought, looking through the glazed door. The moon was shining through the window, and he was gazing at a figure which lay in the bath.

His description of what he saw reminds me of what I once beheld myself in the famous vaults of St. Michan's Church in Dublin, which possess the horrid property of preserving corpses from decay for centuries. A figure inexpressibly thin and pathetic, of a dusty leaden colour, enveloped in a shroud-like garment, the thin lips crooked into a faint and dreadful smile, the hands pressed tightly over the region of the heart.

As he looked upon it, a distant, almost inaudible moan seemed to issue from its lips, and the arms began to stir. The terror of the sight forced Stephen backwards, and he awoke to the fact that he was indeed standing on the cold boarded floor of the passage in the full light of the moon. With a courage which I do not think can be common among boys of his age, he went to the door of the bathroom to ascertain if the figure of his dream were really there. It was not, and he went back to bed.

Mrs. Bunch was much impressed next morning by his story, and went so far as to replace the muslin curtain over the glazed door of the bathroom. Mr. Abney, moreover, to whom he confided his experiences at breakfast, was greatly interested, and made notes of the matter in what he called "his book."

The spring equinox was approaching, as Mr. Abney frequently reminded his cousin, adding that this had been always considered by the ancients to be a critical time for the young: that Stephen would do well to take care of himself, and to shut his bedroom window at night; and that Censorinus had some valuable remarks on the subject. Two incidents that occurred about this time made an impression upon Stephen's mind.

The first was after an unusually uneasy and oppressed night that he had passed—though he could not recall any particular dream that he had had.

The following evening Mrs. Bunch was occupying herself in mending his nightgown.

"Gracious me. Master Stephen!" she broke forth rather irritably, "how do you manage to tear your nightdress all to flinders this way? Look here, sir, what trouble you do give to poor servants that have to darn and mend after you!"

There was indeed a most destructive and apparently wanton series of slits or scorings in the garment, which would undoubtedly require a skilful needle to make good. They were confined to the left side of the chest—long, parallel slits, about six inches in length, some of them not quite piercing the texture of the linen. Stephen could only express his entire ignorance of their origin: he was sure they were not there the night before.

"But," he said, "Mrs. Bunch, they are just the same as the scratches on the outside of my bedroom door; and I'm sure I never had anything to do with making *them*."

Mrs. Bunch gazed at him open-mouthed, then snatched up a candle, departed hastily from the room, and was heard making her way upstairs. In a few minutes she came down.

"Well," she said, "Master Stephen, it's a funny thing to me how them marks and scratches can 'a' come there—too high up for any cat or dog to 'ave made 'em, much less a rat: for all the world like a Chinaman's finger-nails, as my uncle in the tea-trade used to tell us of when we was girls together. I wouldn't say nothing to master, not if I was you, Master Stephen, my dear; and just turn the key of the door when you go to your bed."

"I always do, Mrs. Bunch, as soon as I've said my prayers."

"Ah, that's a good child: always say your prayers, and then no one can't hurt you."

Herewith Mrs. Bunch addressed herself to mending the injured nightgown, with intervals of meditation, until bed-time. This was on a Friday night in March, 1812.

On the following evening the usual duet of Stephen and Mrs. Bunch was augmented by the sudden arrival of Mr. Parkes, the butler, who as a rule kept himself rather *to* himself in his own pantry. He did not see that Stephen was there: he was, moreover, flustered and less slow of speech than was his wont.

"Master may get up his own wine, if he likes, of an evening," was his first remark. "Either I do it in the daytime or not at all, Mrs. Bunch. I don't know what it may be: very like it's the rats, or the wind got into the cellars; but I'm not so young as I was, and I can't go through with it as I have done."

"Well, Mr. Parkes, you know it is a surprising place for the rats, is the Hall."

"I'm not denying that, Mrs. Bunch; and, to be sure, many a time I've heard the tale from the men in the shipyards about the rat that could speak. I never laid no confidence in that before; but to-night, if I'd demeaned myself to lay my ear to the door of the further bin, I could pretty much have heard what they was saying."

"Oh, there, Mr. Parkes, I've no patience with your fancies! Rats talking in the wine-cellar indeed!'

"Well, Mrs. Bunch, I've no wish to argue with you: all I say is, if you choose to go to the far bin, and lay your ear to the door, you may prove my words this minute."

"What nonsense you do talk, Mr. Parkes—not fit for children to listen to! Why, you'll be frightening Master Stephen there out of his wits."

"What! Master Stephen?" said Parkes, awaking to the consciousness of the boy's presence. "Master Stephen knows well enough when I'm a-playing a joke with you, Mrs. Bunch."

In fact, Master Stephen knew much too well to suppose that Mr. Parkes had in the first instance intended a joke. He was interested, not altogether pleasantly, in the situation; but all his questions were unsuccessful in inducing the butler to give any more detailed account of his experiences in the wine-cellar.

We have now arrived at March 24, 1812. It was a day of curious experiences for Stephen: a windy, noisy day, which filled the house and the gardens with a restless impression. As Stephen stood by the fence of the grounds, and looked out into the park, he felt as if an endless procession of unseen people were sweeping past him on the wind, borne on resistlessly and aimlessly, vainly striving to stop themselves, to catch at something that might arrest their flight and bring them once again into contact with the living world of which they had formed a part. After luncheon that day Mr. Abney said:

"Stephen, my boy, do you think you could manage to come to me to-night as late as eleven o'clock in my study? I shall be busy until that time, and I wish to show you something connected with your future life which it is most important that you should know. You are not to mention this matter to Mrs. Bunch nor to anyone else in the house; and you had better go to your room at the usual time."

Here was a new excitement added to life: Stephen eagerly grasped at the opportunity of sitting up till eleven o'clock. He looked in at the library door on his way upstairs that evening, and saw a brazier, which he had often noticed in the corner of the room, moved out before the fire; an old silver-gilt cup stood on the table, filled with red wine, and some written sheets of paper lay near it. Mr. Abney was sprinkling some incense on the brazier from a round silver box as Stephen passed, but did not seem to notice his step.

The wind had fallen, and there was a still night and a full moon. At about ten o'clock Stephen was standing at the open window of his bedroom, looking out over the country. Still as the night was, the mysterious population of the distant moonlit woods was not yet lulled to rest. From time to time strange cries as of lost and despairing wanderers sounded from across the mere. They might be the notes of owls or water-birds, yet they did not quite resemble either sound. Were not they coming nearer? Now they sounded from the nearer side of the water, and in a few moments they seemed to be floating about among the shrubberies. Then they ceased; but just as Stephen was thinking of shutting the window and resuming his reading of *Robinson Crusoe*, he caught sight of two figures standing on the gravelled terrace that ran along the garden side of the Hall—the figures of a boy and girl, as it seemed; they stood side by side, looking up at the windows. Something in the form of the girl recalled irresistibly his dream of the figure in the bath. The boy inspired him with more acute fear.

Whilst the girl stood still, half smiling, with her hands clasped over her heart, the boy, a thin shape, with black hair and ragged clothing, raised his arms in the air with an appearance of menace and of unappeasable hunger and longing. The moon shone upon his almost transparent hands, and Stephen saw that the nails were fearfully long and that the light shone through them. As he stood with his arms thus raised, he disclosed a terrifying spectacle. On the left side of his chest there opened a black and gaping rent; and there fell upon Stephen's brain, rather than upon his ear, the impression of one of those hungry and desolate cries that he had heard resounding over the woods of Aswarby all that evening. In another moment this dreadful pair had moved swiftly and noiselessly over the dry gravel, and he saw them no more.

Inexpressibly frightened as he was, he determined to take his candle and go down to Mr. Abney's study, for the hour appointed for their meeting was near at hand. The study or library opened out of the front-hall on one side, and Stephen, urged on by his terrors, did not take long in getting there. To effect an entrance was not so easy. It was not locked, he felt sure, for the key was on the outside of the door as usual. His repeated knocks produced no answer. Mr. Abney was engaged: he was speaking. What! why did he try to cry out? and why was the cry choked in his throat? Had he, too, seen the mysterious children? But now everything was quiet, and the door yielded to Stephen's terrified and frantic pushing.

On the table in Mr. Abney's study certain papers were found which explained the situation to Stephen Elliott when he was of an age to understand them. The most important sentences were as follows:

> It was a belief very strongly and generally held by the ancients—of whose wisdom in these matters I have had such experience as induces me to place confidence in their assertions—that by enacting certain processes, which to us moderns have something of a barbaric complexion, a very remarkable enlightenment of the spiritual faculties in man may be attained; that, for example, by absorbing the personalities of a certain number of his fellow-creatures, an individual may gain a complete ascendancy over those orders of spiritual beings which control the elemental forces of our universe.
>
> It is recorded of Simon Magus that he was able to fly in the air, to become invisible, or to assume any form he pleased, by the agency of the soul of a boy whom, to use the libellous phrase employed by the author of the "Clementine Recognitions," he had "murdered." I find it set down, moreover, with considerable detail in the writings of Hermes Trismegistus, that similar happy results may be produced by the absorption of the hearts of not less than three human beings below the age of twenty-one years. To the testing of the truth of this receipt I have devoted the greater part of the last twenty years, selecting as the *corpora vilia* of my experiment such persons as could conveniently be removed without occasioning a sensible gap in society. The first step I effected by the removal of one Phoebe Stanley, a girl of gipsy extraction, on March 24, 1792. The second, by the removal of a wandering Italian lad, named Giovanni Paoli, on the night of March 28, 1805. The final "victim"—to employ a word repugnant in the highest degree to my feelings—must be my cousin, Stephen Elliott. His day must be this March 24, 1812.
>
> The best means of effecting the required absorption is to remove the heart from the *living* subject, to reduce it to ashes, and to mingle them with about a pint of some red wine, preferably port. The remains of the first two subjects, at least, it will be well to conceal: a disused bath-room or wine-cellar will be found convenient for such a purpose. Some annoyance may be experienced from the psychic portion of the subjects, which popular language dignifies

> with the name of ghosts. But the man of philosophic temperament—to whom alone the experiment is appropriate—will be little prone to attach importance to the feeble efforts of these beings to wreak their vengeance on him. I contemplate with the liveliest satisfaction the enlarged and emancipated existence which the experiment, if successful, will confer on me; not only placing me beyond the reach of human justice (so-called), but eliminating to a great extent the prospect of death itself.

Mr. Abney was found in his chair, his head thrown back, his face stamped with an expression of rage, fright, and mortal pain. In his left side was a terrible lacerated wound, exposing the heart. There was no blood on his hands, and a long knife that lay on the table was perfectly clean. A savage wild-cat might have inflicted the injuries. The window of the study was open, and it was the opinion of the coroner that Mr. Abney had met his death by the agency of some wild creature. But Stephen Elliott's study of the papers I have quoted led him to a very different conclusion.

The Man with No Face

G. M. Robins

"I am no raconteur. This is not a story; it is a case. I choose it from among many very strange experiences, because it is, to me, inexplicable; and some of you, in the plenitude of youth and knowledge, may feel able to explain it to me.

"Ten years ago, the North of England was horrified by a crime the circumstances of which may be in the memories of some of you. One of the *dramatis persona* was a patient of mine; and of his share in the matter I will tell you what I know.

"A young man named Shirley, who had, I believe, made money in Australia, married a Scotch girl, a Miss Violet Rothesay; and they arrived, in course of their honeymoon travels, at Riley, the popular inland watering-place where I was then in practice. One day I received a visit from Mrs. Shirley, an interesting-looking girl, whose appearance, though not was indicative of perfect health, her general air that of birth and breeding, her dress and manners attractive—decidedly attractive.

"We had hardly shaken hands before she blurted out abruptly:

"'Are you good at mental cases?'

"'I am not a specialist, but I am interested in the study of brain disease,' I replied.

"'I come to ask you to do a curious thing,' she said, with some hesitation and a little added colour. 'I want you to come and dine at the hotel with my husband and me to-night. We have been married ten days. I want you to pretend to be an old friend of my family, to account naturally for my inviting you. My husband knows none of my friends, so there is no likelihood of his being suspicious. I have here written down a few details to guide you, in case of your being able to do as I wish,—such as my name, and those of my family, the place we live in, and so on. Do you think you could come?'

"I was surprised, of course; but it was by no means the first curious request that had been made to me, and I confess that my interest was stimulated.

"'I must, of course, ask what would be the real object of my visit,' I said.

"She waited a little before replying.

"'I don't want to say anything that might give you a clue,' said she at last. 'I want you to be quite unbiassed,—simply to watch Mr. Shirley and me, and to report to me faithfully afterwards anything that seems to be unusual. After dining with us, you will naturally call upon me next day; and, if you come between eleven and twelve, my husband will be drinking the waters, and you can see me alone. Then we can talk.'

"I said I would come. I felt sure she was sincere; her looks declared her to be in every sense a lady, and her manner betrayed an amount of controlled agitation which called out my sympathy.

"'Whatever you may notice,' said she, as she thanked me, 'pretend to see nothing unusual.'

"I promised. We made the necessary arrangements, and I went to the hotel that night. We dined in a private room. The husband was a heavily built man, about thirty-five years old. He was rather handsome, in a rough-hewn way, but without his wife's air of distinction. He was taking the waters for rheumatism, and had a slight stiffness of the right shoulder. His eyes were clear, steady, very blue, impressing you at first with the idea of great candour; but I very soon began to feel that this appearance was delusive. The first thing I was able to feel sure of about him was his devotion to his wife—the devotion of a man who is past his youth, and loves, as one might say, irretrievably. Whatever else in his life might have lacked the element of devotion—and I thought there might be much—he was at least a devout lover; there is no mistaking the symptoms.

"I felt her watching me as I watched him. I could see her eyes following mine. I could feel, and more strongly as the evening wore on, that she was wishing, or expecting, that I should become aware of something which eluded me. I studied the man 'for all I was worth,' as the modern youth has it. I felt myself weighing each word as he let it fall, so as to focus it upon his soul and get a clue. He was reticent, but not unpleasantly so. His manner impressed me favourably; but his eyes—his eyes were cruel . . . or relentless . . . or was it only dauntless?

"Why were they so guarded? Why was the portcullis so manifestly down? Did danger threaten the citadel?

"So by degrees I shaped out the notion that the man was on the defensive. There was something he wanted to hide, and more especially from the girl he loved.

"I had found out no more than this when I took my leave. I had purposely led him on to speak of his life abroad, and he had responded simply and easily, displaying not the least unwillingness to be questioned, and giving some interesting information. But his entire preoccupation—that of the married lover in the earlier stages—was a little evident as the evening wore on. I left early on account of it, and made my call next morning, a good deal perplexed as to Mrs. Shirley's reasons for inviting me.

"She was alone, as she had promised to be, and took no pains to hide the eagerness with which her eyes questioned me.

"'You noticed nothing—nothing?' she cried in a sort of fear. 'Once I thought you must have seen it—it was so close to you!'

"'It?'

"Quick as thought I glanced over my shoulder.

"She laughed.

"'Oh, it's not there now; it goes with him.'

"I looked searchingly at her; she motioned to me to sit down.

"'We must talk it out,' she said, in a sort of desperation. 'Is there something the matter with my brain?'

"'There does not seem to be; but illusions, you know, are neither uncommon nor dangerous. Is yours of a very unpleasant character?'

"She looked at me with a terrible look in her lovely eyes.

"'You shall judge. It is a man without a face.'

"'My dear lady!'

"I always see it following Randall about—ever since the day after our wedding-day, that is. I never saw it before.'

"She paused. I waited. She continued in a minute.

"'It was there yesterday evening standing behind his chair. It is very horrible, for where its face ought to be is only a mass of scars. It wears a kind of white mask.'

"She broke off.

"'Have you had illusions before?" I asked, feeling, I own, a trifle sick.

"'Oh, never—never!'

"'Have you mentioned it to him?'

"She shook her head.

"'Why not?'

"'Because'—she rose and went to ascertain that the door was closed; then, coming back—'because I think he knows.'

"'You think he knows?'

"'I will tell you why I think so.' For a moment she deliberated, turning her wedding-ring round and round her finger; and her colour rose—she was a charming girl. 'On the morning after my marriage,' she said, 'Randall got up early and went out to bathe. We were at Scarborough. I dressed and went down to the coffee-room; and as I sat at a little table near the window, he came in through the window, which opened on a verandah. This creature followed him into the room. It gave me a shock, it was so hideous. I began to say, "Oh, they ought not to let such creatures into the hotel," but the sight of Randall and his happy face and some roses which he had brought me made me forget. Then, as we sat down I saw it was close—close behind his chair. There was something in its hand, I could not see what—I have never been able to see yet; and at that very moment the waiter brought a hot dish to Randall, and walked clean through the creature, taking no notice whatever. Then I knew suddenly that the thing was not substantial—I had merely taken it to be some afflicted creature stopping at the hotel; but now—what could it be? A dreadful feeling of faintness and oppression came over me, and I fainted dead away, falling on the floor in the sight of everybody. When I revived, the thing was gone, and I would not speak of it to Randall, because I thought it was mere over-excitement of the nerves. Presently I went to get ready for a walk, and when I came back into our sitting-room, with my hat on, there was the thing standing behind him as he sat reading on a sofa. I went slowly up to him—nearer—nearer, trying to understand what it could be. His eyes were on his book, and he did not see where my gaze was fixed; and, as I approached, it slipped its hands round his neck, over his mouth and nose, and he gave a choking gasp, as if something were strangling him.

"'His own hands went up to his collar, he staggered to his feet, and went over to the open window, as if to get air. The thing was gone; but as I noticed Randall's face and the look in his eyes as they searched mine, I suddenly remembered that once during our engagement this had happened before. I remembered how terribly shaken he had been, how anxious to reassure me; I felt certain then, looking back upon it, that he wanted to find out whether I had seen anything. All in a moment knowledge flashed into me. He knew about this awful thing, but did not want me to know. Until we were married I could not see; now that I was his wife, I saw. . . . And I felt that, to save him, I must pretend I saw nothing.

"'"What a curious little catch in the breath you have!" I said gaily. "Do you remember, you choked in that manner once before, when we were sitting in Glen Birken?'"

"'It was wonderful to see the blessed relief stealing over his face. His look searched me through, as if he could hardly believe that I was safe from having seen the horror he knew of; and he glanced apprehensively behind him in the sunny room, but it was not there then.

"'"It's a muscular spasm," he said apologetically. "Don't take any notice; I was afraid you would be frightened."

"'"Oh," I said, very tranquilly, "my nerves are good, as you know. I am not going to begin by being nervous whenever you seem to ail anything; that would be to prepare a rod for my own back." I said it saucily, to make him laugh and kiss me, and we went out for a walk; but all that day I was thinking, "Are we both mad? What will be the end?" And I made up my mind to come to you.'

"'Last night the creature did not appear till you had been with us some time. Randall grows restless when it comes. Can medicine exorcise such a fiend, or had I better go to a priest?'

"I felt her pulse; it was calm and steady. I asked her several professional questions, and her answers confirmed me in the opinion I had already formed.

"The illusion, I feel sure,' said I, 'exists in your husband's brain, and is merely transferred to yours by the power of a strong sympathy. You *are* strongly in sympathy with him?'

"She assented without speaking; it was a very emphatic assent.

"'Then,' said I, 'it is he who should be my patient; and, short of examining him, I fear I can give you no help.'

"'If I could induce him to come to you!' she said. 'But how can I, without telling him that I know?'

"But that afternoon he came to me of his own accord.

"'Since you are a doctor, and Violet's friend,' he prefaced his confidence, 'I am going to tell you my case, on condition that you do not tell her, unless we both consider it advisable.'

"He then told me that for the past two years he had been more or less haunted by the sinister apparition, which he described in almost exactly the same terms that his wife had used—a strong point in favour of my opinion that the whole thing was simply conveyed from his brain to hers.

"He told me that he had never in his life seen such a creature in the flesh. He had no enemies that he knew of; there was nothing on his mind. He had certainly never mutilated, assisted to mutilate, or allowed to be mutilated the face of any human being.

"I fully believed his assurances; the more I saw of the man, the better I liked him.

"I could but treat the whole matter medically. I made him up a prescription, gave him advice, and bade him consider the whole thing purely as a matter of health, mentioning to him several cases in which overwrought nerves had been responsible for hideous delusions. They were leaving Riley next day, but he promised to write and let me know whether my medicine had done him good. I managed to convey to his wife the message that he had consulted me, and it comforted her considerably.

"From Riley they returned to Scarborough, as the air there seemed to suit Shirley better, and ten days later the whole of the north of England was full of the Scarborough hotel horror.

"Two of the visitors to the hotel were murdered in their beds in the course of the same night. They were perfect strangers to each other; they had never seen each other; they slept in rooms on different floors, numbered respectively two and eleven. One was the just returned manager of a sugar estate in the West Indies—his name was Gabbett; the other was Randall Shirley.

"The murderer was caught entirely through the description of him given to the police by the young widow. He was a half-caste, and his face was eaten away by vitriol. His motive in murdering the man Gabbett was clear enough. He owed his disfigurement and much other brutal ill-treatment to him. He had followed him to England to be revenged upon him.

"The murder of Randall Shirley was simply a blunder. The figures on the doors of the hotel rooms were in Roman numerals. The intended victim's number was eleven, and the miscreant mistook 'II.' for that number. After murdering the wrong man, he had the diabolical self-possession and resolution to go on and murder the right one.

"The method adopted in both cases was strangulation, but of a peculiar kind. The doctors who examined the bodies thought that some small curious tool had been used to close the nostrils and mouth; and a remarkable feature in the gruesome tale is, that so silently was the work accomplished that the young wife, asleep in the same room, was not awakened.

"There you have it—the only case I ever heard of in which second sight was actually transferred from one brain to another; and, like all instances of this incomprehensible gift, the premonition totally failed to accomplish the one purpose for which one can conceive it to have existed.

"It foreshadowed, it could not prevent, the tragedy."

The Mass of Shadows

Anatole France

This tale the sacristan of the church of St. Eulalie at Neuville d'Aumont told me, as we sat under the arbor of the White Horse, one fine summer evening, drinking a bottle of old wine to the health of the dead man, now very much at his ease, whom that very morning he had borne to the grave with full honors, beneath a pall powdered with smart silver tears.

"My poor father who is dead" (it is the sacristan who is speaking), "was in his lifetime a gravedigger. He was of an agreeable disposition, the result, no doubt, of the calling he followed, for it has often been pointed out that people who work in cemeteries are of a jovial turn. Death has no terrors for them: they never give it a thought. I, for instance, Monsieur, enter a cemetery at night as little perturbed as though it were the arbor of the White Horse. And if by chance I meet with a ghost, I don't disturb myself in the least about it, for I reflect that he may just as likely have business of his own to attend to as I. I know the habits of the dead, and I know their character. Indeed, so far as that goes, I know things of which the priests themselves are ignorant. If I were to tell you all I have seen, you would be astounded. But a still tongue makes a wise head, and my father, who, all the same, delighted in spinning a yarn, did not disclose a twentieth part of what he knew. To make up for this he often repeated the same stories, and to my knowledge he told the story of Catherine Fontaine at least a hundred times.

"Catherine Fontaine was an old maid whom he well remembered having seen when he was a mere child. I should not be surprised if there were still, perhaps, three old fellows in the district who could remember having heard folks speak of her, for she was very well known and of excellent reputation, though poor enough. She lived at the corner of the Rue aux Nonnes, in the turret which is still to be seen there, and which formed part of an old half-ruined mansion looking on to the garden of the Ursuline nuns. On that turret can still be traced certain figures and half-obliterated inscriptions. The late Curé of St. Eulalie, Monsieur Levasseur, asserted that there are the words in Latin, *Love is stronger than death*, 'which is to be understood,' so he would add, 'of divine love.'

"Catherine Fontaine lived by herself in this tiny apartment. She was a lacemaker. You know, of course, that the lace made in our part of the world was formerly held in high esteem. No one knew anything of her relatives or friends. It was reported that when she was eighteen years of age she had loved the young Chevalier d'Aumont-Cléry, and had been secretly affianced to him. But decent folk didn't believe a word of it, and said it was nothing but a tale concocted because Catherine Fontaine's demeanor was that of a lady rather than that of a working woman, and because, moreover, she possessed beneath her white locks the remains of great beauty. Her expression was sorrowful, and on one finger she wore one of those rings fashioned by the goldsmith into the semblance of two tiny hands clasped together. In former days folks were accustomed to exchange such rings at their betrothal ceremony. I am sure you know the sort of thing I mean.

"Catherine Fontaine lived a saintly life. She spent a great deal of time in churches, and every morning, whatever might be the weather, she went to assist at the six o'clock Mass at St. Eulalie.

"Now one December night, whilst she was in her little chamber, she was awakened by the sound of bells, and nothing doubting that they were ringing for the first Mass, the pious woman dressed herself, and came downstairs and out into the street. The night was so obscure that not even the walls of the houses were visible, and not a ray of light shone from the murky sky. And such was the silence amid this black darkness, that there was not even the sound of a distant dog barking, and a feeling of aloofness from every living creature was perceptible. But Catherine Fontaine knew well every single stone she stepped on, and, as she could have found her way to the church with her eyes shut, she reached without difficulty the corner of the Rue aux Nonnes and the Rue de la Paroisse, where the timbered house stands with the tree of Jesse carved on one of its massive beams. When she reached this spot she perceived that the church doors were open, and that a great light was streaming out from the wax tapers. She resumed her journey, and when she had passed through the porch she found herself in the midst of a vast congregation which entirely filled the church. But she did not recognize any of the worshipers and was surprised to observe that all of these people were dressed in velvets and brocades, with feathers in their hats, and that they wore swords in the fashion of days gone by. Here were gentlemen who carried tall canes with gold knobs, and ladies with lace caps fastened with coronet-shaped combs. Chevaliers of the Order of St. Louis extended their hands to these ladies, who concealed behind their fans painted faces, of which only the powdered brow and the patch at the corner of the eye were visible! All of them proceeded to take their places without the slightest sound, and as they moved neither the sound of their footsteps on the pavement, nor the rustle of their garments could be heard. The lower places were filled with a crowd of young artisans in brown jackets, dimity breeches, and blue stockings, with their arms round the waists of pretty blushing girls who lowered their eyes. Near the holy water stoups peasant women, in scarlet petticoats and laced bodices, sat upon the ground as immovable as domestic animals, whilst young lads, standing up behind them, stared out from wide-open eyes and twirled their hats round and round on their fingers, and all these silent countenances seemed centred irremovably on one and the same thought, at once sweet and sorrowful. On her knees, in her accustomed place, Catherine Fontaine saw the priest advance towards the altar, preceded by two servers. She recognized neither priest nor clerks. The Mass began. It was a silent Mass, during which neither the sound of the moving lips nor the tinkle of the bell was audible. Catherine Fontaine felt that she was under the observation and the influence also of her mysterious neighbour, and when, scarcely turning her head, she stole a glance at him, she recognized the young Chevalier d'Aumont-Cléry, who had once loved her, and who had been dead for five-and-forty years. She recognized him by a small mark which he had over the left ear, and, above all, by the shadow which his long black eyelashes cast upon his cheeks. He was dressed in his hunting clothes, scarlet with gold lace, the very clothes he wore that day when he met her in St. Leonard's Wood, begged of her a drink, and stole a kiss. He had preserved his youth and good looks. When he smiled, he still displayed magnificent teeth. Catherine said to him in an undertone—

"'Monseigneur, you who were my friend, and to whom in days gone by I gave all that a girl holds most dear, may God keep you in His grace! O, that He would at length inspire me with regret for the sin I committed in yielding to you; for it is a fact that, though my hair is white and I approach my end, I have not yet repented of having loved you. But, dear dead friend and noble seigneur, tell me, who are these folk, habited after the antique fashion, who are here assisting at this silent Mass?'

"The Chevalier d'Aumont-Cléry replied in a voice feebler than a breath, but none the less crystal clear—

"'Catherine, these men and women are souls from purgatory who have grieved God by sinning as we ourselves sinned through love of the creature, but who are not on that account cast off by God, inasmuch as their sin, like ours, was not deliberate.

"'Whilst separated from those whom they loved upon earth, they are purified in the cleansing fires of purgatory, they suffer the pangs of absence, which is for them the most cruel of tortures. They are so unhappy that an angel from heaven takes pity upon their love-torment. By the permission of the Most High, for one hour in the night, he reunites each year lover to loved in their parish church, where they are permitted to assist at the Mass of Shadows, hand clasped in hand. These are the facts. If it has been granted to me to see thee before thy death, Catherine, it is a boon which is bestowed by God's special permission.'

"And Catherine Fontaine answered him—

"'I would die gladly enough, dear, dead lord, if I might recover the beauty that was mine when I gave you to drink in the forest.'

"Whilst they thus conversed under their breath, a very old canon was taking the collection and proffering to the worshipers a great copper dish, wherein they let fall, each in his turn, ancient coins which have long since ceased to pass current: écus of six livres, florins, ducats and ducatoons, jacobuses and rose-nobles, and the pieces fell silently into the dish. When at length it was placed before the Chevalier, he dropped into it a louis which made no more sound than had the other pieces of gold and silver.

"Then the old canon stopped before Catherine Fontaine, who fumbled in her pocket without being able to find a farthing. Then, being unwilling to allow the dish to pass without an offering from herself, she slipped from her finger the ring which the Chevalier had given her the day before his death, and cast it into the copper bowl. As the golden ring fell, a sound like the heavy clang of a bell rang out, and on the stroke of this reverberation the Chevalier, the canon, the celebrant, the servers, the ladies and their cavaliers, the whole assembly vanished utterly; the candles guttered out, and Catherine Fontaine was left alone in the darkness."

Having concluded his narrative after this fashion, the sacristan drank a long draught of wine, remained pensive for a moment, and then resumed his talk in these words——

"I have told you this tale exactly as my father has told it to me over and over again, and I believe that it is authentic, because it agrees in all respects with what I have observed of the manners and customs peculiar to those who have passed away. I have associated a good deal with the dead ever since my childhood, and I know that they are accustomed to return to what they have loved.

"It is on this account that the miserly dead wander at night in the neighborhood of the treasures they conceal during their lifetime. They keep a strict watch over their gold; but the trouble they give themselves, far from being of service to them, turns to their disadvantage; and it is not a rare thing at all to come upon money buried in the ground on digging in a place haunted by a ghost. In the same way deceased husbands come by night to harass their wives who have made a second matrimonial venture, and I could easily name several who have kept a better watch over their wives since death than they ever did while living.

"That sort of thing is blameworthy, for in all fairness the dead have no business to stir up jealousies. Still I do but tell you what I have observed myself. It is a matter to take into account if one marries a widow. Besides, the tale I have told you is vouchsafed for in the manner following:

"The morning after that extraordinary night Catherine Fontaine was discovered dead in her chamber. And the beadle attached to St. Eulalie found in the copper bowl used for the collection a gold ring with two clasped hands. Besides, I'm not the kind of man to make jokes. Suppose we order another bottle of wine? . . ."

The Medium's End

Ford Madox Ford

A man called Edward White was talking to a man called Charles Fowler at the Embankment Club. White was a man of thirty-eight and Fowler was thirty-nine, having just returned to London after seven years in Burma.

"So you're still in the Bank?" Fowler asked.

"I am one of the Directors," White answered; "though that is no particular credit to me, as most of my family are directors, and I just stepped in. It isn't, I mean, like making a career. It was just waiting for me."

"Then South . . ." the other began.

"Oh, you remember South?" White asked.

"You'd nothing else but South on your mind just when I went away," Fowler said. "I thought you were going clean mad—both you and Milly."

The banker looked gravely at the point of his evening slippers.

"I think we were both going mad," he said; "but it wasn't we who did it in the end, it was South."

"Oh, South," Charles Fowler said; "I thought there was more in him than that. I thought he was a tremendous swindler—what's the word?—charlatan? But I certainly thought he had some sort of powers."

"He had," the banker declared grimly. "I don't want to talk about it, but I may as well. If I don't you'll hear some silly version from some other chap. It was like this:

"Just about after you left, Milly and I really did go practically off our heads. It wasn't only that we were prepared to stake all we had on that wretched medium's wretched tricks. I use the word 'wretched' quite carefully, because that was what they were. The whole thing was a wretched business. It wasn't, as I've said, that Milly and I were prepared to stake our whole fortunes, but we were trying—we were succeeding—in roping the whole fortunes of a lot of people—unfortunate old maids and servants and people.

"You can't understand that sort of madness. I can't understand it myself, though I've been through it. Why, I mean, should the fact that a tambourine jangles in the air in a dark room or a phosphorescent hand touches you on the face—why in the world should that seem the most important thing in the whole world? There's no knowing. It's just a madness. It's like seeing an enormously bright ray of light and being convinced that it's a diamond sparkling. And then suddenly, lo! and behold it's just a bit of broken bottle glass.

"Anyhow, there was this man South—a weird looking creature, with nasty, shifty eyes. You remember him. You used to think he had powers, you say? Well, he had powers.

"But the point is that the powers he had weren't, if you understand me, the powers we thought he had. They weren't even the power *he* thought he had.

"Anyhow, we were getting together a large sum of money for him—quite a large sum. There was mine, and Milly's, and old odd Williamson's, and twenty or thirty other people's. Why there might have been forty to fifty thousand pounds in it for him. And after this—his collapse—we discovered that he had forged another old woman's name for just about forty thousand, and lost the money on the Stock Exchange. So that our money would just have gone to make up that sum. You understand, he was an arrant swindler. He thought he was an arrant swindler. After his collapse I found in his pocket all the usual paraphernalia of these fellows—the rubber glove with the tube, the fishing-lines with the small hooks, the bird-lime, the patent reflecting spectacles—but just the very cheapest sort of swindler he was. It was nothing short of amazing that he hadn't been found out, for every one of his tricks had been exposed thirty or forty times, even at that date.

"And then came his extraordinary triumph—what you might call his hour of victory and death. What I am going to tell you is absolute truth—perfect and exact truth.

"It was the day before our cheque was to have been handed over to South. And South was going to give us all a manifestation in the afternoon. He preferred the night himself, as a rule, because it was easier to get darkness. But there was an old general, Sir Neville Beville, who was to catch a 6:20 train to his place near Southhampton, and we wanted to get some money out of him, so the séance was to take place at half-past four, at Lady Arundale Maxwell's. You remember her?

"I daresay you remember her room, a big ordinary drawing-room, with a terrific lot of Indian stuff about it, in Queen Anne's Mansions. Not in the least bogeyfied as far as the house went; but of course there was that disagreeable skeleton of the old West Indian *Obi* worker in front of the fireplace. And there were other unpleasant things in the room, though I've rather forgotten what they were. I daresay South rather liked to have them about. They increased the feeling of mystery.

"Well, the meeting began about four. There might have been twenty of us. General Sir Neville Beville himself tied South into the ordinary bentwood American chair. South wasn't looking at all well that day. Extraordinarily pale he was, and with his eyes unusually big.

"The General tied and tied, and then South winced, and said: 'Hi! I can't stand that.' The old General said: 'Ah! I thought you wouldn't be able to. That was a knot I used for tying up some of those Yogi fellows that did the murders in the Deccan.'

"'But confound it,' South exclaimed, 'I'm not a murderer. There's no need to tie the ropes until they eat into the flesh right through my skin. Damn it, you untie them!'

"The General grumbled a good deal; then he undid the knot, and South began to shake his hands and slap them together. They were perfectly blue. He began to explain to the General that he could not be expected to make any manifestations when he was in acute pain; he wouldn't be able to keep his mind on the subject. And then he asked whether the General hadn't brought the pair of police handcuffs that he had suggested using. The General went and got the handcuffs. They were put on South's wrists behind the chair. Then the General took a piece of rope and tied it, from the cuffs, under the seat of the chair, to the front legs and round and round South's legs and arms and body in all sorts of ways.

"South said he didn't mind that, but he still complained that his hands hurt him, and he really appeared to be extraordinarily irritable.

"It came out most when the General began to press him to make a demonstration in open daylight. You understand the General was an absolute novice at the sort of thing. He had never been to a séance of any kind before, and he was one of those chaps who say they have an absolutely open mind. Usually South refused to answer many questions of that sort. He used to say he needed the darkness in order to be able to concentrate his mind. If he looked at any other objects they took his thoughts away. And usually that was taken to be sufficient. But the General went on pressing him and pressing him.

"'Can't you give an exhibition in the daylight?' he kept on saying. 'Can't you? Can't you?'"

"And the South exclaimed with exasperation—almost in a sort of scream:

"'By God, I can!'"

"He must have been in a really extraordinary state of irritation; indeed, he looked as if he might be going mad. Almost positively epileptic. He sat leaning forward on the ropes that tied him to the chair, and glared furiously at the General.

"'Well, then, do it!'" the General said.

"Then fell a singular silence on us all. You see, we all believed in South. We all believed that he could make manifestations in the daylight, and we began to think he was going to do it then. It was decidedly the most unpleasant thing I've ever been in. The room, as I've pointed out, was quite commonplace. We could hear the rumble of the Underground if we listened carefully, and a chap a long way down below crying daffodils, and, occasionally, a muffin-bell, as one of the windows was open.

"I forgot to tell you what we really had come there for was to get a manifestation of the spirit of Anne Boleyn. She was an ancestress of General Neville Beville, and he was always talking about her. South kept staring at the General, and the General kept quiet. He explained afterwards that he didn't want to interfere with the chap, who he supposed was praying or something.

"I daresay South was a good deal upset, if only because he had to find the forty thousand next day, or it would mean seven years for him. I've no doubt, swindler that he was, he was praying for a miracle as hard as he could go. After all, his whole life was in the balance, and I daresay his whole life was as important to him as anyone else's is to anyone else. At any rate, no doubt he was willing it as hard as he could.

"One of the bones of the old skeleton in front of the fireplace—it was decorated with bits of brass wire and scarlet flannel—creaked in the oddest possible manner. There was nothing very mysterious about that. South used to insist on its being stood in front of the fire whenever he was going to manifest, though it usually stood in the corner of the room. When it got near the heat, of course, the wood it was hung on used to give a little, and so the bones moved. I've seen them move a dozen times.

"But South's condition was so strained that he really gave a high squeak.

"Then the tambourine at South's elbow moved. It jumped up and down perfectly plainly and visibly before all our eyes. It jingled and thumped, and South's jaw just hung open, and he just gazed at it. It began to hop about the table from edge to edge. Then it fell over on the floor, and jingled away towards the skeleton.

"South said in a husky voice, 'Who's doing that?'"

"His face was towards the window, and all our backs were to it. Then he screamed—the most agonised beastly scream that I've ever heard outside of a lunatic asylum. Our eyes all followed his—a hand was coming in at the open window. You remember it was Anne Boleyn that we'd come there to meet. Well, this was Anne Boleyn's hand. There was a distinct rudimentary, extra little finger. Anne Boleyn had six fingers on her right hand. That was why she was always drawn with her hands folded. She was very much ashamed of the defect.

And the hand just came in at the window. It was dark against the light at first, then it looked white enough. It passed close to old Lady Arundale Maxwell's face, and she exclaimed:

"'How cold! How extraordinarily cold!'"

"We weren't any of us particularly moved—not extra moved. We'd all of us been to a good many séances, and had felt cold hands passing near our faces. But, of course, it was a sufficiently exciting thing to have it happen in broad daylight.

"But South's mouth was hanging open; his eyes were starting out of his head, and there was perspiration all over his forehead. It was really most disagreeable to look at him.

"The hand stopped just beside General Neville Beville, at about a level with his chest. It was pointing towards South, with the first finger stretched out as if the person behind it were addressing him. He shrank back right against the back of his chair, huddling into it. The General slowly, and with a timidity that was singular in him, raised his own hand and just touched the other with his little finger. He drew his hand back sharply, as if he had had an electric shock. The hand began very slowly to move towards South. Then the medium screamed; he screamed very highly, and then exclaimed:

"'Cut me loose! For God's sake cut me loose. I shall go mad if it touches me.'"

"It shows the state of agitation that he must have been in in that he made no attempt whatever to wriggle himself out of the handcuffs. In ordinary circumstances he could have done that as easily as you or I could take our waistcoats off. He went on imploring the General personally to let him loose. He abjured him, by his braveness as a soldier, to cut the ropes. I daresay it only took a moment or so, but this thing seemed to last for hours.

"The General certainly started towards the medium; he put his hand into his pocket to take out a penknife. Then the hand moved right across the General's chest as if to bar his progress. He lifted up his left arm to push the hand away. And then we didn't see any more of the General. I don't mean to say that he disappeared in a flash, but it was as if we had forgotten him. You understand, he wasn't there.

"He was found that afternoon wandering about Putney without a hat. He didn't remember how he got there; he didn't even remember who he was. It was a case of complete failure of the memory. The only thing that he could remember at the moment was Anne Boleyn's hand; and he did want to talk about that for fear of being laughed at. He never has talked about it except just one to me. The police took him home all right, of course, because he had his card-case in his pocket, and he was all right again in a month or so.

"As for the hand, it just got nearer and near to the medium, and he continued screaming until touched him. Then he became dead silent, and, after the contact, he exclaimed 'Cold! cold!'"

"That's all he's ever done from that day to this. He walks about the grounds of a private lunatic asylum in Chiswick, shivering pitifully; but he will never be cured."

"And what do you make of it all?" Charles Fowler asked.

"I don't make anything at all," Edward White answered. "Perhaps it was only the Grace of God. I mean that his collapse certainly saved quite a number of poor people from ruin, and possibly it saved me from becoming the accomplice—the quite unwilling accomplice, of course—of an atrocious charlatan. On the other hand, there's the other possible view—the view that Spiritualists are trying to make fashionable today—that mediums who are perfectly genuine sometimes have their days of failure, and reinforce themselves with bits of fishing-line and inflatable rubber gloves.

"But for myself I'm perfectly convinced that the poor beast was a swindler just at the end of his tether, and that, in his agony, his will, which he didn't really believe in, suddenly worked. He didn't I the least believe in ghosts; he had to pretend that he did. And then suddenly the ghost came. That was why he was so horribly afraid. I think some of these chaps wouldn't go on playing these tricks if they knew what it might let them in for."

Monsieur de Guise

Perley Poore Sheehan

That any one should live in the center of Cedar Swamp was in itself so singular as to set all sorts of queer ideas to running through my head.

A more sinister morass I had never seen. It was as beautiful and deadly as one of its own red moccasins, as treacherous and fascinating.

It was a tangle of cypress and cedar almost thirty miles square, most of it under water—a maze of jungle-covered islands and black bayous. There were alligators and panthers, bear and wild pig. There were groans and grunts and queer cries at night, and silence, dead silence by day.

That was Cedar Swamp as I knew it after a week of solitary hunting there. I no longer missed the sun. My eyes had become used to the perpetual twilight. My nerves no longer bothered me when I stepped into opaque water, or watched a section of gliding snake. But the silence was getting to be more than I could bear. It was too uncanny.

And now, just after I had noticed it, and wondered at it for the hundredth time, I heard a voice.

It was low and clear—that of a woman who sings alto. There were four or five notes like the fragment of a strange song. And then, before I had recovered from the shock of it, there was silence again.

I was up to my knees in water at the time, wading a narrow branch between two islands. I must have stood there for a full minute waiting for the voice to resume, but the silence closed in on me deeper than ever. With a little shiver creeping over one part of my body after another, I stole ashore.

The island was one of the highest I had yet encountered. I had not taken a dozen steps up through the dank growth of its shelving shore before I found a deeply worn path.

This, I could see, ran down to the water-front on one direction, where I caught a glimpse of a boat-house masked by trees. I turned and followed the path in the other direction up a gentle slope.

As I advanced, the jungle around me thinned out and became almost park-like. There were open stretches of meadow and clumps of trees, suggesting a garden. But I was so intent on discovering the owner of the voice that the wonder of this did not at first impress me. I had, moreover, an eery, uneasy sensation of being watched.

I walked slowly. I carried my gun with affected carelessness. I looked around me as though I were a mere tourist dropped in to see the sights.

I had thus covered, perhaps, a quarter of a mile, when the path turned into an avenue of cabbage-palmetto, at the further end of which I saw a house.

It was large and white with a pillared porch, such as they used to build before the war. It was shaded by a magnificent grove of live-oak trees. There were beds of geranium and roses in front, and clusters of crepe-myrtle and flowering oleander on a well-clipped lawn.

It all gave an impression of infinite care, of painstaking upkeep, of neatness and wealth, yet, there was not a soul in sight. Not a servant was there. No dog barked, I saw no horses, no chickens, no pigeons, nor sheep; no familiar animate emblem whatever of the prosperous farm.

I stood in the presence of this silent and lonely magnificence with a feeling that was not exactly fear, but rather stupefaction. For a moment I was persuaded that I had emerged from the great swamp into some unknown plantation of its littoral.

But a moment was enough to convince me that this could not be. I was, without the slightest doubt, almost at the exact center of the morass. I was too familiar with its circumference and general contour to be wrong as to that. For a dozen miles at least, in every direction, Cedar Swamp surrounded this island of mystery with its own mysterious forests and bayous.

Once again I was acutely aware of being stared at. Almost at the same instant a man's voice addressed me from behind my back.

"Monsieur," it asked, "why do you hesitate?"

I might as well confess it right away—I believe in ghosts. I have seen too many things in my life that were not to be explained by the commonly accepted laws of nature. I have lived too much among the half-civilized and learned too much of their odd wisdom to recognize any hard and fast definition of what is real and what is not.

From the moment I heard that bit of song in the swamp, I felt that I was passing from the commonplace into the weird. My succeeding impressions had confirmed this feeling.

And now, when I heard the voice behind me: "Monsieur, why do you hesitate?"—I was not sure that it was the voice of a human being at all. I turned slowly, my mind telling me that I should see no one.

It was with a distinct feeling of relief, therefore, that I saw a small, pale, well-dressed old man smiling at me as though he had read my secret thoughts.

His face was cleanly shaven and bloodless. His head, partly covered by a black velvet skull-cap, was extremely large. His snow-white hair was silky and long. His eyes, which were deeply sunken, were large and dark. His appearance, as well as the question which he had just put to me suggested the foreigner. He was not alone un-American; he appeared to be of another century, as well.

I said something about intruding. He made a brusk gesture, almost of impatience, and, telling me to follow him, started for the house.

It was as though I was an expected guest. Only the absence of servants maintained that feeling of the bizarre, which never left me.

The interior of the house was in keeping with its outward appearance—sumptuous and immaculate. My host led me to the door of a vast chamber on the first floor, motioned me to enter, and, standing at the door, said:

"Monsieur, luncheon will be served when you reappear. Pray, make yourself at home."

Then he left me.

Two details of this room impressed me: the superlative richness of the toilet articles, all of which were engraved with a coat-of-arms, and the portrait of a woman, by Largilliére. All women were beautiful to Largilliére, but in the present instance he had surpassed himself.

The gentle, aristocratic face, with its tender, lustrous eyes, was the most alluring thing I had ever seen. At the bottom of the massive frame was the inscription: "*Anne-Marie, Duchesse de Guise. Anno 1733.*"

I was still marveling at the miracle which had brought such an apparition to the heart of an American swamp when I heard a light step in the hallway, and I knew that my host was awaiting me.

The luncheon, which was served cold in a splendid dining-room, had been laid for two. I wondered at this, for still no servant appeared, and surely I could not have been expected. And my host added to my mystification rather than lessened it when he said: "Monsieur, I offer you the place usually reserved for my wife."

Apart from this simple statement, the meal was completed in silence. Now and then I thought I surprised him, nodding gravely, as though someone else were present.

I suspected him several times of speaking in an undertone. But, my mind was so preoccupied with the inexplicable happenings of the preceding hour that I was not in a condition to attack fresh mysteries now.

He scarcely touched his food. Indeed, his presence there seemed to be more in the nature of an act of courtesy than for the purpose of taking nourishment. As soon as I had finished he arose and invited me to follow him.

Across the hall was a music-room, with high French windows, opening on the porch. He paused at one of these windows now and plucked the flower from a potted heliotrope. The perfume of it seemed to stimulate him strangely. He at once became more animated. A slight trace of color mounted to his waxen cheeks. Turning to me, abruptly, he remarked:

"I mentioned just now my wife. Perhaps you noticed her portrait?"

As he spoke, a faint breath of the heliotrope came to me, and with it, by one of those odd associations of ideas, the portrait by Largilliére. I saw again the gentle face and the lustrous eyes, but the date—1733. Surely, this was not the portrait he referred to.

But he had seen the perplexity in my face, and he broke out in French: "*Oui, oui; c'est moi, monsieur de Guise*." And then, in English: "It was the portrait of my wife you saw, *madame la duchesse par monsieur Largillière.*"

"But then, *madame*, your wife," I stammered, "is dead."

He was still smelling the heliotrope. He looked up at me with his somber eyes for a moment as though he had failed to grasp my meaning. Then he said:

"No, no. There is no such thing as death—only life. For, what is life?—the smile, the perfume, the voice. Ah, the voice! Will you hear her sing?"

For a brief instant my head turned giddily. The world I had always known, the world of tragedies, of sorrows, of physical joys and pains, the world of life and death, in short, was whirling away from beneath my feet.

And I began to recall certain old stories I had heard about the visible servants of the invisible, the earthly agents of the unearthly. Such things have been known to exist.

M. de Guise was walking up and down the room murmuring to himself in French. I could catch an occasional word of endearment. Once I saw him distinctly press the heliotrope to his lips. He had forgotten my presence, apparently. He was in the company of some one whom he alone could see. And then he seated himself at the piano.

I had a presentiment of what was coming. I dropped into a chair and closed my eyes.

Again the heliotrope perfumed the air around me. I saw the smooth brow, the sympathetic eyes, the magic smile of the Duchesse de Guise, and then a voice—that voice I had heard in the swamp—began to sing, so soft, so sweet, that a little spasm twitched at my throat and a chill crept down my back.

It was a love song, such as they sang centuries ago. I know little French, but it told of love in life and death—"*Moi, je t'ai, vive et morte, incessament aimée.*"

And when I opened my eyes again, all that I saw was the shrivelled black figure of Monsieur de Guise, his silvered head thrown back with the air of one who has seen a vision.

Subconsciously I had heard something else while listening to the song. It was the swift, muffled throb of an approaching motor-boat. M. de Guise had heard it, too, for now he left the piano and approached the window. Presently, I could see a dozen negroes approaching along the avenue of palms. They seemed strangely silent for their race.

"These are my people," said my host. "Once a week I send them to the village. They will carry you away."

The afternoon was far advanced when I bade M. de Guise farewell. As I looked back for the last time the sunset was rapidly dissolving the great white house and its gardens in a golden haze.

His figure on the porch was all that linked it to the world of man.

Late that night I was landed at a corner of Cedar Swamp, adjacent to my home. My black boatman, who had spoken never a word immediately backed his barge away into the darkness, leaving me there alone.

And, although I have since made several efforts to repeat my visit to M. de Guise, I have never been successful. Once, indeed, I found again what I believed to be his island, but it was covered entirely with a dense, forbidding jungle. Which will doubtless discredit this story, as it has caused even me to reflect.

But grant that the story is true, and that M. de Guise was merely mad. Why, then in a certain event, which I need not mention, may God send me madness, too!

Mrs. Morrel's Last Séance

Edgar Jepson

I had attended all of the séances of Mrs. Joaquine Morrel during the two previous winters; and of all the mediums I have sat with, in the States or in Europe, she was the best. Sometimes, of course, she was not in the right mood or condition, or whatever it is; and the phenomena were trivial; sometimes we got mere trickery, and that poorly done. Like most other mediums, public or even private, if real phenomena did not come, Mrs. Morrel would do her best to produce imitations. Sometimes she would quite deliberately use trickery rather than endure the exhaustion and nausea which always followed the genuine exercise of her powers.

But often at her séances I had seen phenomena which I did not believe to have been produced by trickery. I did not profess to be able to find any explanation of them; and I was profoundly sceptical about their having to do with the spirits of the dead. I inclined to the theory that they were produced by the obscure and mysterious action of the subconscious, or if you prefer it, the subliminal self. But whatever their cause, I saw phenomena which I accounted genuine; and, as I say, after these Mrs. Morrel was in a state of utter prostration. She seemed not only to have lost vital force, but actually to have lost blood, so weak and pale and shrunken was she.

I came to the séance on the fourth of last December with no great expectations: for it was a mere chance whether the phenomena would be interesting, or more or less trickery. Besides, the night was very cold, and the weather had been abominable; and that was against Mrs. Morrel's being in a favourable condition for the best exercise of her powers. But I had not been in the room with her three minutes before I was sure that she was in uncommonly good spirits; and I began to expect a good sitting.

I was the first to arrive; and we chatted for a few minutes about what she had been doing since the last séance I had attended, and about the members of the circle which was to sit that night. I had become aware that one of the reasons of her good spirits was that she was wearing a new dress, a black, watered silk. I complimented her on it; and she made me feel the material, what a good, thick, serviceable silk it was. She was plainly so proud of it that I again complimented her on her taste, and congratulated her on having got so exactly what she wanted and such an excellent fit. Indeed, the dress suited her very well, for she was a dark, almost swarthy black-haired, biggish woman, and stout, weighing over eleven stone. Her rather heavy face lighted up and grew quite animated at my compliments.

The other members of the circle began to arrive, singly or two at a time. There was Eric Magnus, who was even more sceptical than I, though for the last year he had ceased to deny, in anything like his old tone of conviction, that we did sometimes get genuine, inexplicable phenomena at Mrs. Morrel's séances. There were Harold Beveridge and Walters, the Professor of Mathematics, both of them very careful and shrewd observers of psychical phenomena; and there were Dr. and Mrs. Paterson, Mrs. Grant, Admiral Norton, and a man of the name of Thompson of whom I know very little, since he had only lately attended the séances. These five were of the credulous type which sees, or makes itself see, anything, and were of very little account in matters psychical.

Of course, the circle was rather too large. I have always seen the best phenomena when the circle has been composed of three men and two women.

Last of all came two strangers, who, I gathered, had never sat with Mrs. Morrel, or with anyone else—a Mr. and Mrs. Longridge. Longridge was a man of about forty-five, of a short, square, stout figure, clean-shaven, with a heavy, masterful jaw, thin lips, and keen black eyes, deep-set, under projecting brows. He looked a man of uncommon force of character; and I hoped the Mrs. Morrel would keep off trickery, for he was the very man, if he detected it, to make a row. I fancied that I had seen his face among a set of portraits of captains of industry in a magazine.

His wife was a very pretty, even beautiful, woman of about twenty-eight, with large dark-brown eyes and dark-brown hair. Her cheeks were pale and she looked fragile; she gave me the impression of having been broken down by some great trouble. It was plain that she was strung up to the highest pitch; her eyes were restless and excited, and her lips kept twitching. Longridge looked rather bored.

Mrs. Morrel welcomed them with great deference, and Mrs. Longridge came into the room wearing a cloak of sables over her black evening gown. All the members of the circle, except Professor Walters, are rich people, but not to the point of being able to pay two thousand pounds for a sable cloak. I took it that Longridge was a millionaire. When his wife found that the room was quite warm, she gave him the cloak, and he laid it on the little writing-table, against the wall, by the door.

We were all assembled by a quarter to nine; and I explained to the Longridges the conditions of the séance, especially begging them on no account, whatever happened, to break the circle by loosing the hand of the person on either side of them. Then we settled down on our chairs in a half-circle before the cabinet, which was formed by a curtain hung on a rod across a corner of the room. The curtain was drawn back and it was quite plain that but for Mrs. Morrel's chair the cabinet was empty.

Mrs. Morrel went into it and drew the curtain. Magnus turned out two of the gas-jets of the chandelier, and left the third burning about three quarters of an inch. It gave less light than a candle would have done.

We joined hands, and Mrs. Grant went to the piano and began to play softly. We talked quietly. I had placed myself between Mr. and Mrs. Longridge. Magnus sat on the other side of Longridge. I realised even more clearly that Mrs. Longridge was strung up to a pitch of extraordinary tenseness. She answered my occasional remarks to her in strained tones; and her hand was rigid, and so cold that it kept mine chilled. Two or three times I begged her to let herself relax, but it was no use.

Every now and then I felt her quiver. Longridge was relaxed enough; he was leaning back in his chair, his hand was warm and limp in mine, two or three times I heard him sigh impatiently. It was plain that he had only come to please his wife, and expected nothing.

We sang the hymn "Lead Kindly Light," and then we went on talking. It was about half an hour after we had sat down that I heard in the cabinet the sound of scratching which always preceded Mrs. Morrel's going into a trance.

The talk died down in a momentary hush; Mrs. Grant left the piano and sat down on her chair at the end f the half-circle nearest the piano; and Mrs. Longridge said, in a shaky whisper:

"Is it going to begin?"

"Very soon," I said, and I felt that she was quivering, or, to be exact, trembling violently; and after that she was trembling most of the time.

The first phenomenon was a ball of light. It began in a faint luminousness about three feet from the floor in front of the curtain of the cabinet, and grew stronger and stronger until it was a ball of greenish, phosphorescent light, some six inches in diameter, and about the strength of the light given out by those marine *animalculae* which are called sea-stars; not, that is, as bright as the light of a glow-worm. Longridge sat upright in his chair.

The ball of light disappeared suddenly, and from beyond the end of the half-circle a voice began to speak, the voice of Thomas. We were familiar with it; sometimes he would materialise and move about the room, an odd dwarfish figure; sometimes we only heard his voice. Mrs. Longridge was still, no longer trembling, but breathing quickly.

I knew that we were going to have an interesting sitting. But it seemed to me that the atmosphere was different from that of any other sitting at which I had been present. There was a sense of strain in it, rather oppressive and unnerving. I thought Mrs. Longridge's emotions had infected me.

Two or three lights floated across the room and faded; as one of them passed it, I caught a glimpse of Thomas's rather impish face—only his face.

He talked for a while, the usual aimless, trivial, and rather tiresome talk, chiefly to Admiral Norton, who wanted to know what would be the upshot of a naval scandal which was agitating the public mind. Thomas's views on it were those of a schoolboy of fourteen.

Then he said: "Sister Sylvia is coming."

There came from the cabinet the figure of a nun, a familiar figure at Mrs. Morrel's séances. She went by the name of Sister Sylvia. She talked to one another of us. There was very little more to her talk than to that of Thomas. Mrs. Longridge was panting softly, and holding my hand tighter; Longridge, too, had tightened his grip and was leaning forward.

There was a breath of cold air (a very common phenomenon at séances), then Sister Sylvia said: "There's a little girl here. She wants——"

I heard Mrs. Longridge gasp, and without finishing her sentence, Sister Sylvia went back into the cabinet with quite unusual swiftness. It was almost, if one might say so, as if she had been sucked back into it.

Another light floated across the room and faded. Then the rings of the curtain grated softly along the rod, and there came out of the cabinet the figure of a child, a little girl. Then I saw that the curtain was half-drawn, a thing which had never happened at one of Mrs. Morrel's séances before, and I could see dimly the figure of Mrs. Morrel on her chair in the cabinet.

The child came straight to Mrs. Longridge. Mrs. Longridge sank back in her chair, gasping painfully, and her nerveless hand would have slipped from mine had I not held it firmly.

The child stood before her, and said in a faint, shrill voice: "Oh, mummy!"

Mrs. Longridge burst out sobbing, tried vainly to tear her hand from mine, and cried wildly: "Oh, Maisie! Maisie!"

I heard Mrs. Morrel shuffle in the cabinet. Then suddenly Longridge's hand gripped mine with a vicelike, crushing grip. He said: "Don't go back, Maisie! Stay with us—try to stay with us—hard!" then he hissed: "Will her to stay, grace. Hold her! Will her to stay!"

He crouched forward, and I saw the glimmer of his eyes staring at the dim figure of Mrs. Morrel.

Mrs. Longridge and the child were murmuring to one another in broke, staccato voices, just repeating one another's names. When Longridge had spoken, Mrs. Longridge was silent. She seemed to stiffen, and her breathing was slower, coming in long-drawn gasps; plainly she was concentrating herself in the effort of will.

Longridge was crushing my hand; I thought that the bones would go. The pain was confusing. I thought the child had her arms around Mrs. Longridge's neck.

There were some seconds, perhaps fifteen, of tense stillness. It seemed to me that the air of the room grew more and more oppressive with the sense of straining, silent struggle, but that feeling might have been caused by the pain of Longridge's grip. Then I felt rather than saw that the child was being drawn back to the cabinet. Longridge crouched forward in his intense effort, never stirred, never loosened his crushing grip.

Mrs. Grant burst out crying; Magnus cried in a high-pitched, squeaky whisper: "Keep still! Keep still! Don't break the circle!" I heard the Admiral rasp out an oath; then I saw that Mrs. Morrel was swaying on her chair.

The child seemed to be about two feet from Mrs. Longridge, bent forward as though her arms were around her neck and she was holding onto it.

Then Mrs. Morrel rose from her chair, swaying, clutching at the air with twisting arms; then she pitched forward on her face, half in the cabinet and half out of it.

As she came to the ground the child cried in quite another voice, a deeper, louder voice:

"I can't get back!"

We were all on our feet at once.

Longridge cried: "Come along! Come along!" thrust me aside, and picked up the child.

Magnus sprang to the gas, but in his excitement, instead of turning it up, he turned it off, and we were in pitch darkness. The door opened; a sheet of light from the hall fell into the room, and in it I saw Longridge's face, very white and glistening with sweat. He was carrying the child in his arms, wrapped in his wife's sable cloak. I only caught a glimpse of them as he hurried out of the room. His wife followed him quickly, and slammed the door after her.

I made for the door. I ran into a chair; then I ran into Professor Walters. Just as my hand touched the wall I heard the house door bang.

The Admiral struck a match. I opened the door, ran down the hall, and opened the house door. A big, closed motor-car was gliding swiftly down the street.

I came quickly back to the room. The gas had been lighted, and everyone was talking at once, wildly. I hurried to Mrs. Morrel, who still lay where she had fallen, and raised her. To my amazement it was no more than if I were lifting a child of twelve. As I laid her on the sofa my sleeve-link caught in her dress. I tore a patch out of that strong new silk as if it had been tissue-paper. The bodice had fitted like a glove; it was hung about her shrunken bust in great wrinkles. Her face was bloodless and shrunken; her black hair and eyebrows were a curious, dead, lusterless white; and, oddest of all, the iris, and even the black pupils of her eyes, had gone grey, as if the colour had been bleached out of them.

Mrs. Grant had a bottle of strong-smelling salts, the Admiral got some brandy from the servant, and we tried our best to revive her. Our efforts were useless. She was dead.

We sent for a doctor. He could do nothing. He talked about heart-failure, and seemed to have it firmly in his mind that Mrs. Morrel was an albino.

Eric Magnus and I were the last to leave, and we came away together.

As we turned up the street he said:

"It was a good thing that I noticed the draught when the door of the room was opened to let the child slip in."

"I noticed a breath of cold air; in fact, I noticed several during the evening," I said. "But if the door was opened, why didn't the light from the lamp fall into the room? It was burning brightly."

"Oh, it was turned down, and then up again," he said confidently.

"It might have been," said I; and for the next twenty yards he said nothing.

Then he broke out:

"It was a splendid fake—splendid! I never saw better! What accomplices! It was first rate acting—absolutely first-rate!"

"Yes; acting that turned the lady's hands icy. And accomplices? An accomplice of Mrs. Morrel in a two-thousand pound sable cloak! That is a bit hard to swallow," I said.

"Hired, my dear fellow—hired," he said confidently.

"It might be," I said. "A hired cloak and a form of heart disease which turns a swarthy woman into an albino."

"Oh, yes, that was odd; but I have no doubt that it sometimes acts like that."

"Haven't you?" I said.

We separated at the end of the street, and I was glad to be rid of him. I wanted to think it out quietly. I could not; my mind was in a whirl, and it would not clear.

The next day I set about trying to find out something about the Longridges. I was quite unsuccessful; I could not find a trace of them. They were unknown in spiritist circles by name; no medium of my acquaintance recognised either of them from my description. Also, I could find no one of the name Longridge among our captains of industry. I was forced to the conclusion that, like so many other people, they had come to the séance under false names. So many people are ashamed of their interest in spiritism.

The Murderer's Violin

Erckmann-Chatrian

Karl Hâfitz had spent six years in mastering counterpoint. He had studied Haydn, Glück, Mozart, Beethoven, and Rossini; he enjoyed capital health, and was possessed of ample means which permitted him to indulge his artistic tastes—in a word, he possessed all that goes to make up the grand and beautiful in music, except that insignificant but very necessary thing—inspiration!

Every day, fired with a noble ardour, he carried to his worthy instructor, Albertus Kilian, long pieces harmonious enough, but of which every phrase was "cribbed." His master, Albertus, seated in his armchair, his feet on the fender, his elbow on a corner of the table, smoking his pipe all the time, set himself to erase, one after the other, the singular discoveries of his pupil. Karl cried with rage, he got very angry, and disputed the point; but the old master quietly opened one of his numerous music-books, and putting his fingers on the passage said, "Look there, my boy."

Then Karl bowed his head and despaired of the future.

But one fine morning, when he had presented to his master as his own composition a fantasia of Boccherini, varied with Viotti, the good man could no longer remain silent.

"Karl," he exclaimed, "do you take me for a fool? Do you think I cannot detect your larcenies? This is really too bad!"

And then perceiving the consternation of his pupil, he added: "Listen. I am willing to believe that your memory is to blame, and that you mistake recollection for originality, but you are growing too fat decidedly; you drink too generous a wine, and, above all, too much beer. That is what is shutting up the avenues of your intellect. You must get thinner!"

"Get thinner!"

"Yes, or give up music. You do not lack science, but ideas, and it is very simple; if you pass your whole life covering the strings of your violin with a coat of grease how can they vibrate?"

These words penetrated the depths of Hâfitz's soul.

"If it is necessary for me to get thin," exclaimed he, "I will not shrink from any sacrifice. Since matter oppresses the mind I will starve myself."

His countenance wore such an expression of heroism at that moment that Albertus was touched; he embraced his pupil and wished him every success.

The very next day Karl Hâfitz, knapsack on his back and bâton in hand, left the hotel of The Three Pigeons and the brewery sacred to King Gambrinus, and set out upon his travels.

He proceeded towards Switzerland.

Unfortunately at the end of six weeks he was much thinner, but inspiration did not come any more readily for that.

"Can anyone be more unhappy than I am?" he said. "Neither fasting nor good cheer, nor water, wine, or beer can bring me up to the necessary pitch; what have I done to deserve this? While a crowd of ignorant people produce remarkable works, I, with all my science, all my application, all my courage, cannot accomplish anything. Ah! Heaven is not good to me; it is unjust."

Communing thus with himself, he took the road from Brück to Freibourg; night was coming on; he felt weary and footsore. Just then he perceived by the light of moon an old ruined inn half-hidden in trees on the opposite side of the way; the door was off its hinges, the small window-panes were broken, the chimney was in ruins. Nettles and briars grew around it in wild luxuriance, and the garret window scarcely topped the heather, in which the wind blew hard enough to take the horns off a cow.

Karl could also perceive through the mist that a branch of a fir-tree waved above the door.

"Well," he muttered, "the inn is not prepossessing, it is rather ill-looking indeed, but we must not judge by appearances."

So, without hesitation, he knocked at the door with his stick.

"Who is there? what do you want?" called out a rough voice within.

"Shelter and food," replied the traveller.

"Ah ha! very good."

The door opened suddenly, and Karl found himself confronted by a stout personage with square visage, grey eyes, and his shoulders covered with a great-coat loosely thrown over them, and carrying an axe in his hand.

Behind this individual a fire was burning on the hearth, which lighted up the entrance to a small room and the wooden staircase, and close to the flame was crouched a pale young girl clad in a miserable brown dress with little white spots on it. She looked towards the door with an affrighted air; her black eyes had something sad and an indescribably wandering expression in them.

Karl took all this in at a glance, and instinctively grasped his stick tighter.

"Well, come in," said the man; this is no time to keep people out of doors."

Then Karl, thinking it bad form to appear alarmed, came into the room and sat down by the hearth.

"Give me your knapsack and stick," said the man.

For the moment the pupil of Albertus trembled to his very marrow; but the knapsack was unbuckled and the stick placed in the corner, and the host was seated quietly before the fire ere he had recovered himself.

This circumstance gave him confidence.

"Landlord," said he, smiling, "I am greatly in want of my supper."

"What would you like for supper, sir?" asked the landlord.

"An omelette, some wine, and cheese."

"Ha, ha! you have got an excellent appetite, but our provisions are exhausted."

"You have no cheese, then?"

"No."

"No butter, nor bread, nor milk?"

"No."

"Well, good heavens! what *have* you got?"

"We can roast some potatoes in the embers."

Just then Karl caught sight of a whole regiment of hens perched on the staircase in the gloom, of all sorts, in all attitudes, some pluming themselves in the most nonchalant manner.

"But," said Hâfitz, pointing at his troop of fowls, "you must have some eggs surely?"

"We took them all to market this morning."

"Well, if the worst comes to the worst, you can roast a fowl for me."

Scarcely had he spoken when the pale girl, with dishevelled hair, darted to the staircase, crying: "No one shall touch the fowls! No one shall touch my fowls! Ho, ho, ho! God's creatures must be respected."

Her appearance was so terrible that Hâfitz hastened to say, "No, no, the fowls shall not be touched. Let us have the potatoes. I devote myself to eating potatoes henceforth. From this moment my object in life is determined. I shall remain here three months—six months—any time that may be necessary to make as thin as a fakir."

He expressed himself with such animation that the host cried out to the girl: "Genovéva, Genovéva, look! The Spirit has taken possession of him; just as the other was——"

The north wind blew more fiercely outside; the fire blazed up on the hearth, puffed great masses of grey smoke up to the ceiling. The hens appeared to dance in the reflection of the frame while the demented girl sang in a shrill voice a wild air, and the log of green wood, hissing in the midst of the fire, accompanied her with plaintive sibilations.

Hâfitz began to fancy that he had fallen upon the den of the sorcerer Hecker; he devoured a dozen potatoes and drank a great draught of cold water. Then he felt somewhat calmer; he noticed that the girl had left the chamber, and that only the man sat opposite to him by the hearth.

"Landlord," he said, "show me where I am to sleep."

The host lit a lamp and slowly ascended the worm-eaten staircase; he opened a heavy trap-door with his grey head, and led Karl to a loft beneath the thatch.

"There is your bed," he said, as he deposited the lamp on the floor; "sleep well, and above all things beware of the fire."

He then descended and Hâfitz was left alone, stooping beneath the low roof in front of a great mattress covered with a sack of feathers.

He considered for a few seconds whether it would be prudent to sleep in such a place, for the man's countenance did not appear very prepossessing, particularly as, recalling his cold grey eyes, his blue lips, his wide bony forehead, his yellow hue, he suddenly recalled to mind that on the Golzenberg he had encountered three men hanging in chains, and that one of them bore a striking resemblance to the landlord; that he had also those grave eyes, the bony elbows, and that the great toe of his left foot protruded from his shoe, cracked by the rain.

He also recollected that the unhappy man named Melchior had been a musician formerly, and that he had been hanged for having murdered the landlord of The Golden Sheep with his pitcher, because he had asked him to pay his scanty reckoning.

This poor fellow's music had affected him powerfully in former days. It was fantastic, and the pupil of Albertus envied the Bohemian; but just now when he recalled the figure on the gibbet, his tatters agitated by the night wind, and the ravens wheeling around him with great discordant screams, he trembled violently, and his fears augmented when he discovered, at the farther end of the loft against the wall, a violin decorated with two faded palm-leaves.

Then indeed he was anxious to escape, but at the moment he heard the rough voice of the landlord.

"Put out that light, will you?" he cried; "go to bed. I told you particularly to be cautious about fire."

Those words froze Karl; he threw himself upon the mattress and extinguished the light. Silence fell on all the house.

Now, notwithstanding his determination not to close his eyes, Hâfitz, in consequence of hearing the sighing of the wind, the cries of the night-birds, the sound of the mice pattering over the floor, towards one o'clock fell asleep; but he was awakened by a bitter, deep, and most distressing sob. He started up, a cold perspiration standing on his forehead.

He looked up, and saw crouched up beneath the angle of the roof a man. It was Melchior, the executed criminal. His hair fell down to his emaciated ribs; his chest and neck were naked. One might compare him to a skeleton of an immense grasshopper, so thin was he; a ray of moonlight entering through the narrow window gave him a ghastly blue tint, and all around him hung the long webs of spiders.

Hâfitz, speechless, with staring eyes and gaping mouth, kept gazing at this weird object, as one might be expected to gaze at Death standing at one's bedside when the last hour has come!

Suddenly the skeleton extended its long bony hand and took the violin from the wall, placed it in position against its shoulder, and began to play.

There was in this ghostly music something of the cadence with which the earth falls upon the coffin of a dearly-loved friend—something solemn as the thunder of the waterfall echoed afar by the surrounding rocks, majestic as the wild blasts of the autumn tempest in the midst of the sonorous forest trees; sometimes it was sad—sad as never-ending despair. Then, in the midst of all this, he would strike into a lively measure, persuasive, silvery as the notes of a flock of wild goldfinches fluttering from twig to twig. These pleasing trills soared up with an ineffable tremolo of careless happiness, only to take flight all at once, frightened away by the waltz, foolish, palpitating, bewildering—love, joy, despair—all together singing, weeping, hurrying pell-mell over the quivering strings.

And Karl, notwithstanding his extreme terror, extended his arms and exclaimed: "Oh great, great artist! oh, sublime genius! oh, how I lament your sad fate, to be hanged for having murdered that brute of an innkeeper who did not know a note of music!—to wander through the forest by moonlight!—never to live in the world again—and with such talents! O Heaven!"

But as he thus cried out he was interrupted by the rough tones of his host.

"Hullo up there! will you be quiet? Are you ill, or is the house on fire?"

Heavy steps ascended the staircase, a bright light shone through the chinks of the door, which was opened by a thrust of the shoulder, and the landlord appeared.

"Oh!" exclaimed Hâfitz, "what things happen here! First I am awakened by celestial music and entranced by heavenly strains; and then it all vanishes as if it were but a dream."

The innkeeper's face assumed a thoughtful expression.

"Yes, yes," he muttered, "I might have thought as much. Melchior has come to disturb your rest. He will always come. Now we have lost our night's sleep; it is no use to think of rest any more. Come along, friend; get up and smoke a pipe with me."

Karl waited no second bidding; he hastily left the room. But when he got downstairs, seeing that it was still dark night, he buried his head in his hands and remained for a long time plunged in melancholy meditation. The host relighted the fire, and taking up his position in the opposite corner of the hearth, smoked in silence.

At length the grey dawn appeared through the little diamond-shaped panes; then the cock crew, and the hens began to hop down from step to step of the staircase.

"How much do I owe you?" asked Karl, as he buckled on his knapsack and resumed his walking-staff.

"You owe us a prayer at the chapel of St. Blaise," said the man, with a curious emphasis, "One prayer for the soul of Melchior, who was hanged, and another for his *fiancée*, Genovéva, the poor idiot."

"Is that all?"

"That is all."

"Well, then, good-bye—I shall not forget."

And indeed, the first thing that Karl did on his arrival at Freibourg was to offer up a prayer for the poor man and for the girl he had loved, and then he went to The Grape Hotel, spread his sheet of paper upon the table, and, fortified by a bottle of "rikevir," he wrote at the top of the page *The Murderer's Violin*, and then on the spot he traced the score of his first original composition.

My Friend's Story

Catherine Crowe

"I don't know how often you have promised to tell me a remarkable thing in the ghostly line, that happened to yourself," said I, the other day to my friend; "but something has always come in the way; now I shall be very much obliged to you for the particulars, if you have no objection to my printing the story."

"None," she said, "but as regards names of persons and places; the circumstances are so singular that I think they deserve to be recorded. That part of the affair which happened to myself I vouch for; and I can only say that I have most entire confidence in the truth of the rest, and that all the enquiries I made, tended to confirm the story.

"I remember your asking me once, why I so seldom visited our place in S—, and I told you it was because it was so dreadfully *triste* that I could not inhabit it. You will perhaps suppose that what I am going to relate happened there, but it did not, for the house has not even the recommendation of being haunted—that would at least give it an interest—but I am sorry to say the sole interest it possesses is, that it happens to be ours. Dull as it is, however, we lived there shortly after I was married, for some time. I had no children then, which made it all the duller, particularly when my husband was called away; and on one of these occasions, some acquaintance I had, who were living at a place called the Bellfry, about two miles distant, invited me to visit them for a few days.

"The Bellfry is a common place square house, just such as the doctor or lawyer would inhabit in a provincial town; a little white swing gate, a round grass plot, with a few straggling dahlias, a gravel road leading to the small portico, and a terrible loud bell to ring, when you want to be admitted. So much for the exterior. The interior is not at all more suggestive to the fancy. On the ground floor, there is the usual parlour on one side, and drawing-room on the other, with a long passage leading to the offices at the back; upstairs, a sort of corridor, with dingy bedrooms opening into it. Decidedly not lively, but perfectly prosaic, it was by no means calculated to inspire ghostly terrors; and, indeed, I must confess the supernatural, as it is called, was a subject that, at that time, had never engaged my attention. I mention all this to show you that what happened was not 'the offspring of my excited imagination,' as the learned always tell you these things are. Moreover, I was young; and, to the best of my belief, in very good health.

"The room they gave me was the best. It was plainly but comfortably furnished, with a large four-post bed, and it looked into the churchyard; but this is not an uncommon prospect in country towns, and I thought nothing about it. Now that we understand these things better, I should think it not ghostly, but unhealthy.

"The first two or three nights I slept there, nothing particular occurred; but on the fourth or fifth night, soon after I had fallen asleep, I was awoke by a noise which appeared very near me, and on listening attentively, I heard a rustling sound, and footsteps on the floor. I forgot for the moment that I had looked my door, and concluding it was the housekeeper, who sometimes looked in when I was going to bed, to ask if I was comfortable, I said, 'Is that you Mrs. H?' But there was no answer, upon which I sat up and looked around; and seeing nobody, though I heard the sound still, I jumped out of bed. Then I observed, for if was a bright moonlight night, that there was a large tree in the churchyard, which grew very close to the window, and I concluded that a breeze had arisen, and caused the branches to touch the glass; so I got into bed again quite satisfied, and settled myself to sleep. But scarcely had I closed my eyes, when the footsteps began again, much too distinct this time to be mistaken for anything else; and whilst I was listening in amazement, I heard a heavy, heavy sigh. I had raised myself on my elbow, in order to have my ears freer to listen, and presently I saw the curtains at the foot of the bed, which were closed, slowly and gently opened. I saw no figure, but they we're held apart, apparently by the two hands of some one standing there. I bounded out of bed, and rushed out of the room into the corridor, screaming for help.

All who heard me, got up and came out of their rooms, to enquire what had happened; but I had not courage to tell the truth, I was afraid of giving offence, or incurring ridicule, and I said I had been awakened by a noise in my room, and I was afraid somebody was concealed there. They went in with me and searched; of course, nobody was found; and one suggested that it was a mouse, another that it was a dream, and so forth. But then, and still more the next morning, I fancied, from their manner, they were better acquainted with my midnight visitor than they chose to say. However, I changed my room, and soon after quitted the Bellfry, which I have never slept at since, so there concludes the story, so far as I am concerned; but there is a sequel to the tale.

"I must tell you that I never mentioned these circumstances, because I knew I should only be laughed at; besides I thought it might annoy my hosts, as they had an idea of going abroad for some time, and it might have interfered with their letting the house.

"Now to my sequel.

"Two or three years after this occurrence, I fell desperately ill; first I was confined of an infant which did not survive; and then I was attacked with typhus fever, which raged in the neighbourhood. I was at death's door for eleven weeks, and not expected to recover; but you see, I did, *nonobstant messrs. les medicins*; but I was so long regaining my strength, that I was recommended to try the effects of a sea voyage. Even then, I could not sit up, and was lifted about like a baby; and as a fine lady's maid would have been of no use on board the yacht, a sailor's daughter from the coast was engaged to attend me; a strong, healthy young woman, to whom my weight was a feather. She tended me most faithfully, and I found her simple, truthful, and straightforward; insomuch, that I had thoughts of engaging her in my service permanently. With this view, and also because it helped to pass the time, I questioned her about her family, and the manner of life of her class, in the out of the way part of the country from which she came.

"'I suppose, Mary, you've never been away from home before?'

"'Oh, yes, Ma'am; I was in service as house-maid for a short time at the Bellfry, not far from your place, Ma'am; but I soon left that, and I have never been out again.'

"But why did you leave? Didn't you like the place?'

"'No, Ma'am.'

"'But why? Perhaps you'd too much to do?'

"'No, Ma'am, it wasn't a hard place; but unpleasant things happened, and so I left.'

"'What sort of unpleasant things?' said I, my own adventure there suddenly recurring to my memory.

"She hesitated, and said, that perhaps it would alarm me; she had also made a sort of promise to her master and mistress not to talk about it, and she never had mentioned what happened except to her parents, in order to account for leaving so suddenly. I assured her that I should not be alarmed, and overcame her scruples, and then she told me what follows.

"It appeared that she was engaged as house-maid at the Bellfry about two years before my visit there. Shortly after her arrival, her mistress being taken very unwell, her master went to sleep at the other side of the house, whilst Mary made her bed in the dressing-room, in order to be near at hand if the invalid required any assistance in the night. She had directions to keep some refreshment ready in case it was wanted, and towards two o'clock in the morning, her mistress saying she should like a little broth, Mary rose, and half drest, proceeded down stairs with a candle in her hand, to fetch some which she had left simmering on the kitchen fire. As she descended the last flight of stairs, she was a good deal startled at seeing a bright light issuing from the kitchen—the door of which was open—much brighter than could possibly proceed from the fire, for the whole passage was illuminated by it. Her first and very natural idea was that there were thieves in the house; and she was about to rush upstairs again to her master's room, when it occurred to her that one of the servants might be sitting up for some object of her own, and she stopt to listen, but there was not the least sound—all was silent. It then occurred to her that possibly something might have caught fire; so half-frightened, she advanced on tip-toe and peeped in, when, to her surprise, she saw a lady dressed in white, sitting by the fire, into which she was sadly and thoughtfully gazing. Her hands were clasped upon her knees, and two large greyhounds—beautiful dogs, said Mary—sat at her feet, both looking up fondly in her face. Her dress seemed to be of cambric or dimity, and from Mary's description, was that worn by ladies in the seventeenth century.

"The kitchen was as bright as if illuminated by twenty candles, but this did not strike her she said, till afterwards; so quite reassured by the appearance of a lady instead of a band of robbers, it did not occur to her to question who she was or how she came there; and saying, 'I beg your pardon ma'am,' she entered the kitchen, dropt a curtsey, and was going towards the fire, but as she advanced the vision retreated, till, at last, lady, chair, and dogs, glided through the closed window; and then the figure appeared standing erect in the garden, with its face close to the panes, and the eyes looking sorrowfully and earnestly on poor Mary.

"'And what did you do then, Mary?' said I.

"'Oh, ma'am, then I *fared* to feel very queer, and I fell upon the floor with a scream.'

"Her master heard the cry, and came down to see what was the matter. When she told him what she had seen, he endeavoured to persuade her it was all fancy; but Mary said she knew better than that; however, she promised not to talk of it, as it might frighten her sick mistress.

"Subsequently, she met the same melancholy apparition pacing the corridor into which the room that. I had slept in opened; and not liking these rencontres she gave warning and left the place.

"She knew nothing more, for her home was at some distance from the Belfry, which she had not since revisited; but when I had recovered my health and returned to that part of the country, I found, on enquiry, that this apparition was believed to haunt not only the house, but the neighbourhood; and I conversed with several people who affirmed they had seen her, generally alone, but sometimes accompanied by the two dogs.

"One woman said she had no fear, and that she had determined if she met the ghost, to try and touch her, in order to ascertain if it was positively an apparition; she did meet her in the dusk of the evening on the path that runs by the high road between the Bellfry and G . . . and put out her arm to take hold of her dress. She felt no substance, but she described the sensation as if she had plunged her hand into cold water.

"Another person saw her go through the hedge, and he observed, that he could see the hedge through the figure as she glided into the field.

"It is whispered that this unfortunate lady was an ancestress of the original proprietor of the place, who married a man she adored, contrary to the advice of her friends; and too late she discovered that he had taken her only for her money, which was needed to repair his ruined fortunes; he, the while being deeply enamoured of her younger sister, whose portion was too small for his purpose.

"The sister came to live with the newly married couple; and suspecting nothing, the bride was some time wholly unable to account for her husband's mysterious conduct and total alienation. At length she awakened to the dreadful reality, but unable to overcome her passion, she continued to live under his roof, suffering all the tortures of jealousy and disappointed love. She shunned the world; and the world, who soon learnt the state of affairs, shunned her husband's society; so she dragged on her dreary existence with no companionship but that of two remarkable fine greyhounds, which her husband had given her before marriage. Riding or walking, she was always accompanied by these animals—they and their affection were all she could call her own on earth.

"She died young; not without some suspicions that her end was hastened—at least, passively, by neglect, if not by more active means.

"When she was gone, the husband and the sister married; but the tradition runs, that the union was anything but blest. It is said that on the wedding night, immediately after her attendant had left her, screams were heard proceeding from the bridal chamber; and that on going upstairs, the bride was found in hysterics, and the groom pale, and apparently horror-stricken. After a little while, they desired to be left alone, but in the morning it was evident that no heads had prest the pillows. They had past the night without going to bed, and the next day they left their home—she never to return. She is supposed to have gone out of her mind, and to have died abroad in that state, carefully tended by him to the last. After her decease, he returned once to the Bellfry, a prematurely aged, melancholy man; and after staying a few days, and destroying several letters and papers, to do which appeared the object of his visit, he went away, and was seen no more in that county."

Alas, for poor human nature! How we are cursed in the realisation of our own wishes! How we struggle and sin to attain what we are never to enjoy!

The Mystery of the Semi-Detached

Edith Nesbit

He was waiting for her; he had been waiting an hour and a half in a dusty suburban lane, with a row of big elms on one side and some eligible building sites on the other—and far away to the south-west the twinkling yellow lights of the Crystal Palace. It was not quite like a country lane, for it had a pavement and lamp-posts, but it was not a bad place for a meeting all the same; and farther up, towards the cemetery, it was really quite rural, and almost pretty, especially in twilight. But twilight had long deepened into night, and still he waited. He loved her, and he was engaged to be married to her, with the complete disapproval of every reasonable person who had been consulted. And this half-clandestine meeting was to-night to take the place of the grudgingly sanctioned weekly interview—because a certain rich uncle was visiting at her house, and her mother was not the woman to acknowledge to a moneyed uncle, who might "go off" any day, a match so deeply ineligible as hers with him.

So he waited for her, and the chill of an unusually severe May evening entered into his bones.

The policeman passed him with but a surly response to his "Good night." The bicyclists went by him like grey ghosts with fog-horns; and it was nearly ten o'clock, and she had not come.

He shrugged his shoulders and turned towards his lodgings. His road led him by her house—desirable, commodious, semi-detached—and he walked slowly as he neared it. She might, even now, be coming out. But she was not. There was no sign of movement about the house, no sign of life, no lights even in the windows. And her people were not early people.

He paused by the gate, wondering.

Then he noticed that the front door was open—wide open—and the street lamp shone a little way into the dark hall. There was something about all this that did not please him—that scared him a little, indeed. The house had a gloomy and deserted air. It was obviously impossible that it harboured a rich uncle. The old man must have left early. In which case—

He walked up the path of patent-glazed tiles, and listened. No sign of life. He passed into the hall. There was no light anywhere. Where was everybody, and why was the front door open? There was no one in the drawing-room, the dining-room and the study (nine feet by seven) were equally blank. Every one was out, evidently. But the unpleasant sense that he was, perhaps, not the first casual visitor to walk through that open door impelled him to look through the house before he went away and closed it after him. So he went upstairs, and at the door of the first bedroom he came to he struck a wax match, as he had done in the sitting-rooms. Even as he did so he felt that he was not alone. And he was prepared to see *something*; but for what he saw he was not prepared. For what he saw lay on the bed, in a white loose gown—and it was his sweetheart, and its throat was cut from ear to ear. He doesn't know what happened then, nor how he got downstairs and into the street; but he got out somehow, and the policeman found him in a fit, under the lamp-post at the corner of the street. He couldn't speak when they picked him up, and he passed the night in the police-cells, because the policeman had seen plenty of drunken men before, but never one in a fit.

The next morning he was better, though still very white and shaky. But the tale he told the magistrate was convincing, and they sent a couple of constables with him to her house.

There was no crowd about it as he had fancied there would be, and the blinds were not down.

As he stood, dazed, in front of the door, it opened, and she came out.

He held on to the door-post for support.

"She's all right, you see," said the constable, who had found him under the lamp. "I told you you was drunk, but you *would* know best—"

When he was alone with her he told her—not all—for that would not bear telling—but how he had come into the commodious semi-detached, and how he had found the door open and the lights out, and that he had been into that long back room facing the stairs, and had seen something—in even trying to hint at which he turned sick and broke down and had to have brandy given him.

"But, my dearest," she said, "I dare say the house was dark, for we were all at the Crystal Palace with my uncle, and no doubt the door was open, for the maids *will* run out if they're left. But you could not have been in that room, because I locked it when

I came away, and the key was in my pocket. I dressed in a hurry and I left all my odds and ends lying about."

"I know," he said; "I saw a green scarf on a chair, and some long brown gloves, and a lot of hairpins and ribbons, and a prayer-book, and a lace handkerchief on the dressing-table. Why, I even noticed the almanac on the mantelpiece—October 21. At least it couldn't be that, because this is May. And yet it was. Your almanac is at October 21, isn't it?"

"No, of course it isn't," she said, smiling rather anxiously; "but all the other things were just as you say. You must have had a dream, or a vision, or something."

He was a very ordinary, commonplace, City young man, and he didn't believe in visions, but he never rested day or night till he got his sweetheart and her mother away from that commodious semi-detached, and settled them in a quite distant suburb. In the course of the removal he incidentally married her, and the mother went on living with them.

His nerves must have been a good bit shaken, because he was very queer for a long time, and was always inquiring if any one had taken the desirable semi-detached; and when an old stockbroker with a family took it, he went the length of calling on the old gentleman and imploring him by all that he held dear, not to live in that fatal house.

"Why?" said the stockbroker, not unnaturally.

And then he got so vague and confused, between trying to tell why and trying not to tell why, that the stockbroker showed him out, and thanked his God he was not such a fool as to allow a lunatic to stand in the way of his taking that really remarkably cheap and desirable semi-detached residence.

Now the curious and quite inexplicable part of this story is that when she came down to breakfast on the morning of the 22nd of October she found him looking like death, with the morning paper in his hand. He caught hers—he couldn't speak, and pointed to the paper. And there she read that on the night of the 21st a young lady, the stockbroker's daughter, had been found, with her throat cut from ear to ear, on the bed in the long back bedroom facing the stairs of that desirable semi-detached.

The Occupant of the Room

Algernon Blackwood

He arrived late at night by the yellow diligence, stiff and cramped after the toilsome ascent of three slow hours. The village, a single mass of shadow, was already asleep. Only in front of the little hotel was there noise and light and bustle—for a moment. The horses, with tired, slouching gait, crossed the road and disappeared into the stable of their own accord, their harness trailing in the dust; and the lumbering diligence stood for the night where they had dragged it—the body of a great yellow-sided beetle with broken legs.

In spite of his physical weariness the schoolmaster, revelling in the first hours of his ten-guinea holiday, felt exhilarated. For the high Alpine valley was marvellously still; stars twinkled over the torn ridges of the Dent du Midi where spectral snows gleamed against rocks that looked like solid ink; and the keen air smelt of pine forests, dew-soaked pastures, and freshly sawn wood. He took it all in with a kind of bewildered delight for a few minutes, while the other three passengers gave directions about their luggage and went to their rooms. Then he turned and walked over the coarse matting into the glare of the hall, only just able to resist stopping to examine the big mountain map that hung upon the wall by the door.

And, with a sudden disagreeable shock, he came down from the ideal to the actual. For at the inn—the only inn—there was no vacant room. Even the available sofas were occupied. . . .

How stupid he had been not to write! Yet it had been impossible, he remembered, for he had come to the decision suddenly that morning in Geneva, enticed by the brilliance of the weather after a week of rain.

They talked endlessly, this gold-braided porter and the hard-faced old woman—her face was hard, he noticed—gesticulating all the time, and pointing all about the village with suggestions that he ill understood, for his French was limited and their *patois* was fearful.

"There!"—he might find a room, "or *there*! But we are, *hélas*, full—more full than we care about. To-morrow, perhaps—if So-and-So give up their rooms—!" And then,

with much shrugging of shoulders, the hard-faced old woman stared at the gold-braided porter, and the porter stared sleepily at the schoolmaster.

At length, however, by some process of hope he did not himself understand, and following directions given by the old woman that were utterly unintelligible, he went out into the street and walked towards a dark group of houses she had pointed out to him. He only knew that he meant to thunder at a door and ask for a room. He was too weary to think out details. The porter half made to go with him, but turned back at the last moment to speak with the old woman. The houses sketched themselves dimly in the general blackness. The air was cold. The whole valley was filled with the rush and thunder of falling water. He was thinking vaguely that the dawn could not be very far away, and that he might even spend the night wandering in the woods, when there was a sharp noise behind him and he turned to see a figure hurrying after him. It was the porter—running.

And in the little hall of the inn there began again a confused three-cornered conversation, with frequent muttered colloquy and whispered asides in *patois* between the woman and the porter—the net result of which was that, "If Monsieur did not object—there *was* a room, after all, on the first floor—only it was in a sense 'engaged.' That is to say—"

But the schoolmaster took the room without inquiring too closely into the puzzle that had somehow provided it so suddenly. The ethics of hotel-keeping had nothing to do with him. If the woman offered him quarters it was not for him to argue with her whether the said quarters were legitimately hers to offer.

But the porter, evidently a little thrilled, accompanied the guest up to the room and supplied in a mixture of French and English details omitted by the landlady—and Minturn, the schoolmaster, soon shared the thrill with him, and found himself in the atmosphere of a possible tragedy.

All who know the peculiar excitement that belongs to high mountain valleys where dangerous climbing is a chief feature of the attractions, will understand a certain faint element of high alarm that goes with the picture. One looks up at the desolate, soaring ridges and thinks involuntarily of the men who find their pleasure for days and nights together scaling perilous summits among the clouds, and conquering inch by inch the icy peaks that for ever shake their dark terror in the sky. The atmosphere of adventure, spiced with the possible horror of a very grim order of tragedy, is inseparable from any imaginative contemplation of the scene; and the idea Minturn gleaned from the half-frightened porter lost nothing by his ignorance of the language. This Englishwoman, the real occupant of the room, had insisted on going without a guide. She had left just before daybreak two days before—the porter had seen her start—and . . . she had not returned! The route was difficult and dangerous, yet not impossible for a skilled climber, even a solitary one. And the Englishwoman was an experienced mountaineer. Also, she was self-willed, careless of advice, bored by warnings, self-confident to a degree. Queer, moreover; for she kept entirely to herself, and sometimes remained in her room with locked doors, admitting no one, for days together: a "crank," evidently, of the first water.

This much Minturn gathered clearly enough from the porter's talk while his luggage was brought in and the room set to rights; further, too, that the search partly had gone out and *might*, of course, return at any moment. In which case— Thus the room was empty, yet still hers. "If Monsieur did not object—if the risk he ran of having to turn out suddenly in the night—" It was the loquacious porter who furnished the details that made the transaction questionable; and Minturn dismissed the loquacious porter as soon as possible, and prepared to get into the hastily arranged bed and snatch all the hours of sleep he could before he was turned out.

At first, it must be admitted, he felt uncomfortable—distinctly uncomfortable. He was in some one else's room. He had really no right to be there. It was in the nature of an unwarrantable intrusion; and while he unpacked he kept looking over his shoulder as though some one were watching him from the corners. Any moment, it seemed, he would hear a step in the passage, a knock would come at the door, the door would open, and there he would see this vigorous Englishwoman looking him up and down with anger. Worse still—he would hear her voice asking him what he was doing in her room—her bedroom. Of course, he had an adequate explanation, but still!

Then, reflecting that he was already half undressed, the humour of it flashed for a second across his mind, and he laughed—*quietly*. And at once, after that laughter, under his breath, came the sudden sense of tragedy he had felt before. Perhaps, even while he smiled, her body lay broken and cold upon those awful heights, the wind of snow playing over her hair, her glazed eyes staring sightless up to the stars. . . . It made him shudder. The sense of this woman whom he had never seen, whose name even he did not know, became extraordinarily real. Almost he could imagine that she was somewhere in the room with him, hidden, observing all he did.

He opened the door softly to put his boots outside, and when he closed it again he turned the key. Then he finished unpacking and distributed his few things about the room. It was soon done; for, in the first place, he had only a small Gladstone and a knapsack, and secondly, the only place where he could spread his clothes was the sofa. There was no chest of drawers, and the cupboard, an unusually large and solid one, was locked. The Englishwoman's things had evidently been hastily put away in it. The only sign of her recent presence was a bunch of faded *Alpenrosen* standing in a glass jar upon the washhand stand. This, and a certain faint perfume, were all that remained. In spite, however, of these very slight evidences, the whole room was pervaded with a curious sense of occupancy that he found exceedingly distasteful. One moment the atmosphere seemed subtly charged with a "just left" feeling; the next it was a queer awareness of "still here" that made him turn cold and look hurriedly behind him.

Altogether, the room inspired him with a singular aversion, and the strength of this aversion seemed the only excuse for his tossing the faded flowers out of the window, and then hanging his mackintosh upon the cupboard door in such a way as to screen it as much as possible from view. For the sight of that big, ugly cupboard, filled with the clothing of a woman who might then be beyond any further need of covering—thus his imagination insisted on picturing it—touched in him a startled sense of the Incongruous that did not stop there, but crept through his mind gradually till it merged somehow into a sense of a rather grotesque horror. At any rate, the sight of that cupboard was offensive, and he covered it almost instinctively. Then, turning out the electric light, he got into bed.

But the instant the room was dark he realised that it was more than he could stand; for, with the blackness, there came a sudden rush of cold that he found it hard to explain. And the odd thing was that, when he lit the candle beside his bed, he noticed that his hand trembled.

This, of course, was too much. His imagination was taking liberties and must be called to heel. Yet the way he called it to order was significant, and its very deliberateness betrayed a mind that has already admitted fear. And fear, once in, is difficult to dislodge. He lay there upon his elbow in bed and carefully took note of all the objects in the room—with the intention, as it were, of taking an inventory of everything his senses perceived, then drawing a line, adding them up finally, and saying with decision, "That's all the room contains! I've counted every single thing. There is nothing more. *Now*—I may sleep in peace!"

And it was during this absurd process of enumerating the furniture of the room that the dreadful sense of distressing lassitude came over him that made it difficult even to finish counting. It came swiftly, yet with an amazing kind of violence that overwhelmed him softly and easily with a sensation of enervating weariness hard to describe. And its first effect was to banish fear. He no longer possessed enough energy to feel really afraid or nervous. The cold remained, but the alarm vanished. And into every corner of his usually vigorous personality crept the insidious poison of a *muscular* fatigue—at first—that in a few seconds, it seemed, translated itself into *spiritual* inertia. A sudden consciousness of the foolishness, the crass futility, of life, of effort, of fighting—of all that makes life worth living, shot into every fibre of his being, and left him utterly weak. A spirit of black pessimism that was not even vigorous enough to assert itself, invaded the secret chambers of his heart. . . .

Every picture that presented itself to his mind came dressed in grey shadows: those bored and sweating horses toiling up the ascent to—nothing! that hard-faced landlady taking so much trouble to let her desire for gain conquer her sense of morality—for a few francs! That gold-braided porter, so talkative, fussy, energetic, and so anxious to tell all he knew! What was the use of them all? And for himself, what in the world was the good of all the labour and drudgery he went through in that preparatory school where he was junior master? What could it lead to? Wherein lay the value of so much uncertain toil, when the ultimate secrets of life were hidden and no one knew the final goal? How foolish was effort, discipline, work! How vain was pleasure! How trivial the noblest life! . . .

With a fearful jump that nearly upset the candle Minturn pulled himself together. Such vicious thoughts were usually so remote from his normal character that the sudden vile invasion produced a swift reaction. Yet, only for a moment. Instantly, again, the black depression descended upon him like a wave. His work—it could lead to nothing but the dreary labour of a small headmastership after all—seemed as vain and foolish as his holiday in the Alps. What an idiot he had been, to be sure, to come out with a knapsack merely to work himself into a state of exhaustion climbing over toilsome mountains that led to nowhere—resulted in nothing. A dreariness of the grave possessed him. Life was a ghastly fraud! Religion a childish humbug! Everything was merely a trap—a trap of death; a coloured toy that Nature used as a decoy! But a decoy for what? For nothing! There was no meaning in anything. The only *real* thing was—DEATH. And the happiest people were those who found it soonest.

Then why wait for it to come?

He sprang out of bed, thoroughly frightened. This was horrible. Surely mere physical fatigue could not produce a world so black, an outlook so dismal, a cowardice that struck with such sudden hopelessness at the very roots of life? For, normally, he was cheerful and strong, full of the tides of healthy living; and this appalling lassitude swept the very basis of his personality into Nothingness and the desire for death. It was like the development of a Secondary Personality. He had read, of course, how certain persons who suffered shocks developed thereafter entirely different characteristics, memory, tastes, and so forth. It had all rather frightened him. Though scientific men vouched for it, it was hardly to be believed. Yet here was a similar thing taking place in his own consciousness. He was, beyond question, experiencing all the mental variations of—*some one else*! It was un-moral. It was awful. It was—well, after all, at the same time, it was uncommonly interesting.

And this interest he began to feel was the first sign of his returning normal Self. For to feel interest is to live, and to love life.

He sprang into the middle of the room—then switched on the electric light. And the first thing that struck his eye was—the big cupboard.

"Hallo! There's that—beastly cupboard!" he exclaimed to himself, involuntarily, yet aloud. It held all the clothes, the swinging skirts and coats and summer blouses of the dead woman. For he knew now—somehow or other—that she *was* dead. . . .

At that moment, through the open windows, rushed the sound of falling water, bringing with it a vivid realisation of the desolate, snow-swept heights. He saw her—positively *saw* her!—lying where she had fallen, the frost upon her cheeks, the snow-dust eddying about her hair and eyes, her broken limbs pushing against the lumps of ice. For a moment the sense of spiritual lassitude—of the emptiness of life—vanished before this picture of broken effort—of a small human force battling pluckily, yet in vain, against the impersonal and pitiless Potencies of Inanimate Nature—and he found himself again, his normal self. Then, instantly, returned again that terrible sense of cold, nothingness, emptiness. . . .

And he found himself standing opposite the big cupboard where her clothes were. He wanted to see those clothes—things she had used and worn. Quite close he stood, almost touching it. The next second he had touched it. His knuckles struck upon the wood.

Why he knocked is hard to say. It was an instinctive movement probably. Something in his deepest self dictated it—ordered it. He knocked at the door. And the dull sound upon the wood into the stillness of that room brought—horror. Why it should have done so he found it as hard to explain to himself as why he should have felt impelled to knock. The fact remains that when he heard the faint reverberation inside the cupboard, it brought with it so vivid a realisation of the woman's presence that he stood there shivering upon the floor with a dreadful sense of anticipation: he almost expected to hear an answering knock from within—the rustling of the hanging skirts perhaps—or, worse still, to see the locked door slowly open towards him.

And from that moment, he declares that in some way or other he must have partially lost control of himself, or at least of his better judgment; for he became possessed by such an overmastering desire to tear open that cupboard door and see the clothes within, that he tried every key in the room in the vain effort to unlock it, and then, finally, before he quite realised what he was doing—rang the bell!

But, having rung the bell for no obvious or intelligent reason at two o'clock in the morning, he then stood waiting in the middle of the floor for the servant to come, conscious for the first time that something outside his ordinary self had pushed him towards the act. It was almost like an internal voice that directed him . . . and thus, when at last steps came down the passage and he faced the cross and sleepy chambermaid, amazed at being summoned at such an hour, he found no difficulty in the matter of what he should say. For the same power that insisted he should open the cupboard door also impelled him to utter words over which he apparently had no control.

"It's not *you* I rang for!" he said with decision and impatience, "I want a man. Wake the porter and send him up to me at once—hurry! I tell you, hurry—!"

And when the girl had gone, frightened at his earnestness, Minturn realised that the words surprised himself as much as they surprised her. Until they were out of his mouth he had not known what exactly he was saying. But now he understood that some force foreign to his own personality was using his mind and organs. The black depression that had possessed him a few moments before was also part of it. The powerful mood of this vanished woman had somehow momentarily taken possession of him—communicated, possibly, by the atmosphere of things in the room still belonging to her. But even now, when the porter, without coat or collar, stood beside him in the room, he did not understand *why* he insisted, with a positive fury admitting no denial, that the key of that cupboard must be found and the door instantly opened.

The scene was a curious one. After some perplexed whispering with the chambermaid at the end of the passage, the porter managed to find and produce the key in question. Neither he nor the girl knew clearly what this excited Englishman was up to, or why he was so passionately intent upon opening the cupboard at two o'clock in the morning. They watched him with an air of wondering what was going to happen next.

But something of his curious earnestness, even of his late fear, communicated itself to them, and the sound of the key grating in the lock made them both jump.

They held their breath as the creaking door swung slowly open. All heard the clatter of that other key as it fell against the wooden floor—within. The cupboard had been locked *from the inside*. But it was the scared housemaid, from her position in the corridor, who first saw—and with a wild scream fell crashing against the bannisters.

The porter made no attempt to save her. The schoolmaster and himself made a simultaneous rush towards the door, now wide open. They, too, had seen.

There were no clothes, skirts or blouses on the pegs, but, all by itself, from an iron hook in the centre, they saw the body of the Englishwoman hanging by the neck, the head bent horribly forwards, the tongue protruding. Jarred by the movement of unlocking, the body swung slowly round to face them. . . . Pinned upon the inside of the door was a hotel envelope with the following words pencilled in straggling writing:

"Tired—unhappy—hopelessly depressed. ... I cannot face life any longer. . . . All is black. I must put an end to it. . . . I meant to do it on the mountains, but was afraid. I slipped back to my room unobserved. This way is easiest and best. . . ."

Old Ayah

Alice Perrin

A May morning in the Himalayas, crystal clear, golden with sunshine. Honeysuckle, passion-flower, roses, clung in a perfumed tangle to the red roof of the veranda; and opposite, across the lower hills and the deep purple valley, against the wondrous blue of the sky, the dazzling range of snow peaks looked deceptively, startlingly near. The air was charged with strong scents and gentle sound—voices of the hill-people as they climbed the steep pathway with burdens on their heads and shoulders; strains of the band that practised in a remote compound.

Only within the veranda did there seem to be gloom and distress. An old ayah stood crying helplessly in the corner, and a little English boy danced before her in frenzied concern and remonstrance.

"Must not go, Ayah! Must not go!" he shrieked in Hindustani.

Then he rushed into the dining-room where his mother was breakfasting. "For Ayah a letter has come," he wailed, still in Hindustani, "and she says to-day she must go—to-day! Mamma, give an order that she stays. Give it now, at once."

Mrs. Dring hurried out, but she checked her words of impatience when she saw the trouble in the old woman's faithful eyes, and the pathetic trembling of the hand that held out a flimsy piece of yellow paper scrawled across with Hindi characters.

"Mem-sahib! pardon, my son is very ill—surely he dies. They have written for me, he calls for me, his mother. I must go to him. But quickly will I return. For a certainty, mem-sahib, will I return when my son is better—or maybe dead." She turned away.

The mem-sahib tried to smother her own annoyance and dread of the inconvenience that lay before her. "Poor Ayah!" she said, kindly, "it is very sad for you. Of course you must go. But how am I to get another ayah for Jackie-sahib while you are away—what am I to do? We have only just come up to the hills, and you will be leaving us altogether when we go to England after the rains!"

Old Ayah wept afresh. She was sorely loath to vex her dear mem-sahib and cause her worry; she could not bear the thought of leaving Jackie, the "babba" she had tended from his birth. The final parting was already too near, and every day seemed precious.

Yet she must go to her only son, the son who had never given her trouble or anxiety, who had supported her so bravely, when years ago, his father, bitten by a mad dog, had died a cruel death before she herself went into service; the clever, hardworking son, who at last had risen to the honourable post of chief sweeper to a down-country bazaar, and was such a good father, such a good husband, as well as a model son. All Old Ayah's savings, invested in the heavy silver ornaments that she wore day and night round her neck, and wrists, and ankles, were to go to him and his children at her death as a token of her pride and affection; and now it was he who lay dying. He was calling for her, and she must go, wretched as the separation from Jackie would make her, painfully conscious as she was of the inconvenience her absence would cause her beloved mistress.

As usual, the mem-sahib was kind and good, and said she would manage all right for herself and Jackie, and Ayah was not to worry. She advanced the unhappy old woman a month's wages, and sent her down to the railway station at the foot of the hills in her own dandy; and, if possible, enslaved Ayah's heart to her more than ever.

Jackie saw his nurse off with howls and tears. "Must not go, Ayah! Must not go!" he bellowed to the last.

"Ayah will come back, my little one," she answered. "Ayah will come back quickly."

But Jackie only wept with greater violence until the dandy and its awkwardly seated burden had disappeared down the hill path, and nothing but the promise that he should carry the bearer's lantern about when it grew dark gave him any comfort for the rest of the day.

Old Ayah was terribly missed in the little house with the red veranda roof facing the snows. Jackie felt strange and forlorn without her indulgent yet experienced care, and consequently became a trial to everybody. He bullied the other servants and was naughty and exacting; he defied his mother and screamed himself purple when she corrected him; he would not to go bed, he would not get up, he would not eat what was good for him, and he was continually in mischief. No satisfactory substitute could be found to take Ayah's place for such a short period, and Mrs. Dring counted the days till the old woman should come back. She wrote pages to her husband in the plains, chronicling her woes, and declared that native servants really ought to be born without relations. But a month went by and still Ayah did not come back, neither did she send a line of explanation to her mistress, which caused Mrs. Dring to enlarge on the ingratitude of even the best of native servants. At the same time her experience of India, comparatively short though it was, had familiarized her with the dilatoriness of the people where letters are concerned, and in her heart she excused Ayah, for she knew that the adored son's illness would occupy the old woman's time and attention completely. Also that if the man died the funeral ceremonies and arrangements must be a long and engrossing business. The mem-sahib did not really doubt but that Ayah would come back the moment she was free to do so, only it was certainly very vexing that her absence should last so much longer than anyone had anticipated.

But one day Jackie ceased to be defiant and unmanageable. He played listlessly all the morning and then declared, with little whimpers of self-pity, that he felt tired and wished only to sit on his mother's lap with his head against her shoulder. Mrs. Dring took his temperature, with the result that she put him to bed at once and sent for the doctor, who said it was impossible to tell at present if the fever were ordinary malaria or the prelude to a serious illness.

The doctor came back again late that night, also early the next morning. Jackie had not slept, his mother reported anxiously, and had cried continually for his Ayah, who was away on leave.

"Can't you recall her?" the doctor suggested. "You must have a woman to help you if this goes on, and it would be better to have some one he knows."

So Mrs. Dring telegraphed to Old Ayah, urging her, if possible, to come back, as the child was ill and wanted her. She also telegraphed to Major Dring to hold himself in readiness to take leave if Jackie should grow worse. Then she sat by the little boy's bed through the long hours, fighting the fever according to the doctor's directions, praying that the blue eyes, so unnaturally bright, might close in healing sleep, listening to the ceaseless moan of "Ayah, Ayah! come back; must not go, Ayah!"

Next morning the doctor stayed on and on—he only left the sick child for a still more urgent case—and when he had gone Mrs. Dring telegraphed the necessary summons to her husband.

The hours that followed seemed endless. Now and then she crept into the veranda to see if Ayah, could by any chance be coming up the pathway. She dreaded the night-time. Her husband could not possibly be with her before sunrise. The doctor, overworked, single-handed though he was, stayed late again that evening, and when he left he looked worried and apprehensive. "If the child could only get to sleep naturally," he said.

The mother arranged the room for the night's vigil, set medicine ready, saw that milk and chicken essence were at hand, noted with a sick foreboding that, save for his heavy breathing, Jackie was lying unnaturally still, with eyes wide open yet glazed and unseeing. She sat by the shaded lamp alert and miserable, listening to the tick of the clock, the rustle of the fir-trees outside the window, the thick, difficult breathing that shook the fragile little form on the bed.

Of a sudden a sharp sound rang through the room: "Ayah! Ayah!"

Jackie was holding out his arms and gabbling hoarsely in Hindustani. "Ayah must not go any more. Ayah stay and sing Jackie to sleep. Why did you go? Naughty Ayah!"

Mrs. Dring flew to the bedside, but Jackie paid no heed to her. He mumbled happily in Hindustani, and pushed her hand away when she laid it on his forehead. Reluctantly she sat down again by the shaded lamp, and then, to her everlasting bewilderment, she thought she heard a low, faint sound of singing, the sound of the quaint little crooning chant with which ayahs soothe children to sleep.

Years afterwards, when Mrs. Dring was telling me this story herself, she said that she should never forget the feeling that came over her as she listened to the sound, the feeling of awe and mystery, the conviction that she was listening to something not earthly. She tried to persuade herself that it was one of the servants in the compound, or that the sound came from the public footpath below the house; but all the time she knew that some one who she could not see was there, beside Jackie's bed, singing and soothing him to sleep; and that the voice, though so faint and thin and uncertain, was surely the voice of Old Ayah.

"Ayah!" came from her lips, involuntarily, in a loud whisper.

The singing ceased abruptly, as though startled into silence, and Jackie set up a peevish cry. His mother bent over him, and laid her fingers lightly on his forehead. Was it her fancy, or did the skin feel less dry and burning?

"Ayah must not go! Sing, Ayah, sing," he murmured, and nestled his cheek drowsily into his pillow. "Sing!" he whimpered with impatience; and Mrs. Dring crooned as she had heard Old Ayah croon so often at Jackie's bedtime, and then patted the small shoulder softly.

"No! No!" the child wailed, and flung out his arms. "Ayah, sing— "

Then Mrs. Dring stole back to her seat by the lamp and waited, waited breathless and expectant till the fluttering sound that was more like the echo of a voice, returned, as she had known instinctively that it would return, and hung, hovering, over the bed.

How long it went on she could never say. She thinks she may have fainted, she does not know; she can only remember opening her eyes to find the room full of the yellow dawn-light, and Jackie sleeping quietly, naturally, his breathing regular and easy, his skin moist and cool. Hardly daring to believe the happy truth, she lingered long beside the bed, then slipped quietly into the veranda. Before her rose the chain of white mountains burnished with the crimson and gold of daybreak, glowing and glistening high into the radiant sky.

She stood there, weary, and dishevelled, yet with heart and soul uplifted in thankfulness. All the dread and suspense and longing now might yield to a glad relief. The ghostly fancies of the night had rolled away like a dark cloud; she believed she must have slept to her shame and dreamed of that faint, crooning song, dreamed that it had soothed the sick child into life-giving rest. . . .

The sound of hoofs on the gravel made her turn, and she saw her husband riding up the pathway. The next moment she was clinging to him. "He is better—the fever has gone—he is asleep," she half sobbed.

Together they tiptoed into the room, and bent over the softly sleeping little figure. Then they stole into the next room, where the sound of their voices could not disturb the child, but where Mrs. Dring's strength failed her suddenly; and just as the doctor's voice was heard outside, she slipped from her husband's arm to the ground a huddled, senseless heap.

Before midday a nurse from the hospital was in temporary command of the little house, for though Jackie was practically out of danger, his mother lay on her bed weak and exhausted, forbidden to move for the present, forbidden to talk. So it was not until the next morning that she was able to tell her husband of the weird lullaby that had soothed Jackie to sleep.

"I'm certain I didn't dream it," she added nervously.

"Dearest," he argued, "of course you either dreamt or imagined it."

But Mrs. Dring would not listen to reason. "Something must have happened to poor Old Ayah," she persisted tearfully. "I believe she came back when Jackie called her, and saved his life."

"My dear child, what nonsense!" he interrupted.

"I wish you would write," she urged. "Do write and make inquiries about her; write to the cantonment magistrate of the place where the son lives." She began to cry.

"Yes—yes, I'll write, of course," Major Dring promised hastily. "But I'm sure you needn't worry yourself. You know what natives are—time means nothing to them. She'll turn up in a day or two."

"But I telegraphed to her—"

"Very likely she never got it. Her relations would see to that if they wanted her to stay on. But, anyway, we'll find out. She's been away far too long."

"Something must have happened to her," Mrs. Dring repeated with tearful obstinacy. "Old Ayah would never take advantage."

"Well, I've no doubt she'll turn up the moment I've posted the letter," said the Major cheerfully.

But before the promised letter of inquiry had even been written there came an answer to Mrs. Dring's telegram, signed with the name of Old Ayah's son. It had been sent the cheapest way "*Deferred,*" which means in India that the message must take its chance of delay, and may possibly reach its destination no sooner than a letter.

"*Mother not come*," was the message.

"There now," said Major Dring, "they're not going to let her come back at all, the rascals! and they've got her month's pay into the bargain. I don't suppose that son of hers was ever ill at all. It was just a trick."

Mrs. Dring was looking at the telegram with thoughtful attention and troubled eyes. "I think," she said slowly, "it means that Old Ayah never even arrived!"

Her husband scoffed and contradicted, but was obviously disturbed by the suggestion. He went off and wrote to the proper authority at the place where Old Ayah's son was head sweeper to the bazaar, and asked that the matter might be investigated.

When the answer came, three or four days later, they were all out in the veranda. Major and Mrs. Dring, Jackie, thin and pale but hourly growing stronger, and the pleasant hospital nurse.

The postman came up the path and handed the letters to Major Dring. In anxious silence his wife watched him open them. She was afraid to ask before Jackie if there was news of Old Ayah. Since his recovery the child had not mentioned her; he was engrossed with the hospital nurse, who could draw pictures, and make things out of paper, and play all sorts of games. He found her far more interesting than Old Ayah had ever been.

Presently Major Dring got up and went into the house. A moment later he called his wife, and she joined him hurriedly.

"I'm afraid," he said, "you were right. It seems Old Ayah never did arrive at her son's house. The son was certainly ill, and his mother was sent for, but when she did not come they concluded she was unable to get leave, and, just like natives, never thought of writing again. They had no idea she was not still with us till they got your telegram. The cantonment magistrate says the son is well known and respected, and there's no doubt his story is true. I'm afraid—" he hesitated significantly.

"Oh! I *knew* something had happened," cried his wife in sore distress, "Oh! poor Old Ayah! She had her month's pay with her, and all her jewellery. Of course she was murdered on the way down. You know how many cases there are like that in India—people who are never traced, never discovered. Why didn't I think of it—I shall never forgive myself—and she came back to Jackie just to save his life—she came back and sang him to sleep—" She burst into a storm of tears.

"Hush! Hush!" said the Major. "Don't talk like that. We will do all we can to trace her."

And he went off at once to set inquiries in train, while Mrs. Dring stood at the window staring out with wet eyes at the glittering snows. She felt a sad conviction that Old Ayah would never be seen or heard of again in the flesh or the spirit; and indeed time proved that she was right.

On the Brighton Road

Richard Middleton

Slowly the sun had climbed up the hard white downs, till it broke with little of the mysterious ritual of dawn upon a sparkling world of snow. There had been a hard frost during the night, and the birds, who hopped about here and there with scant tolerance of life, left no trace of their passage on the silver pavements. In places the sheltered caverns of the hedges broke the monotony of the whiteness that had fallen upon the coloured earth, and overhead the sky melted from orange to deep blue, from deep blue to a blue so pale that it suggested a thin paper screen rather than illimitable space. Across the level fields there came a cold, silent wind which blew fine dust of snow from the trees, but hardly stirred the crested hedges. Once above the sky-line, the sun seemed to climb more quickly, and as it rose higher it began to give out a heat that blended with the keenness of the wind.

It may have been this strange alternation of heat and cold that disturbed the tramp in his dreams, for he struggled for a moment with the snow that covered him, like a man who finds himself twisted uncomfortably in the bed-clothes, and then sat up with staring, questioning eyes. "Lord! I thought I was in bed," he said to himself as he took in the vacant landscape, "and all the while I was out here." He stretched his limbs, and, rising carefully to his feet, shook the snow off his body. As he did so the wind set him shivering, and he knew that his bed had been warm.

"Come, I feel pretty fit," he thought. "I suppose I am lucky to wake at all in this. Or unlucky—it isn't much of a business to come back to." He looked up and saw the downs shining against the blue like the Alps on a picture-postcard. "That means another forty miles or so, I suppose," he continued grimly. "Lord knows what I did yesterday. Walked till I was done, and now I'm only about twelve miles from Brighton. Damn the snow, damn Brighton, damn everything!" The sun crept up higher and higher, and he started walking patiently along the road with his back turned to the hills.

"Am I glad or sorry that it was only sleep that took me, glad or sorry, glad or sorry?" His thoughts seemed to arrange themselves in a metrical accompaniment to the steady thud of his footsteps, and he hardly sought an answer to his question. It was good enough to walk to.

Presently, when three milestones had loitered past, he overtook a boy who was stooping to light a cigarette. He wore no overcoat, and looked unspeakably fragile against the snow. "Are you on the road, guv'nor?" asked the boy huskily as he passed.

"I think I am," the tramp said.

"Oh! then I'll come a bit of the way with you if you don't walk too fast. It's a bit lonesome walking this time of day." The tramp nodded his head, and the boy started limping along by his side.

"I'm eighteen," he said casually. "I bet you thought I was younger."

"Fifteen, I'd have said."

"You'd have backed a loser. Eighteen last August, and I've been on the road six years. I ran away from home five times when I was a little 'un, and the police took me back each time. Very good to me, the police was. Now I haven't got a home to run away from."

"Nor have I," the tramp said calmly.

"Oh, I can see what you are," the boy panted; "you're a gentleman come down. It's harder for you than for me." The tramp glanced at the limping, feeble figure and lessened his pace.

"I haven't been at it as long as you have," he admitted.

"No, I could tell that by the way you walk. You haven't got tired yet. Perhaps you expect something the other end?"

The tramp reflected for a moment. "I don't know," he said bitterly, "I'm always expecting things."

"You'll grow out of that," the boy commented. "It's warmer in London, but it's harder to come by grub. There isn't much in it really."

"Still, there's the chance of meeting somebody there who will understand—"

"Country people are better," the boy interrupted. "Last night I took a lease of a barn for nothing and slept with the cows, and this morning the farmer routed me out and gave me tea and toke because I was little. Of course, I score there; but in London, soup on the Embankment at night, and all the rest of the time coppers moving you on."

"I dropped by the roadside last night and slept where I fell. It's a wonder I didn't die," the tramp said. The boy looked at him sharply.

"How do you know you didn't?" he said. "I don't see it," the tramp said, after a pause.

"I tell you," the boy said hoarsely, "people like us can't get away from this sort of thing if we want to. Always hungry and thirsty and dog-tired and walking all the time. And yet if any one offers me a nice home and work my stomach feels sick. Do I look strong? I know I'm little for my age, but I've been knocking about like this for six years, and do you think I'm not dead? I was drowned bathing at Margate, and I was killed by a gipsy with a spike—he knocked my head right in; and twice I was froze like you last night; and a motor cut me down on this very road, and yet I'm walking along here now, walking to London to walk away from it again, because I can't help it. Dead! I tell you we can't get away if we want to."

The boy broke off in a fit of coughing, and the tramp paused while he recovered.

"You'd better borrow my coat for a bit, Tommy," he said, "your cough's pretty bad."

"You go to hell!" the boy said fiercely, puffing at his cigarette; "I'm all right. I was telling you about the road. You haven't got down to it yet, but you'll find out presently. We're all dead, all of us who're on it, and we're all tired, yet somehow we can't leave it. There's nice smells in the summer, dust and hay and the wind smack in your face on a hot day; and it's nice waking up in the wet grass on a fine morning. I don't know, I don't know—" he lurched forward suddenly, and the tramp caught him in his arms.

"I'm sick," the boy whispered—"sick."

The tramp looked up and down the road, but he could see no houses or any sign of help. Yet even as he supported the boy doubtfully in the middle of the road a motorcar suddenly flashed in the middle distance, and came smoothly through the snow.

"What's the trouble?" said the driver quietly as he pulled up. "I'm a doctor." He looked at the boy keenly and listened to his strained breathing.

"Pneumonia," he commented. "I'll give him a lift to the infirmary, and you, too, if you like."

The tramp thought of the workhouse and shook his head. "I'd rather walk," he said.

The boy winked faintly as they lifted him into the car.

"I'll meet you beyond Reigate," he murmured to the tramp. "You'll see." And the car vanished along the white road.

All the morning the tramp splashed through the thawing snow, but at midday he begged some bread at a cottage door and crept into a lonely barn to eat it. It was warm in there, and after his meal he fell asleep among the hay. It was dark when he woke, and started trudging once more through the slushy roads.

Two miles beyond Reigate a figure, a fragile figure, slipped out of the darkness to meet him.

"On the road, guv'nor?" said a husky voice. "Then I'll come a bit of the way with you if you don't walk too fast. It's a bit lonesome walking this time of day."

"But the pneumonia!" cried the tramp aghast.

"I died at Crawley this morning," said the boy.

THE OPEN WINDOW

SAKI

"MY AUNT WILL BE DOWN PRESENTLY, MR. NUTTEL," SAID A VERY SELF-POSSESSED young lady of fifteen; "in the meantime you must try and put up with me."

Framton Nuttel endeavoured to say the correct something which should duly flatter the niece of the moment without unduly discounting the aunt that was to come. Privately he doubted more than ever whether these formal visits on a succession of total strangers would do much towards helping the nerve cure which he was supposed to be undergoing.

"I know how it will be," his sister had said when he was preparing to migrate to this rural retreat; "you will bury yourself down there and not speak to a living soul, and your nerves will be worse than ever from moping. I shall just give you letters of introduction to all the people I know there. Some of them, as far as I can remember, were quite nice."

Framton wondered whether Mrs. Sappleton, the lady to whom he was presenting one of the letters of introduction, came into the nice division.

"Do you know many of the people round here?" asked the niece, when she judged that they had had sufficient silent communion.

"Hardly a soul," said Framton. "My sister was staying here, at the rectory, you know, some four years ago, and she gave me letters of introduction to some of the people here."

He made the last statement in a tone of distinct regret.

"Then you know practically nothing about my aunt?" pursued the self-possessed young lady.

"Only her name and address," admitted the caller. He was wondering whether Mrs. Sappleton was in the married or widowed state. An undefinable something about the room seemed to suggest masculine habitation.

"Her great tragedy happened just three years ago," said the child; "that would be since your sister's time."

"Her tragedy?" asked Framton; somehow in this restful country spot tragedies seemed out of place.

"You may wonder why we keep that window wide open on an October afternoon," said the niece, indicating a large French window that opened on to a lawn.

"It is quite warm for the time of the year," said Framton; "but has that window got anything to do with the tragedy?"

"Out through that window, three years ago to a day, her husband and her two young brothers went off for their day's shooting. They never came back. In crossing the moor to their favourite snipe-shooting ground they were all three engulfed in a treacherous piece of bog. It had been that dreadful wet summer, you know, and places that were safe in other years gave way suddenly without warning. Their bodies were never recovered. That was the dreadful part of it." Here the child's voice lost its self-possessed note and became falteringly human. "Poor aunt always thinks that they will come back some day, they and the little brown spaniel that was lost with them, and walk in at that window just as they used to do. That is why the window is kept open every evening till it is quite dusk. Poor dear aunt, she has often told me how they went out, her husband with his white waterproof coat over his arm, and Ronnie, her youngest brother, singing 'Bertie, why do you bound?' as he always did to tease her, because she said it got on her nerves. Do you know, sometimes on still, quiet evenings like this, I almost get a creepy feeling that they will all walk in through that window—"

She broke off with a little shudder. It was a relief to Framton when the aunt bustled into the room with a whirl of apologies for being late in making her appearance.

"I hope Vera has been amusing you?" she said.

"She has been very interesting," said Framton.

"I hope you don't mind the open window," said Mrs. Sappleton briskly; "my husband and brothers will be home directly from shooting, and they always come in this way. They've been out for snipe in the marshes to-day, so they'll make a fine mess over my poor carpets. So like you men-folk, isn't it?"

She rattled on cheerfully about the shooting and the scarcity of birds, and the prospects for duck in the winter. To Framton it was all purely horrible. He made a desperate but only partially successful effort to turn the talk on to a less ghastly topic; he was conscious that his hostess was giving him only a fragment of her attention, and her eyes were constantly straying past him to the open window and the lawn beyond. It was certainly an unfortunate coincidence that he should have paid his visit on this tragic anniversary.

"The doctors agree in ordering me complete rest, an absence of mental excitement, and avoidance of anything in the nature of violent physical exercise," announced

Framton, who laboured under the tolerably wide-spread delusion that total strangers and chance acquaintances are hungry for the least detail of one's ailments and infirmities, their cause and cure. "On the matter of diet they are not so much in agreement," he continued.

"No?" said Mrs. Sappleton, in a voice which only replaced a yawn at the last moment. Then she suddenly brightened into alert attention—but not to what Framton was saying.

"Here they are at last!" she cried. "Just in time for tea, and don't they look as if they were muddy up to the eyes!"

Framton shivered slightly and turned towards the niece with a look intended to convey sympathetic comprehension. The child was staring out through the open window with dazed horror in her eyes. In a chill shock of nameless fear Framton swung round in his seat and looked in the same direction.

In the deepening twilight three figures were walking across the lawn towards the window; they all carried guns under their arms, and one of them was additionally burdened with a white coat hung over his shoulders. A tired brown spaniel kept close at their heels. Noiselessly they neared the house, and then a hoarse young voice chanted out of the dusk: "I said, Bertie, why do you bound?"

Framton grabbed wildly at his stick and hat; the hall-door, the gravel-drive, and the front gate were dimly-noted stages in his headlong retreat. A cyclist coming along the road had to run into the hedge to avoid an imminent collision.

"Here we are, my dear," said the bearer of the white mackintosh, coming in through the window; "fairly muddy, but most of it's dry. Who was that who bolted out as we came up?"

"A most extraordinary man, a Mr. Nuttel," said Mrs. Sappleton; "could only talk about his illnesses, and dashed off without a word of good-bye or apology when you arrived. One would think he had seen a ghost."

"I expect it was the spaniel," said the niece calmly; "he told me he had a horror of dogs. He was once hunted into a cemetery somewhere on the banks of the Ganges by a pack of pariah dogs, and had to spend the night in a newly dug grave with the creatures snarling and grinning and foaming just above him. Enough to make anyone lose their nerve."

Romance at short notice was her speciality.

The Other Occupant

Ulrich Daubeny

Roger Wayford had never known The Castle to be so packed with visitors. He arrived to find the place in hubbub, a pell mell of scurrying servants and excited guests, everyone in the best of humour, because the occasion for this fancy-dress frivolity was none other than the great Armistice Ball.

"We are absolutely crammed, Wayford," apologised his host, "and as you can only stay the night, we've put a bed for you in the old oak closet. Hope you've no objection."

On the contrary, he was most agreeable, for the Oak Closet, ordinarily used, or rather disused as a study, made a comfortable enough apartment for a bachelor. The panelling was said to date from Queen Elizabeth, but the pictures were smug portraits, mostly Georgian; otherwise, the appearance of the room was not unusual, as bed with a bright quilt now occupying one corner, while the little Jacobean dressing chest, erstwhile the writing table, once again fulfilled its ancient purpose.

Wayford changed hurriedly, and repaired down-stairs, where there was a continuous bustle of arrivals, all gaily disguised parties from the surrounding countryside.

As is the case with most short-notice entertainments, the Armistice Ball was perceptibly behind its scheduled time, and after idling until the band arrived, Wayford seized the opportunity to go upstairs, for more of his particular brand of cigarette. On approaching the Oak Closet, he found the door ajar, and a light within; his footsteps along the passage had been inaudible, nor did the door creak as he pushed it further open, and came to a sudden halt upon the threshold.

A young girl, attired in Puritan costume, was sitting at the dressing chest, putting the finishing touches to her coiffure. A pair of dancing eyes and an attractive mouth, curved in mischievous smile, were reflected in the mirror—but the glimpse was only fleeting, for, undiscovered, he immediately stepped back, softly pulling to the door. The situation was unusual, but easily explained. She was among the late arrivals, who had driven over to the ball, and with visitors so numerous, all or any of apartments were being put to temporary use as cloak-rooms.

Wayford returned downstairs without his cigarettes, but satisfied with the thought of securing as many dances as possible with the pretty Puritan.

Despite this promising commencement, the evening to Wayford proved disappointing. He had set his heart upon dancing with the unknown girl, and on that account, as she was late in coming to the ball-room, he sacrificed his chances with the general favourites. Instead, he wandered anxiously among the groups of chattering guests, for the time was passing and the band already tuning up, while the Puritan costume persisted in its non-appearance. At last he saw it, and with a gratified smile edged forward through the crowd, only to discover that the wearer was somebody quite different. Her eyes lacked lustre, the lips were thin and petulant: there was nothing of that joyous diablerie which had characterised the lady in the Oaken Closet.

Wayford felt keenly disappointed, and not a little puzzled, when his adorable Puritan altogether failed to appear. He searched the faces of the dancers, wondering whether for some reason she could have changed her costume, and he put an indirect question to his hostess, who declared that only one Puritan was at the ball. He had even visited his room, professedly for cigarettes, but inwardly questioning whether his divinity had fainted, or otherwise been taken ill. But although the door was still ajar, the Oak Closet was without the faintest sign of her.

The ball over, Wayford retired upstairs, not waiting to speed the final batch of lingering guests. Being more than usually weary, he was soon asleep, but before long awoke, to find the room illuminated, and the charming Puritan seated before the dressing chest, letting down her hair! A candle burnt on either side of the old mirror, casting a becoming light on the altogether fascinating vision, who, needless to say, appeared supremely unaware that the room was doubly occupied. Wayford lay rigid, partly from surprise and not knowing what to do, partly because he did not wish to cause alarm. No doubt she was preparing for her drive home—yet how came he to have missed her during the evening, and why should she be letting down her hair?

These were problems too abstruse for sleepy brains, and for a while he must have dozed, to be aroused again by a sudden transition in the room from light to darkness. He heard the rustle of silk garments, the pattering of feet; then she was leaving, and if he remained quite still, she would never know—— With a shock he realized that he had missed the direction of the door, and her steps were turned toward the bed. Still nearer, until at its very edge they halted, and there came the sound of slippers shaken off, a faint sigh, and a hand commenced to draw aside the bedclothes.

"Please don't be alarmed!" Wayford exclaimed, jumping out the other side. "There has been some mistake! I will get a light."

He fancied he could hear a stifled laugh, but a moment later the room, flooded with electric light, proved to be quite empty. He blinked around in dazed astonishment, then went to the door, which was fast shut, and peered up and down the silent passage. There was no sign of anyone, although he searched the room, even telling himself that the poor child might, in her alarm, have dived beneath the bed. Neither was there trace of feminine slippers, or disarrangement on the dressing chest—and another curious circumstance occurred to him: there were no candles, not even any candlesticks about the room, nor could he detect that odour of smouldering wick, of which he had been distinctly conscious upon waking.

Vastly puzzled, but still more drowsy, Wayford returned to bed, and did not wake again till morning.

Returning consciousness was haunted by memories of the lovely Puritan, her appearance, and still more extraordinary disappearance from his room; and then, still mazed with sleep, he found his eyes fixed, not on her, but on her picture. It hung in an old gilt frame above the bed, the same bewitching eyes and mouth, the same stiff costume accentuating her shapely, pliant figure. . . . Curious that he had noticed this the night before, when in a comprehensive glance he had classed the pictures as "a lot of stuffy ancestors." But the hour was advanced, and cutting short his pleasing reverie, he went along to the bathroom, where he met his host.

"Can you tell me what became of that fair Puritan last night," he asked. "The merry-eyed girl, like the picture in my room?"

"What do you mean? There *is* no picture of a Puritan!"

"But of course there is—above the bed!" insisted Wayford, surprised by the blank look upon his companion's face.

"My dear fellow, I assure you no such picture hangs in your room—or anywhere else about the house!"

Wayford, insisting that he was right, dragged an incredulous host along the passage, and into the Oak Chamber, where he pointed a triumphant hand—only to let it fall, as he gaped foolishly around. Without exception the painting were of frumpy ancestors in Georgian dress, the one above the bed, if anything, of all the most unlovely!

Several months elapsed before Wayford was again bidden to The Castle. His curious experience had never been long absent from his thoughts; as much as ever it remained a mystery, but he gladly accepted the invitation, clinging obstinately to the belief that the fascinating little Puritan might yet be run to earth in one of the neighbouring country houses.

His host was waiting with the motor, and talked volubly during the long drive from the station.

"I must tell you of the extraordinary happening since you left us, Wayford," be began, almost before the car was started. "Some of the pictures have recently been cleaned, commencing with those in the Oak Closet. You remember the one you termed a 'must Georgian ancestor,' and which a moment earlier you had prepared to swear was the portrait of a lovely Puritan?"

Wayford nodded, a trifle sheepishly.

"By accident the surface of that picture was injured in removal, and we found there was a much older, and a better one beneath. It proved to be that of a Puritan, provoking eyes, tantalizing smile—everything just as you described her! By Jove, old fellow, but however came you to imagine it was there?"

"Can't think!" came the reply, after a short pause. "Except—as you say—just imagination!"

Outside the Door

E. F. Benson

The rest of the small party staying with my friend Geoffrey Aldwych in the charming old house which he had lately bought at a little village north of Sheringham on the Norfolk coast had drifted away soon after dinner to bridge and billiards, and Mrs. Aldwych and myself had for the time been left alone in the drawing-room, seated one on each side of a small round table which we had very patiently and unsuccessfully been trying to turn. But such pressure, psychical or physical, as we had put upon it, though of the friendliest and most encouraging nature, had not overcome in the smallest degree the very slight inertia which so small an object might have been supposed to possess, and it had remained as fixed as the most constant of the stars. No tremor even had passed through its slight and spindle-like legs. In consequence we had, after a really considerable period of patient endeavour, left it to its wooden repose, and proceeded to theorise about psychical matters instead, with no stupid table to contradict in practice all our ideas on the subject.

This I had added with a certain bitterness born of failure, for if we could not move so insignificant an object, we might as well give up all idea of moving anything. But hardly were the words out of my mouth when there came from the abandoned table a single peremptory rap, loud and rather startling.

"What's that?" I asked.

"Only a rap," said she. "I thought something would happen before long."

"And do you really think that is a spirit rapping?" I asked.

"Oh dear no. I don't think it has anything whatever to do with spirits."

"More perhaps with the very dry weather we have been having. Furniture often cracks like that in the summer."

Now this, in point of fact, was not quite the case. Neither in summer nor in winter have I ever heard furniture crack as the table had cracked, for the sound, whatever it was, did not at all resemble the husky creak of contracting wood. It was a loud sharp crack like the smart concussion of one hard object with another.

"No, I don't think it had much to do with dry weather either," said she, smiling. "I think, if you wish to know, that it was the direct result of our attempt to turn the table. Does that sound nonsense?"

"At present, yes," said I, "though I have no doubt that if you tried you could make it sound sense. There is, I notice, a certain plausibility about you and your theories—"

"Now you are being merely personal," she observed.

"For the good motive, to goad you into explanations and enlargements. Please go on."

"Let us stroll outside, then," said she, "and sit in the garden, if you are sure you prefer my plausibilities to bridge. It is deliciously warm, and——"

"And the darkness will be more suitable for the propagation of psychical phenomena. As at séances," said I.

"Oh, there is nothing psychical about my plausibilities," said she. "The phenomena I mean are purely physical, according to my theory."

So we wandered out into the transparent half light of multitudinous stars. The last crimson feather of sunset, which had hovered long in the West, had been blown away with the breath of the night wind, and the moon, which would presently rise, had not yet cut the dim horizon of the sea, which lay very quiet, breathing gently in its sleep with stir of whispering ripples. Across the dark velvet of the close-cropped lawn, which stretched seawards from the house, blew a little breeze full of the savour of salt and the freshness of night, with, every now and then, a hint so subtly conveyed as to be scarcely perceptible of its travel across the sleeping fragrance of drowsy garden-beds, over which the white moths hovered seeking their night-honey. The house itself, with its two battlemented towers of Elizabethan times, gleamed with many windows, and we passed out of sight of it, and into the shadow of a box-hedge, clipped into shapes and monstrous fantasies, and found chairs by the striped tent at the top of the sheltered bowling-alley.

"And this is all very plausible," said I. "Theories, if you please, at length, and, if possible, a full length illustration also."

"By which you mean a ghost-story, or something to that effect?"

"Precisely: and, without presuming to dictate, if possible, first-hand."

"Oddly enough, I can supply that also," said she. "So first I will tell you my general theory, and follow it by a story that seems to bear it out. It happened to me, and it happened here."

"I am sure it will fill the bill," said I.

She paused a moment while I lit a cigarette, and then began in her very clear, pleasant voice. She has the most lucid voice I know, and to me sitting there in the deep-dyed dusk, the words seemed the very incarnation of clarity, for they dropped into the still quiet of the darkness, undisturbed by impressions conveyed to other senses.

"We are only just beginning to conjecture," she said, "how inextricable is the interweaving between mind, soul, life—call it what you will—and the purely material part of the created world. That such interweaving existed has, of course, been known for centuries; doctors, for instance, knew that a cheerful optimistic spirit on the part of their patients conduced towards recovery; that fear, the mere emotion, had a definite effect on the beat of the heart, that anger produced chemical changes in the blood, that anxiety led to indigestion, that under the influence of strong passion a man can do things which in his normal state he is physically incapable of performing. Here we have mind, in a simple and familiar manner, producing changes and effects in tissue, in that which is purely material. By an extension of this—though, indeed, it is scarcely an extension—we may expect to find that mind can have an effect, not only on what we call living tissue, but on dead things, on pieces of wood or stone. At least it is hard to see why that should not be so."

"Table-turning, for instance?" I asked.

"That is one instance of how some force, out of that innumerable cohort of obscure mysterious forces with which we human beings are garrisoned, can pass, as it is constantly doing, into material things. The laws of its passing we do not know; sometimes we wish it to pass and it does not. Just now, for instance, when you and I tried to turn the table, there was some impediment in the path, though I put down that rap which followed as an effect of our efforts. But nothing seems more natural to my mind than that these forces should be transmissible to inanimate things. Of the manner of its passing we know next to nothing, any more than we know the manner of the actual process by which fear accelerates the beating of the heart, but as surely as a Marconi message leaps along the air by no visible or tangible bridge, so through some subtle gateway of the body these forces can march from the citadel of the spirit into material forms, whether that material is a living part of ourselves or that which we choose to call inanimate nature."

She paused a moment.

"Under certain circumstances," she went on, "it seems that the force which has passed from us into inanimate things can manifest its presence there. The force that passes into a table can show itself in movements or in noises coming from the table. The table has been charged with physical energy. Often and often I have seen a table or a chair move apparently of its own accord, but only when some outpouring of force, animal magnetism—call it what you will—has been received by it. A parallel phenomenon to my mind is exhibited in what we know as haunted houses, houses in which, as a rule, some crime or act of extreme emotion or passion has been committed, and in which some echo or re-enactment of the deed is periodically made visible or audible. A murder has been committed, let us say, and the room where it took place is haunted. The figure of the murdered, or less commonly of the murderer, is seen there by sensitives, and cries are heard, or steps run to and fro. The atmosphere has somehow been charged with the scene, and the scene in whole or part repeats itself, though under what laws we do not know, just as a phonograph will repeat, when properly handled, what has been said into it."

"This is all theory," I remarked.

"But it appears to me to cover a curious set of facts, which is all we ask of a theory. Otherwise, we must frankly state our disbelief in haunted houses altogether, or suppose that the spirit of the murdered, poor wretch, is bound under certain circumstances to re-enact the horror of its body's tragedy. It was not enough that its body was killed there, its soul has to be dragged back and live through it all again with such vividness that its anguish becomes visible or audible to the eyes or ears of the sensitive. That to me is unthinkable, whereas my theory is not. Do I make it at all clear?"

"It is clear enough," said I, "but I want support for it, the full-sized illustration."

"I promised you that, a ghost-story of my own experience."

Mrs. Aldwych paused again, and then began the story which was to illustrate her theory.

"It is just a year," she said, "since Jack bought this house from old Mrs. Denison. We had both heard, both he and I, that it was supposed to be haunted, but neither of us knew any particulars of the haunt whatever. A month ago I heard what I believe to have been the ghost, and, when Mrs. Denison was staying with us last week, I asked her exactly what it was, and found it tallied completely with my experience. I will tell you my experience first, and give her account of the haunt afterwards.

"A month ago Jack was away for a few days and I remained here alone. One Sunday evening I, in my usual health and spirits, as far as I am aware, both of which are serenely excellent, went up to bed about eleven. My room is on the first floor, just at the foot of the staircase that leads to the floor above. There are four more rooms on my passage, all of which that night were empty, and at the far end of it a door leads into the landing at the top of the front staircase. On the other side of that, as you know, are more bedrooms, all of which that night were also unoccupied; I, in fact, was the only sleeper on the first floor.

"The head of my bed is close behind my door, and there is an electric light over it. This is controlled by a switch at the bed-head, and another switch there turns on a light in the passage just outside my room. That was Jack's plan: if by chance you want to leave your room when the house is dark, you can light up the passage before you go out, and not grope blindly for a switch outside.

"Usually I sleep solidly: it is very rarely indeed that I wake, when once I have gone to sleep, before I am called. But that night I woke, which was rare; what was rarer was that I woke in a state of shuddering and unaccountable terror; I tried to localise my panic, to run it to earth and reason it away, but without any success. Terror of something I could not guess at stared me in the face, white, shaking terror. So, as there was no use in lying quaking in the dark, I lit my lamp, and, with the view of composing this strange disorder of my fear, began to read again in the book I had brought up with me. The volume happened to be *The Green Carnation*, a work one would have thought to be full of tonic to twittering nerves. But it failed of success, even as my reasoning had done, and after reading a few pages, and finding that the heart-hammer in my throat grew no quieter, and that the grip of terror was in no way relaxed, I put out my light and lay down again. I looked at my watch, however, before doing this, and remember that the time was ten minutes to two.

"Still matters did not mend: terror, that was slowly becoming a little more definite, terror of some dark and violent deed that was momently drawing nearer to me held me in its vice. Something was coming, the advent of which was perceived by the sub-conscious sense, and was already conveyed to my conscious mind. And then the clock struck two jingling chimes, and the stable-clock outside clanged the hour more sonorously.

"I still lay there, abject and palpitating. Then I heard a sound just outside my room on the stairs that lead, as I have said, to the second story, a sound which was perfectly commonplace and unmistakable. Feet feeling their way in the dark were coming downstairs to my passage: I could hear also the groping hand slip and slide along the bannisters. The footfalls came along the few yards of passage between the bottom of the stairs and my door, and then against my door itself came the brush of drapery, and on the panels the blind groping of fingers. The handle rattled as they passed over it, and my terror nearly rose to screaming point.

"Then a sensible hope struck me. The midnight wanderer might be one of the servants, ill or in want of something, and yet—why the shuffling feet and the groping hand? But on the instant of the dawning of that hope (for I knew that it was of the step and that which was moving in the dark passage of which I was afraid) I turned on both the light at my bed-head, and the light of the passage outside, and, opening the door, looked out. The passage was quite bright from end to end, but it was perfectly empty. Yet as I looked, seeing nothing of the walker, I still heard. Down the bright boards I heard the shuffle growing fainter as it receded, until, judging by the ear, it turned into the gallery at the end and died away. And with it there died also all my sense of terror. It was It of which I had been afraid: now It and my terror had passed. And I went back to bed and slept till morning."

Again Mrs. Aldwych paused, and I was silent. Somehow it was in the extreme simplicity of her experience that the horror lay. She went on almost immediately.

"Now for the sequel," she said, "of what I choose to call the explanation. Mrs. Denison, as I told you, came down to stay with us not long ago, and I mentioned that we had heard, though only vaguely, that the house was supposed to be haunted, and asked for an account of it. This is what she told me:

"'In the year 1610 the heiress to the property was a girl Helen Denison, who was engaged to be married to young Lord Southern. In case therefore of her having children, the property would pass away from Denisons. In case of her death, childless, it would pass to her first cousin. A week before the marriage took place, he and a brother of his entered the house, riding here from thirty miles away, after dark, and made their way to her room on the second story. There they gagged her and attempted to kill her, but she escaped from them, groped her way along this passage, and into the room at the end of the gallery. They followed her there, and killed her. The facts were known by the younger brother turning king's evidence.'

"Now Mrs. Denison told me that the ghost had never been seen, but that it was occasionally heard coming downstairs or going along the passage. She told me that it was never heard except between the hours of two and three in the morning, the hour during which the murder took place."

"And since then have you heard it again?" I asked.

"Yes, more than once. But it has never frightened me again. I feared, as we all do, what was unknown."

"I feel that I should fear the known, if I knew it was that," said I.

"I don't think you would for long. Whatever theory you adopt about it, the sounds of the steps and the groping hand, I cannot see that there is anything to shock or frighten one. My own theory you know—"

"Please apply it to what you heard," I asked.

"Simply enough. The poor girl felt her way along this passage in the despair of her agonised terror, hearing no doubt the soft footsteps of her murderers gaining on her, as she groped along her lost way. The waves of that terrible brainstorm raging within her, impressed themselves in some subtle yet physical manner on the place. It would only be by those people whom we call sensitives that the wrinkles, so to speak, made by those breaking waves on the sands would be perceived, and by them not always. But they are there, even as when a Marconi apparatus is working the waves are there, though they can only be perceived by a receiver that is in tune. If you believe in brain-waves at all, the explanation is not so difficult."

"Then the brain-wave is permanent?"

"Every wave of whatever kind leaves its mark, does it not? If you disbelieve the whole thing, shall I give you a room on the route of that poor murdered harmless walker?"

I got up.

"I am very comfortable, thanks, where I am," I said.

Over an Absinthe Bottle

W. C. Morrow

Arthur Kimberlin, a young man of very high spirit, found himself a total stranger in San Francisco one rainy evening, at a time when his heart was breaking; for his hunger was of that most poignant kind in which physical suffering is forced to the highest point without impairment of the mental functions. There remained in his possession not a thing that he might have pawned for a morsel to eat; and even as it was, he had stripped his body of all articles of clothing except those which a remaining sense of decency compelled him to retain. Hence it was that cold assailed him and conspired with hunger to complete his misery. Having been brought into the world and reared a gentleman, he lacked the courage to beg and the skill to steal. Had not an extraordinary thing occurred to him, he either would have drowned himself in the bay within twenty-four hours or died of pneumonia in the street. He had been seventy hours without food, and his mental desperation had driven him far in its race with his physical needs to consume the strength within him; so that now, pale, weak, and tottering, he took what comfort he could find in the savory odors which came steaming up from the basement kitchens of the restaurants in Market Street, caring more to gain them than to avoid the rain. His teeth chattered; he shambled, stooped, and gasped. He was too desperate to curse his fate—he could only long for food. He could not reason; he could not understand that ten thousand hands might gladly have fed him; he could think only of the hunger which consumed him, and of food that could give him warmth and happiness.

When he had arrived at Mason Street, he saw a restaurant a little way up that thoroughfare, and for that he headed, crossing the street diagonally. He stopped before the window and ogled the steaks, thick and lined with fat; big oysters lying on ice; slices of ham as large as his hat; whole roasted chickens, brown and juicy. He ground his teeth, groaned, and staggered on.

A few steps beyond was a drinking-saloon, which had a private door at one side, with the words "Family Entrance" painted thereon. In the recess of the door (which was closed) stood a man. In spite of his agony, Kimberlin saw something in this man's face that appalled and fascinated him. Night was on, and the light in the vicinity was dim; but it was apparent that the stranger had an appearance of whose character he himself must have been ignorant. Perhaps it was the unspeakable anguish of it that struck through Kimberlin's sympathies. The young man came to an uncertain halt and stared at the stranger. At first he was unseen, for the stranger looked straight out into the street with singular fixity, and the death-like pallor of his face added a weirdness to the immobility of his gaze. Then he took notice of the young man.

"Ah," he said, slowly and with peculiar distinctness, "the rain has caught you, too, without overcoat or umbrella! Stand in this doorway—there is room for two."

The voice was not unkind, though it had an alarming hardness. It was the first word that had been addressed to the sufferer since hunger had seized him, and to be spoken to at all, and have his comfort regarded in the slightest way, gave him cheer. He entered the embrasure and stood beside the stranger, who at once relapsed into his fixed gaze at nothing across the street. But presently the stranger stirred himself again.

"It may rain a long time," said he; "I am cold, and I observe that you tremble. Let us step inside and get a drink."

He opened the door and Kimberlin followed, hope beginning to lay a warm hand upon his heart. The pale stranger led the way into one of the little private booths with which the place was furnished. Before sitting down he put his hand into his pocket and drew forth a roll of bank-bills.

"You are younger than I," he said; "won't you go to the bar and buy a bottle of absinthe, and bring a pitcher of water and some glasses? I don't like for the waiters to come around. Here is a twenty-dollar bill."

Kimberlin took the bill and started down through the corridor towards the bar. He clutched the money tightly in his palm; it felt warm and comfortable, and sent a delicious tingling through his arm. How many glorious hot meals did that bill represent? He clutched it tighter and hesitated. He thought he smelled a broiled steak, with fat little mushrooms and melted butter in the steaming dish. He stopped and looked back towards the door of the booth. He saw that the stranger had closed it. He could pass it, slip out the door, and buy something to eat. He turned and started, but the coward in him (there are other names for this) tripped his resolution; so he went straight to the bar and made the purchase. This was so unusual that the man who served him looked sharply at him.

"Ain't goin' to drink all o' that, are you?" he asked.

"I have friends in the box," replied Kimberlin, "and we want to drink quietly and without interruption. We are in Number 7."

"Oh, beg pardon. That's all right," said the man.

Kimberlin's step was very much stronger and steadier as he returned with the liquor. He opened the door of the booth. The stranger sat at the side of the little table, staring at the opposite wall just as he had stared across the street. He wore a wide-brimmed, slouch hat, drawn well down. It was only after Kimberlin had set the bottle, pitcher, and glasses on the table, and seated himself opposite the stranger and within his range of vision, that the pale man noticed him.

"Oh! you have brought it? How kind of you! Now please lock the door."

Kimberlin had slipped the change into his pocket, and was in the act of bringing it out when the stranger said,—

"Keep the change. You will need it, for I am going to get it back in a way that may interest you. Let us first drink, and then I will explain."

The pale man mixed two drinks of absinthe and water, and the two drank. Kimberlin, unsophisticated, had never tasted the liquor before, and he found it harsh and offensive; but no sooner had it reached his stomach than it began to warm him, and sent the most delicious thrill through his frame.

"It will do us good," said the stranger; "presently we shall have more. Meanwhile, do you know how to throw dice?"

Kimberlin weakly confessed that he did not.

"I thought not. Well, please go to the bar and bring a dice-box. I would ring for it, but I don't want the waiters to be coming in."

Kimberlin fetched the box, again locked the door, and the game began. It was not one of the simple old games, but had complications, in which judgment, as well as chance, played a part. After a game or two without stakes, the stranger said,—

"You now seem to understand it. Very well—I will show you that you do not. We will now throw for a dollar a game, and in that way I shall win the money that you received in change. Otherwise I should be robbing you, and I imagine you cannot afford to lose. I mean no offence. I am a plainspoken man, but I believe in honesty before politeness. I merely want a little diversion, and you are so kind-natured that I am sure you will not object."

"On the contrary," replied Kimberlin, "I shall enjoy it."

"Very well; but let us have another drink before we start. I believe I am growing colder."

They drank again, and this time the starving man took his liquor with relish—at least, it was something in his stomach, and it warmed and delighted him.

The stake was a dollar a side. Kimberlin won. The pale stranger smiled grimly, and opened another game. Again Kimberlin won. Then the stranger pushed back his hat and fixed that still gaze upon his opponent, smiling yet. With this full view of the pale stranger's face, Kimberlin was more appalled than ever. He had begun to acquire a certain self-possession and ease, and his marvelling at the singular character of the adventure had begun to weaken, when this new incident threw him back into confusion. It was the extraordinary expression of the stranger's face that alarmed him. Never upon the face of a living being had he seen a pallor so death-like and chilling. The face was more than pale; it was white. Kimberlin's observing faculty had been sharpened by the absinthe, and, after having detected the stranger in an absent-minded effort two or three times to stroke a beard which had no existence, he reflected that some of the whiteness of the face might be due to the recent removal of a full beard. Besides the pallor, there were deep and sharp lines upon the face, which the electric light brought out very distinctly. With the exception of the steady glance of the eyes and an occasional hard smile, that seemed out of place upon such a face, the expression was that of stone inartistically cut. The eyes were black, but of heavy expression; the lower lip was purple; the hands were fine, white, and thin, and dark veins bulged out upon them. The stranger pulled down his hat.

"You are lucky," he said. "Suppose we try another drink. There is nothing like absinthe to sharpen one's wits, and I see that you and I are going to have a delightful game."

After the drink the game proceeded. Kimberlin won from the very first, rarely losing a game. He became greatly excited. His eyes shone; color came to his cheeks. The stranger, having exhausted the roll of bills which he first produced, drew forth another, much larger and of higher denominations. There were several thousand dollars in the roll. At Kimberlin's right hand were his winnings,— something like two hundred dollars. The stakes were raised, and the game went rapidly on. Another drink was taken. Then fortune turned the stranger's way, and he won easily. It went back to Kimberlin, for he was now playing with all the judgment and skill he could command. Once only did it occur to him to wonder what he should do with the money if he should quit winner; but a sense of honor decided him that it would belong to the stranger.

By this time the absinthe had so sharpened Kimberlin's faculties that, the temporary satisfaction which it had brought to his hunger having passed, his physical suffering returned with increased aggressiveness. Could he not order a supper with his earnings? No; that was out of the question, and the stranger said nothing about eating. Kimberlin continued to play, while the manifestations of hunger took the form of sharp pains, which darted through him viciously, causing him to writhe and grind his teeth. The stranger paid no attention, for he was now wholly absorbed in the game. He seemed puzzled and disconcerted. He played with great care, studying each throw minutely. No conversation passed between them now. They drank occasionally, the dice continued to rattle, the money kept piling up at Kimberlin's hand.

The pale man began to behave strangely. At times he would start and throw back his head, as though he were listening. For a moment his eyes would sharpen and flash, and then sink into heaviness again. More than once Kimberlin, who had now begun to suspect that his antagonist was some kind of monster, saw a frightfully ghastly expression sweep over his face, and his features would become fixed for a very short time in a peculiar grimace. It was noticeable, however, that he was steadily sinking deeper and deeper into a condition of apathy. Occasionally he would raise his eyes to Kimberlin's face after the young man had made an astonishingly lucky throw, and keep them fixed there with a steadiness that made the young man quail.

The stranger produced another roll of bills when the second was gone, and this had a value many times as great as the others together. The stakes were raised to a thousand dollars a game, and still Kimberlin won. At last the time came when the stranger braced himself for a final effort. With speech somewhat thick, but very deliberate and quiet, he said,—

"You have won seventy-four thousand dollars, which is exactly the amount I have remaining. We have been playing for several hours. I am tired, and I suppose you are. Let us finish the game. Each will now stake his all and throw a final game for it."

Without hesitation, Kimberlin agreed. The bills made a considerable pile on the table. Kimberlin threw, and the box held but one combination that could possibly beat him; this combination might be thrown once in ten thousand times. The starving man's heart beat violently as the stranger picked up the box with exasperating deliberation. It was a long time before he threw. He made his combinations and ended by defeating his opponent. He sat looking at the dice a long time, and then he slowly leaned back in his chair, settled himself comfortably, raised his eyes to Kimberlin's, and fixed that unearthly stare upon him. He said not a word; his face contained not a trace of emotion or intelligence. He simply looked. One cannot keep one's eyes open very long without winking, but the stranger did. He sat so motionless that Kimberlin began to be tortured.

"I will go now," he said to the stranger—said that when he had not a cent and was starving.

The stranger made no reply, but did not relax his gaze; and under that gaze the young man shrank back in his own chair, terrified. He became aware that two men were cautiously talking in an adjoining booth. As there was now a deathly silence in his own, he listened, and this is what he heard:

"Yes; he was seen to turn into this street about three hours ago."

"And he had shaved?"

"He must have done so; and to remove a full beard would naturally make a great change in a man."

"But it may not have been he."

"True enough; but his extreme pallor attracted attention. You know that he has been troubled with heart-disease lately, and it has affected him seriously."

"Yes, but his old skill remains. Why, this is the most daring bank-robbery we ever had here. A hundred and forty-eight thousand dollars—think of it! How long has it been since he was let out of Joliet?"

"Eight years. In that time he has grown a beard, and lived by dice-throwing with men who thought they could detect him if he should swindle them; but that is impossible. No human being can come winner out of a game with him. He is evidently not here; let us look farther."

Then the two men clinked glasses and passed out.

The dice-players—the pale one and the starving one—sat gazing at each other, with a hundred and forty-eight thousand dollars piled up between them. The winner made no move to take in the money; he merely sat and stared at Kimberlin, wholly unmoved by the conversation in the adjoining room. His imperturbability was amazing, his absolute stillness terrifying.

Kimberlin began to shake with an ague. The cold, steady gaze of the stranger sent ice into his marrow. Unable to bear longer this unwavering look, Kimberlin moved to one side, and then he was amazed to discover that the eyes of the pale man, instead of following him, remained fixed upon the spot where he had sat, or, rather, upon the wall behind it. A great dread beset the young man. He feared to make the slightest sound. Voices of men in the bar-room were audible, and the sufferer imagined that he heard others whispering and tip-toeing in the passage outside his booth. He poured out some absinthe, watching his strange companion all the while, and drank alone and unnoticed. He took a heavy drink, and it had a peculiar effect upon him: he felt his heart bounding with alarming force and rapidity, and breathing was difficult. Still his hunger remained, and that and the absinthe gave him an idea that the gastric acids were destroying him by digesting his stomach. He leaned forward and whispered to the stranger, but was given no attention. One of the man's hands lay upon the table; Kimberlin placed his upon it, and then drew back in terror—the hand was as cold as a stone.

The money must not lie there exposed. Kimberlin arranged it into neat parcels, looking furtively every moment at his immovable companion, and *in mortal fear that he would stir*! Then he sat back and waited. A deadly fascination impelled him to move back into his former position, so as to bring his face directly before the gaze of the stranger. And so the two sat and stared at each other.

Kimberlin felt his breath coming heavier and his heart-beats growing weaker, but these conditions gave him comfort by reducing his anxiety and softening the pangs of hunger. He was growing more and more comfortable and yawned. If he had dared he might have gone to sleep.

Suddenly a fierce light flooded his vision and sent him with a bound to his feet. Had he been struck upon the head or stabbed to the heart? No; he was sound and alive. The pale stranger still sat there staring at nothing and immovable; but Kimberlin was no longer afraid of him. On the contrary, an extraordinary buoyancy of spirit and elasticity of body made him feel reckless and daring. His former timidity and scruples vanished, and he felt equal to any adventure. Without hesitation he gathered up the money and bestowed it in his several pockets.

"I am a fool to starve," he said to himself, "with all this money ready to my hand."

As cautiously as a thief he unlocked the door, stepped out, reclosed it, and boldly and with head erect stalked out upon the street. Much to his astonishment, he found the city in the bustle of the early evening, yet the sky was clear. It was evident to him that he had not been in the saloon as long as he had supposed. He walked along the street with the utmost unconcern of the dangers that beset him, and laughed softly but gleefully. Would he not eat now—ah, would he not? Why, he could buy a dozen restaurants! Not only that, but he would hunt the city up and down for hungry men and feed them with the fattest steaks, the juiciest roasts, and the biggest oysters that the town could supply. As for himself, he must eat first; after that he would set up a great establishment for feeding other hungry mortals without charge. Yes, he would eat first; if he pleased, he would eat till he should burst. In what single place could he find sufficient to satisfy his hunger? Could he live sufficiently long to have an ox killed and roasted whole for his supper? Besides an ox he would order two dozen broiled chickens, fifty dozen oysters, a dozen crabs, ten dozen eggs, ten hams, eight young pigs, twenty wild ducks, fifteen fish of four different kinds, eight salads, four dozen bottles each of claret, burgundy, and champagne; for pastry, eight plum-puddings, and for dessert, bushels of nuts, ices, and confections. It would require time to prepare such a meal, and if he could only live until it could be made ready it would be infinitely better than to spoil his appetite with a dozen or two meals of ordinary size. He thought he could live that long, for he felt amazingly strong and bright. Never in his life before had he walked with so great ease and lightness; his feet hardly touched the ground—he ran and leaped. It did him good to tantalize his hunger, for that would make his relish of the feast all the keener. Oh, but how they would stare when he would give his order, and how comically they would hang back, and how amazed they would be when he would throw a few thousands of dollars on the counter and tell them to take their money out of it and keep the change! Really, it was worth while to be so hungry as that, for then eating became an unspeakable luxury. And one must not be in too great a hurry to eat when one is so hungry—that is beastly. How much of the joy of living do rich people miss from eating before they are hungry—before they have gone three days and nights without food! And how manly it is, and how great self-control it shows, to dally with starvation when one has a dazzling fortune in one's pocket and every restaurant has an open door! To be hungry without money—that is despair; to be starving with a bursting pocket—that is sublime! Surely the only true heaven is that in which one famishes in the presence of abundant food, which he might have for the taking, and then a gorged stomach and a long sleep.

The starving wretch, speculating thus, still kept from food. He felt himself growing in stature, and the people whom he met became pygmies. The streets widened, the stars became suns and dimmed the electric lights, and the most intoxicating odors and the sweetest music filled the air. Shouting, laughing, and singing, Kimberlin joined in a great chorus that swept over the city, and then—

The two detectives who had traced the famous bank-robber to the saloon in Mason Street, where Kimberlin had encountered the stranger of the pallid face, left the saloon; but, unable to pursue the trail farther, had finally returned. They found the door of booth No. 7 locked. After rapping and calling and receiving no answer, they burst open the door, and there they saw two men—one of middle age and the other very young—sitting perfectly still, and in the strangest manner imaginable staring at each other across the table. Between them was a great pile of money, arranged neatly in parcels. Near at hand were an empty absinthe bottle, a water-pitcher, glasses, and a dice-box, with the dice lying before the elder man as he had thrown them last. One of the detectives covered the elder man with a revolver and commanded,—

"Throw up your hands!"

But the dice-thrower paid no attention. The detectives exchanged startled glances. They looked closer into the faces of the two men, and then they discovered that both were dead.

The Pageant of Ghosts

R. Murray Gilchrist

Late twilight in June. A wood-lark rippling in mid-air. Drowsy-scented ladies' bed-straw in a marsh that was once a garden. On the terrace wall, beside the cedar, a stone urn with a lambent flame.

The casement hung open, and the excess of beauty and perfume drugged me: so that, with a sigh, I sank back into a moth-eaten sedan that had borne four generations to Court. Dried dust of lavender and rue filtered through the brocade lining, and grew into a mist, where through the bird's song waxed fainter and fainter. Indeed, I was just closing my eyes when the tuning of fifes and viols roused me with a start.

A shrill titter from the further end of the ballroom drew me from my seat. At the outer extremity of the oriel hung a curtain of Philimot velvet, lined inwardly with pale green silk: behind this I stole, and, parting the draperies from the wall, gazed towards the musicians' gallery. Five men, dressed in styles that ranged from the trunk-hose and collared mantle of Elizabeth's day to the pantaloons and muslin cravats of the third George, were arranging yellow music-sheets on the table. The youngest forced a harsh note from his viol, then struck another's bald pate, and set all a-laughing. A grave silence followed. Then began just such a curious melody as the wind makes in a wood of half-blighted firs.

All the sconces were lighted of a sudden, and the martlets and serpents in the alt-relief above the panelling sprang into a weird life. Resting between the fire-dogs on the open hearth were three logs, one of pine, another of oak, and a third of sycamore. The grey flame licked them hungrily, and the sap hissed and bubbled. The carved work of the walls was distinct: Potiphar's wife wrapped her bed-gown about Joseph, Judith triumphed with the bloody head aloft, and in the centre Lot's daughters paddled with his withered jowls.

I felt but little wonder at the change from stillness to life. As the last of my race, treasurer of a vast hoard of traditions, why should I be disturbed by this return of the creatures of old? I dragged forth the creaking sedan, and sat waiting.

A rusty, half-unstrung zither that hung near quivered and gave one faint note to the melody. Ere its vibration had ceased, Mistress Lenore entered through the arched doorway. Hour after hour had she plucked those wires that cried out in welcome.

Her fox-coloured tresses were wrought into a fantastic web; each separate hair twisted and coiled. A pink flush painted her cheeks, and her lustrous blue eyes were mirthful. She wore opals (unfortunate stones for such as love), and hanging from a black riband below her throat was the golden cross Prince Charles had sent her from Rome.

The legends of her character came in floods. Wantonly capricious at one moment, earnest and devout as a nun's at another, her expression changed a thousand times as I beheld. Now she was racking her soul with jealousy; now pleading—as she alone could plead—for pardon; now, when pardon was won, laughingly swearing that her repentance was only feigned. As she neared my heart beat furiously, and I cried "*Lenore! Lenore!*" My voice was low and broken (the music gave a loud burst then), but she passed without a word, her ivory-like hands almost hidden beneath jewels and lace. The further door stood open, and she disappeared.

Nowell the Platonist followed; a haggard middle-aged man in a long cloak of sable-edged black velvet. Forgetful of all save desire, he bore a scroll of parchment, whereon was written in great letters *To Parthenia*. This was the only outcome of his one passion. At the second window he paused, with a wry mouth, to gaze on that statue of Europa from whose arm he had hanged himself. Then his hands were uplifted to his head to force away the agony of despair; for hurrying towards him came the Mad Maid, who could not love him, being devoted to the memory of one wrecked at sea.

"Why art thou in anguish?" she said. "See my joy; laugh with me, dance with me. He returns to-morrow—the boat's coming in. Ah, darling! ah, heart's delight!" And she held up her arms to a girandole whose candles fluttered; but her face grew long, and thin, and pale, and she rested on a settee and drew from her pocket a dusky lace veil, which, being unfolded, discovered a ring with a burning topaz and a heart of silver. She leaned forward, resting her brow in her hands, and talked to the toys in her lap as if they understood.

To the veil she said, "No bride's joy-blushes shalt thou conceal!"

To the ring, "Thou last gift of him who died and left me!"

To the heart, "O heart, thou hast endured! Thou art not broken!"

After a few tears she refolded all, and unbuttoning her bodice took from the bosom a miniature framed with pearls; but, as if afraid lest it should grow cold, she replaced it hurriedly, and seeing that Nowell beckoned towards her, glided on, sighing, and with downcast looks.

Then passed a cavalier in azure silk and snowy ruffled cravat and long-plumed cap of estate. He was whistling a song that threw all bachelors into humorous ecstasy. Who he was I know not: unless the courtier who had fought a duel with my Lord Brandreth, and had died in the wood near St. Giles's Well, pressing convulsively in his right hand a dainty glove of Spanish kid. A merry fellow, quoth the legend, who loved the world and all in it, but who was over fond of his own jest.

Fidessa, the singer, entered next. She had. brought her little gilt harp, and her lips were parted to join harmonies of voice and instrument. Bright yellow hair plaited in bands that formed a filigrain-bound coronet; eyes half-veiled, with sleepy lashes, hands fragile as sea-shells. It was the *Verdi Pratt*, Mr. Handel's celebrated song, that she adored most, and on the morrow she would sing it at Lincoln's-Inn-Fields Theatre. At least she purposed to sing it then and there. Fate, however, had otherwise ordained: the tomorrow would never come, and the sweetheart at the upland grange might well write on her letters, "Darkness hath overcome me."

Thin and pale Margot, her wanness heightened by dishevelled black curls, came forward in her scarlet cloak. Silent reproach was in her every feature; her eyes were stern and long-suffering. The prophecy that bound up her life with that of her dying twin was rapidly approaching consummation. Another moment and the direst pain filled her; for a loud cry from an outer chamber told her he was dead.

As she disappeared in the gloom, Nabob Darrington, himself in life the lover of a ghost, paced slowly along. A beau of the last century, wearing a satin flowered waistcoat and a coat and breeches of plum-coloured kerseymere, between his finger and thumb he held the diamond which he had brought from the East as a spousal gift for the woman who, unknown to him, had died of waiting. He was anticipating the meeting with her, and his brown cheeks flushed blood-red at the sound of a light footstep. He turned, saw one with violet eyes and tragic forehead; and with one joyous murmur they enfolded each other and passed.

Althea approached; a massive creature gowned in white and gold. In one hand she held a tangle of sops-in-wine, in the other, as symbolical kings hold globes, a bejewelled missal. The contention between the two lovers—the old, who had tyrannised until her life was of the saddest, and the new, who filled her with such wild happiness—was troubling her, and she was pondering as to which should gain the victory. She was just beginning to understand that to wait in passive indecision is to be torn with dragon's teeth.

Barbara, with eyes like moon-pierced amethysts, followed, singing Ben Jonson's *Robin Goodfellow* in a sweet quaver that was only just heard above the music. How strangely her looks changed—from maiden innocence to the awakening of love! from the height of passion to the abyss of despair!

But as she went the horizon was ripped from end to end, and a golden arrow leaped into the ball-room. Dawn had broken. The scent of the ladies' bed-straw was trebly strong; the tired wood-lark sank lower and lower.

The room was empty—the pageant passed and done.

THE QUEER PICTURE

BERNARD CAPES

IT WAS STANDING WITH ITS FACE TO THE WALL IN A DARK CORNER OF THE DINGY OLD shop in Beak Street, whose miscellaneous litter had peered at me through a window so dirty as to make its owner appear rather to wish to baffle custom than to court it. Nor in that respect was its owner's manner reassuring. His eyes peered dimly out of an unwashed face, like the pale blue oriental saucers through the window. He seemed to regard me with indifference and a little weariness, as if the profit of chaffering were hardly worth its trouble. "O, yes!" he said, in a weak, hoarse voice, to my appreciations of this or that, as I edged my way through the labyrinth of Chippendale chairs, bureaux, coffin-stools, and gate-legged tables piled with Staffordshire figures, brass door-knockers, candlesticks, and "genuine antiques" of every sort, description and plausibility.

A little nettled by the creature's apathy, I stooped, somewhat truculently, and turned the picture round for myself. It showed a landscape, pretty dark and mellow in tone, of, I fancied, the Crome or Nasmyth period. A woodland road, receding from the middle foreground of the canvas, presently took a curve round some palings to the left, and disappeared into greenery. Prominent over the near palings towered a huge oak; on the other side was a close medley of foliage gradually dimming into blue distances. The whole was feelingly painted and composed, the large oak tree, quite superbly rendered, forming its predominant feature. It all only suffered slightly to my mind as a composition from the white emptiness of the road and the absence of figures. I said so to the dealer. "O yes!" he answered, with a dry cough, and I shrugged my shoulders.

I have had one or two "finds" in my time—enough to stimulate my adventurous nerve. This thing seemed to me good: there was power in it, and knowledge. The time was evidently near twilight, still and darkling—a lonely, solemn place. The atmosphere was unmistakably suggested. Its canvas measurement was some 34 by 28 inches, and it possessed a frame, a little dingy and battered, but of the right sort. "Whom is it by?" I said.

The dealer made as if to bend, cleared his thin old throat and stood up again. "It's unsigned," he said.

"But don't you know?"

"If you were to ask me," he answered, "I should say—no more than that, mind you—that it was Urquhart's work." Then, in response to my mute inquiry, "He was a follower of John Constable, you know."

I didn't know; I knew nothing about the man; but, whoever he was, his capacity was plain. I decided to risk it. "Well, how much? "I said.

"Twenty pounds," said the dealer.

As a matter of principle I protested—"Unsigned; of disputable origin; preposterous!" "O yes!" he said, in his indifferent way. "Twenty pounds is the price. It's a greatly admired piece. If you change your mind, I will take it back any time within a week, less ten per cent."

That seemed a fair offer, and I ended by carrying the picture home with me in a cab. Alone, I cleared the mantelpiece of my sitting-room, and stood the treasure up on it. I thought it distinctly an admirable piece of work, and so far rejoiced in my bargain. It seemed to reflect the very spirit of the twilight which was even now creeping over my room, to assimilate and conform to it. As I gazed I grew penetrated, possessed, by what I gazed on. I was on the wide, white road, standing or crouching somewhere down here out of the picture, and staring into its diminishing distances. The great oak was motionlessly alive; there seemed "a listening fear in its regard." An expectation, an indescribable awe, held me amazedly entranced. And then my breath caught in a quick gasp. Round by the bend of the road, far away, there occurred a minute stirring, and something came into the picture that was not there before. The thing came on, increasing in regular progression as it advanced—and it was the figure of a young man, in a bygone costume, swinging airily towards me. I sat petrified, dumb-stricken; and all in an instant there arose between me and the illusion, blotting it out, a vague, shadowy shape. That receded quickly, shrinking as it withdrew, until it also was the figure of a man going away from me along the road to meet the other. The two encountered, and had passed, when the second wheeled suddenly in his tracks, and struck the first on the neck, so that the young man fell into the road. I saw something—a running stain of red, and simultaneously broke, with a cry, from my stupefaction and, leaping to the mantelpiece, turned the horror with its face to the wall. As I did so I saw that the canvas was empty of figures.

The old dealer made no demur whatever about my returning the picture. "It always comes back," he said impassively, as he paid me in cash eighteen pounds out of the twenty I had given for it. "It stands me in well, you see, as an investment. It's a fine work. I dare say you'll be the dozenth or more who's been struck by it, and carried it away with the same result. Twilight's the time, they say."

"Don't you know it is?" I responded warmly. "Haven't you seen it yourself?"

"No," he said, with a thin cough, "no." (He had returned the picture to its former place and position.) "I don't bother to look. It wouldn't be policy, and it wouldn't be fair, you know, for me to sell it if I had. I'm not bound to go upon hearsay; and it doesn't trouble me where it stands."

"But"—I turned on my heel indignantly, and came back—"you said it was an Urquhart."

"On its intrinsic evidences," he responded; "not in the least because it happens that Urquhart was hanged for the murder of his wife's paramour on a country road he was engaged in painting at the time. He stuck him in the neck with a palette-knife. That *may* have been the very picture—or it may not—before the figures were filled in. Urquhart generally used sheep and countrymen. But all that's no concern of mine. I say it's an Urquhart because of the style. No one but him, in my opinion, could have painted that oak."

The Readjustment

Mary Austin

Emma Jossylin had been dead and buried three days. The sister who had come to the funeral had taken Emma's child away with her, and the house was swept and aired; then, when it seemed there was least occasion for it, Emma came back. The neighbor woman who had nursed her was the first to know it. It was about seven of the evening, in a mellow gloom: the neighbor woman was sitting on her own stoop with her arms wrapped in her apron, and all at once she found herself going along the street under an urgent sense that Emma needed her. She was half-way down the block before she recollected that this was impossible, for Mrs. Jossylin was dead and buried, but as soon as she came opposite the house she was aware of what had happened. It was all open to the summer air; except that it was a little neater, not otherwise than the rest of the street. It was quite dark; but the presence of Emma Jossylin streamed from it and betrayed it more than a candle. It streamed out steadily across the garden, and even as it reached her, mixed with the smell of the damp mignonette, the neighbor woman owned to herself that she had always known Emma would come back.

"A sight stranger if she wouldn't," thought the woman who had nursed her. "She wasn't ever one to throw off things easily."

Emma Jossylin had taken death, as she had taken everything in life, hard. She had met it with the same hard, bright, surface competency that she had presented to the squalor of the encompassing desertness, to the insuperable commonness of Sim Jossylin, to the affliction of her crippled child; and the intensity of her wordless struggle against it had caught the attention of the townspeople and held it in a shocked, curious awe. She was so long a-dying, lying there in the little low house, hearing the abhorred footsteps going about her house and the vulgar procedure of the community encroach upon her like the advances of the sand wastes on an unwatered field. For Emma had always wanted things different, wanted them with a fury of intentness that implied offensiveness in things as they were. And the townspeople had taken offence, the more so because she was not to be surprised in any inaptitude for their own kind of success. Do what you could, you could never catch Emma Jossylin in a wrapper after three o'clock in the afternoon. And she would never talk about the child—in a country where so little ever happened that even trouble was a godsend if it gave you something to talk about. It was reported that she did not even talk to Sim. But there the common resentment got back at her. If she had thought to effect anything with Sim Jossylin against the benumbing spirit of the place, the evasive hopefulness, the large sense of leisure that ungirt the loins, if she still hoped somehow to get away with him to some place for which by her dress, by her manner, she seemed forever and unassailably fit, it was foregone that nothing would come of it. They knew Sim Jossylin better than that. Yet so vivid had been the force of her wordless dissatisfaction that when the fever took her and she went down like a pasteboard figure in the damp, the wonder was that nothing toppled with her. And as if she too had felt herself indispensable, Emma Jossylin had come back.

The neighbor woman crossed the street, and as she passed the far corner of the gate, Jossylin spoke to her. He had been standing, she did not know how long a time, behind the syringa bush, and moved even with her along the fence until they came to the gate. She could see in the dusk that before speaking he wet his lips with his tongue.

"She's in there," he said at last.

"Emma?"

He nodded. "I been sleeping at the store since—but I thought I'd be more comfortable—as soon as I opened the door, there she was."

"Did you see her?"

"No."

"How do you know, then?"

"Don't you know?"

The neighbor felt there was nothing to say to that.

"Come in," he whispered, huskily. They slipped by the rose tree and the wistaria and sat down on the porch at the side. A door swung inward behind them. They felt the Presence in the dusk beating like a pulse.

"What do you think she wants?" said Jossylin. "Do you reckon it's the boy?"

"Like enough."

"He's better off with his aunt. There was no one here to take care of him, like his mother wanted." He raised his voice unconsciously with a note of justification, addressing the room behind.

"I am sending fifty dollars a month," he said; "he can go with the best of them." He went on at length to explain all the advantage that was to come to the boy from living at Pasadena, and the neighbor woman bore him out in it.

"He was glad to go," urged Jossylin to the room. "He said it was what his mother would have wanted."

They were silent then a long time, while the Presence seemed to swell upon them and encroached upon the garden. Finally, "I gave Zeigler the order for the monument yesterday," Jossylin threw out, appeasingly. "It's to cost three hundred and fifty." The Presence stirred. The neighbor thought she could fairly see the controlled tolerance with which Emma Jossylin threw off the evidence of Sim's ineptitude.

They sat on helplessly without talking after that, until the woman's husband came to the fence and called her.

"Don't go," begged Jossylin.

"Hush!" she said. "Do you want all the town to know? You had naught but good from Emma living, and no call to expect harm from her now. It's natural she should come back—if—if she was lonesome like—in—the place where she's gone to."

"Emma wouldn't come back to this place," Jossylin protested, "without she wanted something."

"Well, then, you've got to find out," said the neighbor woman.

All the next day she saw, whenever she passed the house, that Emma was still there. It was shut and barred, but the Presence lurked behind the folded blinds and fumbled at the doors. When it was night and the moths began in the columbine under the window, it went out and walked in the garden.

Jossylin was waiting at the gate when the neighbor woman came. He sweated with helplessness in the warm dusk, and the Presence brooded upon them like an apprehension that grows by being entertained.

"She wants something," he appealed, "but I can't make out what. Emma knows she is welcome to everything I've got. Everybody knows I've been a good provider."

The neighbor woman remembered suddenly the only time she had ever drawn close to Emma Jossylin touching the child. They had sat up with it together all one night in some childish ailment, and she had ventured a question: "What does his father think?" And Emma had turned her a white, hard face of surpassing dreariness. "I don't know," she admitted; "he never says."

"There's more than providing," suggested the neighbor woman.

"Yes. There's feeling . . . but she had enough to do to put up with me. I had no call to be troubling her with such." He left off to mop his forehead, and began again.

"Feelings," he said; "there's times a man gets so wore out with feelings, he doesn't have them any more."

He talked, and presently it grew clear to the woman that he was voiding all the stuff of his life, as if he had sickened on it and was now done. It was a little soul knowing itself and not good to see. What was singular was that the Presence left off walking in the garden, came and caught like a gossamer on the ivy tree, swayed by the breath of his broken sentences. He talked, and the neighbor woman saw him for once as he saw himself and Emma, snared and floundering in an inexplicable unhappiness. He had been disappointed too. She had never relished the man he was, and it made him ashamed. That was why he had never gone away, lest he should make her ashamed among her own kind. He was her husband; he could not help that, though he was sorry for it. But he could keep the offence where least was made of it. And there was a child—she had wanted a child, but even then he had blundered—begotten a cripple upon her. He blamed himself utterly, searched out the roots of his youth for the answer to that, until the neighbor woman flinched to hear him. But the Presence stayed.

He had never talked to his wife about the child. How should he? There was the fact—the advertisement of his incompetence. And she had never talked to him. That was the one blessed and unassailable memory, that she had spread silence like a balm over his hurt. In return for it he had never gone away. He had resisted her that he might save her from showing among her own kind how poor a man he was. With every word of this ran the fact of his love for her—as he had loved her with all the stripes of clean and uncleanness. He bared himself as a child without knowing; and the Presence stayed. The talk trailed off at last to the commonplaces of consolation between the retchings of his spirit. The Presence lessened and streamed toward them on the wind of the garden. When it touched them like the warm air of noon that lies sometimes in hollow places after nightfall, the neighbor woman rose and went away.

The next night she did not wait for him. When a rod outside the town—it was a very little one—the burrowing owls *whoowhooed*, she hung up her apron and went to talk with Emma Jossylin. The Presence was there, drawn in, lying close. She found the key between the wistaria and the first pillar of the porch; but as soon as she opened the door she felt the chill that might be expected by one intruding on Emma Jossylin in her own house.

"'The Lord is my shepherd!'" said the neighbor woman; it was the first religious phrase that occurred to her; then she said the whole of the psalm, and after that a hymn. She had come in through the door, and stood with her back to it and her hand upon the knob. Everything was just as Mrs. Jossylin had left it, with the waiting air of a room kept for company.

"Em," she said, boldly, when the chill had abated a little before the sacred words—"Em Jossylin, I've got something to say to you. And you've got to hear," she added with firmness as the white curtains stirred duskily at the window. "You wouldn't be talked to about your troubles when . . . you were here before, and we humored you. But now there is Sim to be thought of. I guess you heard what you came for last night, and got good of it. Maybe it would have been better if Sim had said things all along instead of hoarding them in his heart, but, anyway, he has said them now. And what I want to say is, if you was staying on with the hope of hearing it again, you'd be making a mistake. You was an uncommon woman, Emma Jossylin, and there didn't none of us understand you very well, nor do you justice, maybe: but Sim is only a common man, and I understand him because I'm that way myself. And if you think he'll be opening his heart to you every night, or be any different from what he's always been on account of what's happened, that's a mistake, too . . . and in a little while, if you stay, it will be as bad as it always was . . . men are like that . . . you'd better go now while there's understanding between you." She stood staring into the darkling room that seemed suddenly full of turbulence and denial. It seemed to beat upon her and take her breath, but she held on.

"You've got to go . . . Em . . . and I'm going to stay until you do," she said with finality; and then began again:

"'The Lord is nigh unto them that are of a broken heart,'" and repeated the passage to the end. Then, as the Presence sank before it, "You better go, Emma," persuasively: and again, after an interval:

"'He shall deliver thee in six troubles.

"'Yea, in seven there shall no evil touch thee.'" The Presence gathered itself and was still; she could make out that it stood over against the opposite corner by the gilt easel with the crayon portrait of the child.

"'For thou shalt forget thy misery. Thou shalt remember it as waters that are past,'" concluded the neighbor woman, as she heard Jossylin on the gravel outside. What the Presence had wrought upon him in the night was visible in his altered mien. He looked, more than any thing else, to be in need of sleep. He had eaten his sorrow, and that was the end of it—as it is with men.

"I came to see if there was anything I could do for you," said the woman, neighborly, with her hand upon the door.

"I don't know as there is," said he.

"I'm much obliged, but I don't know as there is."

"You see," whispered the woman, over her shoulder, "not even to me." She felt the tug of her heart as the Presence swept past her. The neighbor went out after that and walked in the ragged street, past the schoolhouse, across the creek below the town, out by the fields, over the headgate, and back by the town again. It was full nine of the clock when she passed the Jossylin house. It looked, except for being a little neater, not other than the rest of the street. The door was open and the lamp was lit; she saw Jossylin black against it. He sat reading in a book like a man at ease in his own house.

Reconstruction

Michael Kent

As became the junior of the party, Reggie Chorister stood at the door-handle while the ladies left.

"You've given 'em something to talk over now," said his host, with a grin: "we shall have an evening of spooks. Does it interest you?"

"Neurotic balderdash!" interjected Fenwick, before the young man could reply. "Don't you think so, doctor?"

McLean scrutinised the grey ash on the end of his cigar with deliberation. "I'm a Celt," he said. "You're not denying that the Clintons left Witch-Hazel in three months, and that no one has been found to occupy it since?"

"I'm not denying it anyhow," returned Burrows, ruefully. "I've lost three years' rent." He turned to his youngest guest. "If you can persuade anybody that Witch-Hazels is habitable you will be doing me a good turn."

Chorister shifted round in his chair to face his friend.

"I'd stay the night there now," he said, "if I could find someone to keep me company."

"Wants two to deal with a spook, eh?" jeered Fenwick.

"I don't mean that," protested Reggie. "What would you say if I turned up tomorrow and told you I had spent the night playing crown and anchor with an old gentleman who carried his head under his arm and disappeared at cock crow without settling up?"

"I should call it an unsolicited testimonial to Burrows' port," said Fenwick.

"This old gentleman was shot," added McLean, drily.

"Suicide," Burrows explained.

Fenwick laughed. "Now you've done it!" he said. "Hear McLean on the futility of juries for the rest of the evening."

The doctor reddened, fingering the stem of his glass. "All I say is that the wound might have been self-inflicted or might not," he returned, stubbornly. "they should have brought in an open verdict. I can't get over the fact that when I went in close on one o'clock at night, the front door was on the jar."

"But the letter," began Fenwick. "That letter to me——"

"To come back to the original proposition," interrupted Reggie. "Who's game for a patrol of No Man's Land tonight? Fenwick?"

"It would take more than housemaid's gossip to keep me from my little bed," said Fenwick, as he filled his glass and pushed the decanter on.

Chorister felt that he was getting his reputation rather too cheaply. "We'll excuse you, sir," he said to his host. "A damp floor is no lying for sciatica. Doctor?"

McLean drummed his big fingers on the table. I don't deny I'm interested," he said. "It was I who first found old Scryme, you understand. I think I will."

"And that's that," said the young man, joyfully. "Perhaps Fenwick will come round and collect our remains in the morning."

"If you think I've got the wind up," began Fenwick, a little hotly.

A violent ring at the front door bell stopped him. It was unusual at that hour—eight-thirty in the evening.

"The post, I expect," said Burrows, vaguely.

In a moment a maid came in. "A message for Doctor McLean, sir," she said.

The doctor was in the hall on the instant. Chorister noted how the big lethargic man sprang to life at the call. It reminded him of men he had known in France, placid depths that stirred to furious action at the breath of emergency. "That man's sound," he thought.

"Who'd be a doctor?" murmured Burrows.

McLean's entrance prevented any response.

"A plague on the ladies," he apologised, whimsically. "I'm afraid you must excuse me, Burrows—the new generation. I never knew a woman who would keep to a time table."

Burrows nodded genially.

"Take a cigar with you," he said, indicating the box.

"Thanks." McLean nicked the end and fitted it into his holder. "Sorry our picnic is off, Chorister," he said, and then as an afterthought, "perhaps under the circumstances Fenwick will reconsider."

Fenwick stared at his wineglass.

"Anyhow," resumed McLean, "I'll likely be returning past Witch-Hazels about midnight. If I see a light in the hall-window, I'd look in."

"Right-O," returned Chorister. "These affairs require independent testimony, or I'd carry on alone. I may see you later."

As McLean hurried out, Fenwick looked up to find two pairs of eyes fixed on him questioningly. Burrows seemed amused.

"I don't suppose one would see anything before midnight," mused Chorister, regretfully.

"Put it off till you come down again," suggested Burrows, still with that elusive ironic grin. "I'll keep you company when I'm fit."

"You fellows think I've got the wind up," challenged Fenwick, suddenly. "As a matter of fact, I don't believe a word of the whole thing."

"How about that ghostly pistol shot?" asked his host. "That's what worried the Clintons."

"A door banging."

"At precisely twelve forty-five every night?"

"Material explanations must always be considered," broke in Chorister. "Very likely it is a quite simple matter. I wish I knew where to find the house."

Fenwick finished his port at a gulp. "Well, I don't mind coming along to show you and staying up till midnight," he said, lazily. "I don't generally turn in much before. But if neither McLean nor the lamented Scryme appear by then, I shan't wait up for them. I've got work to do tomorrow. Does that suit you?"

"Very sporting," said Chorister. "Make it so, old bird."

So it was settled.

At ten-thirty Fenwick ran round to his own place for his greatcoat. A little after eleven the two men were on their way to Witch-Hazels. Burrows had given them the key.

"We turn in here," said Fenwick, stopping abruptly at a shadowy gate. "It has one of these semi-circular drives." He pushed the gate open and swung it with a rustle of dead leaves like live things running off in the dark. "Show your flash a second."

In the circle of light Chorister could see a drowned and sodden drive, with points of pebbles and the grey, shrivelled husks of plane-tree leaves. Further off in the shadow, the patched, scaly bark of the trees showed like the bodies of bloodless, big-girthed boa constrictors hanging from above. "You'll have to go carefully," he said. "A false step would land you in a fine old mess."

But the flash-lamp brought them through to the door, up a couple of slimy green steps with grass in the crevices, and Chorister fitted the key into the mouldering plate.

"Is Mr. Scryme in?" asked Fenwick with heavy irony, as the round disc of the flash-light slipped from the opening door, and lengthened into a misty oval on the damp tiles of the inner hall. "Brrr!" he added, as he followed the young man in; "I wish these spooks of yours chose drier billets."

Chorister lit a candle, and turned to close the door.

"Leave it open for McLean," cried Fenwick, sharply. "When he turns up he won't be able to get in." He had a flask in his hand. "A drop of cognac," he explained. "Keep out the cold. Have a pull?"

"No, thanks," said Reggie; "I want to be sure of what I see."

"And I'll tell you whether it's alive or not," Fenwick broke in boisterously. He dipped his hand into his overcoat pocket, and brought out a little black automatic.

"Good Lord!" protested Chorister; "you don't think a pistol is any use against a ghost?"

"I'm taking no chances, and I'll drill holes into anything I see."

It made Reggie thoughtful. Now that Fenwick had come, he wished almost that he had been alone. The older man had certainly primed himself well. If he had been drinking brandy on top of his host's port, there was no saying what he might see. The young man was glad that it was only till twelve o'clock.

They placed the light on the sill of the hall window, and went slowly up the stairs to the first landing. The balustrade was old and rotten, and on the wall side great flakes of paper hung down, heavy with damp and fungoid growth.

Chorister lodged the second candlestick on the broad newel post at the stairhead. "Which is the room?" he asked.

"On the left," said Fenwick. "The old chap's office was on the left anyhow. You should have asked McLean. He was the first to find him." He tramped up the passage to the black window that gave on the leads of the porch, and came back.

"You know I don't know anything about the affair really," said Chorister. "Only what Burrows said, that nobody will stay in the place."

Fenwick took another pull at his flask.

"The old chap was thought to be a miser," he explained. "I did what little legal business he had, and that was not much. I drew up his will—entire estate to charity—and I don't know whether it was worth twenty pounds or twenty thousand. He lived quite alone, not a soul with him. It must be three years ago now. McLean says he was passing on a night, and heard a shot. He found the door ajar, went up, and there was the old chap on the floor, with a bullet in his brain." Fenwick paused, and took another pull at his flask. "His pistol lay beside him, and there was an unfinished letter on his desk addressed to me, only a few words, but pretty conclusive. 'Dear Mr. Fenwick,

I am sorry to have to take so serious a step.' Nothing more. He'd meant to explain—they often do—but the suicidal mania got too strong for him."

"McLean has other opinions?" queried Chorister.

Fenwick laughed.

"I don't think so really," he said. "It is just his Scot's caution, you know. Anyway, if he has he knows best. He was the only person anywhere near him at the time."

"A rum thing," returned the young man, thoughtfully. "But if McLean turns up we shall have a sort of complete reconstruction, light in the hall, door ajar, everything except the murderer."

"And there wasn't one," added Fenwick, "or if there was, you don't expect him to help in the tableau." He smiled contemptuously. "Unless, of course," he added, "it was—the man who found him there."

"I think," remarked Chorister with a cold stare, "I'd give that flask of yours a rest. It's running away with your tongue. Let's get in and look at the room."

"God God!" cried Fenwick; "what's that?"

He flashed out his pistol, and stood trembling with the short black barrel pointing down the stair. Heavy footsteps were slowly mounting the shadowy lower flight.

Chorister laughed lightly. "You're a fine spook hunter," he cried. "Haven't you heard an old staircase spring back after someone has passed over it? If it is damp it sticks down under your weight. Then it dries or cools, something release it, and one step after another jerks back; it's the same with a wicker chair."

"Sorry old man," said Fenwick, "but it got on my nerves a bit. It's the patter of the rain outside, I suppose, and your talk about the parallel circumstances. I swear I expected to see the old man's face. A fellow needn't believe in spooks to get jarred by a wet night and an empty house and a talk about suicides. Is it twelve o'clock yet?"

"Lord," said Chorister, "I hope not. We haven't been into the room yet." He looked at his watch. "Quarter to," he added. "Come along."

He took up the candle and entered. It was a big room, gaunt, but not so dilapidated as the stairs. Outside the light breeze tapped a white twig of plane against the streaming window like a dead finger beckoning. Every now and then a gust swept the rain with a soft patter against the dirty panes. There was no carpet on the floor, and across the middle of the room two new boards stood out whitely from the old grey planking on either side. A dressmaker's model stood in one corner, looking unutterably chilly and deserted.

Chorister put the candle down upon the mantelpiece, and his knuckles touched a cold metal disc. It was a cheap American watch, evidently left there by the Clintons. Somehow these rags of domesticity seemed to emphasise the emptiness and gloom of the place.

Suddenly Fenwick spoke as he stood by the door, jerking the porcelain knob round, and letting it spring back. "The old chap's desk was in front of the window," he said.

"I guessed that," said Chorister. "The new boards." He looked keenly at Fenwick standing hesitant at the door. "Here," he said, "you take the candle and watch outside on the landing; I'll wait here."

"Wait there!" cried Fenwick, wonderingly; "there—in the dark."

"That's what I came for," said Chorister.

Fenwick looked thought and for a moment unwilling.

"Right," he said at length; "I'll see if anybody comes up the stairs. McLean ought to be here soon. Hand over that light."

With a rather dry smile Chorister brought the candlestick across the room to him.

"Don't make fun of spook-hunters again, old man," he said. "It's too cheap." With that he closed the door and left Fenwick to his own reflections.

It was utterly dark in the room now, for no light from the rainy sky penetrated the clouded panes. Switching on his flash for a moment, Chorister found his way to the mantelpiece, took out his watch, and laid it upon the bare stone, then, turning his back to the shelf, switched off and waited.

Gradually as he settled down to his vigil, that preternatural sharpness of bearing and sensibility which comes into play when the brain is no longer busy with sight awoke him. The ticking of his watch behind him was loud and strong. The twig tapping at the window now sounded eager and angry, and in the soft patter of the rain Chorister got a suggestion of a shuffling walk, as of a quite feeble presence that paced the long strip of white new board which split the room. He grew conscious of an increasing cold and of a strange relapse from physical reality, as though the things which in everyday life are manifest by sight and sound and touch were not real, and a new phase of reality, appealing to other deeper-hidden senses, had risen from the welter of the subconscious. Entities shadowy and void pressed upon him. Vague morbid suggestions seemed to tap at him, and he shrank back from them—unfathomed abysses of an unknown land, black and foul, and far from the healthy ordinariness of all things seen.

Suddenly a metallic click drove him back to solid earth. He heard the scroop of a screw, and smiled to know that on the landing outside Fenwick was applying too himself his trusted tonic. Presently the lawyer called wistfully, "Isn't it twelve yet, Chorister?"

Reggie flashed the torch a moment on the mantelpiece.

"Five minutes to," he called; "I'll tell you when it's twelve if the doctor doesn't turn up."

He heard the creak of the balustrade, and the light began to come in meagrely beneath the door as though Fenwick had placed the candle lower down.

In a moment he had dropped back again into the groping land where unheard phantoms seemed to press upon him, as it were, with pitiful dumb mouthings earnest toward speech. Delicately he could sense a new atmosphere. The grim unknown who kept his sentry guard seemed to have weighed an issue and taken a decision. Before had been inactive dumb despair, now positive hate, as real as the wire-skirted bust that stood in the corner, filled the room like crowding mist. Chorister found himself analysing it. Avarice was there, cold and cruel and relentless, bitter dismay and mad black hatred. It occurred to the watcher that if thought alone could kill, he would not care to be the object of that frozen flame. Suddenly his knee cramped and gave way, throwing him forward, and incidentally dragging his mind back again in the region of the real. "Good Lord," thought he, "I ought to have warned Fenwick. It must be twelve." He flashed the light on the mantelshelf once more. The watch still showed five minutes to twelve.

For a second he stared at it blankly, wondering if his senses could have been held so long that its descent into darkness had endured but a fraction of a minute. Then he understood. He had looked at the wrong watch—that broken relic of Clinton's tenancy. His own lay further along the shelf upon his other side. He turned the light on.

It was twelve-forty.

He went softly across the room and pulled the door open. Fenwick, muffled in his greatcoat, was seated on the floor with his back to the wall and the candle by his side. He was snoring soundly.

"That's one way of spook-hunting!" thought Chorister with a grin. "I'll leave him until McLean turns up."

He turned into the room again, leaving the door unlatched. The darkness and malevolence enveloped him more swiftly and more closely than before. It was colder.

It was becoming a dead numbing cold that sapped his vitality, only over his skin there was a tiny electric pricking sensation. When he crossed the centre of the room, where he had imagined that dreadful sentry path, his hand seemed to brush for an instant against a mass of roped and snaky tentacles, dead and cold. It stung more than his sense of touch. It reached his soul with a feeling of utter nauseating horror. He hurried to his place by the hearth, and turned, relieved to find the hard edge of the mantelshelf at his shoulder-blades. Now he was past analysis, swept away as one a wind of unholy malignance. He knew that the presence had increased its pace, padding fearsomely up and down the path with the vain rage of an animal behind bars, an embodied curse. He turned his head now mechanically right and left, right and left, to follow it. Weariness took hold of him. The column of his back could hardly hold up the heavy head.

Then he began to notice that the swish of the rain upon the window had changed subtly to a rhythmic pulse. This had come gradually and unheeded. He looked at the window. The moon showed dimly. There was no rain. The sound was different—quite different. It became more marked at every second. It was the shuffle of slippered feet up and down the room.

Then, with eyes and head twitching to right and left, he saw out of the dark a blacker shadow gather, a cloud that grew denser and started to glow at the edges, a human shape, a man. He could not gauge the passage of time. Seconds it might have been, or minutes, before he stood bloodless and looked into the lean white face with its open, savage mouth and green, glinting, sunken eyes. At last he saw it all quite clearly, down to the detail of the black skull cap and ragged dressing-gown, a wicked and cruel old man pacing the room furiously and spitting unheard curses into the void of the dark.

Suddenly the grim form stopped at the window end of the room. Chorister saw it seat itself upon a chair and with the same savage vehemence open the drawer of a desk. There was a pistol there, and it was flung out on the flat top of the desk unheeding. Chorister noted the action. The old man was angry that the thing impeded him. He was not searching for it.

He found paper and set himself furiously to write.

At that moment a sudden clatter no the stair disturbed the watcher, but he could not move. He heard a panic rush of feet and a whine, high-pitched and hysterical voices below as of question and answer, and a bang. He thought that Fenwick had lost his nerve and fled, banging the door. It had not disturbed the writer at the desk.

So certain was Chorister of Fenwick's flight that it staggered him a moment later to see the lawyer push open the door and enter. "Now you can see for yourself," he began. But Fenwick, taking no notice, strode silently across the room, picked up the pistol from the desk, and fired without pause into the old man's head.

"Stop, stop!" shouted Chorister as the phantom turned to twist sideways in the chair and fall inert. Then all at once it occurred to Chorister that the pistol was not really there.

"Fenwick," he called, "Fenwick!" and with the sound darkness came down and left only the slim oblong of light which came through the door from the candle upon the landing.

He ran out, stunned, to hear a voice from below: "Are you all right, Chorister?" and he went down the stairs three at a time.

"Thank Heaven, it's McLean!" he cried. "Have you seen Fenwick, doctor?"

"He's here," returned the doctor gravely.

Fenwick lay in the shadows where the passage narrowed to admit the lower stairs. He was on his back. His hands lay palms upwards, lightly flexed. The doctor with forethought had thrown the breast of the big overcoat across the white shirt-front.

"Didn't you hear the shot," he asked, "four or five minutes ago?"

"I—I thought it was the door," said Chorister. "He went to sleep up there on the landing. I was in the old man's room. I thought he had woke up and got the jim-jams and had bolted, banging the door."

"You weren't far wrong," McLean said grimly. "I was coming in when he came downstairs nineteen to the dozen. It surprised me. I thought he funked it. 'So you did after all?' I said. 'Yes,' he said whimpering, 'I had to. The old man was going to jail me for playing with his securities.' Then he laughed. 'But you're too late, doctor,' he said and fired."

"Fired!" echoed Chorister. "Impossible. After the bang he came into the room. The old man was there. I'll tell you afterwards. I saw it all. Fenwick shot him. It couldn't have been Fenwick."

"May be," said McLean. "I don't know. Death was instantaneous. If you saw him upstairs after that shot was fired you saw some part of him that I could not hold down here."

He spread a handkerchief over the dead man's face. "Come on, Chorister," he said, "we'd better ring up the police."

The Recrudescence of Imray

Rudyard Kipling

Imray had achieved the impossible. Without warning, for no conceivable motive, in his youth and at the threshold of his career he had chosen to disappear from the world—which is to say, the little Indian station where he lived. Upon a day he was alive, well, happy, and in great evidence at his club, among the billiard-tables. Upon a morning he was not, and no manner of search could make sure where he might be. He had stepped out of his place; he had not appeared at his office at the proper time, and his dog-cart was not upon the public roads. For these reasons and because he was hampering in a microscopical degree the administration of the Indian Empire, the Indian Empire paused for one microscopical moment to make inquiry into the fate of Imray. Ponds were dragged, wells were plumbed, telegrams were dispatched down the lines of railways and to the nearest seaport town—1,200 miles away—but Imray was not at the end of the dragropes nor the telegrams. He was gone, and his place knew him no more. Then the work of the great Indian Empire swept forward, because it could not be delayed, and Imray, from being a man, became a mystery—such a thing as men talk over at their tables in the club for a month and then forget utterly. His guns, horses, and carts were sold to the highest bidder. His superior officer wrote an absurd letter to his mother, saying that Imray had unaccountably disappeared and his bungalow stood empty on the road.

After three or four months of the scorching hot weather had gone by, my friend Strickland, of the police force, saw fit to rent the bungalow from the native landlord. This was before he was engaged to Miss Youghai—an affair which has been described in another place—and while he was pursuing his investigations into native life. His own life was sufficiently peculiar, and men complained of his manners and customs. There was always food in his house, but there were no regular times for meals. He eat, standing up and walking about, whatever he might find on the side-board, and this is not good for the insides of human beings. His domestic equipment was limited to six rifles, three shot-guns, five saddles, and a collection of stiff-jointed masheer rods, bigger and stronger than the largest salmon rods. These things occupied one half of his bungalow, and the other half was given up to Strickland and his dog Tietjens—an enormous Rampour slut, who sung when she was ordered, and devoured daily the rations of two men. She spoke to Strickland in a language of her own, and whenever in her walks abroad she saw things calculated to destroy the peace of Her Majesty the Queen Empress, she returned to her master and gave him information. Strickland would take steps at once, and the end of his labors was trouble and fine and imprisonment for other people. The natives believed that Tietjens was a familiar spirit, and treated her with the great reverence that is born of hate and fear. One room in the bungalow was set apart for her special use. She owned a bedstead, a blanket, and a drinking-trough, and if any one came into Strickland's room at night, her custom was to knock down the invader and give tongue till some one came with a light. Strickland owes his life to her when he was on the frontier in search of the local murderer who came in the gray dawn to send Strickland much further than the Andaman Islands, Tietjens caught him as he was crawling into Strickland's tent with a dagger between his teeth, and after his record of iniquity was established in the eyes of the law, he was hanged. From that date Tietjens wore a collar of rough silver and employed a monogram on her night blanket and the blanket was double-woven Kashmir cloth, for she was a delicate dog.

Under no circumstances would she be separated from Strickland, and when he was ill with fever she made great trouble for the doctors because she did not know how to help her master and would not allow another creature to attempt aid. Macarnaght, of the Indian Medical Service, beat her over the head with a gun, before she could understand that she must give room for those who could give quinine.

A short time after Strickland had taken Imray's bungalow, my business took me through that station, and naturally, the club quarters being full, I quartered myself upon Strickland. It was a desirable bungalow, eight-roomed, and heavily thatched against any chance of leakage from rain. Under the pitch of the roof ran a ceiling cloth, which looked just as nice as a white-washed ceiling. The landlord had repainted when Strickland took the bungalow, and unless you knew how Indian bungalows were built you would never have suspected that above the cloth lay the dark, three-cornered cavarn of the roof, where the beams and the under side of the thatch harbored all manner of rats, bats, ants, and other things.

Tietjens met me in the veranda with a bay like the boom of the bells of St. Paul's, and put her paws on my shoulders and said she was glad to see me. Strickland had contrived to put together that sort of meal which he called lunch, and immediately after it was finished went out about his business. I was left alone with Tietjens and my own affairs. The heat of the summer had broken up and given place to the warm damp of the rains. There was no motion in the heated air, but the rain fell like bayonet rods on the earth, and flung up a blue mist where it splashed back again. The bamboos and the custard apples, the poinsettias the mango-trees in the garden stood still while the warm water lashed through them, and the frogs began to sing among the aloe hedges. A little before the light failed, and when the rain was at its worst, I sat on the back veranda and heard the water roar from the eaves, and scratched myself because I was covered with the thing they call prickly heat. Tietjens came out with me and put her head in my lap, and was very sorrowful, so I gave her biscuits when tea was ready, and I took tea in the back veranda on account of the little coolness I found there. The rooms of the house were dark behind me. I could smell Strickland's saddlery and the oil on his guns, and I did not the least desire to sit among these things. My own servant came to me in the twilight, the muslin of his clothes clinging tightly to his drenched body, and told me that a gentleman had called and wished to see some one. Very much against my will, and because of the darkness of the rooms, I went into the naked drawing-room, telling my man to bring the lights. There might or might not have been a caller in the room—it seems to me that I saw a figure by one of the windows, but when the lights came there was nothing save the spikes of the rain without and the smell of the drinking earth in my nostrils. I explained to my man that he was no wiser than he ought to be and went back to the veranda to talk to Tietjens. She had gone out into the wet and I could hardly coax her back to me—even with biscuits with sugar on top. Strickland rode back, dripping wet, just before dinner, and the first thing he said was:

"Has any one called?"

I explained, with apologies, that my servant had called me into the drawing-room on a false alarm; or that some loafer had tried to call on Strickland, and, thinking better of it, fled after giving his name. Strickland ordered dinner without comment and since it was a real dinner, with white table-cloth attached, we sat down.

At nine o'clock Strickland wanted to go to bed, and I was tired too. Tietjens, who had been lying underneath the table, rose up and went into the least-exposed veranda as soon as her master moved to his own room, which was next to the stately chamber set apart for Tietjens. If a mere wife had wished to sleep out-of-doors in that pelting rain, it would not have mattered, but Tietjens was a dog, and therefore the better animal. I looked at Strickland, expecting to see him flog her with a whip. He smiled queerly, as a man would smile after telling some hideous domestic tragedy. "She has done this ever since I moved in here."

The dog was Strickland's dog, so I said nothing, but I felt all that Strickland felt in being made light of. Tietjens encamped outside my bedroom window, and storm after storm came up, thundered on the thatch, and died away. The lightning spattered the sky as a thrown egg spatters a barn door, but the light was pale blue, not yellow; and looking through my slit bamboo blinds, I could see the great dog standing, not sleeping, in the veranda, the hackles alift on her back, and her feet planted as tensely as the drawn wire rope of a suspension bridge. In the very short pauses of the thunder I tried to sleep, but it seemed that some one wanted me very badly. He, whoever he was, was trying to call me by name, but his voice was no more than a husky whisper. Then the thunder ceased and Tietjens went into the garden and howled at the low moon. Somebody tried to open my door, and walked about and through the house, and stood breathing heavily in the verandas, and just when I was falling asleep I fancied that I heard a wild hammering and clamoring above my head or on the door.

I ran into Strickland's room and asked him whether he was ill and had been calling for me. He was lying on the bed half-dressed, with a pipe in his mouth. "I thought you'd come," he said. "Have I been walking around the house at all?"

I explained that he had been in the dining-room and the smoking-room and two or three other places; and he laughed and told me to go back to bed. I went back to bed and slept till the morning, but in all my dreams I was sure I was doing some one an injustice in not attending to his wants. What those wants were I could not tell, but a fluttering, whispering, bolt-fumbling, luring, loitering some one was reproaching me for my slackness, and through all the dreams I heard the howling of Tietjens in the garden and the thrashing of the rain.

I was in that house for two days, and Strickland went to his office daily, leaving me alone for eight or ten hours a day, with Tietjens for my only companion. As long as the full light lasted I was comfortable, and so was Tietjens; but in the twilight she and I moved into the back veranda and cuddled each other for company. We were alone in the house, but for all that it was fully occupied by a tenant with whom I had no desire to interfere. I never saw him, but I could see the curtains between the rooms quivering where he had just passed through; I could hear the chairs creaking as the bamboos sprung under a weight that had just quitted them; and I could feel when I went to get a book from the dining-room that somebody was waiting in the shadows of the front veranda till I should have gone away. Tietjens made the twilight more interesting by glaring into the darkened rooms, with every hair erect, and following the motions of something that I could not see. She never entered the rooms, but her eyes moved, and that was quite sufficient. Only when my servant came to trim the lamps and make all light and habitable, she would come in with me and spend her time sitting on her haunches watching an invisible extra man as he moved about behind my shoulder. Dogs are cheerful companions.

I explained to Strickland, gently as might be, that I would go over to the club and find for myself quarters there. I admired his hospitality, was pleased with his guns and rods, but I did not much care for his house and its atmosphere. He heard me out to the end, and then smiled very wearily, but without contempt, for he is a man who understands things. "Stay on," he said, "and see what this thing means. All you have talked about I have known since I took the bungalow. Stay on and wait. Tietjens has left me. Are you going too?"

I had seen him through one little affair connected with an idol that had brought me to the doors of a lunatic asylum, and I had no desire to help him through further experiences. He was a man to whom unpleasantnesses arrived as do dinners to ordinary people.

Therefore I explained more clearly than ever that I liked him immensely, and would be happy to see him in the daytime, but that I didn't care to sleep under his roof. This was after dinner, when Tietjens had gone out to lie in the veranda.

"'Pon my soul, I don't wonder," said Strickland, with his eyes on the ceiling-cloth. "Look at that!"

The tails of two snakes were hanging between the cloth and the cornice of the wall. They threw long shadows in the lamp-light. "If you are afraid of snakes, of course—" said Strickland. "I hate and fear snakes, because if you look into the eyes of any snake you will see that it knows all and more of man's fall, and that it feels all the contempt that the devil felt when Adam was evicted from Eden Besides which its bite is generally fatal, and it bursts up trouser legs."

"You ought to get your thatch overhauled," I said. "Give me a masheer rod, and we'll poke 'em down."

"They'll hide among the roof beams," said Strickland. "I can't stand snakes overhead. I'm going up. If I shake 'em down, stand by with the cleaning-rod and break their backs."

I was not anxious to assist Strickland in his work, but I took the loading-rod and waited in the dining-room, while Strickland brought a gardener's ladder from the veranda and set it against the side of the room. The snake tails drew themselves up and disappeared. We could hear the dry rushing scuttle of long bodies running over the baggy cloth. Strickland took a lamp with him, while I tried to make clear the danger of hunting roof snakes between a ceiling-cloth and a thatch, apart from the deterioration of property caused by ripping out ceiling-cloths.

"Nonsense!" said Strickland. "They're sure to hide near the walls by the cloth. The bricks are too cold for 'em, and the heat of the room is just what they like." He put his hand to the corner of the cloth and ripped the rotten stuff from the cornice. It gave a great sound of tearing, and Strickland put his head through the opening into the dark of the angle of the roof beams. I set my teeth and lifted the loading-rod, for I had not the least knowledge of what might descend.

"H'm," said Strickland; and his voice rolled and rumbled in the roof. "There's room for another set of rooms up here, and, by Jove! some one is occupying 'em."

"Snakes?" I said down below.

"No. It's a buffalo. Hand me up the two first joints of a masheer rod, and I'll prod it. It's lying on the main beam."

I handed up the rod.

"What a nest for owls and serpents! No wonder the snakes live here," said Strickland, climbing further into the roof. I could see his elbow thrusting with the rod. "Come out of that, whoever you are! Look out! Heads below there! It's tottering."

I saw the ceiling-cloth nearly in the center of the room bag with a shape that was pressing it downward and downward toward the lighted lamps on the table. I snatched a lamp out of danger and stood back. Then the cloth ripped out from the walls, tore, split, swayed, and shot down upon the table something that I dared not look at till Strickland had slid down the ladder and was standing by my side.

He did not say much, being a man of few words, but he picked up the loose end of the table-cloth and threw it over the thing on the table.

"It strikes me," said he, pulling down the lamp, "our friend Imray has come back. Oh! you would, would you?"

There was a movement under the cloth, and a little snake wriggled out, to be back-broken by the butt of the masheer rod. I was sufficiently sick to make no remarks worth recording.

Strickland meditated and helped himself to drinks liberally. The thing under the cloth made no more signs of life. "Is it Imray?" I said.

Strickland turned back the cloth for a moment and looked. "It is Imray," he said, "and his throat is cut from ear to ear."

Then we both spoke together and to ourselves: "That's why he whispered about the house."

Tietjens, in the garden, began to bay furiously. A little later her great nose heaved upon the dining-room door.

She sniffed and was still. The broken and tattered ceiling-cloth hung down almost to the level of the table, and there was hardly room to move away from the discovery.

Then Tietjens came in and sat down, her teeth bared and her forepaws planted. She looked at Strickland.

"It's bad business, old lady," said he. "Men don't go up into the roofs of their bungalows to die, and they don't fasten up the ceiling-cloth behind 'em. Let's think it out."

"Let's think it out somewhere else," I said.

"Excellent idea! Turn the lamps out. We'll get into my room."

I did not turn the lamps out. I went into Strickland's room first and allowed him to make the darkness. Then he followed me, and we lighted tobacco and thought. Strickland did the thinking. I smoked furiously because I was afraid.

"Imray is back," said Strickland. "The question is, who killed Imray? Don't talk—I have a notion of my own. When I took this bungalow I took most of Imray's servants. Imray was guileless and inoffensive, wasn't he?"

I agreed, though the heap under the cloth looked neither one thing nor the other.

"If I call the servants they will stand fast in a crowd and lie like Aryans. What do you suggest?"

"Call 'em in one by one," I said.

"They'll run away and give the news to all their fellows," said Strickland.

"We must segregate 'em. Do you suppose your servant knows anything about it?"

"He may, for aught I know, but I don't think it's likely. He has only been here two or three days."

"What's your notion?" I asked.

"I can't quite tell. How the dickens did the man get the wrong side of the ceiling-cloth?"

There was a heavy coughing outside Strickland's bedroom door. This showed that Bahadur Khan, his body-servant, had waked from sleep and wished to put Strickland to bed.

"Come in," said Strickland. "It is a very warm night, isn't it?"

Bahadur Khan, a great, green-turbaned, six-foot Mohammedan, said that it was a very warm night, but that there was more rain pending, which, by his honor's favor, would bring relief to the country.

"It will be so, if God pleases," said Strickland, tugging off his boots. "It is in my mind, Bahadur Khan, that I have worked thee remorselessly for many days—ever since that time when thou first earnest into my service. What time was that?"

"Has the heaven-born forgotten? It was when Imray Sahib went secretly to Europe without warning given, and I—even I—came into the honored service of the protector of the poor."

"And Imray Sahib went to Europe?"

"It is so said among the servants."

"And thou wilt take service with him when he returns?"

"Assuredly, sahib. He was a good master and cherished his dependents."

"That is true. I am very tired, but I can go buck-shooting to-morrow. Give me the little rifle that I used for black buck; it is in the case yonder."

The man stooped over the case, handed barrels, stock, and fore-end to Strickland, who fitted them together. Yawning dolefully, then he reached down to the gun-case, took a solid drawn cartridge, and slipped it into the breech of the .360 express.

"And Imray Sahib has gone to Europe secretly? That is very strange, Bahadur Khan, is it not?"

"What do I know of the ways of the white man, heaven-born?"

"Very little, truly. But thou shalt know more. It has reached me that Imray Sahib has returned from his so long journeyings, and that even now he lies in the next room, waiting his servant."

"Sahib!"

The lamp-light slid along the barrels of the rifle as they leveled themselves against Bahadur Khan's broad breast.

"Go, then, and look!" said Strickland. "Take a lamp. Thy master is tired, and he waits. Go!"

The man picked up a lamp and went into the dining-room, Strickland following, and almost pushing him with the muzzle of the rifle. He looked for a moment at the black depths behind the ceiling-cloth, at the carcass of the mangled snake under foot, and last, a gray glaze setting on his face, at the thing under the table-cloth.

"Hast thou seen?" said Strickland, after a pause.

"I have seen. I am clay in the white man's hands. What does the presence do?"

"Hang thee within a month! What else?"

"For killing him? Nay, sahib, consider. Walking among us, his servants, he cast his eyes upon my child, who was four years old. Him he bewitched, and in ten days he died of the fever. My child!"

"What said Imray Sahib?"

"He said he was a handsome child, and patted him on the head; wherefore my child died. Wherefore I killed Imray Sahib in the twilight, when he came back from office and was sleeping. The heaven-born knows all things. I am the servant of the heaven-born."

Strickland looked at me above the rifle, and said, in the vernacular: "Thou art witness to this saying. He has killed."

Bahadur Khan stood ashen gray in the light of the one lamp. The need for justification came upon him very swiftly.

"I am trapped," he said, "but the offense was that man's. He cast an evil eye upon my child, and I killed and hid him. Only such as are served by devils," he glared at Tietjens, crouched stolidly before him, "only such could know what I did."

"It was clever. But thou shouldst have lashed him to the beam with a rope. Now, thou thyself wilt hang by a rope. Orderly!"

A drowsy policeman answered Strickland's call. He was followed by another, and Tietjens sat still.

"Take him to the station," said Strickland. "There is a case toward."

"Do I hang, then?" said Bahadur Khan, making no attempt to escape and keeping his eyes on the ground.

"If the sun shines, or the water runs, thou wilt hang," said Strickland. Bahadur Khan stepped back one pace, quivered, and stood still. The two policemen waited further orders.

"Go!" said Strickland.

"Nay; but I go very swiftly," said Bahadur Khan. "Look! I am even now dead a man."

He lifted his foot, and to the little toe there clung the head of the half-killed snake, firm fixed in the agony of death.

"I come of land-holding stock," said Bahadur Khan, rocking where he stood. "It were a disgrace for me to go to the public scaffold, therefore I take this way. Be it remembered that the sahib's shirts are correctly enumerated, and that there is an extra piece of soap in his wash-basin. My child was bewitched, and I slew the wizard. Why should you seek to slay me? My honor is saved, and—and—I die."

At the end of an hour he died as they die who are bitten by the little kariat, and the policemen bore him and the thing under the table-cloth to their appointed places. They were needed to make clear the disappearance of Imray.

"This," said Strickland, very calmly, as he climbed into bed, "is called the nineteenth century. Did you hear what that man said?"

"I heard," I answered. "Imray made a mistake."

"Simply and solely through not knowing the nature and the coincidence of a little seasonal fever. Bahadur Khan had been with him for four years."

I shuddered. My own servant had been with me for exactly that length of time. When I went over to my own room I found him waiting, impassive as the copper head on a penny, to pull off my boots.

"What has befallen Bahadur Khan?" said I.

"He was bitten by a snake and died; the rest the sahib knows," was the answer.

"And how much of the matter hast thou known?"

"As much as might be gathered from one coming in the twilight to seek satisfaction. Gently, sahib. Let me pull off those boots."

I had just settled to the sleep of exhaustion when I heard Strickland shouting from his side of the house:

"Tietjens has come back to her room!"

And so she had. The great deerhound was couched on her own bedstead, on her own blanket, and in the next room the idle, empty ceiling-cloth wagged light-heartedly as it flailed on the table.

The Return

R. Murray Gilchrist

Five minutes ago I drew the window curtain aside and let the mellow sunset light contend with the glare from the girandoles. Below lay the orchard of Vernon Garth, rich in heavily flowered fruit-trees—yonder a medlar, here a pear, next a quince. As my eyes, unaccustomed to the day, blinked rapidly, the recollection came of a scene forty-five years past, and once more beneath the oldest tree stood the girl I loved, mischievously plucking yarrow, and, despite its evil omen, twining the snowy clusters in her black hair. Again her coquettish words rang in my ears: "Make me thy lady! Make me the richest woman in England, and I promise thee, Rupert, we shall be the happiest of God's creatures. And I remembered how the mad thirst for gold filled me; howl trusted in her fidelity, and without reasoning or even telling her that I would conquer fortune for her sake, I kissed her sadly and passed into the world. Then followed a complete silence until the *Star of Europe*, the greatest diamond discovered in modern times, lay in my hand—a rough, unpolished stone not unlike the lumps of spar I had often seen lying on the sandy lanes of my native country. This should be Rose's own, and all the others that clanked so melodiously in their leather bulse should go toward fulfilling her ambition. Rich and happy I should be soon, and should I not marry an untitled gentlewoman, sweet in her prime? The twenty years' interval of work and sleep was like a fading dream, for I was going home. The knowledge thrilled me so that my nerves were strung tight as iron ropes and I laughed like a young boy. And it was all because my home was to be in Rose Pascal's arms.

I crossed the sea and posted straight for Halkton village. The old hostelry was crowded. Jane Hopgarth, whom I remembered as a ruddy-faced child, stood on the box-edged terrace, courtesying in matronly fashion to the departing mail-coach. An alteration in the sign-board attracted my attention: the white lilies had been painted over with a mitre, and the name changed from the *Pascal Arms* to the *Lord Bishop*. Angrily, aghast at this disloyalty I cross-questioned the ostlers, who hurried to and fro, but failing to obtain any coherent replies I was fain to content myself with a mental denunciation of the times.

Twilight had fallen before I reached the cottage at the entrance of the park. This was in a ruinous condition; here and there sheaves in the thatched roof had parted and formed crevices through which smoke filtered. Some of the tiny windows had been walled up, and even where the glass remained snake-like ivy hindered any light falling into their thick recesses.

The door stood open, although the evening was chilly. As I approached, the heavy autumnal dew shook down from the firs and fell upon my shoulders. A bat, swooping in an undulation, struck between my eyes and fell to the grass, moaning querulously. I entered. A withered woman sat beside the peat fire. She held a pair of steel knitting-needles which she moved without cessation. There was no thread upon them, and when they clicked her lips twitched as if she had counted. Some time passed before I recognized Rose's foster-mother, Elizabeth Carless. The russet colors of her cheeks had faded and left a sickly gray; those sunken, dimmed eyes were utterly unlike the bright black orbs that had danced so mirthfully. Her stature, too, had shrunk. I was struck with wonder. Elizabeth could not be more than fifty-six years old. I had been away twenty years; Rose was fifteen when I left her, and I had heard Elizabeth say that she was only twenty-one at the time of her darling's weaning. But what a change! She had such an air of weary grief that my heart grew sick.

Advancing to her side I touched her arm. She turned, but neither spoke nor seemed aware of my presence. Soon, however, she rose, and helping herself along by grasping the scanty furniture, tottered to a window and peered out. Her right hand crept to her throat; she untied the string of her gown and took from her bosom a pomander set in a battered silver case. I cried out; Rose had loved that toy in her childhood; thousands of times had we played ball with it. . . . Elizabeth held it to her mouth and mumbled it, as if it were a baby's hand. Maddened with impatience, I caught her shoulder and roughly bade her say where I should find Rose. But something awoke in her eyes, and she shrank away to the other side of the house-place: I followed; she cowered on the floor, looking at me with a strange horror. Her lips began to move, but no sound issued. Only when I crossed to the threshold did she rise; and then her head moved wildly from side to side, and her hands pressed close to her breast, as if the pain there were too great to endure.

I ran from the place, not daring to look back. In a few minutes I reached the balustraded wall of the Hall garden. The house looked as if no careful hand had touched it for years. The elements had played havoc with its oriels, and many of the latticed frames hung on single hinges. The curtain of the blue parlor hung outside, draggled and faded, and half hidden by a thick growth of bindweed.

With an almost savage force I raised my arm high above my head and brought my fist down upon the central panel of the door. There was no need for such violence, for the decayed fastenings made no resistance, and some of the rotten boards fell to the ground. As I entered the hall and saw the ancient furniture, once so fondly kept, now mildewed and crumbling to dust, quick sobs burst from my throat. Rose's spinet stood beside the door of the withdrawing-room. How many carols had we sung to its music! As I passed my foot struck one of the legs and the rickety structure groaned as if it were coming to pieces; I thrust out my hand to steady it, but at my touch the velvet covering of the lid came off and the tiny gilt ornaments rattled downward.

By now the full moonlight pierced the window and quivered on the floor. As I gazed on the tremulous pattern it changed into quaint devices of hearts, daggers, rings, and a thousand other tokens. All suddenly another object glided among them so quickly that I wondered whether my eyes had been at fault—a tiny satin shoe, stained crimson across the lappets. A revulsion of feeling came to my soul and drove away all my fear. I had seen that selfsame shoe white and unsoiled twenty years before, when vain, vain Rose danced among her reapers at the harvest-home. And my voice cried out in ecstasy: "Rose, heart of mine! Delight of all the world's delights!"

She stood before me, wondering, amazed. Alas, so changed! The red and yellow silk shawl still covered her shoulders; her hair still hung in those eldritch curls. But the beautiful face had grown wan and tired, and across the forehead were drawn lines like silver threads. She threw her arms around my neck and pressing her bosom heavily on mine sobbed so piteously that I grew afraid for her and drew back the long masses of hair which had fallen forward, and kissed again and again those lips that were too lovely for simile. Never came a word of chiding from them. "Love," she said, when she had regained her breath, "the past struggle was sharp and torturing—the future struggle will be crueller still. What a great love yours was, to wait and trust for so long. Would that mine had been as powerful! Poor, weak heart that I could not endure!"

The tones of a wild fear throbbed through all her speech, strongly, but yet with insufficient power to prevent her from feeling the tenderness of those moments. Often, timorously raising her head from my shoulder, she looked around, and then turned with a soft, inarticulate, and glad murmur to hide her face on my bosom. I spoke fervently; told of the years spent away from her; how, when working in the diamond-fields, she had ever been present in my fancy; how at night her name had fallen from my lips in my only prayer; how I had dreamed of her among the greatest in the land—the richest, and, I dare swear, the loveliest woman in the world. I grew warmer still: all the gladness which had been constrained for so long now burst wildly from my lips; a myriad of rich ideas resolved into words which, being spoken, wove one long and delicious fit of passion. As we stood together the moon brightened and filled the chamber with a light like the day's. The ridges of the surrounding moorland stood out in sharp relief.

Rose drank in my declarations thirstily, but soon interrupted me with a heavy sigh. "Come away," she said softly. "I no longer live in this house. You must stay with me to-night. This place is so wretched now; for time, that in you and me has only strengthened love, has wrought much ruin here."

Half leaning on me she led me from the precincts of Bretton Hall. We walked in silence over the waste that crowns the valley of the Whitelands, and being near the verge of the rocks saw the great pine-wood sloping downward, lighted near us by the moon, but soon lost in density. Along the mysterious line where the light changed into gloom, intricate shadows of withered summer bracken struck and receded in a mimic battle. Before us lay the Priests' Cliff. The moon was veiled here by a grove of elms, whose ever-swaying branches alternately increased and lessened her brightness. This was a place of notoriety—a veritable Golgotha—a haunt fit only for demons. Murder and theft had been punished here, and to this day fireside stories are told of evil women dancing around that Druids' circle, carrying hearts plucked from gibbeted bodies.

"Rose," I whispered, "why have you brought me here?"

She made no reply, but pressed her head more closely to my shoulder. Scarcely had my lips closed than a sound like a hiss of a half-strangled snake vibrated among the trees. It grew louder and louder. A monstrous shadow hovered above.

Rose from my bosom murmured: "Love is strong as Death! Love is strong as Death!"

I locked her in my arms, so tightly that she grew breathless. "Hold me," she panted. "You are strong."

A cold hand touched our foreheads so that, benumbed, we sank together to the ground, to fall instantly into a dreamless slumber.

When I awoke the clear gray light of the early morning had spread over the country. Beyond the Hall garden the sun was just bursting through the clouds, and had already spread a long golden haze along the horizon. The babbling of the streamlet that runs down to Halkton was so distinct that it seemed almost at my side. How sweetly the wild thyme smelt! Filled with the tender recollections of the night, without turning I called Rose Pascal from her sleep.

"Sweetheart, sweetheart, waken! waken! waken! See how glad the world looks—see the omens of a happy future."

No answer came. I sat up, and looking round me saw that I was alone. A square stone lay near. When the sun was high I crept to read the inscription carved thereon: *"Here, at four cross-paths, lieth, with a stake through the bosom, the body of Rose Pascal, who in her sixteenth year wilfully cast away the life God gave."*

Rose Rose

Barry Pain

Sefton stepped back from his picture. "Rest now, please," he said.

Miss Rose Rose, his model, threw the striped blanket around her, stepped down from the throne, and crossed the studio. She seated herself on the floor near the big stove. For a few moments Sefton stood motionless, looking critically at his work. Then he laid down his palette and brushes and began to roll a cigarette. He was a man of forty, thick-set, round-faced, with a reddish moustache turned fiercely upwards. He flung himself down in an easy-chair, and smoked in silence till silence seemed ungracious.

"Well," he said, "I've got the place hot enough for you to-day, Miss Rose."

"You 'ave indeed," said Miss Rose.

"I bet it's nearer eighty than seventy."

The cigarette-smoke made a blue haze in the hot, heavy air. He watched it undulating, curving, melting.

As he watched it Miss Rose continued her observations. The trouble with these studios was the draughts. With a strong east wind, same as yesterday, you might have the stove red-hot, and yet never get the place, so to speak, warm. It is possible to talk commonly without talking like a coster, and Miss Rose achieved it. She did not always neglect the aspirate. She never quite substituted the third vowel for the first. She rather enjoyed long words.

She was beautiful from the crown of her head to the sole of her foot; and few models have good feet. Every pose she took was graceful. She was the daughter of a model, and had been herself a model from childhood. In consequence, she knew her work well and did it well. On one occasion, when sitting for the great Merion, she had kept the same pose, without a rest, for three consecutive hours. She was proud of that. Naturally she stood in the first rank among models, was most in demand, and made the most money. Her fault was that she was slightly capricious; you could not absolutely depend upon her. On a wintry morning, when every hour of daylight was precious, she might keep her appointment, she might be an hour or two late, or she might stay away altogether. Merion himself had suffered from her, had sworn never to employ her again, and had gone back to her.

Sefton, as he watched the blue smoke, found that her common accent jarred on him. It even seemed to make it more difficult for him to get the right presentation of the "Aphrodite" that she was helping him to paint. One seemed to demand a poetical and cultured soul in so beautiful a body. Rose Rose was not poetical nor cultured; she was not even businesslike and educated.

Half an hour of silent and strenuous work followed. Then Sefton growled that he could not see any longer.

"We'll stop for to-day," he said. Miss Rose Rose retired behind the screen. Sefton opened a window and both ventilators, and rolled another cigarette. The studio became rapidly cooler.

"To-morrow, at nine?" he called out.

"I've got some way to come," came the voice of Miss Rose from behind the screen. "I could be here by a quarter past."

"Right," said Sefton, as he slipped on his coat.

When Rose Rose emerged from the screen she was dressed in a blue serge costume, with a picture-hat. As it was her business in life to be beautiful, she never wore corsets, high heels, nor pointed toes. Such abnegation is rare among models.

"I say, Mr. Sefton," said Rose, "you were to settle at the end of the sittings, but—"

"Oh, you don't want any money, Miss Rose. You're known to be rich."

"Well, what I've got is in the Post Office, and I don't want to touch it. And I've got some shopping I must do before I go home."

Sefton pulled out his sovereign-case hesitatingly.

"This is all very well, you know," he said.

"I know what you are thinking, Mr. Sefton. You think I don't mean to come to-morrow. That's all Mr. Merion, now, isn't it? He's always saying things about me. I'm not going to stick it. I'm going to 'ave it out with 'im."

"He recommended you to me. And I'll tell you what he said, if you won't repeat it. He said that I should be lucky if I got you, and that I'd better chain you to the studio."

"And all because I was once late—with a good reason for it, too. Besides, what's once? I suppose he didn't 'appen to tell you how often he's kept me waiting."

"Well, here you are, Miss Rose. But you'll really be here in time to-morrow, won't you? Otherwise the thing will have got too tacky to work into."

"You needn't worry about that," said Miss Rose, eagerly. "I'll be here, whatever happens, by a quarter past nine. I'll be here if I die first! There, is that good enough for you? Good afternoon, and thank you, Mr. Sefton."

"Good afternoon, Miss Rose. Let me manage that door for you—the key goes a bit stiffly."

Sefton came back to his picture. In spite of Miss Rose's vehement assurances he felt by no means sure of her, but it was difficult for him to refuse any woman anything, and impossible for him to refuse to pay her what he really owed. He scrawled in charcoal some directions to the charwoman who would come in the morning. She was, from his point of view, a prize charwoman—one who could, and did, wash brushes properly, one who understood the stove, and would, when required, refrain from sweeping. He picked up his hat and went out. He walked the short distance from his studio to his bachelor flat, looked over an evening paper as he drank his tea, and then changed his clothes and took a cab to the club for dinner. He played one game of billiards after dinner, and then went home. His picture was very much in his mind. He wanted to be up fairly early in the morning, and he went to bed early.

He was at his studio by half-past eight. The stove was lighted, and he piled more coke on it. His "Aphrodite" seemed to have a somewhat mocking expression. It was a little, technical thing, to be corrected easily. He set his palette and selected his brushes. An attempt to roll a cigarette revealed the fact that his pouch was empty. It still wanted a few minutes to nine. He would have time to go up to the tobacconist at the corner. In case Rose Rose arrived while he was away, he left the studio door open. The tobacconist was also a news-agent, and he bought a morning paper. Rose would probably be twenty minutes late at the least, and this would be something to occupy him.

But on his return he found his model already stepping onto the throne.

"Good-morning, Miss Rose. You're a lady of your word." He hardly heeded the murmur which came to him as a reply. He threw his cigarette into the stove, picked up his palette, and got on excellently. The work was absorbing. For some time he thought of nothing else. There was no relaxing on the part of the model—no sign of fatigue. He had been working forever an hour, when his conscience smote him. "We'll have a rest now, Miss Rose," he said cheerily. At the same moment he felt human fingers drawn lightly across the back of his neck, just above the collar. He turned round with a sudden start. There was nobody there. He turned back again to the throne. Rose Rose had vanished.

With the utmost care and deliberation he put down his palette and brushes. He said in a loud voice, "Where are you, Miss Rose?" For a moment or two silence hung in the hot air of the studio.

He repeated his question and got no answer. Then he stepped behind the screen, and suddenly the most terrible thing in his life happened to him. He knew that his model had never been there at all.

There was only one door out to the back street in which his studio was placed, and that door was now locked. He unlocked it, put on his hat, and went out. For a minute or two he paced the street, but he had got to go back to the studio.

He went back, sat down in the easy-chair, lit a cigarette, and tried for a plausible explanation. Undoubtedly he had been working very hard lately. When he had come back from the tobacconist's to the studio he had been in the state of expectant attention, and he was enough of a psychologist to know that in that state you are especially likely to see what you expect to see. He was not conscious of anything abnormal in himself. He did not feel ill, or even nervous. Nothing of the kind had ever happened to him before. The more he considered the matter, the more definite became his state. He was thoroughly frightened. With a great effort he pulled himself together and picked up the newspaper. It was certain that he could do no more work for that day, anyhow. An ordinary, commonplace newspaper would restore him. Yes, that was it. He had been too much wrapped up in the picture. He had simply supposed the model to be there.

He was quite unconvinced, of course, and merely trying to convince himself. As an artist, he knew that for the last hour or more he had been getting the most delicate modelling right from the living form before him. But he did his best, and read the newspaper assiduously. He read of tariff, protection, and of a new music-hall star. Then his eye fell on a paragraph headed "Motor Fatalities."

He read that Miss Rose, an artist's model, had been knocked down by a car in the Fulham Road about seven o'clock on the previous evening; that the owner of the car had stopped and taken her to the hospital, and that she had expired within a few minutes of admission.

He rose from his place and opened a large pocket-knife. There was a strong impulse upon him, and he felt it to be a mad impulse, to slash the canvas to rags. He stopped before the picture. The face smiled at him with a sweetness that was scarcely earthly.

He went back to his chair again. "I'm not used to this kind of thing," he said aloud. A board creaked at the far end of the studio. He jumped up with a start of horror. A few minutes later he had left the studio, and locked the door behind him. His commonsense was still with him. He ought to go to a specialist. But the picture—

"What's the matter with Sefton?" said Devigne one night at the club after dinner.

"Don't know that anything's the matter with him," said Merion. "He hasn't been here lately."

"I saw him the last time he was here, and he seemed pretty queer. Wanted to let me his studio."

"It's not a bad studio," said Merion, dispassionately.

"He's got rid of it now, anyhow. He's got a studio out at Richmond, and the deuce of a lot of time he must waste getting there and back. Besides, what does he do about models?"

"That's a point I've been wondering about myself," said Merion. "He'd got Rose Rose for his 'Aphrodite,' and it looked as if it might be a pretty good thing when I saw it. But, as you know, she died. She was troublesome in some ways, but, taking her all round, I don't know where to find anybody as good today. What's Sefton doing about it?"

"He hasn't got a model at all at present. I know that for a fact, because I asked him."

"Well," said Merion, "he may have got the thing on further than I thought he would in the time. Some chaps can work from memory all right, though I can't do it myself. He's not chucked the picture, I suppose?"

"No; he's not done that. In fact, the picture's his excuse now, if you want him to go anywhere and do anything. But that's not it: the chap's altogether changed. He used to be a genial sort of bounder—bit tyrannical in his manner, perhaps—thought he knew everything. Still, you could talk to him. He was sociable. As a matter of fact, he did know a good deal. Now it's quite different. If you ever do see him—and that's not often—he's got nothing to say to you. He's just going back to his work. That sort of thing."

"You're too imaginative," said Merion. "I never knew a man who varied less than Sefton. Give me his address, will you? I mean his studio. I'll go and look him up one morning. I should like to see how that 'Aphrodite's' getting on. I tell you it was promising; no nonsense about it."

* * * * *

One sunny morning Merion knocked at the door of the studio at Richmond. He heard the sound of footsteps crossing the studio, then Sefton's voice rang out.

"Who's there?"

"Merion. I've travelled miles to see the thing you call a picture."

"I've got a model."

"And what does that matter?" asked Merion.

"Well, I'd be awfully glad if you'd come back in an hour. We'd have lunch together somewhere."

"Right," said Merion, sardonically. "I'll come back in about seven million hours. Wait for me."

He went back to London and his own studio in a state of fury. Sefton had never been a man to pose. He had never put on side about his work. He was always willing to show it to old and intimate friends whose judgment he could trust; and now, when the oldest of his friends had travelled down to Richmond to see him, he was told to come back in an hour, and that they might then lunch together!

"This lets me out," said Merion, savagely.

But he always speaks well of Sefton nowadays. He maintains that Sefton's "Aphrodite" would have been a success anyhow. The suicide made a good deal of talk at the time, and a special attendant was necessary to regulate the crowds round it, when, as directed by his will, the picture was exhibited at the Royal Academy. He was found in his studio many hours after his death; and he had scrawled on a blank canvas, much as he left his directions to his charwoman: "I have finished it, but I can't stand any more."

The Shell of Sense

Olivia Howard Dunbar

It was intolerably unchanged, the dim dark-toned room. In an agony of recognition my glance ran from one to another of the comfortable, familiar things that my earthly life had been passed among. Incredibly distant from it all as I essentially was, I noted sharply that the very gaps that I myself had left in my bookshelves still stood unfilled; that the delicate fingers of the ferns that I had tended were still stretched futilely toward the light; that the soft agreeable chuckle of my own little clock, like some elderly woman with whom conversation has become automatic, was undiminished.

Unchanged—or so it seemed at first. But there were certain trivial differences that shortly smote me. The windows were closed too tightly; for I had always kept the house very cool, although I had known that Theresa preferred warm rooms. And my work-basket was in disorder: it was preposterous that so small a thing should hurt me so. Then, for this was my first experience of the shadow-folded transition, the odd alternation of my emotions bewildered me. For at one moment the place seemed so humanly familiar, so distinctly my own proper envelope, that for love of it I could have laid my cheek against the wall; while in the next I was miserably conscious of strange new shrillnesses. How could they be endured—and had I ever endured them?—those harsh influences that I now perceived at the window; light and color so blinding that they obscured the form of the wind, tumult so discordant that one could scarcely hear the roses open in the garden below?

But Theresa did not seem to mind any of these things. Disorder, it is true, the dear child had never minded. She was sitting all this time at my desk—at *my* desk—occupied. I could only too easily surmise how. In the light of my own habits of precision it was plain that that sombre correspondence should have been attended to before; but I believe that I did not really reproach Theresa, for I knew that her notes, when she did write them, were perhaps less perfunctory than mine. She finished the last one as I watched her, and added it to the heap of black-bordered envelopes that lay on the desk. Poor girl! I saw now that they had cost her tears. Yet, living beside her day after day, year after year, I had never discovered what deep tenderness my sister possessed.

Toward each other it had been our habit to display only a temperate affection, and I remember having always thought it distinctly fortunate for Theresa, since she was denied my happiness, that she could live so easily and pleasantly without emotions of the devastating sort. . . . And now, for the first time, I was really to behold her. . . . Could it be Theresa, after all, this tangle of subdued turbulences? Let no one suppose that it is an easy thing to bear, the relentlessly lucid understanding that I then first exercised; or that, in its first enfranchisement, the timid vision does not yearn for its old screens and mists.

Suddenly, as Theresa sat there, her head, filled with its tender thoughts of me, held in her gentle hands, I felt Allan's step on the carpeted stair outside. Theresa felt it, too,—but how? for it was not audible. She gave a start, swept the black envelopes out of sight, and pretended to be writing in a little book. Then I forgot to watch her any longer in my absorption in Allan's coming. It was he, of course, that I was awaiting. It was for him that I had made this first lonely, frightened effort to return, to recover. . . . It was not that I had supposed he would allow himself to recognize my presence, for I had long been sufficiently familiar with his hard and fast denials of the invisible. He was so reasonable always so sane—so blindfolded. But I had hoped that because of his very rejection of the other that now contained me I could perhaps all the more safely, the more secretly, watch him, linger near him. He was near now, very near,—but why did Theresa, sitting there in the room that had never belonged to her, appropriate for herself his coming? It was so manifestly I who had drawn him, I whom he had come to seek.

The door was ajar. He knocked softly at it. "Are you there, Theresa?" he called. He expected to find her, then, there in my room? I shrank back, fearing, almost, to stay.

"I shall have finished in a moment," Theresa told him, and he sat down to wait for her.

No spirit still unreleased can understand the pang that I felt with Allan sitting almost within my touch. Almost irresistibly the wish beset me to let him for an instant feel my nearness. Then I checked myself, remembering—oh, absurd, piteous human fears!—that my too unguarded closeness might alarm him. It was not so remote a time that I myself had known them, those blind, uncouth timidities. I came, therefore, somewhat nearer—but I did not touch him. I merely leaned toward him and with incredible softness whispered his name. That much I could not have forborne; the spell of life was still too strong in me.

But it gave him no comfort, no delight.

"Theresa!" he called, in a voice dreadful with alarm—and in that instant the last veil fell, and desperately, scarce believingly, I beheld how it stood between them, those two.

She turned to him that gentle look of hers.

"Forgive me," came from him hoarsely. "But I had suddenly the most—unaccountable sensation. Can there be too many windows open? There is such a—chill—about."

"There are no windows open," Theresa assured him. "I took care to shut out the chill. You are not well, Allan!"

"Perhaps not." He embraced the suggestion. "And yet I feel no illness apart from this abominable sensation that persists—persists. . . . Theresa, you must tell me: do I fancy it, or do you, too, feel—something—strange here?"

"Oh, there is something very strange here," she half sobbed. "There always will be."

"Good heavens, child, I didn't mean that!" He rose and stood looking about him. "I know, of course, that you have your beliefs, and I respect them, but you know equally well that I have nothing of the sort! So—don't let us conjure up anything inexplicable."

I stayed impalpably, imponderably near him. Wretched and bereft though I was, I could not have left him while he stood denying me.

"What I mean," he went on, in his low, distinct voice, "is a special, an almost ominous sense of cold. Upon my soul, Theresa,"—he paused—"if I *were* superstitious, if I *were* a woman, I should probably imagine it to seem—a presence!"

He spoke the last word very faintly. but Theresa shrank from it nevertheless.

"*Don't* say that, Allan!" she cried out. "Don't think it, I beg of you! I've tried so hard myself not to think it—and you must help me. You know it is only perturbed, uneasy spirits that wander. With her it is quite different. She has always been so happy—she must still be."

I listened, stunned, to Theresa's sweet dogmatism. From what blind distances came her confident misapprehensions, how dense, both for her and for Allan, was the separating vapor!

Allan frowned. "Don't take me literally, Theresa," he explained; and I, who a moment before had almost touched him, now held myself aloof and heard him with a strange untried pity, new born in me. "I'm not speaking of what you call—spirits. It's something much more terrible." He allowed his head to sink heavily on his chest. "If I did not positively know that I had never done her any harm, I should suppose myself to be suffering from guilt, from remorse. . . . Theresa, you know better than I, perhaps. Was she content, always? Did she believe in me?"

"Believe in you?—when she knew you to be so good!—when you adored her!"

"She thought that? She said it? Then what in Heaven's name ails me?—unless it is all as you believe, Theresa, and she knows now what she didn't know then, poor dear, and minds—"

"Minds what? What do you mean, Allan?"

I, who with my perhaps illegitimate advantage saw so clear, knew that he had not meant to tell her: I did him that justice, even in my first jealousy. If I had not tortured him so by clinging near him, he would not have told her. But the moment came, and overflowed, and he did tell her—passionate, tumultuous story that it was. During all our life together, Allan's and mine, he had spared me, had kept me wrapped in the white cloak of an unblemished loyalty. But it would have been kinder, I now bitterly thought, if, like many husbands, he had years ago found for the story he now poured forth some clandestine listener; I should not have known. But he was faithful and good, and so he waited till I, mute and chained, was there to hear him. So well did I know him, as I thought, so thoroughly had he once been mine, that I saw it in his eyes, heard it in his voice, before the words came. And yet, when it came, it lashed me with the whips of an unbearable humiliation. For I, his wife, had not known how greatly he could love.

And that Theresa, soft little traitor, should, in her still way, have cared too! Where was the iron in her, I moaned within my stricken spirit, where the steadfastness? From the moment he bade her, she turned her soft little petals up to him—and my last delusion was spent. It was intolerable; and none the less so that in another moment she had, prompted by some belated thought of me, renounced him. Allan was hers, yet she put him from her; and it was my part to watch them both.

Then in the anguish of it all I remembered, awkward, untutored spirit that I was, that I now had the Great Recourse. Whatever human things were unbearable, I had no need to hear. I ceased, therefore. to make the effort that kept me with them. The pitiless poignancy was dulled, the sounds and the light ceased, the lovers faded from me, and again I was mercifully drawn into the dim, infinite spaces.

There followed a period whose length I cannot measure and during which I was able to make no progress in the difficult, dizzying experience of release. "Earth-bound" my jealousy relentlessly kept me. Though my two dear ones had forsworn each other, I could not trust them, for theirs seemed to me an affectation of a more than mortal magnanimity. Without a ghostly sentinel to prick them with sharp fears and recollections, who could believe that they would keep to it? Of the efficacy of my own vigilance, so long as I might choose to exercise it, I could have no doubt, for I had by this time come to have a dreadful exultation in the new power that lived in me. Repeated delicate experiment had taught me how a touch or a breath, a wish or a whisper, could control Allan's acts, could keep him from Theresa. I could manifest myself as palely, as transiently, as a thought. I could produce the merest necessary flicker, like the shadow of a just-opened leaf, on his trembling, tortured consciousness. And these unrealized perceptions of me he interpreted, as I had known that he would, as his soul's inevitable penance. He had come to believe that he had done evil in silently loving Theresa all these years, and it was my vengeance to allow him to believe this, to prod him ever to believe it afresh.

I am conscious that this frame of mind was not continuous in me. For I remember, too, that when Allan and Theresa were safely apart and sufficiently miserable I loved them as dearly as I ever had, more dearly perhaps. For it was impossible that I should not perceive, in my new emancipation, that they were, each of them, something more and greater than the two beings I had once ignorantly pictured them. For years they had practised a selflessness of which I could once scarcely have conceived, and which even now I could only admire without entering into its mystery. While I had lived solely for myself, these two divine creatures had lived exquisitely for me. They had granted me everything, themselves nothing. For my undeserving sake their lives had been a constant torment of renunciation—a torment they had not sought to alleviate by the exchange of a single glance of understanding. There were even marvellous moments when, from the depths of my newly informed heart, I pitied them:—poor creatures, who, withheld from the infinite solaces that I had come to know, were still utterly within that

Shell of sense
So frail, so piteously contrived for pain.

Within it, yes; yet exercising qualities that so sublimely transcended it. Yet the shy, hesitating compassion that thus had birth in me was far from being able to defeat the earlier, earthlier emotion. The two, I recognized, were in a sort of conflict; and I, regarding it, assumed that the conflict would never end; that for years, as Allan and Theresa reckoned time, I should be obliged to withhold myself from the great spaces and linger suffering, grudging, shamed, where they lingered.

It can never have been explained, I suppose, what, to devitalized perception such as mine, the contact of mortal beings with each other appears to be. Once to have exercised this sense-freed perception is to realize that the gift of prophecy, although the subject of such frequent marvel, is no longer mysterious. The merest glance of our sensitive and uncloyed vision can detect the strength of the relation between two beings, and therefore instantly calculate its duration. If you see a heavy weight suspended from a slender string, you can know, without any wizardry, that in a few moments the string will snap; well, such, if you admit the analogy, is prophecy, is foreknowledge. And it was thus that I saw it with Theresa and Allan. For it was perfectly visible to me that they would very little longer have the strength to preserve, near each other, the denuded impersonal relation that they, and that I, behind them, insisted on; and that they would have to separate. It was my sister, perhaps the more sensitive, who first realized this. It had now become possible for me to observe them almost constantly, the effort necessary to visit them had so greatly diminished; so that I watched her, poor, anguished girl, prepare to leave him. I saw each reluctant movement that she made. I saw her eyes, worn from self-searching; I heard her step grown timid from inexplicable fears; I entered her very heart and heard its pitiful, wild beating. And still I did not interfere.

For at this time I had a wonderful, almost demoniacal sense of disposing of matters to suit my own selfish will. At any moment I could have checked their miseries, could have restored happiness and peace. Yet it gave me, and I could weep to admit it, a monstrous joy to know that Theresa thought she was leaving Allan of her own free intention, when it was I who was contriving, arranging, insisting. . . . And yet she wretchedly felt my presence near her; I am certain of that.

A few days before the time of her intended departure my sister told Allan that she must speak with him after dinner. Our beautiful old house branched out from a circular hall with great arched doors at either end; and it was through the rear doorway that always in summer, after dinner, we passed out into the garden adjoining. As usual, therefore, when the hour came, Theresa led the way. That dreadful daytime brilliance that in my present state I found so hard to endure was now becoming softer. A delicate, capricious twilight breeze danced inconsequently through languidly whispering leaves. Lovely pale flowers blossomed like little moons in the dusk, and over them the breath of mignonette hung heavily. It was a perfect place—and it had so long been ours, Allan's and mine. It made me restless and a little wicked that those two should be there together now.

For a little they walked about together, speaking of common, daily things. Then suddenly Theresa burst out:

"I am going away, Allan. I have stayed to do everything that needed to be done. Now your mother will be here to care for you, and it is time for me to go."

He stared at her and stood still. Theresa had been there so long, she so definitely, to his mind, belonged there. And she was, as I also had jealously known, so lovely there, the small, dark, dainty creature, in the old hall, on the wide staircases, in the garden. . . . Life there without Theresa, even the intentionally remote, the perpetually renounced Theresa—he had not dreamed of it, he could not, so suddenly, conceive of it.

"Sit here," he said, and drew her down beside him on a bench, "and tell me what it means, why you are going. Is it because of something that I have been—have done?"

She hesitated. I wondered if she would dare tell him. She looked out and away from him, and he waited long for her to speak.

The pale stars were sliding into their places. The whispering of the leaves was almost hushed. All about them it was still and shadowy and sweet. It was that wonderful moment when, for lack of a visible horizon, the not yet darkened world seems infinitely greater—a moment when anything can happen, anything be believed in. To me, watching, listening, hovering. there came a dreadful purpose and a dreadful courage. Suppose, for one moment, Theresa should not only feel, but see me—would she dare to tell him then?

There came a brief space of terrible effort, all my fluttering, uncertain forces strained to the utmost. The instant of my struggle was endlessly long and the transition seemed to take place outside me—as one sitting in a train, motionless, sees the leagues of earth float by. And then, in a bright, terrible flash I knew I had achieved it—I had attained visibility. Shuddering, insubstantial, but luminously apparent, I stood there before them. And for the instant that I maintained the visible state I looked straight into Theresa's soul.

She gave a cry. And then, thing of silly, cruel impulses that I was, I saw what I had done. The very thing that I wished to avert I had precipitated. For Allan, in his sudden terror and pity, had bent and caught her in his arms. For the first time they were together; and it was I who had brought them.

Then, to his whispered urging to tell the reason of her cry, Theresa said:

"Frances was here. You did not see her, standing there, under the lilacs, with no smile on her face?"

"My dear, my dear!" was all that Allan said. I had so long now lived invisibly with them, he knew that she was right.

"I suppose you know what it means?" she asked him, calmly.

"Dear Theresa," Allan said, slowly, "if you and I should go away somewhere, could we not evade all this ghostliness? And will you come with me?"

"Distance would not banish her," my sister confidently asserted. And then she said. softly: "Have you thought what a lonely, awesome thing it must be to be so newly dead? Pity her, Allan. We who are warm and alive should pity her. She loves you still,—that is the meaning of it all, you know—and she wants us to understand that for that reason we must keep apart. Oh, it was so plain in her white face as she stood there. And you did not see her?"

"It was your face that I saw," Allan solemnly told her—oh, how different he had grown from the Allan that I had known!—"and yours is the only face that I shall ever see." And again he drew her to him.

She sprang from him. "You are defying her, Allan!" she cried. "And you must not. It is her right to keep us apart, if she wishes. It must be as she insists. I shall go, as I told you. And, Allan, I beg of you, leave me the courage to do as she demands!"

They stood facing each other in the deep dusk, and the wounds that I had dealt them gaped red and accusing. "We must pity her," Theresa had said. And as I remembered that extraordinary speech, and saw the agony in her face, and the greater agony in Allan's, there came the great irreparable cleavage between mortality and me. In a swift, merciful flame the last of my mortal emotions—gross and tenacious they must have been—was consumed. My cold grasp of Allan loosened and a new unearthly love of him bloomed in my heart.

I was now, however, in a difficulty with which my experience in the newer state was scarcely sufficient to deal. How could I make it plain to Allan and Theresa that I wished to bring them together, to heal the wounds that I had made?

Pityingly, remorsefully, I lingered near them all that night and the next day. And by that time I had brought myself to the point of a great determination. In the little time that was left, before Theresa should be gone and Allan bereft and desolate, I saw the one way that lay open to me to convince them of my acquiescence in their destiny.

In the deepest darkness and silence of the next night I made a greater effort than it will ever be necessary for me to make again. When they think of me, Allan and Theresa, I pray now that they will recall what I did that night, and that my thousand frustrations and selfishnesses may shrivel and be blown from their indulgent memories.

Yet the following morning, as she had planned, Theresa appeared at breakfast dressed for her journey. Above in her room there were the sounds of departure. They spoke little during the brief meal, but when it was ended Allan said:

"Theresa, there is half an hour before you go. Will you come up-stairs with me? I had a dream that I must tell you of."

"Allan!" She looked at him, frightened, but went with him. "It was of Frances you dreamed," she said, quietly, as they entered the library together.

"Did I say it was a dream? But I was awake—thoroughly awake. I had not been sleeping well, and I heard, twice, the striking of the clock. And as I lay there, looking out at the stars, and thinking—thinking of you, Theresa,—she came to me, stood there before me, in my room. It was no sheeted spectre, you understand; it was Frances, literally she. In some inexplicable fashion I seemed to be aware that she wanted to make me know something, and I waited, watching her face. After a few moments it came. She did not speak, precisely. That is, I am sure I heard no sound. Yet the words that came from her were definite enough. She said: 'Don't let Theresa leave you. Take her and keep her.' Then she went away. Was that a dream?"

"I had not meant to tell you," Theresa eagerly answered, "but now I must. It is too wonderful. What time did your clock strike, Allan?"

"One, the last time."

"Yes; it was then that I awoke. And she had been with me. I had not seen her, but her arm had been about me and her kiss was on my cheek. Oh, I knew; it was unmistakable. And the sound of her voice was with me."

"Then she bade you, too—"

"Yes, to stay with you. I am glad we told each other." She smiled tearfully and began to fasten her wrap.

"But you are not going—*now*!" Allan cried. "You know that you cannot, now that she has asked you to stay."

"Then you believe, as I do, that it was she?" Theresa demanded.

"I can never understand, but I know," he answered her. "And now you will not go?"

I am freed. There will be no further semblance of me in my old home, no sound of my voice, no dimmest echo of my earthly self. They have no further need of me, the two that I have brought together. Theirs is the fullest joy that the dwellers in the shell of sense can know. Mine is the transcendent joy of the unseen spaces.

The Soul of Laploshka

Saki

Laploshka was one of the meanest men I have ever met, and quite one of the most entertaining. He said horrid things about other people in such a charming way that one forgave him for the equally horrid things he said about oneself behind one's back. Hating anything in the way of illnatured gossip ourselves, we are always grateful to those who do it for us and do it well. And Laploshka did it really well.

Naturally Laploshka had a large circle of acquaintances, and as he exercised some care in their selection it followed that an appreciable proportion were men whose bank balances enabled them to acquiesce indulgently in his rather one-sided views on hospitality. Thus, although possessed of only moderate means, he was able to live comfortably within his income, and still more comfortably within those of various tolerantly disposed associates.

But towards the poor or to those of the same limited resources as himself his attitude was one of watchful anxiety; he seemed to be haunted by a besetting fear lest some fraction of a shilling or franc, or whatever the prevailing coinage might be, should be diverted from his pocket or service into that of a hard-up companion. A two-franc cigar would be cheerfully offered to a wealthy patron, on the principle of doing evil that good may come, but I have known him indulge in agonies of perjury rather than admit the incriminating possession of a copper coin when change was needed to tip a waiter. The coin would have been duly returned at the earliest opportunity—he would have taken means to ensure against forgetfulness on the part of the borrower—but accidents might happen, and even the temporary estrangement from his penny or sou was a calamity to be avoided.

The knowledge of this amiable weakness offered a perpetual temptation to play upon Laploshka's fears of involuntary generosity. To offer him a lift in a cab and pretend not to have enough money to pay the fair, to fluster him with a request for a sixpence when his hand was full of silver just received in change, these were a few of the petty torments that ingenuity prompted as occasion afforded. To do justice to Laploshka's resourcefulness it must be admitted that he always emerged somehow or other from the most embarrassing dilemma without in any way compromising his reputation for saying "No." But the gods send opportunities at some time to most men, and mine came one evening when Laploshka and I were supping together in a cheap boulevard restaurant. (Except when he was the bidden guest of some one with an irreproachable income, Laploshka was wont to curb his appetite for high living; on such fortunate occasions he let it go on an easy snaffle.) At the conclusion of the meal a somewhat urgent message called me away, and without heeding my companion's agitated protest, I called back cruelly, "Pay my share; I'll settle with you to-morrow." Early on the morrow Laploshka hunted me down by instinct as I walked along a side street that I hardly ever frequented. He had the air of a man who had not slept.

"You owe me two francs from last night," was his breathless greeting.

I spoke evasively of the situation in Portugal, where more trouble seemed brewing. But Laploshka listened with the abstraction of the deaf adder, and quickly returned to the subject of the two francs.

"I'm afraid I must owe it to you," I said lightly and brutally. "I haven't a sou in the world," and I added mendaciously, "I'm going away for six months or perhaps longer."

Laploshka said nothing, but his eyes bulged a little and his cheeks took on the mottled hues of an ethnographical map of the Balkan Peninsula. That same day, at sundown, he died. "Failure of the heart's action" was the doctor's verdict; but I, who knew better, knew that he had died of grief.

There arose the problem of what to do with his two francs. To have killed Laploshka was one thing; to have kept his beloved money would have argued a callousness of feeling of which I am not capable. The ordinary solution, of giving it to the poor, would by no means fit the present situation, for nothing would have distressed the dead man more than such a misuse of his property. On the other hand, the bestowal of two francs on the rich was an operation which called for some tact. An easy way out of the difficulty seemed, however, to present itself the following Sunday, as I was wedged into the cosmopolitan crowd which filled the side-aisle of one of the most popular Paris churches. A collecting-bag, for "the poor of Monsieur le Curé" was buffeting its tortuous way across the seemingly impenetrable human sea, and a German in front of me, who evidently did not wish his appreciation of the magnificent music to be marred by a suggestion of payment, made audible criticisms to his companion on the claims of the said charity.

"They do not want money," he said; "they have too much money. They have no poor. They are all pampered."

If that were really the case my way seemed clear. I dropped Laploshka's two francs into the bag with a murmured blessing on the rich of Monsieur le Curé.

Some three weeks later chance had taken me to Vienna, and I sat one evening regaling myself in a humble but excellent little Gasthaus up in the Währinger quarter. The appointments were primitive, but the Schnitzel, the beer, and the cheese could not have been improved on. Good cheer brought good custom, and with the exception of one small table near the door every place was occupied. Half-way through my meal I happened to glance in the direction of that empty seat, and saw that it was no longer empty. Poring over the bill of fare with the absorbed scrutiny of one who seeks the cheapest among the cheap was Laploshka. Once he looked across at me, with a comprehensive glance at my repast, as though to say, "It is my two francs you are eating," and then looked swiftly away. Evidently the poor of Monsieur le Curé had been genuine poor. The Schnitzel turned to leather in my mouth, the beer seemed tepid; I left the Emmenthaler untasted. My one idea was to get away from the room, away from the table where *that* was seated; and as I fled I felt Laploshka's reproachful eyes watching the amount that I gave to the piccolo—out of his two francs. I lunched next day at an expensive restaurant which I felt sure that the living Laploshka would never have entered on his own account, and I hoped that the dead Laploshka would observe the same barriers. I was not mistaken, but as I came out I found him miserably studying the bill of fare stuck up on the portals. Then he slowly made his way over to a milk-hall. For the first time in my experience I missed the charm and gaiety of Vienna life.

After that, in Paris or London or wherever I happened to be, I continued to see a good deal of Laploshka. If I had a seat in a box at a theatre I was always conscious of his eyes furtively watching me from the dim recesses of the gallery. As I turned into my club on a rainy afternoon I would see him taking inadequate shelter in a doorway opposite. Even if I indulged in the modest luxury of a penny chair in the Park he generally confronted me from one of the free benches, never staring at me, but always elaborately conscious of my presence. My friends began to comment on my changed looks, and advised me to leave off heaps of things. I should have liked to have left off Laploshka.

On a certain Sunday—it was probably Easter, for the crush was worse than ever—I was again wedged into the crowd listening to the music in the fashionable Paris church, and again the collection-bag was buffeting its way across the human sea. An English lady behind me was making ineffectual efforts to convey a coin into the still distant bag, so I took the money at her request and helped it forward to its destination. It was a two-franc piece. A swift inspiration came to me, and I merely dropped my own sou into the bag and slid the silver coin into my pocket. I had withdrawn Laploshka's two francs from the poor, who should never have had that legacy. As I backed away from the crowd I heard a woman's voice say, "I don't believe he put my money in the bag. There are swarms of people in Paris like that!" But my mind was lighter than it had been for a long time.

The delicate mission of bestowing the retrieved sum on the deserving rich still confronted me. Again I trusted to the inspiration of accident, and again fortune favoured me. A shower drove me, two days later, into one of the historic churches on the left bank of the Seine, and there I found, peering at the old wood-carvings, the Baron R., one of the wealthiest and most shabbily dressed men in Paris. It was now or never. Putting a strong American inflection into the French which I usually talked with an unmistakable British accent, I catechised the Baron as to the date of the church's building, its dimensions, and other details which an American tourist would be certain to want to know. Having acquired such information as the Baron was able to impart on short notice, I solemnly placed the two-franc piece in his hand, with the hearty assurance that it was "pour vous," and turned to go. The Baron was slightly taken aback, but accepted the situation with a good grace. Walking over to a small box fixed in the wall, he dropped Laploshka's two francs into the slot. Over the box was the inscription, "Pour les pauvres de M. le Curé."

That evening, at the crowded corner by the Café de la Paix, I caught a fleeting glimpse of Laploshka. He smiled, slightly raised his hat, and vanished. I never saw him again. After all, the money had been *given* to the deserving rich, and the soul of Laploshka was at peace.

The Specter

Guy de Maupassant

In speaking of a recent lawsuit, our conversation had turned on sequestration, and each of us, thereupon, had a story to tell — a story affirmed to be true. We were a party of intimate friends, who had passed a pleasant evening, now drawing to a close, in an old family residence in the Rue de Grenelle. The aged Marquis de la Tour-Samuel, bowed 'neath the weight of eighty-two winters, at last rose, and leaning on the mantelpiece, said, in somewhat trembling tones:

"I also know something strange, so strange that it has been a haunting memory all my life. It is now fifty-six years since the incident occurred, and yet not a month has passed in which I have not seen it again in a dream, so great was and is the impression of fear it left on my mind. For ten minutes I experienced such horrible fright that, ever since, a sort of constant terror has made me tremble at unexpected noises, and objects half-seen in the gloom of night inspire me with a mad desire to take flight. In short I am afraid of the dark!

"Ah, no! I would not have avowed that before having reached my present age! Now I can say anything. I have never receded before real danger. So at eighty-two years of age, I do not feel compelled to be brave over an imaginary danger.

"The affair upset me so completely, and caused me such lasting and mysterious uneasiness, that I never spoke of it to anyone. I will now tell it to you exactly as it happened, without any attempt at explanation.

"In July, 1827, I was in garrison at Rouen. One day, as I was walking on the quay, I met a man whom I thought I recognized, without being able to recall exactly who he was. Instinctively, I made a movement to stop; the stranger perceived it and at once extended his hand.

"He was a friend to whom I had been deeply attached as a youth. For five years I had not seen him, and he seemed to have aged half a century. His hair was quite white, and he walked with a stoop as though completely worn out. He apparently comprehended my surprise, for he told me of the misfortune which had shattered his life.

"Having fallen madly in love with a young girl he had married her, but, after a year of more than earthly happiness, she died suddenly of heart failure. He had left his château on the very day of her burial and had come to live at Rouen. There he still dwelt, more dead than alive, desperate and solitary, exhausted by grief, and so miserable that he thought constantly of suicide.

"'Now that I have found you again,' said he, 'I will ask you to render me an important service. It is to go to my old home and get for me, from the desk of my bedroom—our bedroom—some papers which I greatly need. I cannot send a servant or an agent, as discretion and absolute silence are necessary. As for myself, nothing on earth would induce me to re-enter that house. I will give you the key of the room, which I myself locked on leaving, and the key of my desk—also a note to my gardener, telling him to open the château for you. But come and breakfast with me to-morrow, and we will arrange all that.'

"I promised to do him the slight favor he asked. For that matter, it was nothing of a trip, his property being but a few miles distant from Rouen and easily reached in an hour on horseback.

"At ten o'clock the following day I breakfasted, tête-à-tête, with my friend, but he scarcely spoke.

"He begged me to pardon him; the thought of the visit I was about to make to that room, the scene of his dead happiness, overwhelmed him, he said. He, indeed, seemed singularly agitated and preoccupied, as though undergoing some mysterious mental combat.

"At length he explained to me exactly what I had to do. It was very simple. I must take two packages of letters and a roll of papers from the first drawer on the right of the desk of which I had the key. He added, 'I need not beg you to refrain from glancing at them.'

"I was wounded at that remark, and told him so somewhat sharply. He stammered, 'Forgive me, I suffer so,' and tears came to his eyes.

"At about one o'clock I took leave of him to accomplish my mission.

"The weather was glorious, and I cantered over the turf, listening to the songs of the larks and the rhythmical striking of my sword against my boot. Then I entered the forest and walked my horse. Branches of the trees caressed my face as I passed, and, now and then, I caught a leaf with my teeth, from sheer gladness of heart at being alive and strong on such a radiant day.

"As I approached the château, I took from my pocket the letter I had for the gardener, and was astonished at finding it sealed. I was so irritated that I was about to turn back without having fulfilled my promise, but reflected that I should thereby display undue susceptibility. My friend's state of mind might easily have caused him to close the envelope without noticing that he did so.

"The manor seemed to have been abandoned for twenty years. The open gate was dropping from its hinges; the walks were overgrown with grass, and the flower-beds were no longer distinguishable.

"The noise I made by tapping loudly on a shutter brought an old man from out a door near by, who seemed stunned with astonishment at seeing me. On receiving my letter, he read it, reread it, turned it over and over, looked me up and down, put the paper in his pocket, and finally asked:

"'Well! what is it you wish?'

"I replied shortly: 'You ought to know, since you have just read your master's orders. I wish to enter the château.'

"He seemed overcome. 'Then you are going in—in her room?'

"I began to lose patience and said sharply: 'Of course; but is that your affair?'

"He stammered in confusion: 'No—sir—but it is because—that is, it has not been opened since—since the—death. If you will be kind enough to wait five minutes, I will go to—to see if—'

"I interrupted him, angrily: 'Look here, what do you mean with your tricks? You know very well you cannot enter the room, since I have the key!'

"He no longer objected. 'Then, sir, I will show you the way.'

"'Show me the staircase and leave me. I'll find my way without you.'

"'But—sir—indeed—'

"This time I silenced him effectually, pushed him aside, and went into the house.

"I first traversed the kitchen; then two rooms occupied by the servant and his wife; next, by a wide hall, I reached the stairs, which I mounted, and recognized the door indicated by my friend.

"I easily opened it and entered. The apartment was so dark that, at first, I could distinguish nothing. I stopped short, my nostrils penetrated by the disagreeable, moldy odor of long-unoccupied rooms. Then, as my eyes slowly became accustomed to the darkness, I saw plainly enough, a large and disordered bedroom, the bed without sheets, but still retaining its mattresses and pillows, on one of which was a deep impression, as though an elbow or a head had recently rested there.

"The chairs all seemed out of place. I noticed that a door, doubtless that of a closet, had remained half open.

"I first went to the window, which I opened to let in the light; but the fastenings of the shutters had grown so rusty that I could not move them. I even tried to break them with my sword, but without success. As I was growing irritated over my useless efforts, and could now see fairly well in the semi-obscurity, I renounced the idea of getting more light and went over to the writing-table.

"Seating myself in an armchair and letting down the lid of the desk, I opened the designated drawer. It was full to the top. I needed but three packages, which I knew how to recognize, and began searching for them.

"I was straining my eyes in the effort to read the superscriptions, when I seemed to hear, or rather feel, something rustle back of me. I paid no attention, believing that a draught from the window was moving some drapery. But, in a minute or so, another movement, almost imperceptible, sent a strangely disagreeable little shiver over my skin. It was so stupid to be affected, even slightly, that self-respect prevented my turning around. I had then found the second packet I needed and was about to lay my hand on the third when a long and painful sigh, uttered just over my shoulder, made me bound like a madman from my seat and land several feet away. As I jumped I had turned about, my hand on the hilt of my sword, and, truly, had I not felt it at my side, I should have taken to my heels like a coward.

"A tall woman, dressed in white, stood gazing at me from the back of the chair where I had been sitting an instant before.

"Such a shudder ran through all my limbs that I nearly fell backward. No one can understand unless he has felt it, that frightful, unreasoning terror! The mind becomes vague; the heart ceases to beat; the entire body grows as limp as a sponge.

"I do not believe in ghosts, nevertheless I completely gave way to a hideous fear of the dead; and I suffered more in those few moments than in all the rest of my life, from the irresistible anguish of supernatural fright. If she had not spoken, I should have died, perhaps! But she spoke, she spoke in a sweet, sad voice, that set my nerves vibrating. I dare not say that I became master of myself and recovered my reason. No! I was so frightened that I scarcely knew what I was doing; but a certain innate pride, a remnant of soldierly instinct, made me, almost in spite of myself, maintain a creditable countenance.

"She said: 'Oh! sir, you can render me a great service.'

"I wanted to reply, but it was impossible for me to pronounce a word. Only a vague sound came from my throat.

"She continued: 'Will you? You can save me, cure me. I suffer frightfully. I suffer, oh! how I suffer!' and she slowly seated herself in the armchair, still looking at me.

"'Will you?' she said.

"I replied 'Yes' by a nod, my voice still being paralyzed.

"Then she held out to me a tortoise-shell comb, and murmured:

"'Comb my hair, oh! comb my hair; that will cure me; it must be combed. Look at my head—how I suffer; and my hair pulls so!'

"Her hair, unbound, very long and very black, it seemed to me, hung over the back of the chair and touched the floor.

"Why did I receive that comb with a shudder, and why did I take in my hands the long, black hair which gave to my skin a gruesomely cold sensation, as though I were handling snakes? I cannot tell.

"That sensation has remained in my fingers and I still tremble when I think of it.

"I combed her hair. I handled, I know not how, those icy locks. I twisted, knotted, and plaited, and braided them. She sighed and bowed her head, seeming to be happy. Suddenly she said: 'Thank you!' snatched the comb from my hands, and fled by the door that I had noticed ajar.

"Left alone, I experienced for several seconds the horrible agitation of one who awakens from a nightmare. At length I regained my full senses; I ran to the window, and with a mighty effort burst open the shutters, letting a flood of light into the room. Immediately I sprang to the door by which she had departed. I found it closed and immovable!

"Then a mad desire to flee came on me like a panic, the panic which soldiers know in battle. I seized the three packets of letters on the open secretary; ran from the room, dashed down the stairs, found myself outside, I know not how, and seeing my horse a few steps off, leaped into the saddle and galloped away.

"I stopped only when I reached Rouen and my lodgings. There I shut myself into my room to reflect. For an hour I anxiously strove to convince myself that I had been the victim of a hallucination. I was about ready to believe that all I had seen was a vision, an error of my senses, when, as I approached the window, my eyes fell, by chance, upon my chest. Around the buttons of my uniform were entwined a quantity of long, black hairs! One by one, with trembling fingers, I plucked them off and threw them away.

"I then called my orderly, feeling unable to see my friend that day; wishing, also, to reflect more fully upon what I ought to tell him. I had his letters carried to him, for which he gave the messenger a receipt. He asked after me most particularly, and, on being told I was ill—had had a sunstroke—appeared exceedingly anxious. Next morning I went to him, determined to tell him the truth. He had gone out the evening before and not yet returned. I called again during the day; my friend was still absent.

After waiting a week longer without news of him, I advised the authorities, and a judicial search was instituted. Not the slightest trace of his whereabouts or manner of disappearance was discovered.

"A minute inspection of the abandoned château revealed nothing of a suspicious character. There was no indication that a woman had been concealed there.

"After these fruitless researches all further efforts were abandoned, and in the fifty-six years that have elapsed since then I have heard nothing more."

A Spectral Collie

Elia W. Peattie

William Percy Cecil happened to be a younger son, so he left home—which was England—and went to Kansas to ranch it. Thousands of younger sons do the same, only their destination is not invariably Kansas.

An agent at Wichita picked out Cecil's farm for him and sent the deeds over to England before Cecil left. He said there was a house on the place. So Cecil's mother fitted him out for America just as she had fitted out another superfluous boy for Africa, and parted from him with an heroic front and big agonies of mother-ache which she kept to herself.

The boy bore up the way a man of his blood ought, but when he went out to the kennel to see Nita, his collie, he went to pieces somehow, and rolled on the grass with her in his arms and wept like a booby. But the remarkable part of it was that Nita wept too; big, hot dog tears which her master wiped away. When he went off she howled like a hungry baby, and had to be switched before she would give any one a night's sleep.

When Cecil got over on his Kansas place he fitted up the shack as cosily as he could, and learned how to fry bacon and make soda biscuits. Incidentally, he did farming, and sunk a heap of money, finding out how not to do things. Meantime, the Americans laughed at him, and were inclined to turn the cold shoulder, and his compatriots, of whom there were a number in the county, did not prove to his liking. They consoled themselves for their exiled state in fashions not in keeping with Cecil's traditions. His homesickness went deeper than theirs, perhaps, and American whiskey could not make up for the loss of his English home, nor flirtations with the gay American village girls quite compensate him for the loss of his English mother. So he kept to himself and had nostalgia as some men have consumption.

At length the loneliness got so bad that he had to see some living thing from home, or make a flunk of it and go back like a cry baby. He had a stiff pride still, though he sobbed himself to sleep more than one night, as many a pioneer has done before him. So he wrote home for Nita, the collie, and got word that she would be sent. Arrangements were made for her care all along the line, and she was properly boxed and shipped.

As the time drew near for her arrival, Cecil could hardly eat. He was too excited to apply himself to anything. The day of her expected arrival he actually got up at five o'clock to clean the house and make it look as fine as possible for her inspection. Then he hitched up and drove fifteen miles to get her. The train pulled out just before he reached the station, so Nita in her box was waiting for him on the platform. He could see her in a queer way, as one sees the purple centre of a revolving circle of light; for, to tell the truth, with the long ride in the morning sun, and the beating of his heart, Cecil was only about half-conscious of anything. He wanted to yell, but he didn't. He kept himself in hand and lifted up the sliding side of the box and called to Nita, and she came out.

But it wasn't the man who fainted, though he might have done so, being crazy homesick as he was, and half-fed and overworked while he was yet soft from an easy life. No; it was the dog! She looked at her master's face, gave one cry of inexpressible joy, and fell over in a real feminine sort of a faint, and had to be brought to like any other lady, with camphor and water and a few drops of spirit down her throat. Then Cecil got up on the wagon seat, and she sat beside him with her head on his arm, and they rode home in absolute silence, each feeling too much for speech. After they reached home, however, Cecil showed her all over the place, and she barked out her ideas in glad sociability.

After that Cecil and Nita were inseparable. She walked beside him all day when he was out with the cultivator, or when he was mowing or reaping. She ate beside him at table and slept across his feet at night. Evenings when he looked over the *Graphic* from home, or read the books his mother sent him, that he might keep in touch with the world, Nita was beside him, patient, but jealous. Then, when he threw his book or paper down and took her on his knee and looked into her pretty eyes, or frolicked with her, she fairly laughed with delight.

In short, she was faithful with that faith of which only a dog is capable—that unquestioning faith to which even the most loving women never quite attain.

However, Fate was annoyed at this perfect friendship. It didn't give her enough to do, and Fate is a restless thing with a horrible appetite for variety. So poor Nita died one day mysteriously, and gave her last look to Cecil as a matter of course; and he held her paws till the last moment, as a stanch friend should, and laid her away decently in a pine box in the cornfield, where he could be shielded from public view if he chose to go there now and then and sit beside her grave.

He went to bed very lonely, indeed, the first night. The shack seemed to him to be removed endless miles from the other habitations of men. He seemed cut off from the world, and ached to hear the cheerful little barks which Nita had been in the habit of giving him by way of good night. Her amiable eye with its friendly light was missing; the gay wag of her tail was gone; all her ridiculous ways, at which he was never tired of laughing, were things of the past.

He lay down, busy with these thoughts, yet so habituated to Nita's presence, that when her weight rested upon his feet, as usual, he felt no surprise. But after a moment it came to him that as she was dead the weight he felt upon his feet could not be hers. And yet, there it was, warm and comfortable, cuddling down in the familiar way. He actually sat up and put his hand down to the foot of the bed to discover what was there. But there was nothing there, save the weight. And that stayed with him that night and many nights after.

It happened that Cecil was a fool, as men will be when they are young, and he worked too hard, and didn't take proper care of himself; and so it came about that he fell sick with a low fever. He struggled around for a few days, trying to work it off, but one morning he awoke only to the consciousness of absurd dreams. He seemed to be on the sea, sailing for home, and the boat was tossing and pitching in a weary circle, and could make no headway. His heart was burning with impatience, but the boat went round and round in that endless circle till he shrieked out with agony.

The next neighbors were the Taylors, who lived two miles and a half away. They were awakened that morning by the howling of a dog before their door. It was a hideous sound and would give them no peace. So Charlie Taylor got up and opened the door, discovering there an excited little collie.

"Why, Tom," he called, "I thought Cecil's collie was dead!"

"She is," called back Tom.

"No, she ain't neither, for here she is, shakin' like an aspin, and a beggin' me to go with her. Come out, Tom, and see."

It was Nita, no denying, and the men, perplexed, followed her to Cecil's shack, where they found him babbling.

But that was the last of her. Cecil said he never felt her on his feet again. She had performed her final service for him, he said. The neighbors tried to laugh at the story at first, but they knew the Taylors wouldn't take the trouble to lie; and as for Cecil, no one would have ventured to chaff him.

The Spectre Bride

William Harrison Ainsworth

The castle of Hernswolf, at the close of the year 1655, was the resort of fashion and gaiety. The baron of that name was the most powerful nobleman in Germany, and equally celebrated for the patriotic achievements of his sons, and the beauty of his only daughter. The estate of Hernswolf, which was situated in the centre of the Black Forest, had been given to one of his ancestors by the gratitude of the nation, and descended with other hereditary possessions to the family of the present owner. It was a castellated, gothic mansion, built according to the fashion of the times, in the grandest style of architecture, and consisted principally of dark winding corridors, and vaulted tapestry rooms, magnificent indeed in their size, but ill-suited to private comfort, from the very circumstance of their dreary magnitude. A dark grove of pine and mountain ash encompassed the castle on every side, and threw an aspect of gloom around the scene, which was seldom enlivened by the cheering sunshine of heaven.

The castle bells rung out a merry peal at the approach of a winter twilight, and the warder was stationed with his retinue on the battlements, to announce the arrival of the company who were invited to share the amusements that reigned within the walls. The Lady Clotilda, the baron's only daughter, had but just attained her seventeenth year, and a brilliant assembly was invited to celebrate the birth-day. The large vaulted apartments were thrown open for the reception of the numerous guests, and the gaieties of the evening had scarcely commenced when the clock from the dungeon tower was heard to strike with unusual solemnity, and on the instant a tall stranger, arrayed in a deep suit of black, made his appearance in the ballroom. He bowed courteously on every side, but was received by all with the strictest reserve. No one knew who he was or whence he came, but it was evident from his appearance, that he was a nobleman of the first rank, and though his introduction was accepted with distrust, he was treated by all with respect. He addressed himself particularly to the daughter of the baron, and was so intelligent in his remarks, so lively in his sallies, and so fascinating in his address, that he quickly interested the feelings of his young and sensitive auditor. In fine, after some hesitation on the part of the host, who, with the rest of the company, was unable to approach the stranger with indifference, he was requested to remain a few days at the castle, an invitation which was cheerfully accepted.

The dead of the night drew on, and when all had retired to rest, the dull heavy bell was heard swinging to and fro in the grey tower, though there was scarcely a breath to move the forest trees. Many of the guests, when they met the next morning at the breakfast table, averred that there had been sounds as of the most heavenly music, while all persisted in affirming that they had heard awful noises, proceeding, as it seemed, from the apartment which the stranger at that time occupied. He soon, however, made his appearance at the breakfast circle, and when the circumstances of the preceding night were alluded to, a dark smile of unutterable meaning played round his saturnine features, and then relapsed into an expression of the deepest melancholy. He addressed his conversation principally to Clotilda, and when he talked of the different climes he had visited, of the sunny regions of Italy, where the very air breathes the fragrance of flowers, and the summer breeze sighs over a land of sweets; when he spoke to her of those delicious countries, where the smile of the day sinks into the softer beauty of the night, and the loveliness of heaven is never for an instant obscured, he drew tears of regret from the bosom of his fair auditor, and for the first time she regretted that she was yet at home.

Days rolled on, and every moment increased the fervour of the inexpressible sentiments with which the stranger had inspired her. He never discoursed of love, but he looked it in his language, in his manner, in the insinuating tones of his voice, and in the slumbering softness of his smile, and when he found that he had succeeded in inspiring her with favourable sentiments, a sneer of the most diabolical meaning spoke for an instant, and died again on his dark featured countenance. When he met her in the company of her parents, he was at once respectful and submissive, and it was only when alone with her, in her ramble through the dark recesses of the forest, that he assumed the guise of the more impassioned admirer.

As he was sitting one evening with the baron in the wainscotted apartment of the library, the conversation happened to turn upon supernatural agency. The stranger remained reserved and mysterious during the discussion, but when the baron in a jocular manner denied the existence of spirits, and satirically mocked their appearance, his eyes glowed with unearthly lustre, and his form seemed to dilate to more than its natural dimensions. When the conversation had ceased, a fearful pause of a few seconds and a chorus of celestial harmony was heard pealing through the dark forest glade. All were entranced with delight, but the stranger was disturbed and gloomy; he looked at his noble host with compassion, and something like a tear swam in his dark eye. After the lapse of a few seconds, the music died gently in the distance, and all was hushed as before. The baron soon after quitted the apartment, and was followed almost immediately by the stranger. He had not long been absent, when an awful noise, as of a person in the agonies of death, was heard, and the Baron was discovered stretched dead along the corridors. His countenance was convulsed with pain, and the grip of a human hand was visible on his blackened throat. The alarm was instantly given, the castle searched in every direction, but the stranger was seen no more. The body of the baron, in the meantime, was quietly committed to the earth, and the remembrance of the dreadful transaction, recalled but as a thing that once was.

After the departure of the stranger, who had indeed fascinated her very senses, the spirits of the gentle Clotilda evidently declined. She loved to walk early and late in the walks that he had once frequented, to recall his last words; to dwell on his sweet smile; and wander to the spot where she had once discoursed with him of love. She avoided all society, and never seemed to be happy but when left alone in the solitude of her chamber. It was then that she gave vent to her affliction in tears; and the love that the pride of maiden modesty concealed in public, burst forth in the hours of privacy. So beauteous, yet so resigned was the fair mourner, that she seemed already an angel freed from the trammels of the world, and prepared to take her flight to heaven.

As she was one summer evening rambling to the sequestered spot that had been selected as her favourite residence, a slow step advanced towards her. She turned round, and to her infinite surprise discovered the stranger. He stepped gaily to her side, and commenced an animated conversation. "You left me," exclaimed the delighted girl; "and I thought all happiness was fled from me for ever; but you return, and shall we not again be happy?"

"Happy," replied the stranger, with a scornful burst of derision, "Can I ever be happy again—can the—but excuse the agitation, my love, and impute it to the pleasure I experience at our meeting. Oh! I have many things to tell you; aye! and many kind words to receive; is it not so, sweet one? Come, tell me truly, have you been happy in my absence? No! I see in that sunken eye, in that pallid cheek, that the poor wanderer has at least gained some slight interest in the heart of his beloved. I have roamed to other climes, I have seen other nations; I have met with other females, beautiful and accomplished, but I have met with but one angel, and she is here before me. Accept this simple offering of my affection, dearest," continued the stranger, plucking a heath-rose from its stem; "it is beautiful as the wild flowers that deck thy hair, and sweet as is the love I bear thee."

"It is sweet, indeed," replied Clotilda, "but its sweetness must wither ere night closes around. It is beautiful, but its beauty is short-lived, as the love evinced by man. Let not this, then, be the type of thy attachment; bring me the delicate evergreen, the sweet flower that blossoms throughout the year, and I will say, as I wreathe it in my hair, 'The violets have bloomed and died—the roses have flourished and decayed; but the evergreen is still young, and so is the love of heart!'—you will not—cannot desert me. I live but in you; you are my hopes, my thoughts, my existence itself: and if I lose you, I lose my all—I was but a solitary wild flower in the wilderness of nature, until you transplanted me to a more genial soil; and can you now break the fond heart you first taught to glow with passion?"

"Speak not thus," returned the stranger, "it rends my very soul to hear you; leave me—forget me—avoid me for ever—or your eternal ruin must ensue. I am a thing abandoned of God and man—and did you but see the scared heart that scarcely beats within this moving mass of deformity, you would flee me, as you would an adder in your path. Here is my heart, love, feel how cold it is; there is no pulse that betrays its emotion; for all is chilled and dead as the friends I once knew."

"You are unhappy, love, and your poor Clotilda shall stay to succour you. Think not I can abandon you in your misfortunes. No! I will wander with thee through the wide world, and be thy servant, thy slave, if thou wilt have it so. I will shield thee from the night winds, that they blow not too roughly on thy unprotected head. I will defend thee from the tempest that howls around; and though the cold world may devote thy name to scorn—though friends may fall off, and associates wither in the grave, there shall be one fond heart who shall love thee better in thy misfortune, and cherish thee, bless thee still."

She ceased, and her blue eyes swam in tears, as she turned it glistening with affection towards the stranger. He averted his head from her gaze, and a scornful sneer of the darkest, the deadliest malice passed over his fine countenance. In an instant, the expression subsided; his fixed glassy eye resumed its unearthly chillness, and he turned once again to his companion.

"It is the hour of sunset," he exclaimed; "the soft, the beauteous hour, when the hearts of lovers are happy, and nature smiles in unison with their feelings; but to me it will smile no longer—ere the morrow dawns I shall very far, from the house of my beloved; from the scenes where my heart is enshrined, as in a sepulchre. But must I leave thee, dearest flower of the wilderness, to be the sport of a whirlwind, the prey of the mountain blast?"

"No, we will not part," replied the impassioned girl; "*where thou goest, will I go; thy home shall be my home; and thy God shall be my God.*"

"Swear it, swear it," resumed the stranger, wildly grasping her by the hand; "swear to the fearful oath I shall dictate."

He then desired her to kneel, and holding his right hand in a menacing attitude towards heaven, and throwing back his dark raven locks, exclaimed in a strain of bitter imprecation with the ghastly smile of an incarnate fiend, "May the curses of an offended God," he cried, "haunt thee, cling to thee for ever in the tempest and in the calm, in the day and in the night, in sickness and in sorrow, in life and in death, shouldst thou swerve from the promise thou hast here made to be mine. May the dark spirits of the damned howl in thine ears the accursed chorus of fiends—may the air rack thy bosom with the quenchless flames of hell! May thy soul be as the lazar-house of corruption, where the ghost of departed pleasure sits enshrined, as in a grave: where the hundred-headed worm never dies where the fire is never extinguished. May a spirit of evil lord it over thy brow, and proclaim, as thou passest by, 'This is the abandoned of god and man'; may fearful spectres haunt thee in the night season; may thy dearest friends drop day by day into the grave, and curse thee with their dying breath: may all that is most horrible in human nature, more solemn than language can frame, or lips can utter, may this, and more than this, be thy eternal portion, shouldst thou violate the oath that thou has taken."

He ceased—hardly knowing what she did, the terrified girl acceded to the awful adjuration, and promised eternal fidelity to him who was henceforth to be her lord. "Spirits of the damned, I thank thee for thine assistance," shouted the stranger; "I have wooed my fair bride bravely. She is mine—mine for ever.—Aye, body and soul both mine; mine in life, and mine in death. What in tears, my sweet one, ere yet the honeymoon is past? Why! indeed thou hast cause for weeping: but when next we meet we shall meet to sign the nuptial bond."

He then imprinted a cold salute on the cheek of his young bride, and softening down the unutterable horrors of his countenance, requested her to meet him at eight o'clock on the ensuing evening in the chapel adjoining to the castle of Hernswolf. She turned round to him with a burning sigh, as if to implore protection from himself, but the stranger was gone.

On entering the castle, she was observed to be impressed with deepest melancholy. Her relations vainly endeavoured to ascertain the cause of her uneasiness; but the tremendous oath she had sworn completely paralysed her faculties, and she was fearful of betraying herself by even the slightest intonation of her voice, or the least variable expression of her countenance. When the evening was concluded, the family retired to rest; but Clotilda, who was unable to take repose, from the restlessness of her disposition, requested to remain alone in the library that adjoined her apartment.

All was now deep midnight; every domestic had long since retired to rest, and the only sound that could be distinguished was the sullen howl of the ban-dog as he bayed, the waning moon Clotilda remained in the library in an attitude of deep meditation. The lamp that burnt on the table, where she sat, was dying away, and the lower end of the apartment was already more than half obscured. The clock from the northern angle of the castle tolled out the hour of twelve, and the sound echoed dismally in the solemn stillness of the night. Suddenly the oaken door at the farther end of the room was gently lifted on its latch, and a bloodless figure, apparelled in the habiliments of the grave, advanced slowly up the apartment. No sound heralded its approach, as it moved with noiseless steps to the table where the lady was stationed. She did not at first perceive it, till she felt a death-cold hand fast grasped in her own, and heard a solemn voice whisper in her ear, "Clotilda."

She looked up, a dark figure was standing beside her; she endeavoured to scream, but her voice was unequal to the exertion; her eye was fixed, as if by magic, on the form which, slowly removed the garb that concealed its countenance, and disclosed the livid eyes and skeleton shape of her father. It seemed to gaze on her with pity and regret, and mournfully exclaimed—"Clotilda, the dresses and the servants are ready, the church bell has tolled, and the priest is at the altar, but where is the affianced bride? There is room for her in the grave, and to-morrow shall she be with me."

"To-morrow?" faltered out the distracted girl; "the spirits of hell shall have registered it, and to-morrow must the bond be cancelled." The figure ceased—slowly retired, and was soon lost in the obscurity of distance.

The morning—evening—arrived; and already as the hall clock struck eight, Clotilda was on her road to the chapel. It was a dark, gloomy night, thick masses of dun clouds sailed across the firmament, and the roar of the winter wind echoed awfully through the forest trees. She reached the appointed place; a figure was in waiting for her—it advanced—and discovered the features of the stranger.

"Why! this is well, my bride," he exclaimed, with a sneer; "and well will I repay thy fondness. Follow me."

They proceeded together in silence through the winding avenues of the chapel, until they reached the adjoining cemetery. Here they paused for an instant; and the stranger, in a softened tone, said, "But one hour more, and the struggle will be over. And yet this heart of incarnate malice can feel, when it devotes so young, so pure a spirit to the grave. But it must—it must be," he proceeded, as the memory of her past love rushed on her mind; "for the fiend whom I obey has so willed it. Poor girl, I am leading thee indeed to our nuptials; but the priest will be death, thy parents the mouldering skeletons that rot in heaps around; and the witnesses to our union, the lazy worms that revel on the carious bones of the dead. Come, my young bride, the priest is impatient for his victim."

As they proceeded, a dim blue light moved swiftly before them, and displayed at the extremity of the churchyard the portals of a vault. It was open, and they entered it in silence. The hollow wind came rushing through the gloomy abode of the dead; and on every side were piled the mouldering remnants of coffins, which dropped piece by piece upon the damp mud. Every step they took was on a dead body; and the bleached bones rattled horribly beneath their feet. In the centre of the vault rose a heap of unburied skeletons, whereon was seated, a figure too awful even for the darkest imagination to conceive. As they approached it, the hollow vault rung with a hellish peal of laughter; and every mouldering corpse seemed endued with unholy life. The stranger paused, and as he grasped his victim in his hand, one sigh burst from his heart—one tear glistened in his eye. It was but for an instant; the figure frowned awfully at his vacillation, and waved his gaunt hand.

The stranger advanced; he made certain mystic circles in the air, uttered unearthly words, and paused in excess of terror. On a sudden he raised his voice and wildly exclaimed—"Spouse of the spirit of darkness, a few moments are yet thine; that thou may'st know to whom thou hast consigned thyself. I am the undying spirit of the wretch who curst his Saviour on the cross. He looked at me in the closing hour of his existence, and that look hath not yet passed away, for I am curst above all on earth. I am eternally condemned to hell! and I must cater for my master's taste till the world is parched as is a scroll, and the heavens and the earth have passed away. I am he of whom thou may'st have read, and of whose feats thou may'st have heard. A million souls has my master condemned me to ensnare, and then my penance is accomplished, and I may know the repose of the grave. Thou art the thousandth soul that I have damned.

I saw thee in thine hour of purity, and I marked thee at once for my home. Thy father did I murder for his temerity, and permitted to warn thee of thy fate; and myself have I beguiled for thy simplicity. Ha! the spell works bravely, and thou shall soon see, my sweet one, to whom thou hast linked thine undying fortunes, for as long as the seasons shall move on their course of nature—as long as the lightning shall flash, and the thunders roll, thy penance shall be eternal. Look below! and see to what thou art destined."

She looked, the vault split in a thousand different directions; the earth yawned asunder; and the roar of mighty waters was heard. A living ocean of molten fire glowed in the abyss beneath her, and blending with the shrieks of the damned, and the triumphant shouts of the fiends, rendered horror more horrible than imagination. Ten millions of souls were writhing in the fiery flames, and as the boiling billows dashed them against the blackened rocks of adamant, they cursed with the blasphemies of despair; and each curse echoed in thunder cross the wave. The stranger rushed towards his victim. For an instant he held her over the burning vista, looked fondly in her face and wept as he were a child. This was but the impulse of a moment; again he grasped her in his arms, dashed her from him with fury; and as her last parting glance was cast in kindness on his face, shouted aloud, "Not mine is the crime, but the religion that thou professest; for is it not said that there is a fire of eternity prepared for the souls of the wicked; and hast not thou incurred its torments?"

She, poor girl, heard not, heeded not the shouts of the blasphemer. Her delicate form bounded from rock to rock, over billow, and over foam; as she fell, the ocean lashed itself as it were in triumph to receive her soul, and as she sunk deep in the burning pit, ten thousand voices reverberated from the bottomless abyss, "Spirit of evil! here indeed is an eternity of torments prepared for thee; for here the worm never dies, and the fire is never quenched."

The Spectre of Rislip Abbey

Dick Donovan

[The particulars of this story have been supplied by a well-known member of Parliament from his own experience. The story is told almost in his own words. He is the owner of a broad and fair estate in central England, and has gained an enviable reputation for his high intelligence, his administrative ability—which on more than one occasion has been of great advantage to his party—as well as for his princely hospitality.]

Up to about twenty years ago I was a comparatively poor man, and had to supplement my income by literary work, which, being of a scientific character, had not a very wide market. However, at that time, I succeeded to a snug patrimony, which freed my mind at once from all anxiety about the future. I had been married for seventeen years, and had two daughters, Cynthia and Phyllis, aged thirteen and fifteen respectively. My wife was an invalid, and our medical attendant had frequently told me that her restoration to health depended to a large extent on her living in the country, and indulging in country pursuits. But want of adequate means had prevented our giving effect to this advice, for circumstances rendered it important that I should reside in London, and my wife resolutely refused to leave me. Consequently, we had been living in a modest flat, and made the best we could of its inconveniences and drawbacks.

It was not surprising, therefore, that one of my first cares as soon as I was in possession of my fortune was to seek for some suitable country residence. We were all fond of the country, and my tastes inclined to the life of a gentleman farmer. I therefore called one morning on my friend, the late Mr. George R——, the well-known West-End auctioneer and estate agent. He had a connection all over Great Britain, and I knew that if anyone could find me the place I wanted he could. After we had chatted for some time, and I had made known my requirements, he began to discuss the pros and cons of several estates he had on his books, but against all there was some objection to urge as far as I was concerned, until at last he exclaimed with a chuckle:

"By Jove, I have it. Rislip Abbey, that's the place for you." Then, calling his head clerk, he desired him to bring the printed particulars of Rislip, which were read out as follows:—

"Rislip.—Containing about three thousand acres arable land, five hundred acres pasture, one thousand timber (mostly oak and beech), the rest park and ornamental grounds. The house is a quaint, old-fashioned, turreted mansion, believed to have been built about the end of the reign of Henry VIII. The place is without any historical interest. Most of the land lies well. The house stands high, and commands splendid views, but is in a dilapidated condition, not having had a tenant for the last thirty years. The property has been the subject of litigation, but the rightful ownership has now been determined."

The foregoing were the crude particulars, so to speak, in outline, and having listened to them I questioned my friend further, and asked him if he had personally surveyed the property.

"I have," he answered.

"And what is your opinion about it?"

"Well, at present it is a wilderness, and the house is well nigh a ruin. Chancery, as you know, is like a blight and a curse—it ruins every property it has anything to do with, as well as breaks the hearts of men and women. Of course, the lawyers have done well while Rislip has been going to decay, and now the owners are too poor to spend any money on it, nor can they sell any portion of it for the next twenty-five years. But they would grant you a lease for that period for a merely nominal rent, and give you the option of purchase. It would want a good deal of money laid out on it in the first instance, but my opinion is you could soon bring the land under cultivation, and make it profitable. Anyway, go down and see the property. I'll go with you, if you like. You will soon see if it is likely to suit you, and, of course, you can get the ghost and all thrown in."

"Ghost!" I exclaimed, with a laugh.

"Oh, yes. I understand there is a real, genuine ghost, according to local tradition. The yokels swear that the place is haunted. But I should say the only spirits you will find there are bats and owls."

I laughed at the ghost idea. I was pleased to think myself a hard-headed man, and my disposition was to view most things from a severely critical and scientific point of view; while as for spiritualism, I had nothing but contempt for those who professed to believe in it.

Now, the result of my interview with my friend the auctioneer was that a week later we journeyed down to Rislip together, and spent three or four days in examining the estate. It was certainly not an exaggeration to call it a wilderness, while the house itself was crumbling to decay; but I saw at once the potentialities of the place, and as the situation of the house would have been hard to beat, while the rental asked was little more than nominal, I secured the refusal of the property for a fortnight. During that time I consulted my lawyers, took my wife and daughter down to Rislip, and as they confessed themselves charmed, and I found I could secure it almost on my own terms, I lost no time in closing, and at once proceeded to get estimates for putting the house in habitable condition.

As may be imagined, I was very busy for the next three months, and by means of a liberal expenditure and ample labour, a very different aspect was imparted to the erstwhile wilderness, and the house was ready for occupation by the early part of November. Though the prospect of moving at such a period wasn't very pleasant, we faced it boldly, and by the end of the month were comfortably installed in our new quarters. In carrying out the repairs and alterations in the house I had been careful not to interfere in any way with its structural arrangements, as its quaintness and rambling character appealed very forcibly to my antiquarian instincts. One of the features of the house was most certainly the dining-room. It was a room of really noble proportions, unusually lofty for a building of that date, with three straight windows on one side, and at one end a very deep bay, from which there was a view second to none in the country.

The floor, which had been laid with oak, was as level as a billiard table, and in a perfect state of preservation. The walls were all wainscoted from floor to ceiling, and as some of this had decayed, it had been found necessary to restore it during the process of renovating the house. In the course of this work the men discovered a sliding door so artfully let in as a panel that anyone unacquainted with its existence would never have found it out. Behind the sliding panel was a narrow passage, leading to a flight of stone steps that descended to a second passage, closed by a door. This door gave access to a short tunnel that had its exit in the grounds, near a lake of considerable dimensions.

Romantic no doubt as all this may seem, there was really nothing very remarkable in it, as very few country houses were built in Henry VIII's time, and, indeed, for long after his reign, without a secret passage, the object being to afford the occupants a means of escape in case of need. The contractor who carried out the work for me suggested that the passage should be blocked up, to this I would not give my consent, but insisted on its being left in its original state, and in this decision I was supported by my wife and daughters. I ought to add that running parallel with the dining-room, and communicating by a doorway, was another room of smaller dimensions, but so conveniently situated and well lighted that I at once appropriated it as a library, as I had a valuable collection of books.

By the middle of December we had quite settled down, and all felt charmed with our new home, then we began to send out invitations very freely to our friends and relatives for Christmas, as we were desirous of having a good housewarming.

Of course, during the short time I had been in possession I had heard much gossip and gathered a good many interesting anecdotes about the property. The fact of its having at last changed hands aroused a great deal of interest and curiosity over a very extended area, for the history of Rislip was pretty well known, and the story of the Chancery suit and the ruin it had brought about had caused general regret, as it was regarded as a shame that so good a property should be allowed to run to waste. I found that there was a very curious belief that Rislip had its familiar spirit—in other words, that it was haunted. I tried to find out the foundation for this belief, but, as is usually the case, I was met with the reply—

"Oh, I've never seen anything myself, but I've heard of people who have."

When I tried to find out these people who, by common account, had had ocular demonstration of the existence of disturbed spirits, I need scarcely say I failed. It is always so. Neither my wife nor I attached the slightest serious importance to the current stories. We were amused by them, and possibly there was just a tendency on our part to regard people who expressed belief in the supernatural as being far from what is generally termed "strong minded," to use a mild term.

But now, to come to the strangest part of my narrative. I had been dining one night with my family, and we had had a neighbouring gentleman and his wife as guests. They had departed, and my wife and the girls had retired. I had remained to indulge in a final cigar, and enjoy the comfort of the brightly burning fire and the warm room. Outside the weather was murky, cold, and dismal. My butler had been to inquire if I wished for anything more, and my wants having been attended to, he bade me good night and went to his room. After that I fell into a reverie. Possibly I may have dozed. Anyway, I was aroused to a sense of things mundane by a cold draught of air blowing upon me, and glancing round I saw, to my amazement, that the secret door or panel in the wall to which I have already alluded was wide open. Then I was still further amazed—I might almost say dumfounded—by *seeing a hand*, only a hand, slowly draw the panel into its place again.

It is almost impossible for me to describe the extraordinary sensation that crept over me. There was something so uncanny in the whole proceeding. Now, I have already said I was not a superstitious man, and I think I may also assert that I was by no means lacking in courage. Nevertheless, for the moment I was the prey to a feeling of absolute funk. Then suddenly I thought that a trick was being tried upon me, and anger got the better of my funk. I seized the poker from the fireplace, rushed to the panel, got it open with some little difficulty, and peered into the darkness, but saw nothing; listened intently, but heard nothing. Next I snatched a candle from the table and proceeded down the passage, but found no living thing, and the doors were properly fastened. Returning to the dining-room, I sat down to think, and came to the conclusion that I had been the victim of a trick of the brain, and laughed at my own folly. But when a quarter of an hour later I went upstairs to my bedroom I experienced an unaccountable and absolutely unusual feeling of nervousness. The next day my first impulse was to tell my wife of the remarkable incident of the night previous; my second to do nothing of the sort, but keep it a locked secret in my own breast. A week later my daughter Phyllis had been with me in the library. She was a clever shorthand writer, and had been taking some important letters down from my dictation. As the clock on the mantelpiece chimed out midnight I told her to cease work and go to her bed. She wished me good night, and trotted off.

A few minutes passed, then the door of the library was flung violently open, and Phyllis, half fainting, looking ghastly pale, and with a "scared-to-death" appearance of face, rushed in and clung wildly to me.

"What's the matter, child; what's the matter?" I cried in alarm; but she remained speechless. Moments, perhaps minutes, slipped by, during which I kept urging her to speak. She found her voice at last sufficient to jerk out in a breathless way:

"Oh, pa, I've had such a fright. When I got up to the first landing such a strange-looking man was standing there. I was about to ask him what he was doing, when he raised his hand in a sort of warning way and disappeared."

I laughed, but it wasn't a genuine laugh, and I pretended to speak lightly, as I said: "My dear child, I've been overworking you and your poor tired brain has seen visions. Come, let me take you upstairs to your room. You must try and get a good night's rest. You will be all right to-morrow."

She gave me a look that was full of meaning. She said with her eyes as plainly as possible, "Don't try to turn it off in that way. I have seen what I have seen." She had mastered her feelings by this time, and though she spoke no words, she went upstairs with me until we reached the first landing, which was lighted in the day time by a long stained-glass window. Edging a little closer to me, she whispered, "This was where I saw him."

"Nonsense, nonsense," I answered, though I was far from believing it was nonsense, but I wanted to reassure her. I escorted her to her door, saw that her lamp was burning, then kissed her good night and descended, and as I went down the last flight of stairs I turned suddenly, for I was sure I heard footsteps. And close behind me was a weird-looking man dressed in the costume of a gentleman of Charles II's reign. He appeared to be about sixty-five years of age. Long, grey, ringleted hair hung about his shoulders. His face wore an expression of awful anguish.

For a moment I experienced a shock, but I quickly recovered myself and tried to grasp him, but he was as unsubstantial as the air, and the uncanniness of the whole business made me involuntarily shrink back. Then he raised his hands, and drawing down the large lace collar from his neck, he bared his throat, showing me a tremendous gash that had severed the windpipe, and from which the blood seemed to pour in a stream. It was a fearsome sight, I must confess, and I had never before in the whole course of my existence experienced such an utterly "gone" and helpless feeling as I did in the presence of that supernatural visitant, and before I had pulled myself together, as the saying is, the weird spectre raised his hand, pointed upward with an extended finger, and in an instant had disappeared.

I returned to my library and flung myself into a chair, and I asked myself seriously whether the incidents of the last quarter of an hour were not the result of some morbid condition of my own brain. That is to say, I was disposed to doubt whether my daughter had really rushed pale and fainting into the room, as I have described, or whether it wasn't a figment of my own imagination. But here let me say that I had always been regarded as an unimaginative person, with, as I have before said, a scientific mind, which required hard, stern facts to convince it. How was it then I had come to see visions?

I asked myself this question, and mentally argued the whole thing out, trying to explain away the vision; but, firstly, there were the mysterious hand and the sliding panel, and now here was a man of a bygone age who had horrified me by showing me his throat gashed, and rent, and bleeding.

I don't know really how long I sat revolving the problem in my brain, but I do know that I crept up to bed at last feeling terribly fagged mentally and physically.

I slept far beyond my usual hour the following morning. My family had already breakfasted, but Phyllis came and sat with me, and recounted her previous night's experiences. There was an unwonted paleness in her pretty face and a scared look in her eyes. I felt it wise not to say anything to her about what I myself had seen; but, moved by a sudden impulse, I said I was going up to London by the next train and would take her with me.

It was no unusual thing for me to be called away from home at a moment's notice, so that my wife was not surprised. Phyllis expressed her delight at going, and two hours later we were seated in the up express. On arriving at our destination, I quartered Phyllis at the house of my sister, while I went to an hotel where I was in the habit of staying when in town. The following day I called on an old and esteemed medical friend—a man not only eminent as a physician, but famous as an author of several erudite works dealing with all forms of mental disease. I detailed the experiences of myself and daughter to him, and he looked very grave and puzzled, but before venturing to express any opinion he said he would like to see Phyllis. So I drove off at once to my sister's, and took Phyllis back with me, and without entering into any particulars I simply remarked that I wanted the doctor to see her. She expressed surprise by her face, but remained silent. On arriving at the doctor's house I requested her to tell him what she had seen, which she did in a plain, intelligent way. My friend appeared more than ever puzzled, and, having sent Phyllis out of the room, he delivered himself somewhat as follows:

"Well, now, my dear fellow, the facts of the case are these. Both you and Phyllis are more impressionable than you imagine, and you have gone through a great deal of excitement lately in connection with your new quarters. Last night you overtaxed the girl's brain, and what she thought she saw was a pure fancy. Her sudden appearance in your room in a state of nervous agitation, her story, her manner, made a great impression on you, and what she told you she had seen suggested the same thing to you."

"But how about the hand and the sliding panel?" I asked.

"The result also of a morbid condition of the mind," he answered. "Fancy, fancy, all fancy, my dear sir. Now you and Phyllis go and make a little journey somewhere. A trip to the South of France, a month at Monte Carlo, will do you all the good in the world."

I left my friend's house far from satisfied. I knew he was sincere in his belief, but he was wrong in his diagnosis. Nevertheless, I began to think of carrying out his suggestion and visiting the Riviera. No doubt I should have done that if it hadn't been for the fact that three days later I received a telegram from home, summoning me back at once, as my wife had been taken ill.

I began to fear now that Rislip was to prove a curse instead of a blessing to me; and, depressed by an anxiety I had never known before, I caught the next train out. Phyllis, of course, accompanied me, and we reached Rislip about ten o'clock at night. I learnt that my wife had had a fit. The cause nobody knew, but she told me. She had been sitting in the dining-room alone, when she felt a draught as I had done. Then to her horror she saw a deathly-white hand sliding the panel back. Suddenly a quaintly-dressed man, with a haggard, anguished face, appeared before her, and, baring his throat, displayed it gashed and bleeding as he had done to me. She was conscious of uttering a loud, shrill scream of terror. Then all was blank until she awoke to find a doctor attending her.

As she finished telling me her story, she expressed great anxiety lest her brain was giving way, and she only grew calm when I assured her that I had seen what she had seen, and that Phyllis had also met the ghostly man on the stairs. My medical friend's theory would not now hold water, because my wife had been ignorant of my own and Phyllis's experiences, so that she was not influenced by a recital which might have set up a morbid set of conditions in her own brain.

Up to this time I had always regarded spiritualism so-called as abominable quackery, and it always made me angry when I heard of the antics and silly pranks which the spirits called up at the *séances* of the professional humbugs indulged in. But now I myself had seen a spirit, my daughter had also seen it, and my wife had seen it. We all three claimed to be people of common sense, free from morbid taint, and not given to conjuring up bogeys out of every shadow that came in our path. And yet it seemed to me that the spirit that had made itself manifest unto us had behaved in a very idiotic way, for if it had a grievance why did it try to frighten us all to death. Of course, the matter was too serious to be pooh-poohed with a scornful laugh and a sceptical toss of the head. The statement of three persons, not quite fools, could not be ignored. I began to feel deeply interested in the psychological problem that was suggested to me, and after much cogitation I mentally asked myself whether the ghostly visitor had any particular reason for pointing upward. Anyway, I was prompted to try and find out, and made my way to the top of the house, where there was a range of garrets. Here I began to pry about in a very inquisitive way, and after long and patient searching for I knew not what, I chanced to strike a portion of the wall in a back garret with a stick

I carried, and was rather astonished to find that it gave out a hollow sound. I rapped it again. The same sound; but a yard on either side and there was solidity.

I lost no time in getting the assistance of two of my men servants. I simply told them that I had accidentally discovered what I believed to be a door, and, prompted now more by curiosity than anything else, I, with their help, tore off the paper, then a lining of canvas, then more paper, till we got to some wood that had once been painted. Close examination revealed that it was a door, and not without considerable trouble we got it open, disclosing a deep recess. Lights were procured, and from out the recess we dragged a heavy mass of dusty and time-stained metal. It was apparently a bundle of lead rolled up. We unrolled it, and brought to light a quantity of human bones, including a singularly well preserved skull, to which a mass of hair still adhered.

What my feelings were I will not attempt to describe. Of course the servants were amazed. I sent them to their duties, again cautioning them to say nothing at present of our find. My next step was to lodge information with the county police, and in due course the inevitable coroner's inquiry was held, but elicited nothing beyond the medical opinion that the bones must have been where they were found for generations. Whose bones they were no one could even conjecture. Why they had been wrapped in lead, and hidden in the secret cupboard was no less inscrutable. The coroner's jury could return but one verdict. The remains were those of some person unknown, and how he had met his death it was impossible to say. The bones were ordered to be buried in consecrated ground, and with Christian burial, and that was done. At my own expense I placed a slab over the grave, bearing this line:

"Sacred to the memory of a stranger. Date of birth and death unknown."

With the finding and burial of those bones the spectre of Rislip Abbey departed, and troubled us no more.

Now, the story I have told you is a true one. There is the independent testimony of my wife and daughter to corroborate mine. My theory is that in some far off time a brutal crime had been committed, and the murdered man's body had been rolled in a sheet of lead and thrust in the secret closet; but while the murderers could confine his body they could not confine his spirit. Though why, after so many generations had passed, I should have been selected to bring the matter to light I know not, and cannot even possibly suggest a theory, nor can the mystery of the crime be cleared up. Who the murdered man was, and why he was murdered, will never be known until the secrets of all hearts are revealed in the burning light of the Judgment Day.

The Spectre Spiders

William L. Wintle

The fog hung thickly over London one morning in late autumn. It was not the dense compound of smoke and moisture, pea-souplike in colour and pungent to eyes and nose, that is known as a "London peculiar"; but a fairly clean and white mist that arose from the river and lay about the streets and squares in great wisps and wreaths and banks.

The passing crowd shivered and thought of approaching winter; while a few optimistic souls looked upward to the invisible sky and predicted a warm day when the sun had grown in strength. A little child remarked to a companion that it smelled like washing day: and the comparison was not without its point. It was as if the motor machinery of the metropolis had blown off steam in preparation for a fresh start.

People passed one another in the mist like sheeted ghosts and did not speak. Friend failed to recognise friend; or, if he did, he took for granted that the other did not. Apart from the steady rumble of the traffic and the long deep note that the great city gives forth to hearing ears all the day long, the world seemed strangely silent and unfriendly.

Certainly this applied with truth to one member of the passing crowd whose business brought abroad that misty morning when home and the fireside gained an added attraction. Ephraim Goldstein was silent by nature and unfriendly by profession. For him language was an ingenious device for the concealment of thought; and when there was no special reason for such concealment, why should he trouble to speak?

It was not as if people were over desirous to hear him speak. He was naturally unattractive: and where nature had failed to complete her task, Ephraim had brought it to perfection. A habit of scowling had effectually removed any trace of amiability that might have survived the handicap of evil eyes and unpleasing features. When strangers saw Ephraim for the first time, they looked quickly around for a pleasant face to act by way of antidote.

We have said that he was unfriendly by profession. But the unwary and innocent would never have suspected this from his professional announcements in the personal column of the morning papers. The gentleman of fortune who was wishful, without security or inquiry, to advance goodly sums of money to his less fortunate fellow-creatures on nominal terms and in the most delicate manner possible, was surely giving the best of all proofs of a soul entirely immersed in the milk of human kindness.

Yet those who had done business with Ephraim spoke of him in terms not usual in the drawing-room: men of affairs who knew the world of finance called him a blood-sucking spider: and Scotland Yard had him noted down as emphatically a wrong 'un. Ephraim was not popular with those who knew him. He had in fact only one point of character that could be commended. He had never changed his name to Edward Gordon or even to Edwin Goldsmith: he was born Ephraim Goldstein—and Ephraim Goldstein he was content to remain to the end. A rose by any other name smells just as sweet—but people did not express it quite like that when Ephraim was under discussion.

He had not always been a gentleman of fortune, nor had he always been wishful to share his fortune with others. People with inconveniently long memories recalled a youth of like name who got into trouble at Whitechapel for selling Kosher fowls judiciously weighted with sand: and there was also a story about a young man who manipulated three thimbles and a pea on Epsom Downs.

But why drag in these scandals of the past? In the case of any man it is unfair to thus search the record of his youth for evidence against him; and in the case of Ephraim it was quite unnecessary. He was a perennial plant: however lurid the past, he blossomed forth afresh every year in renewed vigor and in equally glowing colours.

How fortune had come to him seemed to be known by no one save himself; but certainly it had come, for it is difficult to lend money if you do not possess it. And with its coming Ephraim had migrated from Whitechapel to Haggerston, then to Kilburn, and finally to Maida Vale where he now had his abode. But it must not be supposed that he indulged in either ambition or luxury. He was content with very modest comfort, and lived a simple bachelor existence; but he found a detached villa with some garden behind it more convenient for his purposes than a house in a terrace with an inquisitive neighbor on either side. His visitors came on business and by no means for pleasure: and privacy was as congenial to them as it was to him.

The business that had brought him out on this foggy morning was of an unusual character in that it had nothing to do with money making. It in fact involved spending money to the extent of two guineas now, with a probability of further sums; and he did not at all relish it. Ephraim was on his way to Cavendish Square to consult a noted oculist.

For some weeks past, he had been troubled with a curious affliction of his sight. He was still on the sunny side of fifty, and hitherto he had been very sharp-sighted in more senses than one. But now something seemed to be going wrong. His vision was perfect during the day, and usually through the evening as well; but twice recently he had been bothered with a curious optical delusion. On each occasion he had been sitting quietly reading after dinner, when something had made him easy. It was the same sort of disquiet that he always felt if a cat came into the room. So strong had been this feeling that he had sprung out of his chair without quite knowing why he did it and each time had fancied that a number of shadows streamed forth from his chair and ran across the carpet to the walls, where they vanished. They were evidently nothing but shadows, for he could see the carpet through them; but they were fairly clear and distinct. They seemed to be about the size of a cricket ball. Though he attached no meaning to the coincidence, it was a little odd that on each occasion he had been reluctantly compelled during the day to insist upon his pound of flesh from a client. And when Ephraim insisted, he did not stick at a trifle. But obviously this could have nothing to do with a defect of vision.

The great specialist made a thorough examination of Ephraim's eyes, but could find nothing wrong with them. So he explored further and investigated the state of his patient's nervous aid digestive systems; but found that these were perfectly sound.

Then he embarked upon more delicate matters, and sought to learn something of the habits of Ephraim. A bachelor in the forties may be addicted to the cup that cheers and occasionally inebriates as well: he may be fond of the pleasures of the table: he may be attracted by the excitement of gambling: in fact he may do a great many things that a man of his years should not do. The physician was a man of tact and diplomacy. He asked no injudicious questions; but he had the valuable gift of inducing conversation in others. Not for years had Ephraim talked so freely and frankly to any man. The result was that the doctor could find no reason for suggesting that the trouble was due to any kind of dietary or other indiscretion.

So he fell back on the last refuge of the baffled physician. "Rest, my dear Sir," he said; "that is the best prescription. I am happy to say that I find no serious lesion or even functional disturbance; but there is evidence of fatigue affecting the brain and the optic nerve. There is no reason to anticipate any further or more serious trouble; but a wise man always takes precautions. My advice is that you drop all business for a few weeks and spend the time in golf or other out-of-door amusement—say at Cromer or on the Surrey Downs. In that case you may be pretty confident that no further disturbance of this kind will occur."

Ephraim paid his two guineas with a rather wry face. He had the feeling that he was not getting much for his money; still it was reassuring to find that there was nothing the matter. Rest! Rubbish! He was not overworked. Surrey Downs indeed! Hampstead Heath was just as good and a great deal cheaper: he might take a turn there on Sunday mornings. Golf? You would not catch him making a fool of himself in tramping after a ridiculous ball! So he simply went on much the same as before, and hoped that all would be well.

Yet, somehow, things did not seem to be quite right with him. Business was prosperous, if you can speak of business in connection with the pleasant work of sharing your fortune with the less fortunate—always on the most reasonable terms possible. Ephraim would have told you that he lost terribly through the dishonesty of people who died or went abroad or whose expectations did not turn out as well as they should; and yet, in some mysterious way, he had more money to lend than ever. But he was worried.

One evening, after an unusually profitable day, he was sitting in his garden, smoking a cigar that had been given him by a grateful client who was under the mistaken impression that Ephraim's five per cent was to be reckoned per year, whereas it was really per week. It was a good cigar; and the smoker knew how to appreciate good tobacco. He was lying back in a hammock chair, and idly watching the rings of smoke as they rose on the quiet air and floated away.

Then he suddenly started and stared. The rings were behaving in a very odd fashion. They seemed to form themselves into globes of smoke; and from each of them protruded eight waving filaments that turned and bent like the legs of some uncanny creature. And it seemed as if these trailing limbs of smoke turned and reached towards him. It was curious and not altogether pleasant. But it was no case of an optical delusion. The evening light was good, and the thing was seen clearly enough. It must have been the result of some unusual state of the atmosphere at the time.

He was aroused by hearing conversation on the other side of the wall. The occupant of the next-door house was in his garden with a friend, and their talk was of matters horticultural. It did not interest Ephraim, who paid a jobbing gardener the smallest possible amount to keep the place tidy, and concerned himself no further about it. He did not want to hear of the respective virtues of different local seed-vendors. But the talk was insistent, and he presently found himself listening against his will. They were talking about spiders; and his neighbor was saying that he had never known such a plague of them or such large-sized specimens. And he went on to say that they all seemed to come over the wall from Ephraim's side! The listener discovered that his cigar had gone out; and he went indoors in disgust.

It was only a few days later when the next thing happened. Ephraim had gone to bed rather earlier than usual, being somewhat tired, but was unable to sleep. For some hours he tossed about wearily and angrily—for he usually slept well—and then came a spell of disturbed and restless slumber. Dream after dream passed through his mind; and somehow they all seemed to have something to do with spiders. He thought that he fought his way through dense jungles of web; he walked on masses of soft and yielding bodies that crushed and squished beneath his tread; multitudinous hairy legs waved to and fro and clung to him; fanged jaws bit him with the sting of fiery fluids; and gleaming eyes were everywhere staring at him with a gaze of unutterable malignancy. He fell, and the webs wrapped him round in an embrace of death; great woolly creatures flung themselves upon him and suffocated him with their foul stink; unspeakable things had him in their ghastly grip; he was sinking in an ocean of unimaginable horror.

He awoke screaming, and sprang out of bed. Something caught him in the face and clung round his head. He groped for the switch and turned on the light. Then he tore off the bandage that blinded him, and found that it was a mass of silky threads like the web that a giant spider might have spun. And, as he got it clear of his eyes, he saw great shadows run up the walls and vanish. They had grown since he saw them first on the carpet; they were now the size of footballs.

Ephraim was appalled by the horror of it. Unrestful sleep and persistent nightmare were bad enough; but here was something worse. The silky wisps that still clung about his head were not such stuff as dreams are made of. He wondered if he was going mad. Was the whole thing a hallucination? Could he pull himself together and shake it off? He tried; but the bits of web that waved from his fingers and face were real enough. No dream spider could have spun them; mere imagination could not have created them. Moreover, he was not a man of imagination. Quite the opposite. He dealt in realities: real estate was the security he preferred.

A stiff glass of brandy and soda pulled him together. He was not addicted to stimulants—it did not pay in his profession—but this was a case that called for special measures. He shook off the obsession, and thought there might be something in the golf suggestion after all. And when a client called during the morning to negotiate a little loan, Ephraim drove a shrewd bargain that surprised even himself.

The next incident that caused considerable disquiet to the gentleman of fortune seems to have occurred about a month later. He was no lover of animals, but he tolerated the presence of a Scots terrier in the house. It occasionally happened that he had large sums of money on the premises—not often, but sometimes it could not be helped—and the alert little dog was a good protection against the intrusive burglar. So he treated the animal as a sort of confidential servant, and was, after his fashion, attached to it. If he did not exactly love it, he at any rate appreciated and valued it. He did not even grudge the veterinarian charges when it was ill.

At night the terrier had the run of the house, but usually slept on a mat outside Ephraim's door. On this particular occasion Ephraim dreamed that he had fallen over the dog, and that it gave a loud yelp of pain. So vivid was the impression that it woke him, and the cry of the animal seemed to still linger on his ear. It was as if the terrier outside the door had really cried out. He listened, but all was quiet save for a curious clicking and sucking sound that he heard at intervals. It seemed to come from just outside the door; but that could not be, for the dog would have been roused and would have given the alarm if anything was wrong.

So he presently went to sleep again, and did not wake until his usual time for rising. As he dressed, it struck him as unusual that he heard nothing of the dog, which was accustomed to greet the first sounds of movement with a welcoming bark or two. When he opened his door, the terrier lay dead on the mat.

Ephraim was first shocked, then grieved, and next alarmed. He was shocked because it was simply natural to be shocked under the circumstances; he was grieved because it then dawned upon him that he was more fond of the animal than he could have believed possible; and he was alarmed because he knew that the mysterious death of a watch dog is often the preliminary to a burglary.

He hurried downstairs and made a hasty examination of the doors and windows, and particularly of a safe that was hidden in the wall behind what looked like a solid piece of furniture. But everything was in good order, and there was no sign of any attempt on the premises. Then he went upstairs to remove the body of the dog, wondering the while if it would be worth the expense to have a post-mortem. Ephraim disliked mysteries, especially when they happened in the house.

He picked up the dead terrier, and at once met with a bad shock. It was a mere feather-weight, and collapsed in his hands! It was little more than a skeleton, rattling loose in a bag of skin. It had been simply sucked dry!

He dropped it in horror, and as he did so he found some silky threads clinging to his hands. And there were threads waving in the air, for one of them twined itself about his head and clung stickily to his face. And then something fell with a soft thud on the floor behind him, and he turned just in time to see a shadow dart to the wall and disappear. He had seen that shadow form before; but it somehow seemed to be less shadowy and more substantial now.

It seems to have been about this time that a rumor circulated in Maida Vale that a monkey had escaped from the Zoological Gardens in Regent's Park and had been seen climbing on Ephraim's house.

It was first seen early in the morning by a milkman, who mentioned it to a policeman, and soon afterwards by a housemaid who was cleaning the steps of a house opposite. It was a rather dark and misty morning, which doubtless accounts for a certain vagueness in the descriptions of the animal. But, so far as they went, all the descriptions agreed.

The monkey was described as a very fat specimen, almost like a football in size and rotundity, with very long arms. It was covered with thick, glossy, black hair, and was seen to climb up the front of the house and enter by an open window. The milkman, who was fond of reading, said that he thought it was a spider monkey; but his only reason for this seems to have been some fancied resemblance to a very large spider.

Later in the morning, the policeman called on Ephraim to mention the matter, and to ask if the monkey was still there. His reception was not polite; and he retired in disorder. Then he rang up the Zoological Gardens, but was informed that they knew nothing about it. The incident was duly recorded at the police station, and there it ended, for no more was ever heard of it.

But another occurrence in the following week gave rise to much more talk, especially among the ladies of the neighbourhood. The empty skin of a valuable Persian cat was found in the shrubbery of the house next to Ephraim's—empty, that is, except for the bones of the animal. The skin was quite fresh; as it well might be, for the cat had been seen alive the evening before. The mystery formed a nine days' wonder, and was never solved until an even more shocking mystery came to keep it company. The cat's skin had been sucked dry and the local theory was that a stoat or other beast of prey had escaped from the Zoo and done the dire deed. But it was proved that no such escape had occurred: and there the matter had to stop.

Although it seems to have no significance, it may be well to place on record a trifling incident that happened a week or two later. A collector for some charitable institution called upon Ephraim under the mistaken impression that he was a person who wanted to get rid of his money. He was speedily undeceived, and was only in the house for a few minutes. But he told his wife afterward that Mr. Goldstein was evidently a great cat fancier, for he had noticed several fine black Persians curled up asleep in the house. But it was curious that they were all in the darkest and most obscure corners, where they could not be seen very clearly. He had made some passing reference to them to Mr. Goldstein, who did not seem to understand him. Indeed he stared at him as if he thought him the worse for drink!

Another incident at this time was made the subject of remark among Ephraim's neighbors. For reasons best known to himself, he had long been in the habit of sleeping with a loaded revolver at his bedside; and one morning, about daybreak, the sound of a shot was heard. The police were quickly on the spot and insisted upon entering the house. Ephraim assured them that the weapon had been accidentally discharged through being dropped on the floor; and, after asking to see his gun licence, the police departed.

But what had really happened was much more interesting. Ephraim had woke up without apparent cause, but with a vague sense of danger; and was just in time to see a round black body, covered with a dense coat of hair, climb up the foot of his bed and make its way cautiously toward his face. It was a gigantic spider; and its eight gleaming eyes blazed with lambent green light like a cluster of sinister opals.

He was paralysed with horror; then, summoning all his force of will, he snatched up the revolver and fired. The flash and the noise of the report dazed him for a moment; and when he saw clearly again the spider was gone. He must have hit it, for he fired point blank; but it had left no sign. It was just as well, for otherwise his tale would not have passed muster with the police. But, later in the morning, he found a trail of silky threads running across the carpet from the bed to the wall.

But the end was now very near. Only a few days later, the police were again in the house. This time they had been called in by the gardener, who said that he could not make Mr. Goldstein hear when he knocked at his door, and that he thought he must be ill. The door was locked, and had to be forced.

What the police found had better not be described. At the funeral, the undertaker's men said that they had never carried a man who weighed so little for his size.

The Steps

Amyas Northcote

The following story purports to be the actual experience of one of our leading medical men, who, during the late war, attained considerable eminence in the treatment of nervous diseases and affections of the brain. The earlier part of the tale has been collected from other sources for the purpose of bringing about the necessary explanations of the experience itself.

At the beginning of the war, Sir Arthur H. was living with his wife and only unmarried daughter at their place in Hampshire. Sir Arthur was a soldier, and soon after the outbreak of hostilities was despatched to a command Overseas, leaving Lady and Miss H. in charge of Atherfield Court, which is situated in an accessible and pleasant part of Hampshire. The advantages of the neighbourhood caused it to be selected by the War Office as the site for an instructional camp for the new Army, and the quiet lanes around Atherfield were soon alive with khaki-clad men, exotic looking mules and motor vehicles of every type and size. Lady and Miss H. were both of them anxious to take their place in giving pleasure to our young soldiers, and besides occasional entertainments for the men, they threw open the doors of the Court to the officers of their acquaintance, who were cordially invited to bring their friends with them.

Among the officers so brought was a certain Captain X, a man slightly older than most of the officers of his rank and an agreeable, cultivated and travelled man. He was very popular in his Mess and had the reputation of being a capable officer, but no one knew much about him. Like so many other of the men who came to the aid of the old country from Overseas, he had no friends in England and if he had family ties here he never spoke of them.

At first he was very much liked by both Lady and Miss H., and was a very welcome visitor; but after a time the two ladies reached the conclusion that, charming and well-educated as he was, he lacked that indescribable something which characterises a gentleman. However, they did not vary their hospitality towards him on that account, and he became gradually one of their most frequent visitors.

This state of things was interrupted after a time by Captain X proposing marriage to Miss H., a proposal which she promptly and emphatically declined. Thereupon he ceased for awhile to visit the Court, but after a certain interval once more reappeared there and gradually resumed his old habit of frequent visits. The ladies did not greatly like this, and endeavoured by a colder manner towards him to discourage any intimacy; and matters remained on this slightly strained footing until Lady H. learned that the battalion to which Captain X was attached, having completed its training, was about to proceed to France.

A few days before it left Captain X called, ostensibly to make his farewells, but to the surprise and annoyance of Miss H. he seized an opportunity and once more offered himself as a suitor for her hand. She repulsed him firmly and finally, and a somewhat unpleasant scene took place, Captain X vowing that come what might he intended to marry her and that, though she might refuse him now, a time would come when he would carry his point. Naturally angered, Miss H. replied equally emphatically that no earthly power would force her to marry him, and the two parted on very strained terms. A few days later the battalion went abroad, nothing further having been heard at Atherfield of Captain X, and in fact nothing more was heard from him.

For some little time various officers of the battalion who had been entertained by the H.'s kept up a desultory correspondence with them, and very occasionally one or other of them mentioned Captain X's name, but he himself neither wrote nor sent any message to Atherfield, and gradually the memory of him became dim, to Lady H. at any rate. Miss H., if indeed she ever thought of him, never spoke of him, and the whole episode of his acquaintance seemed in a fair way to be forgotten.

About a year later Lady H. and her daughter were sitting in the drawing-room at Atherfield, the former busily writing letters for the afternoon post and the latter immersed in a book. Both were silent and deeply intent on their respective occupations. Suddenly Miss H. started and, laying down her book, exclaimed: "Who can that be coming down the passage?" adding after a moment's pause, "It sounds like that horrid Captain X's footsteps."

Lady H., who had heard nothing, looked up from her letters, saying placidly:

"That is quite impossible, my dear, and I do not think there is anybody in the passage, at least I hear no one."

Miss H. listened for a moment or so longer and then said: "No, I was mistaken, but I certainly thought I heard some one walking quickly and rather uncertainly along the passage, and for a second the idea that it was Captain X came into my head. I cannot think why I should have thought it was him, I fancied I had forgotten him.

Anyway," she went on, "I was quite wrong because evidently there was nobody at all and I must have been dreaming."

Saying this, she picked up her book and Lady H. resumed her letters and thought no more about the occurrence.

Two days later Lady H. when looking through the list of Killed in Action in the *Times* noticed the name of Captain X. She did not associate this event in any way with the recent occurrence in the drawing-room, which she had completely forgotten, neither did she mention the notice to her daughter. The latter probably saw it herself, however, although she did not speak of it to Lady H. Both mother and daughter appeared anxious to avoid any allusion to the dead man of whom neither had any pleasant recollection.

About a week after the notice in the paper, Lady H. began to observe a change in her daughter's usual placid and cheerful manner. She had begun to grow nervous and wore an uneasy look. She made no complaints and at first eluded her mother's efforts to penetrate into what was wrong, but at last a mother's love and anxiety prevailed and Miss H. confessed that at intervals, in fact ever since the afternoon in the drawing-room, she had had an impression of the sound of approaching footsteps. These footsteps, she said, occurred at irregular intervals and at any time and place. They might be heard as she sat with her mother, or when she was out of doors or alone in her room. They always began some way off, approached hastily and, at first especially, rather irregularly and they always ceased at some little distance from her. What agitated her most was that the steps resembled those of the late Captain X of whose memory she now felt a sickening fear and horror. Lady H., a practical, matter-of-fact woman, with no belief in what she called ghost humbug, was somewhat puzzled over her daughter's story, but on consideration put it down to fancy and a disturbed digestion, both of which she proceeded to treat, the former with advice and remonstrance, the latter with various simple remedies.

Miss H. grew no better under this treatment and Lady H. presently called in the services of their local doctor, a man of neither greater nor less ability than the mass of country practitioners. This gentleman also ascribed Miss H.'s trials to the purely physical causes of indigestion and followed in Lady H.'s footsteps in the matter of remedies with as little success as had attended her efforts. Miss H. grew worse and more nervous, and ultimately the local doctor, confessing his inability to deal properly with the case, recommended that the advice of a nerve specialist be asked and gave Lady H. the name and address of the well known physician in London, who may now be left to tell the remainder of the story in his own words.

"On a certain date, which I need not more particularly specify, I received a letter from Dr. B. of Atherfield, Hampshire, saying that he had requested Lady H. to bring her daughter to me for advice. Dr. B.'s letter was not very clearly worded, but I gathered from it that Miss H. believed herself to be suffering from some form of haunting, a belief which Dr. B. did not wholly share. His country medical experience had not afforded him opportunities of studying the numerous subtle varieties of psychic affections, or I might say afflictions, which torment sensitive and receptive minds. While, therefore, he attributed Miss H.'s trouble to physical causes primarily, which causes might affect the mental and nervous system, I was prepared from the first to consider that this was far more likely to be a case of mental disturbance reacting on the body.

"Well, in due course Lady H. wrote for an appointment for herself and her daughter, and presented herself and the young lady in my consulting room on the prescribed date. On a first inspection I was not seriously disturbed by Miss H.'s appearance. She looked in good health and her various organs were in good working order. I listened to her and her mother's stories and came to the conclusion that the probabilities pointed to the first sound of footsteps being genuinely clair-audient, that the late Captain X had at the moment of his death, which I gathered was instantaneous, been deeply absorbed in the thought of Miss H., and that under laws which are known to exist, although by no means understood, had been transported spiritually to her neighbourhood and had become manifest by clair-audience to her during his approach. There are too many well authenticated cases of apparitions at the point of death for us any longer to disbelieve in their possibility, but the continuance of such manifestations for any length of time after bodily extinction are, as has been shown by Mr. Myers, of much more rare and less well-evidenced occurrence.

"Accordingly, whilst prepared to admit that in the first instance Miss H. had been the percipient of a genuine manifestation, I was inclined to believe that the subsequent recurrence of the footsteps was due to an unconscious agitation of her subconscious self and that they were genuine hallucinations, having no real existence. To remove those impressions it appeared to me desirable to prescribe a course of hypnotic suggestion; but I had no sooner hinted at this form of treatment than I found myself strongly opposed by Lady H., who emphatically declared her entire disbelief in and religious revolt from any such proceeding. Obliged to abandon the treatment, owing to this opposition, I fell back upon prescribing a tonic and a complete change of scene, and I advised Lady H. to take her daughter to the sea for a three weeks' stay and to let me know on her return how the patient did.

"The ladies promised to follow my directions and left me, after which I allowed the whole case to fade from my mind.

"Exactly three weeks later it was revived by the receipt of a letter from Lady H. written from her London house and asking me to call and see Miss H. as soon as possible, as they had returned from the sea with the trouble not only unabated but greatly increased.

"At the time I was very busy, but I managed to get round to —— Street fairly early on the following morning. After a brief interview with Lady H., who was extremely agitated, I was shown up alone to Miss H.'s sitting-room, a pleasant apartment at the back of the house and approached by a short, oilcloth-covered passage.

"I was greatly shocked by the change in the young lady's appearance. Physically she had deteriorated greatly, as was apparent at the first glance, but mentally her condition was even more alarming. She had apparently lost all control over herself, trembled violently for no ostensible reason, and appeared to be constantly keenly listening for some dreaded sound. She greeted me eagerly and instantly began: 'Oh, doctor, can you not help me? I know you thought when I saw you before you could do something, if only Mother, would have allowed it; and now I will insist on doing anything you tell me, anything, if only I can be relieved from him.'

"'Tell me more of your trouble,' I said. 'Are you still haunted by the sound of footsteps?

"'Haunted,' she said. 'Haunted, yes, that is just the word. You know I told you I was troubled by footsteps coming from a distance and stopping well away from me. They did not come often then, but they do now; they come all the time,' she went on, 'and come clearer and louder and they come nearer. Nearer, nearer, they come close to me and, oh God, one day he will reach and touch me and then—'"

"She stopped for a moment and I was thinking what I could say to reassure her when she suddenly caught hold of my arm.

"'There they are now,' she cried. 'Listen, they are coming down the passage. Listen, listen.'

"Her distress and agitation were so extreme that I could not control myself for a moment and we both sat in dead silence listening. I am not a nervous or imaginative man and in my cool moments I am sure I was mistaken; but at that instant I could have sworn that I heard a footfall on the oilcloth outside.

"'Do you hear him?' she cried again. 'He is coming, oh, help me.'

"I took her hands in mine and looked her steadily in the face.

"'Control yourself,' I said. 'You are safe, you cannot be harmed.'

"As I spoke her look of she said:

"'He has stopped; he has gone again—but he will come back. He will never really go away till he can take me too.'

"I did my best to reassure her and presently she grew calmer and promised me that she would certainly not listen for the recurrence of the steps, and would endeavour to surround herself with a form of protective envelope, evolved out of her own inner thoughts and will power, so as to ward them off. I was, however, determined at once to commence a course of hypnotic suggestion; with the consent of Lady H. if possible, if not, without. Accordingly I went downstairs and after an earnest conversation with her at last I carried my point. I was then obliged to leave the house to attend to other pressing duties, but I settled to return that afternoon and commence the treatment. In the meantime I arranged with Lady H. that, pending my return, either she or some trusty servant should remain constantly with Miss H.

"That afternoon, in accordance with my promise, I returned to —— Street to find the house in sad trouble, the butler, who opened the door, informing me that Miss H. had died suddenly a short time before. While talking to him about the event, I saw Dr. K., a family physician of my acquaintance, descending the stairs. He greeted me and, telling me that he was the London medical attendant of the H. family, took me into a room on the ground floor to tell me what details he could of the tragedy.

"It appeared that after my visit Miss H. had grown more cheerful and confident of herself. She had been quickly joined by her mother, and the two ladies had remained together till after luncheon, when they went into the drawing-room. A short time after this Lady H. was called to the telephone and, knowing that her absence would be short and thinking Miss H. might, in her happier frame of mind, he left for this brief space of time, she went downstairs to the instrument, leaving Miss H. lying on a sofa alone in the drawing-room. Lady H. had just finished her conversation and was hanging up the receiver when she was startled by hearing a loud scream for help. She rushed upstairs to find Miss H. stretched on the floor in a corner of the room some distance from her sofa, dead.

"After a few questions had been asked and answered, I asked Dr. K. for his opinion as to the cause of death, and he replied, 'Heart failure, undoubtedly caused in my opinion by a shock; but I can form no opinion as to its nature, as there was nothing in Miss H.'s surroundings in the drawing-room of an unusual or alarming character.'

"He presently offered to allow me to inspect the body, and I can only say that I have never seen on any living or dead face such an agonized look of fear and horror as on that of the dead girl."

The Stone Coffin

"B."

I

The year was 1754, the month October. The Chapel at Magdalene had been undergoing renovation all the summer, at the hands of the ingenious Mr. Collins, of Clare Hall—indeed, since the beginning of the Easter Term the College services had been held in St. Giles' Church adjacent.

II

Mr. Dobree the Bursar, a big bluff man, was pacing in the Court in the autumn sunshine. Some workmen were carrying planks and poles out of the doorway of the Chapel staircase. The Bursar's companion, a little meagre figure in rusty black, peering about him through big horn spectacles, was Mr. Janeway, the President of the College. Presently they went in at the Chapel door, and stood regarding the building. "Dear now!" said Mr. Janeway, staring about him, "I hardly see where I am! A great change, no doubt! But it is a chaste design!"

It certainly was a change! but out of a Gothic building with an open roof, much as we see it now, the ingenious Mr. Collins had made a place more like, one would have said, the dining-hall of a Roman consul than a Christian church. The roof was cut off by a flat plaster ceiling, heavily ornamented. A classical arch spanned the sanctuary, and the East window was obliterated by a columned piece of statuary. The floor was elegantly paved with black and white marble.

Mr. Dobree looked complacently about him. "It is not such a change to my eyes," he said, "Because I have watched the work from the beginning. It seems to me a very respectable place!"

"And pray what does the Master think of it all?" said Mr. Janeway.

"That I cannot tell," said Mr. Dobree rather curtly. "Has he seen the progress of the work?" said Mr. Janeway.

"The Master," said Mr. Dobree, "has been, to my knowledge, twice in the chapel since the work began. He ran in once without his wig, in a greasy cassock, and spoke rudely to the workmen about the noise they made—as if such work could be done in silence! He was disturbed at his accounts, he said. Once again he met Mr. Collins in the chapel, when the carved piece over the table was up. He said to Mr. Collins that he was given to understand that the figures were those of saints and angels, but that they appeared to him to be something much more indelicate. Then he laughed, and said he supposed it was the effect of the plaster work, at which Mr. Collins was greatly mortified. But so long as he can find fault and has nothing to pay, the College may go hang for him. He has gotten a Prebend of Durham, they say, by interest, this last week, and that is all he cares for."

"Tut, tut," said Mr. Janeway soothingly.

"Now," said Mr. Dobree, striding up the chapel. "Come hither with me, and I will relate to you a curiosity. About six weeks ago the workmen were laying the floor, and one came to me and said they had found somewhat. It was hereabouts, by this step." He stamped on the pavement, and then continued, "When I came in, they had uncovered and broken in pieces the lid of a stone coffin just here, and I bade them take the bits out. I tell you it was a strange sight underneath! There lay a man, his head in a niche made for it in the stone, robed from head to foot in an embroidered robe, of the colour of a butterfly—one of the orange-brown ones that you may see sitting on summer flowers—with figures and patterns inwrought. The flesh was all perished, and the skull, with its dark eye-holes, stared very dismally out, with something like hair atop of it. I doubt he had lain there since monkish days, and it displeased me very much. I stooped down and picked at the robe, and it all came away in my hands, falling to dust, leaving but a few coloured threads. The bones had mouldered too, all but the thigh-bones, and they were brittle. 'Come,' said I, 'the less we look on this the better!' So I took a besom in my hand and swept the whole carcase, bones and dust and robe and all, to one end of the coffin; and it made but a little heap there. I prodded the skull out of its niche, and that all came to dust too. But while I brushed, I heard a tinkling, and I picked out of the mess a little cup and platter of some metal, very dark, and a big ring with a blue stone—all very Popish and disgraceful to my eyes. I have them in my chamber, and I shall send them to Mr. Gray, at Pembroke Hall, who cares about such oddities. Then I had the coffin broken up, and carried to the stonemasons' yard, and dropt all the dust into the hole thus made, saw that they put soil on the place and battered it well down. A good riddance, I think!"

"Dear now!" said Mr. Janeway, musing. "That is a strange story—a very strange story! But, Mr. Dobree, if you will pardon me, I do not like your action very well. It seems to me that the man, whoever he was, was piously bestowed here, and had a right to his rest—so it appears to me, but I speak under correction!"

"Pish!" said Mr. Dobree. "Here's a pother about a parcel of old Popish bones! I am one who hold by the glorious Reformation, and I would cleanse the temple of all such recusants, if I had my choice. Why, the thought of that ugly figure, under my feet, would have made me very squeamish at my prayers. I wonder at you, Mr. Janeway, indeed I do!"

"Well, well," said Mr. Janeway, "There are many opinions; but I cannot like the business. May be he was a holy man, even if he died in sad error. I doubt if he could have known better."

"A sincere study of the Word would have shown him his abominations," said Mr. Dobree. "I am a Protestant, born and bred, and I have no patience with old mummeries."

Mr. Janeway sighed and said no more, and presently they went away.

III

It might have been a week later that Mr. Dobree awoke suddenly at night in his room, which was in the right-hand corner of the first Court, as you come in by the gate, on the ground floor. He awoke half in terror and half in anger, troubled by a dream, and thought that he heard someone moving very softly about his room; which was lighted only by a little high window in a deep recess that looked out towards the river, on to what was then a little street or lane of houses, running parallel to the College. The window was bare of any curtain, and Mr. Dobree thought that he saw a very faint figure cross the glimmering panes, it being bright moonlight without.

Mr. Dobree was as bold as a lion. He sate up in bed and shouted out in his great voice, Eh, what? Holla-ho! Who is that? Eh, what did you say? What do you there, sirrah?

His voice reverberated in the little bare room, and died away, leaving a shocking silence. Nothing moved or spoke. He felt for his tinder-box and made a light, and then jumping out of bed, in nightcap and nightgown, looked about everywhere, first in his bedroom, then through his two keeping-rooms, and even in his cupboards, but he saw no sign of anything living. After some time he went back to bed, but not to sleep. He was angry with himself for being afraid, and half suspected a trick; but his door was firmly latched, and no one seemed to have come in that way, while the windows into the court were safely shuttered.

In the morning, after a draught of small beer, which he used for his breakfast, and when he had made his toilet, he felt better; but for all that he wished for company, and made his way to Mr. Janeway's rooms in the second Court as soon as might be. He found Mr. Janeway reading in a book, with coffee beside him, and sitting down he told him his adventure rather shamefacedly. Mr. Janeway nodded his head and said very little, save this, that he too, when his stomach was at all disordered, suffered from disturbing dreams. "A little sick fancy, no doubt!" he added comfortably.

"It may be!" said Mr. Dobree moodily; "But I think there was someone with me in the room. Yet what sticks even more in my mind was a dream I had dreamed, which I cannot fully recall."

"What was it like?" said Mr. Janeway.

"What was it?" said Mr. Dobree; "That I cannot quite tell—but it was an ill dream. I was in a dull place, methought between buildings. They were buildings, I believe; and a dark sort of thing poked its head out in front of me in an ugly way. It seems to me now that it had on a parti-coloured robe, of black or white, or both—like a gown, and like a surplice. There was something drawn over the head of it; and the face was very white; now, as I think of it, I believe it had no eyes; it said something to me, which still sounds in my ears like Latin, in a very low voice; and it seemed to be angry—Yes, Sir, it was angry, was that person!"

"Dear now!" said Mr. Janeway, looking over his glasses at Mr. Dobree, "That's a bad story and a confused story! Is it your way to dream like that, Mr. Dobree? It seems to me a dark affair."

"Why, Sir!" said Mr. Dobree with a sudden anger, "It appears to me that you are but very poor company this morning! I come to my old friend to be made cheer with, and you can only shake your head and look dismal. This is not friendly, Sir! You are not speaking your mind!"

"Nay, Sir," said Mr. Janeway, "Be not so peevish! There is something that presses upon my spirits, since you spoke your dream, and I am grown very heavy. You must think no more of it, Sir. It was but a touch of vapours, such as comes to us lonely men, as we get older and more solitary."

Mr. Dobree got up, shaking his head and looking very sullen, and marched off without a word. He went about his business as usual, but found himself day by day in a disordered mood. He ate little and spoke not at all, though he had been ever ready with his tongue. He slept brokenly; and presently as he sate alone in his room, he began to hear whispers in his ear, or he would think that he was called; and his brother Fellows began to be concerned about him, wondering why he peered so often into the corners of the room, and why he wheeled round so sharply in the street to look behind him as he walked alone.

IV

It was a very wet and dull afternoon at the end of November, and Mr. Dobree had sate all day indoors. Just about dusk he remembered that he had a word to say to the stonemason who worked for the College, about some tiling on the roof. He went out of his rooms and found the whole place very still, with a light rain falling. He walked out of the gate, and turned to the left at once, down the lane that ran close by the College, the stonemason's yard being at the end of it, by the water's edge.

When he got there he found the mason with a lantern in his hand looking about among some piled-up stones in the yard. Mr. Dobree went to speak to him, and broke off in the middle. He felt very much displeased to see what was evidently the head-piece of the old stone coffin lying on the ground. "How comes that there?" he said with a sudden sharpness. "Why, Sir," said the mason "You ordered me to take it and break it all up, and it has lain there ever since." "What is that which lies inside it?" said Mr. Dobree in a loud voice. The mason turned his lantern on the piece. It was roughly worked, the strokes of the chisel being visible where the head had lain, and it was pierced with a hole, the use of which Mr. Dobree did not like to guess. "There is nothing here!" said the mason. "No," said Mr. Dobree, "There is not—I see plainly now. I was dazzled—It was but the shadow. Yet I certainly thought . . ." He broke off, turned on his heel and went away, the business being still unsettled. The mason stood, lantern in hand, watching him as he marched out of the yard. Then he shook his head, and went into the house.

A moment later Mr. Dobree was hurrying up the lane. It was very dark, and the rain kept all men at home. On his right, the wall of the College towered up in the misty air, and he could see a few lighted windows, very high above. The houses on his left seemed all dark and comfortless. He went on until he was close outside his own rooms, which lay next the street.

Suddenly out of the window of his own bedroom, just above him, not a yard away, there came with a silent haste the head and shoulders of a man, wrapped up, it seemed to Mr. Dobree, in a parti-coloured robe, black and white, with a hood over the face, but the face itself was visible, a dead yellow-white, like baked clay, with holes for eyes. There came a faint, thin voice upon the air, and words that sounded in Mr. Dobree's agonised ears like "*Quare inquietasti me ut suscitarer?*" But Mr. Dobree heard no more. He fell all his length in the wet road, and presently turned over on his back, where they afterwards found him, still looking upwards.

The Story of the Spaniards, Hammersmith

E. and H. Heron

Lieutenant Roderick Houston, of H.M.S. *Sphinx*, had practically nothing beyond his pay, and he was beginning to be very tired of the West African station, when he received the pleasant intelligence that a relative had left him a legacy. This consisted of a satisfactory sum in ready money and a house in Hammersmith, which was rated at over £200 a year, and was said in addition to be comfortably furnished. Houston, therefore, counted on its rental to bring his income up to a fairly desirable figure. Further information from home, however, showed him that he had been rather premature in his expectations, whereupon, being a man of action, he applied for two months' leave, and came home to look after his affairs himself.

When he had been a week in London he arrived at the conclusion that he could not possibly hope single-handed to tackle the difficulties which presented themselves. He accordingly wrote the following letter to his friend, Flaxman Low:

The Spaniards, Hammersmith, 23-3-1892

Dear Low,

Since we parted some three years ago, I have heard very little of you. It was only yesterday that I met our mutual friend, Sammy Smith ("Silkworm" of our schooldays) who told me that your studies have developed in a new direction, and that you are now a good deal interested in psychical subjects. If this be so, I hope to induce you to come and stay with me here for a few days by promising to introduce you to a problem in your own line. I am just now living at "The Spaniards," a house that has lately been left to me, and which in the first instance was built by an old fellow named Van Nuysen, who married a great-aunt of mine. It is a good house, but there is said to be "something wrong" with it. It lets easily, but unluckily the tenants cannot be persuaded to remain above a week or two. They complain that the place is haunted by something—presumably a ghost—because its vagaries bear just that brand of inconsequence which stamps the common run of manifestations.

It occurs to me that you may care to investigate the matter with me. If so, send me a wire when to expect you.

Yours ever,
Roderick Houston

Houston waited in some anxiety for an answer. Low was the sort of man one could rely on in almost any emergency. Sammy Smith had told him a characteristic anecdote of Low's career at Oxford, where, although his intellectual triumphs may be forgotten, he will always be remembered by the story that when Sands, of Queen's, fell ill on the day before the Varsity sports, a telegram was sent to Low's rooms: "Sands ill. You must do the hammer for us." Low's reply was pithy: "I'll be there." Thereupon he finished the treatise upon which he was engaged, and next day his strong, lean figure was to be seen swinging the hammer amidst vociferous cheering, for that was the occasion on which he not only won the event, but beat the record.

On the fifth day Low's answer came from Vienna. As he read it, Houston recalled the high forehead, long neck—with its accompanying low collar—and thin moustache of his scholarly, athletic friend, and smiled. There was so much more in Flaxman Low than anyone gave him credit for.

My Dear Houston,

Very glad to hear of you again. In response to your kind invitation, I thank you for the opportunity of meeting the ghost, and still more for the pleasure of your companionship. I came here to inquire into a somewhat similar affair. I hope, however, to be able to leave to-morrow, and will be with you some time on Friday evening.

Very sincerely yours,
Flaxman Low

P.S.—By the way, will it be convenient to give your servants a holiday during the term of my visit, as, if my investigations are to be of any value, not a grain of dust must be disturbed in your house, excepting by ourselves?—F. L.

"The Spaniards" was within some fifteen minutes' walk of Hammersmith Bridge. Set in the midst of a fairly respectable neighbourhood, it presented an odd contrast to the commonplace dullness of the narrow streets crowded about it. As Flaxman Low drove up in the evening light, he reflected that the house might have come from the back of beyond—it gave an impression of something old-world and something exotic.

It was surrounded by a ten-foot wall, above which the upper storey was visible, and Low decided that this intensely English house still gave some curious suggestion of the tropics. The interior of the house carried out the same idea, with its sense of space and air, cool tints and wide-matted passages.

"So you have seen something yourself since you came?" Low said, as they sat at dinner, for Houston had arranged that meals should be sent in for them from an hotel.

"I've heard tapping up and down the passage upstairs. It is an uncarpeted landing which runs the whole length of the house. One night, when I was quicker than usual, I saw what looked like a bladder disappear into one of the bedrooms—your room it is to be, by the way—and the door closed behind it," replied Houston discontentedly. "The usual meaningless antics of a ghost."

"What had the tenants who lived here to say about it?" went on Low.

"Most of the people saw and heard just what I have told you, and promptly went away. The only one who stood out for a little while was old Filderg—you know the man? Twenty years ago he made an effort to cross the Australian deserts—he stopped for eight weeks. When he left he saw the house-agent, and said he was afraid he had done a little shooting practice in the upper passage, and he hoped it wouldn't count against him in the bill, as it was done in defence of his life. He said something had jumped on to the bed and tried to strangle him. He described it as cold and glutinous, and he pursued it down the passage, firing at it. He advised the owner to have the house pulled down; but, of course, my cousin did nothing of the kind. It's a very good house, and he did not see the sense of spoiling his property."

"That's very true," replied Flaxman Low, looking round. "Mr. Van Nuysen had been in the West Indies, and kept his liking for spacious rooms."

"Where did you hear anything about him?" asked Houston in surprise.

"I have heard nothing beyond what you told me in your letter; but I see a couple of bottles of Gulf weed and a lace-plant ornament, such as people used to bring from the West Indies in former days."

"Perhaps I should tell you the history of the old man," said Houston doubtfully; "but we aren't proud of it!"

Flaxman Low considered a moment.

"When was the ghost seen for the first time?"

"When the first tenant took the house. It was let after old Van Nuysen's time."

"Then it may clear the way if you will tell me something of him."

"He owned sugar plantations in Trinidad, where he passed the greater part of his life, while his wife mostly remained in England—incompatibility of temper it was said. When he came home for good and built this house they still lived apart, my aunt declaring that nothing on earth would persuade her to return to him. In course of time he became a confirmed invalid, and he then insisted on my aunt joining him. She lived here for perhaps a year, when she was found dead in bed one morning—in your room."

"What caused her death?"

"She had been in the habit of taking narcotics, and it was supposed that she smothered herself while under their influence."

"That doesn't sound very satisfactory," remarked Flaxman Low.

"Her husband was satisfied with it anyhow, and it was no one else's business. The family were only too glad to have the affair hushed up."

"And what became of Mr. Van Nuysen?"

"That I can't tell you. He disappeared a short time after. Search was made for him in the usual way, but nobody knows to this day what became of him."

"Ah, that was strange, as he was such an invalid," said Low, and straightway fell into a long fit of abstraction, from which he was roused by hearing Houston curse the incurable foolishness and imbecility of ghostly behaviour. Flaxman woke up at this. He broke a walnut thoughtfully and began in a gentle voice:

"My dear fellow, we are apt to be hasty in our condemnation of the general behaviour of ghosts. It may appear incalculably foolish in our eyes, and I admit there often seems to be a total absence of any apparent object or intelligent action. But remember that what appears to us to be foolishness may be wisdom in the spirit world, since our unready senses can only catch broken glimpses of what is, I have not the slightest doubt, a coherent whole, if we could trace the connection."

"There may be something in that," replied Houston indifferently. "People naturally say that this ghost is the ghost of old Van Nuysen. But what connection can possibly exist between what I have told you of him and the manifestations—a tapping up and down the passage and the drawing about of a bladder like a child at play? It sounds idiotic!"

"Certainly. Yet it need not necessarily be so. There are isolated facts, we must look for the links which lie between. Suppose a saddle and a horse-shoe were to be shown to a man who had never seen a horse, I doubt whether he, however intelligent, could evolve the connecting idea! The ways of spirits are strange to us simply because we need further data to help us to interpret them."

"It's a new point of view," returned Houston, "but upon my word, you know, Low, I think you're wasting your time!"

Flaxman Low smiled slowly; his grave, melancholy face brightened.

"I have," said he, "gone somewhat deeply into the subject. In other sciences one reasons by analogy. Psychology is unfortunately a science with a future but without a past, or more probably it is a lost science of the ancients. However that may be, we stand today on the frontier of an unknown world, and progress is the result of individual effort; each solution of difficult phenomena forms a step towards the solution of the next problem. In this case, for example, the bladder-like object may be the key to the mystery."

Houston yawned.

"It all seems pretty senseless, but perhaps you may be able to read reason into it. If it were anything tangible, anything a man could meet with his fists, it would be easier."

"I entirely agree with you. But suppose we deal with this affair as it stands, on similar lines, I mean on prosaic, rational lines, as we should deal with a purely human mystery."

"My dear fellow," returned Houston, pushing his chair back from the table wearily, "you shall do just as you like, only get rid of the ghost!"

For some time after Low's arrival nothing very special happened. The tappings continued, and more than once Low had been in time to see the bladder disappear into the closing door of his bedroom, though, unluckily, he never chanced to be inside the room on these occasions, and however quickly he followed the bladder, he never succeeded in seeing anything further. He made a thorough examination of the house, and left no space unaccounted for in his careful measurement. There were no cellars, and the foundation of the house consisted of a thick layer of concrete.

At length, on the sixth night, an event took place, which, as Flaxman Low remarked, came very near to putting an end to the investigations as far as he was concerned. For the preceding two nights he and Houston had kept watch in the hope of getting a glimpse of the person or thing which tapped so persistently up and down the passage. But they were disappointed, for there were no manifestations. On the third evening, therefore, Low went off to his room a little earlier than usual, and fell asleep almost immediately.

He says he was awakened by feeling a heavy weight upon his feet, something that seemed inert and motionless. He recollected that he had left the gas burning, but the room was now in darkness.

Next he was aware that the thing on the bed had slowly shifted, and was gradually travelling up towards his chest. How it came on the bed he had no idea. Had it leaped or climbed? The sensation he experienced as it moved was of some ponderous, pulpy body, not crawling or creeping, but spreading! It was horrible! He tried to move his lower limbs, but could not because of the deadening weight. A feeling of drowsiness began to overpower him, and a deadly cold, such as he said he had before felt at sea when in the neighbourhood of icebergs, chilled upon the air.

With a violent struggle he managed to free his arms, but the thing grew more irresistible as it spread upwards. Then he became conscious of a pair of glassy eyes, with livid, everted lids, looking into his own. Whether they were human eyes or beast eyes, he could not tell, but they were watery, like the eyes of a dead fish, and gleamed with a pale, internal lustre.

Then he owns he grew afraid. But he was still cool enough to notice one peculiarity about this ghastly visitant—although the head was within a few inches of his own, he could detect no breathing. It dawned on him that he was about to be suffocated, for, by the same method of extension, the thing was now coming over his face! It felt cold and clammy, like a mass of mucilage or a monstrous snail. And every instant the weight became greater. He is a powerful man, and he struck with his fists again and again at the head. Some substance yielded under the blows with a sickening sensation of bruised flesh.

With a lucky twist he raised himself in the bed and battered away with all the force he was capable of in his cramped position. The only effect was an occasional shudder or quake that ran through the mass as his half-arm blows rained upon it. At last, by chance, his hand knocked against the candle beside him. In a moment he recollected the matches. He seized the box, and struck a light.

As he did so, the lump slid to the floor. He sprang out of bed, and lit the candle. He felt a cold touch upon his leg, but when he looked down there was nothing to be seen. The door, which he had locked overnight, was now open, and he rushed out into the passage. All was still and silent with the throbbing vacancy of night time.

After searching round, he returned to his room. The bed still gave ample proof of the struggle that had taken place, and by his watch he saw the hour to be between two and three.

As there seemed nothing more to be done, he put on his dressing-gown, lit his pipe, and sat down to write an account of the experience he had just passed through for the Psychical Research Society—from which paper the above is an abstract.

He is a man of strong nerves, but he could not disguise from himself that he had been at handgrips with some grotesque form of death. What might be the nature of his assailant he could not determine, but his experience was supported by the attack which had been made on Filderg, and also—it was impossible to avoid the conclusion—by the manner of Mrs. Van Nuysen's death.

He thought the whole situation over carefully in connection with the tapping and the disappearing bladder, but, turn these events how he would, he could make nothing of them. They were entirely incongruous. A little later he went and made a shakedown in Houston's room.

"What was the thing?" asked Houston, when Low had ended his story of the encounter.

Low shrugged his shoulders.

"At least it proves that Filderg did not dream," he said.

"But this is monstrous! We are more in the dark than ever. There's nothing for it but to have the house pulled down. Let us leave to-day."

"Don't be in a hurry, my dear fellow. You would rob me of a very great pleasure; besides, we may be on the verge of some valuable discovery. This series of manifestations is even more interesting than the Vienna mystery I was telling you of."

"Discovery or not," replied the other, "I don't like it."

The first thing next morning Low went out for a quarter of an hour. Before breakfast a man with a barrowful of sand came into the garden. Low looked up from his paper, leant out of the window, and gave some order.

When Houston came down a few minutes later he saw the yellowish heap on the lawn with some surprise.

"Hullo! What's this?" he asked.

"I ordered it," replied Low.

"All right. What's it for?"

"To help us in our investigations. Our visitor is capable of being felt, and he or it left a very distinct impression on the bed. Hence I gather it can also leave an impression on sand. It would be an immense advance if we could arrive at any correct notion of what sort of feet the ghost walks on. I propose to spread a layer of this sand in the upper passage, and the result should be footmarks if the tapping comes to-night."

That evening the two men made a fire in Houston's bedroom, and sat there smoking and talking, to leave the ghost "a free run for once," as Houston phrased it. The tapping was heard at the usual hour, and presently the accustomed pause at the other end of the passage and the quiet closing of the door.

Low heaved a long sigh of satisfaction as he listened.

"That's my bedroom door," he said; "I know the sound of it perfectly. In the morning, and with the help of daylight, we shall see what we shall see."

As soon as there was light enough for the purpose of examining the footprints, Low roused Houston.

Houston was full of excitement as a boy, but his spirits fell by the time he had passed from end to end of the passage.

"There are marks," he said, "but they are as perplexing as everything else about this haunting brute, whatever it is. I suppose you think this is the print left by the thing which attacked you the night before last?"

"I fancy it is," said Low, who was still bending over the floor eagerly. "What do you make of it, Houston?"

"The brute has only one leg, to start with," replied Houston, "and that leaves the mark of a large, clawless pad! It's some animal—some ghoulish monster!"

"On the contrary," said Low, "I think we have now every reason to conclude that it is a man."

"A man? What man ever left footmarks like these?"

"Look at these hollows and streaks at the sides; they are the traces of the sticks we have heard tapping."

"You don't convince me," returned Hodgson doggedly.

"Let us wait another twenty-four hours, and to-morrow night, if nothing further occurs, I will give you my conclusions. Think it over. The tapping, the bladder, and the fact that Mr. Van Nuysen had lived in Trinidad. Add to these things this single pad-like print. Does nothing strike you by way of a solution?"

Houston shook his head.

"Nothing. And I fail to connect any of these things with what happened both to you and Filderg."

"Ah! now," said Flaxman Low, his face clouding a little, "I confess you lead me into a somewhat different region, though to me the connection is perfect."

Houston raised his eyebrows and laughed.

"If you can unravel this tangle of hints and events and diagnose the ghost, I shall be extremely astonished," he said. "What can you make of the footless impression?"

"Something, I hope. In fact, that mark may be a clue—an outrageous one, perhaps, but still a clue."

That evening the weather broke, and by night the storm had risen to a gale, accompanied by sharp bursts of rain.

"It's a noisy night," remarked Houston; "I don't suppose we'll hear the ghost, supposing it does turn up."

This was after dinner, as they were about to go into the smoking-room. Houston, finding the gas low in the hall, stopped to run it higher; at the same time asking Low to see if the jet on the upper landing was also alight.

Flaxman Low glanced up and uttered a slight exclamation, which brought Houston to his side.

Looking down at them from over the banisters was a face—a blotched, yellowish face, flanked by two swollen, protruding ears, the whole aspect being strangely leonine. It was but a glimpse, a clash of meeting glances, as it were, a glare of defiance, and the face was quickly withdrawn as the two men literally leapt up the stairs.

"There's nothing here," exclaimed Houston, after a search had been carried out through every room above.

"I didn't suppose we'd find anything," returned Low.

"This fairly knots up the thread," said Houston. "You can't pretend to unravel it now."

"Come down," said Low briefly; "I'm ready to give you my opinion, such as it is."

Once in the smoking-room, Houston busied himself in turning on all the light he could procure, then he saw to securing the windows, and piled up an immense fire, while Flaxman Low, who, as usual, had a cigarette in his mouth, sat on the edge of the table and watched him with some amusement.

"You saw that abominable face?" cried Houston, as he threw himself into a chair. "It was as material as yours or mine. But where did he go to? He must be somewhere about."

"We saw him clearly. That is sufficient for our purpose."

"You are very good at enumerating points, Low. Now just listen to my list. The difficulties grow with every fresh discovery. We're at a deadlock now, I take it? The sticks and the tapping point to an old man, the playing with a bladder to a child; the footmark might be the pad of a tiger minus claws, yet the thing that attacked you at night was cold and pulpy. And, lastly, by way of a wind-up, we see a lion-like, human face! If you can make all these items square with each other, I'll be happy to hear what you have got to say."

"You must first allow me to ask you a question. I understood you to say that no blood relationship existed between you and old Mr. Van Nuysen?"

"Certainly not. He was quite an outsider," answered Houston brusquely.

"In that case you are welcome to my conclusions. All the things you have mentioned point to one explanation. This house is haunted by the ghost of Mr. Van Nuysen, and he was a leper."

Houston stood up and stared at his companion.

"What a horrible notion! I must say I fail to see how you have arrived at such a conclusion."

"Take the chain of evidence in rather different order," said Low. "Why should a man tap with a stick?"

"Generally because he's blind."

"In cases of blindness, one stick is used for guidance. Here we have two for support."

"A man who has lost the use of his feet."

"Exactly; a man who has from some cause partially lost the use of his feet."

"But the bladder and the lion-like face?" went on Houston.

"The bladder, or what seemed to us to resemble a bladder, was one of his feet, contorted by the disease and probably swathed in linen, which foot he dragged rather than used; consequently, in passing through a door, for example, he would in the habit of drawing it in after him. Now, as regards the single footmark we saw. In one form of leprosy, the smaller bones of the extremities frequently fall away. The pad-like impression was, as I believe, the mark of the other foot—a toeless foot which he used, because in a more advanced stage of the disease the maimed hand or foot heals and becomes callous."

"Go on," said Houston; "it sounds as if it might be true. And the lion-like face I can account for myself. I have been in China, and have seen it before in lepers."

"Mr. Van Nuysen had been in Trinidad for many years, as we know, and while there he probably contracted the disease."

"I suppose so. After his return," added Houston, "he shut himself up almost entirely, and gave out that he was a martyr to rheumatic gout, this awful thing being the true explanation."

"It also accounts for Mrs. Van Nuysen's determination not to return to her husband."

Houston appeared much disturbed.

"We can't drop it here, Low," he said, in a constrained voice. "There is a good deal more to be cleared up yet. Can you tell me more?"

"From this point I find myself on less certain ground," replied Low unwillingly. "I merely offer a suggestion, remember—I don't ask you to accept it. I believe Mrs. Van Nuysen was murdered!"

"What?" exclaimed Houston. "By her husband?"

"Indications tend that way."

"But, my good fellow——"

"He suffocated her and then made away with himself. It is a pity that his body was not recovered. The condition of the remains would be the only really satisfactory test of my theory. If the skeleton could even now be found, the fact that he was a leper would be finally settled."

There was a prolonged pause until Houston put another question.

"Wait a minute, Low," he said. "Ghosts are admittedly immaterial. In this instance our spook has an extremely palpable body. Surely this is rather unusual? You have made everything else more or less plain. Can you tell me why this dead leper should have tried to murder you and old Filderg? And also how he came to have the actual physical power to do so?"

Low removed his cigarette to look thoughtfully at the end of it. "Now I lapse into the purely theoretical," he answered. "Cases have been known where the assumption of diabolical agency is apparently justifiable."

"Diabolical agency?—I don't follow you."

"I will try to make myself clear, though the subject is still in a stage of vagueness and immaturity. Van Nuysen committed a murder of exceptional atrocity, and afterwards killed himself. Now, bodies of suicides are known to be peculiarly susceptible to spiritual influences, even to the point of arrested corruption. Add to this our knowledge that the highest aim of an evil spirit is to gain possession of a material body. If I carried out my theory to its logical conclusion, I should say that Van Nuysen's body is hidden somewhere on these premises—that this body is intermittently animated by some spirit, which at certain points is forced to re-enact the gruesome tragedy of the Van Nuysens. Should any living person chance to occupy the position of the first victim, so much the worse for him!"

For some minutes Houston made no remark on this singular expression of opinion.

"But have you ever met with anything of the sort before?" he said at last.

"I can recall," replied Flaxman Low thoughtfully, "quite a number of cases which would seem to bear out this hypothesis. Among them a curious problem of haunting exhaustively examined by Busner in the early part of 1888, at which I was myself lucky enough to assist. Indeed, I may add that the affair which I have recently engaged upon in Vienna offers some rather similar features. There, however, we had to stop short of excavation, by which alone any specific results might have been attained."

"Then you are of the opinion," said Houston, "that pulling the house to pieces might cast some further light upon this affair?"

"I cannot see any better course," said Mr. Low.

Then Houston closed the discussion by a very definite declaration.

"This house shall come down!"

So "The Spaniards" was pulled down.

Such is the story of "The Spaniards," Hammersmith, and it has been given the first place in this series because, although it may not be of so strange a nature as some that will follow it, yet it seems to us to embody in a high degree the peculiar methods by which Mr. Flaxman Low is wont to approach these cases.

The work of demolition, begun at the earliest possible moment, did not occupy very long, and during its early stages, under the boarding at an angle of the landing was found a skeleton. Several of the phalanges were missing, and other indications also established beyond a doubt the fact that the remains were the remains of a leper.

The skeleton is now in the museum of one of our city hospitals. It bears a scientific ticket, and is the only evidence extant of the correctness of Mr. Flaxman Low's methods and the possible truth of his extraordinary theories.

A Strange Goldfield

Guy Boothby

Of course nine out of every ten intelligent persons will refuse to believe that there could be a grain of truth in the story I am now going to tell you. The tenth may have some small faith in my veracity, but what I think of his intelligence I am going to keep to myself.

In a certain portion of a certain Australian Colony two miners, when out prospecting in what was then, as now, one of the dreariest parts of the Island Continent, chanced upon a rich find. They applied to Government for the usual reward, and in less than a month three thousand people were settled on the Field. What privations they had to go through to get there, and the miseries they had to endure when they did reach their journey's end, have only a remote bearing on this story, but they would make a big book.

I should explain that between Railhead and the Field was a stretch of country some three hundred miles in extent. It was badly watered, vilely grassed, and execrably timbered. What was even worse, a considerable portion of it was made up of red sand, and everybody who has been compelled to travel over that knows what it means. Yet these enthusiastic seekers after wealth pushed on, some on horseback, some in bullock waggons, but the majority travelled on foot; the graves, and the skeletons of cattle belonging to those who had preceded them punctuating the route, and telling them what they might expect as they advanced.

That the Field did not prove a success is now a matter of history, but that same history, if you read between the lines, gives one some notion of what the life must have been like while it lasted. The water supply was entirely insufficient, provisions were bad and ruinously expensive; the men themselves were, as a rule, the roughest of the rough, while the less said about the majority of the women the better. Then typhoid stepped in and stalked like the Destroying Angel through the camp. Its inhabitants went down like sheep in a drought, and for the most part rose no more. Where there had been a lust of gold there was now panic, terror—every man feared that he might be the next to be attacked, and it was only the knowledge of those terrible three hundred miles that separated them from civilisation that kept many of them on the Field.

The most thickly populated part was now the cemetery. Drink was the only solace, and under its influence such scenes were enacted as I dare not describe. As they heard of fresh deaths, men shook their fists at Heaven, and cursed the day when they first saw pick or shovel. Some, bolder than the rest, cleared out just as they stood; a few eventually reached civilisation, others perished in the desert. At last the Field was declared abandoned, and the dead were left to take their last long sleep, undisturbed by the clank of windlass or the blow of pick.

It would take too long to tell all the different reasons that combined to draw me out into that "most distressful country." Let it suffice that our party consisted of a young Englishman named Spicer, a wily old Australian bushman named Matthews, and myself. We were better off than the unfortunate miners, inasmuch as we were travelling with camels, and our outfits were as perfect as money and experience could make them. The man who travels in any other fashion in that country is neither more nor less than a madman. For a month past we had been having a fairly rough time of it, and were then on our way south, where we had reason to believe rain had fallen, and, in consequence, grass was plentiful. It was towards evening when we came out of a gully in the ranges and had our first view of the deserted camp. We had no idea of its existence, and for this reason we pulled up our animals and stared at it in complete surprise. Then we pushed on again, wondering what on earth place we had chanced upon.

"This is all right," said Spicer, with a chuckle. "We're in luck. Grog shanties and stores, a bath, and perhaps girls."

I shook my head.

"I can't make it out," I said. "What's it doing out here?'

Matthews was looking at it under his hand, and, as I knew that he had been out in this direction on a previous occasion, I asked his opinion.

"It beats me," he replied; "but if you ask me what I think I should say it's Gurunya, the Field that was deserted some four or five years back."

"Look here," cried Spicer, who was riding a bit on our left, "what are all these things—graves, as I'm a living man. Here, let's get out of this. There are hundreds of them and before I know where I am old Polyphemus here will be on his nose."

What he said was correct—the ground over which we were riding was literally bestrewn with graves, some of which had rough, tumbledown head boards, others being destitute of all adornment. We turned away and moved on over safer ground in the direction of the Field itself.

Such a pitiful sight I never want to see again. The tents and huts, in numerous cases, were still standing, while the claims gaped at us on every side like new-made graves. A bullock dray, weather-worn but still in excellent condition, stood in the main street outside a grog shanty whose sign-board, strange incongruity, bore the name of "The Killarney Hotel." Nothing would suit Spicer but that he must dismount and go in to explore. He was not long away, and when he returned it was with a face as white as a sheet of paper.

"You never saw such a place," he almost whispered. "All I want to do is to get out of it. There's a skeleton on the floor in the back room with an empty rum bottle alongside it."

He mounted, and, when his beast was on its feet once more, we went on our way. Not one of us was sorry when we had left the last claim behind us.

Half a mile or so from the Field the country begins to rise again. There is also a curious cliff away to the left, and, as it looked like being a likely place to find water, we resolved to camp there. We were within a hundred yards or so of this cliff when an exclamation from Spicer attracted my attention.

"Look!" he cried. "What's that?"

I followed the direction in which he was pointing, and, to my surprise, saw the figure of a man running as if for his life among the rocks. I have said the figure of a man, but, as a matter of fact, had there been baboons in the Australian bush, I should have been inclined to have taken him for one.

"This is a day of surprises," I said. "Who can the fellow be? And what makes him act like that?"

We still continued to watch him as he proceeded on his erratic course along the base of the cliff—then he suddenly disappeared.

"Let's get on to camp," I said, "and then we'll go after him and endeavour to settle matters a bit."

Having selected a place we offsaddled and prepared our camp. By this time it was nearly dark, and it was very evident that, if we wanted to discover the man we had seen, it would be wise not to postpone the search too long. We accordingly strolled off in the direction he had taken, keeping a sharp look-out for any sign of him. Our search, however, was not successful. The fellow had disappeared without leaving a trace of his whereabouts behind him, and yet we were all certain that we *had* seen him. At length we returned to our camp for supper, completely mystified. As we ate our meal we discussed the problem and vowed that, on the morrow, we would renew the search. Then the full moon rose over the cliff, and the plain immediately became well-nigh as bright as day. I had lit my pipe and was stretching myself out upon my blankets when something induced me to look across at a big rock, some half-dozen paces from the fire. Peering round it, and evidently taking an absorbing interest in our doings, was the most extraordinary figure I have ever beheld. Shouting something to my companions, I sprang to my feet and dashed across at him. He saw me and fled. Old as he apparently was, he could run like a jack-rabbit, and, though I have the reputation of being fairly quick on my feet, I found that I had all my work cut out to catch him. Indeed, I am rather doubtful as to whether I should have done so at all had he not tripped and measured his length on the ground. Before he could get up I was on him.

"I've got you at last, my friend," I said. "Now you just come along back to the camp, and let us have a look at you."

In reply he snarled like a dog and I believe would have bitten me had I not held him off. My word, he was a creature, more animal than man, and the reek of him was worse than that of our camels. From what I could tell he must have been about sixty years of age—was below the middle height, had white eyebrows, white hair and a white beard. He was dressed partly in rags and partly in skins, and went barefooted like a black fellow. While I was overhauling him the others came up—whereupon we escorted him back to the camp.

"What wouldn't Barnum give for him?" said Spicer. "You're a beauty, my friend, and no mistake. What's your name?"

The fellow only grunted in reply—then, seeing the pipes in our mouths, a curious change came over him, and he muttered something that resembled "Give me."

"Wants a smoke," interrupted Matthew's. "Poor beggar's been without for a long time, I reckon. Well, I've got an old pipe, so he can have a draw."

He procured one from his pack saddle, filled it and handed it to the man, who snatched it greedily and began to puff away at it.

"How long have you been out here?" I asked, when he had squatted himself down alongside the fire.

"Don't know," he answered, this time plainly enough.

"Can't you get back?" continued Matthews, who knew the nature of the country on the other side.

"Don't want to," was the other's laconic reply. "Stay here."

I heard Spicer mutter, "Mad—mad as a March hare."

We then tried to get out of him where he hailed from, but he had either forgotten or did not understand. Next we inquired how he managed to live. To this he answered readily enough, "Carnies."

Now the carny is a lizard of the iguana type, and eaten raw would be by no means an appetizing dish. Then came the question that gives me my reason for telling this story. It was Spicer who put it.

"You must have a lonely time of it out here," said the latter. "How do you manage for company?"

"There is the Field," he said, "as sociable a Field as you'd find."

"But the Field's deserted, man," I put in. "And has been for years."

The old fellow shook his head.

"As sociable a Field as ever you saw," he repeated. "There's Sailor Dick and 'Frisco, Dick Johnson, Cockney Jim, and half a hundred of them. They're taking it out powerful rich on the Golden South, so I heard when I was down at 'The Killarney,' a while back."

It was plain to us all that the old man was, as Spicer had said, as mad as a hatter. For some minutes he rambled on about the Field, talking rationally enough, I must confess—that is to say, it would have seemed rational enough if we hadn't known the true facts of the case. At last he got on to his feet, saying, "Well, I must be going—they'll be expecting me. It's my shift on with Cockney Jim."

"But you don't work at night," growled Matthews, from the other side of the fire.

"We work always," the other replied. "If you don't believe me, come and see for yourselves."

"I wouldn't go back to that place for anything," said Spicer.

But I must confess that my curiosity had been aroused, and I determined to go, if only to see what this strange creature did when he got there. Matthews decided to accompany me, and, not wishing to be left alone, Spicer at length agreed to do the same. Without looking round, the old fellow led the way across the plain towards the Field. Of all the nocturnal excursions I have made in my life, that was certainly the most uncanny. Not once did our guide turn his head, but pushed on at a pace that gave us some trouble to keep up with him. It was only when we came to the first claim that he paused.

"Listen," he said, "and you can hear the camp at work. Then you'll believe me."

We *did* listen, and as I live we could distinctly hear the rattling of sluice-boxes and cradles, the groaning of windlasses—in fact, the noise you hear on a goldfield at the busiest hour of the day. We moved a little closer, and, believe me or not, I swear to you I could see, or thought I could see, the shadowy forms of men moving about in that ghostly moonlight. Meanwhile the wind sighed across the plain, flapping what remained of the old tents and giving an additional touch of horror to the general desolation. I could hear Spicer's teeth chattering behind me, and, for my own part, I felt as if my blood were turning to ice.

"That's the claim, the Golden South, away to the right there," said the old man, "and if you will come along with me, I'll introduce you to my mates."

But this was an honour we declined, and without hesitation. I wouldn't have gone any further among those tents for the wealth of all the Indies.

"I've had enough of this," said Spicer, and I can tell you I hardly recognised his voice. "Let's get back to camp."

By this time our guide had left us, and was making his way in the direction he had indicated.

We could plainly hear him addressing imaginary people as he marched along. As for ourselves, we turned about and hurried back to our camp as fast as we could go.

Once there, the grog bottle was produced, and never did three men stand more in need of stimulants. Then we set to work to find some explanation of what we had seen, or had fancied we saw. But it was impossible. The wind might have rattled the old windlasses, but it could not be held accountable for those shadowy grey forms that had moved about among the claims.

"I give it up," said Spicer, at last. "I know that I never want to see it again. What's more, I vote that we clear out of here to-morrow morning."

We all agreed, and then retired to our blankets, but for my part I do not mind confessing I scarcely slept a wink all night. The thought that that hideous old man might be hanging about the camp would alone be sufficient for that.

Next morning, as soon as it was light, we breakfasted, but, before we broke camp, Matthews and I set off along the cliff in an attempt to discover our acquaintance of the previous evening. Though, however, we searched high and low for upwards of an hour, no success rewarded us. By mutual consent we resolved not to look for him on the Field. When we returned to Spicer we placed such tobacco and stores as we could spare under the shadow of the big rock, where the Mystery Man would be likely to see them, then mounted our camels and resumed our journey, heartily glad to be on our way once more.

Gurunya Goldfield is a place I never desire to visit again. I don't like its population.

A Strange Messenger

Mrs. Molesworth

Late in the afternoon of a dull autumn day a man was walking briskly along a hilly road in one of the northern Welsh counties. It was at all times a gloomy part of the world, yet not without a certain picturesqueness of its own, enhanced perhaps by its very grimness—grimness more the work of human hands than of nature, for it was a mining district.

The man, a fairly young man—my story dates back fully twenty years—stood still for a moment and looked about him. He was not a native of the place, and, comparatively speaking, a newcomer. But he was growing to feel at home in it, and he was grateful for the position he had come thither to hold, that of manager to the important mine not far from where he stood—a position which had enabled him to marry sooner than at one time he had dared to hope would be possible.

"Yes," he thought, "it has turned out very well. Margaret is so sensible and adaptable. She never seems to feel it dull, as I feared she might. I remember how I felt like a fish out of water at first, scarcely understanding what the people said, nor their queer ways"; then a shadow crossed his face. "It is very sad about Brough," he went on thinking. "I wonder if I shall find him any better to-day. I fear not. He has been such a good steady fellow, and being an Englishman, made him enter into my difficulties, in his quiet way," and with these thoughts he hurried on again, till he reached a row of small houses occupied by some of the many miners, at a short distance from the pit's mouth.

At the door of one of these he stopped and knocked. It was opened by a tidy-looking elderly woman, the wife of the man to whom the cottage belonged, and with whom Brough, unmarried and with no relations in the place, had lodged for several years.

She shook her head in reply to the manager's unspoken inquiry.

"No better, sir. Step in; he'll be pleased to see you. It's the master, Brough," she went on in a louder voice as she showed Mr. Heald into a small room opening out of the kitchen.

"No better" was plainly written on the worn thin face of the man who tried to raise himself on his pillows as the manager entered, and gently, very gently, shook the big hand, once brown and rough, now pathetically smooth and white, held out to him.

"So good of you, sir," the sick man murmured. "Indeed, I don't know how to thank you for coming so regular, and you so busy," a cough stopped him and he lay back exhausted.

"I wish I could do more for you," said Mr. Heald very kindly, with a sigh.

"Nay, sir," Brough went on again, and his honest blue eyes gazed into his friend's face with the indescribable, mysterious intentness of the dying, "Nay, sir, if I could but have done something in return—you and the lady too—sending me soup and fruit and the best of everything—if I could have done something for you, I feel as if I'd die easier."

Mr. Heald gently touched the thin hand again.

"Don't speak that way, my dear fellow," he said. "If we have been able to cheer you a little, we are only too glad."

But Brough's expression did not change. He murmured something inaudible, and lay still. The manager did not stay long; he saw that the patient was very weak. He just waited to tell the poor fellow that a few details as to his little possessions—the sending some money that the miner had saved, to a sister in Australia, and so on, were all carefully noted and should be attended to, and then with a "I'll come again to-morrow," he left, the blue eyes, faithful and devoted, following him to the door.

And when, true to his promise, he came again next day, Brough was dead.

Time passed. The winter—a very severe one that year—came on, and now and then, when the thought of Brough crossed his mind, the manager would say to his wife that he was glad the poor fellow had not lingered; "it would have been terribly trying for him in that cottage in such weather."

Then slowly and half reluctantly, as it were, followed the spring. The snowdrops, and, later on, the primroses and violets— faithful little friends as ever—began to peep out in the lanes and copses among the valleys between the great grim hills—for there were still green oases even in that black country. Then a short but glowing summer, and "again," said Margaret Heald to herself, with a little sigh, as she stood one dull morning looking after her husband as he set off to his day's work, "again it is autumn and the long winter before us." But the sigh was quietly replaced by a smile. "We are so happy," she murmured, "so very happy. What do outside things like the weather matter?"

That very afternoon, as the doctor of the district returned to his own house after a long round, he was met at the door by an unexpected summons. He was tired and hungry, and, being no longer a young man, these sensations were less easy to bear with philosophy than formerly. And his work was arduous, for he was the only medical man within a circuit of five miles, and, excepting for the cluster of dwellings in the neighbourhood of the mine, his patients were scattered at considerable distances, in that sparsely-populated corner of the world.

"I really think I shall have to get a partner, or at least a thoroughly efficient assistant," he was saying to himself, as he got down from his dog-cart at the gate, and his 'Well, what's the matter, Eliza?' to the servant who opened the door before he had time to take out his latch-key, was perhaps, excusably, a little irritable.

Eliza was a newcomer—a capable and intelligent girl, for she came from a suburb of London and was not without "cockney" acuteness, but as yet unaccustomed to the conditions of a doctor's house and scarcely acclimatised to the place.

"What's the matter now?' said her master, for the girl looked startled and anxious.

"Oh, if you please, sir, will you go at once, *at once*," with emphasis, "to the manager's house, Mr. Heald's. I've been watching to catch you before the horse was taken out. The messenger's not been gone five minutes."

Dr. Warden's face lengthened.

"Did he not say what was wrong? Who brought the message?" he inquired, sharply.

"Oh yes, sir. It's an accident—very bad he seemed to think—to the manager himself. He was one of the workmen, the miners, I mean. He said his name was—," but by this time she was speaking to the air, for the doctor had rushed to the stable-yard, calling to his man that he must have the trap again at once—yes, *at once*— Eliza's emphasis on the words seemed to have pressed them on to his brain.

He had a most hearty and sincere regard—affection indeed, one might say—for both Heald and his sweet wife, but as he drove along, his anxiety had time to cool a little, for his destination was between two and three miles away.

"I daresay that girl has exaggerated," he thought. "She's nervous and excitable, though sharp enough. It was a fad of the missus's to have a servant from such a distance, because the girls hereabouts are rough and clumsy—however, this air will put some colour into Eliza's cheeks. I daresay there's not much wrong with Heald —it may be all a mistake, and they will laugh at me for coming."

But as he entered the village—for village of a kind had grown up near the mine—his fears returned. For, grouped round the gate of the manager's pretty little house at the far end of the street, stood a number of men—miners of course, with grave faces and apprehensive looks. They would have spoken to the doctor, but he, springing from his cart with the alacrity of twenty years ago, pushed his way through them, eager to get to headquarters at once.

The door was closed, but almost before his knock had ceased sounding, it was opened, and at the same moment Margaret Heald came out into the little hall. Her face was deadly pale, her eyes full of anguish, but at the sight of the newcomer a look of intense relief overspread her whole countenance; she almost smiled.

"Oh Dr. Warden, oh dear doctor," she exclaimed. "What a mercy! Thank God, what a blessed chance! Come in at once. You may, you *must* be in time. He is scarcely conscious; he is bleeding to death. We have done all we could, but we *cannot* stop it. Oh come."

She caught hold of the doctor's sleeve and pulled him into the room, where, on a couch, for they had not dared to take him upstairs, lay poor Robert Heald—more dead than alive, for in fact it was getting to be a question of minutes for him. And yet the actual accident had not been a very serious one. He had caught his foot somehow when examining some new tools or machinery just being unpacked, and had fallen, cutting his wrist on a piece of sharp jagged iron lying about, and all but completely severing the artery. But had medical skill been instantly available, he need scarcely have run any risk. As it was, the more experienced as to wounds and injuries, among the miners, had done their best, and temporarily stopped the bleeding, which had, however, burst out again as they carried him to his home, fortunately close at hand.

It took but a short time for Dr. Warden's clever surgery to save the situation, and with an ejaculation of profoundest thankfulness, Margaret saw her husband open his eyes and try to smile at her, while a little colour came back into his face.

"He will do now," said the doctor, "give him what I have ordered from time to time," referring to certain restoratives, "and keep him absolutely quiet and still, till I look in again this evening. He will probably sleep a good deal. Don't talk to him more than you can help."

Margaret followed the doctor out into the hall. Her eyes were full of tears, yet shining with happiness.

"You have saved his life," she said. "But oh, how unspeakably grateful we should be that you happened to be passing! I suppose you saw the men at the gate. Collins"—

the Healds' groom—"was just starting on the pony to fetch you. But," and she shivered, "it would have been too late, I feel certain."

"Yes," was the reply," there was assuredly terrible risk. I was only just in time, but—" and he looked puzzled. "How do you mean that I happened to be passing? I came all the way from home—as soon as I got your message, of course?"

The puzzled expression moved on to Margaret's face and intensified there.

"I did not send for you," she exclaimed. "There had not been time. Robert had not been five minutes in the house when you came."

"Then one of the men must have gone straight from the mine the moment it happened," the doctor replied, but Mrs. Heald still shook her head.

"No, no, impossible," she maintained. "For you to have got a message to bring you here so soon, you must have heard of the accident almost simultaneously with its occurring. It must have been a brain-wave, doctor," and she smiled.

"A very substantial one," he said. "It *was* one of the men, sent, I understood, by you. Still," he added, reflectively, "*you* wouldn't have sent on foot. Ah well," as he went off, "I'll inquire about it and tell you this evening."

He returned within a few hours, and much to Margaret's delight volunteered to stay all night, "just in case of anything going wrong."

But nothing did go wrong, though both doctor and wife sat up; in turn watching by the patient, who slept fairly quietly.

And at breakfast the next morning Dr. Warden told his hostess a strange story.

"I waited till the night was over—not to excite or startle you, my dear," he began, "to tell you the result of my cross-questioning of Eliza, my servant. I had not misunderstood what she said. It *was* one of the miners—a workman, she called him, who summoned me, and by putting things together, he must have been at my door *almost*, as you said, simultaneously with Heald's accident—"

"But," interrupted Margaret, "how—how *could*—"

Dr. Warden in his turn broke into her speech.

"Stay," he said, "I must remind you of the old quotation 'More things in heaven and earth.' Yes, it was one of the miners, or should I say one who *had* been such—but," and he half murmured the next words—"rest his soul, he's dead." "Margaret," he went on, "the girl described him closely. He was pale—'delicate-like, for a rough sort of man, and he had a nice voice and very blue eyes,' etc. 'To make it still surer, as he turned to go, something seemed to strike him, "Tell them," he added, "tell them as it was Brough, Laurence Brough, that fetched the doctor." 'Then,' continued Eliza, 'I was going to ask him to say it again, but he was gone—I don't know how he managed to slip off so quickly—and I said the name over to myself, not to forget it.' That is all she has to tell, and all *she* need ever know. It might upset her."

Margaret had grown very, very white; but it was the whiteness of awe, not of fear.

"Doctor," she said in a whisper, "what do you think? *Can* such things be?"

His voice was very reverent as he replied, "Far be it from me to say they cannot."

It was not till some days' quiet had completely restored Robert Heald to his usual health that they told him the story. And after a moment or two's deep silence he looked up and said gently, "I remember the last words I heard him speak, 'If I could do something in return for you, I feel as if I'd die easier.'"

"And how little we had done, or been able to do," added Margaret. "Such faithfulness of gratitude makes one ashamed—gratitude reaching not till, but beyond, death."

Like the Last Minstrel,

> I say the tale as 'twas said to me,

but as to its truth, I go further. The facts of the incident I have related are facts, not fiction.

The Stranger

Ambrose Bierce

A man stepped out of the darkness into the little illuminated circle about our failing campfire and seated himself upon a rock.

"You are not the first to explore this region," he said, gravely.

Nobody controverted his statement; he was himself proof of its truth, for he was not of our party and must have been somewhere near when we camped. Moreover, he must have companions not far away; it was not a place where one would be living or traveling alone. For more than a week we had seen, besides ourselves and our animals, only such living things as rattlesnakes and horned toads. In an Arizona desert one does not long coexist with only such creatures as these: one must have pack animals, supplies, arms—"an outfit." And all these imply comrades. It was perhaps a doubt as to what manner of men this unceremonious stranger's comrades might be, together with something in his words interpretable as a challenge, that caused every man of our half-dozen "gentlemen adventurers" to rise to a sitting posture and lay his hand upon a weapon—an act signifying, in that time and place, a policy of expectation. The stranger gave the matter no attention and began again to speak in the same deliberate, uninflected monotone in which he had delivered his first sentence:

"Thirty years ago Ramon Gallegos, William Shaw, George W. Kent and Berry Davis, all of Tucson, crossed the Santa Catalina mountains and traveled due west, as nearly as the configuration of the country permitted. We were prospecting and it was our intention, if we found nothing, to push through to the Gila river at some point near Big Bend, where we understood there was a settlement. We had a good outfit but no guide—just Ramon Gallegos, William Shaw, George W. Kent and Berry Davis."

The man repeated the names slowly and distinctly, as if to fix them in the memories of his audience, every member of which was now attentively observing him, but with a slackened apprehension regarding his possible companions somewhere in the darkness that seemed to enclose us like a black wall; in the manner of this volunteer historian was no suggestion of an unfriendly purpose. His act was rather that of a harmless lunatic than an enemy. We were not so new to the country as not to know that the solitary life of many a plainsman had a tendency to develop eccentricities of conduct and character not always easily distinguishable from mental aberration. A man is like a tree: in a forest of his fellows he will grow as straight as his generic and individual nature permits; alone in the open, he yields to the deforming stresses and tortions that environ him. Some such thoughts were in my mind as I watched the man from the shadow of my hat, pulled low to shut out the firelight. A witless fellow, no doubt, but what could he be doing there in the heart of a desert?

Having undertaken to tell this story, I wish that I could describe the man's appearance; that would be a natural thing to do. Unfortunately, and somewhat strangely, I find myself unable to do so with any degree of confidence, for afterward no two of us agreed as to what he wore and how he looked; and when I try to set down my own impressions they elude me. Anyone can tell some kind of story; narration is one of the elemental powers of the race. But the talent for description is a gift.

Nobody having broken silence the visitor went on to say:

"This country was not then what it is now. There was not a ranch between the Gila and the Gulf. There was a little game here and there in the mountains, and near the infrequent water-holes grass enough to keep our animals from starvation. If we should be so fortunate as to encounter no Indians we might get through. But within a week the purpose of the expedition had altered from discovery of wealth to preservation of life. We had gone too far to go back, for what was ahead could be no worse than what was behind; so we pushed on, riding by night to avoid Indians and the intolerable heat, and concealing ourselves by day as best we could. Sometimes, having exhausted our supply of wild meat and emptied our casks, we were days without food or drink; then a water-hole or a shallow pool in the bottom of an *arroyo* so restored our strength and sanity that we were able to shoot some of the wild animals that sought it also. Sometimes it was a bear, sometimes an antelope, a coyote, a cougar—that was as God pleased; all were food.

"One morning as we skirted a mountain range, seeking a practicable pass, we were attacked by a band of Apaches who had followed our trail up a gulch—it is not far from here. Knowing that they outnumbered us ten to one, they took none of their usual cowardly precautions, but dashed upon us at a gallop, firing and yelling. Fighting was out of the question: we urged our feeble animals up the gulch as far as there was footing for a hoof, then threw ourselves out of our saddles and took to the *chaparral* on one of the slopes, abandoning our entire outfit to the enemy. But we retained our rifles, every man—Ramon Gallegos, William Shaw, George W. Kent and Berry Davis."

"Same old crowd," said the humorist of our party. He was an Eastern man, unfamiliar with the decent observances of social intercourse. A gesture of disapproval from our leader silenced him and the stranger proceeded with his tale:

"The savages dismounted also, and some of them ran up the gulch beyond the point at which we had left it, cutting off further retreat in that direction and forcing us on up the side. Unfortunately the *chaparral* extended only a short distance up the slope, and as we came into the open ground above we took the fire of a dozen rifles; but Apaches shoot badly when in a hurry, and God so willed it that none of us fell. Twenty yards up the slope, beyond the edge of the brush, were vertical cliffs, in which, directly in front of us, was a narrow opening. Into that we ran, finding ourselves in a cavern about as large as an ordinary room in a house. Here for a time we were safe: a single man with a repeating rifle could defend the entrance against all the Apaches in the land. But against hunger and thirst we had no defense. Courage we still had, but hope was a memory.

"Not one of those Indians did we afterward see, but by the smoke and glare of their fires in the gulch we knew that by day and by night they watched with ready rifles in the edge of the bush—knew that if we made a sortie not a man of us would live to take three steps into the open. For three days, watching in turn, we held out before our suffering became insupportable. Then—it was the morning of the fourth day—Ramon Gallegos said:

"'Señores, I know not well of the good God and what please him. I have live without religion, and I am not acquaint with that of you. Pardon, señores, if I shock you, but for me the time is come to beat the game of the Apache.'

"He knelt upon the rock floor of the cave and pressed his pistol against his temple. 'Madre de Dios,' he said, 'comes now the soul of Ramon Gallegos.'

"And so he left us—William Shaw, George W. Kent and Berry Davis.

"I was the leader: it was for me to speak.

"'He was a brave man,' I said—'he knew when to die, and how. It is foolish to go mad from thirst and fall by Apache bullets, or be skinned alive—it is in bad taste. Let us join Ramon Gallegos.'

"'That is right,' said William Shaw.

"'That is right,' said George W. Kent.

"I straightened the limbs of Ramon Gallegos and put a handkerchief over his face. Then William Shaw said: 'I should like to look like that—a little while.'

"And George W. Kent said that he felt that way, too.

"'It shall be so,' I said: 'the red devils will wait a week. William Shaw and George W. Kent, draw and kneel.'

"They did so and I stood before them.

"'Almighty God, our Father,' said I.

"'Almighty God, our Father,' said William Shaw.

"'Almighty God, our Father,' said George W. Kent.

"'Forgive us our sins,' said I.

"'Forgive us our sins,' said they.

"'And receive our souls.'

"'And receive our souls.'

"'Amen!'

"'Amen!'

"I laid them beside Ramon Gallegos and covered their faces."

There was a quick commotion on the opposite side of the campfire: one of our party had sprung to his feet, pistol in hand.

"And you!" he shouted—"*you* dared to escape?—you dare to be alive? You cowardly hound, I'll send you to join them if I hang for it!"

But with the leap of a panther the captain was upon him, grasping his wrist. "Hold it in, Sam Yountsey, hold it in!"

We were now all upon our feet—except the stranger, who sat motionless and apparently inattentive. Some one seized Yountsey's other arm.

"Captain," I said, "there is something wrong here. This fellow is either a lunatic or merely a liar—just a plain, every-day liar whom Yountsey has no call to kill. If this man was of that party it had five members, one of whom—probably himself—he has not named."

"Yes," said the captain, releasing the insurgent, who sat down, "there is something—unusual. Years ago four dead bodies of white men, scalped and shamefully mutilated, were found about the mouth of that cave. They are buried there; I have seen the graves—we shall all see them to-morrow."

The stranger rose, standing tall in the light of the expiring fire, which in our breathless attention to his story we had neglected to keep going.

"There were four," he said—"Ramon Gallegos, William Shaw, George W. Kent and Berry Davis."

With this reiterated roll-call of the dead he walked into the darkness and we saw him no more.

At that moment one of our party, who had been on guard, strode in among us, rifle in hand and somewhat excited.

"Captain," he said, "for the last half-hour three men have been standing out there on the *mesa*." He pointed in the direction taken by the stranger. "I could see them distinctly, for the moon is up, but as they had no guns and I had them covered with mine I thought it was their move. They have made none, but, damn it! they have got on to my nerves."

"Go back to your post, and stay till you see them again," said the captain. "The rest of you lie down again, or I'll kick you all into the fire."

The sentinel obediently withdrew, swearing, and did not return. As we were arranging our blankets the fiery Yountsey said: "I beg your pardon, Captain, but who the devil do you take them to be?"

"Ramon Gallegos, William Shaw and George W. Kent."

"But how about Berry Davis? I ought to have shot him."

"Quite needless; you couldn't have made him any deader. Go to sleep."

The Terror by Night

E. F. Benson

The transference of emotion is a phenomenon so common, so constantly witnessed, that mankind in general have long ceased to be conscious of its existence, as a thing worth our wonder or consideration, regarding it as being as natural and commonplace as the transference of things that act by the ascertained laws of matter. Nobody, for instance, is surprised, if when the room is too hot, the opening of a window causes the cold fresh air of outside to be transferred into the room, and in the same way no one is surprised when into the same room, perhaps, which we will imagine as being peopled with dull and gloomy persons, there enters some one of fresh and sunny mind, who instantly brings into the stuffy mental atmosphere a change analogous to that of the opened windows. Exactly how this infection is conveyed we do not know; considering the wireless wonders (that act by material laws) which are already beginning to lose their wonder now that we have our newspaper brought as a matter of course every morning in mid-Atlantic, it would not perhaps be rash to conjecture that in some subtle and occult way the transference of emotion is in reality material too. Certainly (to take another instance) the sight of definitely material things, like writing on a page, conveys emotion apparently direct to our minds, as when our pleasure or pity is stirred by a book, and it is therefore possible that mind may act on mind by means as material as that.

Occasionally, however, we come across phenomena which, though they may easily be as material as any of these things, are rarer, and therefore more astounding. Some people call them ghosts, some conjuring tricks, and some nonsense. It seems simpler to group them under the head of transferred emotions, and they may appeal to any of the senses. Some ghosts are seen, some heard, some felt, and though I know of no instance of a ghost being tasted, yet it will seem in the following pages that these occult phenomena may appeal at any rate to the senses that perceive heat, cold, or smell. For, to take the analogy of wireless telegraphy, we are all of us probably "receivers" to some extent, and catch now and then a message or part of a message that the eternal waves of emotion are ceaselessly shouting aloud to those who have ears to hear, and materialising themselves for those who have eyes to see. Not being, as a rule, perfectly tuned, we grasp but pieces and fragments of such messages, a few coherent words it may be, or a few words which seem to have no sense. The following story, however, to my mind, is interesting, because it shows how different pieces of what no doubt was one message were received and recorded by several different people simultaneously. Ten years have elapsed since the events recorded took place, but they were written down at the time.

Jack Lorimer and I were very old friends before he married, and his marriage to a first cousin of mine did not make, as so often happens, a slackening in our intimacy. Within a few months after, it was found out that his wife had consumption, and, without any loss of time, she was sent off to Davos, with her sister to look after her. The disease had evidently been detected at a very early stage, and there was excellent ground for hoping that with proper care and strict regime she would be cured by the life-giving frosts of that wonderful valley.

The two had gone out in the November of which I am speaking, and Jack and I joined them for a month at Christmas, and found that week after week she was steadily and quickly gaining ground. We had to be back in town by the end of January, but it was settled that Ida should remain out with her sister for a week or two more. They both, I remember, came down to the station to see us off, and I am not likely to forget the last words that passed:

"Oh, don't look so woebegone, Jack," his wife had said; "you'll see me again before long."

Then the fussy little mountain engine squeaked, as a puppy squeaks when its toe is trodden on, and we puffed our way up the pass.

London was in its usual desperate February plight when we got back, full of fogs and still-born frosts that seemed to produce a cold far more bitter than the piercing temperature of those sunny altitudes from which we had come. We both, I think, felt rather lonely, and even before we had got to our journey's end we had settled that for the present it was ridiculous that we should keep open two houses when one would suffice, and would also be far more cheerful for us both.

So, as we both lived in almost identical houses in the same street in Chelsea, we decided to "toss," live in the house which the coin indicated (heads mine, tails his), share expenses, attempt to let the other house, and, if successful, share the proceeds. A French five-franc piece of the second empire told us it was "heads."

We had been back some ten days, receiving every day the most excellent accounts from Davos, when, first on him, then on me, there descended, like some tropical storm, a feeling of indefinable fear. Very possibly this sense of apprehension (for there is nothing in the world so virulently infectious) reached me through him: on the other hand both these attacks of vague foreboding may have come from the same source. But it is true that it did not attack me till he spoke of it, so the possibility perhaps inclines to my having caught it from him. He spoke of it first, I remember, one evening when we had met for a good-night talk, after having come back from separate houses where we had dined.

"I have felt most awfully down all day," he said; "and just after receiving this splendid account from Daisy, I can't think what is the matter."

He poured himself out some whisky and soda as he spoke.

"Oh, touch of liver," I said. "I shouldn't drink that if I were you. Give it me instead."

"I was never better in my life," he said.

I was opening letters, as we talked, and came across one from the house agent, which, with trembling eagerness, I read.

"Hurrah," I cried, "offer of five guas—why can't he write it in proper English—five guineas a week till Easter for number 31. We shall roll in guineas!"

"Oh, but I can't stop here till Easter," he said.

"I don't see why not. Nor by the way does Daisy. I heard from her this morning, and she told me to persuade you to stop. That's to say, if you like. It really is more cheerful for you here. I forgot, you were telling me something."

The glorious news about the weekly guineas did not cheer him up in the least.

"Thanks awfully. Of course I'll stop."

He moved up and down the room once or twice.

"No, it's not me that is wrong," he said, "it's It, whatever It is. The terror by night."

"Which you are commanded not to be afraid of," I remarked.

"I know: it's easy commanding. I'm frightened: something's coming."

"Five guineas a week are coming," I said. "I shan't sit up and be infected by your fears. All that matters, Davos, is going as well as it can. What was the last report? Incredibly better. Take that to bed with you."

The infection—if infection it was—did not take hold of me then, for I remember going to sleep feeling quite cheerful, but I awoke in some dark still house and It, the terror by night, had come while I slept. Fear and misgiving, blind, unreasonable, and paralysing, had taken and gripped me. What was it? Just as by an aneroid we can foretell the approach of storm, so by this sinking of the spirit, unlike anything I had ever felt before, I felt sure that disaster of some sort was presaged.

Jack saw it at once when we met at breakfast next morning, in the brown haggard light of a foggy day, not dark enough for candles, but dismal beyond all telling.

"So it has come to you too," he said.

And I had not even the fighting-power left to tell him that I was merely slightly unwell. Besides, never in my life had I felt better.

All next day, all the day after that fear lay like a black cloak over my mind; I did not know what I dreaded, but it was something very acute, something that was very near. It was coming nearer every moment, spreading like a pall of clouds over the sky; but on the third day, after miserably cowering under it, I suppose some sort of courage came back to me: either this was pure imagination, some trick of disordered nerves or what not, in which case we were both "disquieting ourselves in vain," or from the immeasurable waves of emotion that beat upon the minds of men, something within both of us had caught a current, a pressure. In either case it was infinitely better to try, however ineffectively, to stand up against it. For these two days I had neither worked nor played; I had only shrunk and shuddered; I planned for myself a busy day, with diversion for us both in the evening.

"We will dine early," I said, "and go to the 'Man from Blankley's.' I have already asked Philip to come, and he is coming, and I have telephoned for tickets. Dinner at seven."

Philip, I may remark, is an old friend of ours, neighbour in this street, and by profession a much-respected doctor.

Jack laid down his paper.

"Yes, I expect you're right," he said. "It's no use doing nothing, it doesn't help things. Did you sleep well?"

"Yes, beautifully," I said rather snappishly, for I was all on edge with the added burden of an almost sleepless night.

"I wish I had," said he.

This would not do at all.

"We have got to play up!" I said. "Here are we two strong and stalwart persons, with as much cause for satisfaction with life as any you can mention, letting ourselves behave like worms. Our fear may be over things imaginary or over things that are real, but it is the fact of being afraid that is so despicable. There is nothing in the world to fear except fear. You know that as well as I do. Now let's read our papers with interest. Which do you back, Mr. Druce, or the Duke of Portland, or the Times Book Club?"

That day, therefore, passed very busily for me; and there were enough events moving in front of that black background, which I was conscious was there all the time, to enable me to keep my eyes away from it, and I was detained rather late at the office, and had to drive back to Chelsea, in order to be in time to dress for dinner instead of walking back as I had intended.

Then the message, which for these three days had been twittering in our minds, the receivers, just making them quiver and rattle, came through.

I found Jack already dressed, since it was within a minute or two of seven when I got in, and sitting in the drawing-room. The day had been warm and muggy, but when I looked in on the way up to my room, it seemed to me to have grown suddenly and bitterly cold, not with the dampness of English frost, but with the clear and stinging exhilaration of such days as we had recently spent in Switzerland. Fire was laid in the grate but not lit, and I went down on my knees on the hearth-rug to light it.

"Why, it's freezing in here," I said. "What donkeys servants are! It never occurs to them that you want fires in cold weather, and no fires in hot weather."

"Oh, for heaven's sake don't light the fire," said he, "it's the warmest muggiest evening I ever remember."

I stared at him in astonishment. My hands were shaking with the cold. He saw this.

"Why, you are shivering!" he said. "Have you caught a chill? But as to the room being cold let us look at the thermometer."

There was one on the writing-table.

"Sixty-five," he said.

There was no disputing that, nor did I want to, for at that moment it suddenly struck us, dimly and distantly, that It was "coming through." I felt it like some curious internal vibration.

"Hot or cold, I must go and dress," I said.

Still shivering, but feeling as if I was breathing some rarefied exhilarating air, I went up to my room. My clothes were already laid out, but, by an oversight, no hot water had been brought up, and I rang for my man. He came up almost at once, but he looked scared, or, to my already-startled senses, he appeared so.

"What's the matter?" I said.

"Nothing, sir," he said, and he could hardly articulate the words. "I thought you rang."

"Yes. Hot water. But what's the matter?"

He shifted from one foot to the other.

"I thought I saw a lady on the stairs," he said, "coming up close behind me. And the front-door bell hadn't rung that I heard."

"Where did you think you saw her?" I asked.

"On the stairs. Then on the landing outside the drawing-room door, sir," he said. "She stood there as if she didn't know whether to go in or not."

"One—one of the servants," I said. But again I felt that It was coming through.

"No, sir. It was none of the servants," he said.

"Who was it then?"

"Couldn't see distinctly, sir, it was dim-like. But I thought it was Mrs. Lorimer."

"Oh, go and get me some hot water," I said.

But he lingered; he was quite clearly frightened.

At this moment the front door bell rang. It was just seven, and already Philip had come with brutal punctuality while I was not yet half dressed.

"That's Dr. Enderly," I said. "Perhaps if he is on the stairs you may be able to pass the place where you saw the lady."

Then quite suddenly there rang through the house a scream, so terrible, so appalling in its agony and supreme terror, that I simply stood still and shuddered, unable to move. Then by an effort so violent that I felt as if something must break, I recalled the power of motion, and ran downstairs, my man at my heels, to meet Philip who was running up from the ground floor. He had heard it too.

"What's the matter?" he said. "What was that?"

Together we went into the drawing-room. Jack was lying in front of the fireplace, with the chair in which he had been sitting a few minutes before overturned. Philip went straight to him and bent over him, tearing open his white shirt.

"Open all the windows," he said, "the place reeks."

We flung open the windows, and there poured in so it seemed to me, a stream of hot air into the bitter cold. Eventually Philip got up.

"He is dead," he said. "Keep the windows open. The place is still thick with chloroform."

Gradually to my sense the room got warmer, to Philip's the drug-laden atmosphere dispersed. But neither my servant nor I had smelt anything at all.

A couple of hours later there came a telegram from Davos for me. It was to tell me to break the news of Daisy's death to Jack, and was sent by her sister. She supposed he would come out immediately. But he had been gone two hours now.

I left for Davos next day, and learned what had happened. Daisy had been suffering for three days from a little abscess which had to be opened, and, though the operation was of the slightest, she had been so nervous about it that the doctor gave her chloroform. She made a good recovery from the anesthetic, but an hour later had a sudden attack of syncope, and had died that night at a few minutes before eight, by Central European time, corresponding to seven in English time. She had insisted that Jack should be told nothing about this little operation till it was over, since the matter was quite unconnected with her general health, and she did not wish to cause him needless anxiety.

And there the story ends. To my servant there came the sight of a woman outside the drawing-room door, where Jack was, hesitating about her entrance, at the moment when Daisy's soul hovered between the two worlds; to me there came—I do not think it is fanciful to suppose this—the keen exhilarating cold of Davos; to Philip there came the fumes of chloroform. And to Jack, I must suppose, came his wife. So he joined her.

The Three Sisters

W. W. Jacobs

Thirty years ago on a wet autumn evening the household of Mallett's Lodge was gathered round the death-bed of Ursula Mallow, the eldest of the three sisters who inhabited it. The dingy moth-eaten curtains of the old wooden bedstead were drawn apart, the light of a smoking oil-lamp falling upon the hopeless countenance of the dying woman as she turned her dull eyes upon her sisters. The room was in silence except for an occasional sob from the youngest sister, Eunice. Outside the rain fell steadily over the steaming marshes.

"Nothing is to be changed, Tabitha," gasped Ursula to the other sister, who bore a striking likeness to her although her expression was harder and colder; "this room is to be locked up and never opened."

"Very well," said Tabitha brusquely, "though I don't see how it can matter to you then."

"It does matter," said her sister with startling energy. "How do you know, how do I know that I may not sometimes visit it? I have lived in this house so long I am certain that I shall see it again. I *will* come back. Come back to watch over you both and see that no harm befalls you."

"You are talking wildly," said Tabitha, by no means moved at her sister's solicitude for her welfare. "Your mind is wandering; you know that I have no faith in such things."

Ursula sighed, and beckoning to Eunice, who was weeping silently at the bedside, placed her feeble arms around her neck and kissed her.

"Do not weep, dear," she said feebly. "Perhaps it is best so. A lonely woman's life is scarce worth living. We have no hopes, no aspirations; other women have had happy husbands and children, but we in this forgotten place have grown old together. I go first, but you must soon follow."

Tabitha, comfortably conscious of only forty years and an iron frame, shrugged her shoulders and smiled grimly.

"I go first," repeated Ursula in a new and strange voice as her heavy eyes slowly closed, "but I will come for each of you in turn, when your lease of life runs out. At that moment I will be with you to lead your steps whither I now go."

As she spoke the flickering lamp went out suddenly as though extinguished by a rapid hand, and the room was left in utter darkness. A strange suffocating noise issued from the bed, and when the trembling women had relighted the lamp, all that was left of Ursula Mallow was ready for the grave.

That night the survivors passed together. The dead woman had been a firm believer in the existence of that shadowy borderland which is said to form an unhallowed link between the living and the dead, and even the stolid Tabitha, slightly unnerved by the events of the night, was not free from certain apprehensions that she might have been right.

With the bright morning their fears disappeared. The sun stole in at the window, and seeing the poor earthworn face on the pillow so touched it and glorified it that only its goodness and weakness were seen, and the beholders came to wonder how they could ever have felt any dread of aught so calm and peaceful. A day or two passed, and the body was transferred to a massive coffin long regarded as the finest piece of work of its kind ever turned out of the village carpenter's workshop. Then a slow and melancholy cortege headed by four bearers wound its solemn way across the marshes to the family vault in the grey old church, and all that was left of Ursula was placed by the father and mother who had taken that self-same journey some thirty years before.

To Eunice as they toiled slowly home the day seemed strange and Sabbath-like, the flat prospect of marsh wilder and more forlorn than usual, the roar of the sea more depressing. Tabitha had no such fancies. The bulk of the dead woman's property had been left to Eunice, and her avaricious soul was sorely troubled and her proper sisterly feelings of regret for the deceased sadly interfered with in consequence.

"What are you going to do with all that money, Eunice?" she asked as they sat at their quiet tea.

"I shall leave it as it stands," said Eunice slowly. "We have both got sufficient to live upon, and I shall devote the income from it to supporting some beds in a children's hospital."

"If Ursula had wished it to go to a hospital," said Tabitha in her deep tones, "she would have left the money to it herself. I wonder you do not respect her wishes more."

"What else can I do with it then?" inquired Eunice.

"Save it," said the other with gleaming eyes, "save it."

Eunice shook her head.

"No," said she, "it shall go to the sick children, but the principal I will not touch, and if I die before you it shall become yours and you can do what you like with it."

"Very well," said Tabitha, smothering her anger by a strong effort; "I don't believe that was what Ursula meant you to do with it, and I don't believe she will rest quietly in the grave while you squander the money she stored so carefully."

"What do you mean?" asked Eunice with pale lips. "You are trying to frighten me; I thought that you did not believe in such things."

Tabitha made no answer, and to avoid the anxious inquiring gaze of her sister, drew her chair to the fire, and folding her gaunt arms, composed herself for a nap.

For some time life went on quietly in the old house. The room of the dead woman, in accordance with her last desire, was kept firmly locked, its dirty windows forming a strange contrast to the prim cleanliness of the others. Tabitha, never very talkative, became more taciturn than ever, and stalked about the house and the neglected garden like an unquiet spirit, her brow roughened into the deep wrinkles suggestive of much thought. As the winter came on, bringing with it the long dark evenings, the old house became more lonely than ever, and an air of mystery and dread seemed to hang over it and brood in its empty rooms and dark corridors. The deep silence of night was broken by strange noises for which neither the wind nor the rats could be held accountable. Old Martha, seated in her distant kitchen, heard strange sounds upon the stairs, and once, upon hurrying to them, fancied that she saw a dark figure squatting upon the landing, though a subsequent search with candle and spectacles failed to discover anything. Eunice was disturbed by several vague incidents, and, as she suffered from a complaint of the heart, rendered very ill by them. Even Tabitha admitted a strangeness about the house, but, confident in her piety and virtue, took no heed of it, her mind being fully employed in another direction.

Since the death of her sister all restraint upon her was removed, and she yielded herself up entirely to the stern and hard rules enforced by avarice upon its devotees. Her housekeeping expenses were kept rigidly separate from those of Eunice and her food limited to the coarsest dishes, while in the matter of clothes, the old servant was by far the better dressed. Seated alone in her bedroom this uncouth, hard-featured creature revelled in her possessions, grudging even the expense of the candle-end which enabled her to behold them. So completely did this passion change her that both Eunice and Martha became afraid of her, and lay awake in their beds night after night trembling at the chinking of the coins at her unholy vigils.

One day Eunice ventured to remonstrate. "Why don't you bank your money, Tabitha?" she said; "it is surely not safe to keep such large sums in such a lonely house."

"Large sums!" repeated the exasperated Tabitha, "large sums! what nonsense is this? You know well that I have barely sufficient to keep me."

"It's a great temptation to housebreakers," said her sister, not pressing the point. "I made sure last night that I heard somebody in the house."

"Did you?" said Tabitha, grasping her arm, a horrible look on her face. "So did I. I thought they went to Ursula's room, and I got out of bed and went on the stairs to listen."

"Well?" said Eunice faintly, fascinated by the look on her sister's face.

"There was *something* there," said Tabitha slowly. "I'll swear it, for I stood on the landing by her door and listened; something scuffling on the floor round and round the room. At first I thought it was the cat, but when I went up there this morning the door was still locked, and the cat was in the kitchen."

"Oh, let us leave this dreadful house," moaned Eunice.

"What!" said her sister grimly; "afraid of poor Ursula? Why should you be? Your own sister who nursed you when you were a babe, and who perhaps even now comes and watches over your slumbers."

"Oh!" said Eunice, pressing her hand to her side, "if I saw her I should die. I should think that she had come for me as she said she would. O God! have mercy on me, I am dying."

She reeled as she spoke, and before Tabitha could save her, sank senseless to the floor.

"Get some water," cried Tabitha, as old Martha came hurrying up the stairs, "Eunice has fainted."

The old woman, with a timid glance at her, retired, reappearing shortly afterwards with the water, with which she proceeded to restore her much-loved mistress to her senses. Tabitha, as soon as this was accomplished, stalked off to her room, leaving her sister and Martha sitting drearily enough in the small parlour, watching the fire and conversing in whispers.

It was clear to the old servant that this state of things could not last much longer, and she repeatedly urged her mistress to leave a house so lonely and so mysterious. To her great delight Eunice at length consented, despite the fierce opposition of her sister, and at the mere idea of leaving gained greatly in health and spirits. A small but comfortable house was hired in Morville, and arrangements made for a speedy change.

It was the last night in the old house, and all the wild spirits of the marshes, the wind and the sea seemed to have joined forces for one supreme effort. When the wind dropped, as it did at brief intervals, the sea was heard moaning on the distant beach, strangely mingled with the desolate warning of the bell-buoy as it rocked to the waves. Then the wind rose again, and the noise of the sea was lost in the fierce gusts which, finding no obstacle on the open marshes, swept with their full fury upon the house by the creek. The strange voices of the air shrieked in its chimneys, windows rattled, doors slammed, and even, the very curtains seemed to live and move.

Eunice was in bed, awake. A small night-light in a saucer of oil shed a sickly glare upon the worm-eaten old furniture, distorting the most innocent articles into ghastly shapes. A wilder gust than usual almost deprived her of the protection afforded by that poor light, and she lay listening fearfully to the creakings and other noises on the stairs, bitterly regretting that she had not asked Martha to sleep with her. But it was not too late even now. She slipped hastily to the floor, crossed to the huge wardrobe, and was in the very act of taking her dressing-gown from its peg when an unmistakable footfall was heard on the stairs. The robe dropped from her shaking fingers, and with a quickly beating heart she regained her bed.

The sounds ceased and a deep silence followed, which she herself was unable to break although she strove hard to do so. A wild gust of wind shook the windows and nearly extinguished the light, and when its flame had regained its accustomed steadiness she saw that the door was slowly opening, while the huge shadow of a hand blotted the papered wall. Still her tongue refused its office. The door flew open with a crash, a cloaked figure entered and, throwing aside its coverings, she saw with a horror past all expression the napkin-bound face of the dead Ursula smiling terribly at her. In her last extremity she raised her faded eyes above for succour, and then as the figure noiselessly advanced and laid its cold hand upon her brow, the soul of Eunice Mallow left its body with a wild shriek and made its way to the Eternal.

Martha, roused by the cry, and shivering with dread, rushed to the door and gazed in terror at the figure which stood leaning over the bedside. As she watched, it slowly removed the cowl and the napkin and exposed the fell face of Tabitha, so strangely contorted between fear and triumph that she hardly recognized it.

"Who's there?" cried Tabitha in a terrible voice as she saw the old woman's shadow on the wall.

"I thought I heard a cry," said Martha, entering. "Did anybody call?"

"Yes, Eunice," said the other, regarding her closely. "I, too, heard the cry, and hurried to her. What makes her so strange? Is she in a trance?"

"Ay," said the old woman, falling on her knees by the bed and sobbing bitterly, "the trance of death. Ah, my dear, my poor lonely girl, that this should be the end of it! She has died of fright," said the old woman, pointing to the eyes, which even yet retained their horror. "She has seen something *devilish*."

Tabitha's gaze fell. "She has always suffered with her heart," she muttered; "the night has frightened her; it frightened me."

She stood upright by the foot of the bed as Martha drew the sheet over the face of the dead woman.

"First Ursula, then Eunice," said Tabitha, drawing a deep breath. "I can't stay here. I'll dress and wait for the morning."

She left the room as she spoke, and with bent head proceeded to her own. Martha remained by the bedside, and gently closing the staring eyes, fell on her knees, and prayed long and earnestly for the departed soul. Overcome with grief and fear she remained with bowed head until a sudden sharp cry from Tabitha brought her to her feet.

"Well," said the old woman, going to the door.

"Where are you?" cried Tabitha, somewhat reassured by her voice.

"In Miss Eunice's bedroom. Do you want anything?"

"Come down at once. Quick! I am unwell."

Her voice rose suddenly to a scream. "Quick! For God's sake! Quick, or I shall go mad. *There is some strange woman in the house*."

The old woman stumbled hastily down the dark stairs. "What is the matter?" she cried, entering the room. "Who is it? What do you mean?"

"I saw it," said Tabitha, grasping her convulsively by the shoulder. "I was coming to you when I saw the figure of a woman in front of me going up the stairs. Is it—can it be Ursula come for the soul of Eunice, as she said she would?"

"Or for yours?" said Martha, the words coming from her in some odd fashion, despite herself.

Tabitha, with a ghastly look, fell cowering by her side, clutching tremulously at her clothes. "Light the lamps," she cried hysterically. "Light a fire, make a noise; oh, this dreadful darkness! Will it never be day!"

"Soon, soon," said Martha, overcoming her repugnance and trying to pacify her. "When the day comes you will laugh at these fears."

"I murdered her," screamed the miserable woman, "I killed her with fright. Why did she not give me the money? 'Twas no use to her. Ah! *Look there!*"

Martha, with a horrible fear, followed her glance to the door, but saw nothing.

"It's Ursula," said Tabitha from between her teeth. "Keep her off! Keep her off!"

The old woman, who by some unknown sense seemed to feel the presence of a third person in the room, moved a step forward and stood before her. As she did so Tabitha waved her arms as though to free herself from the touch of a detaining hand, half rose to her feet, and without a word fell dead before her.

At this the old woman's courage forsook her, and with a great cry she rushed from the room, eager to escape from this house of death and mystery. The bolts of the great door were stiff with age, and strange voices seemed to ring in her ears as she strove wildly to unfasten them. Her brain whirled. She thought that the dead in their distant rooms called to her, and that a devil stood on the step outside laughing and holding the door against her. Then with a supreme effort she flung it open, and heedless of her night-clothes passed into the bitter night. The path across the marshes was lost in the darkness, but she found it; the planks over the ditches slippery and narrow, but she crossed them in safety, until at last, her feet bleeding and her breath coming in great gasps, she entered the village and sank down more dead than alive on a cottage door-step.

Told in the Inn at Algeciras

W. Somerset Maugham

I arrived at Algeciras, the little Spanish town opposite Gibraltar, on my way up country; and was taken to its only inn. It was somewhat late at night, and mine host, disturbed at his game at cards, seemed little pleased to see me; he looked me up and down, and without rising, uttered the number of a room to the slatternly maid who led me upstairs, and quietly shuffled his cards for the next deal. I asked for food, inquiring what I could have.

"What you like," replied the servant, shrugging her shoulders.

"What have you in the house?"

I knew well enough the unreality of the seeming profusion.

"You can have eggs and ham."

"Where is the dining-room," I asked.

I had surmised by the typical appearance of the Spanish hostelry that I should get little else, and resigned myself to a meal of boiled eggs and unleavened bread. The girl took me to a narrow room, with whitewashed walls and a low ceiling, in which was a long table, set out already for the next day's luncheon. With his back to me sat a tall man, grey-headed, huddled over a *brasero*, the round brass dish of hot ashes which gives sufficient warmth for the temperate winter of Andalusia. I sat at the head of the table, waiting for my scanty meal, and looked a little curiously at the stranger. He turned his head to glance at me, and then meeting my eyes, rapidly averted his face, as if unwilling to be seen.

But when the servant brought my eggs, he looked up and spoke to he.

"I want you to wake me in time for the first boat tomorrow."

"*Si, señor.*"

His accent told me that English was his native tongue, and the breadth of his build, his strongly marked features, led me to suppose him a northerner; the hardy Scot, indeed, is far more frequently found in Spain than the Englishman. Whether you go to the wealthy mines of Rio Tinto, or to the bodegas of Jerez, to Seville, or to Cadiz, it is the broad and leisurely accents of beyond the Tweed that assail your ears; and you will meet Scotchmen in the olive-groves of Carmona, on the railway between Algeciras and Bobadilla, even in the remote cork-woods of Merida.

But I finished eating and went over to the dish of burning ashes, for it was mid-winter and the windy passage across the bay from Gibraltar had chilled my blood. The Scotchman pushed his chair away as I drew mine forwards.

"Don't move," I said; "there's heaps of room for two."

I lit a cigar and offered him one; in Spain the Havana from Gib is never unwelcome.

"I don't mind if I do," he said, stretching out his hand; and now I had no doubt of his nationality, for I recognized the singing speech of Glasgow.

The stranger was not talkative, and my civil efforts at conversation broke down before his monosyllables. We smoked away in silence. I saw now that my fellow-guest was an even bigger man than at first I thought, with great broad shoulders and ungainly limbs. His face was sunburned, his hair short and grizzly; and his commonest gesture was to pull his ragged, grey moustache. Otherwise he was clean shaven. His features were rather hard, mouth, ears, and nose were large and heavy, and his skin was much wrinkled; his blue eyes were pallid and expressionless.

But I presently felt the Scotchman's eyes upon me, fixed with a singular stare; and the intensity of it was soon so irksome that I glanced up, expecting him, as before, to look away. He did, indeed, momentarily drop his eyelids, but quickly raised them again, appearing then to inspect me through his long bushy eyebrows.

"You've just come from Gib?" he asked suddenly.

"Yes."

"I'm going there tomorrow—on my way home. Thank God!"

The last words he said with such an extraordinary fervour that I was a little startled.

"Have you been long in Spain?" I inquired.

"Too long!—too long!" he cried, with a sudden clutching at his heart, and his voice was almost a gasp.

He sprang to his feet and walked backwards and forwards, the light of the china lamp throwing a glare upon his face. I was astonished at the emotion I had called up. He had forgotten my presence and tramped to and fro like a prisoned beast, pushing aside a chair that stood in his way. And now and again, with a kind of groan, he muttered: "Too long!—too long!" I sat still, taking no notice; and when I stirred the *brasero* to bring the hotter ashes to the top, the strange man stood suddenly still, towering over me, as if my movement had brought back my existence to his notice. Then he sat down heavily on the vacant chair.

"D'you think I'm queer?" he said.

I laughed at the oddness of the question. "No, not more than most people."

"You don't see anything strange in me?" He bent forward as he spoke so that I might see him well.

"No," I shook my head.

"You'd say so if you did, wouldn't you?"

"Certainly," I replied, smiling.

"My name's Robert Morrison."

"Scotch name," I said pleasantly.

"I've been in this country five years. . . . Have you got any baccy?"

I gave him my pouch, and he filled his pipe slowly; I waited while he lit it from a piece of burning charcoal.

"And I can't stay any longer," he added, breaking into his unexpected passion; "I've stayed too long!—too long!"

An impulse took him to spring to his feet and walk up and down, but he resisted, clinging to his chair; I saw a tremor pass over his face as he battled with the emotion, and then he became again perfectly quiet.

"I've been managing some olive-groves," he said, "and making oil. I've been working for the Glasgow and South of Spain Olive Oil Company, Limited."

"Oh yes," I said politely.

"We've got a new process for refining oil, you know. Properly treated, Spanish oil is every bit as good as Lucca; and we can sell it cheaper."

He spoke in a dry, matter-of-fact way, like a sober business man, slowly choosing his words with careful precision. In his longer speeches, the sing-song of the Glasgow intonation was more noticeable.

"You know, Ecija is more or less the centre of the olive trade, and we had a Spaniard there to look after our business; but I found he was robbing us right and left, so I had to turn him out. I used to live in Seville myself, because it was more convenient for shipping the oil. However, I found I couldn't get a trustworthy man to be at Ecija so, last year, I went there myself. D'you know it?"

"Yes," I said; "I rode there once from Seville."

I remembered it well—a little town with many towers, in a valley, right away from civilisation, nestling in the bend of a winding shallow river.

"The firm has got a large estate about two miles from the town, just outside the village of San Lorenzo; and it has a fine house on the crest of the little hill. You know what a Spanish farmhouse is like—a long, white place, straggling, low-built, with a couple of storks perched on the roof. No one lived there, and I thought it would save money if I occupied it rather than a place in town."

"I must have been lonely," I remarked.

"It was."

Robert Morrison paused a while and smoked. I wondered where the point of his reminiscence was coming, and even if there was one.

"I suppose you didn't see many people?" I said.

"Hardly a soul. I lived there with an old man and his wife, who looked after me; and now and then I used to go down to the village to play *tresillo* with the apothecary, Fernandez, and one or two more who met at his shop. I used to shoot a bit, and ride a good deal. . . . Last spring I'd been there about a year. It was hotter last May in Spain than I've ever known it. No one could work: the labourers just lay about in what shade they could find in the olive-groves, and slept through half the day. The sheep died in the heat, and some of the beasts went mad; even the oxen couldn't work, but stood with their backs humped up, gasping for breath. Day after day the sun beat down, dazzling, so that I felt my eyes would shoot out of my head. The brown earth became dry and unfertile, and cracked and crumbled into dust; the crops frizzled in the windless heat; and the olives went to rack and ruin. I couldn't sleep. I went from room to room, trying to get a breath of air; I kept the windows closed, and had the flowers watered, but nothing served. The nights were no cooler than the day; it was like living in an oven.

"At last I had a bed made up for me downstairs on the north side of the house, in a room that was never used, because in ordinary weather it was very damp. But even here I couldn't sleep. I turned and tossed, and my bed was so hot that I could stand it no longer. I got up and opened the doors that led to the verandah and walked out. The night was glorious. I leant against the parapet, looking down on the plain below, dark with the countless olive-trees; and above, the heavens were richer than velvet; the stars were wonderful, and the air so clear that I saw more than I had ever seen before. The sky was like the train of a woman's dress, sparkling with fiery beads. And then somehow I began thinking of home, of the soft cool breeze that now must be sighing through the fir-trees; I thought of the noisy streets of Glasgow; the strong smell of the town and the salt of the sea came to my nostrils. I would have given all I had in the world for an hour of that biting air, and to see the swirling clouds, grey and ragged, chase one another towards the ocean. And I love the northern sea, and the stormy wind, lashing the heavy, yellow waves. I forgot that I was in Spain, in the middle of olive country; and I thought I was home again, and I raised my arms to greet the cold sea-fog.

"But suddenly, creeping through the silence I heard a low sound, the sound of a man's voice. I was astonished. Who could be among the olives at that hour? It was past midnight. I heard the sound of a man laughing; it was a quiet, odd laughter, a long chuckle that seemed to crawl disjointedly up the hill to my ears. I leaned forwards, looking down in the darkness, but could see nothing; the sound stopped, but I still kept all alert to detect some movement. And in a minute it began again, the long laughter of a deep-voiced man; and it became louder: it was no longer a chuckle of amusement, but a hearty peal. And now it rang through the night joyously like the mirth of some whole-hearted drunkard: the very air danced at the shouting. I wondered it did not wake my servants.

"'Who's there?' I shouted.

"But my only reply was a roar of laughter, rippling along the stillness with inextinguishable humour. And then the stream of merriment suddenly broke off in a yell of pain so that I started, and my limbs shook. The deep voice was riven, and now horrible cries of agony tore the air in a terrified falsetto.

"'O God! what can it be?' I cried, and I jumped over the low parapet into the olive-grove. I ran towards the sound. There was a silence, and then one piercing shriek; and as if the pain had been suddenly removed and the wretch were utterly exhausted, it was followed by the sound of sobbing, an anguished gasping for breath and low moans. And the sobs became quieter, dying away; and the moaning was like that of a man at the point of death; and there was a long groan; and there was silence.

"I ran from place to place, but I found nothing, saw no one; and at last I climbed the hill again, and let myself into my room.

"I could not sleep, and, when the day broke, looked out of my window in the direction from which had come those ghostly noises; and to my surprise I saw a little white house in a sort of dell, among the olives. The ground on that side did not belong to us, and I had never been through it; I went to that part of the house so seldom that it was no wonder I had not before seen the little hut, half-hidden by the trees. I asked Jose who lived there. . . . He told me that a madman had inhabited it with his brother and a servant."

"That, of course, explains the whole thing. But you must have found him a very undesirable neighbour."

The Scotchman bent over quickly and seized my wrist. He thrust his face into mine, and his eyes were starting out of his head with terror.

"But the madman," he whispered hoarsely—"the madman had been dead for twenty years!"

He let go my wrist and leant back in his chair, panting.

"I went down to the cottage," he continued at last, "and walked all around it. The windows were barred and shuttered, as in pretty nearly all the houses about Ecija, and the door was locked. I knocked, but got no answer. I shook the handle and rang the bell. I heard the ringing tinkle inside a room, but no one came. I looked up; the house was built in two low storeys, but the upper part was shut as fastly as the rest, and there was no sign of inhabitants."

"Did the place look dilapidated?"

"Yes. The whitewash had worn off the walls, and the door and shutters were void of paint; a few of the tiles on the roof were lying on the ground, blown down in some hurricane. . . . I went to my friend Fernandez, the apothecary; and he repeated to me Jose's story that the house had been inhabited by a maniac with his brother and a keeper. I asked about the madman, and heard that he was never seen by any one; the report went that most of his time was spent in a state of apathy, but now and then he was seized with attacks of frenzy, and then could be heard through the whole country-side, laughing and crying by turns. He died in one of the attacks, and his keepers immediately left the neighbourhood. Since then no one has dared live in the white cottage.

"I did not tell Fernandez what I had heard, but went home; and that night again kept watch. But the night passed silently, no shadow of a sound even disturbed the stillness. The light of the stars waned before the day and the sun mounted the cloudless heavens."

"And you never heard anything more?" I asked.

"Not for five weeks and four days. . . . The drought continued, and I slept in the lumber-room at the back; and one night I was sleeping soundly, when something appeared to pass through me, some indescribable sensation, and I was suddenly wide awake. And then as I lay there in my bed, in the same way as before the long, low gurgle crept up from the valley, the deep chuckle of the madman. And just before it lengthened into the fiendish laugh, bellowing through the air grotesquely. I sprang to my feet and went to the window, but then my legs began to tremble; there was the same pause as before, and then rang through the air cries of pain of the dead man. They were not human; they were the anguished yells of some living thing of uncouth, horrible shape. I could not move, I was afraid; and again, with one last shriek of agony, came the pitiful, passionate sobbing, that wailed along the breeze with ghastly clearness. And all was silence, and I crept back to bed, and hid my face.

"I remember that Fernandez had told me that the frenzies of the dead man came only at intervals; all the rest of the time he lay there only half-conscious, imbecile, demented, and it occurred to me that the attacks returned regularly. I waited three weeks, four weeks, five weeks. And on the thirty-ninth day I prepared myself to find out the cause of the fiendish sounds. I'm not a nervous man, I had got over the first uneasiness, and made up my mind to find an explanation.

"The night came and I did not go to bed. I cleaned my revolver and put new cartridges in it; I had got into the habit of many Spaniards always to carry some arm or other. I prepared a lantern, and sat on the parapet of my house to wait. The wind was blowing, and it whistled about the roof, and rustled over the leaves of the olive-trees like waves sishing on the pebbles of the beach. The moon was full, casting black shadows, and it glistened like shining silver on the white walls of the little house in the hollows.

"At last my quick ears caught the beginning of a sound—of the sound I knew, and I threw myself over the wall into the olive-grove, I ran straight to the house; and as I approached the chuckle louder, and I could not doubt from where it came. I reached the house and looked up; no glimmer of a light came from the shuttered windows. I put my ears to the door and heard the madman's laughter growing hilariously. I knocked loudly and I pulled the bell; the cracked tinkling seemed to rouse him to greater mirth, for he roared with laughter, bellowing in his deep voice. I knocked louder again and again, and my only answer was the peal of laughter. I shouted at the top of my voice:

"'Open the door—open, or I shall break it!'"

"And then I stepped back and kicked the latch with all my might; I flung myself at the door with the whole weight of my body. It creaked and grumbled; I exerted my whole strength, and it smashed open.

"I took up my lantern and seized my revolver. The laughter sounded louder now, but so unnatural within those closed walls, musty and evil-smelling with their long confinement, that I shuddered. The shouting rang out so that I was confused and did not know which way to turn. I pushed open a door by my side and entered a room, bare and white, without a stick of furniture. But the sound grew louder, and I rushed into another room; there was nothing there, and the sound grew ever louder. I burst open a door, and I was at the foot of the staircase. The madman was laughing just over my head; I ran up through a corridor, and was about to burst into the last room—when I stopped, for I knew that he was there. I was only separated from the sound by a thin door.

"A shiver passed through me, and I began to shake so that I could hardly stand. I wanted to run away from the awful mirth; it was Satanic, unearthly—it wasn't the sound of a human being; but I forced myself to stay.

"And then, as before, the laughter broke into a groan; and I heard a little hiss of pain, too low for me to have heard from my house; and I heard a gasp:

"'Ay,' I heard the man speak in Spanish, '*you're killing me!—you're killing me! Take it away! O God, help me!*'

"And then the scream of anguish, as if the wretch were being put to some horrible torture. I could bear it no longer; I flung open the door and leapt in. The wind blew back the loose shutter and the moon streamed in, dimming my lantern. In my ears, as clearly as I hear you speak and as close, rang the madman's sobs, gasps of pain, and an anguished moaning, and groans as if in trouble a man's soul were parting from his body. I tell you I heard the passionate crying and the broken, choking sobs right in my ears.

"And the room was empty."

Robert Morrison sat back, exhausted by his story.

"And then?" I asked.

"Since then I hear it always," he said. "Every forty days—save one—it comes an hour after midnight. . . . I felt I could sleep no longer in that room, where first I heard the ghastly noise; and I shut it up and moved into another wing of the house, far away, where no sound could reach me. But again, when time came, I was wakened by the low chuckle of the madman almost at my elbow; and I screamed with terror.

"The weeks passed by, and when the time returned I got Fernandez, the apothecary, to sleep with me that night. I told him nothing, but kept him playing cards till one in the morning; and then I heard it again. I asked him what he heard, but he said 'Nothing!' He looked at me as if he thought me drunk; I had touched nothing all day. Then, as the laughing grew louder, I put my hands to my ears and cried out. He thought I was mad; but he dared not say so, because he knew I should kill him.

"Then I couldn't bear to live in Ecija. I put a factor there and went to Seville. I felt myself safe for a while, but as the days went by the awful fear came that the sounds had followed me; and I knew that if I heard them in Seville I should never lose them as long as I lived. The agony was so awful that I began to drink, and I used to lie awake at night counting the days; and at last I *knew* it would come. And on the fortieth day save one I heard it in Seville—sixty miles away from Ecija.

"And now I shall never cease to hear the madman's ravings, each time his frenzy takes him."

"When are your thirty-nine days up?" I asked.

"Tonight," cried the Scotchman hoarsely.

And ever as he spoke, a ghastly fear darkened his face; he started to his feet like a man in sudden panic. He looked at me wildly.

"D'you hear?" he cried.

And a strange light came into his blue, expressionless eyes, so that I seemed to see through the pupils, and they shone red, like two dull spots of fire.

"O God! it's come!"

He put his hands to his ears, pressing them with all his might; and, strong man as he was, he trembled as if seized with ague. And the agony of his face was so intense, with those awful frightened eyes, that I too seemed dimly to hear the ghostly chuckling which he had described—the laughter of the madman like the laughter of a devil in hell.

And Robert Morrison filled in the silence with the words that were inaudible: "*You're killing me!—you're killing me! Take it away! God help me!*"

And the wretched man started as if he had been struck some sudden blow when he heard the last shrill yell of anguish.

"D'you hear?—d'you hear?" he cried.

And again, dimly, I almost fancied that I too could hear the pitiful sobbing of the maniac, and the final moan of pain as death eased him of his suffering.

The Tomb

H. P. Lovecraft

Sedibus ut saltem placidis in morte quiescam.

Virgil

In relating the circumstances which have led to my confinement within this refuge for the demented, I am aware that my present position will create a natural doubt of the authenticity of my narrative. It is an unfortunate fact that the bulk of humanity is too limited in its mental vision to weigh with patience and intelligence those isolated phenomena, seen and felt only by a psychologically sensitive few, which lie outside its common experience. Men of broader intellect know that there is no sharp distinction betwixt the real and the unreal; that all things appear as they do only by virtue of the delicate individual physical and mental media through which we are made conscious of them; but the prosaic materialism of the majority condemns as madness the flashes of super-sight which penetrate the common veil of obvious empiricism.

My name is Jervas Dudley, and from earliest childhood I have been a dreamer and a visionary. Wealthy beyond the necessity of a commercial life, and temperamentally unfitted for the formal studies and social recreations of my acquaintances, I have dwelt ever in realms apart from the visible world; spending my youth and adolescence in ancient and little-known books, and in roaming the fields and groves of the region near my ancestral home. I do not think that what I read in these books or saw in these fields and groves was exactly what other boys read and saw there; but of this I must say little, since detailed speech would but confirm those cruel slanders upon my intellect which I sometimes overhear from the whispers of the stealthy attendants around me. It is sufficient for me to relate events without analysing causes.

I have said that I dwelt apart from the visible world, but I have not said that I dwelt alone. This no human creature may do; for lacking the fellowship of the living, he inevitably draws upon the companionship of things that are not, or are no longer, living. Close by my home there lies a singular wooded hollow, in whose twilight deeps I spent most of my time; reading, thinking, and dreaming. Down its moss-covered slopes my first steps of infancy were taken, and around its grotesquely gnarled oak trees my first fancies of boyhood were woven. Well did I come to know the presiding dryads of those trees, and often have I watched their wild dances in the struggling beams of a waning moon—but of these things I must not now speak. I will tell only of the lone tomb in the darkest of the hillside thickets; the deserted tomb of the Hydes, an old and exalted family whose last direct descendant had been laid within its black recesses many decades before my birth.

The vault to which I refer is of ancient granite, weathered and discoloured by the mists and dampness of generations. Excavated back into the hillside, the structure is visible only at the entrance. The door, a ponderous and forbidding slab of stone, hangs upon rusted iron hinges, and is fastened *ajar* in a queerly sinister way by means of heavy iron chains and padlocks, according to a gruesome fashion of half a century ago. The abode of the race whose scions are here inurned had once crowned the declivity which holds the tomb, but had long since fallen victim to the flames which sprang up from a disastrous stroke of lightning. Of the midnight storm which destroyed this gloomy mansion, the older inhabitants of the region sometimes speak in hushed and uneasy voices; alluding to what they call "divine wrath" in a manner that in later years vaguely increased the always strong fascination which I felt for the forest-darkened sepulchre. One man only had perished in the fire. When the last of the Hydes was buried in this place of shade and stillness, the sad urnful of ashes had come from a distant land; to which the family had repaired when the mansion burned down. No one remains to lay flowers before the granite portal, and few care to brave the depressing shadows which seem to linger strangely about the water-worn stones.

I shall never forget the afternoon when first I stumbled upon the half-hidden house of death. It was in mid-summer, when the alchemy of Nature transmutes the sylvan landscape to one vivid and almost homogeneous mass of green; when the senses are well-nigh intoxicated with the surging seas of moist verdure and the subtly indefinable odours of the soil and the vegetation. In such surroundings the mind loses its perspective; time and space become trivial and unreal, and echoes of a forgotten prehistoric past beat insistently upon the enthralled consciousness. All day I had been wandering through the mystic groves of the hollow; thinking thoughts I need not discuss, and conversing with things I need not name. In years a child of ten, I had seen and heard many wonders unknown to the throng; and was oddly aged in certain respects. When, upon forcing my way between two savage clumps of briers, I suddenly encountered the entrance of the vault, I had no knowledge of what I had discovered. The dark blocks of granite, the door so curiously ajar, and the funereal carvings above the arch, aroused in me no associations of mournful or terrible character. Of graves and tombs I knew and imagined much, but had on account of my peculiar temperament been kept from all personal contact with churchyards and cemeteries. The strange stone house on the woodland slope was to me only a source of interest and speculation; and its cold, damp interior, into which I vainly peered through the aperture so tantalisingly left, contained for me no hint of death or decay. But in that instant of curiosity was born the madly unreasoning desire which has brought me to this hell of confinement. Spurred on by a voice which must have come from the hideous soul of the forest, I resolved to enter the beckoning gloom in spite of the ponderous chains which barred my passage. In the waning light of day I alternately rattled the rusty impediments with a view to throwing wide the stone door, and essayed to squeeze my slight form through the space already provided; but neither plan met with success. At first curious, I was now frantic; and when in the thickening twilight I returned to my home, I had sworn to the hundred gods of the grove that *at any cost* I would some day force an entrance to the black, chilly depths that seemed calling out to me. The physician with the iron-grey beard who comes each day to my room once told a visitor that this decision marked the beginning of a pitiful monomania; but I will leave final judgment to my readers when they shall have learnt all.

The months following my discovery were spent in futile attempts to force the complicated padlock of the slightly open vault, and in carefully guarded inquiries regarding the nature and history of the structure. With the traditionally receptive ears of the small boy, I learned much; though an habitual secretiveness caused me to tell no one of my information or my resolve. It is perhaps worth mentioning that I was not at all surprised or terrified on learning of the nature of the vault. My rather original ideas regarding life and death had caused me to associate the cold clay with the breathing body in a vague fashion; and I felt that the great and sinister family of the burned-down mansion was in some way represented within the stone space I sought to explore. Mumbled tales of the weird rites and godless revels of bygone years in the ancient hall gave to me a new and potent interest in the tomb, before whose door I would sit for hours at a time each day. Once I thrust a candle within the nearly closed entrance, but could see nothing save a flight of damp stone steps leading downward. The odour of the place repelled yet bewitched me. I felt I had known it before, in a past remote beyond all recollection; beyond even my tenancy of the body I now possess.

The year after I first beheld the tomb, I stumbled upon a worm-eaten translation of Plutarch's *Lives* in the book-filled attic of my home. Reading the life of Theseus, I was much impressed by that passage telling of the great stone beneath which the boyish hero was to find his tokens of destiny whenever he should become old enough to lift its enormous weight. This legend had the effect of dispelling my keenest impatience to enter the vault, for it made me feel that the time was not yet ripe. Later, I told myself, I should grow to a strength and ingenuity which might enable me to unfasten the heavily chained door with ease; but until then I would do better by conforming to what seemed the will of Fate

Accordingly my watches by the dank portal became less persistent, and much of my time was spent in other though equally strange pursuits. I would sometimes rise very quietly in the night, stealing out to walk in those churchyards and places of burial from which I had been kept by my parents. What I did there I may not say, for I am not now sure of the reality of certain things; but I know that on the day after such a nocturnal ramble I would often astonish those about me with my knowledge of topics almost forgotten for many generations. It was after a night like this that I shocked the community with a queer conceit about the burial of the rich and celebrated Squire Brewster, a maker of local history who was interred in 1711, and whose slate headstone, bearing a graven skull and crossbones, was slowly crumbling to powder. In a moment of childish imagination I vowed not only that the undertaker, Goodman Simpson, had stolen the silver-buckled shoes, silken hose, and satin small-clothes of the deceased before burial; but that the Squire himself, not fully inanimate, had turned twice in his mound-covered coffin on the day after interment.

But the idea of entering the tomb never left my thoughts; being indeed stimulated by the unexpected genealogical discovery that my own maternal ancestry possessed at least a slight link with the supposedly extinct family of the Hydes. Last of my paternal race, I was likewise the last of this older and more mysterious line. I began to feel that the tomb was *mine*, and to look forward with hot eagerness to the time when I might pass within that stone door and down those slimy stone steps in the dark. I now formed the habit of *listening* very intently at the slightly open portal, choosing my favourite hours of midnight stillness for the odd vigil. By the time I came of age, I had made a small clearing in the thicket before the mould-stained facade of the hillside, allowing the surrounding vegetation to encircle and overhang the space like the walls and roof of a sylvan bower. This bower was my temple, the fastened door my shrine, and here I would lie outstretched on the mossy ground, thinking strange thoughts and dreaming strange dreams.

The night of the first revelation was a sultry one. I must have fallen asleep from fatigue, for it was with a distinct sense of awakening that I heard the *voices*. Of those tones and accents I hesitate to speak; of their *quality* I will not speak; but I may say that they presented certain uncanny differences in vocabulary, pronunciation, and mode of utterance. Every shade of New England dialect, from the uncouth syllables of the Puritan colonists to the precise rhetoric of fifty years ago, seemed represented in that shadowy colloquy, though it was only later that I noticed the fact. At the time, indeed, my attention was distracted from this matter by another phenomenon; a phenomenon so fleeting that I could not take oath upon its reality. I barely fancied that as I awoke, a *light* had been hurriedly extinguished within the sunken sepulchre. I do not think I was either astounded or panic-stricken, but I know that I was greatly and permanently *changed* that night. Upon returning home I went with much directness to a rotting chest in the attic, wherein I found the key which next day unlocked with ease the barrier I had so long stormed in vain.

It was in the soft glow of late afternoon that I first entered the vault on the abandoned slope. A spell was upon me, and my heart leaped with an exultation I can but ill describe. As I closed the door behind me and descended the dripping steps by the light of my lone candle, I seemed to know the way; and though the candle sputtered with the stifling reek of the place, I felt singularly at home in the musty, charnel-house air. Looking about me, I beheld many marble slabs bearing coffins, or the remains of coffins. Some of these were sealed and intact, but others had nearly vanished, leaving the silver handles and plates isolated amidst certain curious heaps of whitish dust. Upon one plate I read the name of Sir Geoffrey Hyde, who had come from Sussex in 1640 and died here a few years later. In a conspicuous alcove was one fairly well-preserved and untenanted casket, adorned with a single name which brought to me both a smile and a shudder. An odd impulse caused me to climb upon the broad slab, extinguish my candle, and lie down within the vacant box.

In the grey light of dawn I staggered from the vault and locked the chain of the door behind me. I was no longer a young man, though but twenty-one winters had chilled my bodily frame. Early-rising villagers who observed my homeward progress looked at me strangely, and marvelled at the signs of ribald revelry which they saw in one whose life was known to be sober and solitary. I did not appear before my parents till after a long and refreshing sleep.

Henceforward I haunted the tomb each night; seeing, hearing, and doing things I must never reveal. My speech, always susceptible to environmental influences, was the first thing to succumb to the change; and my suddenly acquired archaism of diction was soon remarked upon. Later a queer boldness and recklessness came into my demeanour, till I unconsciously grew to possess the bearing of a man of the world despite my lifelong seclusion. My formerly silent tongue waxed voluble with the easy grace of a Chesterfield or the godless cynicism of a Rochester. I displayed a peculiar erudition utterly unlike the fantastic, monkish lore over which I had pored in youth; and covered the flyleaves of my books with facile impromptu epigrams which brought up suggestions of Gay, Prior, and the sprightliest of the Augustan wits and rimesters. One morning at breakfast I came close to disaster by declaiming in palpably liquorish accents an effusion of eighteenth-century Bacchanalian mirth; a bit of Georgian playfulness never recorded in a book, which ran something like this:

Come hither, my lads, with your tankards of ale,
And drink to the present before it shall fail;
Pile each on your platter a mountain of beef,
For 'tis eating and drinking that bring us relief:
So fill up your glass,
For life will soon pass;
When you're dead ye'll ne'er drink to your king or your lass!

Anacreon had a red nose, so they say;
But what's a red nose if ye're happy and gay?
Gad split me! I'd rather be red whilst I'm here,
Than white as a lily—and dead half a year!
So Betty, my miss,
Come give me a kiss;
In hell there's no innkeeper's daughter like this!

Young Harry, propp'd up just as straight as he's able,
Will soon lose his wig and slip under the table;
But fill up your goblets and pass 'em around—
Better under the table than under the ground!
So revel and chaff
As ye thirstily quaff:
Under six feet of dirt 'tis less easy to laugh!

The fiend strike me blue! I'm scarce able to walk,
And damn me if I can stand upright or talk!
Here, landlord, bid Betty to summon a chair;
I'll try home for a while, for my wife is not there!
So lend me a hand;
I'm not able to stand,
But I'm gay whilst I linger on top of the land!

About this time I conceived my present fear of fire and thunderstorms. Previously indifferent to such things, I had now an unspeakable horror of them; and would retire to the innermost recesses of the house whenever the heavens threatened an electrical display. A favourite haunt of mine during the day was the ruined cellar of the mansion that had burned down, and in fancy I would picture the structure as it had been in its prime. On one occasion I startled a villager by leading him confidently to a shallow sub-cellar, of whose existence I seemed to know in spite of the fact that it had been unseen and forgotten for many generations.

At last came that which I had long feared. My parents, alarmed at the altered manner and appearance of their only son, commenced to exert over my movements a kindly espionage which threatened to result in disaster. I had told no one of my visits to the tomb, having guarded my secret purpose with religious zeal since childhood; but now I was forced to exercise care in threading the mazes of the wooded hollow, that I might throw off a possible pursuer. My key to the vault I kept suspended from a cord about my neck, its presence known only to me. I never carried out of the sepulchre any of the things I came upon whilst within its walls.

One morning as I emerged from the damp tomb and fastened the chain of the portal with none too steady hand, I beheld in an adjacent thicket the dreaded face of a watcher. Surely the end was near; for my bower was discovered, and the objective of my nocturnal journeys revealed. The man did not accost me, so I hastened home in an effort to overhear what he might report to my careworn father. Were my sojourns beyond the chained door about to be proclaimed to the world? Imagine my delighted astonishment on hearing the spy inform my parent in a cautious whisper *that I had spent the night in the bower outside the tomb*; my sleep-filmed eyes fixed upon the crevice where the padlocked portal stood ajar! By what miracle had the watcher been thus deluded? I was now convinced that a supernatural agency protected me. Made bold by this heaven-sent circumstance, I began to resume perfect openness in going to the vault; confident that no one could witness my entrance. For a week I tasted to the full the joys of that charnel conviviality which I must not describe, when the *thing* happened, and I was borne away to this accursed abode of sorrow and monotony.

I should not have ventured out that night; for the taint of thunder was in the clouds, and a hellish phosphorescence rose from the rank swamp at the bottom of the hollow. The call of the dead, too, was different. Instead of the hillside tomb, it was the charred cellar on the crest of the slope whose presiding daemon beckoned to me with unseen fingers. As I emerged from an intervening grove upon the plain before the ruin, I beheld in the misty moonlight a thing I had always vaguely expected. The mansion, gone for a century, once more reared its stately height to the raptured vision; every window ablaze with the splendour of many candles. Up the long drive rolled the coaches of the Boston gentry, whilst on foot came a numerous assemblage of powdered exquisites from the neighbouring mansions. With this throng I mingled, though I knew I belonged with the hosts rather than with the guests. Inside the hall were music, laughter, and wine on every hand. Several faces I recognised; though I should have known them better had they been shrivelled or eaten away by death and decomposition. Amidst a wild and reckless throng I was the wildest and most abandoned. Gay blasphemy poured in torrents from my lips, and in my shocking sallies I heeded no law of God, Man, or Nature. Suddenly a peal of thunder, resonant even above the din of the swinish revelry, clave the very roof and laid a hush of fear upon the boisterous company. Red tongues of flame and searing gusts of heat engulfed the house; and the roysterers, struck with terror at the descent of a calamity which seemed to transcend the bounds of unguided Nature, fled shrieking into the night. I alone remained, riveted to my seat by a grovelling fear which I had never felt before. And then a second horror took possession of my soul. Burnt alive to ashes, my body dispersed by the four winds, *I might never lie in the tomb of the Hydes!* Was not my coffin prepared for me? Had I not a right to rest till eternity amongst the descendants of Sir Geoffrey Hyde? Aye! I would claim my heritage of death, even though my soul go seeking through the ages for another corporeal tenement to represent it on that vacant slab in the alcove of the vault. *Jervas Hyde* should never share the sad fate of Palinurus!

As the phantom of the burning house faded, I found myself screaming and struggling madly in the arms of two men, one of whom was the spy who had followed me to the tomb. Rain was pouring down in torrents, and upon the southern horizon were flashes of the lightning that had so lately passed over our heads. My father, his face lined with sorrow, stood by as I shouted my demands to be laid within the tomb; frequently admonishing my captors to treat me as gently as they could. A blackened circle on the floor of the ruined cellar told of a violent stroke from the heavens; and from this spot a group of curious villagers with lanterns were prying a small box of antique workmanship which the thunderbolt had brought to light. Ceasing my futile and now objectless writhing, I watched the spectators as they viewed the treasure-trove, and was permitted to share in their discoveries. The box, whose fastenings were broken by the stroke which had unearthed it, contained many papers and objects of value; but I had eyes for one thing alone. It was the porcelain miniature of a young man in a smartly curled bag-wig, and bore the initials "J. H." The face was such that as I gazed, I might well have been studying my mirror.

On the following day I was brought to this room with the barred windows, but I have been kept informed of certain things through an aged and simple-minded servitor, for whom I bore a fondness in infancy, and who like me loves the churchyard. What I have dared relate of my experiences within the vault has brought me only pitying smiles. My father, who visits me frequently, declares that at no time did I pass the chained portal, and swears that the rusted padlock had not been touched for fifty years when he examined it. He even says that all the village knew of my journeys to the tomb, and that I was often watched as I slept in the bower outside the grim facade, my half-open eyes fixed on the crevice that leads to the interior. Against these assertions I have no tangible proof to offer, since my key to the padlock was lost in the struggle on that night of horrors. The strange things of the past which I learnt during those nocturnal meetings with the dead he dismisses as the fruits of my lifelong and omnivorous browsing amongst the ancient volumes of the family library. Had it not been for my old servant Hiram, I should have by this time become quite convinced of my madness.

But Hiram, loyal to the last, has held faith in me, and has done that which impels me to make public at least a part of my story. A week ago he burst open the lock which chains the door of the tomb perpetually ajar, and descended with a lantern into the murky depths. On a slab in an alcove he found an old but empty coffin whose tarnished plate bears the single word "*Jervas*". In that coffin and in that vault they have promised me I shall be buried.

The Transferred Ghost

Frank R. Stockton

The country residence of Mr. John Hinckman was a delightful place to me, for many reasons. It was the abode of a genial, though somewhat impulsive, hospitality. It had broad, smooth-shaven lawns and towering oaks and elms; there were bosky shades at several points, and not far from the house there was a little rill spanned by a rustic bridge with the bark on; there were fruits and flowers, pleasant people, chess, billiards, rides, walks, and fishing. These were great attractions; but none of them, nor all of them together, would have been sufficient to hold me to the place very long. I had been invited for the trout season, but should, probably, have finished my visit early in the summer had it not been that upon fair days, when the grass was dry, and the sun was not too hot, and there was but little wind, there strolled beneath the lofty elms, or passed lightly through the bosky shades, the form of my Madeline.

This lady was not, in very truth, my Madeline. She had never given herself to me, nor had I, in any way, acquired possession of her. But as I considered her possession the only sufficient reason for the continuance of my existence, I called her, in my reveries, mine. It may have been that I would not have been obliged to confine the use of this possessive pronoun to my reveries had I confessed the state of my feelings to the lady.

But this was an unusually difficult thing to do. Not only did I dread, as almost all lovers dread, taking the step which would in an instant put an end to that delightful season which may be termed the ante-interrogatory period of love, and which might at the same time terminate all intercourse or connection with the object of my passion; but I was, also, dreadfully afraid of John Hinckman. This gentleman was a good friend of mine, but it would have required a bolder man than I was at that time to ask him for the gift of his niece, who was the head of his household, and, according to his own frequent statement, the main prop of his declining years. Had Madeline acquiesced in my general views on the subject, I might have felt encouraged to open the matter to Mr. Hinckman; but, as I said before, I had never asked her whether or not she would be mine. I thought of these things at all hours of the day and night, particularly the latter.

I was lying awake one night, in the great bed in my spacious chamber, when, by the dim light of the new moon, which partially filled the room, I saw John Hinckman standing by a large chair near the door. I was very much surprised at this for two reasons. In the first place, my host had never before come into my room; and, in the second place, he had gone from home that morning, and had not expected to return for several days. It was for this reason that I had been able that evening to sit much later than usual with Madeline on the moonlit porch. The figure was certainly that of John Hinckman in his ordinary dress, but there was a vagueness and indistinctness about it which presently assured me that it was a ghost. Had the good old man been murdered? and had his spirit come to tell me of the deed, and to confide to me the protection of his dear ——? My heart fluttered at what I was about to think, but at this instant the figure spoke.

"Do you know," he said, with a countenance that indicated anxiety, "if Mr. Hinckman will return tonight?"

I thought it well to maintain a calm exterior, and I answered,—

"We do not expect him."

"I am glad of that," said he, sinking into the chair by which he stood. "During the two years and a half that I have inhabited this house, that man has never before been away for a single night. You can't imagine the relief it gives me."

And as he spoke he stretched out his legs, and leaned back in the chair. His form became less vague, and the colors of his garments more distinct and evident, while an expression of gratified relief succeeded to the anxiety of his countenance.

"Two years and a half!" I exclaimed. "I don't understand you."

"It is fully that length of time," said the ghost, "since I first came here. Mine is not an ordinary case. But before I say any thing more about it, let me ask you again if you are sure Mr. Hinckman will not return to-night."

"I am as sure of it as I can be of any thing," I answered. "He left to-day for Bristol, two hundred miles away."

"Then I will go on," said the ghost, "for I am glad to have the opportunity of talking to some one who will listen to me; but if John Hinckman should come in and catch me here, I should be frightened out of my wits."

"This is all very strange," I said, greatly puzzled by what I had heard. "Are you the ghost of Mr. Hinckman?"

This was a bold question, but my mind was so full of other emotions that there seemed to be no room for that of fear.

"Yes, I am his ghost," my companion replied, "and yet I have no right to be. And this is what makes me so uneasy, and so much afraid of him. It is a strange story, and, I truly believe, without precedent. Two years and a half ago, John Hinckman was dangerously ill in this very room. At one time he was so far gone that he was really believed to be dead. It was in consequence of too precipitate a report in regard to this matter that I was, at that time, appointed to be his ghost. Imagine my surprise and horror, sir, when, after I had accepted the position and assumed its responsibilities, that old man revived, became convalescent, and eventually regained his usual health. My situation was now one of extreme delicacy and embarrassment. I had no power to return to my original unembodiment, and I had no right to be the ghost of a man who was not dead. I was advised by my friends to quietly maintain my position, and was assured that, as John Hinckman was an elderly man, it could not be long before I could rightfully assume the position for which I had been selected. But I tell you, sir," he continued, with animation, "the old fellow seems as vigorous as ever, and I have no idea how much longer this annoying state of things will continue. I spend my time trying to get out of that old man's way. I must not leave this house, and he seems to follow me everywhere. I tell you, sir, he haunts me."

"That is truly a queer state of things," I remarked. "But why are you afraid of him? He couldn't hurt you."

"Of course he couldn't," said the ghost. "But his very presence is a shock and terror to me. Imagine, sir, how you would feel if my case were yours."

I could not imagine such a thing at all. I simply shuddered.

"And if one must be a wrongful ghost at all," the apparition continued, " it would be much pleasanter to be the ghost of some man other than John Hinckman. There is in him an irascibility of temper, accompanied by a facility of invective, which is seldom met with. And what would happen if he were to see me, and find out, as I am sure he would, how long and why I had inhabited his house, I can scarcely conceive. I have seen him in his bursts of passion; and, although he did not hurt the people he stormed at any more than he would hurt me, they seemed to shrink before him."

All this I knew to be very true. Had it not been for this peculiarity of Mr. Hinckman, I might have been more willing to talk to him about his niece.

"I feel sorry for you," I said, for I really began to have a sympathetic feeling toward this unfortunate apparition. "Your case is indeed a hard one. It reminds me of those persons who have had doubles, and I suppose a man would often be very angry indeed when he found that there was another being who was personating himself."

"Oh! the cases are not similar at all," said the ghost. "A double or doppelganger lives on the earth with a man; and, being exactly like him, he makes all sorts of trouble, of course. It is very different with me. I am not here to live with Mr. Hinckman. I am here to take his place. Now, it would make John Hinckman very angry if he knew that. Don't you know it would?"

I assented promptly.

"Now that he is away I can be easy for a little while," continued the ghost; "and I am so glad to have an opportunity of talking to you. I have frequently come into your room, and watched you while you slept, but did not dare to speak to you for fear that if you talked with me Mr. Hinckman would hear you, and come into the room to know why you were talking to yourself."

"But would he not hear you?" I asked.

"Oh, no!" said the other: "there are times when any one may see me, but no one hears me except the person to whom I address myself."

"But why did you wish to speak to me?" I asked.

"Because," replied the ghost, "I like occasionally to talk to people, and especially to some one like yourself, whose mind is so troubled and perturbed that you are not likely to be frightened by a visit from one of us. But I particularly wanted to ask you to do me a favor. There is every probability, so far as I can see, that John Hinckman will live a long time, and my situation is becoming insupportable. My great object at present is to get myself transferred, and I think that you may, perhaps, be of use to me."

"Transferred!" I exclaimed. "What do you mean by that?"

"What I mean," said the other, "is this: Now that I have started on my career I have got to be the ghost of somebody, and I want to be the ghost of a man who is really dead."

"I should think that would be easy enough," I said. "Opportunities must continually occur."

"Not at all! not at all!" said my companion quickly. "You have no idea what a rush and pressure there is for situations of this kind. Whenever a vacancy occurs, if I may express myself in that way, there are crowds of applications for the ghostship."

"I had no idea that such a state of things existed," I said, becoming quite interested in the matter. "There ought to be some regular system, or order of precedence, by which you could all take your turns like customers in a barber's shop."

"Oh dear, that would never do at all!" said the other. "Some of us would have to wait forever. There is always a great rush whenever a good ghostship offers itself—

while, as you know, there are some positions that no one would care for. And it was in consequence of my being in too great a hurry on an occasion of the kind that I got myself into my present disagreeable predicament, and I have thought that it might be possible that you would help me out of it. You might know of a case where an opportunity for a ghostship was not generally expected, but which might present itself at any moment. If you would give me a short notice, I know I could arrange for a transfer."

"What do you mean?" I exclaimed. "Do you want me to commit suicide? Or to undertake a murder for your benefit?"

"Oh, no, no, no!" said the other, with a vapory smile. "I mean nothing of that kind. To be sure, there are lovers who are watched with considerable interest, such persons having been known, in moments of depression, to offer very desirable ghostships; but I did not think of any thing of that kind in connection with you. You were the only person I cared to speak to, and I hoped that you might give me some information that would be of use; and, in return, I shall be very glad to help you in your love affair."

"You seem to know that I have such an affair," I said.

"Oh, yes!" replied the other, with a little yawn. "I could not be here so much as I have been without knowing all about that."

There was something horrible in the idea of Madeline and myself having been watched by a ghost, even, perhaps, when we wandered together in the most delightful and bosky places. But, then, this was quite an exceptional ghost, and I could not have the objections to him which would ordinarily arise in regard to beings of his class.

"I must go now," said the ghost, rising: "but I will see you somewhere to-morrow night. And remember—you help me, and I'll help you."

I had doubts the next morning as to the propriety of telling Madeline any thing about this interview, and soon convinced myself that I must keep silent on the subject. If she knew there was a ghost about the house, she would probably leave the place instantly. I did not mention the matter, and so regulated my demeanor that I am quite sure Madeline never suspected what had taken place. For some time I had wished that Mr. Hinckman would absent himself, for a day at least, from the premises. In such case I thought I might more easily nerve myself up to the point of speaking to Madeline on the subject of our future collateral existence; and, now that the opportunity for such speech had really occurred, I did not feel ready to avail myself of it. What would become of me if she refused me?

I had an idea, however, that the lady thought that, if I were going to speak at all, this was the time. She must have known that certain sentiments were afloat within me, and she was not unreasonable in her wish to see the matter settled one way or the other. But I did not feel like taking a bold step in the dark. If she wished me to ask her to give herself to me, she ought to offer me some reason to suppose that she would make the gift. If I saw no probability of such generosity, I would prefer that things should remain as they were.

That evening I was sitting with Madeline in the moonlit porch. It was nearly ten o'clock, and ever since supper-time I had been working myself up to the point of making an avowal of my sentiments. I had not positively determined to do this, but wished gradually to reach the proper point, when, if the prospect looked bright, I might speak. My companion appeared to understand the situation—at least, I imagined that the nearer I came to a proposal the more she seemed to expect it. It was certainly a very critical and important epoch in my life. If I spoke, I should make myself happy or miserable forever; and if I did not speak I had every reason to believe that the lady would not give me another chance to do so.

Sitting thus with Madeline, talking a little, and thinking very hard over these momentous matters, I looked up and saw the ghost, not a dozen feet away from us. He was sitting on the railing of the porch, one leg thrown up before him, the other dangling down as he leaned against a post. He was behind Madeline, but almost in front of me, as I sat facing the lady. It was fortunate that Madeline was looking out over the landscape, for I must have appeared very much startled. The ghost had told me that he would see me some time this night, but I did not think he would make his appearance when I was in the company of Madeline. If she should see the spirit of her uncle, I could not answer for the consequences. I made no exclamation, but the ghost evidently saw that I was troubled.

"Don't be afraid," he said—"I shall not let her see me; and she cannot hear me speak unless I address myself to her, which I do not intend to do."

I suppose I looked grateful.

"So you need not trouble yourself about that," the ghost continued; "but it seems to me that you are not getting along very well with your affair. If I were you, I should speak out without waiting any longer. You will never have a better chance. You are not likely to be interrupted; and, so far as I can judge, the lady seems disposed to listen to you favorably; that is, if she ever intends to do so. There is no knowing when John

Hinckman will go away again; certainly not this summer. If I were in your place, I should never dare to make love to Hinckman's niece if he were anywhere about the place. If he should catch any one offering himself to Miss Madeline, he would then be a terrible man to encounter."

I agreed perfectly to all this.

"I cannot bear to think of him!" I ejaculated aloud.

"Think of whom?" asked Madeline, turning quickly toward me.

Here was an awkward situation. The long speech of the ghost, to which Madeline paid no attention, but which I heard with perfect distinctness, had made me forget myself.

It was necessary to explain quickly. Of course, it would not do to admit that it was of her dear uncle that I was speaking; and so I mentioned hastily the first name I thought of.

"Mr. Vilars," I said.

This statement was entirely correct; for I never could bear to think of Mr. Vilars, who was a gentleman who had, at various times, paid much attention to Madeline.

"It is wrong for you to speak in that way of Mr. Vilars," she said. "He is a remarkably well educated and sensible young man, and has very pleasant manners. He expects to be elected to the legislature this fall, and I should not be surprised if he made his mark. He will do well in a legislative body, for whenever Mr. Vilars has any thing to say he knows just how and when to say it."

This was spoken very quietly, and without any show of resentment, which was all very natural, for if Madeline thought at all favorably of me she could not feel displeased that I should have disagreeable emotions in regard to a possible rival. The concluding words contained a hint which I was not slow to understand. I felt very sure that if Mr. Vilars were in my present position he would speak quickly enough.

"I know it is wrong to have such ideas about a person," I said, "but I cannot help it."

The lady did not chide me, and after this she seemed even in a softer mood. As for me, I felt considerably annoyed, for I had not wished to admit that any thought of Mr. Vilars had ever occupied my mind.

"You should not speak aloud that way," said the ghost, "or you may get yourself into trouble. I want to see every thing go well with you, because then you may be disposed to help me, especially if I should chance to be of any assistance to you, which I hope I shall be."

I longed to tell him that there was no way in which he could help me so much as by taking his instant departure. To make love to a young lady with a ghost sitting on the railing near by, and that ghost the apparition of a much-dreaded uncle, the very idea of whom in such a position and at such a time made me tremble, was a difficult, if not an impossible, thing to do; but I forbore to speak, although I may have looked my mind.

"I suppose," continued the ghost, "that you have not heard any thing that might be of advantage to me. Of course, I am very anxious to hear; but if you have any thing to tell me, I can wait until you are alone. I will come to you to-night in your room, or I will stay here until the lady goes away."

"You need not wait here," I said; "I have nothing at all to say to you."

Madeline sprang to her feet, her face flushed and her eyes ablaze.

"Wait here!" she cried. "What do you suppose I am waiting for? Nothing to say to me indeed!—I should think so! What should you have to say to me?"

"Madeline," I exclaimed, stepping toward her, "let me explain." But she had gone.

Here was the end of the world for me! I turned fiercely to the ghost.

"Wretched existence!" I cried. "You have ruined every thing. You have blackened my whole life. Had it not been for you"—

But here my voice faltered. I could say no more.

"You wrong me," said the ghost. "I have not injured you. I have tried only to encourage and assist you, and it is your own folly that has done this mischief. But do not despair. Such mistakes as these can be explained. Keep up a brave heart. Good-by."

And he vanished from the railing like a bursting soap-bubble.

I went gloomily to bed, but I saw no apparitions that night except those of despair and misery which my wretched thoughts called up. The words I had uttered had sounded to Madeline like the basest insult. Of course, there was only one interpretation she could put upon them.

As to explaining my ejaculations, that was impossible. I thought the matter over and over again as I lay awake that night, and I determined that I would never tell Madeline the facts of the case. It would be better for me to suffer all my life than for her to know that the ghost of her uncle haunted the house. Mr. Hinckman was away, and if she knew of his ghost she could not be made to believe that he was not dead. She might not survive the shock! No, my heart could bleed, but I would never tell her.

The next day was fine, neither too cool nor too warm; the breezes were gentle, and nature smiled. But there were no walks or rides with Madeline. She seemed to be much engaged during the day, and I saw but little of her. When we met at meals she was polite, but very quiet and reserved. She had evidently determined on a course of conduct, and had resolved to assume that, although I had been very rude to her, she did not understand the import of my words. It would be quite proper, of course, for her not to know what I meant by my expressions of the night before.

I was downcast and wretched, and said but little, and the only bright streak across the black horizon of my woe was the fact that she did not appear to be happy, although she affected an air of unconcern. The moonlit porch was deserted that evening, but wandering about the house I found Madeline in the library alone. She was reading, but I went in and sat down near her. I felt that, although I could not do so fully, I must in a measure explain my conduct of the night before. She listened quietly to a somewhat labored apology I made for the words I had used.

"I have not the slightest idea what you meant," she said, "but you were very rude."

I earnestly disclaimed any intention of rudeness, and assured her, with a warmth of speech that must have made some impression upon her, that rudeness to her would be an action impossible to me. I said a great deal upon the subject, and implored her to believe that if it were not for a certain obstacle I could speak to her so plainly that she would understand every thing.

She was silent for a time, and then she said, rather more kindly, I thought, than she had spoken before:

"Is that obstacle in any way connected with my uncle?"

"Yes," I answered, after a little hesitation, "it is, in a measure, connected with him."

She made no answer to this, and sat looking at her book, but not reading. From the expression of her face, I thought she was somewhat softened toward me. She knew her uncle as well as I did, and she may have been thinking that, if he were the obstacle that prevented my speaking (and there were many ways in which he might be that obstacle), my position would be such a hard one that it would excuse some wildness of speech and eccentricity of manner. I saw, too, that the warmth of my partial explanations had had some effect on her, and I began to believe that it might be a good thing for me to speak my mind without delay. No matter how she should receive my proposition, my relations with her could not be worse than they had been the previous night and day, and there was something in her face which encouraged me to hope that she might forget my foolish exclamations of the evening before if I began to tell her my tale of love.

I drew my chair a little nearer to her, and as I did so the ghost burst into the room from the door-way behind her. I say burst, although no door flew open and he made no noise. He was wildly excited, and waved his arms above his head. The moment I saw him, my heart fell within me. With the entrance of that impertinent apparition, every hope fled from me. I could not speak while he was in the room.

I must have turned pale; and I gazed steadfastly at the ghost, almost without seeing Madeline, who sat between us.

"Do you know," he cried, "that John Hinckman is coming up the hill? He will be here in fifteen minutes; and if you are doing any thing in the way of love-making, you had better hurry it up. But this is not what I came to tell you. I have glorious news! At last I am transferred! Not forty minutes ago a Russian nobleman was murdered by the Nihilists. Nobody ever thought of him in connection with an immediate ghostship. My friends instantly applied for the situation for me, and obtained my transfer. I am off before that horrid Hinckman comes up the hill. The moment I reach my new position, I shall put off this hated semblance. Good-by. You can't imagine how glad I am to be, at last, the real ghost of somebody."

"Oh!" I cried, rising to my feet, and stretching out my arms in utter wretchedness, "I would to Heaven you were mine!"

"I *am* yours," said Madeline, raising to me her tearful eyes.

The Water Ghost of Harrowby Hall

John Kendrick Bangs

The trouble with Harrowby Hall was that it was haunted, and, what was worse, the ghost did not content itself with merely appearing at the bedside of the afflicted person who saw it, but persisted in remaining there for one mortal hour before it would disappear.

It never appeared except on Christmas Eve, and then as the clock was striking twelve, in which respect alone was it lacking in that originality which in these days is a *sine qua non* of success in spectral life. The owners of Harrowby Hall had done their utmost to rid themselves of the damp and dewy lady who rose up out of the best bedroom floor at midnight, but without avail. They had tried stopping the clock, so that the ghost would not know when it was midnight; but she made her appearance just the same, with that fearful miasmatic personality of hers, and there she would stand until everything about her was thoroughly saturated.

Then the owners of Harrowby Hall calked up every crack in the floor with the very best quality of hemp, and over this was placed layers of tar and canvas; the walls were made water-proof, and the doors and windows likewise, the proprietors having conceived the notion that the unexercised lady would find it difficult to leak into the room after these precautions had been taken; but even this did not suffice. The following Christmas Eve she appeared as promptly as before, and frightened the occupant of the room quite out of his senses by sitting down alongside of him and gazing with her cavernous blue eyes into his; and he noticed, too, that in her long, aqueously bony fingers bits of dripping sea-weed were entwined, the ends hanging down, and these ends she drew across his forehead until he became like one insane. And then he swooned away, and was found unconscious in his bed the next morning by his host, simply saturated with sea-water and fright, from the combined effects of which he never recovered, dying four years later of pneumonia and nervous prostration at the age of seventy-eight.

The next year the master of Harrowby Hall decided not to have the best spare bedroom opened at all, thinking that perhaps the ghost's thirst for making herself disagreeable would be satisfied by haunting the furniture, but the plan was as unavailing as the many that had preceded it.

The ghost appeared as usual in the room—that is, it was supposed she did, for the hangings were dripping wet the next morning, and in the parlor below the haunted room a great damp spot appeared on the ceiling. Finding no one there, she immediately set out to learn the reason why, and she chose none other to haunt than the owner of the Harrowby himself. She found him in his own cosey room drinking whiskey—whiskey undiluted—and felicitating himself upon having foiled her ghostship, when all of sudden the curl went out of his hair, his whiskey bottle filled and overflowed, and he was himself in a condition similar to that of a man who has fallen into a water-butt. When he recovered from the shock, which was a painful one, he saw before him the lady of the cavernous eyes and sea-weed fingers. The sight was so unexpected and so terrifying that he fainted, but immediately came to, because of the vast amount of water in his hair, which, trickling down over his face, restored his consciousness.

Now it so happened that the master of Harrowby was a brave man, and while he was not particularly fond of interviewing ghosts, especially such quenching ghosts as the one before him, he was not to be daunted by an apparition. He had paid the lady the compliment of fainting from the effects of his first surprise, and now that he had come to he intended to find out a few things he felt he had a right to know. He would have liked to put on a dry suit of clothes first, but the apparition declined to leave him for an instant until her hour was up, and he was forced to deny himself that pleasure. Every time he would move she would follow him, with the result that everything she came in contact with got a ducking. In an effort to warm himself up he approached the fire, an unfortunate move as it turned out, because it brought the ghost directly over the fire, which immediately was extinguished. The whiskey became utterly valueless as a comforter to his chilled system, because it was by this time diluted to a proportion of ninety per cent of water. The only thing he could do to ward off the evil effects of his encounter he did, and that was to swallow ten two-grain quinine pills, which he managed to put into his mouth before the ghost had time to interfere. Having done this, he turned with some asperity to the ghost, and said:

"Far be it from me to be impolite to a woman, madam, but I'm hanged if it wouldn't please me better if you'd stop these infernal visits of yours to this house. Go sit out on the lake, if you like that sort of thing; soak the water-butt, if you wish; but do not, I implore you, come into a gentleman's house and saturate him and his possessions in this way. It is damned disagreeable."

"Henry Hartwick Oglethorpe," said the ghost, in a gurgling voice, "you don't know what you are talking about."

"Madam," returned the unhappy householder, "I wish that remark were strictly truthful. I was talking about you. It would be shillings and pence—nay, pounds, in my pocket, madam, if I did not know you."

"That is a bit of specious nonsense," returned the ghost, throwing a quart of indignation into the face of the master of Harrowby. "It may rank high as repartee, but as a comment upon my statement that you do not know what you are talking about, it savors of irrelevant impertinence. You do not know that I am compelled to haunt this place year after year by inexorable fate. It is no pleasure to me to enter this house, and ruin and mildew everything I touch. I never aspired to be a shower-bath, but it is my doom. Do you know who I am?"

"No, I don't," returned the master of Harrowby. "I should say you were the Lady of the Lake, or Little Sallie Waters."

"You are a witty man for your years," said the ghost.

"Well, my humor is drier than yours ever will be," returned the master.

"No doubt. I'm never dry. I am the Water Ghost of Harrowby Hall, and dryness is a quality entirely beyond my wildest hope. I have been the incumbent of this highly unpleasant office for two hundred years to-night."

"How the deuce did you ever come to get elected?" asked the master.

"Through a suicide," replied the spectre. "I am the ghost of that fair maiden whose picture hangs over the mantel-piece in the drawing-room. I should have been your great-great-great-great-great-aunt if I had lived, Henry Hartwick Oglethorpe, for I was the own sister of your great-great-great-great-grandfather."

"But what induced you to get this house into such a predicament?"

"I was not to blame, sir," returned the lady. "It was my father's fault. He it was who built Harrowby Hall, and the haunted chamber was to have been mine. My father had it furnished in pink and yellow, knowing well that blue and gray formed the only combination of color I could tolerate. He did it merely to spite me, and, with what I deem a proper spirit, I declined to live in the room; whereupon my father said I could live there or on the lawn, he didn't care which. That night I ran from the house and jumped over the cliff into the sea."

"That was rash," said the master of Harrowby.

"So I've heard," returned the ghost. "If I had known what the consequences were to be I should not have jumped; but I really never realized what I was doing until after I was drowned. I had been drowned a week when a sea-nymph came to me and informed me that I was to be one of her followers forever afterwards, adding that it should be my doom to haunt Harrowby Hall for one hour every Christmas Eve throughout the rest of eternity. I was to haunt that room on such Christmas Eves as I found it inhabited; and if it should turn out not to be inhabited, I was and am to spend the allotted hour with the head of the house."

"I'll sell the place."

"That you cannot do, for it is also required of me that I shall appear as the deeds are to be delivered to any purchaser, and divulge to him the awful secret of the house."

"Do you mean to tell me that on every Christmas Eve that I don't happen to have somebody in that guest-chamber, you are going to haunt me wherever I may be, ruining my whiskey, taking all the curl out of my hair, extinguishing my fire, and soaking me through to the skin?" demanded the master.

"You have stated the case, Oglethorpe. And what is more," said the water ghost, "it doesn't make the slightest difference where you are, if I find that room empty, wherever you may be I shall douse you with my spectral pres—"

Here the clock struck one, and immediately the apparition faded away. It was perhaps more of a trickle than a fade, but as a disappearance it was complete.

"By St. George and his Dragon!" ejaculated the master of Harrowby, wringing his hands. "It is guineas to hot-cross buns that next Christmas there's an occupant of the spare room, or I spend the night in a bath-tub."

But the master of Harrowby would have lost his wager had there been any one there to take him up, for when Christmas Eve came again he was in his grave, never having recovered from the cold contracted that awful night. Harrowby Hall was closed, and the heir to the estate was in London, where to him in his chambers came the same experience that his father had gone through, saving only that, being younger and stronger, he survived the shock. Everything in his rooms was ruined—his clocks were rusted in the works; a fine collection of water-color drawings was entirely obliterated by the onslaught of the water ghost; and what was worse, the apartments below his were drenched with the water soaking through the floors, a damage for which he was compelled to pay, and which resulted in his being requested by his landlady to vacate the premises immediately.

The story of the visitation inflicted upon his family had gone abroad, and no one could be got to invite him out to any function save afternoon teas and receptions. Fathers of daughters declined to permit him to remain in their houses later than eight o'clock at night, not knowing but that some emergency might arise in the supernatural world which would require the unexpected appearance of the water ghost in this on nights other than Christmas Eve, and before the mystic hour when weary churchyards, ignoring the rules which are supposed to govern polite society, begin to yawn. Nor would the maids themselves have aught to do with him, fearing the destruction by the sudden incursion of aqueous femininity of the costumes which they held most dear.

So the heir of Harrowby Hall resolved, as his ancestors for several generations before him had resolved, that something must be done. His first thought was to make one of his servants occupy the haunted room at the crucial moment; but in this he failed, because the servants themselves knew the history of that room and rebelled. None of his friends would consent to sacrifice their personal comfort to his, nor was there to be found in all England a man so poor as to be willing to occupy the doomed chamber on Christmas Eve for pay.

Then the thought came to the heir to have the fireplace in the room enlarged, so that he might evaporate the ghost at its first appearance, and he was felicitating himself upon the ingenuity of his plan, when he remembered what his father had told him—how that no fire could withstand the lady's extremely contagious dampness. And then he bethought him of steam-pipes. These, he remembered, could lie hundreds of feet deep in water, and still retain sufficient heat to drive the water away in vapor; and as a result of this thought the haunted room was heated by steam to a withering degree, and the heir for six months attended daily the Turkish baths, so that when Christmas Eve came he could himself withstand the awful temperature of the room.

The scheme was only partially successful. The water ghost appeared at the specified time, and found the heir of Harrowby prepared; but hot as the room was, it shortened her visit by no more than five minutes in the hour, during which time the nervous system of the young master was well-nigh shattered, and the room itself was cracked and warped to an extent which required the outlay of a large sum of money to remedy. And worse than this, as the last drop of the water ghost was slowly sizzling itself out on the floor, she whispered to her would-be conqueror that his scheme would avail him nothing, because there was still water in great plenty where she came from, and that next year would find her rehabilitated and as exasperatingly saturating as ever.

It was then that the natural action of the mind, in going from one extreme to the other, suggested to the ingenious heir of Harrowby the means by which the water ghost was ultimately conquered, and happiness once more came within the grasp of the house of Oglethorpe.

The heir provided himself with a warm suit of fur under-clothing. Donning this with the furry side in, he placed over it a rubber garment, tightfitting, which he wore just as a woman wears a jersey. On top of this he placed another set of under-clothing, this suit made of wool, and over this was a second rubber garment like the first. Upon his head he placed a light and comfortable diving helmet, and so clad, on the following Christmas Eve he awaited the coming of his tormentor.

It was a bitterly cold night that brought to a close this twenty-fourth day of December. The air outside was still, but the temperature was below zero. Within all was quiet, the servants of Harrowby Hall awaiting with beating hearts the outcome of their master's campaign against his supernatural visitor.

The master himself was lying on the bed in the haunted room, clad as has already been indicated, and then—

The clock clanged out the hour of twelve.

There was a sudden banging of doors, a blast of cold air swept through the halls, the door leading into the haunted chamber flew open, a splash was heard, and the water ghost was seen standing at the side of the heir of Harrowby, from whose outer dress there streamed rivulets of water, but whose own person deep down under the various garments he wore was as dry and as warm as he could have wished.

"Ha!" said the young master of Harrowby. "I'm glad to see you."

"You are the most original man I've met, if that is true," returned the ghost. "May I ask where did you get that hat?"

"Certainly, madam," returned the master, courteously. "It is a little portable observatory I had made for just such emergencies as this. But, tell me, is it true that you are doomed to follow me about for one mortal hour—to stand where I stand, to sit where I sit?"

"That is my delectable fate," returned the lady.

"We'll go out on the lake," said the master, starting up.

"You can't get rid of me that way," returned the ghost. "The water won't swallow me up; in fact, it will just add to my present bulk."

"Nevertheless," said the master, firmly, "we will go out on the lake."

"But, my dear sir," returned the ghost, with a pale reluctance, "it is fearfully cold out there. You will be frozen hard before you've been out ten minutes."

"Oh no, I'll not," replied the master. "I am very warmly dressed. Come!" This last in a tone of command that made the ghost ripple.

And they started.

They had not gone far before the water ghost showed signs of distress.

"You walk too slowly," she said. "I am nearly frozen. My knees are so stiff now I can hardly move. I beseech you to accelerate your step."

"I should like to oblige a lady," returned the master, courteously, "but my clothes are rather heavy, and a hundred yards an hour is about my speed. Indeed, I think we would better sit down here on this snowdrift, and talk matters over."

"Do not! Do not do so, I beg!" cried the ghost. "Let me move on. I feel myself growing rigid as it is. If we stop here, I shall be frozen stiff."

"That, madam," said the master slowly, and seating himself on an ice-cake—"that is why I have brought you here. We have been on this spot just ten minutes, we have fifty more. Take your time about it, madam, but freeze, that is all I ask of you."

"I cannot move my right leg now," cried the ghost, in despair, "and my overskirt is a solid sheet of ice. Oh, good, kind Mr. Oglethorpe, light a fire, and let me go free from these icy fetters."

"Never, madam. It cannot be. I have you at last."

"Alas!" cried the ghost, a tear trickling down her frozen cheek. "Help me, I beg. I congeal!"

"Congeal, madam, congeal!" returned Oglethorpe, coldly. "You have drenched me and mine for two hundred and three years, madam. To-night you have had your last drench."

"Ah, but I shall thaw out again, and then you'll see. Instead of the comfortably tepid, genial ghost I have been in my past, sir, I shall be iced-water," cried the lady, threateningly.

"No, you won't, either," returned Oglethorpe; "for when you are frozen quite stiff, I shall send you to a cold-storage warehouse, and there shall you remain an icy work of art forever more."

"But warehouses burn."

"So they do, but this warehouse cannot burn. It is made of asbestos and surrounding it are fire-proof walls, and within those walls the temperature is now and shall forever be 416 degrees below the zero point; low enough to make an icicle of any flame in this world—or the next," the master added, with an ill-suppressed chuckle.

"For the last time let me beseech you. I would go on my knees to you, Oglethorpe, were they not already frozen. I beg of you do not doo—"

Here even the words froze on the water ghost's lips and the clock struck one. There was a momentary tremor throughout the ice-bound form, and the moon, coming out from behind a cloud, shone down on the rigid figure of a beautiful woman sculptured in clear, transparent ice. There stood the ghost of Harrowby Hall, conquered by the cold, a prisoner for all time.

The heir of Harrowby had won at last, and to-day in a large storage house in London stands the frigid form of one who will never again flood the house of Oglethorpe with woe and sea-water.

As for the heir of Harrowby, his success in coping with a ghost has made him famous, a fame that still lingers about him, although his victory took place some twenty years ago; and so far from being unpopular with the fair sex, as he was when we first knew him, he has not only been married twice, but is to lead a third bride to the altar before the year is out.

The Will of Luke Carlowe

Clive Pemberton

Mr. Jonas Fenwick, the lawyer, unclasped his bony, wrinkled hands as he came to the end of the short document he had perused for the third time, and carefully placing it in a convenient pigeon-hole in his bureau, peered sharply over his gold-rimmed *pince-nez* at Mr. Reuben Tunny, his confidential clerk.

"It is quite the most extraordinary document that has ever come under my notice," he said, slowly. "A little more than eccentric, eh, Reuben, eh?" and the lawyer chuckled—a dry, eminently legal chuckle in which mirth found no place. Mr. Reuben Tunny—an angular, sallow-faced man of middle age who had grown up in Mr. Fenwick's service—slowly and gravely shook his head.

"I don't understand it, sir," he said, solemnly. "I don't understand it at all."

"What don't you understand, Reuben?" returned the lawyer, quizzically. "This,"—laying his hand on the document under discussion—"is plain enough for a child to comprehend."

"I did not mean that I could not understand the meaning of Professor Luke Carlowe's last written words, sir," said Mr. Tunny, slowly. "As you rightly say, a child could comprehend the meaning of that document, for it is a perfectly plain statement. Now, what I *cannot understand* is a sane man doing such an extraordinary thing. It—it is almost uncanny!"

"*Almost* uncanny!" echoed the lawyer, laying a strong emphasis on the first word. "I call it *very* uncanny, and with a hint of the devilish in it, too, Reuben! Of course, I—in common with everybody acquainted with Luke Carlowe—knew that he was very eccentric, and expected him to do something extraordinary before he died; but this matter relating to his will—Well, well! We will hear presently what the young man has to say about it."

"You appointed twelve o'clock in your letter, and I do not doubt that he will be punctual," and with a dry smile at his employer, the sedate old clerk withdrew to the outer office with a sheaf of parchments. Precisely at twelve o'clock the outer door of Mr. Fenwick's office opened, and a tall, good-looking young man of about twenty-five years of age quickly entered.

"I have an appointment with Mr. Fenwick," he said, handing Mr. Tunny a card on which was neatly engraved the name "Cyril Carlowe." "I suppose—I presume he is in?"

"If you will be so good as to wait one moment, I will inform Mr. Fenwick that you are here," returned Mr. Tunny, and a moment later he ushered Mr. Cyril Carlowe into the lawyer's presence.

"Good morning, Mr. Carlowe," said Mr. Fenwick briskly, bowing his visitor to a chair.

"I daresay—I expect you are wondering why I have asked you to see me this morning?"

The other shifted in his chair a little; then he gave the lawyer a frank, clear look.

"I will confess that I am most curious to learn the reason, Mr. Fenwick," he replied quickly, "for I can think of nothing to—to—"

"Well, well, Mr. Carlowe, I will set the matter before you at once. I have sent for you with regard to your uncle's will. You are aware, of course," he went on, slightly hesitating as he looked at the other, "that your uncle, Professor Carlowe, died just a month ago."

Cyril Carlowe nodded disinterestedly, and the lawyer proceeded:

"I think I may say that I enjoyed the fullest confidence of my late client, and I never knew him to take a step or do anything important without first consulting me. Of course, I need not say that I am cognizant of the strange and, now that I have seen you,"—with a courtly little bow—"inexplicable dislike he bore towards his brother—your father—and you."

Cyril Carlowe nodded gloomily.

"I always told the guv'nor he was mad," he rejoined slowly. "Before he refused to see either of us again, he used to talk the wildest rot you ever heard by the hour. All about the spirits of the dead returning from the grave—supernatural agencies and intermediate states—that kind of mad foolery! I verily believe it was our scepticism and—and ridicule that turned him so violently against us, Mr. Fenwick."

The lawyer nodded quietly.

"He was eccentric—most eccentric, I agree with you; but to return to what I was saying. With regard to his will, I drew it up, he kept it, and—"

"And, of course, left all his money—a good bit it must be too—to some society for the furthering of his mad theories, eh?"

"Yes—and no," answered the lawyer, paradoxically. He took a paper from the pigeon-hole and turned it about thoughtfully in his hand. "That will he left in my care, and in it he bequeathed his fortune to a—a society. This paper,"—holding it up—"contains his last written instructions, and leads me to believe that he made a later will, leaving everything instead to—to you."

"To—me?" If a thunderbolt had fallen at his feet, Cyril Carlowe could not have looked more astounded. "Good heavens! Mr. Fenwick, what do you mean? What—what is that paper? Where is the last will?"

"Ah! Where, indeed?" rejoined the lawyer, handing him the paper. "Just read that, Mr. Carlowe, and you will know as much as I know."

There was a space of silence while Cyril Carlowe, with amazed eyes, read the following few lines—the last words of the late Professor Luke Carlowe, written but a few hours before his death.

> This message, which I leave in the care of my trusted friend and lawyer, Jonas Fenwick, is to be read by him one month after my decease, and then handed to my nephew, Cyril Carlowe. I now state that I have made a later will, in which I leave everything I possess to my nephew, Cyril Carlowe, on certain conditions. The whereabouts of this will only I know, and it is to prove my life theory—that is, that there is a means of communication between the dead and the living—that I have planned this proof. On a certain night—to be arranged by the members of the "Occult Association"—my nephew, Cyril Carlowe, is to descend into the vault where I am buried, and I—from the spirit world—will return and reveal where the will is. A committee of ten of my colleagues will wait outside, and a lasting proof will be given to the world of that which is now treated with ignorant scepticism. If the said Cyril Carlowe will not undertake the test, the will now existent, which Jonas Fenwick holds, will be proved.

"He must have been mad when he wrote this, Mr. Fenwick," said Cyril Carlowe, looking up from the amazing document. "I can't quite grasp it. He says here that in his last will he left me everything. That will, nobody, save himself, knows the whereabouts of, and unless I—I—Good heavens! Am I awake or dreaming?"

"What it means is this, Mr. Carlowe," replied the lawyer, looking keenly at him. "The will which I hold, and which I thought was the only one and the last, is evidently not so. That document distinctly states that he drew up a fresh will, leaving you his sole heir. To find that will and establish your right, he states what I candidly confess is beyond my powers of credulity—that is, that he himself will reveal to you—alone—where it is."

"But—but it is too—too monstrously fantastic!" cried the other excitedly. "A dead man reveal where his will is hidden?"

"It was his pet theory, remember," put in the lawyer, "the theory that there is a means of communicating between the dead and the living—a bridge of communication I think they call it."

There was another long silence. Professor Carlowe had ended an eccentric life by an eccentricity which almost passed belief.

Cyril Carlowe spoke at last, slowly and thoughtfully.

"What is your opinion about it, Mr. Fenwick?" he said. The lawyer coughed and deliberated before replying.

"If you were rich, I would say, 'don't do it,'" he replied slowly; "but as things are—you are young, you don't seem nervous—"

"What is the law on the point?"

The lawyer chuckled.

"There is no point of law in it," he said drily. "It is purely an optional matter as far as you are concerned. You can carry out the—er—instructions, or—you need not."

"And if I don't?"

"Then the will I hold—in which everything is left to the 'Occult Association'—will be proved, and the money will go to further more—ahem!—extraordinary theories."

"I see!"

There was another long silence—a thoughtful one on Mr. Cyril Carlowe's part, judging from his facial expression.

He looked up suddenly, and his firm chin set in a determined manner. "I shall do it, Mr. Fenwick," he said in a decisive tone.

The lawyer looked sharply at him

"You will—?" he began, then stopped abruptly.

"I shall carry out the instructions left in that document," said Cyril Carlowe, firmly. "I am not afraid, and to show that I am not afraid I will do it. You will make all the formal arrangements?"

"I will," replied the lawyer, and a strange light—a light of admiration—flickered in his dull eyes for one moment.

In the large, comfortably-appointed room where the "Occult Association" held its spiritualistic and psychological séances, a group of men were gathered round the solid mahogany table. At one end sat the chairman—Professor Michael Andover—

and ranged along either side were six of the association's foremost members. At the other end, facing the chairman, sat Mr. Fenwick, the lawyer, and Cyril Carlowe. The former's face was expressive of dry cynicism; the latter looked slightly pale, but perfectly calm and self-possessed. The room was very still, for the hour was late—ten o'clock—and the quiet street was empty and deserted. Amid perfect silence, the chairman rose to speak.

"Gentlemen," he began, "the purpose for which we are gathered here tonight is known to you all. Our valued and deeply lamented colleague, Professor Luke Carlowe, has left in our hands the proving of a much discussed and—and scepticised theory. Everything is arranged, and I have only to ask Mr. Cyril Carlowe if he wishes—to say anything before a start is made."

"I have nothing to say—no comment to make," replied Cyril Carlowe, "save to have done with this matter as speedily as possible."

"Very good! Then a start had better be made, for the drive to the cemetery will occupy a full hour."

Four carriages were waiting without, and in a few minutes they were progressing at a fair speed toward the distant cemetery. The night was heavy and overcast—a sullen sky and a peculiar oppressiveness in the air suggesting that thunder was not far distant. Indeed, before the cemetery was reached, a few large drops of rain fell, and a distant muttering of thunder joined the rumbling of the carriage wheels.

"This is a strange project, Mr. Fenwick," said Cyril Carlowe, breaking the silence for the first time. He and the lawyer had the last carriage to themselves. "Even now, I half wish—"

The lawyer look sharply at him.

"It is not too late to draw back if you wish," he said, quietly. "As you say, the whole thing is—er—very strange!"

"I cannot understand how they have arranged it," went on the other, thoughtfully. "The access to the vault at this time of night, I mean."

"Enthusiasts can do anything with money to help them," he said, drily. "I don't know how they have worked it—it is no concern of yours and mine. Suffice to say they have, by bribing the keeper, I suppose."

At that moment the carriages came to a stop, and the party alighted. The cemetery, dark and gloomy, was barred by heavy gates; but, as the carriages withdrew, a man came quickly out of the lodge and unlocked the side gate. The party quickly filed through, and the gate clanged behind them. Led by Professor Andover, they proceeded down a side path which led to a vault. The silence of death was over everything, and only the pattering of the hurrying rain and crunching of their footsteps broke the intense hush. Now and again, arrows of lightning darted from the black sky, lighting up the white stones and lending an added weirdness to the scene. In a few minutes they were standing opposite the vault wherein the body of Professor Luke Carlowe was interred. It was a huge stone mausoleum, square in shape, and guarded by a massive black iron-studded door. Lighting a lamp, the leader of the party unlocked the door, and all descended the short flight of stone steps. In a niche on the level with their heads was the massive coffin with its velvet pall. Flowers still withered on the ledge of the stained-glass window, and a dank atmosphere pervaded the echoing interior.

"We shall leave you now, Mr. Carlowe," said Professor Andover, in a hushed voice. "The conditions you know—that you wait here until the last stroke of twelve has sounded. It is now quarter to twelve."

The young man inclined his head, but said nothing, and one by one they filed up the steps. Mr. Fenwick, with the lantern, was the last to go, and he hung back to say a last word.

"I feel that I advised you wrong," he said in a hurried whisper. "Have done with this mad business—no good can come of it!"

But Cyril Carlowe shook his head.

"I shall go through with it now, Mr. Fenwick," he said firmly. "I am not afraid. I have my revolver, and I will see it through."

The lawyer said nothing further, but holding his hand for a moment, hurried up the steps.

The gate shut with a dull clang, and Cyril Carlowe found himself in the dank darkness—alone!

The moments passed slowly—very slowly. Without, the storm was coming up fast. The rain rattled dully on the roof of the vault; a bright flash of lightning darted through the stained-glass window and revealed the coffin for a fleeting second. High up in domed space of the roof, a harsh screech sounded, followed by a whirr of beating wings as a bat flew round and round, and then clung panting to the groin. Strange, wild fancies crowded on his brain. With the revolver gripped in his hand, he turned slowly round, and once he was certain something touch him. Yet he was alone, save for the dead in the massive casket. Alone! was he alone? A strange sinking sensation suddenly crept over him; a deadly nausea shook him, and he slowly sank on the stone floor. A crash of thunder split the air—a blinding flash of lightning suddenly illumined the whole vault as with the light of day, and in that moment he saw—

Above the war of thunder, the waiting group heard it—a cry that none had ever heard the like of before, and that would ring in their ears for ever.

"Great heaven!" cried the lawyer, looking into the others' white faces; "that was—that was Cyril Carlowe's voice!"

He waited for no reply, but dashed headlong into the open, and made for the vault at frantic speed. In less than ten seconds he was at the gate and tugging at the iron handle. Holding the lamp high above his head, he paused and peered into the darkness below with a horrible presage of evil.

"Carlowe!" he cried, "are you all right?"

No answer—only the dull, reverberating echo of his own voice. With the others pressing behind him, he cleared the steps in two bounds, then fell back, half fainting with a horrible dread, for this is what he saw.

A huddled body on the stone floor—the body of Cyril Carlowe—dead! He knelt down beside him and looked into a face so distorted as to be hardly recognizable. But it was not that which sent the creeping chill of fear—the one frantic desire to be clear of the place—pressing on him. In the clenched hand of the dead man was a roll of paper—the missing will of Professor Luke Carlowe!

A Wireless Message

Ambrose Bierce

In the summer of 1896 Mr. William Holt, a wealthy manufacturer of Chicago, was living temporarily in a little town of central New York, the name of which the writer's memory has not retained. Mr. Holt had had "trouble with his wife," from whom he had parted a year before. Whether the trouble was anything more serious than "incompatibility of temper," he is probably the only living person that knows: he is not addicted to the vice of confidences. Yet he has related the incident herein set down to at least one person without exacting a pledge of secrecy. He is now living in Europe.

One evening he had left the house of a brother whom he was visiting, for a stroll in the country. It may be assumed—whatever the value of the assumption in connection with what is said to have occurred—that his mind was occupied with reflections on his domestic infelicities and the distressing changes that they had wrought in his life.

Whatever may have been his thoughts, they so possessed him that he observed neither the lapse of time nor whither his feet were carrying him; he knew only that he had passed far beyond the town limits and was traversing a lonely region by a road that bore no resemblance to the one by which he had left the village. In brief, he was "lost."

Realizing his mischance, he smiled; central New York is not a region of perils, nor does one long remain lost in it. He turned about and went back the way that he had come. Before he had gone far he observed that the landscape was growing more distinct—was brightening. Everything was suffused with a soft, red glow in which he saw his shadow projected in the road before him. "The moon is rising," he said to himself. Then he remembered that it was about the time of the new moon, and if that tricksy orb was in one of its stages of visibility it had set long before. He stopped and faced about, seeking the source of the rapidly broadening light. As he did so, his shadow turned and lay along the road in front of him as before. The light still came from behind him. That was surprising; he could not understand. Again he turned, and again, facing successively to every point of the horizon. Always the shadow was before—always the light behind, "a still and awful red."

Holt was astonished—"dumfounded" is the word that he used in telling it—yet seems to have retained a certain intelligent curiosity. To test the intensity of the light whose nature and cause he could not determine, he took out his watch to see if he could make out the figures on the dial. They were plainly visible, and the hands indicated the hour of eleven o'clock and twenty-five minutes. At that moment the mysterious illumination suddenly flared to an intense, an almost blinding splendor, flushing the entire sky, extinguishing the stars and throwing the monstrous shadow of himself athwart the landscape. In that unearthly illumination he saw near him, but apparently in the air at a considerable elevation, the figure of his wife, clad in her night-clothing and holding to her breast the figure of his child. Her eyes were fixed upon his with an expression which he afterward professed himself unable to name or describe, further than that it was "not of this life."

The flare was momentary, followed by black darkness, in which, however, the apparition still showed white and motionless; then by insensible degrees it faded and vanished, like a bright image on the retina after the closing of the eyes. A peculiarity of the apparition, hardly noted at the time, but afterward recalled, was that it showed only the upper half of the woman's figure: nothing was seen below the waist.

The sudden darkness was comparative, not absolute, for gradually all objects of his environment became again visible.

In the dawn of the morning Holt found himself entering the village at a point opposite to that at which he had left it. He soon arrived at the house of his brother, who hardly knew him. He was wild-eyed, haggard, and gray as a rat. Almost incoherently, he related his night's experience.

"Go to bed, my poor fellow," said his brother, "and—wait. We shall hear more of this."

An hour later came the predestined telegram. Holt's dwelling in one of the suburbs of Chicago had been destroyed by fire. Her escape cut off by the flames, his wife had appeared at an upper window, her child in her arms. There she had stood, motionless, apparently dazed. Just as the firemen had arrived with a ladder, the floor had given way, and she was seen no more.

The moment of this culminating horror was eleven o'clock and twenty-five minutes, standard time.

"With What Measure Ye Mete . . ."

Ethel Lina White

Extract from the Diary of Desmond Clay

17 November: Had a most extraordinary and startling experience two days ago—so utterly inexplicable that I have not written it up until today. Took car on Friday at Kennington Gate to Steatham. Felt pretty much the same as usual. Passed Brixton Station, and remember looking at the clock. Time was 4:45. Next thing I knew was that I was near Streatham Common, taking the turning to the left. On consulting watch, found it was 5:25. The intervening time is an absolute blank. Try as I will, I cannot piece it together. It is impossible to conclude that I fell asleep, as I had evidently got out of the car at Streatham Hill Station, as I originally intended. Am worried and perplexed at this strange lapse, and, at first recurrence, shall consult a specialist. Saw Enid; she grows dearer every day. A compensation, I suppose, for my past bitter experience of treachery and pain. However, *de mortuis*—for I hear Mrs. Laflèche is dead; something sudden. Forty minutes wiped clean out—sponged away from my memory. Wish I could remember—or else forget all about it.

When Iris Devine married Syd Laflèche with his £12,000 a year, the world said she was a lucky girl. It made the identical remark seven years later, when she became his widow—but with a sympathising accent this time. Yet, regarding the affair from its purely commercial aspect, it was not without its points. Iris had given youth, a moderate portion of good looks, and little else beside, in exchange for a gentleman of agreeable characteristics, very shady antecedents, and an unimpeachable banking account. The flaw in the transaction was the fact that Iris was not a free asset. Yet this item had been quickly discounted by the girl. Born into a struggling theatrical family, her life had been played out, to a considerable degree, in the fierce glow of limelight, which had dried up the dews of youth too soon. The fact that the path that led to her union with Laflèche was paved by a human heart, only made the way for her feet softer.

Yet among the many parts she had played she did not look forward to dismissing her quondam lover. However, she counted on Desmond's gentleness and lack of emotion, feeling she would score heavily through his hatred of a scene. There would be no disagreeable reproaches, she argued—Desmond would not forget that he was a gentleman.

But in this she was mistaken. Desmond *did* forget, and when he passed out of Iris's life as a personal element it was to remain there as a vaguely disquieting memory.

Then the great Wheel of Change snatched her up and whirled her through a cycle of prosperity, excitement, and disillusionment, finally shaking her off and dropping her suddenly into the Kennington Road one foggy November day, just at four o'clock. The fog was creeping on with the stealthy advance of a foe—swelling and darkening in the shadows, and gathering in the corners, only to shrink back before the glow of the street lights. The cars whirled by in an intermittent procession, their red eyes gleaming through the mist. Irish watched them with fascination. They represented her old life—the car and omnibus era. Seven years of carriages and motors had ousted them from a willing memory, but today they seemed to regain their old ascendancy. Each name revived old recollections—the struggle to capture this, the easy conquest of that.

Suddenly yielding to an impulse, Iris halted the next car, and climbing the narrow stair with difficulty, as the car lurched on, she groped along the shaking platform on the top and dropped heavily into the nearest seat.

"Free!" she cried, and then laughed out again into the chill air. "Free!"

The mean houses slid by, yellow patches gleaming through the fan-lights. Iris hailed them with delight. She held up her muff, to ward off the damp air, and laughed again, as the soft fur caressed her face. The six brief weeks of widowhood had found her stunned; today, for the first time, she realised her position, and her liberty.

She nodded familiarly to a beer-palace, resplendent with flaring lights. "Seven years' penal servitude," she whispered. "Free!"

"All fares." The man came to take her ticket. Iris had not troubled to notice the destination of the car.

"All the way," she sad recklessly, and then the woman of wealth, suddenly smitten by habit, found herself keenly counting the coppers that the man had given her for change. That made her laugh again, and she gripped her hands tightly in an ecstasy. "Free! Seven years' hard!" Then she frowned slightly. "Now, am I really free, or—ticket-of-leave?" The thought amused her, and she toyed with it.

"Ticket-of-leave! Then I must really be good, for a bit, or else—back again! And it may be a life-sentence next time. Oh, lucky woman! Free!"

But the car refused to run to this tune now, and it whirred along rapping out in uneven jerks: "Ticket of leave! Ticket of leave!"

Iris laid back dreamily, soothed by the sway of the motion. Imperceptibly, her thoughts slipped away to the crime that held the sentence.

Suddenly, a thick curtain of blue shot down, blotting out the grey world, and spreading over the fog. It hung there for a fraction of a second, and then split in two pieces, and half was the calm turquoise sky, and half the restless, heaving sea. The tide of Memory, in sweeping round the world, had, in a momentary back-wash, left Iris stranded high and dry on the recollection of her parting scene with Desmond.

Well she remembered it! The bold cliff, the winding path, and Desmond swinging along by the foam, hurrying to meet her. She shuddered when she saw the light in his eyes, for she knew it was hers to darken it, hers to kill the faith, and banish the joy—hers to murder youth, and imperil her soul—and all in the sacred name of Mammon! She felt so utterly sorry for herself, that she thought he must be sorry, too, and she could hardly understand it, when she saw the joy in the boy's eyes fade to bewilderment, and then as the baleful light broke through the cloud of doubt, a storm of anger, fierce, ungovernable rage, that blotted the calm face. Iris hardly recognised his voice, though she shrank beneath his reproaches, and bent her head to the tempest, praying for the lull. It seemed to Iris that he raved on interminably, but only one sentence stayed with her.

"It's a monstrous thing you've done, inhuman! To win my heart, and then trample on it. Oh, I know it has been done before. And it will be done again. But it is no small thing. It is murder! I tell you, it is murder! You have killed the best part of me. I can feel it. And you can't do it with impunity. There will be a reckoning, I tell you—you must . . ." The voice dragged incoherently, and then Desmond pulled himself together. He had remembered the fact on which Iris had counted, that he was a gentleman, to whom were barred the rights of primeval man. His face flamed, and in shame-faced manner, he apologised humbly for his tirade. The anger faded from his face, and only dull pain was there. The victory was with Iris. Raising his hat, he left her, and she watched him go into the setting sun, his white-clad form cutting the purple of the heather. Even as he went, she wanted him. She wanted one last look, one smile, even if grudged; in short, she wanted a conscience-salve.

She bent her brows and tightened her mouth under the strain of will-force, and tugged at his consciousness—willing him to look back once more. Desmond had never proved unresponsive to that mute appeal, and even now his head turned involuntarily and their eyes met.

Iris cried out in a sudden panic of terror. For the first time, she saw Murder look out of a man's eyes, and the sight rooted her to the spot, panic-stricken.

She saw his profile sharply outlined against the blue, and then the car jolted to the points, and slithered on to another track. For one minute, the Past still tore desperately at her skirts. The next second the shutter of grey had slammed down, and she was again in the grip of the Present.

Only the profile had not vanished. She found that she was still looking at it, and with a thrill suddenly awoke to the fact that Desmond was on the same car.

Where and when he had got on, she did not know. Leaning forward, she scanned his face with interest. Just the same old Desmond, in every respect. He sat forward, looking in front of him, with a dreamy unconscious smile on his face—absolutely oblivious to his surroundings. Iris's glance was almost a caress, as she scanned each feature. Nothing changed! The calm brow—the clear eyes—the dear mouth! A man who was clearly under petticoat government. Dame Fashion has a thrall in him, as was evident in every detail of his well-groomed appearance, starting from the crown of his hat, down to the tips of his fashionable boots, while a point was scored with every detail of his costume. And Mrs. Grundy plainly had him under her thumb, and had stamped his whole appearance with the Seal of Conventionality.

Iris studied his face yet longer, and then she almost laughed the gentleness and well-bred repose imprinted thereon. Yet, for one brief moment, she had been afraid of this man, and had thought she had seen the ugly specter or murder peeping from his eyes.

The car glided on. Desmond still smiled absently at the mist. At last, Irish grew impatient. She wished he would turn and notice her. Desmond was sitting three seats in front, to the left. A stout policeman by her side hedged her in with the same majesty of Law, while across the gangway to her left sat a portly City man. They seemed to represent obstacles, and she grew yet more restless. She found herself counting the roses that clustered on the hat of a girl who sat in front. Five roses of a pinky mauve shade. And the girl had red hair. Iris shuddered.

Then she remembered her old powers. Should she *will* him to once look at her? She set her hat—whose white strings alone marked her widowhood—straight and pondered. She knew that during the past seven years Dame Fortune had only ripened and embellished her charms, though, perhaps, at the last, as if suddenly repenting of her lavish generosity, with a dash of feminine spite, she had pecked out a few lines in the smooth face.

Iris struggled with the temptation. *Ought* she to try to revive the old fascination? Once, Desmond had suffered bitterly through her action. His face seemed tranquil now. True, there were lines round mouth and eyes, but Iris was unskilled in reading emotions, and placed them as a tribute to time. If the old game of Candle and the Moth were to be revived, would the end this time be total extinction of the Moth?

The woman wavered, and then the love of admiration proved too strong, and the fierce flame of Vanity licked up the last scruples in a glow of desire. Iris had always met a lover's advances halfway, and if he showed no desire to even approach the line of demarcation, then she sallied forth alone, to reveal to him his destination. And she longed for Desmond's other wing. So, with a soulful look in her eyes, she leaned forward—her pretty white chin nestling her dark furs, calling to Desmond—calling, calling.

And he heard. Seven years of disuse had not blunted her old powers. Desmond slowly, reluctantly, fell under the spell, and, in the old way, he turned his head, and looked at her.

The calm blue eyes looked at her quietly. Then, a sudden chill seized Iris, as, to her amazement, she saw the red lamp of murder kindle in them. She watched the light glow and blaze, as though fed by a Devil's torch, and then Desmond rose from his seat, and came towards her—his head thrust forward, his lower lip hanging, and his whole body bent, and moving with a curious undulating slope.

She gripped her seat in alarm, and then the groundlessness of her fears reassured her. The policeman's warm cape caressed her, and the red calico faces of the roses looked at her cheerfully. The City man turned the leaves of his paper with a brisk rustle. This was no isolated spot, where murder stalks unchallenged. The absolute safety of her position filled her with a sense of comfort.

Desmond came yet closer; she could see his fingers quivering and wrapping themselves around each other, with an undefined sense of coming horror. She watched them with fascination, as they twisted and curled, but even as she looked, they shot out, and she felt her throat held in a bony grip.

One minute of shock, and then the terror died away before the comforting assurance that help was at hand. The policeman coughed noisily, and a man behind broke out in a whistle. The fingers pressed tighter.

A sling singing began in Iris's ears, yet to her amazement *nothing happened*. She cast her eyes desperately round the car, and saw, to her bewilderment, that no one had stirred. It was as though everyone was quite unconscious of what had befallen. Iris reeled before this stunning fact. She could not grasp the significance. A wave of utter incredulity swamped her whole being. Even while the murderous fingers were tightening each minute, even while the man was swaying above her, in the force of his convulsive fury, the every-day world read calmly on, while a tragedy was being enacted.

Indignation ran hot through her veins. Then it was met by a returning current of so icy a horror, that she collapsed into a powerless heap.

Still in his seat, two yards away, was Desmond—looking dreamily into space, his eyes absolutely unconscious. She took in every detail of his form and costume; she noted that his tie was grey crêpe de Chine, and that he wore violets in his buttonhole. And yet, standing over her, glowering with inhuman ferocity, was the other Desmond.

Iris looked, and something caught her strained sight. It was something bright, that glittered and swayed in circles and hoops—something as fine as spun glass, and as dazzling as silver—something like a silken cord. She saw with a thrill that this united the two Desmonds.

A jumbled mass of psychological facts heaped themselves up in the woman's brain. Articles she had read on astral bodies, sub-consciousness, second personalities, all blended together, but the one terrible truth seemed to stand out clearly. The injured personality, the spiritual part of Desmond, that she had wounded, so mortally, had suddenly remembered its slumbering wrongs, and had slipped out of its corporeal envelope, to avenge its violated individuality. And stinging her brain like a hornet was the thought that she alone had called for this Minister of Vengeance.

Broad iron bands seemed now to fasten round Iris's head, as the grip pressed more closely. She could feel the blood foaming like a mill-stream through her veins, seeking to find an outlet, and driven back by the encircling hoops.

The pity of her position filled her with anguish. She felt that she was in the thrall of some monstrous nightmare. She struggled to cry out, and tell the people on the car of her danger. The scream "Murder!" rose to her blue lips, but the cruel hands pressed it back, and sent it down to echo in the depths of her hopeless heart—"Murder!" With the strong arms near—with the kind faces round her—"Murder!" And to Iris the horror and pity culminated in the knowledge that Desmond sat and dreamed on, all unconscious of the price that was being paid as Blood Penalty for slaughtered Truth and Faith. His sensitive mouth was set in a smile. His whole being was a mute protest against violence of word or act.

Now the lights began to dance around her, till they joined with the street-lamps in a cluster of golden bulbs. Faster they went, round and round, till a circle was formed, and lamp melted into lamp in a fiery ring. Round and round it spun. Then it suddenly swooped up into the air, while Iris felt herself sinking down—down. She saw the ring grow smaller and smaller, till it flickered to a star—dwindled to pin-prick—and went out.

Iris now became conscious of a strange conflict that was raging within her. She could feel her reeling brain sending down agonised signals to her heart, which sent back an answering "thud." It seemed as if it were holding fortress against the assaults of Death. The beats grew feebler each minute, like the blows from the picks of entombed miners. The roar of a great sea sounded in Iris's ears. The signals from the brain, running down the jangled nerves, grew more desperate and despairing, but the answering "thud" was weaker.

Then suddenly something almost imperceptible broke through the roar. It was so faint, so far away, that it seemed like the very last vibration of sound. The sense, rather than the words, fell on Iris's ears. "Lady—seems—ill."

They were the very last echoes that reached her from the Finite World. The last heart-beat was followed by silence, and she slipped away into the Infinite.

The next minute, the car seemed to break up, like the pieces of a kaleidoscope. Instead of a compact whole of quietly ranked people, forms passed hurriedly to and fro, pushing each other in excited confusion. Only one was unmoved, a man, who remained in his seat, wrapped in dreamy abstraction.

The forms clustered round, and drew closer to the centre. Then they parted, and Something was borne down the steep stairs. The car went on.

But the man on the seat never stirred.

The Woman's Ghost Story

Algernon Blackwood

"Yes," she said, from her seat in the dark corner, "I'll tell you an experience if you care to listen. And, what's more, I'll tell it briefly, without trimmings—I mean without unessentials. That's a thing story-tellers never do, you know," she laughed. "They drag in all the unessentials and leave their listeners to disentangle; but I'll give you just the essentials, and you can make of it what you please. But on one condition: that at the end you ask no questions, because I can't explain it and have no wish to."

We agreed. We were all serious. After listening to a dozen prolix stories from people who merely wished to "talk" but had nothing to tell, we wanted "essentials."

"In those days," she began, feeling from the quality of our silence that we were with her, "in those days I was interested in psychic things, and had arranged to sit up alone in a haunted house in the middle of London. It was a cheap and dingy lodging-house in a mean street, unfurnished. I had already made a preliminary examination in daylight that afternoon, and the keys from the caretaker, who lived next door, were in my pocket. The story was a good one—satisfied me, at any rate, that it was worth investigating; and I won't weary you with details as to the woman's murder and all the tiresome elaboration as to *why* the place was *alive*. Enough that it was.

"I was a good deal bored, therefore, to see a man, whom I took to be the talkative old caretaker, waiting for me on the steps when I went in at 11 p.m., for I had sufficiently explained that I wished to be there alone for the night.

"'I wished to show you *the* room,' he mumbled, and of course I couldn't exactly refuse, having tipped him for the temporary loan of a chair and table.

"'Come in, then, and let's be quick,' I said.

"We went in, he shuffling after me through the unlighted hall up to the first floor where the murder had taken place, and I prepared myself to hear his inevitable account before turning him out with the half-crown his persistence had earned. After lighting the gas I sat down in the arm-chair he had provided—a faded, brown plush arm-chair—and turned for the first time to face him and get through with the performance as quickly as possible. And it was in that instant I got my first shock. The man was *not* the caretaker. It was not the old fool, Carey, I had interviewed earlier in the day and made my plans with. My heart gave a horrid jump.

"'Now who are *you*, pray?' I said. 'You're not Carey, the man I arranged with this afternoon. Who are you?'

"I felt uncomfortable, as you may imagine. I was a 'psychical researcher,' and a young woman of new tendencies, and proud of my liberty, but I did not care to find myself in an empty house with a stranger. Something of my confidence left me. Confidence with women, you know, is all humbug after a certain point. Or perhaps you don't know, for most of you are men. But anyhow my pluck ebbed in a quick rush, and I felt afraid.

"'Who are you?' I repeated quickly and nervously. The fellow was well dressed, youngish and good-looking, but with a face of great sadness. I myself was barely thirty. I am giving you essentials, or I would not mention it. Out of quite ordinary things comes this story. I think that's why it has value.

"'No,' he said; 'I'm the man who was frightened to death.'

"His voice and his words ran through me like a knife, and I felt ready to drop. In my pocket was the book I had bought to make notes in. I felt the pencil sticking in the socket. I felt, too, the extra warm things I had put on to sit up in, as no bed or sofa was available—a hundred things dashed through my mind, foolishly and without sequence or meaning, as the way is when one is really frightened. Unessentials leaped up and puzzled me, and I thought of what the papers might say if it came out, and what my 'smart' brother-in-law would think, and whether it would be told that I had cigarettes in my pocket, and was a freethinker.

"'The man who was frightened to death!' I repeated aghast.

"'That's me,' he said stupidly.

"I stared at him just as you would have done—any one of you men now listening to me—and felt my life ebbing and flowing like a sort of hot fluid. You needn't laugh! That's how I felt. Small things, you know, touch the mind with great earnestness when terror is there—*real terror*. But I might have been at a middle-class tea-party, for all the ideas I had: they were so ordinary!

"'But I thought you were the caretaker I tipped this afternoon to let me sleep here!' I gasped. 'Did—did Carey send you to meet me?'

"'No,' he replied in a voice that touched my boots somehow. 'I am the man who was frightened to death. And what is more, I am frightened *now*!'

"'So am I!' I managed to utter, speaking instinctively. 'I'm simply terrified.'

"'Yes,' he replied in that same odd voice that seemed to sound within me. 'But you are still in the flesh, and I—*am not*!'

"I felt the need for vigorous self-assertion. I stood up in that empty, unfurnished room, digging the nails into my palms and clenching my teeth. I was determined to assert my individuality and my courage as a new woman and a free soul.

"'You mean to say you are not in the flesh!' I gasped. 'What in the world are you talking about?'

"The silence of the night swallowed up my voice. For the first time I realized that darkness was over the city; that dust lay upon the stairs; that the floor above was untenanted and the floor below empty. I was alone in an unoccupied and haunted house, unprotected, and a woman. I chilled. I heard the wind round the house, and knew the stars were hidden. My thoughts rushed to policemen and omnibuses, and everything that was useful and comforting. I suddenly realized what a fool I was to come to such a house alone. I was icily afraid. I thought the end of my life had come. I was an utter fool to go in for psychical research when I had not the necessary nerve.

"'Good God!' I gasped. 'If you're not Carey, the man I arranged with, who are you?'

"I was really stiff with terror. The man moved slowly towards me across the empty room. I held out my arm to stop him, getting up out of my chair at the same moment, and he came to halt just opposite to me, a smile on his worn, sad face.

"'I told you who I am,' he repeated quietly with a sigh, looking at me with the saddest eyes I have ever seen, 'and I am frightened *still*.'

"By this time I was convinced that I was entertaining either a rogue or a madman, and I cursed my stupidity in bringing the man in without having seen his face. My mind was quickly made up, and I knew what to do. Ghosts and psychic phenomena flew to the winds. If I angered the creature my life might pay the price. I must humor him till I got to the door, and then race for the street. I stood bolt upright and faced him. We were about of a height, and I was a strong, athletic woman who played hockey in winter and climbed Alps in summer. My hand itched for a stick, but I had none.

"'Now, of course, I remember,' I said with a sort of stiff smile that was very hard to force. 'Now I remember your case and the wonderful way you behaved. . . .'

"The man stared at me stupidly, turning his head to watch me as I backed more and more quickly to the door. But when his face broke into a smile I could control myself no longer. I reached the door in a run, and shot out on to the landing. Like a fool, I turned the wrong way, and stumbled over the stairs leading to the next story. But it was too late to change. The man was after me, I was sure, though no sound of footsteps came; and I dashed up the next flight, tearing my skirt and banging my ribs in the darkness, and rushed headlong into the first room I came to. Luckily the door stood ajar, and, still more fortunate, there was a key in the lock. In a second I had slammed the door, flung my whole weight against it, and turned the key.

"I was safe, but my heart was beating like a drum. A second later it seemed to stop altogether, for I saw that there was some one else in the room besides myself. A man's figure stood between me and the windows, where the street lamps gave just enough light to outline his shape against the glass. I'm a plucky woman, you know, for even then I didn't give up hope, but I may tell you that I have never felt so vilely frightened in all my born days. I had locked myself in with him!

"The man leaned against the window, watching me where I lay in a collapsed heap upon the floor. So there were two men in the house with me, I reflected. Perhaps other rooms were occupied too! What could it all mean? But, as I stared something changed in the room, or in me—hard to say which—and I realized my mistake, so that my fear, which had so far been physical, at once altered its character and became *psychical*. I became afraid in my soul instead of in my heart, and I knew immediately who this man was.

"'How in the world did you get up here?' I stammered to him across the empty room, amazement momentarily stemming my fear.

"'Now, let me tell you,' he began, in that odd faraway voice of his that went down my spine like a knife. 'I'm in different space, for one thing, and you'd find me in any room you went into; for according to your way of measuring, I'm *all over the house*. Space is a bodily condition, but I am out of the body, and am not affected by space. It's my condition that keeps me here. I want something to change my condition for me, for then I could get away. What I want is sympathy. Or, really, more than sympathy; I want affection—I want *love*!'

"While he was speaking I gathered myself slowly upon my feet. I wanted to scream and cry and laugh all at once, but I only succeeded in sighing, for my emotion was exhausted and a numbness was coming over me. I felt for the matches in my pocket and made a movement towards the gas jet.

"'I should be much happier if you didn't light the gas,' he said at once, 'for the vibrations of your light hurt me a good deal. You need not be afraid that I shall injure you. I can't touch your body to begin with, for there's a great gulf fixed, you know;

and really this half-light suits me best. Now, let me continue what I was trying to say before. You know, so many people have come to this house to see me, and most of them have seen me, and one and all have been terrified. If only, oh, if only some one would be *not* terrified, but kind and loving to me! Then, you see, I might be able to change my condition and get away.'

"His voice was so sad that I felt tears start somewhere at the back of my eyes; but fear kept all else in check, and I stood shaking and cold as I listened to him.

"'Who are you then? Of course Carey didn't send you, I know now,' I managed to utter. My thoughts scattered dreadfully and I could think of nothing to say. I was afraid of a stroke.

"'I know nothing about Carey, or who he is,' continued the man quietly, 'and the name my body had I have forgotten, thank God; but I am the man who was frightened to death in this house ten years ago, and I have been frightened ever since, and am frightened still; for the succession of cruel and curious people who come to this house to see the ghost, and thus keep alive its atmosphere of terror, only helps to render my condition worse. If only some one would be kind to me—laugh, speak gently and rationally with me, cry if they like, pity, comfort, soothe me—anything but come here in curiosity and tremble as you are now doing in that corner. Now, madam, won't you take pity on me?' His voice rose to a dreadful cry. 'Won't you step out into the middle of the room and try to love me a little?'

"A horrible laughter came gurgling up in my throat as I heard him, but the sense of pity was stronger than the laughter, and I found myself actually leaving the support of the wall and approaching the center of the floor.

"'By God!' he cried, at once straightening up against the window, 'you have done a kind act. That's the first attempt at sympathy that has been shown me since I died, and I feel better already. In life, you know, I was a misanthrope. Everything went wrong with me, and I came to hate my fellow men so much that I couldn't bear to see them even. Of course, like begets like, and this hate was returned. Finally I suffered from horrible delusions, and my room became haunted with demons that laughed and grimaced, and one night I ran into a whole cluster of them near the bed—and the fright stopped my heart and killed me. It's hate and remorse, as much as terror, that clogs me so thickly and keeps me here. If only some one could feel pity, and sympathy, and perhaps a little love for me, I could get away and be happy. When you came this afternoon to see over the house I watched you, and a little hope came to me for the first time. I saw you had courage, originality, resource—*love*. If only I could touch your heart, without frightening you, I knew I could perhaps tap that love you have stored up in your being there, and thus borrow the wings for my escape!'

"Now I must confess my heart began to ache a little, as fear left me and the man's words sank their sad meaning into me. Still, the whole affair was so incredible, and so touched with unholy quality, and the story of a woman's murder I had come to investigate had so obviously nothing to do with this thing, that I felt myself in a kind of wild dream that seemed likely to stop at any moment and leave me somewhere in bed after a nightmare.

"Moreover, his words possessed me to such an extent that I found it impossible to reflect upon anything else at all, or to consider adequately any ways or means of action or escape.

"I moved a little nearer to him in the gloom, horribly frightened, of course, but with the beginnings of a strange determination in my heart.

"'You women,' he continued, his voice plainly thrilling at my approach, 'you wonderful women, to whom life often brings no opportunity of spending your great love, oh, if you only could know how many of *us* simply yearn for it! It would save our souls, if but you knew. Few might find the chance that you now have, but if you only spent your love freely, without definite object, just letting it flow openly for all who need, you would reach hundreds and thousands of souls like me, and *release us*! Oh, madam, I ask you again to feel with me, to be kind and gentle—and if you can to love me a little!"

"My heart did leap within me and this time the tears did come, for I could not restrain them. I laughed too, for the way he called me 'madam' sounded so odd, here in this empty room at midnight in a London street, but my laughter stopped dead and merged in a flood of weeping when I saw how my change of feeling affected him. He had left his place by the window and was kneeling on the floor at my feet, his hands stretched out towards me, and the first signs of a kind of glory about his head.

"'Put your arms round me and kiss me, for the love of God!' he cried. 'Kiss me, oh, kiss me, and I shall be freed! You have done so much already—now do this!'

"I stuck there, hesitating, shaking, my determination on the verge of action, yet not quite able to compass it. But the terror had almost gone.

"'Forget that I'm a man and you're a woman,' he continued in the most beseeching voice I ever heard. 'Forget that I'm a ghost, and come out boldly and press me to you with a great kiss, and let your love flow into me. Forget yourself just for one minute and do a brave thing! Oh, love me, *love me*, love me! and I shall be free!'

"The words, or the deep force they somehow released in the center of my being, stirred me profoundly, and an emotion infinitely greater than fear surged up over me and carried me with it across the edge of action. Without hesitation I took two steps forward towards him where he knelt, and held out my arms. Pity and love were in my heart at that moment, genuine pity, I swear, and genuine love. I forgot myself and my little tremblings in a great desire to help another soul.

"'I love you! poor, aching, unhappy thing! I love you,' I cried through hot tears; 'and I am not the least bit afraid in the world.'

"The man uttered a curious sound, like laughter, yet not laughter, and turned his face up to me. The light from the street below fell on it, but there was another light, too, shining all round it that seemed to come from the eyes and skin. He rose to his feet and met me, and in that second I folded him to my breast and kissed him full on the lips again and again."

All our pipes had gone out, and not even a skirt rustled in that dark studio as the story-teller paused a moment to steady her voice, and put a hand softly up to her eyes before going on again.

"Now, what can I say, and how can I describe to you, all you skeptical men sitting there with pipes in your mouths, the amazing sensation I experienced of holding an intangible, impalpable thing so closely to my heart that it touched my body with equal pressure all the way down, and then melted away somewhere into my very being? For it was like seizing a rush of cool wind and feeling a touch of burning fire the moment it had struck its swift blow and passed on. A series of shocks ran all over and all through me; a momentary ecstasy of flaming sweetness and wonder thrilled down into me; my heart gave another great leap—and then I was alone.

"The room was empty. I turned on the gas and struck a match to prove it. All fear had left me, and something was singing round me in the air and in my heart like the joy of a spring morning in youth. Not all the devils or shadows or hauntings in the world could then have caused me a single tremor.

"I unlocked the door and went all over the dark house, even into kitchen and cellar and up among the ghostly attics. But the house was empty. Something had left it. I lingered a short hour, analyzing, thinking, wondering—you can guess what and how, perhaps, but I won't detail, for I promised only essentials, remember—and then went out to sleep the remainder of the night in my own flat, locking the door behind me upon a house no longer haunted.

"But my uncle, Sir Henry, the owner of the house, required an account of my adventure, and of course I was in duty bound to give him some kind of a true story. Before I could begin, however, he held up his hand to stop me.

"'First,' he said, 'I wish to tell you a little deception I ventured to practice on you. So many people have been to that house and seen the ghost that I came to think the story acted on their imaginations, and I wished to make a better test. So I invented for their benefit another story, with the idea that if you did see anything I could be sure it was not due merely to an excited imagination.'

"'Then what you told me about a woman having been murdered, and all that, was not the true story of the haunting?'

"'It was not. The true story is that a cousin of mine went mad in that house, and killed himself in a fit of morbid terror following upon years of miserable hypochondriasis. It is his figure that investigators see.'

"'That explains, then,' I gasped—

"'Explains what?'

"I thought of that poor struggling soul, longing all these years for escape, and determined to keep my story for the present to myself.

"'Explains, I mean, why I did not see the ghost of the murdered woman,' I concluded.

"'Precisely,' said Sir Henry, 'and why, if you had seen anything, it would have had value, inasmuch as it could not have been caused by the imagination working upon a story you already knew.'"